Silver Star, Red Dragon

Book One of "The Soulbound Song"

C.A. Chaplin

Copyright © 2024 Vaeda Publishing

All rights reserved.

No part of this publication may be reproduced, distributed, or transmitted in any form or by any means, including photocopying, recording, and/or other electronic or mechanical methods, without the prior written permission of the publisher, except as permitted by U.S. copyright law.

For permission requests, contact authorcachaplin@gmail.com

The story, all names, characters, and incidents portrayed in this production are fictitious. No identification with actual persons (living or deceased), places, buildings, or products is intended or should be inferred.

Cover by Prokaryarts LLC

1st edition 2024

For my Silver Star.

Table of Contents

Author's Note & Content Warnings

This book contains explicit depictions of sex between consenting adults, graphic violence, graphic language, dark humor, psychological coercion/manipulation, mental illness relating to childhood trauma, and unhealthy relationship dynamics. It's important to remember that the main characters are not human. Their psychology and physiology differ from ours, sometimes in major ways. Dark fantasy means dark, y'all.

As an author, I have both ADHD and Autism, and there is evidence of it in certain characters. I don't call it by name because these concepts do not exist in the same framework in this world and they may manifest a little differently. Cultural context matters.

The elves have a culture of permissive non-monogamy. Sometimes it resembles polyamory, sometimes not. They do not view the world through the lens of compulsive monogamy or follow the sexual mores of Western society. The central relationships are fraught and not intended to depict the polyamorous community or healthy polyamorous relationships.

One of the main characters is demisexual, but he is not meant to represent the asexual/demisexual community at large. No community or identity is a monolith.

Some BDSM practices are depicted but they do not represent the BDSM community or lifestyle, and some practices are definitely unsafe for those without immortal bodies.

If you see occasional UK spellings like "grey," just know that I will die on this hill because "gray" makes my brain itch. "Glamour" is specific to fae magic.

Because this is the first of a trilogy, the story continues in a following book.

Sexual

Explicit sexual contact (consenting adults only), mild dub-con, rope bondage, impact play, toy insertion, fellatio, cunnilingus, dominance/submission, anal sex, sadism/masochism, teratophilia (that's monster fucking to the uninitiated), monster foot fetish-adjacent, cum worship (I really hate that spelling, you'll never see it again), knife play, blood play

Social/Violence

Physical violence, general gore, murder, death, war and battle, evisceration, dismemberment, eye injury, mention of child physical/sexual abuse (off-page), xenophobia, prejudice, misogyny, sexual jealousy, slut-shaming, blood consumption (from people), consumption of sentient beings, necrophagia, medical descriptions of injuries, mention of fertility & pregnancy, emesis, ableism/internalized ableism, revenge porn, rape joke, animal harm/death (brief mentions with unnamed warhorses, ponies, elk)

Psychological

Complex and single event Post-Traumatic Stress Disorder (both PTSD & C-PTSD), Antisocial Personality Disorder (ASPD), Attention-Deficit Hyperactivity Disorder (ADHD), Autism Spectrum Disorder (ASD), Depression, casual drug use (non-needle), hallucinations, loss of autonomy, demons/demon possession, psychotic episodes, self-harm that draws blood, self-destructive behavior, psychological manipulation, graphic language (they say fuck a lot)

Pronunciation Guide

Notes on Elvish:

"C" sounds are hard in elvish words, as in "cat"
Accent marks indicate a rising inflection.

"Ë" is pronounced like the "e" in words like "extra" and "error," and if it follows a consonant, I will pronounce the letter as a full syllable.

"Ä" indicates that the letter should be pronounced separately, and sounds like the "a" in "father"

"Î" is held slightly longer, and sounds like the "i" in "slick"

"Þ"(and "þ") is a soft th or dh sound, such as in "feather" and "the"

"Ea" together without a trema over either letter in elvish indicates two syllables, with the "e" being a long sound such as "bee" and the "a" such as "aim"

"Û" is a long "u" such as "vacuum"

Generally, every vowel is pronounced separately.

Elvish Names
- Cúraniel "Maeliaressë": KOO-rah-nee-ell MAY-lee-ah-rehs-she
- Celebel Elhalanros: KEL-eb-el eh-lah-LAHN-ros
- Rafael: rah-fah-EL
- Nemohee: NEHM-oh-hee
- Feanim: fee-AY-nim

- Araglin: AIR-ah-glen
- Beredhel: BEHR-eh-thell
- Eäriel: ee-AH-ree-ell
- Nimthil Tinunith: NIM-thill tin-OO-nith
- Feledhor: FELL-eh-thor
- Liriadis: LIR-ee-a-diss
- Carafindrien: care-ah-FINN-dree-ehn
- Cael: KAH-el
- Eledom: ELL-eh-dom
- Lámirië: LAH-meer-ree-AYE
- Silfanië: sill-FAH-nee-aye
- Recarmial: reh-KAR-me-all
- Melranim: mel-RAH-nim
- Galdir: GAL-deer
- Galaron: GAL-ah-ron
- Maelial: MY-lee-ahl
- Dhraxael: THRACKS-ah-el
- Dûemer: DOO-ey-mehr
- Lumetala: loo-may-TAHL-ah
- Polilcórë: poh-leel-KOH-ray
- Unarimë: oo-nah-REE-may
- Pulalvea: pool-AHL-vay-ah

Elvish Nations

- Talithiri: tahl-eh-THEE-ree
- Lachanaur: LAHK-ah-nawr
- Duedellen: Dway-del-ehn
- Astolar: AHS-toh-lahr
- Siltaur: SEEL-tawr
- Maraiya: mah-RAH-ee-yah

Elvish Places

- Velúara: vell-OOH-ah-rah
- Férioth: FEH-ree-oth
- Amrún: am-RUNE
- Thraeneleth: THRAY-neh-leth
- Leyúduin: Lay-U-duin
- Sirelon: SEER-eh-lohn
- Seregond: SEHR-eh-gond
- Rimbaras: reem-BAHR-as
- Orfain: OR-fa-een
- Faelen: FAY-len

Elvish Vocabulary

- Pîntellum: PIN-tell-oom – term for specialized armor membrane
- Þilvor: THEEL-vore – star-blessed metal ore
- Þey/Þem/Þeir: they/them/their – nonbinary pronoun
- Moranga – more-ANG-ah – demon ore
- Fallëvaethil – FAHL-eh-VAY-thil – "Rain Jewel" an important gem
- Atani – AH-tah-nee – "the Fifth Kindred" humans with spirit power
- Tárthanë: TAHR-thah-nay – "Long-Walkers" an extinct predecessor of ancient humans

Notes on Draconian

"Rr" is a deep, guttural, rolled "r," started at the base of the throat and led up to the mouth. No equivalent exists in English, though the uvular "r" is a similar concept

All "r" sounds are a trilled "r" as in Spanish

Other double consonants indicate an elongated consonant sound, like a pause.

Draconian Names

- Marron: MEH-rr-on
- Xyxs: ZICKS-ss - closer to one syllable than two
- Boshkt: BAHSHKT, one syllable
- Abrrys: AB-rrees
- Grenyk: GREH-nik
- Byxldurr: BEESH-ill-doo-rr
- Vaerra: VIE-eh-rrah
- Skeffynthir: SKEH-fin-theer
- Itreynith: ih-TREY-nith

Draconian Vocabulary

- Nekarazzi: neh-ka-RAHTS-ze - striped pest
- Inuriterrege: in-OO-ree-teh-rreh-geh - anthill king
- Rraysth e: RR-aysth eh - "The Red" or "Red One"
- Xuatae Aitzindrerrelehen – shu-AH-tie eye-tzin-DREH-rr-eh-en - Title meaning "Progenitor of the First Flame," referring to the first dragon, Dhraxael.

Horse Names

- Machi – MAH-chee
- Helicos – HEL-eh-cos
- Iruwher – EE-roo-whir
- Lettai – LET-tye

regions of VAEDA
Alma
Aureth
Aurel
Órma
Inelmoneth
Amrun
Ferioth
R. Emalen
Armon Elayan
Almatherin
Narinmoneth
R. Erelen
R. Süvalen
Seregonci
Aurelmoneth
Rimbaras
The Broken Lands
The Great Tree
The Orfain Tree
R. Faelen
R. Gliralen
Velvara
Vormoneth
Atatherin
R. Coralaen

Part 1

Chapter 1

84 years ago

When dragons fight, the world trembles.

An expansive thunderhead rolled in from the south. Moving uncannily against the wind, it seethed with lightning and cast the world in eerie twilight. My stomach turned with the wrongness of it, fine hairs raised in alarm on the back of my neck.

The roiling cloud burst open with a roar and dumped two hostile behemoths. An enormous creature of iridescent indigo feathers wheeled and flashed across the sky with a shriek, pursued by an impossibly massive, red-scaled beast. Its wingspan alone blotted out the heavens. It caught the feathered one's tail in its jaws, and they locked together in furious battle, biting and clawing. A rain of steaming blood scorched the vegetation beneath.

The sudden cacophony leveled me. A bed of artemisia cushioned my fall, its scent clinging to my skin.

"Forgive me, little ones," I said to the plants; I'd been prepping the garden when the storm hit. Scrambling to collect my tools, I could hardly react to the sight of fucking *dragons* squabbling over my head.

A wind shear snatched my long, black braid, whipping it across my body with an audible crack. An angry red stripe rose on the curve of my moon-pale hip. Bad timing for my usual naked-gardening. Unsteady and rubbing the welt, I clambered to my feet.

My long ears flattened, throbbing with the onset of a riotous headache. For the first time in my thousands of years of life, I cursed the sensitivity of elvish hearing. I gathered my strength and sprinted. The meager protections I'd left for the poor garden would simply have to suffice. Pausing at the hill's base, I dismantled the wards on the ring of halite crystals to prevent their incessant chiming.

At the crest of the steep slope, the Great Tree had never looked so far away. The spread of its branches nearly blocked out the dragons battling overhead, giving the illusion of safety until a streak of flame lit up the clouds. Fear consumed me as I imagined the Tree catching fire. I'd always loved the view from the hill, but now that monsters threatened the skies, I wished it weren't quite so tall.

A thunderous clap of wings echoed across the valley. Hurricane winds nearly swept me off my feet.

"Gather your gods damned wits, Cúraniel," I snarled to myself, and ran as hard as I could up the incline to my bower. The next echoing bellow ruptured my ear tympanies with such force that blood trickled down my neck. As I dove inside the opening in the trunk, a blinding flash of dragon fire seared through the air behind me. The Tree wrenched closed, sealing me inside.

Shaking, I curled on my soft linen pallet and forced myself to calm down. Deep breaths, centering my spirit to the roots. Between the headache and the stuffy ear pain, a wave of nauseating vertigo grabbed me. Another roar shook the hill. The Tree groaned and my head throbbed. I crawled over to my workbench, grabbed a handful of angelica and lovage roots, and chewed them raw. The bitter plant alkaloids eased my headache enough for me to concentrate on healing my poor ears.

Finding my center, I directed my spirit power to knit the ruptured membranes back together. My hearing cleared as the agony subsided. I ran my hand along the outer helix of my abused ears. Longer than my forearm, I'd always been proud of them.

A loud crack startled me, then another. Hail bounced off the calcites in the bower wall. It had never damaged the thick panes of crystal before, but the next piece was almost as large as my head. I risked a peek outside through the translucent window. Doubled by the crystal's refraction and obscured by the vast spread of the Tree's branches, I caught only a lash of a tail or the swipe of a wing here and there.

These couldn't be true dragons. They'd departed ages ago,

fled or became mountains or glaciers or some such. Their return was said to herald the end of the world. The beasts had brought a nasty storm, true, but the ground itself remained intact, and I'd lived long enough to flee. Hardly the cataclysmic death stroke predicted by the sages. Therefore, these must be the dragon forms of their children, the drakes.

Notorious for mating with a wide variety of species and promptly abandoning the resulting offspring, the true dragons had sprinkled their get across all of Vaeda. The remaining drakes were now many generations removed from their progenitors.

Despite various historic clashes with elves, I had no personal experience with drakes. I knew only that they possessed a bellicose reputation, awful strength, and the ability to shapeshift into full-sized dragons for a limited time. Gods, that red one alone took up the entire sky. It certainly *looked* like a true dragon.

A shriek, a boom, another roar, and the Tree shook again. I doubted I'd get any sleep until this was over. No one had ever mentioned just how damned *loud* dragons were.

Shadows dripped from the ceiling, coalescing into a familiar, vaguely feline shape. Two yellow eyes bobbed to the surface, and the creature promptly made itself comfortable in my lap. Its little feet left no indentations on my plush thighs, and its form drank in the light to make it even blacker than my hair.

"I'll never understand what draws you here, but I'm grateful for the company." I stroked its soft head, my fingers buzzing with its strange energies. "Can you explain why these big beasties chose *my* hill to stage their epic battle? All I've ever wanted was a peaceful life. Perhaps you could kindly ask them to move along before they destroy my home?"

The shadow blinked, circled three times, and settled down again. Not that I expected the odd creature to cooperate. I had a sense that it held immense power, but it seemed content to abide in my presence from time to time.

I prayed and called to her, but the goddess Dûemer, the Night Mother, was curiously unresponsive. She sent none of the usual visions. I grumbled to myself about the utter lack of warning.

The titans fought for days. Each time the noise of their battle drifted, and I thought they'd moved on, another clash of their mighty bodies quaked the ground, announcing their return. The weather went wild with their unleashed power. Torrential rains, high winds, and lightning accompanied the random bouts of hail. Even small tornadoes ripped across the landscape, churning up the ground and flinging debris into the sky. The calcite panes cast brilliant flashes of color and heaving shadows across the bower in a weird show.

Lack of sleep and anxiety clenched my belly like a fist, allowing me little appetite. The Great Tree stood strong through it all, hiding me away in its bower. As it always had and always would.

After six days of violent chaos, an echoing *boom* knocked all the books and bottles from my shelves. The aftershock threw me to the floor, then all went still. I crawled to a clear pane. The dragons had gone. In their place, two people-shaped figures grappled, clawing at each other.

Definitely drakes. End of the world or otherwise, they heralded *trouble*. At least they made less fucking noise in those forms.

With the calcite's distortion and their blurring speed, I could barely follow the action. The larger showed streaming flashes of red. Shifting blue-purple feathers like a scarab's wing crowned the smaller drake. At a pause, the feathered one hooked a taloned foot into the larger one's midsection with a brutal, disemboweling kick. Screeching in victory, it shredded the flesh of its foe. I pressed a sympathetic hand to my gut.

The injured drake rolled forward, taking them both down with an echoing thud. A prolonged shriek had me clapping hands over my ears once more. I looked away just as a head flew free in a gout of blood, whispering a prayer that the end was at hand.

No further sounds assaulted my hearing. Ever unpredictable, my little shadow friend also disappeared, melding into a dark corner under my workbench. After counting to twelve dozen, I dressed in a linen shift and emerged to pregnant silence. The surrounding forest held its collective breath in fear. Not a single fae approached. The more predatory among them were usually quick to swarm any creature unlucky enough to fall outside the halites. I scrambled down the hill to examine the scene.

Melted rocks in a long burn scar cast an eerie glow from the lingering heat. The red drake, a big male, lay in a tangled mess of viscera at the apex of that scar. The acrid tang of blood stung my nose as I approached. He looked much more like a person under all the gore than the reptilian beast I'd expected. One less drake to worry about.

Following the shape of the blast in the opposite direction, I found the feathered drake flung over a nearby cliff. What remained of her on the rocks below, at any rate. Her head was distinctly missing.

I almost left without checking the red one again. Almost. But the Night Mother chose that moment to remind me of my healer's oath with a sharp twinge. Grumbling to myself, I obliged.

To my shock, he drew a rasping gurgle of breath. Heart-struck, eviscerated, his body cracked open and ruined, he should have been dead many times over. Somehow, the stubborn blighter clung to life. He'd made it to my territory, and I owed him healing for it.

The crest of the hill rose far above us. I groaned. The Great Tree would help keep my patient stable while I worked, easing his distress and funneling vitality back into him. With the extent of the injuries, I would need all the help I could get.

Ripping away the hem of my filmy dress, I bound his opened gut as best I could, tucking viscera back where it belonged. With a sigh, I hooked my hands under the drake's arms from behind.

I dragged his immensely heavy carcass to the top at a snail's pace, grateful that he hadn't fallen on the creek side, even farther down the slope. Taking the extra time to haul a rapidly expiring patient all the way to the Great Tree filled me with anxiety, but I made it with him still clinging faintly to life. Only for the Tree to rustle with disapproval. It allowed me to nest the battered drake amongst its roots just outside the bower entrance but refused to provide any direct succor.

"Ancestor, please! The Night Mother will revoke her blessing!" Frustrated tears, from the wasted effort and sheer physical exhaustion, trickled down my cheeks. "Please, help me save him."

Gentle wreaths of branches wrapped me, and the Tree strengthened me in my patient's stead.

Scrambling up the slope of corpses, I slipped and slid on slick bowels and putrid flesh in my effort to reach the clear sky I knew must be somewhere overhead. The fetid stench of cadaverine shoved its way down my throat despite my efforts to not breathe it in. As I reached the peak, I fell through the crust of squelching limbs. I screamed, and the rot gagged my cry. The dead raked at me as I plummeted.

A strong hand caught my arm, stopping my descent. I clung to it, weeping. That hand lifted me out of the horror and set me on a grassy meadow where the bodies had once lain. My savior was none other than my patient, backlit and dressed in black armor. Blood dripped from the hand that caught me.

I blinked, gasping, and the vision scattered. *Now, you send me a vision?*

The goddess ignored my attitude. Her message was obvious, though disorienting as usual. If I saved this brute, someday he would save me. Perhaps more than only me. I dug my bare feet into the earth, reaching for the center I desperately needed. After a moment, the answering hum of nature calmed me, and I could return to my work.

I hacked away the tattered remains of his clothing with

my braid knife to assess the damage, feeding spirit into him as I progressed. Even filthy and mangled as he was, I sucked in an awed breath at his physique. Here were the powerful shoulders and chest of a man able to crush my skull in one hand, tapering to a narrow waist and long, corded legs. Every handspan of him was carved as if from stone; a living weapon.

Ducking briefly into my bower, I picked up a rag and a bucket of cool water. With gentle swipes, I washed away the dirt, crusted blood, and bits of stuck grass and leaves. As carefully as I could, I rinsed the exposed organs, tucking them back into place. Steam rose where I splashed him.

His distinct mane of loose curls, red as freshly spilled blood, gave away his identity. I'd tried, unsuccessfully, to scrub the gore away as I checked for head wounds. It turned out to be the actual hue of his hair.

No, it couldn't be!

My ears flattened. I should have known from the color alone. There was only one drake with solid red scales and a mane to match. But he hadn't been heard from since… gods, since before I'd left Leyúduin! I'd never expected him to look like a man at all.

Legend had it, the Red Dragon dyed his hair with the blood of kings. Or was it virgins? Perhaps infants, according to that one version… I shook myself.

Supposedly, he had the visage of evil incarnate. I did not know what evil's visage should be, but my patient had quite a scowl permanently etched on his narrow, light bronze face. High, hollow cheekbones, a long, hooked nose, and sharply arched eyebrows made for a harsh, yet somehow regal appearance. Short, pointed ears hid under all that hair. He might never be called handsome, but he was certainly striking.

His heavily muscled body lacked the expected scalation, though the digitigrade joints of his legs resembled a beast more than a person. When upright, he would surely walk balanced on his toes. Draconic feet each held three long, splayed toes ending in curved, white talons, a small inner dewclaw, and a vicious heel spur. More long talons tipped each finger, the only other obvious sign of his nature.

If I hadn't seen that dragon form, or his feet, I might not have taken him for a drake at all. Given all the lives those talons had ended, the blood and flesh caked under them took on a nauseating connotation.

My people named him 'Rafael,' meaning 'God of Carnage' in the ancient tongue; 'Rafa' for carnage, and 'Ael' meaning god, or godlike. Also called the 'Bloody Drake,' and by far the most powerful, the most feared, of all those abandoned children. He was said to have razed the great elvish city of Ilitherin, as well as decimating the ancient human Tárthanë kingdom. He'd even slaughtered his way to power amongst his own kind. A murderer on a scale that beggared comprehension, and my hand rested casually on his forehead as though he were any other patient.

I froze. Gods, I was a fucking fool. I'd been so focused on my pondering of true dragons versus drakes that I'd completely overlooked all the glaring signs. How could I rescue such a monster? How many more lives would he take if I saved his?

So notorious for his overwhelming strength and ferocity, some younger elves doubted his very existence. They called the fall of Ilitherin the exaggerated result of a battle with many drakes, rather than one godlike legend. Others claimed the Red Dragon had passed from Vaeda along with his progenitors. Most supposed he simply slumbered with the other ancients. I'd been inclined to agree with those speculations, right up until he landed at my feet. Wonderful.

I stared at him, hands twitching. Something about witnessing such a mighty warrior brought low tugged at my heart, and I reassessed my moralizing. Who was I to decide whether any patient deserved their healing? Surely he warranted as much compassion as any other sword-slinger I'd saved in the past. The Night Mother certainly seemed to think so. After that extended absence, perhaps he'd already reformed.

I pulled at the tips of my ears in distress. *Focus*, I admonished myself. *He is a patient like any other.* A patient who had slaughtered thousands. Perhaps even hundreds of thousands. My gut churned.

The Night Mother remained aloof. Dûemer always kept her aims obscured. It was enough that the goddess had deemed him worthy of salvation. I found it a hard melody to follow that he may someday return the favor. I could wait no longer and began the healing with a heavy heart and her mantle an anchor about my shoulders. No more time to dwell on my personal fears.

Nine days and nine nights passed as I toiled to save the Red Dragon's life. His steaming blood scalded the skin from my hands each time I plunged them into his ravaged body, more volcano on the inside than man. I gritted my teeth through the pain and spared some healing for myself as I went. Gloves only interfered with the delicate work.

His musculature presented a further complication. The unnatural, stonelike hardness prevented me from manually closing his wounds. No needle would pierce his hide, no amount of pressure would budge his flesh. Herbs crisped black in his heat. I threw all my energy into him, and the Great Tree lent me aid where it could. So did my goddess. I'd never before channeled such a flood of healing power.

My strange patient held his own power in tight check, preventing me from coaxing his body to repair itself. Each patient I'd ever healed mingled their spirit with mine, doing their own work from within. Not this one. He walled me out, and I threw myself at his barriers as his life slipped away.

On the ninth night, I found the tiniest crack in his energetic armor, just inside his wounded heart. Begging the Night Mother for aid, I flowed into him, filling him with spirit, hardly conscious of blurring together in my desperation to save him. All at once, that resistance broke with staggering force. My breath filled his weakened lungs, my heart beat for his, my blood guided his home. My power tingled, finding the damage, sealing burst vessels, repairing organs, generating fresh blood.

In response, his spirit rose like a dragon taking flight. The force of him knocked me backwards, stealing my breath, spearing directly into my heart to mesh with the spirit woven throughout my being.

No! No, this can't happen. Not like this, not with this one! Panic clawed at the edges of my mind. The very day I'd left Leyúduin, I'd had a vision of my soulmate's eyes. The soft blue of gentle skies, fringed with sooty, sweeping lashes. Kind. *Definitely* not the eyes of a murderous warlord.

I denied the melody. Fatigue delirium. I'd merely sunk too much of myself into him, nothing more. Gods, what was I to do with this man when he awoke? Would he consider rehabilitation of the soul as well as the body? The absurdity of the idea allowed me to catch my breath.

The Red Dragon's power surged then, around and through me, raising the small hairs on my body, shivering across my skin like a hiss. Wounds I'd spent days trying to close knitted themselves before my eyes. The racing thoughts fled as I watched in awe.

With the dam finally broken, exhaustion overtook my feverish focus. I flopped down beside him, admonishing myself not to touch him unnecessarily. The compulsion grew to drag my fingers over the odd texture of his skin, smooth in one direction and rough in the other. The contact made my hands tingle all the way up my arms. Gods only knew what kind of influence he may exert, even in his unconscious state.

Perhaps it was simply the comfort of his intense body heat that drew me. I'd kept him wrapped in woolen blankets and furs as much as possible. Otherwise, he shivered in the crisp night air of early spring. Tall and broad-shouldered as he was, it took everything I owned to keep him covered. I tugged the edge of a quilt around me and curled up in the roots, dropping into sleep like a rock into a pond.

The sun hadn't moved in the sky when I woke, more refreshed than I expected. I perched on the roots and combed out my abundance of hair. Loose, it fell to my ankles. I admired the flash of my mother-of-pearl comb against my raven's wing locks as I worked, laddering a complex braid around a simple central plait.

An almost physical blow struck my back—the hurled weight of a furious gaze. My hands stilled. With a deep, centering breath, I turned into the full force of the Red Dragon's glare. Reality itself bent and shivered around him as if it, too, feared his attention.

Those fierce eyes belied none of his ordeal. Brilliant flames danced there, flickering with resentment. Pupils narrowed to thin slits, like a venomous snake. That bloody mane of curls sparked to life, the thick strands taking on an ember glow from within, becoming liquid fire. Would it burn to the touch? I shook off the foolish urge to find out.

The Red Dragon opened his mouth to speak, showing the tips of needle-pointed teeth, and a croak issued forth. Coughing, he cleared his throat, his irises flaring red-rimmed hellfire.

"Who the fuck are you?" he demanded in razor-edged elvish.

Weak as he was, he spoke with a voice like the rumbling crack of distant thunder. It held an underlying chorus of a growl so deep and resonant it rattled my sternum and shivered down my spine. So this was the voice of a dragon! Rising heat distorted the already tenuous air into wavy lines.

"I am a healer, and this is my Tree." I kept my tone neutral, formal.

The Tree rustled acknowledgement, a single leaf floating down to meet us. It swirled around the Red Dragon, crisping brown. I imagined my body twisting like scorched parchment. The tip of a root lifted and surreptitiously tapped my foot for mutual comfort, just past the drake's line of sight.

The tension in the Red Dragon's body spoke volumes about his willingness to visit violence upon me. Could I unheal his wounds faster than he could attack? Not without the strength of my lineage to draw upon. Crow, I'd never regretted breaking it until now. I breathed a silent prayer to the Night Mother for protection and kept my voice steady.

"All who reach my hill receive my aid."

"Recognition lights your eyes. Why would an elf save my life?" His words dripped scorn.

I'd worked with enough injured animals to recognize that kind of aggression, and kept my approach gentle, calm, and absolutely firm. I dared not drop my gaze, though he seemed to peer straight into my very soul.

"You needed assistance, my lord." With effort, I calmed myself. "You were gravely wounded."

"Did you also assist my foe?" His scowl deepened. Was that the issue? Or was he simply a vicious, ungrateful blighter?

"She was beyond my power to save, Lord Dragon. You beheaded her." The image of her crumpled, headless body flashed behind my eyes. Where *had* her head gone?

He panted for a moment, considering. Speech put an obvious strain on his limited reserves.

"Be calm, my lord. No harm will come to you in my care." I tried to sound reassuring.

His eyes narrowed to slits, and he pulled the blankets tight around himself. "Where *the fuck* are my clothes?"

The obvious discomfort with his body surprised me. I'd never met a fighter who wasn't proud of their physique, often to an absurd degree. Those furious eyes burned over my ample, bare breasts, the curve of my hips, and his lips pulled back from jagged teeth.

"Where the fuck are yours?" he snarled. Vicious and ungrateful indeed.

"Forgive me, my lord. I had to cut your clothing away to tend your wounds." I waved a hand over my torso. "For myself, I prefer not to be restricted by clothing in my home. Nothing untoward, I swear to you. Now, rest. You need to recover from this ordeal."

He growled low in his throat, the sound shuddering through me. I'd once encountered the mighty crocodiles of the southern Lachanaur lands. They made a similar deep, resonant bellow of a growl. I sighed. This was going to be a long, rocky path.

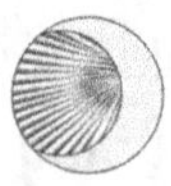

The pinprick of teeth on my throat stilled me. I'd made the mistake of stretching over the slumbering drake to reach for a clean rag. I swallowed hard, and my pulse jumped like a panicked creature seeking escape. His near-scalding breath came even and slow. Deliberate. I willed myself to calm, quieting my rabbit heart.

A test, then. He would have already torn out my throat if he truly wanted my death. Only the growling undercurrent of his breath disturbed the taut silence. The trickling blood itched terribly, the puncture wounds stung, and it took every bit of my control not to squirm.

Did he enjoy the tang of my blood? The taste of my nerve? My muscles quivered as I held myself in that unnatural position, waiting for his teeth to close. Or for his arms to crush me against him. I certainly had a preference. The press of my breasts against that stony shoulder was not entirely unwelcome.

So close, I scented his skin—leather, a hint of smoke, and a distinctive spiced musk, very like a rare aromatic resin called dragon's blood. How appropriate. He breathed me in as well, tasting my scent. What secrets did it tell him? What judgments would he pass?

After a maddening amount of time, measured only in his rumbling breath, he relaxed his jaws. I sprang back from his reach, hands flying to my neck to staunch the bleeding.

The Dragon's eyes crinkled in mockery at the outer corners. Perfectly calm, piercing blue rather than the previous flames. Near white by the elliptical pupils, the bright azure darkened almost to black at the outer ring of the iris. They yet flickered with some internal fire. That hint of smugness infuriated me. He seemed to enjoy the small revenge for the undignified position I'd put him in. I dabbed at my throat with the ill-omened cloth and eyed him levelly.

"Some manners you have."

No more 'my lord' or honorifics from me. Not if he was to be so deliberately rude. I should have been frightened, but all I felt was irritation. It wasn't the first bluff charge I'd faced down from a big predator. If he'd wanted to play rough, he could have at least gotten me off.

He hissed in response, showing jagged teeth stained with my blood.

"Would you like some water to wash out your mouth?" I maintained an air of cool indifference, healing the puncture wounds as he watched. The skin itched as it closed, and I resisted the urge to scratch it, lest he spot the tremor in my hands.

"Your blood is sweet wine," he rumbled, swiping a long tongue over those sharp teeth. Stories of all the elves he'd eaten sprang to mind. I rejected the fear trembling in those thoughts.

"Yours is like boiling oil." I flicked my long ears for emphasis.

He harrumphed, which grew into a wracking cough. I leaned in to lift his head so that he would not choke, showing him I did not fear his threats. Trying to growl made his cough worse. So determined to be awful.

"Turn your head away and spit."

He did, and a thick clot of blood spattered and steamed on the ground beside him. The Tree rustled with displeasure, moving a root away.

I sighed. "You will not heal if you cannot keep your hackles down long enough to rest. I am not your enemy."

Perhaps it was my calm, direct tone, or his own exhaustion, but he exhaled in a shimmering gust of heat and closed his eyes.

The Red Dragon remained wakeful for longer periods, his heavy-lidded eyes always on me. Hoping to soothe and acclimate him to my presence, I sang while I went about my daily routines. He'd erected such a barrier between us that I doubted the veracity of my initial reaction. Which came with its own sense of relief. The thought of being bound to a mass murderer quivered my insides with dread.

I leaned in to wash his face with a damp rag, and he snapped at me, teeth clicking a hairsbreadth from my wrist. I jerked my hand back just in time.

"You are the most irascible patient I've ever encountered." I flicked the rag at him. "Is that why the other drake tried so hard to kill you?"

No response.

"Perhaps I saved the wrong one," I grumbled, and his eyes narrowed. "I may yet stick her head back on her shoulders and call it good."

Although he feigned utter indifference, from the way his eyes flickered, the Red Dragon cataloged my every word. I reached for his hand, intending to dip it in the water bucket. His talons flexed, digging into the earth, and he hissed. With a frustrated groan, I tossed the rag at him.

"Fine. Clean yourself, if my touch is so very threatening."

A flash in his eyes caught my attention, just before he turned his head away. Despair? I watched his face, intent. Something rooted much deeper in him; some horrifying wound cut into his soul. There it was again, flitting across his face like birds taking wing. I knew that sign all too well.

He'd *wanted* to die. Well. That explained his reaction.

Healing the body paled in effort compared to delving into the mind and soul. Suspicion coiled in the Red Dragon's every breath, and the walls erected around his true self had been there since long before my conception. Daunting.

Deciding to grant him a little space, I went hunting for the first time in months. Rare for me to consume meat, but my patient would need heavier fare than my usual diet of roots and buds. Locating an elderly, stumbling doe, I sang to her, lulling her into a deep sleep as I took her life. With reverence, I thanked her and strung up the carcass to skin and quarter it. Working quickly, I bundled up my catch and lugged it back to my bower.

"Your accent is strange," the Red Dragon rumbled, and I nearly dropped the hide I was scraping.

"So, you haven't forgotten how to speak. No disrespect intended," I added hastily, at the red flash in his eyes. "Your elvish accent is flawless."

"Language interests me."

My ears perked at the tidbit of personal information. "I've been in the hills a long time, and the hillspeech burr has taken over." The local cadences charmed me from the very start, and I'd leaned in.

"Hrrm. This hillspeech is unfamiliar."

"There's no surprise. It's a dialectical mix of a few common local languages. If you've never been here before, you won't have heard it. Everyone who lives around here uses it, even the humans."

A storm cloud gathered on his brow. "Humans?" he hissed, leaning hard on the sibilant.

Crow. "Do not trouble yourself over them. It's only a small village, simple people. They're harmless."

An ugly snarl gripped the Red Dragon's face, and he bared those sharp teeth. "Where are they?" he demanded, and the naked hatred in his voice could have boiled the creek.

"Why do you need to know?" Alarm pricked my ears.

His lips peeled back, heat rolling off his body in waves. "I hunger."

Crow! That was worse than mere hatred. Immensely worse. "No, eat this venison instead." Grabbing the haunch, I brandished it like a torch. "I cannot allow you to hurt those people! Besides, you cannot even stand—"

He cut me off with a slashing motion, talons splayed, and sat up. He shouldn't have been able to do even that much. Every muscle in his body strained with effort as he pulled himself unsteadily to his feet, to my utter amazement. My patient towered head and shoulders above me; the top of my head barely clearing the center of his broad chest. I was not a short woman by any measure of elves and taller than most humans as well. I sucked in a breath at the sheer size of him and changed tactics.

"Look at yourself! Wrapped only in a blanket, barely upright. Are you truly going to smite those poor people?"

Consternation replaced the awful rage on his face, and the Red Dragon sagged heavily against the trunk of the Tree. Vowing never to underestimate his strength again, I gestured for him to sit beside me.

"Come on, down you go, you big beast. You're in no shape for this. *Please!*" I was not above begging. When he sank to his knees with a sigh, I gave silent thanks to the Night Mother. "What kind of healer would I be if I let my patient go charging off in such a state? Trying to besmirch my reputation, are you?"

Silence stretched between us, only punctuated by his rumbling, labored breath. After a few heartbeats, he settled down, curling around himself. His fiery eyes remained far away and contemptuous. Whether of the villagers, me, or himself, I could not tell.

His walls fell and a buzzing wave of pain hit me. It ripped through my senses, plummeting to the pit of my belly, and nauseating me to the point of gagging before I could shut him out. A mighty need filled me in place of that anguish, to calm him and soothe his aching soul. Beneath the armor of all that rage and power, he was a raw, gaping wound.

I leaned into him, moving slowly.

He watched with growing suspicion, and finally snapped, "What are you doing?"

"Be calm. This is a healing technique." I moved closer and his eyes widened. "It will seem intimate and strange, but I mean no harm or untoward gesture. I can go only as deep as you allow, but I truly believe I can help you. If you will permit me?"

He said nothing, but he did not growl or otherwise threaten me as I leaned over him. I took it as encouragement. His pupils thinned as I placed my hands on either side of his face, but he made no move to push me away. The connection between us flared, a gravity I couldn't escape. My hands tingled.

"May I?"

He rumbled something that sounded like encouragement. When I pressed a healing kiss to his lips, his body went rigid. Under normal circumstances, the kiss itself remained surface level; merely easing the synchronization of breath and heartbeat. It allowed me a gentle intimacy, meeting the patient's spirit with my own. After melding, I entered the realm of subconscious to perform the deeper healing of trauma at its root.

I had no time to match breath before abject horror swept me away. Red agonies ripped and slashed at my psyche, punctuated by a soul-deep wail. A terrified child shrieked from the depths of his mind, tangled in the matted curtain of his own bloody hair. Blistering hatred. Faceless humans. Unspeakable acts of torture.

He thrashed hard, throwing me off of him. Disoriented, I landed with a painful thump and skidded to a halt. Rolling onto my knees, I vomited, sick to my very soul.

"*WHAT HAVE YOU DONE?*" the Red Dragon roared. The sheer force of it knocked me flat again, shaking the Tree and quaking the ground beneath us. His eyes blistered red as he surged upright once more. His hair came alight with flame, lips peeled back in a rictus grin, baring teeth like broken glass. There was that demonic visage of legend.

Grey smoke billowed from the Red Dragon's nose and mouth. His throat swelled, and he spat a gout of white-hot dragon fire at me.

Chapter 2

Current day

hy do they never reach the top of the hill before collapsing? I sighed to myself as I skidded down the steep eastern slope. Passing the halite ring, I slowed at the creek. Recent rain slicked the rocks, turning my walk into a squelching slog. Swooping and shrieking their excitement, the local jays led me to the crumpled form of a fellow Talithiri elf.

Dressed in fine—if somewhat mangled—armor, he lay face-down in the muck. Slow bubbles formed from his shallow breath. The heady scent of the lilies hung in the air where he'd crushed them along the bank. I plucked a surviving flower and tucked it behind my ear, grateful for the aroma to mask the stench of old blood.

"How did you get all the way out here?" I muttered, frowning at his apparent lack of provisions. My bower was, by design, far from civilization.

The shaft of a broken arrow protruded from a muscular thigh. Various fractures distorted his limbs. Severe swelling and bruising ruined the lines of him. The forest had given me no warning of danger, and his wounds were not fresh. Too much blood seeped into the surrounding mud.

I wanted to get him inside the halites as quickly as I could. That the smell of blood hadn't already drawn the fae in droves was a small miracle. Good thing I'd reached him before dusk, otherwise the sluagh would be upon him. Their malevolent presence fluttered in the growing shadows, seemingly stronger as of late.

I kneeled, heedless of the sucking mud, and drew a small knife from its hidden sheath in my braid. Cutting away the leather straps holding his pauldrons and backplate in place was simple enough. Sawing through the thick gambeson and linens beneath proved a bit more strenuous. Grasping the edges, I gave them a quick tear and ripped the garments.

The moment I laid hands on his bared skin, a jolt ran up my arms and shivered through my core. I jumped backward. Ears twitching, I shook the tingling sensation from my arms. Better to examine that later. Methodically probing my way down his back told me the cord of his spine was intact. Thank the gods.

With a heave, I flipped him face-up and cut away the rest of his armor. His chest rose in a weak rhythm, and each inhalation whistled faintly through a broken nose. I leaned in close, sharing breath with him as I looked him over.

Like most Talithiri, myself included, his hair was long, straight, and black as a moonless ocean. Barely visible under the matted blood and filth, thin streaks of silver shot throughout his inky tresses, as though he'd been kissed by falling stars.

Face pulped into a swollen, purpled mess, his eyelids were barely visible. His long, graceful ears showed only cosmetic damage, with a few earrings torn away from the right lobe. An injury that would doubtless be upsetting, but also a simple repair. I resisted the urge to touch my own ears. Potential issues ranged from simple hearing loss, to burning nerve pain, to severance from the shared song itself.

That last bit was a curse no elf deserved. Not even the banished. I might have removed myself from my people, but the song resonated through my spirit if I held very still. Stronger now, with this newcomer's arrival.

Blood loss left a deathly pallor on his skin. I signed a thanks to the Night Mother that I'd found him in time. This much exsanguination would have killed any human patient. Not that I'd encountered any humans on the hill in at least a century.

The Talithiri's wrist pulses were weak, thin, and deep, with a hollow quality that I expected from the blood loss, but steady enough. His substantial power, humming just under the surface, held him in a stasis. I hummed back as I examined him, matching pitch, and his spirit reached to mine. That instinctive cooperation made elves easier to heal than most of my other patients.

Gathering my strength, I grabbed his uninjured thigh and rolled forward. Heaving him up onto my shoulders, he pulled free from the mud with a *pop*. The sudden movement startled away a deer licking a halite. My patient's greater height, on a slim frame dense with muscle in the way of all fighters, complicated matters. At least he was significantly lighter than that damned drake. Though, to be fair, he had fallen on the higher southern meadow. I planted my feet, centering the elf's weight, and began the long trudge up the hill.

The light dimmed early under the massive spread of the Great Tree's branches, shadowing the hill long before the surrounding area. Just as well, my power grew stronger after dark.

I settled my patient, pushing through the fatigue. Nestled in the Tree's roots and freed of armor and clothing, I found another broken-off shaft buried in his side. He boasted an awful number of badly broken ribs, and both ankles were swollen beyond recognition. Stripping off my filthy dress, I took a deep breath and worked furiously to stabilize him. The Tree cradled him, supplementing my efforts. A nice change from last time.

Following his song, I directed his body to push out the embedded arrows and heal the tissue. With the bleeding staunched, I delved deeper. His power rose to mingle with mine, and I breathed another sigh of thanks to be working on a familiar elvish constitution. Indeed, I found it difficult to pry myself away from him long enough to give my efforts the chance to take hold.

While I waited for his body to respond to my work, I assembled an herbal decoction to replenish the blood he'd lost and speed up regeneration. Picking over my stock of blood-tonifying and external injury herbs, I put together a formula. Angelica root, rehmannia, peony root and bark, lovage, peach kernel, and safflower balanced the base. I added others to direct the impact to various parts of his body, along with an infusion of my power and vitality. He would eventually need some external poultices, but that could wait.

Picking up the dragon's blood resin, I thoughtlessly inhaled its spicy, complex aroma. As always, it brought to mind a distraction I could not afford. Even in a moment of reverie, that burning awareness attuned sharply to me. Disquieted, I set the resin aside, shaking off the phantom gaze and the lingering memories, and pulled out my flat warming stone. Placing my kettle on the spirit-driven heat, I dumped in the herbs and let the decoction brew. With a weary sigh, I turned back to the labor of convincing my patient's body not to surrender.

Dawn's light woke me, bleary-eyed, with my head pillowed uncomfortably on the wash bucket. I glanced over to see if my patient still lived. *Ah, good.* His chest rose and fell much more evenly. I stretched and took his pulses. Stronger, but not as much as I wanted.

I forced another draught of the blood-building tea down his throat, dribbling it carefully so as not to choke him. A gripping urge to stroke his cheek stole my good sense. Sharply admonishing myself, I refocused my attention.

Shoving a biscuit in my mouth, I pieced him back together; cleaning, knitting, guiding tissues to expel the foreign and accept the healthy. The purely mechanical act of cleaning the surface of the wounds came as a welcome break.

A couple of days later, my patient looked a lot more like a proper elf. Once I reduced the swelling in his face and repaired the damaged tissue, he turned out to be strikingly handsome. Straight, dark brows framed large eyes, fringed with luscious, equally dark lashes. He had a straight nose, full shapely lips over a defined jaw, and high cheekbones that were still a touch too hollow after his ordeal. All identified his lineage, even if I hadn't already seen his talisman earring.

How did such high-level nobility even make it all the way out here? The last thing I needed in my life was another king. His body was nicely muscled yet lithe; he just needed a little more flesh on his bones. And I was borrowing trouble. *Gods*, I couldn't let this happen. Even unconscious and battered beyond recognition, the draw of his presence was near-physical in its strength. I erected walls in my mind, tightening my thoughts and feelings.

With a deep breath, I leaned in to give him a healing kiss, to connect and see to the core of him. Many of my seriously injured patients also suffered mental, emotional, or soul-deep wounds. Oh, his lips were so soft. *Crow! Stop that, focus!* I matched breath with him and my soul lit up like the dawn the moment it touched his.

A strange relief flooded me. His soul held a certain melancholy, likely due to whatever event had led him here, but I found no enduring injury. No layers of hidden trauma or madness. His presence buoyed me like a warm, tranquil ocean. Familiar and safe. We swirled around each other, and I lent him my strength as his song mingled with my own. Perfect harmony, like coming home.

I released him with reluctance, sitting back.

As his eyelids fluttered open and we gazed at each other for the first time, I could not deny it. Gentle, sky-blue eyes swept me away. The very day I left elvish society behind, I had seen those eyes in a vision and known my fate awaited.

I could barely continue to breathe. My heart beat in time with his. We drank in the sight of each other as the clouds passed, throwing gentle shadows in their wake. In that vision, those eyes had regarded me exactly as they did now. During my long isolation, and given other circumstances, I had assumed that vision would never come to life. Here he was, impossibility made flesh.

He beamed at me, flashing his white, even teeth. I couldn't help but mirror that infectious smile. To sit in comfortable silence with him in pleasant, shared warmth. He watched me for a short time; his gaze a balm to my weariness. Much less surprisingly, he could not maintain consciousness for long, and his eyes fluttered closed. His hand grasped at mine for comfort, and I took it while he slept.

My mind abuzz with conflicting thoughts, slumber stayed far from me. What did it mean to find those eyes now? But I already knew, didn't I? That inexorable draw. Shaking my head to clear it, I told myself it couldn't be possible. Not again. Not like this. Fate certainly had a cruel sense of timing.

Chapter 3

84 years ago

With all my strength, I drew in my goddess's power. Channeling it through my hands and outward, I formed a protective bubble of the Moon's light around me. Not a moment too soon. Dragon fire seared over the edges, lapping at the straining shield. The Moon wavered, and I squeezed my eyes shut, heart pounding.

The Red Dragon's rage burned as hot as the fire he breathed. The flames dissipated just before my shield collapsed, and so did the last of his strength. He crumpled back against the Tree, panting. The trunk groaned as it bent away from him. Roots lifted from the ground, rolling him outward so that he no longer made direct contact. He offered no resistance, staring blankly at the limbs thrashing over his head.

Taking a moment to regain my bearings and douse the fear, I went to his side. As I kneeled by the exhausted drake, the Great Tree's leaves rustled with agitation. I laid a gentle hand on the nearest root, sending soothing energy into the bark. Understandable, that my long-suffering ancestor would be upset at the proximity of such destructive flames. Normal forest fires it could weather without issue; we'd endured some intense blazes together over the centuries. Dragon fire was an entirely different threat. After a moment, an answering hum of acceptance caressed my palm.

Trees I understood, but how did one mollify a traumatized drake? "Forgive me, please. I did not mean to upset you, I—"

"Be still," he snarled. His hands shook.

The way my heart clenched at the haunted look on his face surprised me, despite the knowledge granted by my brief kiss. Knowledge that disoriented and troubled me beyond his agonized past.

The extreme rarity of gaining two soulmates was enough

to make me question my sanity. Perhaps I would never meet the person with the sky blue eyes from my vision. The very idea of having a *drake* as a soulmate was absurd. Impossible! Not once, in all of our extensive histories, had such a wild bond occurred. And yet, I could not deny the snare of his spirit. It slithered through the interstices of my being like a constricting serpent. Beautiful, deadly, and wrapped with impenetrable strength around my very soul. Crow!

I cast aside my concerns to tend to my patient. Ever so softly, I sang gentle melodies of wind and night. Eventually, his eyes closed and he fell into a heavy, fitful sleep. I kept up my song until the tremors stopped. The Tree succumbed to my pleas and gathered him back into its roots, and I covered him with blankets once more.

Upon waking with the dawn, he begrudgingly accepted my offer of venison.

"I prefer to hunt my own prey." The way he said it chilled me, thinking of the village.

He bit directly into the deer femur, cracking it in half with no visible effort. I ducked into my bower while he ate. No need to imprint more images of those teeth tearing into flesh. While inside, I threw on a light linen shift. Perhaps less nudity would appease my spiky patient.

When I emerged, the Red Dragon had also clothed himself anew. Shadows drawn into solid black garments created a thousand burning questions in me. My fingers itched to touch the clothing and determine if it truly held the texture of the fabrics it appeared to be. He wore an unadorned, sleeveless leather tunic over a wool shirt, leather trousers, and soft boots held in place with crisscrossed straps. The boots forced his feet into a decidedly un-draconic shape; an odd affectation.

I brushed my hands across my skirt and sat near him. "How do you prefer to be addressed?"

He propped himself up on his elbows. All the better to glare at me. "Rafael will suffice." The elvish name and the lack of honorific surprised me.

"What do you call yourself in your language?"

A glimmer of something like amusement lit his eyes. He said a perplexing combination of syllables. I caught mostly sibilants and a confusion of vowels. My ears twitched, trying to discern the individual sounds. Part of it dropped below even the range of my sensitive hearing. I hadn't known that was possible.

"I apologize, I... I did not understand that. Will you repeat it, slower?"

He said it again, dragging out the name, something like "*Jxssdfynn.*"

My traitorous ears flattened and my cheeks flushed hot. I'd never been utterly incapable of comprehending a spoken word. "I ah... I still cannot... May I call you 'Jax'?"

He snorted. "You may not."

I huffed, but conceded the point. "Very well then, Rafael, may I ask how you ended up all the way out here? My people thought you'd passed into legend long ago."

He stretched, displaying an impressive reach, and examined his talons. "Byxldurr thought to claim me. I disagreed."

"The other drake you fought?" My ears twitched in fascination, trying to capture the sounds.

He rumbled assent.

"What do you mean, 'claim'?" I wished I'd attempted to learn about drake customs before all of this landed in my lap.

Rafael regarded me for a moment before answering. "We claim mates for power and martial alliance."

"Ah, and you did not wish to be claimed. Hence that very loud battle." It certainly ranked as the worst romantic rejection I'd ever heard. Who exactly was the War Crow, and why had Rafael reacted so poorly? A myriad of questions crowded my mind, most of them invasive.

"Nor have I ever," he snorted.

That sentiment echoed something I'd discovered with the kiss. Despite his great age and all that amassed power, the mighty

Red Dragon was alone, and had always been.

"What do you call yourself?" His deep voice dispelled my thoughts.

I blinked. "Cúraniel, of the Crescent Moon." I hadn't expected him to care.

"You wear no lineage marker, Cúraniel, of the Crescent Moon." His eyes were sharp, and I tugged at the place where the talisman earring had once adorned my ear. "You have the look of Maelial about you."

"You know far more of our ways than I do of yours." Given how many Talithiri elves had similar coloration, his ability to pick out my exact family line impressed me. What else did he know? "Yes, I was of that lineage, though I broke with it long ago. I find elvish society… stifling."

His gaze slid over my body, to my bare feet, and back to my face. "Indeed."

"You are almost pleasant when you aren't trying to kill me." I arched a brow at him.

"I may yet." His conversational tone made me laugh in spite of myself. He watched my face, a corner of his mouth quirking ever so slightly. "Your lack of fear is… hrrm, refreshing."

"Hard to be afraid of someone after you've been up to your elbows in their guts," I said, and his eyes glittered.

Pressure on my throat woke me. I'd nestled into the roots near Rafael to sleep, wishing to remain close in the event he took an unexpected turn. Not uncommon, for those patients who'd undergone extensive physical trauma. Such healing depleted the body's reserves in ways that did not always make themselves known immediately.

Rafael did indeed take a turn, though in a direction I did not anticipate. Moonlight bathed him in silver as he loomed over me, with his hand at my throat. The points of his talons pricked just at the arterial pulse on either side of my neck. No hint of regard showed in those burning eyes, in that cruel mask of a face.

I should have been afraid. Or angry, at the very least, to go through this a second time. Instead, the heat of his palm on the tender flesh of my throat spread through me. My lips parted with my quickening breath.

His eyes flickered, the press of his talons relenting ever so slightly. '*What have you done?*' The words landed in my mind, laced with conflicted emotion. A desire to understand warred with resentment.

'*You feel it, too,*' I whispered back, internally.

The drake snatched his hand back, shaking it as if stung. His walls snapped into place, shutting me out. When he turned away, it left me strangely cold. I wanted to reach for him, but decided not to press.

Eventually, I settled into a fitful sleep. Rafael took his leave during my slumber. It shouldn't have been possible. I'd gauged him as needing at least another week of convalescence, based on his rate of recovery. Ideally, an entire moon's worth.

My unusual patient left no trace of his presence apart from the scars on the land. When I visited the battle site a few days later, the tattered remains of cloth, armor, shed scales, and feathers were all gone. Not even a single drop of blood remained hidden under a blackened leaf. How had he done all of that so quietly? No sign of the War Crow's corpse, either, but the sluagh may have finally worked up their courage to feast. The entire experience held a surreal quality.

Only a worrying ache in my heart remained. If I concentrated, I felt a tug in the direction he'd gone. The vision said I would surely see the Red Dragon again someday. Had I saved him only to speed the ruin of my people? Had I put my villagers in mortal danger? The thoughts chilled me, and the Night Mother offered no comfort.

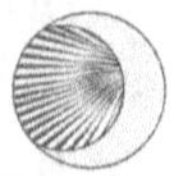

Moons passed, then a year. Whatever lay between us stretched thin, and my spirit dwindled with it. I found it harder and harder to draw on my power. Just as I finally made peace with the unrequited pull on my heart, Rafael reappeared. The forest murmured uneasily, halite ring chiming in alarm as I spied him emerging from the tree line on a sunny afternoon.

I slid off my perch on a root, setting aside the herbs I'd been grinding with my mortar and pestle. Poultices for the villagers made a neat row beside me. No telling when I'd be able to deliver them, now.

The Red Dragon strode with purpose up the slope toward the Great Tree. Toward me. No hint of previous injury hitched his step. Even from the top of the hill, the stiff set of his broad shoulders communicated annoyance.

My heart sped up, anxious over his intent. And for… other reasons. Gods, the way he *moved*. Like a panther; all rippling, predatory grace. I'd never seen such a big man move like that. Every instinct told me to run, to hide, warring with the fascination rooting me to the spot. His hair was flame, and his eyes flickered yellow-orange warning. I rubbed my tingling arms.

With no greeting whatsoever, he shoved an ancient elvish scroll in my face, unrolling it and tapping a single word with a long talon. I took it from him and read over the text. No direct contemporary translation existed for that word, as the cultural practice it referenced had died out thousands of years ago. Just before I'd left elvish civilization.

When he'd recognized my former lineage, he must have understood my age. Last true scion of the family, I was only three generations removed from my ancestral stars—and one of the few remaining who would recall such a thing. I got the distinct sense that not much escaped his burning gaze.

I gave him the best approximation I could; essentially 'the honor of self-sacrifice to preserve tradition.' It described a courtly dance popular when I was still in my youthful serving years, but had fallen from favor as I reached majority. He nodded once and made no move to take back the scroll.

"Good," he said.

"Good? Shall we try, 'you have my thanks, Cúraniel'?" I mimicked his bass growl as best I could. "Or 'I appreciate your invaluable help'? Perhaps 'you are amazing for saving my life and I've returned to sing your praises'?" I bit my lip with the belated realization that my sass might get me killed.

He merely arched one of those pointed brows. At least he was acting civil. More or less.

"Right. *Good.* Where did you find this scroll?" From the patina of its case and the texture of the parchment, it must be the original. Priceless to my people.

"You would not like the answer."

No doubting the truth of his words.

"Did you have a particular interest in ancient elvish dance?"

Rafael's lip curled in a sneer. "It is a tactical manual. Your supposed 'dance' describes a cavalry maneuver, couched in typical elvish fancy." He did not add 'you fucking fool,' but his tone heavily implied it.

I blinked, examining the page again from a different perspective. My ears flushed. Oh.

He snorted, the arrogant blighter. "Keep it. I have no further use for it."

"Thank you. I think?"

He turned to leave, and I decided to take a chance. Why, exactly, did I want this villain to remain in my presence? I hushed my unquiet mind.

"Are you a collector of linguistic knowledge, or is your focus only upon war?"

Rafael paused, looking over his shoulder and arching that imperious brow again.

"I suppose herbalism may bore you, but I have some very old and rare tomes in my bower. They are written in this same iteration of elvish." I'd painstakingly copied them into my own journals for study and annotation, so I'd suffer no loss if he did not return them.

That got his attention. "Show me."

This was a man well acquainted with issuing commands and having those commands obeyed without question. And here he was, trading reading materials with me in the most grating possible way.

Closing my mouth on my irritation, I ducked inside the Tree. The trunk slammed shut behind me, refusing admittance to the Dragon. No amount of wheedling or cajoling would change its stance. It rustled at me defiantly. Defeated, I quit arguing, and the Tree relaxed, allowing me to emerge with the books in tow. Thankfully, Rafael remained impassive in the face of the Tree's insult.

Given his interest in language, it was no wonder that he'd fixated on ancient elvish. We guarded most of these works with zeal, and very few ever left our walled cities. My books held no cultural secrets, and I believed in sharing medicinal knowledge. Perhaps they would help us establish some kind of peace.

He accepted the tomes and opened one, eyes flitting rapidly down the page. Flipping through first one, then the other, he made a satisfied noise and stowed them in the satchel where the scroll had rested. I waited in vain for his recognition of my gift.

"Well? Are you going to thank me?"

His pupils thinned to a knife edge. "I would not offer such insult."

"Insult? Why would I be insulted?" My ears twitched with my confusion.

After a moment's consideration, a faint, catlike smile tugged at the corner of his mouth. "Hrrm, giving thanks is a show of weakness. How very elvish, placing your customs as the standard while knowing nothing of mine." The smile took on an edge.

"Interesting, to select *me* as your cultural ambassador."

I exhaled through my nose, unsure if I should be amused or wary. "I seem to have little choice in the matter. You are the only drake I've ever met, and I didn't invite you here. What is the protocol for receiving a gift?"

Gratitude played such a huge role among elves that we devoted our entire adolescence to serving our elders as thanks for their wisdom and teaching. The stark difference fascinated me.

"We accept tribute as our due, an acknowledgement of our strength."

That explained much. "Do you expect tribute from me? Even after I healed you?"

He tilted his head, eyes glittering with a sudden intensity. "You won that battle."

I considered his word choice. "A battle, was it? Is that how you hear everything, through the drums of war?"

Rafael turned his palms over, one at a time. The elegance of the motion captivated me. "There is battle and battle. Not all are won with might." His words followed the same measured deliberation as his movements. "Shall I instead view the world through medicine? I am hardly suited." Fingers undulating, his talons flashed in the sun.

I laughed. "No, I suppose not. None of your legends mentioned a healer's skill, though you did impressive work on yourself once you decided to cooperate."

"Legends." He snorted. "At least you did not ask if I dye my hair with the blood of kings."

"Oh, is it virgins? No? Now I am disappointed," I teased. "Truthfully, I think it rather obvious from the color of your scales."

"You are smarter than you look." He grinned wickedly, and I exclaimed in mock offense.

"You are a rude fucking blighter!" I tried to bite back the words the moment they left my mouth. Too casual, too complacent! In the rhythm of the banter, I'd forgotten who Rafael truly was.

He growled, low in his chest. "You are a bold little thing."

It had an immediate, unwarranted effect on my body. I found myself nose-to-sternum with him, close enough to feel his heat, and cricked my neck to look him in the eye. By my estimation, he outweighed me by at least a factor of three. In steely, solid muscle. My breath hitched for a moment.

"So I have been told." I held his eyes longer than comfort allowed, before he rumbled acknowledgement.

"You entertain me, Cúraniel. I shall return your books. Eventually."

With a contorted flex of his shoulders, huge leathern wings erupted from his back, red as his hair. Somehow, his clothing remained intact; perhaps an effect of being hewn from shadows? Before I could ask, he turned, took two long steps to the left, and made a great leap over the sheer side of the hill. I rushed to the edge to see him give those wings a mighty flap, and he disappeared rapidly into the blue sky.

That initial conversation about language sparked Rafael's erratic pattern of visits. A scant week later, he returned with a new stack of books in tow. The Great Tree still refused him access to the bower, which he took in stride. He settled across from me on the roots, his hair cooled to red and his viperine eyes bright blue. The summer breeze caressed us both as I teased him about talking to elves instead of eating them.

"You have changed my estimation of your people," he said, perking my ears. "I shall exclude them from my feeding in the future."

I blinked, unsure of my response. He seemed sincere, but I had a hard time reading his facial expressions.

"Solely to preserve knowledge," he added, with the barest hint of his catlike smile, hands to his heart.

I swallowed. "Have you eaten elves in the past?"

Rafael leaned forward and caught my chin with a talon tip. I fought the urge to writhe like a fish on a line. His lips parted, showing off jagged teeth.

"Many elves."

An involuntary tremor ran through me. Fear, with an unexpected surge of lust following close on the tips of its ears. What the fuck was wrong with me?

The Dragon caught the change, nostrils flaring as he inhaled. He drew me closer, and my skin prickled with anticipation. The walls dropped, a brief tangle of emotions. Push, pull. He closed me out again, releasing me from the talon.

"Calm yourself, Moon Woman." His velvety bass shivered down my spine. The growling undertone did interesting things to my body. "I always keep my word. If it eases your mind, it has been a very long time since I last devoured an elf. Immortal flesh is not to my taste, and your kind is far too sweet."

The anxiety passed, taking the unexpected wave of perverse desire with it. Fixated on the flames dancing in his eyes, I stared. He had such an interesting face. Even the rare, laconic blink of his heavy eyelids was a calculated choice, usually for emphasis.

I rubbed the underside of my chin, trying to wipe away my discomfort. "You are not at all what I expected, oh mighty Red Dragon." Any ancient and powerful being had a certain amount of charisma, but what did it mean for me, to be so charmed by violent overtures?

Rafael sobered, his aura growing spiky again. "What did you expect? A mindless barbarian?"

Yes. "Well, certainly not a book-hoarding Dragon."

"Do elvish warriors create no art, no music, in all their long lives?" He gave me an arch look. Considering his great age, it harmonized that he would fill all of that time with more than just bloodshed.

The tips of my ears heated. "Forgive my ignorance, please. My preconceptions were based in hearsay."

My gaze dropped to the book in my lap. A Lachanaur elf

warrior had penned the tome on spiritual intervention for maladies. Emphasizing Rafael's point. Turning it in my hands, I mulled over his words. The tooled leather binding, though well cared for, had the brittle texture of age. Unadorned on its cover, the illuminated script in the pages remained brilliant. Had Rafael killed for this?

"Preconceptions, hrrm. I did not expect a naked, feral elf woman to drag me stubbornly back from the brink of oblivion." On the surface, it sounded like a jest, but something melancholy in his voice caught my attention. The walls eased again, allowing a trickle of spirit to flow between us.

Wind snagged an errant lock of his hair, streaming it in waves across his face like a bloody slash. Thoughtless, I reached out to tuck it behind his ear. He caught my hand with a growl.

"May I?" I breathed.

He released my hand, eyes wary. Cautious, I brushed the hair back from his face with a feather-light touch. For an instant, he leaned into my hand. An endless chasm of isolation yawned around me; loneliness, touch starvation, despair. He pulled away and closed off again, expression distant and guarded.

"Do you regret meeting me?" I asked. Gods only knew how long he'd kept the rest of the world at a distance.

His eyes, flickering with their otherworldly light, snapped to my face. "I have not yet decided."

"You are, by far, my most interesting patient." I could only imagine Nemohee's reaction to all of this, and longed to speak to þem. My friend had been absent for some time.

"Your courage is either commendable or incredibly foolhardy."

"Probably both," I said.

It seemed to intrigue him, but he said nothing, returning to his book. I opened mine in response. We lapsed into an almost comfortable silence, and the bond hummed between us. Surely he felt it, too. Reading helped to distract me from the urge to move closer. Reason reminded me of what had happened the first time I'd thoughtlessly drifted into his reach. I rubbed my throat and flipped the page.

As twilight dusted the hill and fireflies rose, Rafael paced a short distance away and drew his greatsword. The legend sprang to life. He flowed through forms like water, hypnotic, with almost unnaturally perfect muscle control and flexibility. The knowledge that these very motions had ended countless lives blew in like an ominous cloud. Sighing, I pushed the notions away and allowed myself to appreciate a master at work. Not even the layers of leather and wool could disguise the sculpted body beneath. My thoughts strayed to the memory of my hands on his hot skin, my palms sliding over his impressive musculature.

Crow, I *did* find this razor-tongued blighter attractive. While healing, I could easily turn off that part of my mind—bodies were bodies—but after it was all over? Well. I pressed my thighs together.

"Critiquing my form?" His deep rumble caught me out, and the tips of my ears heated once again. If only he knew.

"Just admiring your skill. I have no head for such things," I called, feeling sheepish. "How are you so flexible?"

"More spinal and shoulder girdle muscles than elves have. Too busy to notice while you were 'up to your elbows in my guts' then?"

The frankness surprised a laugh out of me. "I supposed the occasional presence of wings confers certain advantages. Was that display for me?"

The Dragon huffed. "Do you never practice your craft?" Fireflies drifted around him, lazy on the evening breeze. Sheathing the sword, he approached me. "How do you defend your territory?"

My ears twitched. "The Great Tree shelters me and the forest directs would-be threats away from here. The halite ring provides early warning and a layer of protection from certain fae."

"All this so-called protection. And yet, here I am." He folded arms corded with muscle across a broad chest.

"How could the forest have prevented your crash-landing? Besides, I heard you are no longer eating elves."

His mouth twitched into a possible smirk. Gods, I wished I could check his ears for cues.

"Unacceptable. If I can reach you, others will as well. I will rectify this."

"Are you going to station some of your companions around the hill as a guard?" I imagined a ring of stony-faced dragon people, all facing outward from the Tree.

"I have no companions."

The bare truth of his words struck me like a physical blow. "No companions? No friends at all?"

Rafael snorted. "Hah, *friends*. Do not be absurd." He cloaked it with disdain, but his loneliness threatened to choke me.

"Am I not your friend?" I asked softly. "We have done each other good turns. I enjoy your company, as you seem to enjoy mine. You must have some care for my well-being, otherwise my safety wouldn't matter."

He stared for so long I decided to return the conversation to fighting.

I kept my tone light. "So, are you going to bring me a polearm and shield and force me to learn soldiery?" The very thought of wearing armor made me snicker. "You have strange ways of demonstrating care."

Rafael ignored the comment and eyed me, assessing. "Theory first. Then hand-to-hand. You lack the conditioning for weapons."

My ears drooped in dismay. "Oh gods, you're serious."

Seating himself again on the roots, he produced a journal, quill, and pot of ink from somewhere in his cloak and scratched away. The last fading light transformed the highlights of his mane from deep garnet to brilliant ruby.

"May I braid your hair?" I reached toward him. "The color is captivating."

He leaped to his feet with a snarl, hair and eyes sparking. "What is wrong with you?"

What a bizarre reaction. The rejection stung my pride. "Do

you not find me lovely?" I tried and failed to keep the pout from my voice. Perhaps drakes held a concept of beauty as different from mine as their notions of gratitude.

Rafael looked down his long nose as though I'd asked him to fly me to the moon. "I find you mad."

Chapter 4

Current day

"Death is beauty?" My Talithiri patient signed, hands trembling with fatigue, when he woke again.

The version of the language he used struck me as odd, the shapes his fingers formed slightly different from what I remembered. Though, it was bound to have gone through some changes in all the time I'd been away. His eyes traveled appreciatively over my unclothed body.

"Barely conscious and already flirting. You're going to be trouble." I flicked my ears, but couldn't completely suppress my smile as I tugged his blankets higher. *Oh, definitely trouble.* "Be at ease in your speech. No enemies have followed you here."

"Ah, I would hear it from your lips then." His voice was a weak but warm and melodic baritone. "Is this what Death looks like? Much lovelier than I ever presumed."

He should have been sleeping instead of wasting energy on flirtation. My resolve weakened in the face of his considerable charm. Once I'd washed off the caked blood and grime, starsong wreathed my senses; a distinct, lingering gift of his lineage. Now that he was awake, it rose all around us. Chiming bells echoed faintly, and a sweet flavor caressed my tongue. A gentle glimmer clung to his smooth skin, sparkling along with the delicate scents of sweet pea and memory and night.

My patient coughed and grimaced, cupping his ribcage. The starlight fled.

"You've got quite a bit of damage there," I said drolly.

"I see Death has a snarky sense of humor."

"Death hasn't visited here in a while." The realization that I consciously had to refrain from caressing him made me unreasonably cross. Taking a breath, I relaxed with an effort. How could I have forgotten the potential consequences already?

He smiled again. "Forgive me, beautiful lady. I was ambushed and truly thought I would die from those wounds. I'd thought to follow the river to the estuary and find my companions among the Maraiya, but trees led me here instead. Where are we?"

"Far enough from civilization for you not to worry about it. I am Cúraniel. This hill, the Great Tree upon it, and the surrounding forest is my home." I indicated the general area with a casual hand.

The Tree itself shivered in acknowledgement, a single curling leaf floating down to land beside him. He turned it over in his hands, then looked up in wonder at the behemoth that stretched over us, its wide boughs filtering out most of the sunlight. After a few breaths, his gaze landed back on my face, and that brilliant smile returned.

"Well met, beautiful Cúraniel of the Crescent Moon. I am Celebel Elhalanros." That was a smile accustomed to garnering its owner anything he wanted. It was definitely working on me.

"Of course you are. Now go back to sleep."

Celebel's brow creased, his smile fading. "Have I offended, lady?"

I sighed. "No, not at all. Please forgive my lack of manners. I have been alone here for a very long time and I forget how to be social. You need to rest." I could not tell him the other, more pressing reason for my impatience. Not yet, anyway. "I will watch over your slumber."

It was good enough for Celebel, who was sound asleep again in moments. I brushed his silver-shot black hair from his face and wondered exactly what I was getting myself into. His breath hitched occasionally. I made a note to include some lung-clearing herbs, like trichosanthes fruit and balloon flower root, in his next decoction. Maybe a little ginseng too, for support. I entered the Tree, rummaging in my bower for the medicine while he slept.

★★★★★

The next time Celebel woke, I fed him a nutritious broth. The Tree lent its aid where it could, but he still had a long path to recovery. I brewed more of the blood building-tea as he tipped back the bowl.

"Tell me about yourself," he said between sips, watching me avidly.

"Not much to tell. I grew weary of society and fucked off out here quite some time ago. The solitude suits me." I smiled at him to soften my words.

"But you're a powerful healer, and Talithiri at that!" Celebel's eyes were round as the moon.

"Quite astute, my lord."

"Ssst, ouch, she bites!" He pantomimed pulling an injured hand away and waving it to relive the sting.

I snickered despite myself. Good, he had a sense of humor. Too many elves were overly uptight and self-important.

"Any who reach my hill receive my aid. That is the oath I made to Dûemer in exchange for her blessing. The creek counts." I followed his gaze all the way down the steep trail of kicked up grass and mud to where I'd found him. "You are lucky the birds saw you when they did. You nearly bled out."

"Please give them my thanks as well."

I nodded. Definitely nobility; he had that familiar cadence and formality to his words. Yet, I could sense genuine kindness in him. Lacking in most of the scions of the great lineages.

"Surely there is more to you than merely a beautiful healer all alone on this big hill." He waved at the grassy slope.

I took his pulse again as I considered my words. Stronger, good. "What would you like to know?" I'd been very careful to conceal my presence from society at large. Gratifying to know it had mostly worked.

"What was it about 'society' that tired you?" Celebel scooted up to a position that let him watch me more intently, pressing his back against the twisting roots. I handed him a cup of the blood-building tea. He took a deep swallow without looking at it and nearly spewed it all over his lap. "Phaugh, this is awful! Sorry, I mean no offense, but it is truly vile."

I laughed. "No offense taken. The peony I've cultivated here is quite potent and bitter, especially when combined with cyathula root. Here, let me add some cinnamon and honey to mask it."

He accepted the cup back with a big show of inspecting it from all angles. Dramatically smelling it, then coughing again. He made a stoic face and knocked back the whole thing. I appreciated his lack of gravity. Also unusual for nobility.

"It is good that you are relaxed," I said with a smile.

"Should I be otherwise?" He peered at me with open curiosity.

"Not at all. Only, I've had no critical patients in years. The last one was… very unlike you. Nothing to concern yourself over." Or so I hoped. I kept my thoughts, my heart, tightly guarded.

He accepted my words with a shrug." You have yet to truly reveal anything about yourself."

"Surely you know the name of Maelial." I studied his face carefully for his reaction.

"Of course." Every elf knew Maelial. She had ruled Leyúduin for thousands of years, and her power was legendary. Much more surprising if he didn't know of her.

"She was my grandmother." I kept my expression neutral.

His eyebrows shot up. "Maelial? But that would make you…" He did the math frantically, comically, on his fingers.

"Old as bones."

"It has been *ages* since you left, and not just society. You left the court. *You're* Silfanië's missing sibling! We all thought you lost, surely dead! You were myth long before I was even born." The possibilities practically floated in front of his face. He took a hard look at the braid patterns in my hair. Patterns I no longer had a right to, but still used out of habit. I waited for him to question the use, but he blinked and changed melodies. "Have you truly been out here alone all this time?"

"Most of it, yes." I tried to repress the amusement twitching my ears.

"My arrival must seem a most fortunate break in your solitude." He grasped my hand to his chest with a dramatic sigh.

I grinned at the transparent gesture. His smooth skin warmed my palm, and I resisted the urge to caress him. "Indeed. Though the Tree keeps me company, as well as the occasional visitor or patient. I have my herbs to tend, my books to read, and my meditations on the Night Mother. Never had much need for society."

His ears drooped, crestfallen. Such a flirt.

"I do not mean to diminish the quality of your company," I said. "It has been quite some time since I shared song with another Talithiri."

Mollified, he smiled that dazzling smile again, ears perking. "While I am selfishly grateful that you did not follow the elders' melody, why did you decide not to become a tree?"

My own mother had grown into a graceful willow well before I left the court. The Great Tree rustled around us, and three more leaves spiraled lazily down.

I shrugged. "My solitude has perhaps kept me from suffering the same fatigue of this life. I like it here, and the stars haven't yet called me home. So, I continue to learn and grow." And hopefully find some answers about what games fate played with me.

His eyes widened, and a beatific smile split his face. "I have happened upon a fine lost treasure."

I snorted. "Only if you consider me a shiny bauble to possess," *not unlike certain others*.

"Who could be so presumptuous? What a failure of our society to drive you away. Was there a particular event that sparked your exodus? Does this mean you have renounced your family name? Your lineage? Gods, you could have claimed the throne. You could still!" The thought clearly distressed him. "Forgive me for prying, but you are simply fascinating to me."

I nodded to show that I did not mind the barrage of questions. Rare was the chance to explain my position, and his reaction would tell me much about his character.

"It was more of a string of smaller events that built up over time to a larger picture that I did not care for. I have never harmonized well with the structure of the court, but it goes far beyond my preferences. The arrogance, the ethnocentricity, the utter unwillingness to accept the untamable or help anyone outside of our high walls. We are incurably inflexible, and it is our downfall. This was a slow-growing realization for me.

"One day, the council refused to acknowledge a desperate family of kobolds seeking aid for a poisoned child. The kobolds knew enough to find our general vicinity, and I thought it absurd that we must remain hidden in our lofty towers. I broke the law, revealing our location by leaving the walls to help that poor family. Had quite the row about it in the grand hall." I paused, studying Celebel's face. His brow knit, eyes shining. Good.

"I simply could not bear it any longer and took my leave, breaking my lineage rather than accepting banishment. I wish them no ill will, but I have no desire to be a part of such ignorance." The contention of my departure cast a pall on me, and I shrugged it away. "Yes, I have renounced my name. Not out of shame or pettiness; simply a desire to truly separate myself from the court. I'll happily heal our people if they reach me, but I have no wish to rejoin society or claim any status."

He shook his head in bemused wonder. Celebel took my hand again, raising it to his lips, and kissed it reverently. I rather enjoyed the sudden tone shift.

Chapter 5

75 years ago

Wrongness permeated my connection to Rafael, lashing chaotic and wild. The moment he emerged from the trees, I skidded down to the base of the hill, halting just out of reach. Dried blood and gore caked him from ear to toe. The stench of rot clung to him in a noxious cloud, gagging me. His eyes shone brilliantly and disturbingly blank through the curtain of clotted filth. None of the blood appeared to be his.

Murder. The thought pulsed in my mind, but I could not determine a true sense from him. That much blood, though. Someone had surely died.

"What happened?" I hesitated to touch him, revulsion mingling with dread. "Rafael, what have you done?"

Rather than answer, a shudder ran through him. In a single, vicious motion, he raked himself from shoulder to wrist, rending his flesh with his own talons. I cried out. His talons flashed again, cutting to the bone this time. Foolishly in my panic, I threw my arms around him, fully aware that I lacked the strength to restrain him. Aware of the danger. And yet, the urge to be as physically close to him as possible overcame my good sense. His blood splashed and burned holes in my skin. I bit my tongue to keep from whimpering and held tighter.

He slumped against me. I struggled to lower him to the ground without letting him fall. I couldn't tell if he was unconscious or merely still, but I murmured comfort to him all the same. He curled around me, and I cradled his head in my lap. The moon set, and I drifted, lulled by his heat despite the cloying odor of decaying blood.

A movement snapped me to wakefulness. Rafael crouched a short distance away, a stony expression hewn on his face. At least the pull on my heart relaxed, no longer fluttering like a wounded bird. Hollow exhaustion took its place. I wanted to approach him, but his energy bristled with thorns. I had witnessed him, yet again, at his most vulnerable. Yet, he had trusted me to take care of him in that state. I shelved my probing questions for later.

Wrinkling my nose, I stood and held a hand out. "Let's get you cleaned up."

He glared at my hand for a moment before rising. Without waiting for him to follow, I headed to the creek, peeling off my stained linen dress as I went. He moved in perfect silence, appearing at my elbow. It unnerved me. No one should be able to creep up on an elf that way. Especially not a person of his size.

I rinsed and wrung out my dress, holding it to him. Rafael narrowed his eyes and snatched the damp cloth from my hands. I sighed as he scrubbed his face with my ruined dress. He kneeled on the bank, dipping the linen into the creek to cleanse it when he finished.

"Shall I wash your hair for you? Please?" I sat beside him, keeping my tone neutral and movements slow. "I can feel your fatigue."

His hands came to rest on his knees, but he did not look my way.

"I am going to touch your shoulder, if that is acceptable."

His head inclined a fraction, and I laid a cautious hand on him. The Dragon sighed like a forge bellows and relaxed all at once. To my surprise, he turned and laid his head again on my lap, settling on his back. I cupped the cool water in my hands and cautiously rinsed his matted mane.

When a droplet splashed on his face, he winced and trembled, squeezing his eyes shut. Trauma with water? I paused until he calmed and proceeded with more caution. Little by little, I teased the tangles of grime from his hair, luxuriating in the chance to run my fingers through it. With strands nearly as thick as a horse's mane, it was softer than it looked. Resisting the temptation to braid it made me grind my teeth, but that was an unearned intimacy. The creek ran murky by the time I finished.

"Come, rest in the bower." I laid a gentle hand on his forehead. Perhaps I could wrap him in a blanket to keep the gore from contaminating my home.

Rafael got to his feet. His eyes cleared, but still held a haunted quality. A shimmer of heat passed over him and burned away the lingering filth. Somehow, his clothing did not ignite. My ears twitched with surprise. If he could have done that at any time, had he wanted me to touch him but lacked the ability to ask?

For the first time, the Great Tree opened to him without protest. It merely rustled a few leaves at his approach. Interesting that it took pity on him in this state.

"You may sleep on my pallet. I changed the rushes just a few days ago."

He lingered in the entrance, nostrils flaring, eyes fixed on a single point. I followed his gaze to the bundles of herbs drying on a line. Lavender, calendula, thyme…? His pupils thinned. I grabbed the whole string of herbs and tossed them outside.

That seemed to appease the Dragon, and he crept along the far side of the bower as I discreetly warmed a little aromatic resin to help cover the scent of the offending herbs. He arranged himself sitting upright with his back to the wall, taking in my belongings with pointed suspicion. As far from the offered place of rest as he could get.

"Why will you not take the pallet? Have you never slept in a proper bed?"

Offense animated him. His brows shot up, hair sparking into furious, liquid flame. "You live in a tree and you dare insinuate that *I* am the barbarian?" His deep voice reverberated in the small space.

"I'm not insinuating anything! You're so precious with any form of personal information that I have to make up my own stories!" I frowned mightily. He must have been feeling better to give me the usual sass. "You and your mysterious ways."

Rafael made a strange coughing, almost choking sound far down in his chest. It took me a few heartbeats to realize he was laughing. So he *could* laugh!

He stretched to untie the crisscrossed straps of his boots. The way he unfolded and stretched those draconic feet fascinated me. Silvery-white talons flashed in the dim glow of the faerie lights. Some deep part of my mind murmured that I should probably feel more threatened, muttering uneasily about all that blood, and allowing a killer into my haven. Mentally, I touched the bond anchored within, and it soothed away the anxiety.

"Why do you contort your feet into those boots? It looks so uncomfortable."

"Habit. When I was young, it was advantageous to hide my more draconic features. Now, foes tend to forget I have these." He rapped the talons of his feet on the hard-packed earth floor. "There, a tribute; one 'mystery' solved." That last bit was not without a tinge of sarcasm, but the corner of his mouth quirked. "As though elves are not equally precious with their cultural practices."

"Oh, indeed!"

He gave me a sidelong look. "Do you actually fuck the trees?"

Startled, I barked out a laugh. "The gestational groves? No, we don't fuck the trees." I wiped a tear of mirth away. "The pregnancy is planted through ceremony. The would-be parents couple beneath the trunk in the gestation chamber. Their combined essence and spirit forms a seed. It takes a soulbond to create a viable one. If the Tree accepts it, the parents emerge and the Tree will gestate their child. Usually takes about a century to produce an infant."

"Hrrm. So they fuck *inside* the trees. *Vastly* different." That was a definite spark of amusement in his eyes.

"To put it entirely too simplistically, yes, they fuck inside the tree. Of course, we can gestate children in our own wombs as well, but it's fallen out of favor. Much safer with the trees."

"Are the groves for convenience?" He plucked one of my illustrations from the wall, a view of the hill and Great Tree from the valley floor, and studied it.

"The groves are necessary for support. They bolster each other through their roots and a special mycelium that connects them and shares nutrients. Does that answer your question?"

Rafael shrugged, returning my drawing to its place. Remarkably delicate, considering what I'd just witnessed from those long, wicked talons. Something about the precise use of his hands warmed me uncomfortably.

"Explains why your people are so attached to trees. I could only find flowery sagas of tree-praise, never concrete reasons." He slunk over beside me, settling on his side, with his back yet again toward the wall of the trunk. Was this his strange way of flirting?

"We also become trees once we've lived long enough. As this Tree did. As I likely will someday." I waved at the bower. "Wouldn't you rather unpin your cloak?"

"Stop pushing me, Cúraniel. And keep your hands to yourself."

I snatched back the hand that I'd been slowly snaking across the blankets. "May I lie down next to you?" Fluttering my eyelashes at him never had an effect, but I tried it regardless.

"No."

When I awakened in the morning to the bright sun peeking through the open trunk of the Tree, I'd curled up beside his head. Or rather, where it had lain. He was gone.

Nemohee finally showed up, a season after I last saw the Dragon. In typical Nemohee fashion, þey came loaded with whiskey and gossip. Þeir long, wild hair, white blonde at the roots and deep auburn at the tips, streamed behind þem like a flag as þey rode up the southern slope. Machi whickered a greeting, and I patted the blue roan stallion's soft nose.

"Good old Machi. You've got, what, a century behind you

now?"

"He'll outlive us all, you mark it. Best elvish horse ever bred." Nem slid off, flashing pointed canine teeth in a face as pale as mine. Together, we tended to the horse's needs first, removing tack and rubbing him down, then we retired. Kicking off þeir boots, my friend followed me inside my bower.

"Now, where've you got off to? Tumbling some poor unwitting creatures and slurping up their blood when they aren't looking?" I teased, lapsing comfortably into hillspeech.

"Blighting jays must've dropped my last letter in the creek." Þey tossed þeir sword belt aside, flopped onto my pallet, and uncorked the whiskey bottle with þeir teeth. With great ceremony, I produced a pair of earthenware cups carved in the form of mulberry leaves. Þey poured, careful not to splash any of the amber liquid over the sides.

"I've gone and got a soulmate, if you can believe it." Nem's stentorian contralto boomed in the small space. Þey'd already tossed back the first draught.

"You? *You?* I thought you didn't believe in such things your own self." I laughed, taking a cup from my friend and sitting on the stool at my workbench. "What irony brings us both such a curse at the same old time?"

Nemohee sat bolt upright, faerie lights floating around þeir head like a halo. "What shite are you spitting?"

I tipped my cup back, savoring the bite, and waved þem down. "Nah, nah, nah. You first!"

If anyone could hear of my situation without judgment, it would be Nemohee. With one vampiric leanan sidhe parent and one Lachanaur elf parent, my friend understood what it meant to be an outcast. Though þey leaned more fully into the Lachanaur bloodline, elvish society had never fully accepted þem. The impenetrable underhill courts of the sidhe had their own exclusionary ways. As far as I knew, þey'd never entered the halls of the fae.

Nemohee's silver eyes flashed with suspicion for a moment,

swirling whiskey in þeir mouth as þey considered my reaction. "All riiiight. Mine's name of Cael. Minor nobility, if you believe it. Big arms, you ken I like the muckle arms. Astolar, too, got a blondie."

"Big blonde muscles, eh? Does he fight?"

"You ken he does," þey laughed. "No soulmate of mine's gonna be a weak-arm shite. No offence. If he can't wrestle me down, I'm not taking him."

"None taken. I'm perfectly content to live my life a weak-arm shite." Perhaps Rafael would wish it otherwise. The thought made me snort.

"All right, rattle out those words. Ah can see them swirling around in there. Who's this soulmate of yours?" Þeir green leathers creaked as þey leaned forward.

"Nah, nah, your candle still burns. We don't need to light mine yet. How did you meet?"

"Not much of a telling. Our paths crossed during his travel to an outpost 'round the edges of Velúara. Apparently, they've been having some problems with elves going missing in those parts. I did an assist on the scouting and we bided together for a time. We've met up since. Cheerful sort. Easy. Dare I say I'm actually feeling… happy?"

Easy. What must that be like? "Brightens my heart to hear it." Nem's eyes sharpened, and I sighed in resignation. "All right, quit burning holes in me. Do you recall that drake I healed a while back?"

"Big Red Menace, aye. He's still about?"

"He comes and goes, as always." I took a deep breath, but before I could speak, Nemohee cut in.

"If you're about to tell me that your soulmate is a fecking shapeshifting *dragon*, don't." Þeir muscular shoulders flexed, shorter ears flattening.

"Nem—"

"Nem nothing. You're courting death and you ken it."

I rubbed my eyes. "As though I have any choice in the matter. Still, just a strong suspicion at this stage."

"The fecking God of fecking Carnage, his own self. Surprised he hasn't left a blood trail. Crow, I reckon it's a boon he hasn't eaten you yet."

"Ease off. I'd be thoroughly dead by now if he were so inclined." Understandable concern, and I loved my friend all the more for it. "Why do you think he continues to seek me out?"

Nemohee tapped þeir lips thoughtfully. "Mmm, a conundrum. Never knew elves could have non-elvish soulmates apart from some of the greater fae, or humans. Does he at least have some elvish parentage somewhere?"

"Not that I ken. He's chary about all of it. I'd have a much gentler melody if we could simply speak about it." I shook my head. "Loves his secrets and not his emotions, that one. Rage comes easily, guardian for the melancholy just beneath. Everything else is difficult."

My friend's eyebrows waggled suggestively. "Angsty one, eh? What's he like in a tumble?"

I groaned, plucking at the tips of my ears. "No ease there neither. He's closed down harder than a hibernating cicada's song. Some great soul wound holds him hostage. Betimes, he'll aaalmost reach out, then he snaps back like I'm fit to bite."

"You must be fit to bite through this here Tree." Nemohee held out the bottle, and I refreshed my drink.

"I could gnaw down the entire forest at this rate."

"Aye, I'll drink to that. Imagine, the two of us, with fecking *soulmates!*" Þeir boisterous laugh caught me and before long, we were both rolling in mirth. We clinked our cups together and knocked back the contents.

"When d'you plan to introduce me to this mysterious menace of yours?"

"Soon as you bring your big blondie 'round these parts. Nah, don't follow that melody," I added quickly, at the mischievous glint in Nemohee's eyes. "Rafael is unpredictable at best. I don't know that you'd be safe."

"Let the scaly blighter just try and tussle me." Þey made a

show of flexing þeir arms hard enough to strain the leather of þeir sleeveless tunic.

"You've more muscle than sense, Nem."

Nemohee struck an absurd pose, hopping to þeir feet and flexing as hard as þey could. I threw my empty cup at þem, followed by a peal of laughter.

Chapter 6
Current day

As the days passed and Celebel grew stronger, so did his hold over me. His easy comfort in my presence encouraged me to relax. With his clothes ruined, I dressed him in soft, undyed linens I kept stashed away for just that purpose. He had to beg a length of rope to knot about his waist to keep the trousers up on his slim hips, and teased me with outrageous "accidental" slips.

I found simple joy in combing and braiding his lovely hair after washing it; any excuse to touch him, really. The comfort and sense of safety that came with being in another elf's presence breathed a lightness into me that no amount of foreboding could ruin. Hardly feeling in control of myself at all, I pushed the coming storm to the back of my mind.

Resting his head on my thighs as he reclined, I wove intricate patterns into those moon-kissed, inky tresses, braiding in small twinkling shells. The reminders of the sea suited him well.

"How did you get these streaks?" I idly twirled an argent lock in my fingers. "Were you born with them? My half-sister's hair is a fine shining curtain like this, but she has no striping. I suppose you know her."

He nodded. Eyes closed in bliss, he answered lazily. "No, the streaks were not present at my birth. I received them in battle not so long ago."

"Battle!" I'd heard some wild stories over the years, but never anything like that. My own hair shivered with discomfort at the thought. Opening up the sensitive core of the hair seemed painful.

"Mmm, keep scratching my scalp," he purred. "During the Last War—what we thought would be the last war at any rate—Leyúduin was washed away in a tremendous outpouring of power. The backlash caught me, and it partially stripped my hair. Left me in a terrible state for a time. I could have used your aid then as well."

He'd said it gently, but the last statement hit me hard. I paused my ministrations. Even so removed, I'd heard about the tragic destruction of Leyúduin. Despite my departure, I'd wished no ill upon them, especially not the loss of the gestational grove there, and so much history. Nemohee's news that my half-sister, Silfanië, had fled to safety before the city fell brought a surprising amount of tears.

"I can only imagine what a blow that must have been. So few of our cities remain."

Celebel sobered. "We mourned many beautiful lives that dark day. Lovers, companions, family. My dearest friend lost his own twin brother. Worse, we fear that the catastrophe sparked the awakening of malevolent ancient powers, just as it called these old lands of Rimbaras from their slumber in the sea"

Could that explain Rafael's reappearance? He was irritatingly close-mouthed about his previous location and activities. The Dragon's attention brushed over me again, and I reined in my thoughts, shifting back to the topic. I could barely fathom witnessing such an event, let alone catching the energetic repercussions. The earth had shuddered in violence as the land transformed rapidly over centuries. My little hidden archipelago became a hillscape above the ancient lands I knew from my youth, now covered in a sea of young forest. My respect for Celebel increased.

"You sprouted from a tough burl," I said.

"You could test me on that." He stretched and arched his back, ensuring I could see his willingness to be tested.

"Go back to sleep, Celebel Elhalanros." I laughed to distract myself from my growing desire. Denying the temptation proved increasingly difficult. All the years of tormented frustration made themselves known in an insistent heat between my legs.

"Will you sing me to sleep, my lady?" That brilliant smile again. He knew exactly what he was doing.

As I settled him in to rest, I sang an old nursery song of

our people. I leaned forward to tuck the blankets around him and made the mistake of looking at his face. He watched me intently, lips parted ever so slightly, his breathing rate speeding up. Those full lips invited me to kiss them. I shook the fool notion out of my head, interrupting my song.

"Now you stop that. You're in no state."

His eyes sparkled with mischief. Crow, he caught me.

"My lady, it is impossible not to drink in your voluptuous beauty up close. Skin pale as the moon herself, eyes of deepest sapphire, hair black as a raven's wing. Your scent is intoxicating; lilies and earth after a good rain. Exquisite. I confess, the proximity of your luscious, bared curves fully unspools my senses."

"Save your flattery, Silver Star. I know what I look like. I'll be naked as much as I please in my own home, so do try your best to re-spool your senses," I said with an indulgent laugh. "Call me Cúraniel, please. No need to be so formal. And that," I gestured at the impressive peak in his blankets, "is a common side-effect of healing. You'll recover soon enough."

"Perhaps I will, but what about you?" His voice was pure velvet.

"I am quite capable of handling my own needs." I tossed my thick braid back over my shoulder to keep his questing fingers away from it.

"I should very much like to see that."

The imp! I couldn't decide if I wanted to slap him or kiss him. "Everyone at court falls at your feet, don't they?"

His brow furrowed. Damn, even his pout was attractive. "I am not so frivolous, lady."

I arched an eyebrow. "Regardless, you need rest more than you need to slake your lust. Sleep now." I touched the space between his brows with a gentle fingertip and willed him to slumber.

★☆★☆★

When Celebel gained the strength to walk, he requested a full tour of my bower. His wide-eyed exploration was absurdly endearing. I also didn't mind the opportunity to observe his body. He had the shapeliest buttocks I'd ever seen on a man.

Stepping through the opening in the Tree's trunk, he exclaimed with wonder. "It is even larger on the inside!"

I showed him how the trunk could open and close at will, and he practically clapped with delight. He fawned over the calcite 'windows,' casting their colorful glow over the interior. As his lineage hailed from the grandeur of Velúara, his reactions charmed me beyond reason.

"They are both like and unlike our witchlights." He gazed at the faerie lights dancing like tiny stars above our heads.

"They are remnants of an ancient precursor to will o' the wisps and have been here longer than I know. It's been quite some time since I've summoned a witchlight thanks to these. I hardly remember how at this point."

"I doubt that very much. It's quite simple." He flicked a small witchlight into being above his index finger and sent it floating over to my face.

I extinguished it with a gentle breath and then flicked my own over to him. He swept it onto his brow like a diadem. I grinned, and he answered with a broad smile.

Celebel admired the various drawings and tapestries hung from the trunk walls. A shiver of dread ran down my spine at a thoughtful purse of his lips as his gaze landed on a portrait of the Dragon. *Please, I'm not ready.* I murmured a small prayer of thanks to the Night Mother when he moved on without comment. He studied the books and scrolls lining every crevice and stacked haphazardly along the floor.

"This is quite a collection on herbology, but I must confess my surprise to see treatises on swordplay and fighting tactics. You hardly seem the type, or am I mistaken?" He thumbed the cover of one of the aforementioned tomes.

"I'll happily accept any books that come my way," I said,

airily redirecting his attention. It was mostly true. "I prefer to be widely read."

Celebel's favorite item was my workbench, formed of inwardly grown roots and strung with drying herbs and healing implements. Trailing his fingers across the surface, he examined it from every angle.

My heart stuttered again when he lingered over the red rose perched in its carved moonstone bottle. What would happen if he touched a petal? He merely sniffed it instead, and I could breathe again.

"This looks and smells remarkably like the Sirelon rose, only the color is wrong. Where did you find it?"

"A-a friend brings them to me. They are charmed to stay fresh." Thankfully, he didn't seem to catch the hitch in my voice, smiling and moving on. The enthusiasm he showed warmed my heart.

"This Tree is a marvel! I cannot seem to pinpoint its type, however. Strange, most like a great oak, but with the essence of dawn redwood. You said it was one of your own ancestors?"

The Great Tree rustled an acknowledgement.

"It is, and it has no like." I ran my fingers lovingly over the bark. "This Tree has provided comfort and shelter to many, and its roots assist me in keeping my patients stable while I work on them. It was the Tree itself who called me here."

"I've never before met one of the transformed ancients that yet remained alert in any capacity. And to think, one of your very own! No wonder at all that this place feels so comforting. It reminds me of my own birth tree."

I offered him a cup of the cool water, decanted from the Tree's roots, and he accepted it gratefully.

"Very helpful on a hill that remembers when it was once a mountain," I said, and his eyes sparkled with glee.

"Brilliant! Truly a marvel," he reiterated. "It may be very different from our splendid palaces, but the comfort and consideration here—living and working as one with this magnificent

Tree—oh, it is unmatched."

"I quite agree."

He looked around, appraising. "The Tree is much older than the surrounding lands, and the ground here lacks the salts of the valley floor. I've never seen it marked on a map. How have you kept it so hidden all this time? I've worked extensively with our Maraiya kindred in their dives for artifacts, and they've never mentioned you, either."

"When everything else was underwater, this little island wasn't much to bother with. It took longer than I expected for humans to trickle in and settle around here, even after the ocean receded. When the forest seeded, I simply asked those trees to redirect anyone wishing to cause me trouble. It… mostly worked."

"You've been here that long?"

I answered with a smile. After a moment, he nodded thoughtfully.

"I'm surprised that I'm not swatting away faeries. Normally, the minor fae are drawn to the light of my hair, and they delight in tormenting me. A tree this old must be crawling with them. Where have they all gone?"

I laughed. "We have an understanding. The fae are not to interfere when I have a patient. They'll return when I let them know we are finished with your healing. There are numerous pixies, sprites, and pookas about. The creek even has a small naiad. And sluagh lurking about, naturally. Something about this area attracts them in numbers."

He shuddered at the mention of the voracious sluagh. "No other sidhe under this hill?" It was a nervous question, and not out of line.

"None. The greater fae generally do not occupy this area. The Tree maintains that halite ring by pushing the excess salt out of the soil, infusing it with power. It keeps them away."

Celebel sighed. I missed the occasionally troublesome company of the local fae, but I could certainly understand his reaction. With the starsong clinging to him, he would be a candle flame to the moths of their attention. He certainly had that effect on me.

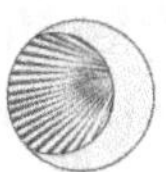

The next morning Celebel watched my every move like a man starved. I prepared the coffee, grinding the beans with my mortar and pestle and heating the water on my flat cooking slate that I brought outside for that purpose. It took only the smallest of cantrips to warm the stone evenly enough for all of my purposes.

While the coffee brewed, I fried up some starchy roots with a couple of fresh quail eggs. I sprinkled them liberally with both angelica and astragalus root powders. Celebel would require the extra energy for proper recovery, and I attempted to redirect his obvious admiration onto the food itself. He chewed on his lip for a moment. Quietly amused, I watched him struggle to think of an appropriate question.

Finally, he came up with, "This is an unusual drink. I've never encountered it before, but I'm intrigued by the scent. How did you find it?"

I laughed. "It's called coffee. Would you like some? I add a bit of honey to mine, to soften the bitterness. The villagers in the valley introduced me to it a couple of centuries ago, having acquired it from a Maraiya trader, and I've been enamored ever since. They were so excited, they actually made a big show of gifting me a bag of these roasted seeds. They also forged this sweet little pot for me to brew it with." I showed him the hammered copper pot, lined with tin, and crowned with an offset brass handle. It had held up surprisingly well. "Most charming little humans I've ever met."

He nodded, and I poured him a cup, handing it over with a plate of steaming food.

"And you can still acquire these seeds?" he asked after an experimental sip.

"I trade for them with various friends and acquaintances who pass through here. You may not have noticed the herbs, but I cultivate many rarer species; both for my own use and for barter. The bush that produces the coffee fruit is easy to grow, but the soil here does not produce the best-tasting seeds."

"Fascinating." He swished the coffee around in his mouth.

"Do you like it? It has some internal heating properties. Humans, in particular, can be very excitable when they drink too much." I smiled at the thought. "They taught me to brew it in the mornings, claiming that it wakes them up. I actually prefer to drink it at night, as it soothes me."

"It's quite pleasant, yes. Richer and heavier than most teas. My thanks!" He seemed pleased, and his approval warmed me in ways I didn't expect. "It pairs well with this fine, hearty breakfast you've prepared for me."

"You are quite welcome, but you didn't want to talk to me about coffee." So much for my attempts to distance myself. He pulled at the very core of me.

"You are distractingly beautiful," he admitted. "I have intended to begin a serious conversation with you many times, but I keep getting lost in your eyes."

I couldn't keep the grin off of my face. "You, sir, are a terrible flirt." He knew exactly how charming he was.

"Perhaps." Celebel shook his head as though trying to clear his thoughts. "I need to speak of a dire matter, all flirting aside." He sighed, looking down at the coffee cup cradled in his hands. "It hurts my heart to invite cruel reality into this dreamlike place, but I must ask. Are you aware of the war that has ravished our people for the last several years?"

"Vaguely. Nemohee, my dear friend, tells me tales."

I tried to stay out of external affairs as a general rule. Just like Celebel, there was the occasional war wound to patch up, but otherwise I remained stubbornly insulated. In fact, how was Nemohee doing? Þey hadn't sent a message in ages.

"I am bound by duty to return to my place in it," Celebel

said.

My cup clanged down. "War is anathema to me." One day, the sheer irony of my life would consume me.

"This one is different."

"Every warmonger says that."

"Cúraniel," his tone was deadly serious, "this conflict will spread here eventually, no matter how you feel about such things. My very presence here is proof."

"Well, before you can run off back to your war, you need a bath, and so do I." I helped him carefully to his feet. "Lean on me. I'm stronger than I look. We're going down to my wading pool in the creek. Just take it slowly." The last thing I wanted was to get embroiled in elvish politics again, and a calm patient healed faster. I would hear his war song, but on my terms.

We hobbled together down to the fresh water of the creek. As he shed the linen clothing, I led him to the shallow, slow-flowing offshoot pool I used for bathing. I preferred the mat of soft algae under my feet to the jumble of rocks in some of the deeper areas. Mild guilt washed over me as I used a cantrip to heat the water. A very useful trick. And learned from someone I distinctly refused to think about. Fortunately, Celebel's sleek, muscular form provided plenty of distraction.

"Now, Celebel Elhalanros, explain everything. Who are you? How did you come to be here? Where are you going?" I demanded, scrubbing his back with a mild-scented soap gifted to me by those same villagers.

"I command the war council with Feanim, a lifelong friend and confidant. Named Consulate together, we share the duties of rulership equally. You must know our powers and our people have dwindled over the last age." He paused, waiting for my acknowledgement.

I nodded. It had been a topic of concern even before my departure. A slow creep gaining momentum.

"Divided opinion on how to manage our fading influence has led to a divide in our people, leaving us terribly weakened.

I, and others in my camp, wish to consolidate what remains and preserve our legacy. The others wish to reclaim our power by force. It has not yet come to blows, but we all hear the notes of that awful melody."

I grimaced. The very concept of civil war amongst elves made my belly quiver with dread.

Celebel continued. "Then there is the matter of the Fomorians. We do not know whence they came or what force drives them, but they are deliberately targeting elves. I have never seen their like; great hulking monsters that vary wildly in appearance. They rise swiftly from seemingly nowhere, in immense numbers, and are utterly relentless in their onslaught. These are no opportunistic raids, but well-considered and organized attacks. We've tried to parley with them. We've even attempted to capture and question a few, but so far could not communicate at all. And so these assaults continue, with each one further weakening us."

With a troubled sigh, he splashed the water. "I despise war, too. I know that may surprise you, but these aren't petty squabbles. The enemy does not merely want us dead, they want us *annihilated*. Make no mistake, we are losing this fight.

"Either of these issues alone are overwhelming in their own right, but there is more. The last war raised ancient sites from the deep, and other powers begin to awaken, powers better left to slumber. It bodes ill for every living creature."

Here was a man who cared deeply about the well-being of others. Singing of ancient powers better left to slumber; what a contrast with the Dragon. I forced myself to end that refrain with a shiver of portent before it could garner unwanted attention.

"You're aware of the ambush that brought me here," he continued. "We left our fortress on a pilgrimage to Orfain."

"Ah, the famous Shining Tree! Ancestor of yours, yes?"

He nodded. "I sought guidance from the lineage. Unfortunately, we were caught out, which makes me suspect foul play. I'm sure it was a targeted attack. I can show you if you'd like?"

"Please."

Celebel turned to face me, weaving light between his hands. He cast a complex illusion between us, painting his memory of the events with broad strokes of color and sound. Unfamiliar voices and birdsong bloomed from his hands. Some figures cut clean lines where others drew foggier shapes, like parting a mist. It took form with impressive speed, and I leaned in to observe.

Celebel and a small group of similarly dressed, lightly armored elves approached Orfain on foot from the south. It gleamed like crystal in the bright afternoon sun, its delicate branches chiming in the slight breeze as they draped over the sheer cliff edge. The famous scintillating Tree stood like a beacon of light over the headwaters of the mighty Faelen River far below. The sound of its rushing currents was barely discernible from such altitude.

Just as Celebel kneeled to offer obeisance, an arrow whistled through the air. Striking the elf standing directly behind him, it speared her through the throat with a loud thump. A single breath's difference in timing and it would have been Celebel skewered on that arrow. It was a wicked thing, with a barbed head and a shaft marked with sickly grey fletching. More of those arrows rained from the sky as the party raised their shields and formed a tight circle facing outward.

Monsters—the aforementioned Fomorians—boiled up from a hidden site over the nearby crest, vastly outnumbering the few elves. They ranged from nearly elvish in appearance to towering heights over three times the size of any elf. Horns crowned some, others had long, flopping ears, and a few sported a trunk and tusks like a boar. Wings, tails, hooves, and even tentacles scattered throughout the mob. Through gaps in their enameled bronze armor, grey, pebbled skin showed. Many of them had pink or yellow eyes.

The elves fought valiantly, cutting down the Fomorians with admirable ferocity. Inevitably, the defenders could not match the monsters' greater weight and numbers. The Fomorians pushed their prey to the brink.

Celebel turned, diving over the cliff edge. Cries of dismay followed him down. Plunging into the icy waters of the Faelen, he lost consciousness.

Drifting in and out of lucidity as his body floated down the river, somehow he gathered himself enough to climb out of the water. Orfain was no longer visible, not even its cliff in the distance, and dark woods closed around him on both banks. With a mighty effort, he limped through the forest until he found another, much smaller river, and followed it until he had no more strength.

"Finding your hill was purest luck." Celebel released me from his memories and turned his back to me once more, ostensibly so I could continue washing his hair. "I roamed for days, utterly lost and rapidly losing strength. Truly, I am very grateful that you found me. For many reasons."

"I'm very grateful that I found you as well. That was quite a fall!" Impulsively, I kissed the back of his head. He pulled my arms forward, folding them around him. We lingered that way for a long moment, and I relished the press of my breasts against his back.

As I rinsed the soap from his hair and combed it back with my fingers, I considered his grave words. If he spoke true, and I knew he did, I was doing a great disservice by hiding away here.

"May I wash your hair in return?" He interrupted my thoughts.

I turned, offering him my back as an answer. He combed my hair back with his fingers, deliberately letting them brush over the length of my ears. The contact thrilled straight to my sex. I sighed, leaning back into him, and he kissed my temple, light as a moth's wing. As I relaxed in his arms, he massaged my shoulders with capable hands. Easing strain I hadn't realized was present, and making me want his hands everywhere.

I drew his arms around me, as he had done with mine, enjoying the sensation of his supple muscles and silky skin against my own. My heart flipped over in my chest at his nearness, not to mention the delicious erection pressing hot and heavy against my buttocks. I had to clamp down on every instinct urging for more.

After clambering back up the hill, and the high emotion of the day, Celebel immediately fell sound asleep, face-down on his blanket under the Tree. I squeezed the last of the water from my long hair and methodically dragged my comb through it. Knotting a bolt of silk around my shoulders and waist to keep the night air off my skin, I admired his ability to knock out so fast.

I brooded long into the night. How could I return to a society I had so thoroughly rejected? Though few who survived of the old court at Leyúduin, they would still know me at once, and judge me harshly for my perceived abandonment. At the very least, I had to consider my half-sister's reaction. Her opinion of me had never been stellar.

The idea of Celebel departing without me, perhaps never to be seen again, chewed at my gut. The vision of his eyes flashed repeatedly as my thoughts chased each other round and round in my mind. Damned visions and portents. The combination made me at once exhausted and restless.

How could I leave my friends behind, my beautiful old tree, and… well, *that one*? I had been fortunate enough to avoid war and violence in all my long life, and yet here I was, contemplating wading right into the thick of it. I simply needed more information to decide, but I couldn't stop worrying at it, like a wild beast picking at a wound.

Chapter 7

72 years ago

The Dragon often brought gifts. Of all the 'trinkets,' as he called them, the most surprising was the rose he handed to me without comment. I'd never seen such a robust bloom, with twice the petals. It put the coastal wild rock roses to shame. It was also the exact sanguine shade of his hair when he relaxed.

We sat together on the Great Tree's roots. Its foliage had already flared to brilliant golds, oranges, and a red almost as deep as the rose, as his own hair. I crunched the fallen leaves under my toes. The crisp air promised a swift turn to winter, and Rafael let me huddle close. After years of snapping and snarling at me for invading his space, he'd finally relented. The man wore his loneliness like a second cloak, and every visit strengthened that atavistic pull. My skin hummed with the need to touch him. I settled for leaning against his shoulder.

"Wherever did you find this?" Just as thorny as its wild counterparts, I held the flower gingerly in one hand, inhaling its rich, cloying scent.

Rafael looked away. "I grew it."

I almost dropped the stem into the duff. My ears twitched as he ran a hand backwards through his hair. Was that embarrassment? I found his sudden shyness terribly endearing.

"You… grow roses." Try as I might, I could not imagine the Dragon on his knees digging in a garden.

That catlike smile ghosted across his lips.

"You had to find this root stock somewhere," I prodded.

"You will not like the answer." His standard 'I killed for this' response. I knew better than to push, as he was always right, and I couldn't unmake the past.

"Very well, keep your secrets. Will you at least tell me why you chose roses?" I fingered the silky edge of a petal and he took the flower from my grasp with delicate precision to avoid snagging my skin. The thorns made no imprint in his hand.

"I find them pleasing, drawing their strength from blood where other plants may not. Thorn, flower, scent, and fruit. A sensual flower." He thumbed the thorns and plucked a single petal. "Open your mouth."

Sensual indeed. I complied, and he placed the petal on my tongue, careful not to touch me directly. Stilling my suddenly galloping heart took effort, and I wondered if he knew what he was doing to me. *Surely he knows!*

"The rose helps me to integrate during periods of… hrrm, call it disquietude, without dulling my awareness. I enjoy the taste as well."

Centering. He'd described a centering technique, using a heart tonic herb rather than a sedative. I'd made rose tea for many a distraught patient, but it had never occurred to me to have a patient hold the petal directly on their tongue. This, however, was no ordinary rose. The petal thrummed with power, diffusing its essence throughout my being. I hoped the blood he'd mentioned was his own.

Surely he noticed the acceleration of my breath. He could have seduced me effortlessly, and yet he remained aloof. I desperately wanted him to kiss me, which filled me with a bit of daring. Plucking another petal, I held it expectantly to his lips. He looked at me slant for a moment. A long, pointed tongue snaked out from in-between jagged teeth and curled around the offering, slipping it into his mouth.

I laid my hand against the Dragon's cheek, trying very hard not to think about his apparently *prehensile* tongue and the way my palm tingled at the contact. The soulbond swelled, humming with intensity. With need. A muscle in his jaw jumped, but he allowed my hand to rest there for a few heartbeats before turning his face away. I stifled my disappointed sigh and crunched the dead leaves under my feet to help with my own centering.

"The rose will last until I return." He looked everywhere

except at me.

I watched him until I could no longer resist the thoughts tumbling through my mind. "Do you prefer men? Or other genders, perhaps? There are those who experience no attraction at all—"

He rasped out a snarl and turned that blistering glare on me. "Why do you speak such nonsense?"

Time to be daring. "You continue to visit. With gifts. Most suitors would have made some kind of overture by now."

He snorted. "You have a very high opinion of yourself, Crescent Moon Woman."

I smiled indulgently. "Should I not? You didn't answer my question. You complain of my impudence and yet you always return. Why *do* you keep coming back, wicked beast?"

"Entertainment." His eyes glittered. "And I suppose you are not *entirely* horrible to gaze upon."

"You *blighter!*"

69 years ago

Dûemer dropped a vision of Rafael into my dreams. He battled a swarm of dark figures. As though cast from shadows, their features obscured in a blurring mist. The cacophony of roars, bellows, and clashing weapons overwhelmed my hearing. Though Rafael fought with a deadly ferocity, he bled from tooth, fang, and blade. It ended abruptly with his foes swarming in a dark wave. Our bond remained, but I could glean no answers from it.

The Dragon hadn't visited in well over a year prior to that vision. When I finally spotted that familiar silhouette striding up the hill toward me, I did the only sensible thing. I burst into tears, bounded down the slope, and flung myself at him. Throwing my arms around his waist, I buried my face in his chest. He stiffened immediately, but did not cast me away.

"Are you hurt? What has happened?" Rafael asked, a little wildly, his deep voice rattling through my skeleton. I hugged him tighter, like embracing a kiln-heated marble statue.

"No, I'm unharmed. Just relieved and happy to see you," I sniffled. "I had a vision that you were fighting, that you were hurt. I was so worried!"

"You have visions?" The thunderstruck look on his face, along with his rigid posture, would have been hilarious to me in other circumstances. "Why are you weeping if you are happy? That makes no sense."

"The Night Mother sends me visions. Part of her influence in exchange for her assistance. They are often vague and confusing—" *much like you*, I almost added. "And I weep with any sufficiently potent emotion." I wiped the tears from my cheeks. "Will you let me touch your face? It helps me to see." That 'seeing' would only work with a soulmate, but I couldn't say so. It accompanied the ability to speak mind-to-mind; another aspect I hadn't tested, but he was so perceptive it often seemed as if he heard my thoughts.

He stared in bewildered discomfort, but eventually nodded. I placed careful hands on his temples, closing my eyes and finding the rhythm of his breath.

Rafael fought alone against a large group of other drakes. They flashed iridescent where the light hit their indigo scales and they came at him from all angles. His thoughts whirled in a cyclone, multiple voices each speaking a different language. Scent and sight, along with an odd air pressure sensitivity of his skin, led his action over sound. His body seemed to move almost without conscious direction; violence enacted by pure instinct.

He wore his full drake form; long dragon jaws better suited to crushing limbs and ripping out throats. For every drake he cut down, two more took its place. The crush of scaly bodies trying to bite and claw him to ribbons left no room for swordplay. Blood, talons, and teeth flashed in a maelstrom. Neither broken bones nor grievous wounds could stop the Red Dragon.

The attackers surged forward and briefly overwhelmed Rafael, dragging him to the ground. Another drake, clad in green scales, wandered into the fray. That newcomer took his own share of assailants and Rafael fought his way free. His battered body lit from within. Hellfire engulfed him, and his enemies burned.

I opened my eyes, shaking off the disorientation of his perspective. The Dragon wore an intense, unreadable expression. Heedless in my awe, I brushed my thumb over his lips and he snatched my hands away from his face.

"You truly have no fear of me," he rumbled, a hint of bemusement in his voice.

"If you wished to kill me, you would have by now." I wrapped my arms around his waist again.

Self-indulgent, I nuzzled his leather-clad chest and lost myself in his scent, his heat, the press of our bodies. I'd been restraining the urge to plant my face into those impressive pectoral muscles since the very start. It was every bit as satisfying as I'd imagined, though I wished his body had even the slightest give to it. I'd had muscular lovers before, but he seemed truly forged from steel. I resisted the childish urge to knock on him just to hear the sound.

The fear that he'd hear my thoughts sobered me, but he did not push me away. The soulbond twinged, drawing us closer.

"You are a strange creature." The heavy buzzing of his voice through his chest sent a thrill down my spine.

"And yet you keep coming back for more. Put your arms around me and relax," I commanded. A slight tremor rattled me as he tensed further. As though readying to throw me. I looked up. "Rafael, please. You're safe here. Do I even own a blade that could part your skin?" Oh, the irony of having to say such a thing to *him*, of all people.

He frowned. "I have brought you plenty of blades—"

"Oh hush. You hear this melody. Do you think all the little ways you find to touch me escape my notice?"

I wished he would simply meld to me and hold me close. No, my true wish was for him to throw me to the ground and fuck me senseless, but I couldn't let him catch even the slightest tendril of that thought. Instead, he gradually let his hands come to rest on the small of my back. He did not relax one bit, though he did rest his chin on the top of my head.

"Were you truly so concerned for my well-being?" he asked after a long moment.

"I care about you! Can you not tell?" I'd have smacked him if I thought it would do anything other than hurt my hand.

He rumbled but otherwise remained silent, discomfort growing. I sighed and released him from my clutches. I led him to the Great Tree, and he trailed out of my reach. I climbed up and perched on a low branch in order to look him in the eye.

"I know this is all new to you, the concept of friendship, sharing a connection," I said. He arched a brow but did not disagree. "I want to make something clear to you, and I say this with no pressure or expectation. You are welcome to take whatever comfort in me, in my body, that you desire." I stretched my arms up and over my head, giving him a good view of my breasts.

His eyes sparked at that, lips parting slightly as he drew a deep, rumbling breath. Ah, he *did* want me! All that time, he had kept such a tight grip on his sexuality that I'd remained unsure of his attraction. Except that he kept returning, and bringing gifts. All those fleeting touches, the taunting 'threats' that held such an undercurrent of need. Those rare moments when he dropped his guard enough for me to feel the truth of him.

All the while, the soulbond hummed insistently between us. His stubborn resistance was like nothing I'd ever known. I welcomed his friendship, but my heart and libido screamed for more. I wished I could speak my lascivious thoughts openly, but he'd never tolerate that.

He looked away, crossing his arms, stifling his growing desire. Dismayed, I reached out, but he dodged my hand.

"Dragon, come now. There is no shame in this, but I will not push you."

He was silent for a long time, leaning against the Tree with his eyes closed. His expression didn't budge from the usual scowl, but I could sense the emotions warring just under the surface. Finally, he shifted his weight.

"Do you… offer yourself… to all of your patients?" Rafael cast a sidelong look at me. Vulnerable rather than judgmental, as if he were afraid of the answer. I wanted to embrace him again.

"Sometimes I forget how innocent you can be," I said, and his eyes flashed in warning. "That is not a criticism! No, I do not, although I have lain with many former patients over the years. It has been a long time and I miss the companionship. There are no others currently, if that is your concern. Nor have there been any since you landed in my lap." I wasn't quite sure how I would handle the opportunity for intimacy should it arise, but it hardly mattered. Solitude blanketed my little pocket of Vaeda.

Something about that thought begged attention. I'd had no other patients reach my hill ever since Rafael crashed into my life, only Nemohee. I still traveled to the village on occasion, to aid the humans and their livestock, but not a single one had approached me. It wasn't unusual to go a dozen years without a new arrival, but over half a century? Had he been chasing them away? Or worse?

I'd done my duty by the Night Mother and saved his life. But how could I reconcile these fucking *feelings* with everything I knew of him? He was utterly unapologetic for his murderous ways. I'd almost rather we became like those who only came together to replenish their spirits and otherwise avoided each other.

No, that wasn't true. I genuinely liked the big blighter, in spite of all my better instincts. Those rare moments of sweetness peeked through the darkness enshrouding him. There was goodness seeded deep down in his soul. Perhaps he only needed sunlight for it to grow.

Finally, I said, "You are unlike anyone I have ever met. Do you visit any others in this way when you leave here?"

I felt no jealousy, though the idea that he would grant another the attention that he denied me ached more than expected. If only I could acknowledge our powerful connection without driving him away. Flighty as he was, he may not stay the night.

"There is no one else. I have always been alone." Cagey, still watching me from the corner of his eye.

"Ah, so you do care for me," I teased, and he turned to face me.

"Hrrm. I would be... saddened. If you died," he said in a deep growl.

I bit down on the instinct to laugh at his odd sincerity. Hard to tell if that was how all drakes expressed care, or if it was simply another of Rafael's many quirks. He would probably never tell me.

"It is indeed a strange hold you have over me." I gave him a wry smile. "I would also be sad if you died. Try not to do that and ruin all my hard work, my bellicose friend."

Rafael exhaled sharply, but the corner of his mouth twitched. "You won that battle."

Someday, he would have to explain the meaning behind those words. I could almost sense it, like a shadow that fled my eyes whenever I looked at it directly. Every time I asked, he closed off.

I was wrong. The Dragon stayed most of the night, sitting close beside me while I drowsed. He disappeared some time before sunrise.

Chapter 8
Current day

Celebel and I talked all throughout the next day, long into the night. Then the following day. And the one after. His presence put me at an ease I'd never realized I was lacking. I luxuriated in gaining his acquaintance. He told me tales of his martial exploits, and I traded for stories of healing and my family. The way he spoke of Velúara—indeed his ancestral home—with such love and reverence, made me dearly wish to visit the majestic city again. I hadn't seen it since the early days of my youth. Although I'd never felt like I truly belonged in any of our cities, its glorious beauty was undeniable.

He enjoyed having his hair braided more than any other person I'd ever met, so I obliged him often. It was a good excuse to keep my hands on him, and we chatted while I worked, perched on the roots outside the bower. The sun warmed us.

"I gained a bit of a reputation as a feckless youth," Celebel said, "for trysting in untoward places."

"Untoward?" I paused mid-braid.

"The kitchens, the hallways, the library. I had quite the public castigation after my fathers caught me hosting a small orgy in the grand throne room. They extended my serving years by a dozen!" He laughed at the memory, and I joined him in mirth. I tried to envision a young Celebel draped in lovers across the sparkling quartz throne of Velúara.

"Gods, I thought you were going to say the gestation groves. Do they still have those plush purple carpets in the throne room? I imagine that would be a nightmare to clean," I teased and the tips of his ears flushed. Celebel reminded me of myself; a born troublemaker.

"I would never," he exclaimed in mock horror. "And yes, I should have planned my aim a bit better."

"Any current grand affairs I should know about?" I wove tiny braids back from his temples, lacing them with delicate shells, to join into a larger central wheat braid.

Celebel was thoughtful for a moment. "Galaron was possibly my most serious tryst. A sweet soul, that one, especially for an Astolar."

"How did it end?"

"Mutually. He's a quiet man and wants a quiet life."

I tugged at his braid. "You mean boring. I also wanted a quiet life and yet here I am, healing an elvish king."

He laughed. "Perhaps. And you? What of your past lovers?"

I swallowed, stilling my hands. I couldn't speak of the Dragon yet, couldn't even speak his name without garnering his attention. The irony of being ignored all that time, only to feel his scrutiny now.

"Varied. Nemohee and I used to roam about together before I settled permanently on the hill, fielding lovers for each other. Occasionally trading them. I once accidentally got entangled with twins; a brother and sister. When I preferred one over the other, the wronged party was furious. Nemohee had to hide me and make up tales until it all blew over."

Celebel laughed merrily. "Holy terrors, the two of you."

I grinned. "You could say that. I like to sample broadly. Various lycanthropes, some giantsblood, humans—though I do not recommend them. Sidhe as well—though I *very much* do not recommend them. That one time with a centaur was interesting."

"Humans!" He twisted to look at me, pulling loose a braid I'd almost finished. "I have considered it in the past, but I find them unsavory, despite the tendencies of my lineage." A few of his progenitors had soulbonded and produced offspring with humans. Despite our exclusionary ways, with our limited fertility and the ability to subsume mortal blood, some considered it a mark of pride.

Celebel made a moue of disdain. "That constant human need to eat, drink, and subsequently relieve themselves puts me off."

"My decision to avoid them has more to do with the human tendency to get far too attached, far too quickly." I gave myself a moment to consider the irony of that statement, given my present situation. Either he didn't pick up on the nuance, or he chose not to acknowledge it. "After a few ill-fated liaisons where my partner held an unrequited heartflame for me through their entire brief lives, I swore off humans for good."

That, and most humans couldn't safely handle some of my more aggressive appetites. They were simply too fragile. Even most of their biggest, burliest folk were still shorter than I, and generally weaker. I had a moment of wondering how a much larger, stronger drake might similarly perceive me before I closed off the thought.

Celebel wasn't the first to express misgivings over my unusual entanglements, and he wouldn't be the last. My heart was a wild and wary creature. Or so it had been once. Gods, what a mess.

"I *was* dallying with a Lachanaur woman before I left for the pilgrimage that brought me here. An idle fling for both of us," he clarified, seeing my questioning look.

I tugged playfully at his hair. "Does she look like me?"

He barked a sharp laugh. "Aha, no, she is nothing like you. No one is. Everyone maneuvers at court. I know she has held designs on ascension in the past as well. I've been relentlessly pressured to marry and forge a soulbond. The intentions are pure, but it's exhausting. Very hard to tell if anyone is truly interested in me for myself, or only for my position."

I murmured assent. Long ago, I'd been similarly pressured to forge a soulbond and have children. Now that I knew what a weak melody a forged soulbond was compared to that of a true soulmate, I especially appreciated my choice to refrain. As the last to inherit my grandmother's considerable power, I'd been expected to take up her mantle of rulership. A role I was uniquely unsuited to assume. Prestige drew plenty of followers, but rarely with any sincerity.

Celebel continued. "She is taller than you and freckled, with long, curling auburn hair, if you must know. She holds some position, but not enough to garner the same type of pressure that I do." He paused for a moment, ears twitching. "I am also well-acquainted with your half-sister. Quite a few voices clamored for us to join our lineages. Everyone on both sides wished for us to forge a soulbond and attempt to produce heirs."

I frowned at that, perplexed. "Silfanië is the last remaining scion, but she has none of Maelial's power."

Running my fingers through a moon-bright lock of his hair, I recalled the initial excitement at the birth of a Full Moon child. That branch produced strong dreamwalkers. When silver-haired Silfanië took after her Astolar mother instead, the ensuing disappointment had been quite vocal. No doubt that played a loud note in her character.

He nodded. "The hope was that together we would unlock some manner of latent power. Not the joyous partnership I had envisioned. Beautiful as the dawn but quite icy-hearted, your sister. I cannot recall ever hearing her laugh. I certainly cannot imagine her ever allowing her feet to muddy in the grass." He gestured at my bare feet for contrast and I wiggled my toes. "One kiss was enough to convince me we would never suit each other as lovers."

My estimation of his character rose. "How unfortunate that in all this time, she is just as stiff-backed as ever. I'd hoped age would soften her edges." I finished his braids with a simple leather tie.

Celebel turned to me, cupping my chin in a gentle hand. "I am realizing how nice it's been to relax and be myself with you."

"Who are you otherwise?" I looked deep into his eyes.

"Ah, well, I suppose I am always myself, but highly restrained for court. There are many expectations placed upon me, many pressures, many responsibilities. I consider myself a balancing force, and it creates a fair amount of strain. I am not looking forward to going back." He gave me a look. "You could join me. We could greatly benefit from your healing prowess."

"I would rather not think about that yet," I said. "Tell me more about your past. Are your progenitors still among us? Who are your friends and enemies?"

He settled his back against me so I could continue playing with his hair while he spoke. "My fathers have both departed this world, but my birth tree yet stands in Velúara. I would very much like to introduce you some day. As for my parents, the formality of the court seemed always between us, but they were kind and good to me."

"My condolences."

He covered my hand with his own. "I have had ample time to mourn, but thank you. Most of my friends do not know me intimately; they are more like acquaintances. I have to be just as careful with friends as I do potential love interests."

I shifted from braiding to massaging his shoulders as he tensed. He sighed with relief and leaned into my hands.

"My closest friend is Feanim. Something of an outcast himself."

The name sounded like one of Melranim's line. Most of his children had names with the '-nim' suffix, meaning 'flame.' One of whom had tried to coerce me into forging a bond with him and reacted poorly to rejection. He took it upon himself to make my courtly life even more miserable. I could still see the hateful glint in those slate-grey eyes, set in a face almost as pale as my own. And the annoying way he tossed his shining, waist-length, chestnut hair in self-righteous fury. His considerable beauty couldn't hide his rancid personality. I'd been so put off by him I'd exclusively bedded women and other non-male genders for the next dozen years.

Celebel huffed at my expression but continued. "I've known Feanim all my life. Rather an intense fellow, brilliant mind. He's not very popular at court, but highly influential. I gained my position by birthright; he gained his by force of will after his brother passed. We work well together. He is aggressive, whereas I am cautious. I am practical, whereas he is lofty. Without his help, the Fomorians might have already overtaken us. He is not without his flaws, but neither am I. Beyond all the rest, he is very loyal, and one of the very few I can trust. Part of my urgency to return is the knowledge that he will not do well on his own without my perspective. He can be… careless with the well-being of others.”

I stifled a sigh. He caught it anyway, and turned to give me a measured look as a light breeze ruffled his hair, making the shells in his fresh braids tinkle softly.

“Without Feanim’s creativity, we very likely would have lost this war already, and I wouldn’t be here causing you problems.” His voice held a note of mild reproach, telling me he was already accustomed to these types of opinions about his friend.

“Very well. I will withhold *most* of my judgment for now. How does he feel about other peoples? How do you?”

Celebel’s expression grew thoughtful. “Feanim has studied other cultures more extensively than I, though his lust for knowledge outpaces his good sense at times.”

“Studied? Or actually spoken to.”

He tapped his fingers on his forearm, thinking. “Both, I think. I’ve done very little of the latter, but I am willing. Our worldview has become far too narrow.”

I kissed his forehead. “Good answer. It is the test by which I judge an elf’s character. In all these years I have been away from the court, I have learned vastly more from non-elves than I ever did from our kind. We limit ourselves so strictly, and cannot see the harm it does.”

“I pass the test?”

“You pass the test. For now.” I pulled him to his feet, and we retired to the bower.

Awakening from pleasant, formless dreams, I found myself curled up at Celebel’s side. He was already alert, propped on one elbow and watching me. When I stretched, he ran a finger over the sensitive length of my ear. I jerked up and out of his reach.

"You are awfully daring." I watched him through narrowed eyes, trying to hide my smile. "I have not yet accepted you as a lover."

He reached for me. I let his hand linger in the air between us for a long moment before accepting it with my own.

"I feel compelled to be daring with you. Forgive my boldness, but I cannot think of anything else, especially after yesterday. You certainly do not make it easier with those filmy, barely-there silks." He tugged playfully at the strip of lavender gauze knotted at my shoulder. "You've fogged my mind with your sensuous presence."

I leaned forward to give him a better view, my instinct to be near him shoving my common sense out of the way. His eyes lit with desire.

"Barely healed and here you are trying to open your wounds again." I watched his reaction.

The knot slipped lower and lower on my shoulder until the lightest pull would undo it completely. He obliged me without a word as my lips brushed over his, and my silks slipped free. *Gods, yes. This is what I need!* The force of my response to him almost drowned out that last, lingering reluctance. Almost.

A pang in my heart dragged me back to reality. I let out an agonized sigh, and Celebel's brow creased, his ears twitching.

"Forgive me." I yanked on my braids to clear my head, pulling my silks to rights and re-knotting them. "There is… something you should see before we grow too entangled. Would you walk with me?"

His eyes grew earnest. "You dodge my advances, yet I can hear your desire plainly in your voice. Do you not feel the same connection? An ache from the very soul?"

I scrubbed a hand over my eyes, unable to look at him. My breath came in shallow sips.

"Cúraniel, please. It is as if I have known you always, and yet we are perfect strangers. I feel a pull as if my heart has been torn in two all my life, and is suddenly made whole. Anchored deep within, an almost physical sensation. I've experienced infatuation many times, and even what I thought was love. This is wholly new; a draw with intensity far beyond anything else. Is this what I think it is?"

Oh, I'm in trouble. I sighed, shoulders drooping in defeat. "I feel it too."

Celebel's brows drew together with concern. He reached to stroke my hair. "Why does that sadden you? I do not wish you to be sad!"

"You are not what saddens me, not at all." I hadn't wished to speak on it so soon, but I disliked holding back even more. "The situation is... complex." I took a deep breath. "I recognized you the moment our eyes met. Ages ago, the day I left Leyúduin, I had a vision of your eyes. I knew you would be my soulmate. We're fated. You are not what weighs on my heart now, certainly not. Only... I have more than one soulmate."

"You have visions? Ah, I am distracting from the more important point. Is this other soulmate such a problem?" His ears twitched. "It is passing rare, yes, but you are hardly the first to have more than one. It is a joyous thing, and I am perfectly happy to share your heart! Let your joy be mine as well. What is it that truly holds you back? The connection between us sings with power. I can tell that you want this as much as I do. Why deny yourself?"

I stood and confusion grew on his face like wild mint. May it be easier to uproot. "Please, just... let me show you."

He grasped my arms as I pulled him to his feet, holding me for a moment to study my eyes. "Your desire is as palpable as the air before a heavy rain. Whatever holds you back must be powerful indeed."

I led him by the hand down the south face of the hill. It was less of an incline than the creek side. The smaller trees of the woods blanketing the valley overtook us at the base, and he followed me through the dappled light and birdsong. We walked in silence, his companionable, and mine buzzing like a hornet trapped in my ribcage.

Before long, the forest opened to a meadow, and the scar came into view. Blackened land in the shape of a narrow wedge spread from a concentrated focal point and stretched back toward the valley floor. A cliff edge provided a far border, hiding a sheer drop off beyond. Completely devoid of vegetation, even the skeletons of trees, the melted rocks contorted into unnatural forms over the ruined surface.

Celebel sucked in his breath at the devastation. Tendrils of green crept cautiously around the edges, but nothing rooted, nothing sprouted from the ruin. I did not like to touch the area, as it made my hands tingle unpleasantly.

"Do you recall that great storm of the last century? The one that altered the weather patterns into absolute nonsense for about a dozen years and raised a new chain of volcanoes along the western coast?" I watched his face.

Celebel's ears twitched as he took in the sight. "This was the epicenter? I've never known lightning to so thoroughly obliterate the land."

"Not lightning. Nor, in fact, a natural storm." *No going back from here.* I swallowed. "Ancient powers clashed."

He spun to face me, eyes widening. "Do you mean to say—"

"Dragons. Or drakes, rather. Nothing would have survived a fight between true dragons, so I'm thankful it was only drakes." I could still hear the awful screech of talons raking over scales. "Here, you see the aftermath of a mighty battle between the two most famous; none other than the Red Dragon himself and the feathered drake called the War Crow." I slowed my heart beat with a minor effort, unusually anxious about his response.

Celebel's eyes went owlish. "We'd had a few sightings of the War Crow in the earlier part of this century, but the *Red Dragon?* Gods, we'd thought he had perhaps passed on—become a volcano himself or some such." He blew out a breath, surveying the scar with sharpened awareness. "Damn, Feanim will be insufferable when he finds out. He's always insisted the Red Dragon still lurked on Vaeda. They truly were *here?*"

"They were. The Red Dragon fell in this very spot." I pointed to the apex of the wedge, just at our feet. "The War Crow was thrown over the cliff edge there."

Celebel kneeled and touched the charred ground with tentative fingers, open wonder flitting across his face. "By the gods, how did you survive such a cataclysm?"

"The Great Tree sheltered me." I chewed on my bottom lip for a moment, procrastinating.

"You have brought me here for a reason. Please speak it." He stood, brushing his hands reflexively against his thighs, but the sooty ash did not cling to his fingertips.

My ears twitched with the effort to keep my voice level. "I've told you of my oath. The Night Mother demands it. If any who need healing should reach me…" I indicated the place where the Red Dragon had fallen.

"You *didn't*," he cried in dismay, his ears flattening.

I ignored the outburst, words rushing from my mouth. "He reached me, Celebel. Look there, my hill is in sight. He was dying! I did not recognize him at first. But I knew I had to save him. The Night Mother—"

"Yes, but the gods-damned *Red Dragon?* Called Rafael, the God of Carnage? The mass-murdering Bloody Drake, with the deaths of *thousands* of our people on his hands? He razed one of our own cities, to say nothing of the downfall of the Tárthanë!"

I winced. Even expecting this response, I'd hoped for a different one. Complex emotions flooded me as Celebel paced, his volume growing alongside his consternation.

"He is evil incarnate, Cúraniel. You must know this. You must, and yet you chose to save that monster?" Pitched just under a shout, his now-strident voice carried across the open space left by the scar.

I covered my ears as his shout echoed through the valley like the disapproval of my ancestors. Like the voices of the Red Dragon's many, many victims. All the same questions I'd asked myself. The breach of decorum made by shouting came as no shock. I occasionally felt like shouting myself.

"I know. Yes, I had to," I said, almost a whisper. Guilt, despair, and painful hope chased each other in circles in my belly.

"Did you save the War Crow as well? Might as well tally up your bloodthirsty monsters. The Lachanaur will be greatly cheered to know that the merciless beast who ravaged her way across their plains lives thanks to you." He paused his incredulous marching to stare me down, tugging his lobes to shake my nonsense free from his ears.

I winced at the volume, ignoring his barb. "She was decapitated. Rather beyond my ability to save. Rafael, however, I could." I'd known going into it that this information would be difficult for anyone to accept, especially another elf. Hopefully Celebel could still accept *me* when he knew the whole of it.

He blinked for a moment, and shook his head, calming himself with a visible effort. "I apologize for shouting. This is a lot to take in. How can you reconcile being a healer, saving lives, with rescuing the most legendary killer of all?"

I remained silent as he paced again, his fingers drumming rapidly on his arms. Thus far, his reaction was actually better than I'd expected. I could easily tolerate a bit of furious ranting. Hopefully, that would be the worst of it.

He paused, ears relaxing. "Did you fear this revelation would change my opinion of you? All considerations aside, you clearly have a more charitable heart than I. Hardly a character flaw."

I took a deep breath, hugging my arms as my heart leaped into my throat. "Not… exactly. There is more."

Celebel's dark brows shot up. "More?"

"Do you promise to try to listen without reacting?" I chewed on my lower lip, trying to calm my rabbit-running heart.

His fingers ceased their tapping. "I've upset you. Forgive me, please. This is a lot to take in, but I do want to hear the rest of it. I shall try very hard not to pass judgment."

"This is difficult. My dearest friend Nemohee is the only other who knows…" I trailed off, sighing as I approached him. After running my hand through his hair, I trailed the pad of my thumb over his full lips. His eyes widened.

"Your other soulmate. A victim of that battle?"

I almost laughed. "In a manner of speaking. But now I must weather the coming storm. And prepare you for it as well." I had to force the words out. Why was this so difficult to speak about?

Celebel's eyes grew wider by the moment, ears akimbo.

Ah, just say it, I chided myself.

"Rafael is my other soulmate."

Chapter 9
65 years ago

Rafael brought me a very fine elvish vintage, one I'd thought long lost to the ravages of time. The long-necked bottle was exquisitely wrought from a single piece of flawless, adularescent moonstone, flashing blue in the light. Carved with flowing script, the vessel was almost as precious as the liquid treasure within. Delicate as it was, most of those bottles had been destroyed over the ages. I was thrilled.

In a deluge of excitement, I explained its significance to the impassive drake. Rafael merely listened, amused by my rambling enthusiasm. After some pleading, he agreed to try it with me after I'd made the proper arrangements.

"As you wish, elvish wine is not to my taste." He promised to return when I was ready, and left me to a flurry of preparation. Eight days, I'd told him, for the eight main phases of the Moon.

When Rafael came back, he found me in the middle of my carefully laid out ceremonial circle preening like a proud bird on a nest. He listened with measured patience as I breathlessly expounded on the significance of every detail of my preparations. The meaning behind the timing of the season, the phase of the moon, the color choices, and so on. I'd never thought to have the chance to share such an important bonding experience with him. His willingness to participate filled me with unexpected joy. Though I suspected he was merely humoring me, I truly appreciated the gesture.

Giddy, I cut the seal on that precious bottle with a flourish, and poured the gleaming, pale wine into a single, small amethyst chalice. The heady floral aroma wreathed us in memory—or perhaps only me, it was difficult to judge the Dragon's stoicism. Taking the chalice, he examined the precious liquid, swirling it in the light before passing it to me.

I drank deeply of the wine, and he followed my lead. Instantly, the star song swept me away. Spooling out into endless nights among the ancient ones, it granted me the light of our ancestral stars newly shining. All of reality breathed my breath, the shared song filling me with sacred unity. As I held back tears from the sheer beauty, I looked over to find him making a face of mild disgust.

"Do you not taste the stars?" I hovered on the verge of devastation.

"It tastes of flower syrup." Gods, he could be so blunt. "And bells. What is this elvish obsession with bells—I warned you that elvish wine is not to my taste," he amended, noting my distress. "Here, it is wasted on me."

When I reached to take back the chalice, he tapped the back of my hand with the pad of one long finger. A rarity for him to touch me voluntarily. My skin tingled.

"I did not intend to bring you sadness." Concern flashed in his eyes as I set the chalice down. He'd shown no such care for my feelings before.

Overcome, I grabbed his hand and kissed the back of it. That sensation stayed with me; the unnatural heat of his skin, and the faint, directional scratching on my lips. A ripple of tension ran through him, but he did not pull away. One minor triumph.

"Forgive my boldness." I pressed my forehead to the back of his hand. "I've perhaps been overeager to share the wine with you. Feeling a bit overwhelmed with the strength of the experience. I only wished you to gain a better understanding of me."

"You are a strange creature," he said. "You watched me pull the head off of the last person who touched me without permission."

The War Crow's decapitated body flashed in my mind, and I released his hand with a shuddering breath.

Rafael's eyes glittered, the cat smile curling his mouth. "I will not hurt you, Cúraniel." To my shock, he took my chin in his hand. "I know you are trying to help. Difficult as it is for me to accept, no one else has ever attempted."

My lip quivered.

"Stop that. None of your nonsense tears." His voice held a rare warmth.

I steadied mine with a breath. "Do you wish for my continued help?"

"I do." He withdrew his hand, and the conversation drifted.

We talked of wine in general and he told me that drakes had no particular customs around imbibing. They did, however, make blood wine. As he spoke, he raised the hand I had dared to sully and, catlike, examined his talons.

"May I try some of this blood wine?" I asked.

He arched one of those peaked brows at me. "Are you certain? It would be... hrrm, *heady* for you."

The emphasis struck me, but I argued in favor.

"Dragon, please. I am heartier than I appear, and I would like to attempt the same cultural sharing from your perspective."

With a long exhale through his nose, he relented. "So be it."

Rafael returned sooner than I expected, barely outpacing a snowstorm. I pulled him into the bower as the flurries started. He shook out his cloak and sat on my pallet beside me, with his back to the trunk. Always with his back to a solid surface, never to open space.

"I have a wine for you, crafted from my blood." He handed me a leather wineskin.

Stunned, I stared at him. "Are you certain you wish to do it this way?" An unusual intimacy.

The Dragon's eyes glowed softly in the dim light, and I squinted, trying to decide if he wore a smirk. "Would you forgive me if I gave you a wine made of elvish blood?"

I closed my mouth on my response.

He uncorked the skin and produced two goblets from the

depths of his cloak. I often wondered what other secrets he kept hidden there. Pouring one, he showed me the thick, dark red liquid.

"I do not recommend the same amount for you."

I poured half that for myself. Before I could raise my goblet to my lips, he stopped me with a simple, "Are you sure?"

"I have experience with various intoxicants." I waved off his concern. "I'm eager to try it!"

With no more preamble, he drank, and I followed his lead. The wine steamed on my tongue, almost startling in its intensity. It had a bold, heavily spiced, and somewhat pungent flavor. Not at all the coppery, choking taste of blood that I'd expected.

Then the first wave hit me.

The wine sparked into flame, racing through my veins and overtaking my senses. I gasped and dropped my cup from nerveless fingers. Rafael's swift reflexes allowed him to catch it before it could spill over my lap. Only a few drops splashed on my knees.

"I did warn you," the Dragon said.

Some fucking warning!

I could only grab hold of his arm as another wave hit. *His essence surged all around me, inside me, my lungs straining with the great bellows of his searing breath. I squeezed my eyes shut, trying to steady myself as scales erupted, sizzling, from my skin. Leathery wings tore free from my back and I screamed.*

"Steady." His voice came from somewhere far away, and reverberated down my spine, rattling my ribs, and settling in the pit of my belly. *Looking down at my hands, they were unchanged. I touched my face. I was myself. Wasn't I?*

A third wave dragged me under completely. The incredible power of his body, the force of his rage, the terror of his past, all of it flooded into me. A fractured chorus of voices pulled me in myriad directions. A child's thin screams. The man's snarling cry. Sibilant, hissing wrath filled my being and threatened to burst me apart. So many languages! The great Red Dragon, the world-ender, stared down into me as I simultaneously peered out through his eyes. He roared—we roared?—and mountains fell. Which one was the true Rafael? All of them? None?

The child screamed again, splintering into me. Hard-bitten faces of ancient humans with cold, uncaring eyes closed in around him. Around us. The Tárthanë. Their sickening jeers echoed as they methodically peeled away the filthy rags covering that starving child's body. Monster. Demon. Changeling, they called him, as they broke him, violated him. Tried their very best to kill a child who could not die. Why couldn't he DIE?

I couldn't escape. He couldn't escape. The horrifying crystalline perfection of his memory swallowed us both. Hard-won freedom from that place led only to novel suffering. Captured again. Starved again. Forced to live in a cage. Forced to fight. Born a weapon or forged?

His brilliant mind cursed him forever, to be lost inside that trauma. To endlessly relive every agonizing moment. I understood it then. Time would never dim the pain for him. Lost with him, I wept as he could not.

Another wave. Breath filled me again, and everything shifted. We shifted. The Red Dragon had finally emerged, awful in his might. Massive wings blotted out the sun, casting the world in crimson darkness. With that freedom came the seething rage and bloodlust. Memory choked him. Hatred spurred him on. The entire village fell at his feet. Drowning in their own blood. Burning to ash, as we burned from the inside.

Unable to distinguish anymore between those who had hurt him, those who had allowed it, and those merely unfortunate enough to exist in proximity, he killed them all. He became the very monster the Tárthanë had named him. I tasted their tears on my tongue. Their cries for mercy rang in my ears. The Red Dragon roared again, and all cowered in fear. Lost in the torment of memory, he hunted them to the very ends of existence.

He couldn't stop. We couldn't stop. I screamed in vain for him, for us, to stop. But his madness, his pain, overcame us both. My mouth filled with blood and embers. He rained fire and death *everywhere his wings took him. Outposts, cities, kingdoms fell. They crumbled alike in the face of his all-encompassing wrath.*

Exhaustion struck, and the great Red Dragon faltered. Finally, we collapsed, shrinking back into the familiar. We slumbered for years. Decades. Perhaps centuries.

Wave. Vengeance achieved rendered him bereft. He discovered his own kind, and the fight began anew. A full spectrum of colorful scales fell beneath our talons. His talons. Until none stood against him. Until they followed him instead. To bring tribute.

Vast, shining hoards. Then came the writing. Languages tumbled together and overlaid each other in palimpsest. The drive to create bloomed. Hammers rang on anvils. Roses whispered to his wounded soul, plucked from the ashes of a city ruined by his hand. His knowledge stretched endlessly before me.

The despair of long, lonely nights stole my breath, wrapped in all the desire he so tightly denied himself. Oh, that tightly controlled sexuality made itself known. It burned like a wildfire, licking right at the boundaries he left in the wake of his fear. Seeking a safe place to take hold. The faces of every person who had ever hurt him flashed in a hateful montage. Safety. Safety was all he'd ever wanted. Not conquest, not riches, not even knowledge. Safety. His loneliness and need blistered through me, hot in the aftermath of self-loathing.

Stretched impossibly thin, I attempted to fill the vastness of him. To comfort him from within. When I failed to reach his edges, I was terrified. I wanted to claw my skin off. I was exhilarated. I was horribly, impossibly aroused.

It could have been hours or days. Or mere moments. It was an eternity of him. Rafael, God of Carnage, the mighty Bloody Drake, the Red Dragon. Wave after wave dragged me under, and all around me the voices hissed. I thought I called his name, scrambling for footing in a world gone completely awry. None of my senses worked as they should.

His hands gripped my shoulders, and I leaped at the chance to cling to him. I crushed myself against his solid body. Drinking in his scent. Pressing my face into his shoulder. Digging my fingers into his hair. Grinding my hips into his. If I could have crawled inside his rib cage and wrapped his bones around me like a cloak, I would have. Perhaps I did.

When I finally came back to myself, the snowstorm had abated, with soft daylight leaking in. My nose was smashed at an odd angle against Rafael's shoulder, my legs locked tight around his waist, and my hands firmly ensnarled in his blood red curls. Moving slowly and carefully, he plucked my hands from their death grip in his hair and eased my knees down to a more reasonable position.

The scent of him filled my nose, along with the smell of arousal. My thighs were uncomfortably damp. Oh gods, what did I do while I was insensate? Was he angry?

"Cúraniel?"

My name spoken in his deep, unusually tentative rumble felt like a caress. Tension melted from me, and I collapsed back into his arms with a shudder. Unwilling to pull away, I stole a furtive glance at his face. His typical scowl was gone, eyes soft and lost as I had never seen them. Flames of yellow worry streaked the brilliant blue, and his slit pupils dilated at the sight of my face. The obvious concern touched me, just as the lack of red rage brought a sigh of relief. It also rekindled the shameless heat between my legs.

"I-I am well. That was." When did speaking become such an effort? My body trembled. "Intense. You are intense." I rubbed my nose and craned my neck to look at him directly.

There was so much more I wanted to say, wanted to ask him, but the words wouldn't form. Not once, in all the legends I'd heard, had any of them mentioned the unspeakable evils visited upon him as a child sparking the slaughter of the Tárthanë. Not that slaughtering an entire people was a reasonable response, but having been inside his mind, I understood how it had happened. And why he hadn't been able to stop himself. Fresh to his dragon form and unfamiliar with his limits, if he hadn't eventually exhausted himself… I shivered.

"You are stronger than I expected," Rafael said. One hand glided over my hair. He'd never done that before. If I could have purred at his touch, I would have.

"What exactly were you expecting?" Part of me wanted to yell at him for the poor preparation, but my voice came out a pitiful croak. I consoled myself by letting my fingers ramble over his powerful chest, relishing the unexpected intimacy. "I'm surprised you are allowing me such familiarity."

His lips twitched. Was that a smile? "I could not remove you without causing harm. You were very… hrrm, *determined* to latch onto me." He opened his mouth as if to say more, but pressed his lips together instead.

I reached a trembling hand up to stroke the hard line of his jaw, and he almost avoided flinching. Almost. So touch-starved, yet still so heavily averse. He sighed, a long exhalation through his nose, and leaned into my hand.

All at once, his previously shrouded thoughts opened up to me. Oh. Oh *gods*. Not only had I immediately climbed on top of him when the hallucinations started, he'd held me through that entire experience. Including a prolonged orgasm at the end. All flirting aside, I'd never intended to force my sexual desire on him. Especially not after—no, I couldn't even name to the atrocities he'd survived. My stomach turned at the thought. The tips of my ears flushed hot, and I withdrew my hand.

"Rafael, I—"

He rumbled, cutting me off. For a moment, I thought he might actually lean in and kiss me as his fingers continued their slow comb through my hair. The air between us hummed with potential, with shared breath. Then he turned his head away, breaking the spell. Was he tacitly accepting my attraction or trying to ignore it? Had he purposefully untangled and strengthened the soulbond? Was this his way of acknowledging its existence? I wished I could simply talk to him about those things. Another rumble rattled my bones.

"I like all your growls and grumbles, especially this close" I traced lazy circles on his chest. "The deep vibrations are soothing."

He didn't look at me, but rumbled again in amusement.

I sighed. "You are one *potent* drug!" I ached to kiss those curling lips, to pull his shirt open, and taste his skin, but it was too soon. He would need time to recover and, perhaps, so did I. For now, I'd consider his willingness to hold me close another small triumph.

Nestled against him and wrapped in his warmth, I fell asleep.

Some amount of time later, I awoke on my pallet, surrounded by cushions and draped with a soft blanket. Rafael was gone, but his presence lingered, almost palpable, on my skin. Almost as if I could still touch him if I pushed hard enough. The space between us stretched as though encapsulated by some metaphysical membrane. A pulse of recognition.

I rolled over to face the wine skin and discovered a small note in a spidery, elegant hand:

"One spoonful!"

Chapter 10
Current day

"How can this be possible?" Celebel's brows knit into a scowl and his nostrils flared. The breeze chose that moment to whip his hair into a dark, silver-shot shadow about his face, emphasizing his stormy expression in dramatic fashion. "You must be mistaken!"

Faster and faster, the words fell from my lips, as though flooding Celebel with knowledge could overwhelm his defensiveness. "I assure you I am not. I, too, thought it impossible, especially in the beginning. Healing Rafael was my greatest challenge. I had never *seen* a drake before! Did you know that their blood is boiling hot?" I rubbed my forearms as I rambled, caught in the sensory memory. "He was far worse off than you when I found him; split open from stem to stern, completely gutted. Took much longer just to get him stabilized." The image of a body cavity trailing steaming viscera like the ribbons of a gory cloak flashed behind my eyes.

"From the moment I first laid hands on him, I felt that same anchor in my soul. When his spirit rose to meet mine, he might as well have harpooned me, the draw was so strong. Gods, he was *such* a shit when he finally woke too, I—"

Celebel shook his head hard enough to whip his ears back and forth. " Forgive me, I mean no disrespect, but know not how to accept this. How is it possible that you, *my* newly discovered soulmate, are also soulbound to the fucking God of Carnage?" He tugged at his earlobes so forcefully I worried they might rip free. Visibly containing himself, he took a deep breath. "No, I vowed to listen without judgment. Please help me understand. Until this revelation, I hadn't truly believed the Red Dragon was even real. The idea that you saved his life, that you know him personally..." His ears twitched. "I am having a hard time imagining my lovely

Moon Woman in the clutches of a beastly drake warrior."

Perhaps I needed to change tactics. "You have seen his likeness already. Many versions of it, actually."

His ears twitched. "I beg your pardon?"

Turning, I climbed back up the hill and he trotted along after me. "I have drawings of Rafael all over my bower. You have seen him; you simply did not know who you were looking at. I cannot blame you for expecting a big scaly beast. Which, yes, he is at times, but he is also much more than that."

He trotted up beside me, landing a light hand on my arm. "No. You don't mean that over-muscled, angry-looking redhead with the rather hawkish nose, do you? *That* is the legendary Red Dragon?" His eyes widened.

I laughed in spite of my tension. "The very same. Excellent way to describe him, actually. Who did you think that was?"

"I had no idea, but admit to curiosity. I assumed all your portraits were of companions and past lovers, but he is... I confess, I am at a loss." Celebel ran his hands through his hair as he glanced back over the scar, seeming to attempt to physically force the concept into his head.

"Your reaction is not so dissimilar to the one he had."

That stopped Celebel in his tracks, crinkling his nose at the comparison as though he'd scented a foul odor. *Ah, how typically elvish.* We were nothing if not predictable in our absurdly stubborn sense of superiority. Disappointment washed over me. He must have caught a look on my face, because he smoothed his own with some effort before continuing up the hill.

"I must apologize for my lack of manners. You are trying to be open and honest with me, and I am not reacting with grace. Please, help me understand. So, the Red Dragon is your other soulmate. Is he aware of this?" He gave me a sidelong glance.

I sighed. "He is... somewhat in denial." Rafael's furious retreat after our last argument on the subject flashed through my mind.

"Do you have any sort of formal, ah, arrangement with

him?" Celebel's voice wavered on the last words and my chest tightened in sympathy.

I leaned against the opening to the bower, faerie lights casting dancing glimmers on my skin. "Quite the opposite. Whenever I broach up the subject, he promptly takes his leave. Years may pass without a word from him. Then one day he will simply show up again without warning and carry on as though nothing has changed." I couldn't keep the edge of bitterness out. "I know he takes no other lovers, and he knows I have taken no lovers since we met, but that is the extent of our discussion. The last time I pressed him on the topic, we had quite a row."

"Ah." Celebel's eyes hooded as he considered my words. "That seems… frustrating."

"Oh, he's infuriating. Like trying to convince a cat to do anything against his will." Thinking of that slight curl at the corner of Rafael's lips lifted my mood.

"A cat. You sincerely compared the God of Carnage to a *cat.*" Celebel rubbed his temples.

I seized the opportunity for levity. "Rafael once told me that cats and dragons are cousins, and he's certainly feline. Often aloof, mostly mistrustful, but every now and then he'll roll over and be charming. Sometimes it's a trap. And sometimes he breaks things simply because he can."

Celebel blinked. "The Red Dragon can be *charming?*"

"Remarkably so." I grinned ruefully and ducked inside, beckoning for him to follow. Crossing to the back, I rummaged through my stock of spirits. No one should have these conversations sober. My fingers closed on an unexpected bottle of my favorite whiskey. I breathed a small sigh of thanks to Nemohee for keeping me stocked. Truest of true friends, that one. Probably Celebel would prefer elvish wine, but I wanted fiery distilled liquor for uncomfortable situations. Fuck the typical stiff, elvish restraint.

I poured two draughts for us and sat on my pallet. He swooped over, snagged the bottle, and downed half the remainder. I would have laughed if I didn't feel so fragile.

Thus infused with whiskey, Celebel scrutinized the art hanging on the bower walls. With care, he plucked my portraits of Rafael and laid them along my work bench for inspection. The images of more unexpected forms I held back. I knew my Dragon well enough not to reveal all of his carefully hoarded secrets. Celebel gave me a sidelong glance, and I handed over the other cup of whiskey. He nodded thanks and returned to his study. He hummed to himself as he pored over my drawings.

The first image was one of my favorites. Backlit and seated in the bower's opening, Rafael glanced over his shoulder with a certain sardonic glint in his eye. I'd thought him fully absorbed in reading a text and paying me no mind, but he'd caught me drawing him. The expression was just so typical I had to include it. Capturing the subtle glow of his eyes always proved a challenge, regardless of the presenting hue. Here, it was the brilliant azure of calm.

While Rafael had originally complained at length about portraits, he'd eventually grown accustomed to my constant sketching. Then he moved on to critique, leaving me wishing he'd simply stuck to his earlier grumbles.

"Well, he certainly has a cruel face," Celebel said, finally. "And you… find him attractive?" His brows flirted with his hairline.

That came as no surprise. All hard lines and sharp angles, my Dragon; much like his personality.

"I do," I said simply. "Rafael has this… it's like a forceful magnetism, as though the whole world holds its breath as he passes. I've never quite managed to capture his sheer intensity." I took the backlit piece from the pile, turning it in my hands.

"Not to pry, but I am surprised you do not have more intimate portraits of him."

"I do, after a fashion, but I keep them hidden. He is rather sensitive about such things. The only time I made the mistake of hanging up a shirtless image of him, he burned it on sight and stormed off in a fit of furious pique." I grinned at the memory of Rafael's theatrics. "The Tree was very upset at having fire so near its core, and refused to allow him entry again for quite a while after that."

"The Great Tree allows him access to your bower?" Celebel's warm baritone colored with surprise.

"It took some time, but yes, Rafael enters the bower freely."

The knowledge seemed to relax my new soulmate. His shoulders softened. "Those viperine eyes, whew. He certainly seems a hard, vicious sort; very much the look of a merciless killer. Does he only ever have the one expression on that long face?"

"He wears a perpetual scowl. And he can certainly be vicious."

"How did you manage to befriend him?" he asked, sitting beside me on my pallet. "Your affection shows in these portraits."

Arranging the blankets and pillows around us for a moment, I considered my response. Taking a deep drink of the peat-rich whiskey, I rolled it around in my mouth.

"He is… complex. I believe I am the first to ever show him any true kindness. A tortured soul, to be sure, but also quite sensual. He loves language and collects all manner of knowledge—"

"Sensual, you say." Celebel arched a brow at me. "Please elaborate."

Here we go. I sighed. "There is something hypnotic about the way he moves, the way he uses his hands. And that impossibly deep voice! Dark and resonant, with a growling chorus, like the voice of thunder itself." I shivered at the thought, growing warm. Rafael's voice was a caress from my ears straight to my sex. At least when he wasn't raging at me. "His presence alone has the tingling pressure of a building storm."

"Your eyes hold all the stars in the night for this… this drake." Celebel's cup sat forgotten beside him. It tempted me to snatch it and down the rest. "You are *singing* your desire!"

"Very much so, as I've already told you. Nem likes to say that he has me in a chokehold. The attraction is mutual." Though Rafael adamantly refused to choke me upon request. He'd narrowly avoided crushing my trachea once when I'd accidentally triggered his prey drive while sparring. I'd been very fortunate to survive with minimal injury, and he'd sworn off ever visiting again while hungry. One more entry in a long book of frustrations.

"Of course he is attracted to you. You're the very vision of beauty, but… a *drake*? Is it the risk of being killed and eaten? Are you drawn to that sort of thing?" Celebel rose again, pacing before the pallet with nervous energy, fingers tapping away on his arms.

I couldn't stifle my laugh. "I admit Rafael has a certain mystique, but I've never swooned over the violent ones." Although I supposed that was no longer precisely true. "The soulbond attracts us, naturally, but we also genuinely enjoy each other's company." Most of the time. "Gods, I miss him." I swallowed the sadness. "It has been almost two years, and I have tried steadfastly *not* to think of him, must as the distance diminishes me. We… did not part on the best of terms. Now, here you are, stealing my heart, and your very presence on this hill puts you in danger. How can I so desperately wish to see him again and also want him to stay away for your safety?"

"You fear for me?"

"Despite all the things I enjoy about him, Rafael is, to his core, a dragon, and they are not known for their sharing nature. He's quite jealous of my attention." I bit my lower lip. "Only my swift intervention prevented a tragedy the last time another sought me out for intimate reasons. His reputation for having a fearsome temper is, unfortunately, well-earned. I fear I may have saved you only to curse you to death at his hands."

Celebel let out a long breath. "No chance of reasoning with him?"

"No! Absolutely not. He would slaughter you." I wrung my braid in my hands until my hair protested the strain.

"It would be an undertaking, but perhaps if I gathered the others—"

"They would all die right beside you! I do not say this to diminish your abilities. Please, believe me. You have never encountered anything like Rafael. He is a fucking force of nature!"

Celebel's face only grew more offended and incredulous as I spoke, so I pressed on. "Please focus your ears! In his man form, Rafael has every bit of the same strength he holds as a full-sized dragon. He could kill any of us with a single blow, with significantly less effort than you'd use strike down an unarmed human. You simply cannot fathom how strong he is, and he moves faster than thought."

"You've witnessed him fight?" He frowned in that particularly universal way certain fighters did when their pride took a bruising.

"Celebel, he *beheaded* the War Crow. Simply wrenched her head off. I've seen him pulverize stone with no more effort than crushing a puff mushroom. I *believe* I can extrapolate." Occasionally, I grew complacent, forgetting the extent of Rafael's awful strength. Until he reminded me, as he always did. "This is not a slight against your prowess. I've sparred with Rafael for years, and know his strength intimately."

"You've… what?" His ears flattened against his skull.

I pulled one of the martial theory tomes from the shelf and handed it to Celebel. "He demanded I learn how to defend myself. In return, I taught him healing arts. So yes, I spar with the Red Dragon. Naturally, he always stomps me into the ground." I winced at the memories.

"He hurts you?"

"He is… not a gentle teacher. However, I accepted his terms and the injuries he inflicts are nothing beyond what I can easily heal. I make a terrible pupil, though. I haven't the natural ability nor much of the inclination. He says I will never be a striker." I grinned ruefully at the memory of breaking fingers trying to punch him, of fractured ribs and split lips. And delicious sexual tension.

Celebel's lips pressed into a thin line, mirroring his flat ears. "I mislike this very much."

"I agreed to it! He told me exactly what to expect well before we began. He taught me a bit of the sword, too, although I'm spectacularly bad at it. I can't get anywhere near him with a blade."

"I am quite well-trained in swordsmanship." Celebel deliberately eyed my soft arms and lush curves.

"I'm sure you are. You survived long enough to reach me. I'm telling you it does not matter. Even if his strength were comparable to an elf's, Rafael is head and shoulders taller than you, and much, much heavier." The Dragon dropped an elbow on me once and it was so painful I'd thought I would die on the spot. It was bad enough that he'd actually expressed contrition and promised he'd never do it again. "Celebel, he can *shapeshift,* and he *breathes fire.* He is a legend for a damned good reason. Give it up, please. I promise I think no less of you."

Celebel flopped backward on the pallet, hugging a pillow to his chest. "I should not assume that I understand more than you."

"On this or any other matter pertaining to my expertise," I said pointedly, and he laughingly agreed.

"I've been an ass, haven't I? Will you allow me to make it up to you?"

"You'll have a lot of making up to do." I folded my arms over my chest.

Celebel watched me for a long moment, weighing some judgment. Finally, he sighed and said, "You *love* him." Not an accusation, but an admission of defeat.

"I… do." It felt strangely vulnerable to speak it aloud. All talk of soulmates aside, I had never dared admit the depth of my feelings. "I do love him." It hurt to say, a clenching pain in my chest that made my belly quiver in response.

I paused, chewing on those words, turning them over in my mind and examining them. I thought of how every time I'd come close to addressing needs, Rafael instantly closed off and disappeared like the morning fog. Or raged at me. How that hatred of vulnerability tied directly into his inability to relinquish even the smallest amount of control. He fought so hard against his own need, the stubborn creature.

And yet, the Dragon always returned, inevitable as the changing seasons, though perhaps our last explosive argument was indeed the end. I hadn't demanded any promises, I'd only wished to speak openly about my feelings. It was enough to send him into a fury. He'd kept me completely closed off, barely able to sense him after that. Prodding the edges of that wound still hurt. *Infuriating man!*

Tentatively, I touched the soulbond with Rafael, and encountered the expected wall. It always came back to this. If we simply talked things through, we could resolve so many problems. Understanding that his avoidant behavior stemmed from trauma made it no easier to deal with the pain he inflicted. The thought of hurting him in turn made my arms tingle with reflexive discomfort. Hiding Celebel from him, whether by default or design, made me uneasy. In contrast to how the Dragon hoarded his secrets, I preferred to live my life out in the sun.

The bower was suddenly much too small, too stifling. I moved outside, sucking in deep breaths and hopping across the roots to calm myself. Celebel followed, watching my face closely. The arch of his brow said that I'd been projecting my thoughts.

I sighed. "I know he loves me as well, but he cannot admit it. He'll come back. He always does."

"The very idea that the Red Dragon is even capable of love…" Celebel paused and rubbed his forehead. "And, naturally, he's the jealous sort. You believe he is going to return soon and murder me, correct?"

"It is a distinct possibility. He can sense when my emotions are running high." He could sense much more than that, but I chose not to divulge that information. Not yet. I rubbed my arms to calm the frissons of dread.

"And are they now?"

I bit my lower lip; Celebel's eyes melted through me. "I think you know the answer to that already."

He was quiet again for a long moment and then smiled prettily. "It seems a shame for you to have put me together, only for your lover to take me apart again. If I am to die, may I at least have a kiss first?"

Chapter 11

64 years ago

Rafael gifted me an exquisite collar of royal blue sapphires, wrought in precious þilvor and festooned with sparkling diamonds. Along with the usual rose stem, of course. I allowed myself to appreciate the decadence of wearing such sumptuous jewelry on my naked body.

"Do you like to adorn me?" I spun for him.

His eyes softened for a moment, indulging me, but he waved away a kingdom's worth of value. "A trinket." Leaning against the trunk of the Great Tree, he scratched notes in a journal.

"Why do you bring me such 'trinkets'?" If this was a trinket, what was a treasure to him? "How do you select them?"

He looked up from the page. "Your bower is full of crystals and books. Thus, you prefer jewels and reading. I would bring herbs, but you already have a strong stock of everything you regularly use."

I flushed with pleasure. "That is remarkably observant."

The Dragon shrugged. "Seems obvious." With that, he sank back into his note-taking.

Deciding to keep the necklace on, I glanced at him as I trotted the steep way down to the stream to bathe. He focused in that intense way of his, the quill flying over the page. Most of his journals, when I could get my hands on them, were written in coded languages. He never settled on just one, and many had an impossible cipher that slid away from the eye. Even his drawings defied focus without his expressed permission. I considered sneaking a nude self-portrait into one of them, just to tease him.

Instead of drying off after bathing in the creek, as the day was unseasonably warm, I danced and let the wind wick away the rest of the moisture. Focusing my ears to the sounds of nature, I found all the music and rhythm I needed, and let it take me.

Moving with abandon, I enjoyed the simple pleasures of the sun on my skin, the soft grass under my feet, and the beat of the world within. The shared song embraced and comforted me.

The heat began as a tickle on my back. I didn't notice its presence as it spread until it suffused me completely with growing warmth. The longing wrapped me and I let it guide my body, spinning and whirling, my hips led the motion. I was too far gone in the pure bliss of dance to consider the source. Only when the heat flared, stifling, did I identify the cause.

Rafael watched me intently. His eyes followed my every move with distinct hunger, lips parted. Every time I looked over at him, his gaze dropped to the journal. Whether he realized it, he was finally ready to accept me, and I could wait no longer. The soulbond's insistent hum reached a fever pitch.

I spun closer and closer, eventually whirling to a stop directly in front of him. Mild consternation lit his eyes as I took the journal from his hands and set it aside. When I pulled his arms around me, his hair and eyes sparked to flame.

"What are you doing?" Anxiety tinged his voice as I stretched upward, sliding my arms around his neck and pressing my body to his.

"Kissing you, if you'll allow it. Bend down, please. You're too tall."

The Dragon obliged, and I pressed my lips to his. He went perfectly still, like a prey animal considering flight. His mouth was hard, unresponsive. I kissed him again, carefully, and his hands trembled on my back.

"What are you *doing?*" he said again, panic rising in his voice, along with an anticipatory tremor in his heavy muscles.

My heart clenched in sorrow for him, and I funneled that emotion into longing.

"Kiss me back," I murmured against his lips, drawing my nails lightly along his scalp and caressing the back of his neck. "Take what you want."

"I do not understand."

I pulled back. "Fucking hells, Dragon. I saw the way you were watching me just now. The same way you've watched me for years. You are not as subtle as you imagine. The heat of your lust is a licking flame, and it's driving me mad."

"But—"

"Kiss me, damn it! Please!" I pounded his chest with a frustrated fist and paused, assessing. "Or at least stop tormenting me. You *know* I can feel your desire!"

He huffed but did not cast me away. Finally, he acquiesced, a little at a time, pressing hard lips to mine. I realized, with another paroxysm of sorrow, that he simply didn't know how to kiss.

"Soften your mouth, relax your jaw." Using my own mouth and stroking his face with my hands, I guided him. Bit by bit, he responded, his lips melding to mine. His rigid posture eased, hands pressing me closer rather than simply weighing on my back.

"What is the purpose of this?" he asked, drawing back when I paused to look into his eyes. His sweet innocence, at odds with his fierce expression, made me laugh. He frowned.

"Oh, my poor Dragon, have you truly never understood it? Lips are quite sensitive, and kissing is a particular intimacy. Sharing breath and taste. Do you like the way it feels? If not, please tell me. I want you to take pleasure in this, in me." I traced the curving bow of his lips with a gentle fingertip.

He gave me a deliberate blink, considering. Then he leaned in and kissed me cautiously. Carefully, so as not to snag my flesh on his pointed teeth, I teased his mouth open. The moment I touched his tongue with my own, a powerful jolt ran through me, hardening my nipples into stinging points. I moaned into his mouth and he shifted his weight, tightening his arms around me.

"You're too tall," I whispered again, pulling him to the ground with me. I curled against him, keeping his arms around me, enjoying his heat on my skin.

Almost painfully bright, the flames danced wildly in his eyes. I had never seen him so unsure of himself and it struck a chord within me. I'd never wanted anything as much as I wanted this man to heal, to find respite in me.

"I am… unaccustomed to kindness." His voice was raw.

"I know." I stroked his hair back, tucking it behind the tip of his ear. The dappled shade softened the harsh angles of his face. "Will you allow me to teach you? You may touch or kiss me however you like, at your pace, so long as you don't bruise or draw blood. Not to say that's never welcome, just not in the beginning. I'll tell you if something is too intense. Will you do the same for me? Show me how you wish to be touched? Is that acceptable?"

Rafael laid a cautious hand on my cheek, the pad of his thumb tracing my lips, as I had touched his. I was acutely aware of his talons so close to my eyes, but he kept perfect control. His touch stoked the fires in me, tingling on my skin.

"You are beautiful," he whispered, almost shyly. Beyond all the lust, his unexpected sweetness created a powerful desire to keep him close, to soothe his aching soul, and perhaps absurdly, to protect him.

"Please, Dragon. You must tell me if you want this." I tilted my face up and closed my eyes.

He took the hint, and his lips brushed my forehead, my eyelids. Intuitive. He hesitated when he got to my mouth, and the heat of his breath made my flesh tingle with anticipation.

"My reticence is… not your fault," he rumbled, low in his throat.

"I know." I didn't want to think of the things I'd seen in his mind, nor did I want him to fixate on them.

"You are utterly mad."

"I am," I agreed, "and I still want clarity. I do not want to force you into—"

He snorted, poking my side with a knuckle. "You are soft as a dove. What force can you muster?"

I ignored the jab. He would bait me in circles if I allowed it. "Speak your needs aloud. Do you want me?" It was a challenge, and one I hoped he would take well.

Rafael shifted me in his strong arms to cradle me in the

crook of an elbow. For a moment, we simply looked at each other.

The fires in his eyes flared. "I have wanted you since I first tasted your blood." His dark growl went straight to my clitoris, flushing my face with desire.

The wetness grew between my legs. What was it about the edge of a threat from him that aroused me with such intensity? A sane person would be terrified. *I* should be terrified. The fucking God of Carnage just said the taste of my blood made him want me. Instead, my lust threatened to strangle me, and the soulbond hummed to a new, higher pitch.

"That is the most disturbing thing a lover has ever said to me." I sighed at the smirk that tugged at his mouth, and the knowledge that I'd willingly let him devour me at this point. "Wicked beast."

He lowered me onto my back, covering my body with his. His heat enveloped me. I'd wanted this for so long I vibrated with need. Trying to let him lead, I resisted the urge to lock my legs around his waist and press my soaking cunt against him. Finally, his lips touched mine again, and I twisted my hands into his hair, reveling in the texture of it. I'd always wondered if it would burn me in that liquid flame state. Happily, the fire seemed contained within the strands.

I let him explore me at his own pace. His kisses gained confidence, his tongue gliding over mine. Trancelike, enrapt, I guided his hands as he placed them on my body. His fascinated wonder was achingly sweet to me, and his touch so gentle, as if fearing I would shatter.

I tugged at the laces of his shirt, but he caught my hands, redirecting them.

"Dragon, please. May I touch your skin? At least remove your jerkin if not your shirt? I want to feel you against me."

He grumbled a bit, pulling off the heavy leather jerkin, but refused to let me unlace the neck of his shirt. I ran my hands greedily over his broad shoulders and powerful chest through the rough wool, like sun-warmed steel under my palms. He caught my hands when they drifted down to stroke the rippling muscle of his abdomen. Surrendering, I twisted them back into his hair.

I sighed when he kissed the helix of my ear. He paused.

"Our ears are highly sensitive," I said, and he stroked a tentative finger up the length of it, watching my reaction. My breath quickened.

"As sensitive as your lips?" He caressed my ear with more confidence.

"M-more so," I panted, and then gasped, arching my back when he rubbed the lobe between thumb and forefinger. If he kept that up, I would climax from my ears alone.

"Hrrm." His eyes flickered with interest, and he bent to kiss my ear.

I turned my head to give him easier access. He surprised me, first by running his tongue along the stiff cartilage of the helix, then by ever-so-gently taking the softer lobe between his teeth. I grabbed the hand he'd rested on my belly and tugged it to my breast, moving his fingers with mine to stroke and lightly squeeze my nipple. He rolled the nipple thoughtfully between his fingers, tugging, and my clitoris throbbed in time with my breathing.

"Your nipples also seem highly sensitive," he murmured in my ear.

"Very m-much so," I stammered. Gods, I wanted him so badly I could barely function.

Continuing to stroke my ear with one hand, he moved down so that he could nuzzle my breasts. He glanced up, measuring my reaction, and then swirled that impossibly long, nimble tongue around one breast. It had to be at least the length of my forearm. When I gasped again, he gave my nipple an experimental flick with the tip of his tongue. I whimpered with pleasure and he made a satisfied noise deep in his throat.

Licking my nipple a few more times, he took it in his mouth and sucked. I arched my back again, pressing my thighs together in a futile attempt to keep my wetness from dripping down to pool underneath me in the grass. Need consumed me. His or mine, I could not tell. As long as his spirit expanded outward, flowing into me, he moved with more confidence. I encouraged it, opening my boundaries wide and allowing him to delve as deep as he wished.

"Show me how to please you," he murmured against my breast, still stroking my ear.

Grabbing his free hand, I moved it down between my legs. Guiding his fingers with mine, I led him to my swollen clit, and he understood what I wanted. The pressure built rapidly at his increasingly assured touch.

Stars exploded behind my eyes. The heat and weight of him, the way he rolled my nipple in his mouth, the confident stroke of his fingers along my ear, the deep buzz of his growling breath, his scent—it overwhelmed me. I could hardly breathe. The shudder started at the base of my spine.

Burning me alive, faster than I would have thought possible, I climaxed with a howling cry. He released my nipple to watch with sharp interest while I writhed and moaned in the grip of a crushing orgasm. Fully caught in the waves, I gasped for breath, winding both fists into his hair and pulling myself up to kiss him with a ravenous fury.

Leaning across me once I came down from the high, he seized my other nipple in his mouth and rubbed my clit with the pad of his thumb. A second climax hit me, then a third shortly after, and a fourth after that. I wanted to grind my aching clit against him, to rip his clothes away and break myself against his body. Instead, all I could do was convulse in the clutches of the successive, brutal orgasms. He pulled back, calculating.

"Are you always this sensitive?" A smile played at his lips.

I slowed my breath with an effort, stroking his face. "N-no, but it has been a-a long time, and I'm incredibly attracted to you. You are very intuitive."

"Simple to observe your breathing and the way you move—pressing against my hand or shying away." He seemed pleased, which made me smile. "The scent of your arousal is delectable. May I..." His gaze dropped as his voice trailed off.

I propped myself up on my elbows, intending to help him voice his desires. "What would you like? Do you want me to touch you?"

Rafael shook his head, a brief toss of his burning hair. "I wish to taste you."

Oh gods. "No biting!"

"No, not that." He raked a hand backward through his hair. "The scent of your sex is intoxicating. May I kiss you there?"

I grinned. "*Please* kiss me there. My clitoris is the most sensitive spot, but all of my cunt responds. Just don't use your teeth. Or your talons."

"I have blunted them," he said with a mild scoff, demonstrating with a hard poke of one forefinger into my lower abdomen. "A bit late to express concern over that, yes?"

The Dragon moved down my body, trailing tentative hands over my thighs. I spread my legs wide to accommodate his broad chest. He spent some time simply breathing in my scent, occasionally gently nuzzling my clit, tugging at my labia with his lips, sucking away my juices. His rapt interest made my heart hammer against my ribs, and the searing exhalation of his breath sent tremors careening through me. I'd never had a lover make such a fascinated study of my vulva. He rumbled, and the vibrations tingled all the way up my spine, making me moan.

"You are lovely, like the glistening petals of a strange flower." He teased apart my labia with a light finger and I shivered at his touch. With agonizing slowness, he pushed a finger inside me. "Interesting, the way you grip my finger. Stronger than I expected." His eyes flicked to my feverish face. "Do you like this?"

"Yes," I hissed, trying in vain to shove his finger deeper inside me. "More!"

"More depth? Or more fingers?" The question made me writhe.

"Both! Thrust with your fingers. Don't worry if you tap my cervix, I like it." The pain peaked the ecstasy, each chasing the other.

With a thoughtful expression, he worked another finger into me, and I shuddered as he slid both in and out, twisting as he did. The dulled talons dragged inside me with uniquely delicious intensity. "Like so?"

"Mmm, yes. Curl them up against—Oh!"

He'd found that interior spot that shattered me and worked it with increasing confidence. I flexed around his fingers in waves as the pleasure rippled through me, trying to imagine how his cock would feel. Oh, how I wanted him to pound me senseless. How I wanted to ride him until I was bruised and bloody all over, until he released so hard inside me I split open. To chain and provoke him until he lost himself in his needful wrath, until he came all over me with his furious heat.

"Dangerous thoughts," he growled. The timbre of his voice made me whimper and grip my nipples, twisting until the pain brought clarity.

"You can hear my thoughts?" I found my voice. Supposedly, soulmates could speak mind-to-mind, but he'd never shown more than keen observation before. "Do they bother you?"

Rafael pulled his fingers out of me, admiring the wet shine of my arousal draped over his talons for a moment, before licking them clean. That long tongue curled around his digits in a way that made my entire cunt ache, dragging a moan from my throat.

We locked eyes for a long moment.

"The darkness in you calls to me," he said. "I cannot... Hrrm, I cannot give you everything. Not... not yet."

"I understand. Should I better hide my fantasies?" I brushed a lock of living embers from his face, trying to think of ways to shut him out of my mind.

He kissed my hand. "You cannot. Nor do I wish it." He exhaled slowly, heat tickling my skin. "I have tasted your lust now. I would have all of it, my dove. Do not hold back." *My dove.* The unexpected affection speared me, making my heart thump in my ears. "If you will grant me patience, I will attempt to grant your desires. It... will be slow."

"You set the pace and I will follow, my Dragon." I would have curled forward to kiss him, but he sank back between my thighs.

The crescendo began anew with the brush of his lips against my clit. I planted my feet on his broad shoulders, grabbing fistfuls of his hair and yanked, admiring the way it glowed through my fingers. He rumbled again, and I squirmed as the vibrations strummed me like a harp. Experimentally, he licked up and around my labia, pulling hissing cries from me. His tongue swirling and dragging over my clit made me wild with need.

"Gods, I want you to fuck me," I blurted. I couldn't help myself. "Use your tongue. If-if you wish, that is."

Rafael looked up at me with brilliant eyes. And thrust that long tongue halfway inside me, undulating it in a rhythmic wave.

I moaned, and my hips bucked against his mouth. He growled and thrust into me again, deeper this time, gripping my thighs with strong hands. Withdrawing his tongue, he flicked the pointed tip over my clit until I hovered, whimpering, right at the brink.

He worked my clit with his mouth and his sinuous tongue curled and rippled inside me. I almost couldn't bear it. The surging force of it stole my breath, my thoughts, my name. I lost all sense of place and time. He growled into my cunt and I went over the edge, crashing into climax with a shriek.

Pinned in place, I screamed and thrashed as I came undone. This most punishing orgasm seemed to go on forever, and the Dragon whipped it along with his tongue. My body exploded into stardust. I cried out until my voice broke. Until I could only keen from the back of my throat. Finally, finally, the waves subsided. He gave my clit a final kiss as his tongue slid free and allowed me to collapse in a heap.

Blearily, I looked up at him. He gave me a smile, genuine if close-lipped, and my juices gleamed on his mouth and chin.

"I like you this way," he said. "Radiant."

"Gods, you're a quick study," I croaked. "What can I do for you?"

He shook his head. "I am… not ready."

I extended my arms, and he gathered me close.

"Why are you doing this?" Rafael idly stroked my ears as I lay cradled against his chest among the roots of the Great Tree. He never did remove his shirt, but he'd unclasped the sapphire collar from my neck.

I raised my head, foggy in the wake of my abated lust. "What do you mean?"

The caresses stopped. "Is it pity?" The question held a hard edge.

"Pity? Wherever did you get that?" I sat up, concerned.

"You know my history." A defensive growl built under the words.

Sighing, I twirled a lock of his bloody hair around a finger. "I do, and it informs my approach, but it in no way puts me off. Jax, you know me better than—"

"Do not call me that."

I bit back my annoyance. He was reacting to the earlier vulnerability, looking for a fight, and I refused to grant his wish. "My friend, I am quite fond of you, despite your standoffish ways. You gave me pleasure, not the other way around—a staggering amount of pleasure!"

His mouth twisted bitterly. "You are an elf."

"What does that mean?" The sudden shift caught me off guard.

"I am not… up to your standards."

I understood in a flash. He thought my ideals were the typical exclusionist sort, as most elves would consider him a far cry from beautiful. Certainly nothing like the lithe or curvy-bodied, serene-featured, long-eared prizes of the elvish court. If he couldn't accept my attraction, it harmonized that he would believe I was somehow using him.

"My standards? My dear Dragon, I have been living out here, far from society, for quite a long time. Fuck elvish 'standards.' I'm hopelessly attracted to you. Surely you've noticed my relentless flirting? Not only do you drive me utterly mad with desire, I also find you fascinating. I've never volunteered to have anyone else beat the shit out of me in the name of teaching, but I'm willing to endure just about anything to get your hands on me." His foreboding expression relaxed as I spoke.

"Your hair is truly lovely." I ran my fingers along the loose garnet curls of his mane. "Your eyes arrest me. I cannot keep my hands off of your body. Gods, the way you move is so sensual. And your voice makes me wet." I grinned impishly as he shifted with discomfort at the barrage of compliments. "You just gave me the most intense orgasms of my life—orgasms, plural!—and you dare accuse me of a pity fuck? I'd slap you if I weren't so wrung out."

A small, wry smile pulled at the corner of his mouth, so I kissed him again, biting his lip. My lust awakened, surging, straining my control to the breaking point, and I released him. Progress needed to happen slowly, as he had said. The actual practice was already maddening. Even though I lay perfectly naked beside him, he still flinched and pulled away if I so much as traced a finger along his stomach.

"What do you want from me?" He pressed his lips to my forehead.

"Only what you're willing to give."

Chapter 12

Current day

I laughed in spite of myself. How had Celebel so easily diffused the tension between us? He was too good at this. As I leaned in to grant his request, he cupped the back of my head, pulling me to him and kissing me like a man drowning and I his only lifeline. That aching, familiar bond fanned to roaring flame, overtaking my senses.

I kissed him back with the full force of eighty-four years of desire denied. I badly needed to fuck with abandon. To fuck without the shadows of ever-present trauma. Without the very real danger of setting off a violent reaction. To simply give myself over to instinct and all-consuming lust.

Celebel's lips were even softer than they looked, his tongue silken on mine. We interlocked as though we'd been forged together from a single billet; two pieces of a burning whole fit perfectly in place. He stole my breath, and I stole his, fingernails raking down his back. Desperate for his skin against mine, to grind my already wet and aching cunt into him. Starsong filled my senses, intoxicating me. I wanted to taste every patch of him. To rake my teeth from the tips of his ears to the tips of his toes. Ravenous.

He tugged the knot loose at my shoulder, and my lavender silks fluttered free. Eagerly cupping my generous breasts in strong hands, he pinched and rolled my sensitive nipples. I nearly orgasmed on the spot with a sharp cry. He ripped his blanket away, pulling me on top of him. I hovered over his body, braced on hands and knees, and looked him over. Well-built, he had developed shoulders and arms from swordplay, a shapely chest, and a flat, nicely defined stomach over narrow hips. *Gods save me from this exquisite creature!*

I'd seen a great many cocks in my life—all shapes, sizes, and shades, and attached to a great variety of people. Celebel's was the most aesthetically pleasing of them all. From his shimmering skin to the graceful flare and taper of the head, the excellent combination of girth and length counterbalanced with his smooth, perfectly proportioned testicles made his genitals appear almost like a painting. An artist's concept of perfection. Forcing myself to slow down, I admired him. I had no preference regarding pubic hair, but he was just as smooth-skinned as any elf, and I liked how no detail was obscured.

His erection was impossible to resist, throbbing with his need for me. I stroked it lightly, running my fingertips up his length. He moaned, and his cock twitched under my hand. Crow, it had been so long! I held myself back from shoving that lovely cock down my throat all at once. Instead, I kissed him hungrily as I caressed the very tip, and it jumped under my hand.

"Do you have the energy for this?" I panted, pulling back. "I want you, but I also want you well."

"I will always have the energy for you," Celebel said, playing with my nipples and sending a thrill ricocheting down my body.

A small part of my mind piped up to question my judgment in further encouraging such activity in his current state. It begged me to consider the troublesome attention I may bring upon myself, but a much larger part was ferociously lustful. The soulbond had me in its teeth; the compulsion to be close to him surged so strongly I could hardly breathe. I compromised between the warring parts of me by guarding my heart just enough to keep my roiling emotions contained. Then I bent and licked the full length of his cock, swirling my tongue around the head.

He bucked and moaned under me. I pulled back, wanting to savor him, and licked my way up his firm abs to bite a nipple. His skin was sweet under my tongue, and he whimpered when I tugged at the small bud clamped in my teeth. I knotted a hand in his hair and yanked, pulling his head back as I moved to the other nipple. He gasped and his cock gave a mighty jump, tapping against my needy clit.

Our lust crashed together in waves.

Holding him in place, I took my time in pleasuring him with my hand. I delighted in the ability to give more than receive, so wholly denied in the recent past. From the way he bucked under me and strained against my grip, I knew he would be all too cheerful to give back as good as he got. He tried to resist; I know he did, but he climaxed anyway. Hot seed gouted onto his chest in thick ropes. He cried out, body rigid in the throes of his pleasure.

Celebel's eyes unfocused and his breath came quick and ragged. I dipped my hands in the pearly spill, painting it on my breasts, massaging it into my skin, relishing in the sensation. Slicking my hands in his come, I worked it into my cunt, and he watched my hands move with rapt hunger. Unable to resist, he grabbed my hand, sucking both my juices and his own from my fingers.

He pulled me in for a kiss and our mingled flavors on his tongue only fanned my flames. I traveled down his body, exploring him with my lips, savoring the taste. Lapping up every bit of him. At the last moment, I gave into my urges and raked my teeth across that beautiful skin. His back arched again, and he moaned for me. His cock sprang back to life, hard and ready.

"Gods, I have needed nothing in my life so much as I need to fuck you," he breathed, clawing at the ground. "I think you could drain me completely dry."

I was beyond words. Every sound he made filled me with a delirious fury; a frantic desire to slake my lust as my arousal flooded down my thighs. I had to force myself to slow, to appreciate each moment, to not just slam down on his cock and fuck him until we both collapsed.

I worked my way back to his ears, gently nibbling to the hollow at the base of his throat. His whimper made my clit throb, and I hissed with need. Licking and biting, I traced a path down to his cock. He took hold of my ears, shivering me with delight.

Nuzzling his shaft dragged a heavy moan from his throat. Kissing the tip made him gasp. Light sucking drew inarticulate sounds. Such a delicious indulgence, the sensation of that velvety skin against my lips, the way his girth strained my jaws. Withdrawing just before bringing him to climax made him whine pitifully, which made me laugh. My wetness pooled beneath me, slicking my thighs, and I slowed myself with a mighty effort.

"Ah, gods," he groaned. "Please, let me pleasure you!"

"Later." With a wicked smile, I deep-throated his cock.

His whine grew into a panting cry. I sucked harder, faster, coaxing the orgasm from the root of his soul. My efforts paid off as a violent spasm rocked me and he spurted down my throat. Stubbornly, I held on and swallowed down every drop. The salty-sweet taste on my tongue, the throb of his passion, his hands massaging my ears—I nearly climaxed with him. Spent, he slipped from my mouth.

Resting against his belly, we both caught our breath. I looked up at him.

"I need you to fuck me now. I want your cock buried deep inside me." Said cock twitched under me. "Give it to me, hard as you can."

His erection grew, and I climbed back over him to kiss his lips. Teasing, I rocked back and forth over his body, just barely grazing the tip of his cock against my clit until I orgasmed with a quick, violent shudder. The speed and force of it took my breath away.

Fully hard again, he made a despairing noise and grabbed my waist, thrusting upward and impaling me. I sat down heavily on him, slamming his cock into my cervix with a strength that made me gasp, and we found a rhythm. I loved the way his cock stretched me, the deep bruising ache of the collision. Forcing him to slow as I had, I wanted to make the moment last as long as possible. Ah, gods, it had been ages!

Working me into another crescendo, he kissed and stroked my breasts as he thrust. I varied the rhythm, speeding and slowing, until I felt his cock give a mighty throb. The sensation made me sing out my glorious climax, pounding down on him as hard as I could. He joined me in bliss, crying out his ecstasy, and the rippling force of his ejaculation pulled a third, quick climax from my body. Such heavenly release!

I didn't realize I was crying until Celebel wiped tears from my cheeks and kissed my eyelids. "Oh, my Moon, why do you weep?"

Rafael's words echoed—*Why are you weeping if you are happy?*—and I cried harder. The emotional intimacy with Celebel filled a yawning chasm of need within me. A chasm I'd been avoiding for years. Perhaps all my life.

Celebel touched his fingers to his tongue, then kissed me. "Your tears taste of freedom. And reverie." We twined together, hearts beating in unison. I drank in the delicious scent of him, and the light taste of sweat drying on his skin. He stroked my hair and hummed to himself as the sun warmed us.

"This is the sweetest convalescence I have ever known," he said.

"Well, I had to be sure all your parts were still in working order." I propped myself on my elbows to look at him, an appreciative smile gilding my face.

My heart lurched then, a powerful tug from another direction, and reality clanged down like an iron portcullis. It doused my blissful afterglow, forcing the breath from my lungs. What had I done? I barely knew this man and already I had abandoned all good sense. I slid off of him, covering my face in my hands with a growing sense of guilt and dread.

"Cúraniel, are you hurt?"

Miserably, I shook my head. "My lust has trodden all over my prudence. I may have signed your death warrant, and you're barely healed! What am I *doing*?" Finally, given relief and genuine connection, I found myself less inclined to chase after the tatters Rafael dangled before me. And yet, and yet…

"If this Dragon truly loves you, would he act in such hurtful ways?"

"It is not his love I question. It's his anger. Once that blistering rage rises to the surface, there is no reasoning with him."

Celebel exhaled in a gusty sigh. "Of all the things I never expected in my life, surely cuckolding the bloody *Red Dragon* tops the list."

I laughed until the tears returned and we held onto each other, sharing anxiety.

"You should be safe if you can get far enough away from me." I selfishly wanted him to stay. Terrified for his safety if he did. "At least I hope you will."

"I've only just found you! I cannot leave now! Surely we have more time."

"Celebel, you have no choice if you want to survive."

"As far as our people are concerned, I'm already dead. Let me enjoy the respite of my death with you, in this little corner of paradise you call home. If your Red Dragon shows up and makes the news official, well, at least I'll die fulfilled."

If I hadn't been drawn so tight, I might have laughed.

He made the sign for 'focus your ears,' "I realize I am an interloper here. Meeting you is a happy accident, but that changes nothing. Obviously you have unfinished business with the... with Rafael. I want to clarify that I have no intention of standing in your way. I apologize if I made it seem shameful. If it's important to you, then it's equally important to me. Do whatever you need to do, just please, do not push me away."

I let him pull me in again for more kisses, our hands crawling over each other's bodies with mutual hunger.

Chapter 13

25 years ago

Inside the bower, I sat with my legs twined around Rafael's waist as he licked my breasts through the silk gauze of my dress. He had a frustrating way of angling his hips to prevent me from grinding against his erection. Worse, he resisted my tug at his arm to draw his hand down between my thighs.

"You're going to ruin this silk." Despite that, I reveled in the heat of his breath on my sensitive flesh.

"I have brought more," he rumbled, taking a nipple in his mouth and sucking hard enough to make me gasp.

He gestured at a glimmering, night-blue bolt of silk peeking from under his folded cloak. His long tongue curled around my breast, squeezing, and I flushed with the memory of how sublime it felt buried deep in my cunt.

"When are you going to take that gods damned shirt off?" I hissed it through clenched teeth, the insistent throb between my legs making it difficult to form words. "I am desperate to feel my skin against yours! You're driving me mad."

"I have already removed my cloak and jerkin. And boots," he murmured against my breast.

Knotting both fists into his hair, I yanked his head up to look at me. "Skin. I want your skin, not that horrible scratchy wool!"

"Hrrm. I suppose you wish me to allow you release as well as giving in to your demands." An evil smile played at his lips. Rafael stood, lifting me by my buttocks, legs still wrapped around his waist.

"What are you—"

The bower opened, and he carried me into the sun, dropping me to my feet. "Earn it. Strike me."

I groaned and shook out the front of my damp dress. "Not this again! Haven't we established that I have no head for the fight?"

Only my instinct to flinch away saved me from the huge fist that grazed past where my face had been. I danced backward, out of the Dragon's reach.

"Fucking hells, Rafael!"

A grin spread, showing the points of his jagged teeth. Then he was on me. It took everything I had not to get crushed into the dirt, scrambling backward in desperation to avoid his lightning-fast strikes. My skirt tangled in my legs, and sweat beaded my brow.

"Defend yourself," he snarled.

I spun around his jabbing punch, locking my arms around him rather than backing away again. As he adroitly broke my hold, I whipped a hand up and slapped his face. Only a light tap, but my palm stung on impact.

"Fucking stop it," I shouted, overcome with the irritation of my defied lust and his sudden aggression.

To my surprise, he coughed out a laugh. "Point to you. Good. You can be taught after all."

I'd learned the hard way to only strike at the most vulnerable areas. Every time I'd hurt myself punching him, he taunted me about it for years. So I slapped him again, and he laughed harder.

In triumph, I grabbed his hand and dragged him back into the bower. The cool interior soothed me. When I pulled him down beside me on the pallet, he hesitated. I stroked his cheek, and he leaned into my hand, closing his eyes.

"Set the pace, but please let's actually move forward. Tell me if you want me to touch you, and what to avoid," I said.

He exhaled slowly, and loosened the laces at his throat, then the ones at his wrists. Finally, with a heavy sigh, he pulled the shirt over his head and clasped it to his chest. So much vulnerability in that gesture. It drew a wistful sigh from my lips. The muscles in his broad shoulders bunched with tension, quivering with anticipatory fear. My heart quivered in response. I wished I could simply kiss it all away.

"Easy, Dragon. I won't touch you unless you invite it," I

murmured.

"I want your touch. I need it, but... pain is far easier to bear." He set the shirt aside and gave me a sidelong look. The sun trickling in from the calcites illuminated his aquiline profile, highlighting the beautiful lines of his torso.

"What if you simply hold me and I don't touch you at all?"

As an answer, Rafael gathered me roughly in his arms, dragging me into his lap. I spun my immediate physical reaction into a tight ball and stuffed it deep in my mind for his comfort. Easy enough to summon again if he initiated anything. Pressing my cheek against his chest, I closed my eyes, inhaling the spiced musk of his skin. His chin rested on the top of my head. After a moment, his rumbling breath took on a soothing, rhythmic quality.

"Are you... are you *purring?*" I couldn't look at his face; I knew my sudden glee would sour his already fraught mood. Gods forfend my calling anything he did *cute,* he'd probably knock my head off my shoulders.

He snorted, tightening his arms around me defensively. "It is called *thrumming.*"

"It's so charming!" I couldn't help myself.

"Shut the fuck up, Cúraniel."

2 years ago

Sleeting rain beat a staccato rhythm on the outer trunk of the Great Tree. Not for the first time, I was grateful for the ability to enclose my bower, preventing the icy water from leaking through and turning the floor to mud. Rafael sat at the opposite end of the space, back to the wall where he could watch both me and the entrance.

He never quite managed to get along with the Tree, but they at least had some kind of truce. He would, of course, decline to thank his host for the shelter. Shadows drew around him as his lambent eyes followed my every move.

I lounged on my pallet, freshly stuffed with clean rushes and fragrant chrysanthemum. Feeling a bit more daring than usual in the comforting warmth, I risked broaching a topic that I'd danced around before, to ill effect. I'd been worrying at it like a gnawed bone ever since.

"Are you familiar with the concepts of soulmates and soulbonding?"

Rafael remained perfectly still, but his eye flicked over to my face. "Fanciful elvish nonsense."

Exactly as I expected. No matter how close we grew—nor how many times he brought me to climax—he took great lengths to avoid the subject of the obvious bond between us. The infuriating man could slay the entire world and still run from his feelings.

"Not at all," I protested. "These are very real states of being, though I can see why you would have that impression. There is a tendency to wax poetic about them in our writings, as though having a soulmate is merely the epitome of romantic love."

He quirked one of those sharply arched eyebrows. Disdainful, but listening.

I took a deep breath. "Soulbonding is the deliberate act of binding your power and very soul to another. It must be done in order to conceive a child," I said, which was perhaps a mistake, "but there are other advantages."

"Oh, indeed." His droll tone held a note of 'where are you going with this?'

With an effort, I controlled my heart rate, knowing he would sense if it sped up. "A strong soulbond gives a sense of the partner's location, as well as their general state of being." I waited for his reaction, trying to prod him into acknowledging the connection I knew he could feel.

He remained silent. Watchful.

"Soulmates are a natural soulbond, much stronger than a forged soulbond, and formed through compatibility of spirit. It's rare, treasured, and occurs immediately upon introduction. It is said that with practice, one may speak mind-to-mind with one's partner." I tapped the center of my bare chest. His eyes followed the movement and flicked back to my face. I continued, hesitant. "I've heard it described as a deep, inexorable pull toward the other person anchored in the heart-mind. When soulmates are apart for too long, the strain on the bond diminishes their power. Easily rectified by spending time in each other's presence."

Rafael's look sharpened into a glare, suspicion writ large on his face. I cursed myself for not taking a more subtle approach, but I couldn't seem to stop talking.

"It… it is possible to sever a forged soulbond," I stammered, "but the stronger the connection, the greater the risk. Soulmate bonds are unbreakable. Losing a soulmate has a high fatality rate."

"Why?" The word was short, clipped.

"Because you have to rend your—"

"Why are you telling me this?" Rafael's expression closed off, a storm brewing on his brow. His burning eyes pinned me in place, and I wondered how long it would take him to leave this time. I couldn't say aloud what he already knew.

"I thought you would find it interesting. Cultural differences." It wasn't exactly a lie. I'd never been able to lie to him. I wasn't much given to prevarication in general, but I knew from experience he would pick up on any dishonesty as easily as scenting blood. "Having a soulmate is no guarantee of harmony. I've known of some who absolutely loathed each other, but they were still drawn together. We are meant to strengthen and aid each other, regardless of other entanglements."

"'We'." It was a flat statement.

"I only meant—"

"Hrrm." His rumble strengthened to an echoing growl, causing the Tree to shiver around us. Rising, the Dragon unfolded his long, powerful legs with ease. At least he wasn't lashing out. Yet.

"Rafael—"

"I have several books and scrolls on the subject, if you would like them. As you say, they are heavily romanticized."

That was not at all the response I'd expected. He was absurdly skilled at knocking me off-balance. "I… thank you, yes, I would like that."

"Stop thanking me. Terrible habit."

"You are the only drake I've ever met!" I tugged my earlobes.

"And I intend for it to remain thus, but you should be prepared, regardless."

I gazed up at him, faerie lights glimmering around his head like stars. "Surely you aren't leaving now, in the freezing rain?" It was a gamble.

He grimaced, shifting his weight as he considered his options. I scooted over on my pallet, making space for him.

"Stay, please. At least wait out the storm. These scrolls will keep. You only arrived last night and you haven't even rested! I know because I woke several times in the early morning to find you watching me. Which, truly, is a bit unsettling."

With an unreadable look, Rafael settled himself beside me. He stared like I might shapeshift into a venomous serpent at any moment. Were drakes immune to venom? Could a viper's fangs even penetrate that hide? I knew so little.

"Rest here with me." I patted the blanket and sighed in consternation at the stubborn set to his mouth. "I know you usually like to flee while I'm asleep after we talk about anything that resembles *feelings*, but you have the option." As soon as I spoke, I regretted the words.

"You are testing me today." The Dragon's voice darkened.

"You're testing yourself. Just lie down!"

He growled then, eyes flashing. The sound reverberated in the bower.

"Now you're being unpleasant for no reason." Familiarity took the edge off of his usual intimidation tactics. I only ever truly feared him when the madness took hold and he lost his sense of time and place, trapped in the prison of his crystalline memory.

"At some point, you have to actually face the reality of what's happening between us."

"With you as the sole arbiter of reason." He rose, heat rising with him in a wavering halo.

"Rafael, the storm—"

"Fuck the storm," he snarled, and the Tree shivered in response. The trunk opened wide. It always reacted this way to his temper; wanting to cast him out.

"Don't do this." I hopped to my feet and snagged the edge of his cloak. "Don't fucking run away again."

He yanked his cloak free with a growl. "What power do you believe you hold over me to make such demands?"

Snow gusted in, sprinkling the carpets with dots of moisture. I shivered, pulling a blanket around me. Winter had truly arrived, with a bite nearly as sharp as Rafael's.

"It's a request. Please, just talk to me. I know you feel the connection between us, no matter how you deny it."

The Dragon paused just outside the opening to the bower. "What proof do you have of this supposed connection?"

Gods, I wanted to slap him. Instead, I focused my thoughts into a sharp point, and drove them into his head.

'If we had no deep connection, could I speak to you thus?' I sent. *'Would you know my desires half so well?'*

His eyes went wide, the pupils thinning to venomous slits. *'Get. The Fuck. Out. Of my HEAD!'*

The response boomed in my thoughts, nearly palpable in its force. I pulled back, guarding myself as he rounded on me. Grey smoke issued from his nose and mouth. Just as his lips pulled back from his teeth, the Tree slammed shut, blocking him out.

I ran to the wall, but the Tree remained sealed. "Let me out, please!"

It rustled, stubborn.

"I cannot have this battle on two fronts. Great Ancestor, please!" I pounded the smooth interior bark with my fists. After a moment, the Tree groaned, a shudder passing from root to crown.

It cracked open just wide enough for me to squeeze out.

Rafael was already stomping off into the flurrying snow. I ran after him, bare feet splashing on the wet grass, dully noting the snow hadn't begun to stick.

"Please stop! Just talk to me, please!" I shouted over a shrieking gust of wind.

Pausing, he glared over his shoulder. Steam drifted around him, snowflakes evaporating before they made contact.

"Leave me be," he snapped. "Is it not enough that I bring you gifts and pleasure? You must own me as well?"

"I make no claims of ownership! And I've never asked for gifts. All I've ever wanted was to be close to you!" I skidded to a halt well outside of his reach. When I focused inward, the soulbond twisted in agony, wringing out my gut like a damp rag. "Fucking hells, Dragon. I *know* you can feel this!"

"Do not speak for me!" His voice echoed down the hill, fury building in each syllable. "You presume *far* too much, and I have tolerated it for too long. Your absurd emotions will not collar me."

Tears pricked my eyes. "Rafa—" A freezing gale ripped the words from my mouth. I tried again. "Rafael, I can't keep doing this. Every time I think we're making some kind of progress, you shy like a nervous horse and disappear again. I can't even speak with honesty! Instead, I must dance unceasing over the hot coals of your avoidance. It hurts! You are *hurting* me."

"Your softness is not my problem."

"Can't you stop being such a fucking insensitive blighter for one heartbeat and simply talk to me?" I swore I wouldn't cry. Not again. It only made him more defensive. A rebellious tear trickled down my cheek, anyway.

"Keep your trinkets." He turned away.

Wings sprouted from his scaly back, and he launched himself into the sky. I sank to my knees in the cold slush and bowed my head, trying to breathe over the hiccoughing pain in my chest.

Chapter 14
Current day

Against my advice, Celebel borrowed a longsword, insisting that he needed to restore his 'conditioning.' As he worked through a series of exercises, I couldn't help but compare. *He moves like a dancer. Rafael moves like a killer.* The thought had me shuddering away from the burning focus that seared into me. What had changed to grab the Dragon's notice so easily? I knew the answer, but stubbornly sent my awareness outward once more.

Celebel caught me watching and grinned, exaggerating his motions. A circling of slim hips, a forward thrust with firm, round buttocks, and he'd captured my full attention. When he finished, he propped the pommel of his sword on those captivating hips, made eye contact with me, and slowly polished the length of his blade with a cloth. I dissolved into much-needed laughter.

The next morning, I admired Celebel's lithe form as he bathed again in the stream, the dappled sun gleaming on his pale skin, lighting up the streaks in his dark hair. He danced in place to his own internal music, the sway of his hips sending ripples across the water. With a cheeky grin, he gyrated deliberately for me, bringing heat between my legs. His ease with his body relaxed something deep within me.

Again, the contrast struck me. I chewed on my lower lip, envisioning Rafael's body and the way his powerful, armor-like musculature flexed and rolled as he moved. His abdomen was like a fitted cobblestone path—I'd never seen anything like it. The yoke of his impossibly broad shoulders held a bundle of highly developed muscles that belonged to only the most devastating strikers. And in his scalier, more overtly draconic forms… Well. I'd claimed I wasn't drawn to danger, but there was something deeply, perversely thrilling about being with someone who could crush me like a butterfly wing.

"What are you so intent on, my dear?" Celebel's smooth voice interrupted my reverie, and my blossoming lust turned to guilt. He caught the shift in my mood. "Ah, *him.* Come now, no need to feel shame. I would have no secrets between us."

I reached for Celebel, and he folded me into his arms. His skin was still slightly damp from the creek and smelled faintly of the sweet, chiming starsong. The inevitable comparisons followed, how different it felt to have my head tucked just under his chin rather than resting on a hard chest. How Celebel's body was firm with supple muscle and yielded nicely to me instead of feeling like stone under my hands. How, instead of unnaturally hot, his skin was pleasantly warm. My frustrated desire was all too happy to find a willing target.

We tumbled in the grass on the bank. He caught me from behind, and I arched my back against him. The fragrance of lilies encircled us.

Celebel slid his hands between my legs, pushing my knees apart. I writhed against him, desperate for his cock.

"Oh gods, you're already wet," he murmured.

"Fuck me hard," I commanded. "I need to be obliterated. Rough, brutal, and quick, to get me out of my head and fully into my body. I need to lose myself in the physicality."

He happily obliged, cupping my breasts in his hands, squeezing. I reached behind me, grabbed two fistfuls of his beautiful hair, and yanked. He gasped and bucked against me, cock throbbing as it slid in deep.

"Harder. I want to feel it in my spine."

This would be the test; if he could fuck me with abandon, or if he would hold back. I wanted all the carnality, the unbridled desire.

Slowly increasing in speed and intensity, he pounded into me, the slap of our skin an aching rhythm. He gripped my hips, digging his fingers in, and we crashed together in bliss. The way I'd longed for. The harder he fucked me, the more I relaxed into it, the more I allowed my pleasure to crest and wash away my concerns.

He came with an abrupt shudder, and I clamped down with all the muscular strength of my cunt, locking him in place. The undulations drew ragged cries as he climaxed inside me. He had done well, but I didn't release him, not yet. I needed to be fucked within moments of death.

Gripping him from within and rocking against him, I coaxed him back into hardness. He took his time for the second round, pulling all the way out between each thrust and burying himself to the hilt with each punishing stab into me. I relished the building sound of his moans, the slap of his testicles against me, the delectable scent of his sweat, his seed dripping down my thighs. Bracing myself with an elbow, I used my free hand to pinch my sensitized nipples, intensifying the pain, intensifying the ecstasy. Glancing down, the sight of my blood mingling with his issue made my spine tingle with wicked glee.

When he took bruising hold of my ears to better guide his next thrust, my orgasm roared up and tore free, taking his second with it. We cried out together, slamming into each other with abandon. His cock rippled inside me, filling me to the brink with his seed, overflowing my capacity to hold him. I screamed to the gods with my release, clawing tufts of grass free.

After, he held me content against his chest and murmured into my hair. "Given how you like to fuck, I believe I can understand the physical attraction to this drake. However, I don't understand the emotional connection at all. He is a famous, ruthless murderer! I know we all have unusual attractions from time to time, but this is something else entirely." He paused, frowning. "Soulmate or otherwise. Are you willing to explain further?"

I turned to meet his eyes. Soft, gentle, sky blue. Tracing a thoughtful finger over the outline of his full lips, I considered the request.

"This feels awkward. Are you sure?" Did I even have the fortitude to discuss my feelings for Rafael in depth, given everything?

Celebel blinked. "Given what?"

I clamped down on my thoughts. Crow. I hadn't expected him to connect so intimately, so fast. The slingshot of emotion between two soulmates already exhausted me. I had to be more careful.

My new lover rubbed my back in lazy circles and made an encouraging noise. "Know thy enemy, yes?" He felt me stiffen, and his hands sped up. "I'm only teasing, love! Please continue."

Love. He seemed to realize it in the same moment I did, hands pausing in their ministrations.

"Am I your love?" I whispered. "You hardly know me and I'm proven to have instincts that are, at best, questionable."

He was still for a long moment. "I should not say so, for the reasons you have given, but I cannot deny what I already know in my deepest heart to be true. I love you. Call it infatuation if you prefer, but my soul says 'love'."

"Your sincerity is evident. I've never once claimed a romantic love for anyone until you pulled that confession from me."

I'd fielded plenty of those confessions, but never returned them. Until now. All the tears and carrying on had seemed so overwrought before it happened to me, and a deep sense of guilt washed over me for some of my past callousness. Given my spectacular arguments with Rafael over emotions, I had no claim to superiority. Perhaps my long absence from the lives of my former lovers meant their good fortune.

"Pity it wasn't for me." Sadness colored Celebel's words, and I settled against him, pulling his arms around me. The woven scents of crushed grass and lilies might linger forever in these memories.

"You seem to convince me despite myself, oh Silver Star of the pretty face and even prettier cock. Can I say that I love you so soon?" The sentiment rang through me like a bell. "I think perhaps my heart understands better than my recalcitrant mind. I feel you anchored there, as you said."

He shifted me in his arms, turning me toward him for a long

kiss. I reveled in his soft mouth and shared breath. Lowering me to the ground, he propped himself on an elbow as he traced the line of my shoulder.

"You gleam like the moon itself. I've never met anyone with quite that tint of violet to their lips… and nipples," he said, brushing a gentle hand over my breast, then it drifted between my legs. "And other places."

I caught his hand, bringing his knuckles to my lips. His eyes shone with tenderness and he kissed my forehead. I stood and stretched, wading into the water, and he joined me. We rinsed away the remainder of our lovemaking. Drying in the sun, we walked to the bower. He moved easily up the hill, pleasing me with the progression of his recovery. The cool interior of the Tree welcomed us.

Celebel gave me a knowing look. "Weren't you going to explain exactly what draws you to this monstrous lover of yours?"

Crow. I'd hoped to distract him away from this conversation, but it pleased me that he was not so easily led. I sat at the stool by my work bench while he paced.

"There is a hidden sensitivity to Rafael that I truly value. I know it seems outlandish." I caught the rise in his eyebrows. "He grows roses. *Roses!* He even taught me a centering technique with them."

I'd always wished Rafael would bring me a rooted seedling, but he guarded his plants as jealously as, well, a dragon. One time I mistakenly mentioned trying to coax one of those cut roses to root. He'd given me such an evil look that I just handed the whole stem back and never spoke of it again.

"*Roses*, really?" Celebel's incredulous voice cut into my thoughts. "A warlord who grows flowers? I would think him more of the scorched earth sort." He glared at the portraits of Rafael he'd collected.

"What kind of mindless killer teaches a centering technique for the dissociation that comes from extreme trauma? The rose petals help to realign the heart-mind. He's sensitive enough to intuit these things without guidance, a rare skill."

"Seems like useful self-preservation when you're extinguishing entire kingdoms." Celebel's voice was snide.

"Perhaps, but *he* taught *me* a healing art I did not know, for no reason other than to share it with me because he knew I would be interested." I picked an errant blade of grass from my hair.

Celebel paused before me, leaning over to pick up the moonstone bottle. "This rose, yes?"

I twisted to watch his face, formless anxiety mounting. "Yes. Please don't touch the flower itself. I do not know if he can sense what it experiences. It holds a significant amount of power."

My new lover tilted and turned the bottle, watching the light shimmer across the petals, inhaling its aroma.

"Could it truly be the Sirelon rose? The fragrance and conformation are exactly the same." Horror crept across his features. "Cúraniel, what if your lover took this plant from the ashes of the city he razed? We had a single specimen in the gardens of Velúara. Gifted before the fall, it was once the symbol of Sirelon. The last bloom faded when I was young, as Sirelon's final remaining elder passed, and it never flowered again." His brow creased. "That rose was an iridescent white."

Celebel's words froze the breath in my lungs. I thought back to all the times Rafael had said, 'you would not like the answer.' The tales of his slaughter were mostly academic to me. Apart from the conflict with the War Crow and a few minor incidents early on, I'd been wholly removed from his violence.

"I hardly know what to say. Rafael claimed he is no longer eating elves out of consideration for me." My voice sounded far away, as though coming from elsewhere. I'd never visited Sirelon, but now I wished I had. "It does not absolve him of past atrocities, but it seems a good place to start."

Celebel's expression softened. "Do you believe him?"

"I do," I said without hesitation. "He is brutally honest, if not particularly forthright. I often find myself combing through his words for hidden meaning, but they always have the taste of truth."

"Fair enough." He set the bottle down. "The roses are potentially fraught, and you simply didn't know. It has been a very long time, after all. At least the Red Dragon may have preserved *something* of the culture he destroyed."

"All of Rafael's gifts are a bit fraught."

Celebel's brows raised. I purposefully did not mention the personal implement Rafael had brought me later on. Or the items we'd argued about.

"May I take a closer look at those pearls in your hair? I assume they're also from him. Fit for dragon's hoard, to be sure."

I unbraided them and handed him the strand. "Yes. His first 'trinket,' as he calls them."

He ran them through his hands, marveling. "No record exists of these that I can recall. Gods, they're spectacular. Surely Maraiya origin?"

"I believe so. He woke me one day by draping them over my neck, and said they reminded him of my face." I warmed at the memory. Rafael had been so earnest, and so startled when I'd shamelessly flirted with him. "I tried to refuse, to insist he return them to their original owners. He told me he'd taken them from another dragon's hoard. A blue dragon, as I recall."

Celebel almost dropped the pearls in shock but made a smooth recovery. "A *dragon?* A true dragon? Not a drake?"

"I said the same thing. He responded with, 'I have slain my share of gods'." I mimicked Rafael's deep rumble to the best of my abilities.

Celebel shuddered and handed back the strand. "He must really want to impress you."

"Hardly." I laughed at the idea of the Red Dragon caring at all about anyone's opinion of him. "It pleases him to make me smile, but he also seems to have some draconic impulse to stash riches away. I never asked to be showered with gifts. It's as though he views my bower as an extension of his hoard."

"Does it follow that he also views you as part of that hoard?"

I blew out a breath. "Perhaps. He certainly believes he

knows my complete melody without practice."

"Charming," Celebel said. I made a face, and he laughed softly, pressing a kiss to my brow. "Be at ease, my dear. I am only teasing you."

"You are alike there. We tease each other frequently." With a pang, I realized I missed the Dragon's caustic sense of humor.

"Hard to imagine *that* face ever smiling."

"Drakes do not emote as we do." How many times had I voiced frustration with Rafael's stony expression? "They have a saying, 'the Dragon who shows his teeth does not smile.' His true smile is subtle; a slight curl of the lips, a devilish glint in the eyes—"

"Ah, good to know. We do not want smiling drakes, only devilish ones." Celebel's own eyes glittered wickedly.

I tried to swat him from my perch, and he laughed, dancing back out of my reach. He settled on my pallet. "You speak his elvish name, Rafael, but what does he call himself?"

I blushed. "I, ah, I cannot pronounce his drake name. Not even close. I've tried, believe me, and I've learned to speak what he says is marginally passable draconian. His name sounds different every time I hear it. It seems to start with a 'j' and contains some 'x' sounds, so I finally asked if I could just call him 'Jax.' He denied me. Still, since it annoys him, I save 'Jax' for when I need to get his attention quickly."

Celebel's expression turned serious, and he rested his chin on my knee. "You do love him. It is plain. The stars twinkle in your eyes when you speak of him. If you are so very enamored with this… person and his idiosyncrasies, what do you see in me?"

I appraised him for a long moment, drinking in his beautifully earnest, open face. "It has been a very long time since I have felt so fully relaxed with a lover," I said, touching his lips, his jawline, tracing down the line of his shoulder. Perhaps it was selfish, but I appreciated not having to navigate an intricate web of emotional trauma. "You put me at ease. He wishes to protect me, but sometimes the one he protects me from is himself."

It felt disloyal to say, but there were things Celebel inherently understood simply because he was also an elf. The 'love' verse still loomed too large for either man, and I wished to nurture it before I added too many refrains.

"Celebel, I know you are my soulmate. I feel the same magnetic pull to you, soul-deep. The ability to speak openly with you about these topics is a relief I can barely express. How can I love a person I've known for such a short time? And yet here I am, enrapt. It intimidates me. I have never expressed romantic love for anyone, and you've drawn it out of me twice in quick succession.

"You are kind, with an easy laugh, and you garner the same from me. You are confident without arrogance, strong without violence. You are not afraid to claim your sexuality. And you are quite delectable."

He kissed the back of my hand and then grabbed it, blowing his lips on my skin to make a loud, rude noise.

"And that as well. You are comfortable being ridiculous," I laughed. "Plus, it *vastly* helps that you let me do this." I slid off the stool to reach between his legs.

"I see, just using me for my body—oh!"

"Is that a complaint?"

"Certainly not. Keep doing that." He closed his eyes in bliss.

"Does it feel more personal, losing your earrings in a battle like that, versus something like an accident?" Curling beside Celebel on the pallet, I touched his right ear where I had mended the damage. "Will you re-pierce?"

He heaved a rueful sigh. "Yes, I suppose I must. That lower one was from my first battle, ironically enough."

"Will you tell me the story of the rest?" I draped myself across his lap and he smiled.

"It would be my honor." He ran his fingers along his left ear, hooking one finger through each small ring as he spoke. "This one is from reaching my majority, of course. There is my first intimate encounter." He gave me a mischievous grin. "This is from the bestowal of the family name, our signifier." It was a beautifully crafted pendant earring set with a fine sapphire, crowned by diamonds in a distinctive star pattern. "Here is where I was named Consul." That one contained a single rose cut diamond, outlined in tiny, ancient script proclaiming his position.

He switched to the right ear, touching the lost piercings and the remainder. "Receiving my first real sword, armor, and horse. The first battle. It also coincides with my first kill, but I pierced that separately. Declaration of war. I'm sorry, this side is rather grim."

I stroked his arm. "No need to apologize. It helps me know you. Perhaps I'll pierce your left ear for your introduction to me. It seems like you could use some protective energy on that side," I said, only half-teasing.

He grew solemn. "I would be greatly honored. May I do the same for you?"

"Of course!" I twitched my ears, making my earrings jangle merrily.

"Tell me your story, please, let me know you." He traced my ears, sending a pleasant tingle down my spine. "I noticed you are not wearing your family signifier."

"The left side is similar to yours, with my majority and first significant intimacy. The empty hole there is where I took the family name. Here is the departure of the last elders. Just above that is where I broke with the lineage and left. This is where I found the hill."

I switched sides, as he had. "This is the first patient healed, and the pact with the Night Mother. Here is the first patient I healed upon arriving at my hill. This is where I met Nemohee..." I paused, reluctant.

"The next is for *him*, isn't it?" His voice was serious, but his eyes were kind.

"That obvious?"

"Well, it is your only gold ring, and dragons love their gold. Does he understand the significance of piercing your ear?" He reached out as if to touch the gold earring, and then withdrew his hand at the last moment.

I sighed. "Yes. He was strange about it at first, but already familiar with the custom."

Rafael had gone still as death when I mentioned piercing my ear to commemorate meeting him. He'd stared long enough for me to grow nervous. Just as I was sure I'd mortally offended him, he blinked and suggested that I use yellow gold.

When I'd said I didn't have any, he'd breezily waved away my concern and produced a coin from somewhere in his clothing. In a casual demonstration of his immense strength, he'd squeezed and rolled the coin in his hand, extruding it into a perfectly even wire. The piercing itself was surprisingly gentle. Once the ring was in place, he'd used a small, tightly directed flame, breathed through pursed lips, to melt the ends together. I'd been nervous, but it had worked beautifully.

I'd asked if he wanted to pierce his ear as well. His answer was such a withering glare that I ended up teasing him about it. Because the whole thing veered dangerously close to emotional territory, he never acknowledged it again.

"May I add mine just above the gold?" Celebel's voice brought me back to the present. The mischievous grin had returned.

I laughed. "What a troublemaker you are! Yes, you may. Would you prefer to use your own material or some of mine? I have a bit of þilvor stashed away." I'd carefully hoarded the star ore over the ages. Rare, incredibly strong, and resonant, it had always been the metal of choice for elvish crafting. We made jewelry and weapons alike with it. I'd never grown accustomed to Rafael's casual gifting of þilvor.

He wrapped his arms around me and kissed my neck. "You are generous to offer. I'm afraid I'm rather short on the basics at the moment, so I'll have to take you up on that."

I disentangled myself from his arms in order to find the þilvor I had stored in a case full of small drawers. He followed me to the entrance of the bower, watching me select the jewelry.

"Seems a starry night with a waxing moon would be the best choice for this," he said.

"Good thing we have such a night coming upon us." I found the pieces I needed and rejoined him outside.

We held each other and watched the sunset cast flaming oranges and deep purples across the forest below. Celebel braided my hair as the moon rose, kissing me often enough that I had to make him stop so my hands would be steady.

With a song, I infused the earring with the breadth of my emotion, pouring all my joy and relief into the þilvor. The precious metal hummed in my hand. Lit from within, the earring gleamed like the moon itself with the resonance of my spirit.

All of it flowed into Celebel as the sharp point bit through skin and cartilage. He sighed, a shiver running down his spine. I hooked the earring closed and breathed on the fresh piercing to heal it and cement the memory. He murmured a pleased sound.

Taking the earring meant for me, he brushed my braid away from my right shoulder and reverently kissed the ear where the piercing would be. He did the same as I had, pouring his heart into the jewelry. The sweetness of his wordless song raised a tear to my eye, and the þilvor glowed.

Swiftly and accurately, he pierced my ear. I hardly felt a thing over the tingle of power. He kissed the fresh piercing, and then we were kissing each other hungrily.

Chapter 15

The rose wilted. Crow, it was so much sooner than I expected. Given the strength of my newfound emotions, and the frequency and force of my newfound orgasms, I really shouldn't have been surprised. Concentrating for a moment, I pinpointed the general direction of the Dragon's approach.

Down by the creek, Celebel tried futilely to hammer the dents out of his armor with a rock by using a larger, flat rock as a makeshift anvil. It would have been entertaining to watch under other circumstances.

"Rafael is coming," I said.

Celebel set his project aside with a frown. "Now?"

"Very soon." I showed him the wilted flower. "This only happens on his imminent return."

We locked eyes for a long moment. He assessed me thoughtfully. "I've thought on this at length. You say the Red Dragon will know I've been here. Even if I return to my people alone, what's stopping him from tracking me down and killing me there? Given what you've told me about his vindictive nature, I wouldn't be surprised if he followed me and murdered us all."

I sucked in a startled breath. He was right. Gods damn it, I had to choose *now*. I wasn't ready. Leave the Great Tree and my quiet life behind, or risk losing Celebel—and possibly my soul. No way to predict what Rafael would do, regardless of my choice. What if he only returned in order to kill me and end my influence over him? Worse, what if he immediately attacked Celebel?

In my dream scenario, the most unlikely by far, Rafael listened with temperance. He would accept the situation, safely allowing me to introduce my new soulmate. No matter the outcome, I had to face the Dragon. He would never forgive me if I fled in cowardice. Neither would I.

Celebel pulled me into a close embrace, murmuring into

my hair, "I do not wish to force you into anything against your will."

"I've only myself to blame for this mess." Taking a steadying breath, I made my decision. "I will go with you when you depart. If these attacks on our people are so dire, I must offer my services as a healer. And… and I cannot bear to lose you. You know the tales of soulmates withering." As I had withered alone on the hill. His arms tightened around me. "We can discuss it later. Now, you must hide in the human village on the far side of the forest. They'll shelter you. It's the only place Rafael will avoid. We'll have to mask your scent somehow. Crow!" I entered the Tree, cursing my foolishness. Rooting around in my storage trunks, I found an amulet and a couple of small vials of ointment.

"This is a strong glamor charm. It will help. Go bathe thoroughly in the stream and then anoint yourself with the scented oils. With these and the charm, it should be enough for now." Or so I hoped.

He accepted the items with a solemnity that made my heart sink. "I don't know that I've ever truly walked amongst humans. I speak their trade languages well enough, but I know nothing of the local dialect."

"It'll be a great cultural exchange experience for you then. These are a simple folk, mostly sheep farmers and wool spinners. Tell them a few stories about your exploits. They'll love it; they get little excitement out here. If they offer you mutton stew with beer, please accept graciously. It is greasy, and the beer is awful, but they are quite proud of it. If you give them any gifts, they'll keep whatever it is for generations and tell the most overwrought stories about them to their children. Ah, it's endearing." I sorted through my store of prepared herbs, handing some packets to him. "Take these with you for their hospitality. Humans always seem to need more medicine. Let them know I sent you, so they won't be afraid."

Celebel watched my face with mild wonder as I spoke. "You care for them."

"They have been kind to me, and they are good stewards of the land." I felt oddly self-conscious. He smiled and stroked my ears.

"It speaks well of your kind heart. But what of your safety?" His eyes crackled with worry.

"I will manage Rafael. I've steered clear of his talons all this time, and we've had more than one heated argument. He may not understand my choices, and he's likely to be *very* dramatic." I barely kept from adding, 'and he will undoubtedly lash out.' "But I also know that he loves me, even if he cannot speak it aloud." My love for Rafael ached like an old wound flaring to life, and my newfound love for Celebel coiled tight with fear for him.

"You are much more confident about all of this than I," Celebel said.

"I'm trying very hard to be confident. Confidence is the best way to handle Rafael. He hones in on weakness like a viper on a mouse."

"That image is not helping." He paled.

"It is his nature. Trust me, my love. We will come through this together." *My spirit might not be whole by the end, but I've made my choices and now I must abide by them.* I held his hands, looking deep into his eyes for several long breaths. Finally, he sighed with something like resignation.

"May I kiss you before I go?" The smallest smile crept onto his face.

"You'd better." I crushed my lips to his.

"It is worth dying for this," he said against my mouth.

"Celebel Elhalanros, I think I'm in love with you." I hated sending him away, but I surely didn't mind watching him leave.

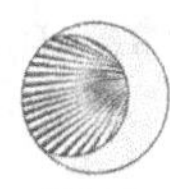

When the Dragon finally appeared, my heart swelled with longing. Then clenched like a fist. I spotted him flying low in the clouds, red wings flashing in the diminishing light. Of course, he would arrive on the leading edge of a thundercloud. Just like him, to time it that way. I carefully clamped the image of Celebel down deep in my mind. My hands trembled, and I stilled myself. In the distance, lightning streaked across the dark sky. Maybe I prayed hard enough, the gods would strike me down before this conversation did.

As Rafael approached me with that deliberate, predatory grace, the wind picked up, whipping his hair into a red cloud like blood mist about his broad shoulders. Those great wings folded away to nothing as he strode up the hill, heavy cloak billowing behind him. The bond between us hummed to life like we'd never been apart, an almost physical force dragging me toward my returning soulmate.

I'd always enjoyed the controlled fluidity of his movement. Now, it only reminded me of his seemingly limitless capacity for violence. I had a moment of small gratitude, noting that Rafael was neither coated in blood nor armored. Armor indicated a recent involvement in conflict. It always brought along a sharper edge to his overall spiky nature. This would be unpleasant enough without having him already primed for combat.

Emotion building faster than I could tolerate, I ran to the Dragon, and he caught me easily in his powerful arms. He lifted me off my feet as though I weighed less than a cloud. Instinctively, I wrapped my arms about his neck and my legs around his waist.

The permanent scowl etched on his face smoothed into something like calm. His eyes flickered blue, lips curling in that catlike smile. I counted any smile on his initial approach a rarity, quivering my gut with dread.

I wanted so badly to kiss him, to wind my fists in his hair and crush my body against him. Instead, I pressed my forehead to his for a long moment. The soulbond wrapped us in a pulsating field of energy, the power of it stealing my thoughts. Breathing in his scent—that heady combination of leather, a hint of smoke, and something akin to dragon's blood resin—oh, it almost made me foolhardy. For a heartbeat, I considered risking that kiss before I unleashed all the hells. Crow, it had been *so long*, but my secret clawed its way out of my throat.

"I have met someone," I choked out, pulling back just before his lips met mine.

Rafael's face closed off immediately, yellow streaking through the blue of his eyes in a warning flash. His gaze flicked to the new earring, and I tried my best not to squirm.

"What does that mean?" That deep rumble held the building threat of destruction, and he bit off each word. His hands slowly tightened their viselike grip.

Knowing how easily he could crush my bones, I sucked in a deep breath, trying unsuccessfully to calm my nerves—and ended up babbling.

"He-he showed up injured, much like you. You know I must heal any who reach the hill. When I laid hands on him, I discovered he's a soulmate, also like you. You *are*, you know. I know we fought about it, but you cannot deny—"

"Where is he?" The Dragon hissed the words so harshly, I almost didn't understand him.

"No, Rafael, we need to talk—"

"WHERE?" He shook me hard enough to snap my jaws together. I narrowly avoided biting my tongue.

My ears went back. I struggled in his grip, trying to kick away from him. "Fucking *stop* that. Put me down! You may storm off all you like, but you will *not* brutalize me." Wind whipped my hair around us.

The Dragon froze. I thought I'd gotten through to him until his nostrils flared. His pupils thinned to razor slashes, and he leaned in close, inhaling deeply. *Crow!*

"You reek of sex." His voice was dangerously quiet.

This wasn't at all how I wanted this discussion to progress. Oh, Night Mother, I was such a fool. Tears welled and threatened to spill down my cheeks.

"You were so angry last we spoke. Not a word in two years! Gods, I've been lonely, to say nothing of my diminished spirit. You closed off the bond, thus I had no way of contacting you. No way to explain what was happening—"

Rafael made a strangled cry and hurled me away. I landed hard on my shoulder and rolled unsteadily back to my feet. A move that, ironically, he had taught me. In another time, he would have mocked me for my poor execution. Instead, he dropped to his haunches and covered his face, his hair sparking into flame.

I wanted to take him in my arms, to comfort and kiss him, but the heat of his body flared so intensely that the grass surrounding him instantly withered and died. The first drops of rain fell, sizzling into steam where they landed on his back. The sky blackened overhead. Why did we always have the worst fights during a storm?

After a long, dreadful silence, he speared me with a glare, eyes blistering red. My breath shuddered. Underneath the rage, those eyes were open wounds. His heartbreak was so much worse than I expected, the agony washing over me in choking waves. Crow, I'd gone about this all wrong. Too late to unsing that melody. I reached for him.

He roared in anguish. The force of it knocked me flat on my back. Shaking his head from side to side, as though trying to clear it, he raked his talons down his face. Slicing his skin to tattered ribbons, his steaming blood splashed the ground. I wanted to run to him, but I had no illusions about my safety. He rose to his feet and roared again, shaking the ground under my feet. Lightning flashed in the distance, and the thunder boomed as though responding to his cry.

Gods, what had I done? The sinews of his hands stood out as he locked them into claws. Scales rippled over his skin, appearing and vanishing in quick succession. His body shivered as he folded forward, wings erupting from his back. I held my breath in the sudden dread he would take on his full dragon form and vent his wrath on the Great Tree, destroying my hill and me along with it.

Mad eyes fixed on to me, his throat swelled, and for a horrible moment I thought he was going to spit fire directly at my face. Instead, he threw his head back and breathed it to the heavens; a discomfiting, roiling flame I'd never seen before. He followed that with another roar that shook the very bedrock of the hill itself. The Great Tree groaned and quaked, the shock rippling through the forest in a wave as Rafael turned from me.

"Wait, don't go," I cried, but he was already moving. Always, always begging him to stay. To be reasonable. To fucking *talk* to me.

Desperate, I lunged forward, grabbing Rafael's sleeve. He whipped an elbow back, simultaneously wrenching his shirt from my grasp and connecting with my cheek. I stumbled backwards and slipped in the wet grass. Sobbing, all I could do was watch him shift into his scaled drake form. He launched himself into the sky with furious wingbeats. A flash of lightning illuminated his retreating figure. I had a brief, wild desire to make a net of that lightning, to catch and pull him back down to the ground. The Dragon disappeared like a phantom into the clouds.

"I love you," I whispered helplessly. "I'm sorry."

Having him turn his fists on me in rage would surely hurt less than witnessing his devastation. I dabbed at the trickle of blood from my split cheek. *It didn't have to be this way. It shouldn't.* He might never speak to me again. Or perhaps he would return to set fire to the hill, and me with it. A queasy, hollow feeling tugged at the soulbond. I yanked the tips of my ears down, wanting to shut it all out.

The blow to my cheek had loosened a tooth. Dazed, I spat it into my hand and pondered the blood that followed before popping it back into the socket. What would Nemohee think? Wretched, I sat out in the pouring rain and cried my heart out. Fully realizing just how much I loved that damned drake, how much I missed him already, and how much I hoped he didn't hate me. That last bit hurt most of all, trembling my very soul in the place where it joined me to him. I wept myself sick. Stomach turning with the force of my heartache, I vomited yellow bile. Only the burned grass remained to mark the Dragon's anguish.

Part 2

Chapter 16

The storm followed in the Dragon's wake, sheeting rain trailing like a veil across the rolling hills. Though I could barely sense him, I waited until Rafael was far away to give Celebel the 'all clear' signal. My elvish soulmate met me on the outskirts, as I'd requested. We'd agreed on a meadowlark call for 'all clear, come out' and a raven croak for 'run for your life.' Despite everything, I was grateful to sing out with the meadowlark.

Celebel's smile faltered when he saw the look on my face. Soul sick and wrung out, I told him of the scene as we returned to the bower, picking our way across the slick stones and muddy ground.

He stopped still, ears flattened in outrage. "What kind of person strikes a lover?"

"If he had done it intentionally, I'd be dead. Rafael turned to leave. I grabbed hold of his sleeve and ran my face into his elbow when he yanked it free."

"But he *struck* you!" Celebel gestured hugely, nostrils flaring with his outrage.

"I struck myself on him, I promise." I clasped my hands together to keep from prodding the healed injury. "You're making me wish I hadn't told you."

"I will find this *monster* and challenge him!" Celebel's normally gentle eyes blazed with anger.

The Night Mother moved, and the vision struck, dragging me under like a stone dropped into a well. *Storms touched down everywhere on devastated lands, ripping entire mountain ranges apart. No trees, no grass, nothing green and growing for as far as my eyes could see. My body stretched too thin, diaphanous as silk gauze. The wind buffeted me helplessly across the broken land. Above me in the turbulent sky, two great cats circled each other— one black and streaked through with silver, the other red with a curling mane of flame. Larger even than the warring dragons, they encompassed all of my reality.*

Lashing tails and flashing claws scattered what little remained of me. The great cats hissed at the same moment and sank their fangs into each other's throats. Blood rained in a monsoon, flooding the ruined plains, and I drowned as they died.

I gasped as I came back to myself, shuddering with horror. Celebel only noticed the hitch in my breath, so swiftly had the vision come and gone. Over the centuries, I'd practiced hiding my reactions from others, though my stomach roiled.

"Celebel Elhalanros, you will do no such thing!" I pulled myself up to my full height, still staring up at his face. "Rafael is very dear to me, despite all of this strife. And we've discussed this at length. He would pick his teeth with your bones. I've had enough of rage, *please!* His anger I expected, but the hurt..." I sighed, my lungs weighted with grief. "Gods, you should see what he did to his own face." The bloody furrows, the wild pain in his eyes. I shivered.

Celebel's lips thinned. No, that would not do. I told him of the vision in detail.

"It was brief but very clear; if you two ever come to blows, all three of us will be lost." And worse. Lacking other context, I did not want to make such sweeping, fatalistic statements. The goddess remained frustratingly silent on the matter.

"I suppose my intent sparked this vision." He frowned. "Very well, I shall try to make the best of it. Forgive my burst of misguided protectiveness. I loathe how upsetting this has been for you." A glance at me. "Truly amazing how quickly these visions come and go. You didn't miss a step!"

"I am not always so fortunate. At times the goddess leans heavily on me." I shook off the lingering dread. "Now, where are we going? We cannot stay here." My gut churned at the thought of Rafael returning to set the Great Tree ablaze. "It will not take long to gather my belongings." Saying it aloud increased the ache in my heart.

Celebel's arm draped across my shoulders was a comforting weight, and I huddled against him. He made forgiveness as easy as his smile. "Férioth, Araglin's fortress, is quite a distance from here, but it is the best choice. More of a miniature walled city than a fortress, really, and quite secure. We've been consolidating our forces there and using it as a safe haven for refugees fleeing the raids. With luck, we may encounter search and rescue parties along the way."

We walked in silence the rest of the way. Celebel stole anxious glances at me. The concern for my well-being touched me, but I didn't have the capacity to dwell on it or comfort him. Once we reached the bower and wiped the muck from our feet, I made some tea for him, a soothing chamomile, and straight whiskey for myself. Then I set about rifling through my things.

He watched me, questions bubbling just under the surface. I wanted none of them. Most of my clothing was useless for travel, and I tossed it outside in the dirt. Digging into an old trunk, I brushed the spine of one of the many books Rafael had brought me over the years. A rare herbal treatise, and a favorite. The tears started anew. Celebel padded to my side, rubbing my back as I sobbed over books.

"Forgive me," he whispered. "I never meant to cause you harm. Have I ruined everything?"

I could only shake my head and cry harder. Celebel pulled me into his arms, singing while he stroked my hair and ears with the back of his hand. I nursed the thought that the awful sound Rafael had made was the literal noise of his heart breaking, and used it to hurt myself.

Shaking off my useless feelings after a moment of self-indulgence, I packed as lightly and quickly as I could. So many gifts from the Dragon. Whatever I left behind would be safe enough. I chose sparingly of the 'trinkets' he had brought me, in the end taking only the original string of pearls and the collar of sapphires.

"We will need weapons. Do you have anything other than the sword I used for practice?" Celebel asked, looking around the bower.

"Take whatever you like." I flipped open a case stuffed full of blades.

His eyes widened in horror. "Why do you have them stored this way?"

I waved a dismissive hand. "I never use them. Nor did I request any of these."

"These are all from *him*? Does he know you keep these fine blades in such disarray?" Celebel gestured broadly.

"Of course he does. He's yelled at me for it more than once." At length.

"And yet he allows you to continue?"

"Considering that Rafael refused to help me arrange them to his liking, yes. He once told me that his muscles are for battle, *not* manual labor. Doesn't like getting *dirt* under his talons, so he has no right to criticize. Vanity manifests in strange ways with that one." I chuckled at the memory of Rafael's face when I'd asked him to help me move my heavy cases outside so I could reorganize them. It tinged around the edges with sadness and I sighed.

Celebel sensed the mood shift and held up a glimmering short sword. "I believe this one has a name. He brought you named blades?"

"If it makes you feel better, I keep the ones I actually practice with over there." I gestured to a pair of crescent swords and my falcata hanging from root hooks, safely sheathed and wrapped. "I've barely looked at the rest."

"Curved blades. Prioritizing defense?" Celebel paused his fussing over my pile of weapons to inspect them.

"Rafael claims they suit me best. Apparently, I am too unwieldy with straight blades, and tend to overreach, throwing myself off balance. I'm terrible with a sword either way, but marginally less terrible with those."

Celebel barked a laugh. "I cannot believe I'm saying this, but I wish I could have witnessed this training."

I smiled ruefully. "A lot of getting immediately disarmed,

smacked with the flat of a blade, and booted face first into the dirt while he taunts me. That reach of his is impossible enough to manage unarmed; with that damned greatsword in hand, it's absurd. He's so damned *fast*. The resulting critique is the worst part." Rafael's tongue held an edge sharper than any sword. "It annoys him that I cannot swing a blade at him with the intent to kill. He once offered to bring me a training form to practice striking. When I realized he meant an actual corpse, I put a stop to that. I'm sure he would have kept up a constant stream of dead bodies otherwise. Very much his sense of humor."

Celebel blanched. "He is… an interesting fellow."

"You could say that. Come now, we do not have time for you to reorganize this whole trunk."

He'd meticulously laid out each and every weapon as we spoke. "I cannot leave them this way," he said, despairing. "And why have you no shields?"

Something about his reaction charmed me, but the thrill of impending danger pushed me to haste. "You should consider that we do not know if Rafael might return. Or when. And he doesn't fight with a shield."

Celebel shuddered, working faster. "Point taken. And you are certain that taking some of these will not further anger him?"

I shrugged. "If he wanted them to be lovingly kept and cared for, he shouldn't have brought them here in the first place."

In the end, Celebel selected the same bright longsword he'd used for training. I'd always admired it but had never been skilled enough to wield it effectively. He also chose the named blade he'd mentioned, a hunting knife stuck in his boot, a fine stiletto, and a shortbow. Citing a potentially dangerous road and a bleak future, he encouraged me to bring my own armament. I settled for the three curved blades, plus the small knife I kept braided into my hair for practicality, and my boot knife. Celebel also insisted on bringing his ruined armor along. I, with my books, could not exactly argue.

We worked quickly, picking through the rest of my things

and packing. How could one collect all the trappings of a long life under duress? The torment dulled my focus, spinning me in helpless circles. I touched each item in the bower, the pain of abandoning my beloved home echoing the ache in my heart, doubling my vision with unshed tears.

Though I barely sensed Rafael through the strangled connection, he remained far off. I still glanced through the calcite panes every few breaths and strained my ears for wingbeats; for what little good it served, considering how often he caught me by surprise.

Sadly, I left my beloved mortar and pestle behind, as Celebel pointed out that the healer's hall would have many. I had made them myself by directing water over river rocks given up by the creek bed. The set had taken quite a while to form, and I was proud of it, but alas. Of my herbal stores, I took only the rarest and most difficult to grow. My fingers grazed the moonstone bottle and the resulting jolt of emotional pain convinced me to leave it as well.

"Where did *this* come from? Hasn't it been lost for centuries?" Celebel's voice cut into my reverie. He held up an ancient scroll case.

"Ah, yes. The first translation we bonded over. I argued for its return later, but Rafael steadfastly maintained that since the elves he took it from were long dead, I might as well keep it." That memory would have ordinarily garnered a smile, but the wounded look in his eyes overlaid all the others.

Celebel blew out an exasperated breath and shook his head, tucking the case into his pack with care. "Unbelievable," he muttered. "An entire trove of cultural antiquities stowed here."

After a moment of consideration, I packed up all my drawings of the Dragon and a single personal implement. Made of deep red, seamless boiled leather wrapped over a heavy core in a strange crafting method, Rafael had dropped it in my lap one day without a word. He'd given me one of his unreadable looks when I'd dared to ask if it accurately represented his cock. Since then, I'd performed quite a few demonstrations with it. The memories made my hands tingle.

I walked around the bower one last time, committing every detail to memory. Perhaps my other drawings would eventually become a part of the trunk itself. A shadow passed overhead, and I ducked instinctively. Only a hawk stooping to catch a rodent in the long grass.

As we took our leave, I kissed the roots before the entrance and thanked the Great Tree for its long years of protection and comfort. With reverence, Celebel repeated the gesture. The branches rustled acceptance.

For the local fae, I left offerings of honey. Finally, I sent a note via jay to the villagers, inviting them to help themselves to my medicinal garden, including a hastily sketched diagram of the various herbs and their uses. The folk knew well enough how to maintain the plants in my absence. I trusted them to be respectful. Another jay carried a brief explanation of events to Nemohee.

"I hope to return some day," I whispered, heartsick, over my shoulder as we departed.

The limbs of the Great Tree bowed low, and the halite ring chimed a mournful note as we passed.

"It is strange to see you so clothed," Celebel said later as we traversed the forest, following narrow deer trails. We kept a rapid pace, almost a jog, to cover as much ground as possible.

"I could say the same for you."

I wore soft woolen trousers with a linen blouse under a light blue, homespun traveling cape, embroidered along the edges with foxglove blossoms. All except the sturdy boots had been gifts from my villagers. It was modest raiment, somewhat roughly made, but sturdy.

It felt right to honor the work. The cape was a gift of thanks for showing them how the judicious use of foxglove could strengthen a failing heart. Leaving the villagers twinged me with guilt. When I returned, would anyone recognize me? I hoped they could manage well enough on their own. Winter months always seemed to bring along respiratory complaints, easily solved with my herbs.

Luckily for Celebel, the villagers had been happy to shower him with more garments than he would ever wear, though everything hung short on him. At least the boots fit.

"The brief time spent with your humans was indeed educational," he said. "How long has it been since you visited? I think they had a difficult time telling you and I apart because I have no beard and superficially resemble you in coloration. They kept using female signifiers despite my corrections. The poor things were so confused."

"This village gets stuck on some inflexible concepts of gender and sexual propriety. Did you bed any of them?" I was curious. They'd never seen an elvish man before, to my knowledge. I steered my non-human patients away from the village for fear of causing conflict.

"Gods, no. Not my type at all. I may have created some entirely new fetishes, though," he said, with a good-natured laugh. "Poor fellows, I wish them luck."

"The first time their ancestors saw me, they mistook my ears for horns and fled. Took them a while to come around. And when they did, so did the ill-fated wooing." I grinned at the memory. "So many of them swore they'd get me with child! It matters not how often I explain we cannot be impregnated by accident, they refuse to accept the idea. I suppose if I popped out a baby every time I sneezed, perhaps I'd feel differently. Fecund creatures, humans. Even limited as they are to procreating only by coupling male and female together. Imagine if they could also use our gestational trees!"

I'd been called upon to assist many a precarious human childbirth, at times too late. Witnessing the damage done to their bodies gave me an appreciation for human fortitude. It also made me grateful to be child free, and for the option of gestational groves if I ever trod that path. Given the complexity of my soulbonds, that possibility seemed highly unlikely.

"Gods, they'd be swarming like ants!" Celebel pulled down on his ears and made a terrible face. "You were right about the beer and mutton, by the way."

I chuckled. "Quite an experience, eh?"

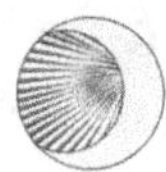

Celebel proved to be an entertaining traveling companion. He asked after every plant's medicinal use, made up little songs as he walked, and occasionally grabbed me for a spontaneous dance. He did an excellent job of distracting me from my angst. It relaxed me to see him at ease; that very moment found him exclaiming at a newt he'd discovered in the stream we'd been following.

"Look at this handsome fellow! I didn't know they lived this far north." He pulled me over to look. The newt gazed up at us impassively.

"They're hard to impress," I said, and lifted a piece of bark for the small amphibian to hide beneath. I knew he was trying his best to cheer me and loved him ever more for it.

We spoke of our personal histories and attachments in whispers and sign as we left my familiar forest, crossing the first river to the northeast. These trees were strangers to me, and I jumped at every new sound. We took to moving through the branches whenever possible, far above the ground in the dark canopy. Could Fomorians climb as we did? Would Rafael burn the forest looking for me?

I talked Celebel into resting first. Normally, we could go for days without deep sleep. The strain of recovery combined with the tension of unknown threat sapped Celebel's strength, and his energy flagged. The opportunity to watch over his slumber, nestled into a tangle of branches, also allowed my aching feet some recovery time. He made soft noises as he dreamed, and woke with the first trickle of dawn through the leaves.

Trying to focus on something other than angst and soulmates as we traveled, I told Celebel of my stunted relationship with my half-sister, Silfanië. Fascinating to consider her connection to him. She'd been barely more than a child, just out of her serving years when I'd left her world. From the sound of it, that aloof girl had grown into a cold, austere woman. With the fall of Leyúduin and Celebel's tales, her presence upon my return to court seemed likely. He confirmed as much, and the growing knot in my stomach tightened that much more.

A crow circled overhead while Celebel spoke of his own past. From his account, he was well-liked. The edges of his stories hinted at loneliness, and I wondered how much of his true self he'd ever been able to share. Another crow joined the first. Soon a small murder of the iridescent black birds careened above us.

"These are Feanim's crows!" Celebel's eyes lit up. "Hopefully that means he's camped somewhere nearby. I should have known he would not give up the search, even after all this time." He extended an arm. A crow landed on it, fixating on his face with sharp interest. "Will you lead us to Feanim?" he asked the bird.

She cawed agreement, fluffing her feathers with excitement. Her comrades echoed the sentiment. He thanked the crow as she took to the wing once more, and the small flock ushered us along.

The Night Mother moved again. A vision doubled over the crows of brightly colored dragons filling the sky. Their hurricane wings blocked out the sun. Snapping back to myself like the twang of a loosed bowstring, the disorientation nearly knocked me from my perch. Fortunately, I'd been stationary when it struck, rather than mid-spring to the next tree. Unable to tell if it was a sight of relief or dread, I chose not to mention it to avoid undue worry.

Rafael had tried to test the visions over time to see if he could get consistent results, but their lack of context made it challenging. Occasionally, I'd been able to warn him about a particular enemy, but that was the extent of the visions' usefulness. The thought of him made my chest squeeze painfully. A distant answering thrum of hurt startled me, and I wrapped my arms around myself.

I tried to shake off my discomfort. "What kind of reception do you think you'll have upon your return from the dead?"

"Incredulity mostly. Perhaps some disappointment." Celebel landed beside me and laughed, teeth flashing in dappled canopy. "No doubt Feanim will insist he knew the truth all along." A crow cawed at the mention of Feanim.

"And I?"

"Possibly a few broken hearts. And some lustful ones." He tried to tweak my ear, and I ducked easily, dropping to a lower branch.

Celebel laughed again. "Truly, you are full of surprises."

"Oh, my love, you have no idea."

Chapter 17

I dreamed of Rafael. Or rather, Rafael thrust a dream of himself upon me, moving through my mind with ease. Much more memory than dream. The moment my eyes closed, the Dragon enveloped my senses, his presence closer than breath.

Rafael's eyes burned with lust, red streaking into the yellow and orange flame, the only light in the dim bower. I'd barely tugged him down beside me on my pallet when he tucked a petal into his mouth. Then gave one to me. Before my lips could close around it, he kissed me fiercely, and I responded in kind. He often greeted me without words, only the heat of desire. However much he denied my attempts to reciprocate, I never questioned his passion. The petals danced as our tongues mingled.

A rosebud brushed my breast, drawing a shuddering breath from me. Rafael held it loosely in one hand. I pulled him over me, wrapping my legs around him. He traced a path with his tongue from my neck to my breast and deftly flicked at my nipple with the petal in his mouth. Pleasure shot through me, arching my back. He watched my face, working that petal in circles around my sensitive nipple until he had me gasping. If he'd asked me to help him raze cities in that moment, I would have agreed.

The rosebud traveled up my thigh and slid back and forth over my swollen clit. I moaned and grabbed fistfuls of his hair, guiding him down my belly. He dropped the teasing rosebud and gripped my thighs with both hands.

The Dragon's searing breath on my tender flesh made my nipples painfully tight. He exhaled, slow and deliberate, working me into a state of desperation. A rumbling growl from him, and I drew taut as a harp string, waiting with trembling anticipation for him to strike the chord. With only the slightest touch of his tongue to my clit, I came, crying out.

Pulling him up to face me again, I tore open his shirt in

a frenzy, licking and biting. I clawed at the laces of his trousers and he grabbed my wrists, pinning my hands above my head so I could not reach for him. He always pinned me when I got carried away. Frustrated, I arched my body to his, grinding my wet cunt against the leather straining to hold back his massive cock. He bent to my breast and sucked hard enough to hurt.

"Rafael, please! I want you," I hissed. "I want to feel you inside me. I want to make you come."

He moaned against my breast. Leather creaked. I grew frantic, struggling in his grip.

"Please, please fuck me, please!"

Rafael sat up, releasing my hands with a dark rumble of amusement. I lurched forward to cling to him. He stopped me with a palm to the center of my chest, easily shoving me back down. Thrashing against this new pin was like trying to lift the Great Tree. He watched me fight until I whined and went limp.

Kissing my mouth again, he slid the tips of his fingers, talons blunted, over my tongue and his. I sucked hard, trying to trap his fingers in my mouth, trying to demonstrate what I wanted to do to him. To show him how good it could feel. The need for him consumed me.

He pulled his fingers free and reached between my legs. Using only two at first, he thrust them into me, building intensity with every push, stretching me. Watching my face the entire time, he added another finger, stretching me again, then another. My arousal ran rivers beneath me, all my awareness pinpointed to his deliberate ministrations. Eventually, he worked his entire hand deep inside me. I thought he would surely split me apart in sweet agony. I bucked against the cone of his fingers, against the pain, clawing at his arms.

No longer needing to press me down, as the hand rhythmically fucking me to pieces weighed me to the floor, he used the other one to thumb my clit. I shuddered under his touch, and he kissed my inner thigh. His hand rotated inside me. Twist and thrust. Aroused beyond comprehension, I flooded him with my juices, ensuring a smooth, constant glide.

I tightened my walls around his hand and tugged from within. Forcing his hand deeper. Rafael smiled. Undulating the fingers inside me, he tapped on my clit with the other hand. Light blows, just enough to make me gasp. The climax tore out of me, long and punishing. He did not relent in his attentions, bringing me to the brink again and again, until I was exhausted and hoarse. Finally, gently, he extricated his hand.

Through eyes heavy with fatigue, I watched a tremor run through him as he sat up. His expression held a strange mixture of desire and despair. That next morning Rafael was gone like a fever dream. For the first time, I wept for him.

I woke with a poignant smile on my face until I remembered the current state of affairs. The sight of Celebel, who was up and cheerfully brewing coffee, brought another smile. My cheek twanged with phantom pain where I'd struck it on Rafael's elbow, bringing my mood right back down. The Dragon had sent me that dream-memory directly, but to what end? To make me miss him, or feel guilty? Simply to torment me?

"Whew, a storm blew over your face." Celebel offered me a steaming cup.

I accepted gratefully. "You made me coffee?"

A grand feat, that far off the ground. He must have used a warming cantrip to avoid a fire; perhaps even copied the one Rafael taught me. I'd used it in front of him often enough.

"I wanted to try my hand at it after you showed me the preparation. You add honey, yes? How is it?" His eyes sparkled with excitement, and also a little apprehension.

I made a big show of inhaling the aroma, taking my first sip, and swirling it thoughtfully in my mouth.

"Excellent, you've a talent for this."

He beamed in triumph. "Now, what has you so stormy upon waking? Dreams?"

I nodded between sips. "This is much more difficult than I anticipated. I can feel Rafael's hurt stretched across the distance between us, like the slow, nauseating throb of blood loss." Even as I spoke, that heartsickness flared again, and I clutched at my chest as it constricted.

Celebel gingerly touched my cheek. "I do not wish you to feel as though you need to hide anything from me. Even if you think it will be upsetting, I want to know all your moods. To know your whole heart. It may take me some time to accept certain things, but please, confide in me."

"I only wish I'd recognized the depth of my own feelings before all this." I gestured back and forth between us. "Now I do not know if I'll ever even see him again, and it's eating me alive." My hands tingled with the force of my heartache. "I'm all twisted up inside."

"I've heard of soulmates existing in disharmony, but never quite to this degree. How do you suppose he has tolerated the distance all this time? Surely he must feel the effects."

I swirled my coffee, considering. "Perhaps his draconic nature protects him from some of the energetic drain. He certainly seemed to suffer little for keeping his distance. I wouldn't call what we had functional or healthy by any means. Barely a relationship. Fucking frustrating, for everything to be at his whim. But at least when he was with me…" My heart constricted, forcing the air out of my lungs. "He can be so very good when he wishes. Otherwise… gods. He *is* a fucking hellbeast." Avoiding both tears and spilling my precious coffee, I leaned forward to kiss Celebel.

"You brought other drawings with you," he said against my lips. "May I see them?"

I hesitated. "Perhaps some of them. Some he would not wish me to share." Digging in my packs, I found what I was looking for, minus a few select images, and handed Celebel the folio.

Feeling more self-conscious than ever in my life, I sipped

my coffee as I watched him slowly flip through some of my more intimate depictions of my Dragon. Images of Rafael in repose, shirtless. Studies of his powerful back, his muscular abdomen, of his taloned hands gripping my thighs, of my nails raking down his broad chest. That look of fierce satisfaction burning in his eyes as his long, sinuous tongue twined over my fingers and into my body.

I didn't mind showing my compromising self-portraits, but I kept certain images under wraps. Drawings of things like blood play, intimacy with his scalier forms, the hollow look in his eyes when he lost himself in memory, and the outline of his impressive cock against his leathers. Those vulnerable moments I did not share. That last one I'd never even shown the Dragon himself.

"He's very jealous about his privacy." My nerves jangled under the weight of Rafael's sudden attention.

Celebel shushed me and kept looking. I twisted my cup in my hands to give them something to do. He lingered over the rare image of Rafael sleeping, curled around me like a big cat, with that slight smile I treasured so much. My breath hitched. All the best sleep I'd ever gotten was lying with him at my back like that, wrapped tightly in his arms and blanketed by his heat.

Finally, Celebel looked up at me. "Thank you for sharing these. I'm beginning to understand what you find attractive in him."

"And that is?" I downed the last of my coffee and wiped the cup clean.

"He's not my preferred type, but damn! That body is a sculptor's masterpiece." Celebel fanned himself dramatically, and I laughed. "All that aside, this is an aspect of the legend I never would have expected. If your hand is true, he really does love you. It's in the softness of his eyes in some of these. Seems like nothing else about him is soft, though, whew. I'm surprised, and rather surprisingly disappointed, that you have no fully nude studies of him."

"I assume your usual type is elvish? Yes, I thought so. See what you've been missing? Nothing here is exaggerated, only slightly stylized." I packed the drawings away once more, sobering at the poignancy. "That soft look was a slow progression. It took a few dozen years to coax it out of him. As far as nudity is concerned, well. He has intense trauma about his body, and would never allow such a portrait."

"What a terrible shame. I never expected to actually pity the Red Dragon." Celebel raised meaningful eyebrows. His face was so open and expressive, so strikingly different. "Is he, ah, scarred?" He waved a demonstrative hand over his groin.

"No, nothing like that. Physically, he is perfectly functional." I weighed how much I should say. "It took twenty years of shameless flirting for him to accept my attention."

"*You* are the aggressor?" Ears akimbo, Celebel's eyes grew larger by the heartbeat.

"You underestimate me, sir. I can be quite persistent when I want something," I said in a husky voice. "Also, I dislike what that term implies."

"I cannot. That is. I mean to say." He closed his eyes, passing a hand across them, and visibly gathered himself. "I assumed the mighty Red Dragon would have no qualms about forcing himself on you."

"Never! Don't look at me like that. He would never tolerate that sort of thing, and neither would I."

Celebel's ears relaxed. "That is somewhat comforting."

I busied myself cleaning up our meager bed site. Easier not to look at my lover directly when I spoke about such things. "I want to be open with you, but some things are not mine to tell. This is a sensitive topic." Guilt suffused me, burning up to the tips of my ears. "Rafael had only known cruel treatment when I met him. Took him years to *begin* to relax in my presence."

"I simply cannot fathom that a famed mass-murderer is such an innocent." He waved a hand in circles in the air, as though expecting to catch an answer with it.

"Not innocent, not at all. He had an utterly horrific past." Rafael's long absence stabbed through me, a sharp pang in my chest. I looked down at the exquisite pearls woven into my braid;

his first 'trinket' gift. Still my favorite. "It is… difficult. We have never consummated in the traditional sense." The Dragon's attention burned into me once more, and my heart thudded painfully in my chest.

Celebel stroked my hair, lightly, cautiously, tucking a stray lock behind my ear. I leaned into the touch, trying to stifle the rising tide of tears.

"I did not mean to upset you. I'm merely trying to understand everything," he cooed, attempting to soothe me. It worked surprisingly well. "Your love for him is clear in your drawings. I hope to be so loved by you."

I kissed him and he kissed back hungrily.

"Tell me of your desire, your need, give me everything," Celebel murmured against my lips with a lusty sigh.

"I cannot. Not yet," I breathed, fighting down my libido. "The wound is too fresh. And we must not draw his attention so soon."

Celebel's ears drooped, but he signed understanding, fist by his face and flicking his index finger upward.

The mild weather made travel easy. Trees thinned into broad meadows as we approached the mountains, forcing us to the ground. I hadn't walked so far in ages; I'd used almost all of my store of pain relief salve on my feet after only the third night. At one point Celebel jokingly offered to carry me. I seriously considered taking him up on it. He kept that brisk trot and I often struggled to match.

"How did you meet Nemohee?" His hand trailed through the graceful branches of a willow. The attempts to quell my stormy moods might be transparent, but I appreciated the effort.

"Same way I meet most of you musclebound rockheads." I said it with enough fondness to make Celebel grin. "I healed þeir wounds."

"Before or after you reached your hill?"

"After. Once every few hundred years or so, I venture out. I cannot recall now exactly how Nem got into that predicament, but I found þem with þeir legs trapped between a rock fall and a tree trunk. No broken bones, thankfully, just some superficial wounds and bad bruising. Took some levering to get þem free and then I healed the damage. We traveled together for a time before I returned to the hill."

"Were you ever lovers?"

I cackled at the thought. "We were never suited. Nemohee is like a sibling. No, we tossed a few lovers back and forth, but never shared a bed. Under different circumstances, Nem might be the only other person mad enough to have a go at Rafael." Nemohee would probably knock my head into a tree for saying so, but would also laugh while doing it. Þey suffered from a similar pathological lack of self-preservation, and a self-avowed weakness for 'big arms.'

Celebel was quiet for a few moments. "I'm still angry with that brute for striking you. Yes, you say it was an accident, but I have difficulty accepting it." He paused, staring me down.

I tugged my earlobes, frustration rising. "Rafael is not and will never be my enemy. Even if he returns in a rage, even if he kills me in the end the way Nemohee seems to think he will." I paused, chewing on the problems in my words. If a friend said such to me… I shook my head. "That is between the two of us, and no one could stop him, regardless. Not you, not your little army, perhaps not even the rest of the drakes combined. That vision was very clear, and I will not have others become collateral damage.

"He told me himself that he used to consider killing me because he misliked the power I had over him. At the end of that tale, he swore he would never hurt me. He also swore that he would come to my aid if I called to him out of dire need. He didn't have to tell me any of that, and he certainly didn't have to swear an oath. I have solicited nothing of the sort from him, but he offered it freely." Agitation sped my steps and Celebel trotted to keep up.

"I know Rafael feels I betrayed his trust. It matters not to him that before all this started, he and I had an awful fight and he stormed off. It matters not that he abandoned me for *years* with no method of contact. Nor that he could never even remotely discuss his true feelings about any of it. He would never be reasonable about any of this. I knew exactly who he was from the start, so I get what I get for the choices I've made. I have no illusions about that. But I *will not* have you or anyone else get involved. Do you understand?" I punctuated the last words by jabbing the air with my finger.

Celebel tentatively reached out, and I allowed him to take my hands.

"You are glorious in your anger," he said. "Please forgive me. I will harbor no more thoughts of vengeance against your Dragon."

I met his gaze, felt for our connection, and *reached*. My spirit touched his and pushed past his outer defenses. Celebel's eyes went wide at my probe, and I peered deep into his soul. He was open, guileless. Fear of the Dragon swirled there, and some resentment, but no malicious intent.

"I accept your apology." I released him. He sat back with a gasp.

"What did you do?"

"I used our connection to determine if you were truly genuine."

"I've heard of this, but the experience is very different. My spirit rippled like you dove through it." His eyes widened further. "You mean you can do that with Rafael as well?"

"Yes, and he can return the favor. My bond with him was strengthened through… special circumstances. I'll tell you about that another time." Something deep within me shuddered away from the thought.

"You really are a wonder." He placed his hands over his heart. "I told you the truth, and I always will."

"I know that now, but I wanted you to feel it, to understand from the inside. I want you to truly know who you're dealing with.

Rafael is not the only one with power," I said, drawing in the surrounding forest, breathing as one with it, as shadows gathered like cobwebs. Sometimes you have to let the young ones know who you are.

"I am Cúraniel of the Crescent Moon. I am both healer and seer. My visions are truths of the future, granted by the Night Mother, Dûemer. That which I can heal, I can also *un*heal." I demonstrated by opening up the wound on my cheek and sealing it again with a wave of my hand. "Know me well, Celebel Elhalanros. I am no less deadly for being a poor swordslinger."

Celebel sat silent, reverent. When I released the gathered power, he bowed low, forehead touching the ground, and then kissed my feet.

"You bless me with the knowledge of your true self. You have my deepest thanks," he said formally.

He held my gaze for a long moment, then removed the family talisman from his ear. "I feel that a simple hoop is not enough to convey your importance to me. Would you do me the great honor of wearing my family signifier in its place?"

I accepted the earring in my palm, hefting the piece and considering. It had been a very long time since any talisman graced my ear, and only ever my own lineage piece. Were we progressing too fast? To wear his talisman wasn't exactly a declaration of intent to marry, but it was close enough.

"If you are amenable, I would like to announce you as my consort. I wish for you to have the social armor it provides."

He watched me anxiously while I mulled over the request. It would certainly grant me a measure of protection from a likely hostile court, but how would Rafael react? Assuming I ever even saw the Dragon again. My back itched, just between my shoulder blades. I wasn't ready for such a move.

"We can discuss the consort idea later. I would prefer anonymity for as long as possible. Your desire to protect me is sweet, but I have no wish to take on any rulership responsibilities." I handed back the talisman and kissed him.

"The others will naturally question your identity. Consort is a coveted position; one step down from marriage," Celebel argued. "It will also help to smooth over, ah, certain other entanglements of yours."

"These are not my people. I am happy to pass along my healing techniques and aid those in need, but that is the extent of the involvement I want. Simple songs, please. I have lived alone for a very long time. If we must, save the consort announcement for the court itself."

Chapter 18

"We are close to the crossroads. I should go ahead alone to make doubly sure the way is safe, as raids have happened in this area. I shall come and collect you when I may. Since you can use your connection so well, you will know how I am faring, correct?" Celebel asked.

I didn't like it, but he was right. We'd been traveling for weeks, and I was more than ready to see the journey's end. "Yes, love. Go swiftly, return to me safely."

I sat in the branches of a tan oak, massaging my dangling calves, relieved to have the pressure off of them. He climbed up just long enough for a farewell kiss and embrace, then left his pack with me and took off at a swift jog into the trees.

The oak bordered the rolling foothills. The sight of more forest ahead comforted me. I leaned back against the trunk, feet swinging from the bough, and willed him all the protective force I could muster.

It struck me just how much of my recent life I'd spent waiting anxiously for a lover to return, and I scowled. That was a habit in need of breaking. Reactive as Rafael was, I'd never once been first to anger and kick him out before he stomped off. At least leaving my hill allowed me to take a more active role in my life. I hated being a mere passenger in the current of time.

Waiting for Celebel, I drowsed. Not quite deep sleep, not enough for Rafael to send me another dream. More of a suspension of awareness. Meditatively, I tapped into the tree's spirit and mingled it with mine, drawing strength through its roots and the attached network of mycelium. Vaeda itself fed and comforted me.

"All is well!" Celebel's sweet baritone broke through my reverie.

The sun had crept halfway across the sky. Refreshed, I slid off the bough into his arms. He set me on my feet.

"That was much faster than I expected."

"Scouts found me first. Evidently, Feanim never stopped searching for me. He has moved on with the others in a planned sweep, but you will meet him later tonight. There is a small encampment close to here devoted to search and rescue for other elves scattered by the Fomorian attacks."

"A camp! How was your reception?" I asked, as we walked together back in the direction he'd come from. I'd have to prepare myself for meeting a lot more elves, all at once. Some part of me looked forward to new faces, but the rest tingled with anxiety.

"Surprised, and emotional. Well, all except for Feanim, who insisted that he knew I must still be alive. 'No body, no death'." He mimicked a clipped accent and gestured dramatically. "Very typical for him, you'll see. I was overjoyed to find that my horse, Helicos, made it back unscathed! I had thought for sure that those beasts had gotten him, my gallant lad, but he escaped. He felt such guilt for leaving me behind that I had to give him many apples to soothe his conscience."

"Is he very beautiful, your horse?"

I loved elvish horses. Barely ever had the chance to interact with them since leaving the court, but those I had known were such fascinating creatures. They were almost unrecognizable compared to the rough, short-lived, and simple-minded beasts of burden my villagers used. Steeped in our power and selectively bred for ages, the stamina, grace, and intelligence of our steeds was unmatched.

"He is the *most* beautiful! Fine featured, shining dappled grey, and so wise. You'll love him. He'll love you even more; he's a sap for a pretty face."

I laughed, imagining. "Just like you, eh?"

Celebel laughed too and pushed me playfully. "I suppose I deserve that. Come, allow me to introduce you."

Much to my delight, we rounded a bend to the glorious sight of those vaunted horses. Celebel bowed low, with a smile, as he led me to them. Their silky coats gleamed in the sun, and they wore saddles in the finely tooled, stirrup-less style of my people. Celebel introduced me to a beautiful blood bay mare to ride alongside his—indeed very handsome—dappled grey stallion. She named herself Iruwher in the gentle way of elvish horses. The stallion whickering a greeting. Although he sidled close to Iruwher, as I would expect, Helicos maintained lovely manners. The horses bobbed their proud heads in acknowledgement.

More of a revelation was the addition of two heavily armored guards, themselves mounted. Despite the extra horse, they seemed just as surprised as I was. Helms hid their faces and hair. Their only identifiers were blue tabards embroidered with the silver tree and stars of Celebel's lineage.

"Oh, he is a beauty!" I approached the stallion with reverence, allowing Helicos to take in my scent. "And these fine folks are…?"

"Tasked with Lord Celebel's safe return," one said flatly.

Lithe and wiry, with dark, hooded eyes and tense shoulders, she glared down from the back of her chestnut courser. Something about the intensity of her gaze lent itself to a Duedellen heritage. A pointed helm hid her ears, otherwise they would likely be flattened against her skull. I had the distinct impression that if I made a feint, she would spring from her horse like a panther.

"Easy, now." The other one had a friendly baritone. Tall and burly—for an elf, I amended. Probably an Astolar with that build. His paint stallion looked almost like a pony under him. "Lord Celebel appears miraculously whole after that fall. I assume you are the one to thank for it?" His hazel eyes roved over my face.

"Lord Celebel's strength carried him all the way to my bower, and my spirit did the rest." Feeling exposed under their scrutiny, I kept my statement vague.

Both of the guards shifted at my words, armored joints chiming softly. Celebel raised his hands, drawing their attention.

"My Lady Cúraniel saved my life," he declared. "Without her aid, I would surely be lost. At my behest, she has agreed to join our cause and aid us. Protect her as you would me. Lady, these are Eledom," he indicated the bulky elf, "and Lámirië, my most trusted guards."

I nodded in greeting, and they tapped their chests.

"Don't mind Lámirië," Eledom said. "She's suspicious of her own shadow."

Lámirië snorted, and I grinned to hide my uncertainty. Celebel gave me a rueful smile and offered a leg up. With an arch look, I swept past him, grabbed Iruwher's mane, and swung myself lightly up onto her back. It might have been centuries since I'd last ridden a horse, but I certainly hadn't forgotten how.

A delighted smile adorned my face; riding was a treat to me. Energetic and sensitive, the mare responded to the slightest shift of my weight and anticipated my movements. Her gaits were smooth as a glass sea and her tack of the finest grain leather. The horses needed no bridles and bits. They followed our direction without such strict measures, and instead wore decorated, protective halters and light barding. I'd grown far too accustomed to the crude equestrian manner of the villagers.

We rode together into the trees in silence. All the while the guards' ears trained on me.

The camp settled in a clearing, tents blending with the surrounding forest. Arranged in a rough circle, a larger tent stood in the protected center, soon to be joined by a second. An artificer rapidly grew and shaped the tent trees from flexible maples, forming a spacious and well-sealed frame. Others hung a canopy from the supports. Mottled browns, greens, and golds merged with the trees, and yet the interior was white as newly fallen snow.

The elves that emerged greeted Celebel with much fanfare and more than a few tears. Apparently, the scouts hadn't yet spread the news. I hung back, chuckling to myself at a couple of particularly hysterical, particularly beautiful young things. A man and a woman threw themselves upon his feet, wailing. Celebel looked embarrassed and quickly introduced his former paramours; the first of many. The sulking that followed was almost as dramatic as the wailing had been. I managed not to laugh aloud, but only just barely, and added more sets of ears to the collection following my every sound.

The amount of rapt attention focused on Celebel at all times made avoiding fanfare difficult. My request for anonymity dampened his excitement, so he introduced me as merely the healer who had saved him. The gathered elves, mostly light-haired Astolar, all touched my hair and my hands. They lobbed rapid questions about my whereabouts, family, past, and alliances. I dodged as many as I could, begging fatigue from our long travels. Their lilting voices blended together in a wearying cacophony, and my skin shivered at so much physical contact. Despite my best intentions, the stacks of names refused to stick in my mind in the wake of my overwhelm.

Once the initial celebration over Celebel's return died down, the familiar sounds of the forest returned. Hands flashed in sign language that overtook the chatter. They shared the same stylistic changes I'd noted with Celebel's signs.

Despite my misgivings about rejoining society, I appreciated the perks of attachment to the Consul. More elves carried furnishings into the tent, casting curious glances at me. When they completed their flurry of activity, I ducked in to discover a large, comfortable bed strewn with cushions and quality furs. Beautiful hand-knotted woolen rugs provided insulation from the hard-packed ground. Intricate witchlight lanterns hung from the walls, and a storage chest nestled beside a walnut writing desk. That they'd had these amenities casually on hand, awaiting Celebel's return, staggered me.

Exhausted from the combination of travel and social bombardment, I made use of a grand, portable wash tub beside his tent. Formed of tightly intertwined fronds, it melded comfortably to my body. I doused myself over and over with heated water, soaking until it cooled. Finally, some respite for my aching feet. I thanked the mossy Siltaur elf, who brought a tray of cut fruit, and popped a slice into my mouth. Ah, heaven in a war camp, who would have thought?

From the sound of Celebel's voice, out near the edge of the camp, Feanim must have returned. It pulled me out of my drowsy relaxation. I listened carefully. The other voice, a sharp tenor, seemed more interested in Celebel's next steps than in the story of how he'd survived.

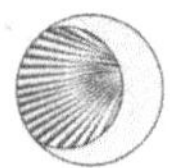

Celebel had just coaxed me into the bed early that first evening when the tent flap blew open and a backlit figure burst through in a gust of cool night air. A dampening field swirled around us, shutting out all outside noise. Humid and buzzing against my skin, it held a faint olivine glow.

"I have it," the stranger declared, completely ignoring my presence.

Celebel groaned and sat up. "This would be my partner in the Consulate, Feanim—"

The newcomer interrupted the introductions with a two-handed wave and I closed my mouth on my greeting. Dressed in forest green leathers, he was shorter than most elves. With dark, curling hair that brushed his collar and intense, algae-green eyes under thick, sardonically arched brows, he might have been handsome if not for the sneering set to his wide mouth. A certain sallow cast to his skin spoke of long hours locked in study away from the sun and moon, but he moved with the particular surety of a fighter.

Feanim held the same tone of Duedellen intensity that Lámirië displayed. They tended toward a particular singularity of focus. I hoped he would prove to be more like the few artificers that I'd known back in my courtly days. Often brusque and off-putting, they also possessed an exquisite sense of aesthetics. I could always find the means to bond with an artist.

"Cel, focus your ears. I know how to bring him to our side. This could be the turning point!" Feanim's tenor held a condescending edge.

I sat up, ears pricking with interest. I might as well have been a wall hanging. Celebel squeezed my forearm under the covers but said nothing.

"Some context, please, Fé." How could he be so patient?

"The fire drake! Are your ears packed with wool? I've been trying to track him for ages and I've had reports of his whereabouts. *Finally!*" Feanim paced around our tent, gesticulating as he spoke, witchlights casting strange shadows on his face. "He is not mere legend, nor has he passed on like we believed. You were mistaken about that cataclysmic storm."

I bit my lip, and Celebel studiously avoided my eyes, shifting under the blankets.

"Oh, indeed?" His voice was mild.

Feanim fluttered a hand at him. "Yes! He played a role in that event, and he's been active since. My crows spotted several drakes on the move recently."

Several drakes? I shuddered internally at the implications.

"If we could harness even a fraction of his might, we need not worry about the Fomorians any longer. We could strike at the heart of their power, root out whatever is coordinating them, and break them once and for all." Feanim made a broad gesture. "I believe we can actually approach the Red Dragon if we go about it the right way. We have something I know he wants. I will offer it to him, just a taste, with the promise of a mutually beneficial trade. What could a warrior such as he possibly desire more than *moranga*?" He raised a clenched fist. Dramatic, this one.

I'd only heard of such things in distant tales. "Moranga is real? I'd thought it only a fancy."

Legend had it that the demon ore, once refined and forged, was nigh indestructible. Supposedly it drank both light and spirit, and spread blight to whatever it touched. But to find it, one must travel deep within the world to the demon realm, and only the hottest fires could smelt it.

The Duedellen hissed at my interruption. "*Some* of us take the histories seriously," he sniffed, without a glance at me.

"*Some* of those histories were written with bias," I countered.

Celebel intervened, directing the conversation back to the demon ore. "You finally have it then. After all your searching." An unreadable look flashed in his eyes.

Feanim sliced a glare at me, brows raised, before turning back to Celebel. "Yes. I told you those negotiations with the spiders would pay off in the end." Spiders? "I manged to refine a bit and forged a knife—"

"You're going to give him the moranga?" Celebel cut in.

"No, *focus your ears,*" Feanim's hands flashed, signing with a jerking slash of irritation. He seemed to talk with his hands just as much as his mouth. "We're going to offer him just a *taste,* and if he agrees to help our cause, we will provide it to him freely. It's perfect!"

"And you're offering this to—"

"To the Red Dragon, lord of the drakes. Who else could I possibly be speaking of? Try to follow the melody!" Feanim tossed his hands up in exasperation. "If we can coax him to our side, we'll never have to worry about the Fomorians again."

I couldn't hold it together anymore, and the smallest giggle escaped my lips. The Duedellen rounded on me with furious eyes. They really were the color of a murky swamp.

"Who the fuck are you?" he demanded, his generous mouth turning down.

"I am a simple healer and a follower of the Night Mother. Now, I'm sorry, did you say you were going to offer the Red Dragon, my Rafael, *a gift*?" I bit my lip harder but couldn't entirely control the building laughter.

Feanim looked past me with an imperious glare. "Cel, I know you can get very… *attached* to your paramours, but this is a serious matter! Our people are dying and I'm trying to save us all."

The way he emphasized 'paramour' made it sound like an epithet.

Celebel stood, looking down at his compatriot. "Feanim, don't condescend to her. She not only saved my life, but she has valuable knowledge we need—"

"Relax, Starshine. I can defend myself." I met Feanim's gaze with a level stare of my own. "You're going to get yourself killed. If you offer the Red Dragon a gift instead of simply showing your strength, he'll murder you, trace it back to the source, and take the rest. Now, you say you have reports of his whereabouts. He was last in the hills southwest of the former Dolorne."

Feanim's ears twitched wildly at hearing his secret intelligence spoken so casually by a nameless woman. His initial reaction suggested he was accustomed to encountering Celebel in bed with different partners and thought nothing of it. Seeming to shake himself, Feanim turned away from me to address my lover.

"Again, who the fuck is she? How the *fuck* does she know—"

Celebel placed one hand on the back of Feanim's neck. "*Listen* to her! Focus your ears! She knows what she's talking about."

Feanim's nostrils flared, and he shot me a venomous look. "You said *your* Rafael. Explain!"

I held the rude elf's gaze and my silence for a moment longer than I should have, just to see if steam would actually come out of his ears. "I know Rafael very well." My heart clenched unexpectedly, and I had to draw a breath. "This is a bad plan."

"You-you… what." His ears went flat with shock.

I cleared my throat, feeling suddenly self-conscious, feeling the judgment coming. "I have known Rafael for the better part of a century. He is… a friend."

Feanim caught the hesitation and looked me up and down with disgust. "A friend. You just so happen to be *friends* with the legendary Red Dragon. Naturally. You seem the type to treat with warlords. And he's certainly the type to keep company with nameless elves. What, do you meet over tea? Is there even a cup large enough to fit his claws?" he sneered. "Do you sit on his tail and polish his scales for him?"

"He drinks blood wine and drakes shed their scales like reptiles," I lobbed back, and Feanim closed his mouth. Celebel grinned at me over his unpleasant friend's head. "He also prefers to be addressed as Rafael, and he is not at all what you imagine. To answer your question, I healed him of grievous injury some eight dozen years ago. Pure happenstance. He has been a friend to me, in his way, ever since." With the notable exception of recent events. I grimaced internally. "Actually, you favor him a bit, in brow shape and hair texture. He's much taller and far more muscular, of course." I couldn't help a spiteful grin at the horrified look on Feanim's face. A vein in his forehead throbbed as Celebel released him.

The Duedellen gestured impotently for a moment, evidently trying to regain his footing. "All right then," *liar*, he did not say, but I heard it in the pause, "how would you, in your great wisdom, seek the Red Dragon's aid?"

"I wouldn't. Those who presume do not live to regret their foolishness. But if you want to find out for yourself, perhaps I could call to him." I smiled prettily and batted my lashes. Not that I should, considering the way things had ended, but Feanim didn't need to know that. His attitude rankled. I thought that forehead vein might burst and lazily considered what wound care I would offer.

Feanim waved at Celebel. "Have I gone mad? Are you hearing this too?"

"Fé, will you stop being an ass for one entire heartbeat and actually listen to her?" From the weary patience in Celebel's voice, this was not an uncommon exchange. Feanim considered Celebel for a long moment and turned back to me with an exaggerated bow.

"Oh, *do* continue. Enlighten me." He folded his arms and arched a brow.

A cruel streak as well as a flair for drama. How typical. I decided not to bait him further. "Rafael may not answer, as we did not part on the best of terms," my eyes flitted to Celebel and back, "but I can sense him. Part of the… healing bond." I hoped Feanim didn't catch the truth in my pause. The wish bubbled up to tell everything all at once. Backlash and judgment be damned. I stifled the reckless urge. "I can give only a vague direction, but if he is in distress, I feel it, and the opposite is true as well. He told me if I were to call to him out of genuine need, he would heed the message."

"You claim you can whistle up the fucking God of Carnage like a dog and he'll heel to you. And you expect me to believe that you have that kind of power?"

"I said he would know if I reached out, that is all. He may not answer. He may even be angry with me, and it's quite possible that drawing his attention is a terrible idea."

Feanim snorted. "Celebel," he snapped, "come with me. We need to have a discussion."

Without waiting for a response, the Duedellen turned on a heel and imperiously stomped out of the tent. Celebel sighed in a gusty exhale and kissed my cheek.

"Forgive the intrusion, my love. These moods take hold of him, and he won't stop until I hear him out."

"Go on, do your Consulate duties," I teased, stretching my arms over my head. "I'll still be here when you return."

Chapter 19

The moment my head hit the pillow, Rafael took over my dreams with another memory. Despite my somnolent state, his influence manifested in force. Wrapped in his presence, he breathed the memories into me as though we shared the same lungs. My unconscious mind belonged entirely to him.

"Rafael, you godsforsaken blighter! Where have you been? You know how I hate it when you slink off in the night like a thief!" I tossed aside the cloak I'd been mending to glare at the approaching red drake. He'd been gone for half a year. Left without a word, as usual, and no communication since.

The Dragon moved in a languorous lope, dressed in his scaly, full drake form. A dragon indeed, on two legs rather than four. He wore no wings, and a long, muscular tail lashed behind him. In that body, he was even more massive, half again my height. I'd always expected drakes to appear thus; as great reptilian beasts. The scales beautifully outlined his muscular body, emphasizing all his hard edges. There was a thought I'd never had before meeting Rafael—that scales could be attractive. The piercing blue of his eyes shone brighter against all the crimson. Rather than his usual layers, he wore only a sleeveless, long jerkin over leather trousers; all black, as usual. His dragon feet remained bare.

"Well? Are you going to answer?"

Silently, he crouched onto all fours, and laid that wedge-shaped, draconic head in my lap. His skull alone was nearly the length of my torso. My hands wandered over him of their own accord, and I cursed myself. Rafael didn't deserve my forgiveness, the unrepentant ass, but he had an instinctive knack for drawing it out of me.

"I'm glad you overcame your reluctance to show me this form," I finally said. Why couldn't I hold onto my anger? I scratched behind a horn. He made a contented sound that relaxed the tension

in my chest, and I sighed in defeat.

The scales rendered his facial expression even more unreadable, but his body language reassured me. As he continued his refusal to receive any form of sexual pleasure from me, I was grateful for the opportunity to touch him in new ways. This form was just as spiky as his personality, but if I stroked down the direction of the scales, I could avoid cutting my hands.

The manner in which the drake still resembled the man I knew fascinated me. His snout had a distinct ridge similar to his aquiline nose, his brow ridges sprouted spikes that mimicked his sharply arched eyebrows. He had those same heavy-lidded eyes and defined, hollow cheekbones. Two long, white horns swept back from behind his temples, nestled amongst other spines. A 'mane' of thinner, significantly longer scales emerged behind his head and extended a third of the way down the S-curve of his neck. He even had the same broad shoulders and comparatively slim waist.

I tugged at the jerkin, wishing to stroke his back. Obliging, he pulled it off. He was no less clothed without it. A row of spines raised where they had previously lain flat under his clothing, trailing down his back to the tip of his sinuous tail. His trousers laced tightly around the base of his tail and crisscrossed out a quarter length. It allowed him modesty without sacrificing mobility.

Most of the shining, blood red scales that covered his body were teardrop-shaped and heavily keeled with serrated edges. Smaller, more pebbled scales allowed finer movements around his face. Pointed, overlapping plates protected his snout. His chest and belly had the most noticeable scalation change. Wider, flatter scales with a pebbled texture curved over his muscular, deep-keeled chest. Perhaps I could wheedle him into removing those trousers, since his scales so thoroughly shielded his body.

He rumbled, the sound vibrating against my thighs and awakening my lust.

"I've never fucked a dragon before," I said. "At least, not like this."

Rafael responded in draconian; a deep, guttural growl. Something about discovery. Or perhaps redundancy. With a glance at my face, he nudged my legs apart with his snout. Hot breath seared my sensitive skin, shivering me with desire. And some small amount of trepidation. All of him seemed designed to rip and tear. To destroy me.

I gripped his horns as he inhaled the scent of my arousal. His long tongue flicked out, swirling my clit in precise circles. He took care not to scrape his scales against my sensitive inner thighs and I relaxed against the Tree. Closing my eyes, I let the pleasure take me. Each lap of his tongue built that exquisite pressure, starting at the base of my spine. He growled again, sending delicious tremors through my flesh.

When his great, scaled hands seized my breasts, I cried out in startlement. He paused in his tasting, tilting his head to look at my face.

"Sorry, sorry," I forced out. "Please continue."

The Dragon resumed his sampling of my cunt, pinching my nipples in the pebbled scales of his fingertips. I moaned and lifted myself by his horns, trying to force his tongue inside me. He hissed, and the blast of hot air made me squirm and whimper.

He shoved me up the trunk of the Tree, bark scraping my back, until my feet dangled in the air. Scaled hands pinned me in place and he stretched to his full height. I whined at the sweet agony, no longer able to reach his horns. A sliding sensation beneath my buttocks and a glance down told me he'd braced me with his tail. I longed to view us from a distance and capture the moment in a drawing. His strength thrilled and frightened me, sharpening my lust to a bleeding edge.

He thrust that impossibly long tongue into me, keeping my tenderest flesh well away from the rending points of his teeth. I cried out as it writhed within me like a serpent. The pressure tipped over into a wave. Between his tongue and hands, throes of bliss coursed through me. The bruising force on my breasts made me want to goad him to bite. To claw. To break me.

His next growl pushed me over the edge and I cried out as my orgasm crested. The tips of his talons bit into my breasts, drawing blood and forcing me to greater heights. Yes! Shuddering ecstasy stole my senses, blotting out all thought, and I writhed in the sheer force of it. His tongue curled and undulated inside me, hitting every sensitive spot.

The tickle of blood, the sharp pain of his talons, the sweet intensity of his tongue. It all conspired to create a staccato melody of smaller climaxes. Each peak and dip took me a little farther until I gasped for breath.

He withdrew his tongue, holding me pinned against the Tree.

"Gods, Rafael," I panted, trying to slow my breathing. "I need you."

Something flashed in his eyes. He unhooked his talons and moved to lick the blood away from the puncture wounds. The lap of his tongue over my nipples threatened to take me right back to orgasm.

Releasing his hold, he caught me in his arms. I wrapped my legs around his waist, wincing as the saw-edged scales cut into me, and pressed my face to his chest. The weight of him, the sheer size of him half-crushing me against the Tree, dizzied me with desire. I licked the pebbled scales of his chest, wondering just how much he could feel, grinding my hips against him as hard as I could.

His muscular thighs spread beneath me, and something teased across my wet cunt. Pulling back, I glanced down at the very tip of his tail curling against my clit.

"Do you want this?" he asked, in clear elvish. His voice was a thunderclap, the depth and timbre threatening to shake me apart. My nipples tightened in response. All I could see was the garnet expanse of his chest, turning my vision to blood.

"Yes." I barely got the words out before his tail teased apart my labia and entered me.

I gasped, rocking against him as he worked it deeper, little by little. Some part of my mind breathed a sigh of relief that he'd smoothed those biting scales and flattened the spines. The rest of me wanted him to fuck me into bloody ribbons.

I moaned, and he growled in response, thrusting with his hips and tail. As that tail stretched me wide, the heated weight of his leather-bound cock pressed into my belly. Gods, it was huge! When I reached down to stroke that impressive erection, he grabbed my wrists and snatched both hands above my head. My clit throbbed painfully in response, and I undulated against him.

"Fill me up, oh gods, I need you," I whimpered. "Ruin me, devour me. Fuck me to pieces!"

The Dragon growled in response, seizing one of my delicate ears in his carnivore teeth. I gasped, and he thrust hard. The tip of his tail slammed into my cervix and stars burst before my eyes. The orgasm tore free from my core, bringing with it a screech. He thrust again and again, each punishing blow knocking me into greater heights of ecstasy. I bit at him as I climaxed, raking my teeth over his impenetrable scales. Shuddering waves ripped more screams from my throat. My legs spasmed. I lost all feeling in my arms. My world pinpointed to the tail bruising my cervix and the shaft of his cock grinding against my sensitized clit.

I thrashed in his grip, shrieking like the dying, in the throes of agonized pleasure. As the last wave of convulsing orgasm finally faded, he slowly withdrew his tail and lowered me to the ground.

I lost my senses for a time. When next I opened my eyes, Rafael wore his usual form and cradled me in his arms. Worried yellow streaks marred the brilliant blue of his eyes, his brows knit with concern.

"There you are." He brushed a strand of hair back from my face. "I feared—" His breath hitched, and he closed his eyes for a moment. "Are you hurt?"

I was a boneless sack of meat. My sex burned with the abuse I'd put it through.

"Not hurt, no." I smiled at him. "I'm sore, but unharmed."

Oh, I would be so deliciously sore in the next few days. I

never healed myself after a proper rough fucking, relishing the lingering reminder. This, however, was perhaps a little beyond my usual definition of 'rough.'

He sighed and kissed my forehead. The tenderness of the gesture brought tears to my eyes. Gods, if only I could get him to speak the thoughts simmering just under the surface. To express that care aloud.

"Be at ease. I thoroughly enjoyed your ferocity. Those scales suit you, my handsome Dragon." I trailed fingers down his cheek and his expression eased.

"As your soft skin suits you, my dove."

Chapter 20

Celebel woke me, padding softly through the tent. Shaking off the intense desire of the dream-memory, I sat up and shifted in the bedding, uncomfortably damp between my legs. I didn't wish to hide my carnality from him, but it left me in a strange haze of unrequited emotion.

His ears twitched in recognition. Staring at me for a long moment, a sly grin crept across his face. "This is the second time you've awoken in such a state, flushed like you've just been fucked. Surely we've enough distance from your hill…" He trailed off, taking my hand and idly caressing my knuckles. "How are you feeling?"

I took in the sight of him. Gone were the homespun clothes from the village. In their place, he wore a grey coat sewn with seed pearls, laced deliciously tight across his chest. It cut away at the waist to reveal a long white skirt with gathers that did little to hide the outline of his cock. I still feared drawing Rafael's attention, but perhaps he would pay no heed if I only gave pleasure.

Rather than speak to my roiling emotion, I pushed Celebel back on the bed and spread his thighs. He gasped with delight as I tugged the skirt up to his waist. Licking my palm, I took hold of that lovely cock.

"Tell me, oh Consul. Have you sued for peace?"

"Truly? Very well, I will enlighten you until I am no longer able." He sighed with pleasure. "Feanim will harmonize eventually."

"And for now?" I stroked him casually and he sprang to attention under my hand.

"Lots of ranting. A bit of naming you a liar and warning that you were trying to take advantage somehow. He wants proof of the connection you claim. I believe he suspects the true nature of it."

"Feanim may receive more proof than he's prepared for if

I call to Rafael and he actually heeds me." I rose from the bed. Celebel whined as I rummaged through a chest for the things I had brought from the hill. "Show him the scroll if you must." I tossed the case to my lover. He caught it one-handed, grimacing at both my causal handling of the relic and my abandonment of his erection.

"I doubt he'll accept any proof other than a face-to-face meeting."

"Your fellow Consul knows not what he asks." Pacing, I shook the disarray from my hair and plaited it into one long tail. "Rafael needs no tribute. He knows very well he's stronger than we'll ever be." A small glimmer of fortune in the darkness that I'd encountered Feanim before the Dragon did. Rafael had only stated that he would no longer consume elves, not that he would stop killing us for good.

"I believe you, love. Feanim can be difficult, but he is not a fool. He will listen. Eventually." Celebel's brow creased.""You've spoken of the gifts the Dragon brought you. How does that factor with this concept of gifts versus tribute?"

"When I asked, Rafael made some vague statement intimating that his 'gifts' still belong to him, as he has the strength to take them back at any time. I do not grasp all the nuance. It's possible that his rank affords him a different set of rules." He certainly seemed to be the consistent exception to said rules. Including the one about how no one had ever made a soulmate of a drake.

My heart fluttered and I pressed a hand to my chest to calm it. "Do you truly think it necessary to have his aid in this fight?" Keeping the two halves of my soulbond completely separate would at least be cleaner, if not any easier. The melancholic assumption that Rafael would not make amends wove throughout my decision-making.

Celebel gave another weary sigh. "Feanim certainly thinks so. I would love to say no, but my dear, this is becoming a war of attrition that we are slowly, inexorably, losing. The Fomorian raids have grown worse in my absence, and we still do not know why they're targeting us. If this pace continues, there will hardly be enough elves left to stand and fight. You are the last known wakeful ancient, and no warrior by your own admission. We need might at our backs."

Celebel took my hand as I paced by, and I let him stop me.

"We should inform Feanim of your past," he said.

I almost opened my mouth to ask why, then closed it on the answer. Foolish, to put such stock in a name rather than individual merit, but wholly unexpected.

"You may tell him. It will come to light eventually, anyway."

He gestured to his crotch. "May I request that we retire the politics for now? I am defeated."

I leaned over him and wrapped my lips around his cock.

I'd expected us to move on quickly after the reunion, but the small camp lingered, planning their next steps with care. Pairs of scouts searched the area for signs of other missing elves in the meantime. They recovered no victims, but reported evidence of recent Fomorian presence in the surrounding area.

Celebel and Feanim spent a lot of time in conference together. Somehow, there were always maps involved. I found them in Feanim's tent. Eledom and Lámirië lurked just outside, always watchful. The Duedellen woman moved to stop me from entering, but Celebel called out. I slipped past the bodyguard as she relaxed.

The dual Consulate sat at a circular table laden with the aforementioned maps, plates of fruit, and bottles of wine. A neglected bedroll had been kicked to a far corner, weighed down with books. Across from them, a rack held a set of armor that had seen abundant use.

"I have had only small news of this conflict. How did it begin?" I asked, moving to Celebel's side to peer at their work.

Feanim looked up sharply at Celebel. "Why the fuck is she

present?"

"She has every right to be here," Celebel countered. He looked at me. "May I tell him your history now?"

I signed surrender.

"Cúraniel is of the line of Maelial. She is the lost daughter." Celebel paused for emphasis. "The one who abdicated and left the court."

"I see no family talisman." Feanim's eyes were shrewd. "And there is no record of a 'Cúraniel' Maelialressë."

"Indeed, I broke with the lineage when I abandoned the court," I said. "I returned the earring to my sister before I left. Send your crows to Silfanië to confirm if you must."

"How convenient that you appear with huge claims of kinship and power, bearing no proof, and wearing naught but a strand of pearls in your hair." The rich yellow gold of his own earrings winked in the light as his ears twitched.

"I've no desire to claim either, only to lend aid where I may." I gave him a twirl, making my braid fly out and the pearls flash in the witchlight. "Since you noticed, aren't they fine? Perfectly matched, white as the moon, flawless nacre, and with such a mirrorlike luster! I've never seen their like. Rafael gave them to me." The memory brought a smile.

"The Red Dragon gives you *gifts?*" If Feanim's eyebrows climbed any higher, they would disappear into his hairline. "You truly expect me to believe that the Red Dragon—the same Bloody Drake who slaughtered an entire ancient human species and murdered *thousands* of elves—gives *you* gifts?" He yanked on his earlobes.

"You saw the scroll, that was another." A fey urge to tweak his ears about a certain *other* gift bubbled up just when Celebel smoothly interrupted.

"My love, you came asking about the attacks." He'd sensed my mischief and gave me a brief, chiding look.

"Thank you, Starshine." I pulled a stool over beside him.

Celebel kissed my hand as I sat. He unsheathed and

examined a small þilvor stiletto dagger. Plucked from the hoard Rafael had kept at my tree, the sapphires set into the pommel sparkled in the light.

"Thank you for lending me this blade, which we believed lost to our house ages ago," Celebel said.

I smiled at Feanim, letting him make the connection about where this other gift must have originated.

"The Lord Consul and I were discussing our position here," my soulmate continued, pointing to a spot on the map with the stiletto. "I was attempting to impress that patience will be a key factor in strategy and successful leadership."

Feanim's scowl hardened. His vision fixed on me, mouth tight with the effort of holding back whatever caustic thought boiled just under the surface. I supposed he had a right to his suspicion, given the circumstances.

"I think Feanim has heard my point, and we may take a moment to inform you of the origins of this conflict, Cúraniel Maeliaressë." Celebel paused dramatically, inviting Feanim to speak. Obviously, he was accustomed to the use of subtext to maneuver the stubborn elf.

Feanim rolled his thumb over his fist so tightly I thought he may break a finger. The silence hung heavy as he considered me.

Celebel intervened again. "Recall our discussion of how all the land surrounding your hill was submerged until a couple thousand years ago. The massive amount of power discharged at the end of the last great war led to that string of earthquakes and volcanic eruptions. They changed our lands and pushed several of the old cities to the surface again. Had that been the extent of it, there would be no true problems, and indeed we had a long period of what we thought was peace. But the Fomorians began to appear in the land. And they immediately sought out and attacked us wherever they could."

He pointed to markers on the map showing where the attacks had occurred. At a glance, they held no discernible pattern. "We've determined that they come from some centralized location, but thus far we've been unable to draw them out into pitched battle. As I've said, we cannot win a war of attrition. Even if every remaining elf in this world united under one banner, we simply do not have the numbers."

"Who are the Fomorians? I saw them in Celebel's memory of the attack that drove him to me, but I have never encountered such creatures in my journeys." I leaned forward with interest.

Feanim frowned, and for a moment I thought I'd somehow offended him again. "We are not entirely sure. They may have some connection to the sidhe, but we cannot yet determine the nature of it. Their language defies our ears, even upon capture. Some obfuscating power." He glanced at Celebel. "We managed to capture one recently, but learned very little. They are not constructs, though their spirit is strange. They bleed just as we do. This one melted away in the shackles after three days, like wax in the sun. We'll have to capture another to determine the cause."

"Oh, the poor thing!" I cried, and they both gave me strange looks.

"Are you... are you really having a fit of compassion for the fucking *Fomorians?*" Feanim asked, ears twitching wildly. He looked at Celebel. "Where did you find her again?"

I shuddered. "How could I not? Imagine being captured by an enemy whose language you do not speak and rotting away in chains!"

"You do realize they are indiscriminately murdering our own people, yes?" Feanim countered.

"Perhaps we have somehow caused them a great ill or offense." Could I ask the sidhe directly? Risky. Their secrets came writ in blood.

"I refuse to have a philosophical argument about the inherent goodness of monsters with a nameless madwoman from the hills." He stood, gathered up a few journals and maps, and stomped off.

"He's a sunbeam," I said, watching him leave. The guards rustled outside, acknowledging the Consul's passage.

Celebel sighed. "He'll warm up, eventually."

"So you claim."

"As it stands, there is some mysterious force guiding these attacks. The Fomorians always seem to know where we'll be in numbers. They've even reclaimed a few of these newly risen cities as their strongholds, just as we were able to take a few. Despite our best efforts, it's been difficult to unite our distinct nations under the Astolar banner without a named leader."

I'd forgotten about the loss of the Astolar queen. "How goes the bid for succession? Who is under consideration?" Poor timing for the spiritual trials.

"It shifts so quickly I am certain that whoever I name would be wildly inaccurate by the time we reach the court. It is not so much contentious as it is difficult with how scattered we've become in our migrations to safety. I favor Araglin for the throne, but he is not much interested in rulership."

"Perhaps that is a note in his favor." At least this Araglin was willing to open his gates to the needy and displaced. It spoke well of his character. "And the others?"

Celebel nodded, thoughtful. "Currently, we have a decent number of Lachanaur thanks to Feanim's partnership with their queen, a few more Talithiri with me, and the rest are a mere peppering. Too many close their minds and their gates, thinking that they will remain unaffected."

I followed him outside, past the wary gaze of his bodyguards, as he continued. "Not only elves are affected. The humans of this area say it is no longer safe for them to venture into the woods. They complain of blighted crops and slaughtered livestock that will surely lead to famine. We were treating with a few of their more prominent leaders when the ambush at Orfain happened. I fear all of Vaeda may eventually become embroiled in this conflict."

He paused, drumming his fingers on his arms. "I still have hope. In spite of it all, I see the potential for us to grow and evolve beyond the confines we've set for ourselves. This conflict does not affect nature, and it will endure. So must we."

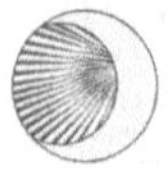

Finally, our camp disbanded. The speed at which the others regrew the trees, broke down their tents, and packed up was truly impressive. My own packing was simple enough. This fortified city lay several days' hard ride to the northeast, depending on the route we chose along the way.

Celebel outfitted me in fitted leather armor, saving the fine, lightweight þilvor for the actual fighters. It took me some time to grow used to the restrictive garments. I hadn't worn anything more limiting than a belt since leaving the court. He helped me braid my hair in a tight coil around my head to keep it from catching on anything.

I hated the idea of abandoning the others in an attack, but my lack of mounted combat experience would make me more of a liability than an asset. My half-moon blades hung from the saddle in their scabbards only as a last resort. The falcata would not be of much use from horseback, so we packed it away. Strange, to consider such things.

We moved in near-silence, the horses stepping with care. Þilvor armor and barding earned its keep, as the valuable metal only chimed when struck with intention. As much as possible, we spoke to each other only in sign. Even that was diminished, as no one wanted sunlight to glint off of a careless gauntlet and alert potential enemies to our location.

My enthusiasm for riding turned quickly to weary acceptance after three solid days in the saddle, resting only long enough to water and feed the mounts. I made the mistake of complaining about saddle soreness once; my inner thighs chafed and my knees burned. Feanim snidely suggested I walk the rest of the way and Celebel's frustration became quickly evident. I vowed at that moment not to become a burden.

Chapter 21

Early in the morning of the fourth day of travel, hands flashed in signs of distress about our path through a high-walled slot canyon called Seregond Pass. To avoid it would either mean abandoning the horses for a climb or riding nearly a moon out of the way. Naive to battle as I was, even I recognized the potential for ambush.

Celebel confirmed that our own forces had in fact staged an ambush in the area during a battle many years ago; it was a known risk. My stomach roiled with unease.

"Why haste if danger?" I signed, concern creasing my brow.

"Other way means battle," he replied, with a modified sign for 'monsters' that I took to indicate the Fomorians. "Many Fomorians."

Around a bend, we came upon an enormous stone fire pit strewn with the charred remains of bones. It was still warm. A pulse of spirit confirmed that none of the bones were elvish, though quite a few were human. Feanim insisted that we could press on, and perhaps even take a few more Fomorians captive. The roiling condensed into a stone, heavy in the pit of my belly.

Two scouts raced ahead as the rest proceeded with caution. The horses sensed the strain, stepping lightly. The soldiers stretched their ears for the slightest hint of enemy presence. Celebel grew apprehensive in a way I had never seen before, and even Feanim was tense. Iruwher danced beneath me, my anxiety transferring to her.

The walls of Seregond cut the wind and birdsong to eerie silence as we rode through. Some areas were tight enough to reduce us to only three across. I had the sensation of rock brushing my shoulders, though in reality the striated sandstone was well out of reach. My spine itched, and I looked over my shoulder to another wall of impassive helms more than once.

A sharp, whistling chorus caught my attention. The other elves had already raised their shields in unison by the time my mind parsed the sound of a loosed arrow. Many loosed arrows. Celebel called for me to raise my shield. He'd hung it from the pommel of my saddle for just this purpose, a long teardrop of polished, painted wood. Blinking stupidly, I raised it just in time for an arrow to skid off of it, drawing a startled shriek from me. They struck the walls, the other shields, the ground. Fear jolted through me, striking true where no arrow had, and I trembled in my saddle.

The archers waited until we were fully walled in to rain down their arrows. Only elvish hearing and reflexes saved us, no thanks to mine. The first volley didn't do much damage against the quality of the elvish shields. I quickly learned to work in tandem with the others to deflect incoming arrows. Though well-made and lightweight for its size, holding the shield aloft made my arms ache before long. I silently cursed Rafael for being right about my lack of conditioning. The focus on my growing physical discomfort kept me from giving in to blatant panic.

Iruwher guided us, her training and instinct taking over. Our smaller company maneuvered forward, finding a space large enough to create a proper defensive formation. It drew into tight rings around the Consulate and a few other noncombatants like myself.

When Fomorians poured down the cliff walls like molten tar and rose from the ground behind us in a wave, we knew exactly how dire the situation truly was. We were hopelessly outnumbered, but why weren't they simply picking us off from a distance? Or throwing boulders down on our heads?

Their howling cries froze my blood. With nowhere to run, all I could do was free my blade from its scabbard and watch the encroaching doom. Just like the memory Celebel showed me, the Fomorians were a strange and varied mishmash of animal and person. Most had grey skin, but other hues showed through their bronze maille.

I tried to draw upon the Night Mother's power and weave a

protective ward of the Moon's light around our group. The speed at which the Fomorians attacked left me no room to gather myself. The resulting clash jarred me from all possibility of concentration.

An enormous Fomorian charged forward and bit through the forelegs of a rearing warhorse with a sweep of its massive tusks. Its rider sliced a desperate blow through the attacker's thick neck. The fight began in earnest and I had no more time to think.

The shriek of metal on metal, the screams, the stench of opened bowels and the foul breath of monsters; it was too much. I clung to Iruwher's back for dear life, trusting her instincts over mine as she wheeled and kicked and bit. A Fomorian leaped, grabbing an elf to my right about her waist—I recognized her in a state of detachment as one of those who'd flung themselves on Celebel's feet. The attacker dragged her halfway off of her horse. An arrow sprouted in the beast's eye, spraying blood, and it released her. I jerked to see Celebel over my shoulder, lowering a shortbow.

I hunkered in my saddle, nervous to strike with the press of horses around me. The Fomorians had no such compunction. They laid about with weapons of bronze, obsidian, and flint, mostly spears and axes, to devastating effect. A surprising number of Fomorians struck their own fellows in their haste to reach us, showing no care at all for the proximity of their comrades.

Slower than us, they made up for the lack with raw power. When their blows landed, they wreaked havoc. Lopping off armored limbs with hacking strikes, staving in breastplates, crushing bones with sickening force. I vomited when a ripped-out eyeball landed on my hand. It all blurred into a hideous cacophony.

A mildly hysterical voice in the back of my head pointed out that the enemy didn't seem to land as many killing blows as they should. Why weren't they slaughtering us? Why did they aim the bulk of their attack at the horses themselves? *Why were they targeting the horses?*

I turned and swung my blades in wild terror at a slavering face looming at my flank. It dodged backward. Iruwher promptly kicked it in the stomach, knocking it to the ground. She trampled it to death with a furious squeal. The squelch of organs and cracking bones made me ill. More of a courser than a destrier, my mare, and yet she matched the heavier chargers in both ferocity and skill.

So much *noise!* My ears ached horribly. I wanted nothing more than to flee to my quiet hill, but the attacking monsters hemmed us in from all sides. I ducked under a club meant for my head. No more time for thought, only action.

Celebel was magnificent. He and Helicos moved as one, flowing through one sword strike to the next in seamless harmony. He swung that bright blade in flashing arcs and Fomorians fell in mounds before them.

Feanim fought like a demon. With a sharp syncopation, his sword stabbed and cut, moving too fast for my eyes to track. His dark liver mare, Lettai, was no exception, her flaxen mane and tail lashing the air as she kicked and bit.

For a moment, I thought perhaps we had a chance, as we seemed to be turning back the tide. But our protective ring buckled. I watched in helpless horror as horses collapsed and soldier after soldier fell to the inexorable, crushing wave. The smell of blood and viscera choked me. An axe caught on my shield, wrenching it from my hands.

A horn blew. The Fomorians lunged as one. Grabbing hold of the closest elves in the outer protective ring, heedless of blows landed, they bore their prey bodily to the ground. Horses fell under the crush of bodies.

One by one, the Fomorians dragged the struggling, screaming elves away. Some were ripped apart in the process.

"Call him," Celebel shouted from somewhere nearby.

Disoriented, I looked for my lover in the press, and finally found him at my rear. When had he gotten behind me? Watching him expertly wheel his stallion and lay about with his sword, I realized he was intercepting the enemy before they could reach me. A sense of gratitude washed over me, despite my terror.

"Cúraniel, call the Dragon! We are going to die here!"

My heart hammered in my throat. *Crow!* "What if—"

"Now is all that matters! Call him," he bellowed.

I looked as deeply into Celebel's desperate eyes as the swell of bodies around us would allow, willing him to feel my love.

"Protect me for as long as you can. I'll be senseless for a moment."

He nodded and signaled to his bodyguards, and the three of them formed a loose circle around me. Eledom blocked a spear aimed at my head as I squeezed my eyes shut and centered the image of Rafael in my mind. Reaching with all my might, I cried out his name. Sending him the scene of violence all around me. Channeling my fear and desperation. Begging. Pleading for him to save us all.

An endless silence breathed between us, vibrating with tension. I lost count of the heartbeats, but the Dragon's presence manifested as surely as if he stood before me, staring me down. I simultaneously wanted to throw myself into his arms, yell at him, and flee his wrath.

I opened my eyes in time to see a huge Fomorian grab Celebel from the rear, pulling him to the ground. Shrieking, I wheeled my horse around and slashed as far as I could with my blade. It didn't connect, but at least made the creature flinch away and land on its back in the churn. Celebel stabbed up under its chin, righted himself quickly, and slashed behind the knees of another Fomorian readying to leap at my head. It crumpled on suddenly useless legs and he chopped it down. Helicos bobbed low, biting another assailant's arm and flinging the beast away. Celebel grabbed the destrier's mane and hopped astride once more.

"Rafael heard me. Let us hope he answers," I yelled through the clamor. Perhaps my hearing had gone. Celebel signaled understanding and urged his horse ahead to stomp a beast closing on a soldier nearby.

I wasn't the overly pious sort, but oh did I pray. Prayers that my request fell on willing ears, that speed was on our side, that none of it was in vain. Prayers that the Night Mother would look upon us all with mercy. It would be the first true test of Rafael's word to me. Was his goodwill greater than his rage? Did he hold any love for me at all?

No one warned me that time seemed to slow in battle. The world shrank to the enemy before me. Deal with that one. Another appeared. Cut them down, another attacked. With luck, they attacked one at a time. Otherwise, my best hope was to break away as quickly as possible. Aid my fellows as they aid me. Stay out of my horse's way. Fatigue leadened my senses and wore on Iruwher. Her proud head began to droop.

Stay alive, keep them alive, hold out, keep going. Swing, cut, dodge, block. Keep going. Stay alive. Keep them alive. I made it a chant.

A blow from a club glanced off my thigh. Barely able to register the shooting pain before one of ours cut the offender down, I was off to backstab a different Fomorian. My connection to Rafael swelled in that moment but I had no time to consider it. Did I have a thousand cuts or no injuries at all? I could hardly feel my body. My arms grew heavy and my strikes weakened.

One more swing. One more block. Keep going, stay alive, keep them alive.

Darkness fell preternaturally fast. Or perhaps I was losing consciousness. Disoriented, I dared a quick glance to the sun. A great shadow took its place. The thunderclap of mighty wings echoed across the canyon. I knew that sound. *I knew that sound!*

"He's coming," I crowed over the din, almost giddy with relief. "Hold fast. The Red Dragon is coming!"

When the first blast of dragon fire hit, it sent a shockwave through the enemy. Those unlucky enough to be in the direct path died instantly. An enormous, shining red form streaked past, blotting all else from my field of vision. More startling were the three dragons on his tail. The others peeled off as he circled back.

He blanketed the canyon walls with fire, and the massed enemy melted before us. No time to even scream. The acrid odor of charred flesh gagged me. The dragons banked up and over us, an awesome sight, and my vision sprang to life.

Panic spread through the Fomorians and their attack faltered as they realized what was happening. Some ran for cover, others clustered together for a hopeless defense. As one, they turned their attention away from their equally awestruck prey.

My heart swelled at the sight of the lead dragon. Red as a pool of fresh blood, with a bristling mane of scales, he was followed closely by a burly green dragon with ram-like horns, then a stockier black-tipped red, and finally a smaller, more serpentine blue. Even the larger newcomers were barely half the size of their leader. They all flew in perfect, elegant unison.

Only the Red Dragon breathed fire, a controlled stream of death that utterly obliterated our foes. It wove past us without burning a single elf, moving in ways I'd never witnessed fire behave. Seeking out Fomorians like a living serpent and swallowing them whole.

The screams, when they had breath before dying, curdled my blood. I blocked my ears, sickened. Closing my eyes did nothing to block out the twisting, blackening bodies. The stench clawed its way into my lungs and I heaved bile. A slightly delirious part of my mind insisted that I might never eat roasted venison again.

Heartened, our soldiers took up the fight with renewed vigor, and the remaining enemy crumpled like tin under a hobnail boot. Cheering, our forces surged forth. Shivering with emotion, my leg beginning to throb, I was not much help in the rout. It was all I could do not to drop my sword to the churned ground.

The dragons made a few more passes, picking off stragglers, before landing in the clearing at the far opening of the canyon. My heart pounded in time with the hoofbeats of my mare, so strongly I wondered if everyone around me could hear it too. Feanim wore an expression of bemusement. Celebel gave me a knowing look as I passed and mouthed 'I love you.' All I could muster was a feeble smile, and then Iruwher was carrying me forward. To *him*.

They shifted into their drake forms as I watched. I barely had eyes for the others. There he was, front and center. Staring right at me. Bristling in black armor, he strode toward me the moment I broke free of the crowd.

I pulled to a stop and slid off my courageous horse, who immediately sidled backward with understandably anxious energy. Eyes fixed on the imposing figure before me, I took a step and my leg buckled. Running on pure nervous fear through the battle had deadened the blow to my thigh, and now the injury flared to life with shooting pain. Strong arms caught me before I hit the ground.

"You called me. Here I am." Rafael's deep voice rattled all the way down my spine and I burst into helpless, relieved tears.

He held me at a wary distance until the tremors passed, tension humming in his muscular body. I dared to find comfort in breathing in his scent; leather, that particular spice recalling dragon's blood resin, and a hint of smoke. If he was to be the end of me, I would seek what small pleasure I could.

"Thank you," I whispered to his chest. Drake customs be damned. "Thank you!"

"I swore to you, did I not?"

I finally summoned the courage to look up at his eyes. Yellow streaked with red, hair lit with flame, and yet his expression was carefully neutral. I wanted to touch his face, but restrained myself, sniffling.

"You saved us!"

"You were certainly in need of it," he rumbled, disdain creeping in. He released me and stepped back, looking over the company gathering behind me. "The Lady calls, I answer." His velvety growl carried easily across the meadow and echoed off the canyon walls. "Her enemies are also mine. We will discuss terms later." Those fiery eyes landed on me once more. "This is for *you*," he hissed for my ears alone before withdrawing.

Chapter 22

We had few gravely wounded to tend, and fewer still of the dead. Far more horses had been killed in those targeted attacks or injured beyond saving. We did what we could for them.

Eerily, many of our number were simply missing. I couldn't spare the fear for what that meant after everything else. We all worked together to bandage, splint, and suture. I had little spirit left for healing, and did what I could. It amounted to mild pain relief at best.

Guilt wracked me at the feeling of uselessness. Useless in battle, and now useless in spite of all my expertise. I spared the very last of my salves for my own aching leg, desperate not to become a burden on our strained resources.

After the grinding stress of battle, setting up a temporary camp was torture. In an interaction necessarily kept as brief as possible, Celebel and I mutually agreed that physical distance was tantamount to his continued safety and the peace of the group. It was a long shot, but better than nothing.

"Stay *downwind*," I admonished as a parting word.

I left Iruwher in his care, with a kiss on her soft nose as thanks. She whickered worriedly after me.

It felt wrong to be away from Celebel after such an ordeal. I wanted nothing more than to search every fingerbreadth of his body for hurt. To curl up in his arms for comfort. To ask a million questions, and process all the horrors I had just seen. Instead, I laboriously pitched a small tent by myself near the outskirts of the campsite.

I stripped off my sweat-soaked leathers and tossed them in a pile outside. Shaking from exhaustion and the growing pain in my leg, by the time I finished undressing I could barely slide inside on my belly. Merciful sleep took me immediately.

The Dragon's unmistakable presence shivered me awake.

Much too soon. I struggled to regain lucidity. How had he gotten past the scouts? Probably the same way he'd crept up on me at the hill. I briefly considered maintaining my comfortable nudity, but he had once told me that drakes took offense to such displays. Something about flaunting weakness. Better not to chance his ire in this state.

Wearily, I dragged a robe around my shoulders. Raking all the hair that had escaped my braid out of my face, I crawled on trembling limbs out to meet him. My leg had marginally improved with rest and the salve, but the throbbing pain hardly registered next to my overwhelming dread.

Rafael stood at the edge of the trees, fiery gaze piercing the shroud of darkness. Straight into my soul. He wore no sword at his hip and stood deceptively still, arms folded over his broad chest. Somewhat encouraging, that his hair had dimmed to its true red. Waiting, tense, looking for all the world like a viper readying to strike. I staggered to my feet and tried to summon a courage I did not feel.

"Hello, Dragon. Have you come to kill me?"

Perhaps he'd only kept his word out of a sense of honor, now satisfied. Surely he would vent that horrible wrath from the confrontation on the hill. Visions of blistering, blackening bodies, and the bloody furrows clawed into his own face flitted through my mind.

His heavy-lidded eyes widened ever so slightly. "I could never," he rumbled. Turning on a heel, he strode off into the gloom, clearly expecting me to follow him. I took a deep, steadying breath and trailed painfully along behind.

A bonfire burned in a small clearing ahead, firelight dancing through the dark ring of trees. As soon as I emerged from the forest a wave of weirdness hit me, and a heavy, vibrational feel to the air blanketed my senses. All birdsong and insect noise, as well as the soft sounds of the nearby camp, cut off abruptly. A dampening field. My ears twitched. I'd always thought it a purely elvish ability. It meant he wanted absolute privacy. *Ah, here comes the storm.*

"I didn't think you would come." Emotion welled, choking my voice. *I thought you hated me.*

"You called." Rafael turned and gave me an openly hurt look. A look that said he hadn't expected that call. I bit my lip, feeling small.

Before I could say anything else, he swept me into his arms, kissing my mouth with fervor, so swift I hadn't even seen him move. His heat seared through me, straight to the soul. I kissed him back with equal desperation. Our tongues twined, limbs interlocked. My spirit meshed with his power and surged around us. His scent intoxicated me. Oh gods, I had missed him. Sliding his hand up my thigh toward the growing wetness between my legs, he pulled away at my wince when his palm grazed the site struck by the club.

"You are still hurt." He gripped my shoulders in his hands to look at me with sharp displeasure.

"I have been too weary to heal myself." I was almost too weary to even stand upright.

"May I?"

I nodded. Rafael laid me on the cool ground, uncovering my right thigh, now purpled and swollen. He ran a light, assessing hand over the injury and I twinged with pain, feeling both the hairline fractures in the bone and a few loosened fragments. I shouldn't have put any weight on the leg. It would take days to restore enough strength to fully heal myself, but what choice did I have?

"I taught you better than to leave yourself so open." The Dragon's customary scowl deepened as he looked over the injury. "Almost a direct hit."

"I don't recall you ever teaching me to fight from horseback," I countered, feeling slightly cross.

He rumbled in disapproval. "Please tell me you at least used the half-moon—"

"Grant me a little faith!" I folded my arms over my ample

chest and glared. I didn't want to admit how good it felt to banter with him again, trading words like blows in a sparring match that we both knew would end locked in a passionate embrace.

He smirked and leaned forward to breathe on my thigh. The heat was almost too much to bear. Pinpointed at the injury site, it raced up my spine and down to my toes, intensifying. I tried not to squirm as the flesh and bone re-knit, pain receding with the warmth.

"You are a better pupil than I ever was." I sat up and stroked his hair, running my fingers over the thick, garnet waves.

"I am a great fool." His voice tightened with emotion, and he lifted his eyes to meet mine. "I never should have left you unprotected."

"Rafael," I began.

He cut me off with a sharp shake of his head, tossing back that curling mane.

"No, focus your own damn ears, as you say. I *hurt* you! I have never felt such regret." He touched my cheek softly where his elbow had struck. The bruise had long faded, but the memory lingered.

"That was an accident, and my own fault. I hold no ill will over it." I clasped my hand over his. "You've broken my nose in training, cracked my ribs, inflicted many other injuries. Why so distraught over this?"

"I was *careless*," he hissed. "I am *never* careless! And here you are, injured again, in the middle of this fucking stupid *shit*. I should have taken you away." Fierce red streaked into the worried yellow of his eyes, burning bright under a stormy brow.

"What do you mean, you should have 'taken me away'?" I kept still, hardly daring to breathe.

"I should have claimed you, made you my mate. Taken you away. Saved you from this nonsense before it could reach you. I saw it coming, but I thought I had more time. I… am a great fucking fool." His eyes shut tight, as though blocking out the sight would take away his regret.

I gasped. He'd never given me the slightest hint of any of this. Was he on the verge of tears? Gods, his voice was so raw.

"Rafael!" I touched his face, trying to smooth away the harsh lines.

"I love you." He said it in a forceful growl, unwilling, or unable, to look at me.

Tears sprang unbidden to my eyes. He couldn't have shocked me more if he'd slapped me in the face. "Rafael, I—"

"*I love you!*" He kissed me then, clasping me to his chest. I wept openly from the enormity of his words, from need, from frustration… from pure, blistering *wrath* so swift and intense it nearly took my breath away.

"How dare you! How *dare* you say this to me *now*, after *everything!*" My voice broke on the words. He kissed my face, my ears, my neck, ignoring my attempts to push him away like they were nothing more than a light breeze.

"I will rectify my mistakes. Carry you away from here and claim you," he said in my ear, stroking my skin. "I will *force* my people to accept you."

"You will do no such bloody gods damned thing, you colossal fucking *blighter!*"

I had never felt such choking rage mingled with so much desire. He kissed me anyway, seizing my lips between his sharp teeth, thrusting that sinful tongue into my mouth. My body's immediate, wantonly lustful response made me even angrier. I swatted at him impotently, and he deepened the kiss.

"Do you hold no affection for me after all?" he murmured when our lips parted. I wanted to howl.

"Are you fucking *serious?*" I slapped his face hard enough to split the skin of my palm. He didn't even have the grace to blink. "I've been in love with you for dozens of years! *Dozens!* And I could never even *tell* you because any time you got too close to feeling anything real, you fucking *ran away*. You gods damned *coward!* You abandoned me over and over. *You broke my heart!* Every! Single! Time!" I pounded on his heavy pectoral muscles with my fists, punctuating my words with strikes.

Might as well bare-knuckle box a stone wall. Knowing that I couldn't physically hurt him, no matter how I might break myself against his body, fed my seething wrath.

"Do you know how often I've cried myself to sleep over you? *Do you?!*" I shrieked, shaking with the force of my emotion.

He accepted both my insults and my tears with enraging stoicism, catching my fists and kissing them. Prying open my bleeding hand, he licked the blood away from my palm, sealing the cut while I struggled like a furious cat in his implacable grip. Satisfied, he laid me once more on my back and trapped me beneath him. The comforting weight and furnace of his body stole some of my fight as I broke down and sobbed.

"I will never leave you again. I swear it. I was naught but a monster, lost in myself when we met. You taught me to be more, granted me permission to be something new." He nuzzled my neck, and I resisted the instinct to open like a flower and grant him whatever nectar he wished.

"Where were these sweet words when I needed them all those years ago? Where were they when I begged you for them?" *Fucking hells, stop crying!* "But you *will* turn away. You will run from my love. I know you, you cannot help yourself. You and your fucking commitment issues."

He pulled back with another sharp shake of his head. "Not commitment, no. Never that. Never have I held affection, nor attraction, for any other. I told you as much, but perhaps I was unclear. You hold power over me that I swore I would never grant another, and I can deny it no longer. I *need* you."

And he did, oh I could feel his need so clearly. Damn him. It took the last of my willpower not to grind my hips into his. Perhaps if I could convince him to fuck me on the spot, it would solve so many of our issues.

"I will not abandon you again," he said with fervor.

"If all this is true, why did you conveniently wait to realize it until I found someone else? Someone ready and willing to meet my needs?" My words landed like a rain of arrows. He flinched as I struck true to the heart. It needed to be said. "I am not trying to hurt you, I swear it. I regret the pain I've caused. If you'd granted me even a single route of communication, even a single letter, I would have happily talked through everything with you before the situation progressed to… where it is now. But after all your bellowing and blowing smoke, and avoidance, did you think I would wait and pine forever? Frozen in time, only existing at your whim?"

He exhaled through his long nose, calming his rising temper. "I know I cannot… give you everything you want from me. Yet. But you have changed me in ways I never thought possible. You are *mine*," he snarled, and I grabbed fistfuls of his hair, yanking his head back before he could kiss me again.

"You hear me now, Dragon. Listen well. I am *my own!* I belong only to myself. I am not a part of your hoard. I do not belong to you or anyone else, and I never will." I managed, just barely, not to scream. "With your great strength, surely you could abduct me against my will, and I could do nothing to stop you. But if you ever disrespect me like that, I will *never* speak to you again. I will never *willingly* touch you again. You may overpower my body all you like, but you will never own me. Do you understand?" A stiff finger poking his chest punctuated each word of that last sentence.

With a growl, deadly promise rippled through his muscles. "I will not allow that little weasel to steal you from me." His voice was low, vicious.

I yanked his hair again. "If you seek my *other soulmate* to hurt or kill him, or send your minions to hurt him, or knowingly allow him to come to harm in any way, you will also do irreparable damage to me. And I will *never* forgive you for it. I had a very clear vision that if you two *ever* come to blows, all three of us will be lost. I love you now. Do not make me hate you."

His lips pressed into a thin line at my speech, anger glimmering in his eyes, and his deep red mane sparked to life with the flames of his fury. Here it was. I had never truly directly tested his feelings for me before. Would his prideful wrath win out over his heart? I held my breath.

The space between us sizzled with his heat, his building thunderous growl shaking me to the core, causing the small pebbles to dance on the ground. My heart hammered in my ears, galloping with abandon. Digging deep into my well of courage, I maintained that scalding eye contact. The air itself shivered with his dread power. Even at his worst, he was beautiful in his fury, and I could not truly fear him.

Abruptly, the growl cut off. He closed his eyes and turned his face from me, sitting back on his haunches. The deadly spell broke. I sat up as well, daring to breathe again. Tentatively, I reached to stroke the corded muscle of his arm with my fingertips and drew a ragged sigh from him.

"Please, Cúraniel, do not leave me," he said in the smallest, most humble tone I'd ever heard him use, still looking away. "I am lost without you, my dove."

My heart broke anew, and I crawled to him, wrapping my arms around his neck. He allowed me to pull him close.

"Oh, my Dragon, you make me want to scream to the heavens, but I forgive you. I hope you can forgive me as well." I kissed a curling lock of living flame, the tip of his ear, his sharp cheekbone. "Foolish, beautiful, infuriating man. You damn overgrown hellbeast of a lizard. I *do* love you. Why can I never stay properly on the outs with you, even at your most vile?"

"Must be my winning personality." He gave me a sidelong glance, startling a laugh out of me.

"Did you really make a joke after all that?" I wanted to hit him again.

"Your smile is a song to my heart." Rafael favored me with a weak grin, the corners of his mouth curling in that subtle, catlike way of his.

"How do you *do* that? You make me *wildly* angry, then you make me laugh, and finally just demolish me with something so achingly sweet. You've got me so twisted up I can't even see the sky. The single most uniquely frustrating person who has ever lived, I swear." I tossed my hands up, and he caught them.

"I accept my punishment." He brought my palm to his lips. The tingle of his kiss ran up my arm and directly to my cunt, flooding me with lust.

"I want you to fuck me, hard," I said, flatly, and he dropped my hand.

"I know." Frustration and need were writ clear upon his face. "Ah, how well do I know."

"Do you *want* to fuck me?" I challenged. "To completely give yourself to me without reserve? We have circled this topic for far too long. I am patient. I understand needing time to heal and progressing slowly. It is not a straightforward, smooth path. But you need to decide exactly what you want from me, and you must give me a direct answer. Even if that answer is 'never.' Even if you change your song in the future. I will not tolerate any more escapes or dodging when the conversation grows uncomfortable."

He exhaled heavily, shimmering heat dancing in his breath.

"Yes." His growling register dropped almost lower than I could hear, but he could not hold my gaze. "*Yes.*" Drawing a deep, shaky inhalation, he steadied himself. "You may belong only to yourself, but I belong to you fully. I wish to prove it someday." His voice was dark, heavy with desire. I held my hand out, and he took it, pressing it to his heart.

Gathering myself for a potential backlash, I sent, '*Will you acknowledge the soulbond between us now, or must I continue to pretend otherwise?*'

His brows raised. '*Bold, pushing into the shadows of my mind in this way. Yes, my dove. I feel the connection just as you say.*' Aloud, he added, "Unthinkable, to have a soulmate after all this time alone. I regret my reaction to that discussion. For many reasons." He sighed. "I am aimless, diminished in your absence."

I drew my thumb across his lips. "When we are apart, I too am stretched thin and raw. My spirit is lessened, my powers made small. I never understood how you could tolerate it."

"Poorly." A night breeze ruffled his hair. "If I win this little elf war for you, will you come with me, be my mate?"

I held his gaze, trying to judge his words. He was absolutely sincere. Manipulative blighter.

"I… will consider it. I am *not* saying yes," I added quickly as he opened his mouth to complicate things. "Only that I will consider it."

He nodded after a moment. "Very well. You alone command my loyalty. I will command my people to fight for you. Will you stay with me tonight?"

My life grew stranger with each passing day. "Yes, my Dragon, I will stay tonight. But tomorrow I must return to my duties."

"Hrrm, and who assigns you these so-called duties?" His eyes narrowed. The bonfire threw shadows across his angular face.

"Leave off. I came here to help, remember? I offered my skills as a healer."

"You cannot resist a lost cause," he said archly.

"*You* are going to make me cross again."

Pulling me into his embrace and wrapping his cloak about me, he laughed his odd, coughing, raspy laugh into my hair. "You are beautiful in your anger."

"Wicked beast." I would have smacked him again for good measure, but the last of my strength had left me. "You must think me very beautiful indeed."

"Mmm," he agreed, petting my hair, stroking the length of my ears.

I laughed and laid my head on his chest. "I've missed your hands on me."

"You will continue to miss them, little minx. You *abandoned* me for another, remember?" When I looked at his face to gauge the severity of the words, his expression held but mild reproach. "Your pleasure awaits your atonement."

I studied him. "You're plotting something wicked. I can tell."

"I cannot help my nature." That 'something wicked' flickered briefly in his eyes.

Very well, let him dodge that question. I could only ask for so much growth in one night. He kissed the frown away from my forehead.

"Rest now. You may admonish my wicked ways tomorrow."

I clung to him, and the horrors of the battle rose, unbidden, in my mind. Tears rose with them. "Gods, Rafael, it was horrible," I said into his chest. "I thought we were all going to be torn apart by those monsters." A sob escaped.

"Whist, my dove. No more tears. You are safe now." He sang to me then, in a language I didn't recognize. The resonance of his voice against the backdrop of the crackling bonfire soothed me to sleep.

Chapter 23

I awoke in the late afternoon back inside my makeshift tent, neatly tucked into my bedroll. Rafael's scent lingered on my pillow. He must have carried me back and stayed for some time. The image of him slinking in and out of the low tent brought a smile. I rolled over and stretched, testing my previously injured thigh. Only a faint echo of the damage remained; all the pain was gone. I wished yet again that he cared more for healing than fighting.

'*Cúraniel, I need you!*' Celebel's words in my mind startled me like a bucket of cold water to the face. He sent an image of his location with a sense of the direction. I raced to meet him, throwing clothes on as I went and ignoring the startled stares from the camp.

A striking scene greeted me, tightening my belly with apprehension. Feanim and Celebel stood speaking to Rafael. The Dragon was backlit, hair and eyes glowing against his black armor. He towered over the elves—who were downwind. Good.

Celebel, with his sleek black and silver hair and long blue robe picked with twinkling patterns, made quite a contrast. Feanim dressed in more practical, and far more casual, forest green leathers, his hair a wild fluff of dark curls. All three stood out against a backdrop of tall golden grasses and high canyon walls in the distance. Seeing both soulmates in one place flooded me with unfamiliar emotion. Dread, perhaps. And hope. And something else, something rooted in pure instinct, deep inside where those soulbonds hummed.

Just as I crested the hill, the wind shifted. Rafael's eyes narrowed. He shot Celebel a venomous look. I sped up and inserted myself bodily between them.

"Hello boys, what'd I miss?" I favored them all with my most winning, insincere smile. It failed to draw Rafael's attention. Celebel kept perfectly still, outwardly serene under the Dragon's blatant hostility. My estimation of my elvish soulmate's fortitude rose.

Feanim similarly ignored me. "Why were none of the other drakes involved in routing the Fomorians?"

Rafael's burning eyes remained locked on Celebel's face. "They fight as they will. I am not their keeper."

"Yet you mustered them to our aid?" the Duedellen persisted. He had some courage along with that caustic personality. Or perhaps foolhardiness.

"*Your* aid?" The Dragon snorted, pupils dilating as he slashed a glare at Feanim. "Was it *your* summons I answered?"

I moved to Rafael's side, placing a hand on his arm. The volatile energies made my hand tingle. "We are eternally grateful that you saved us all." After a long, tense moment, his eyes flicked to my face, assessing.

"You are remarkably attached to these people for someone who chose to abandon them and live as a hermit." A pointed brow raised.

"You are remarkably attached to your own people for someone who murdered his way into power," I countered. His mouth twitched with humor and the set of his broad shoulders relaxed just a hair. I would claim my victories where I could. Stares of disbelief from the other two bore into my back.

Feanim cleared his throat and we turned to him. "Lord Dragon, if I may ask, how did you reach us so quickly?"

"He was following her," Celebel interjected quietly.

A chill ran down my spine. Rafael's gaze snapped back to Celebel's face, shoulders tightening again. *Crow.* I should have asked about that the previous night, but the intensity of the emotions swept away my practicality.

"We should count ourselves fortunate, then." I didn't dare withdraw my hand, as if that small point of contact could hold back the Dragon's threat of violence.

"Indeed." Rafael's low growl raised the fine hair on the back of my neck. "They have no idea how truly *fortunate* they are." His eyes scoured my face, a muscle jumping in his jaw.

'Easy, now. Recall your promises from last night, please.'

A brief curl of the lip provided acknowledgement. "I will aid your cause as I see fit. Cúraniel's well-being will always take precedence; you live and die at her whim. My people will join in as they wish."

"Do they follow no command at all?" Feanim used cautious tone for once. "You are their king!"

Rafael huffed, almost a laugh. "Our progenitors are dead and gone. No gods, no rulers. Only might. My people followed at my request, with no expectation of further commitment." He caught the sly look creeping across Feanim's face. "I agree to confer over tactics, but you will make no demands. Some of us quite like the taste of elf flesh."

Both elvish men blanched, but I'd long been inured to the Dragon's casual threats. "With the way you guided your fire so precisely to our foes, do we need the aid of other drakes?"

"I can only use that attack sparingly. The confines made it ideal." Rafael's candor surprised me.

'You spared it for me?' Realization dawned.

His expression softened a fraction. *'I could not risk losing you.'*

Feanim studied the Dragon's face for a moment. "When did you decide not to kill us all and simply carry her away?"

Celebel made a choking noise, quickly stifled. I shivered with portent.

An evil grin spread across Rafael's face. "How *very* fortunate that Cúraniel specifically asked me to save all of you."

Gods. I hadn't even considered my wording when I'd made that cry for help. He noted the tremor in my hand with a sidelong glance, laden with ominous meaning. Palpable tension flowed from Celebel, and Feanim's face pinched with concern.

The Dragon continued. "We will settle outside your fortifications as space allows, but your gates shall remain open to us. Other drakes will convene once we arrive. My protection from their whims extends only to the individuals I name."

"You would allow your folk to commit acts of violence against allies?" Celebel couldn't quite keep the offense from his voice. Visiting direct harm upon another elf had always been anathema in our culture. Only years of exposure to the Dragon's warlike ways kept me from a similar reaction.

"My folk regularly commit acts of violence against each other," Rafael replied drolly. According to his tales of drake custom, continually testing one's standing through fighting was expected and rarely fatal. "Your folk are simply too fragile to keep pace with dragons." His eyes sharpened. "My cooperation depends on access to your plans and resources. And to her. Deny me at your peril." His voice dropped dangerously low, talons flexing.

Celebel, to his credit, kept his face neutral.

'Peace, please. You promised,' I begged Rafael. *'Let us speak later.'*

He grumbled, but gave me a deliberate, relenting blink. At the periphery of my vision, Feanim's brow furrowed, gaze bouncing from Rafael's face to mine, trying to follow our private communication. Then the Dragon turned and strode off, back to where the other drakes presumably waited.

We breathed a collective sigh of relief.

"At least he departed without throwing a punch or starting any fires," I said. "Small victories."

Celebel waited until Rafael was well out of sight and earshot before rushing to me. He paused just before taking me in his arms, concern marring his smooth features. I longed to embrace him but took a judicious step back for safety's sake.

"You warned me he was intense. I still was not prepared," Celebel said, straightening the collar of his coat. "I believe he was preparing to crush my skull when the wind changed. Very glad you showed up when you did."

"I doubt that shift in the breeze was a coincidence." I surveyed the path the Dragon had taken across the sunny meadow. No birds sang; frozen in fear at the proximity of a large predator.

"He knows you now, and we'll have to deal with that. I made him vow that no harm would come to you, but I don't trust his anger not to overcome his intentions."

"Am I to believe my own senses? From what I'm witnessing, you've not only *fucked* the gods damned *Red Dragon*, but you *jilted* him for *Celebel?*" Feanim's snide, clipped voice cut in. "Do you have a magic pussy?"

"The intimate details of my affairs are none of your concern," I snapped.

"I beg to differ. They are *very much* my concern now." Feanim crossed his arms over his chest with a sneer.

"Interesting, coming from the one who told me I was full of shit just scant nights ago." My palms itched to slap the attitude right off the Duedellen's smug face. It would be so vindicating to slap a man who could actually bleed from it.

Celebel's loud sigh got my attention. "Please, both of you, we have all had enough stress. Might we speak with civility?"

"You're right, my love, forgive me." Weariness overtook me, deflating my indignation. "Did Rafael tell you of our conversation last night?"

They signed denial.

"Ah, well, we resolved some… issues, and he swore to help us win this war. He is quite shrewd. Be cautious in any agreements you make with him." Already I worried about the loopholes he would inevitably find. "Though it seems we have little bargaining power in this arrangement."

"You believe his word is sound?" Celebel spoke quickly over whatever nonsense was about to spew forth from Feanim.

The Duedellen clamped his mouth shut and watched us closely.

"He is not one to make idle vows, nor idle threats. He answered my call, and we owe him a huge debt of gratitude for our lives."

"What does he gain from this?" Celebel finally asked.

I took a deep breath. "Drakes love to fight. They hardly

need encouragement."

His clear blue eyes narrowed. "You're prevaricating."

"Fine. I told him… I told him I would consider letting him claim me as his mate if he wins the war for us." I braced myself.

"Cúraniel!" Shock and hurt. He tugged furiously at his lobes.

"Forgive me, my love. I made it very clear it was only a consideration, and I made no commitment. We should be grateful he didn't spirit me off last night, as he was originally intending. This is much more significant than you may realize. Mate claiming is typically determined by might and it isn't negotiable."

Feanim's ears perked. "What if he claims you anyway and you don't consent?"

I could barely say the words with a straight face. The absurdity loomed large. "According to their custom, I'd have to fight him and win to break the claim."

Celebel's ears drooped, and Feanim looked me over with newly appraising eyes.

"Come, we need to talk." I led Celebel away, leaving the other Consul to brood in the cooling advent of evening.

The return to Celebel's grand tent instead of my tiny one on the outskirts gave me a sense of relief. Perhaps I'd grown a bit spoiled with luxury, but I'd also developed an aversion to sleeping alone after we'd been together near-constantly since our first meeting. To my surprise, the tent flap had already delivered my belongings and waited in a neat bundle. Even my sweaty, filthy leather armor. Exhaustion and a certain red-haired distraction had prevented me from properly addressing the state of it.

My relief quickly transformed to dismay. Our tent held an occupant; Rafael's presence hung like a miasma in the night air. I lifted the flap and entered first, Celebel close on my heels. The Dragon waited for us in the lantern-less shadows, his lambent eyes piercing the darkness.

"Celeb-el, the Silver Star. So, this is the one who would steal *my* mate." He spoke the highly formal, courtly version of elvish, enunciating every syllable with deliberate, deadly calm.

Celebel waved the witchlights to life, and the Dragon immediately snuffed them again.

"Afraid of the dark, are we?" His eyes glittered with evil humor.

"Rafael, what are you doing here?" Even I heard the weariness in my voice, switching to common elvish. I relit the witchlights, and he left them alone this time.

"Simple… conversation." A flash of sharp teeth. "Would you wait outside, my dove?"

"Absolutely not. Whatever you have to say to him, you can say to me as well." I planted my hands on my hips, keeping my body squarely between my opposing soulmates.

"You do not trust me to honor my word?"

"While baring your teeth? No. No, I do not." I had no desire to test the limits of what he considered 'harm' given his current agitation.

"Very well. *You*," he snapped at Celebel, countenance darkening. "You *failed* her! She took injury due to your weakness. Why did you bring her here if you cannot protect her?"

The air in the small space stifled with his heat.

"Oh, be reasonab—" I cut off with a squeak as Rafael grabbed me.

He spun me around to face Celebel, who was decidedly pale but otherwise masking his apprehension. The Dragon drew a rough hand across my clavicle from one shoulder to the other, then down my centerline, splitting my coat and the gown beneath with his talons. It would have been intensely sensual in other circumstances, having one lover forcibly bare my breasts to the other.

"Observe the perfection of her skin. If I find her marred in any way, even a *single* mark left upon her in violence, I will rain down *hellfire* upon all your kind," Rafael hissed, his bloodlust surging through our bond. I didn't have to see his face to know that his visage would be truly terrible.

Celebel steeled himself. "You are correct, my Lord Dragon. I did fail her; I will not make excuses. Yet, we are under attack from an unknown foe, and I cannot be everywhere. You, however, have none of the same restrictions, so may I therefore suggest that you take on the role of her bodyguard?"

Rafael growled, raising the hairs on the back of my neck at his timbre. The air shimmered with heat, beading sweat on my skin.

I twisted to face him. "Stop this. You know Celebel is right."

"This presumptuous little…" he trailed off into unintelligible draconian, low in his throat. The intended insult conveyed clearly enough. His hands clamped on my shoulders, the points of his talons made themselves known through the fabric of my coat.

"I know this situation is difficult," I said, forcing myself to a calm tone, "but your desire to lash out is making it worse. My own kind will not harm me, and you will surely protect me from other threats. Or will you still count it against Celebel if the marks left on my skin come from your own hands?"

His lip curled, but he released me.

Celebel raised placating hands. "Please understand, I never intended to come between you two. I have as little choice in a soulmate bond as either of you, and divisiveness runs contrary to my nature. If she's amenable, you could take her right now on our own bed and I would not protest."

"*DO NOT MOCK ME!*" Rafael's enraged bellow hurt my ears.

Celebel took several steps back, instinctively raising his arms in a guard position for what little good it would do. The Dragon flexed his talons with murderous intent, lips pulling back from his teeth.

"No, no, no, he's sincere, I swear it," I cried, trying desperately to get the angry drake to focus on me instead. "He means no disrespect!"

Rafael snarled again. Pale smoke issued forth from his mouth and flared nostrils with a biting, acrid tang. He took a menacing step toward Celebel, shifting me out of his way like a paper doll.

"I should peel the flesh from your bones." He stared Celebel down.

I pounded on the Dragon's back with balled up fists and yelled at the top of my lungs. "*That's enough!* Gods above and below, Rafael, *get ahold of yourself!* Yes, you are big and strong, and very scary. Could you *please* go do something productive, like finding a Fomorian to punch in the face until you feel better?"

Rafael turned, blistering red eyes speared into me for an uncomfortably long time. Finally, he stalked out of the tent with another smoking hiss.

Chapter 24

Once we were certain the Dragon had moved out of range, Celebel slumped against the center tent pole. A dampening field settled around our temporary quarters with a tingling hush. My ears twitched with appreciation for the wise choice. I should have considered it sooner, given that Rafael's bellowing surely terrified the rest of the camp.

"Cúraniel, what have we done? Promises aside, he certainly would have killed me, and perhaps everyone else as well, if you had not been here!"

My knees buckled, and I angled myself so that I sank onto the bed instead of the floor, too tired even for tears.

"Oh Starshine, I knew this would be a trial, but I never anticipated just how unequipped I would be to navigate these things. I understand if you wish no further involvement with me." I couldn't look him in the eye, afraid of the rejection I was certain to find there. "We can surely find some arrangement…"

Celebel wrapped me in his arms, kissing my ears and my forehead. "Do not be ridiculous. I am not so weak as to abandon you at the first sign of trouble. If I thought stepping back for a time would actually smooth things over, I would consider it. Unfortunately, your Dragon strikes me as the type to tighten his grip and exert more control if given the chance." I murmured assent. Rafael always pressed an advantage. Celebel pulled back to study my face. "I love you, but I do sincerely question your judgment in getting involved with that… *person.*"

"You may call him an asshole. He's certainly been acting the part today."

"…as you say. I prefer not to take the antagonistic approach. I'm truly amazed at his ability to be both petty *and* a tyrant. You, love, are *very* brave." He smoothed my hair out of my face.

"I wish his mood from last night had carried over to today.

I've never seen him so contrite." With a regretful sigh, I traced my fingers along Celebel's jaw. "*You* are a true diplomat. Would you really have stepped back and watched him fuck me in our bed?" I tilted my head up to look into his eyes for the truth. The notion would have fired my passion, were I not so emotionally wrung out.

"According to you, that wouldn't actually be an option, now would it?" He had the nerve to give me a mischievous grin.

"Oh, so you *were* being an asshole, and he was right to be offended." I scowled.

"Not intentionally! I swear! And yes, I would have watched if he'd allowed it. I'm sure it would have been *most informative*." His next smile was all innocence.

"I am *surrounded* by assholes." My ears flattened.

"You seem to enjoy the company of assholes. Perhaps I should practice being rude and pushy." The smile broadened.

"I'm sure Feanim could give you some pointers." I pulled away from him in a huff, arranging the blankets and pillows like a barrier.

Celebel reached for me, and I swatted his hand away. "Come now, do forgive me. I am only teasing. This has been a very long couple of days and I am feeling the strain."

"You are right to question my judgment," I said after a pause. "I have often questioned it myself. Nemohee has as well. Loudly. All I can say is the heart wants what it wants. Unfortunately, mine seems to be fixated on a big, bad fire drake with a murderous attitude problem and severe emotional trauma." I sighed heavily. "At least I know I'm making a good choice with you." Despite it all, I was still happy and relieved to see my Dragon again, and hear him openly acknowledge his feelings for me.

Celebel kissed me then, our first real kiss since Rafael's tumultuous arrival.

"Would he really have abducted you and made you his mate against your will?" he asked when we parted, worry knitting his brow.

"He was strongly considering it. It took the threat of never speaking to him again for him to relent. There is much he simply doesn't understand because he has no frame of reference for how a relationship should work. At least he told me about it first, before just doing it."

"Oh, how grand of him."

"I know, believe me. I gave him a thorough tongue lashing for that. He understands my reaction, I think. But he also healed my leg." I bared my unblemished thigh.

"Very nice, a fair exchange for threatening to abduct you and kill us all." Celebel's expression was sour.

"I'm only trying to demonstrate that he genuinely cares for me. It's not all possessiveness and rage. Much easier for him to yell and storm about my being physically hurt than it is to admit that he's jealous of you and feeling vulnerable. He's unaccustomed to challenges from people he cannot simply cow with fear or beat to a bloody pulp."

Celebel nodded, thoughtful, tapping fingers on his arm. "That melody harmonizes. For a moment, I truly thought he would renege on his vow to you and devour me on the spot!"

"I did as well. His temper is, unfortunately, a truthful part of his legend. I cannot apologize for him, but I will do my best to stay out of harm's way. Causing you more stress than I already have is the last thing I desire." I pulled him close again, resting his head on my breast. "Often have I wished that I cared less for him than I do, and questioned my wisdom in saving his life. Why, of all the great powers in the world, did it have to be the bloody God of Carnage who landed in my lap? But my own life would be much poorer without his presence in it. I only truly wish that it did not cause me so much gods damned *trouble.*"

Celebel stifled my self-pitying sighs with kisses, lowering me to the bed on my back and peeling my clothes away. An image of a Fomorian peeling open the ribcage of an elf flashed in my mind and I whimpered, trying to cast it off.

"How do you manage it? Surviving these horrors, with all that death all around you?" I couldn't fathom the experiences that had brought him to me.

He paused, taking my hands and kissing them. "One note at a time. Focus your ears on the now, on that which you may control. Concentrate on the life you have, the small joys where you can find them."

My shoulders unknit; tension I hadn't realized I was holding. "Wise words, thank you."

"No more thoughts, no more stress. Let us simply enjoy what peace we may find in each other. It keeps us vital," he said. "Will you deny me the taste of your glory on my tongue?"

Since Rafael had learned Celebel's identity, I found no reason to maintain the distance between us. One way or another, my Dragon would have to grow accustomed to this. I closed off my connection to my troublesome soulmate and focused on the one before me.

With a weary smile, I acquiesced. Celebel bent to push my knees apart. I held back only for a moment, fatigue washing over me. When he licked his way down my inner thigh, the sudden jolt of need wiped the fog from my mind. I twisted my hands into his hair as he found my clit. Somehow, ages had passed since he was last between my legs. Relief and lust rose as twin serpents, twining through me.

"I want your pleasure to flood my mouth," he said into my cunt and I moaned, releasing his hair to tug at his ears. He murmured joyful sounds and my body responded at once.

I climaxed quickly under his tender ministrations, all the pain and dread and heartache washing away with a few sharp jerks of my hips. When I reached for him to do the same, he danced out of reach.

"If he can tease you thus, so can I," Celebel sang, dodging my hands with ease.

I shrieked in frustration and tackled him. We rolled, laughing, off of the bed. I landed under him, and he looked me steadily in the eye as he lowered his hips. With agonizing slowness, he penetrated me. No amount of cursing or bucking under him could convince him to speed up. He grinned, pumping casually in and out of me.

I slapped his lovely round ass repeatedly, leaving red handprints. Little by little, he increased his speed and force. I clawed rivulets into his back, trying to pull him deeper. He hissed when my nails broke the skin.

"Slow down, temptress! I want to savor this," he laughed.

"You'll have to restrain me." I arched my back and seated him deep with a slap of skin on skin.

"Oh, is that the way of it?" Abruptly, he pulled out, making me gasp, and stood.

"Celebel, come back!" I fingered myself as I begged, trying to coax the next fluttering orgasm to the surface. He turned his back to me, rummaging in his things. "Cel!"

His hand raised, signing, "Wait."

I groaned and flopped backwards. After a moment, he made a triumphant noise and turned, brandishing a shining length of silvery rope. Spidersilk. Impossibly strong, rare, and valuable. He must have picked it up upon his return.

"Since you have no restraint of your own," he purred, and it was my turn to laugh.

Obliging, I sat up and he tied my hands together with swift precision. Tugging me to my feet, he led me back to the bed where he anchored my hands to the branches forming the bedframe. My legs, he left free.

"Now I may tease you to my heart's content." Wicked glee lit his face, and he leaned to breathe over my prickling skin. His long, silky hair tickled across my breasts as he moved back down to my cunt. "If the bonds grow too tight, say 'spidersilk' or tap three times with your foot."

"Yes, perfect."

Situating himself between my legs, he watched my face as he penetrated me with fingers and tongue. I growled, thrashing against my bonds, which only heightened my pleasure. He had me climaxing again in moments.

Pushing my legs up, he teased my clit with the tip of his cock until I was breathless.

"Shall I fuck you, or shall I merely use these lovely breasts?"

I writhed against my bonds. "Fuck! Fuck me. *Please!*" I wanted him inside me so badly I could barely form a coherent word.

"Hmm… no. Not yet." Watching me for a moment, instead of thrusting his cock into my needy cunt, he straddled my waist. My breath caught at the sight of him looming over me, hard and ready. Witchlights floated around his head in an ethereal crown.

"Suck my cock, lather it well," he commanded, raising his hips to press the tip of his erection into my mouth. I did as I was bid, enjoying the velvety skin on my lips and tongue. Just as I worked into a rhythm, he pulled back again.

Seating his cock in my cleavage, he gripped my breasts and pressed them into his shaft, working his hips to slide back and forth. His abdominal muscles stood out in relief with his efforts, making my clit throb painfully. Beneath me, the blankets grew sodden with my arousal.

"Gods, yes! Spill yourself all over me," I panted.

He moaned and worked faster, masturbating himself with my breasts. Throwing his head back in a cry, he shuddered and orgasmed hard, cock pulsing and painting me with his issue.

Just when I'd thought he finished, he climbed back between my legs. Grabbing my thighs from underneath, he pushed my legs up until my ankles rested beside my ears. Holding my buttocks in firm hands, he parted my labia with a newly hardened cock. Slowly at first, until he sheathed fully inside, he yanked back and then slammed into me. The contact of his flesh with mine made me howl, dragging another climax up from the base of my spine.

"Harder," I begged. "As hard as you can!"

He obliged with gleeful force until we panted in unison. Unable to do much more than accept the delicious pounding, I closed my eyes and let the ecstasy sweep me away. Celebel's cries of climax rang beautifully in my ears.

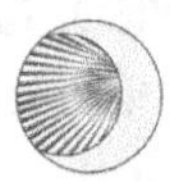

Rafael's talk of the energy needed to maintain dragon forms had me wondering where the drakes would end up feeding. Until I accidentally witnessed the battlefield clean up. I wished I hadn't. The few remaining unburned bodies belonged to warhorses, not elves and Fomorians, but it still turned my stomach to see the other drakes rip into them. My Dragon, at least, kept his dining preferences a mystery. A small kindness.

The scaly warriors remained apart from us as we traveled. They made no attempt to move with the same silence, and we often glimpsed hulking forms through the trees. Their looming presence made the other elves understandably tense and upset the horses. I did not know how Rafael kept his people under control, or how much control was even needed. Thankfully, we had no incidents.

We rode for several days, as before, stopping only to water and feed our horses. I fared better this time, slowly growing accustomed to life in the saddle. I kept my sword handy, and an ear toward Rafael's location, just in case. Surely, I was the only one comforted by his proximity. I was also thankful that the time spent on horseback meant no more tents to share, and thus fewer opportunities for conflict.

When Feanim pulled his mare, Lettai, alongside mine, I should not have been surprised. She snapped waspishly at Iruwher. Like rider, like horse.

"I think it would be wise to have you with us whenever we meet with Rafael," the Duedellen said. He had dark circles under his eyes and unkempt hair.

"Likely so." I smoothed the braid coiled at my nape.

"We must present him to the court. It will not be a popular choice, as there are many with personal grudges against him. So then, how do we prevent him from striking them down?"

"As far as I know, we cannot. Advising them in advance not

to provoke him would be the wisest action."

He rode beside me in silence, brow furrowing. The furious thoughts racing through his mind might as well be spoken aloud, so well did he announce them.

"I need Rafael focused on the war, not this little rivalry. What would it take for you to withdraw your claim on Celebel but remain with us to ensure the Dragon's cooperation?"

Iruwher reacted to my immediate mood shift and stopped dead in her tracks. "It is too late for that, son of Melranim. It was too late when he first appeared on my hill, bleeding and dying. Celebel is my soulmate, as Rafael is. I am bound to both and there is no changing it without true death," I said coldly. "Backing away only diminishes both Celebel and myself. For one who ostensibly values our histories, surely you understand this?"

An assessing look crawled over Feanim's face. "And what if you have doomed Celebel to an early death at the Dragon's hands with your selfishness?"

"Surely you will nobly volunteer to take his place when the time comes since you are so concerned." Could I get away with pushing him off his horse? Iruwher danced under me, and Lettai lowered her head, ears going back defensively.

Feanim laughed darkly, reining in his mare. "What hold do you truly have over the Dragon? Unfettered for millennia, and now he willingly falls at your feet? Does he simply have a fetish for moon elves with blue eyes and big tits?"

"Ask him yourself," I snapped, and nudged my horse away. "I'll be sure to let him know you have all the probing questions ready for him. He'll love that."

Feanim's mocking laugh followed me.

Chapter 25

The trees thinned out, turning to tall granite pillars and deep ravines. Rafael leaned against one of those massive formations as we approached; Feanim, Celebel, and myself. Easily three times the Dragon's height, it overlooked a drop off to his left. A steep wall of scree rose to his right. Rafael's chosen meeting place left just enough room for all of us to stand comfortably, but not quite enough for anyone to escape his reach with ease.

Feanim and Celebel both dressed in light armor. I wore only my traveling clothes, scrubbed clean during one of our brief rests. The Dragon held out a taloned hand, and I went to his side. Celebel tried, unsuccessfully, to hide his frown, but it was better to appease Rafael than start the conversation with antagonism.

The tall drake wrapped a possessive arm around my shoulders. "What is your plan?" He addressed Feanim, pointedly ignoring Celebel's presence.

"My Lord Dragon, we must introduce you to the court," Feanim said.

Rafael startled us all with his coughing laugh. A handful of pebbles tumbled down the slope, scattering across the ground. "*That* will be entertaining."

"Before we begin—Feanim, didn't you have some *questions* for Rafael?" I asked sweetly, leaning into my draconic lover.

Why should everyone else get to make all the trouble? The Dragon's hand twitched on my arm; he knew I was up to something. Celebel looked troubled, but the way Feanim blanched nearly made me laugh aloud.

"Indeed," Rafael rumbled, eyes narrowing.

"Yes, he wanted to know what kind of hold I have over you, wasn't that it? What was it you said, Feanim, that he must have a fetish for—"

"This is hardly the place for petty squabbles," Feanim

snapped.

'*Shall I kill him for you?*' Rafael asked, deep in my mind. His talons pricked my skin ever so lightly, without drawing blood.

'*No, only scare him. He's an arrogant little shit, but please do not actually hurt him,*' I responded silently. '*We need him, unfortunately.*'

'*As you wish.*' He rumbled again and more rocks bounced down. "If you have upset her, I will crush your skull in my teeth, little shade." Rafael made a show of turning to me, tilting my chin up to look at him. I pouted my best pout and his eyes glittered wickedly.

"He asked if I had a magic pussy," I said, immediately regretting it.

That angered the Dragon in truth. He turned to Feanim with a snarl, baring his teeth, eyes sparking red, and the hapless elf took a step back. The wind whistled through the ravine below.

"I meant it only in jest." Feanim raised supplicating hands, eyes wide.

"You will *learn*, little elf. Insult to her is insult to *me*." Rafael's bass growl raised the small hairs on the nape of my neck and pebbles cascaded from the slope, nearly burying our feet. He took a threatening step forward and Feanim scrambled back out of his considerable reach.

"My lord Dragon, she is only a nameless *woman*, she—"

"*ONLY* a woman," the Dragon roared, and punched the granite pillar he'd been leaning against, splitting it cleanly in half lengthwise. All three of us elves ducked in awe. Knowing of his strength and seeing it demonstrated effectively were two very different things. "She holds more power than you ever will," he snarled again, advancing.

I quickly caught his arm.

"That's enough. He understands the lesson." I rubbed my poor ears. Rafael looked at me for a long moment, and visibly relaxed.

"As you wish." He touched my cheek and temple with a

gentle hand, easing my headache, then turned back to Feanim. With an evil glare, he pulled me into his arms, protective. I may have swooned, just a little. Despite insisting on fighting my own battles, it was nice to have someone else step in for once.

"My-my apologies, my lord—" Feanim stammered, clearly unaccustomed to losing the upper hand.

"Apologize to *her*," Rafael hissed, pale smoke issuing from his mouth with the same sharp scent as before.

When Feanim's nostrils flared slightly in anger, I knew I had pushed things too far. The Duedellen made a show of bowing deeply. "Please forgive me for any slight you may have perceived, Lady Cúraniel." He leaned on the honorific just enough to add ambiguous sarcasm.

"Yes, accepted." I waved away to his non-apology, and he gave me a dark scowl. '*Simple, but effective,*' I sent to Rafael, and he caressed my back in response. I slid my arms around him.

Celebel watched the exchange in silence, worry straining his eyes. I hoped he would forgive me for being petty, and for demonstrating clear affection for Rafael despite his intimidation tactics. The Dragon practically hummed with the urge to hurt someone. It wasn't the first time my desire to disrupt the melody had gotten away from me.

"If I may," Celebel ventured. "We need to consider the impact this will have on the court. Most of the remaining nobility are young and inexperienced, refugees from beleaguered regions. Some may have a very poor reaction to the Lord Dragon's presence. There may be unrest."

"Your pretty boy is smarter than he looks," Rafael said, and I scowled up at him. Which, of course, he found amusing. Better to be amused than angry. I leaned into him. After all the time apart, the proximity fed my spirit and restored my meager reserves. I'd have to take care not to lean too heavily on him and accidentally encourage his violent possessiveness.

"May we request you do not fight the nobles?" Strain thinned Celebel's melodic baritone.

"You may not," he countered flatly. "But I will not start the fight."

"I suppose it will have to suffice." Celebel sighed. "Feanim, whenever you're done sulking, we could use your input." His hands flashed, signing to the Duedellen, "You deserved for disrespect." Rafael followed the signs with marked interest.

Feanim set his jaw and clasped his hands together. "You stated you would keep your soldiers outside the gates."

"Yes," the Dragon replied. "Keep them fed if you wish to avoid trouble. Shapeshifting has a high energy demand."

"Again, are they not under your command?" Feanim asked, incredulous.

"How typically elvish." Rafael stroked my hair as he spoke. "I have convinced them to fight for you. We will guard your walls. Some will join your ranks in battle. The rest is your problem."

"What provisions do they need?" the Duedellen ventured.

"Cattle, sheep, goats, wild game, it does not matter. Give them what they ask for. They can speak for themselves. If you need to purchase livestock, I will cover the cost."

I looked up at him, startled. "That's quite generous of you." The enormity of his offer to help was sinking in.

"I am not *only* here to make trouble." Rafael ruffled my hair.

'*He is mocking us,*' Celebel sent, souring my gratitude. He cleared his throat, garnering a flat stare from the Dragon. "So it is settled. Later today, when we reach the fortress and have had time to prepare our people, we will introduce you to the court. Will you be remaining outside the walls as well?" Celebel asked delicately.

"Of course not. I go where she goes." Rafael kissed me deeply before I could protest. '*You do indeed have a magic pussy.*' With a wicked glint in his eye, he flicked a hand between my legs, releasing me before I could react.

Blushing furiously, I consciously had to slow the pounding of my heart as he took his leave. I turned just in time to see Celebel folding his arms, nostrils flared in irritation.

Feanim squinted in the direction Rafael had taken. "He is

not an attractive man, but there is something undeniably sexy about him."

"I should reproach you for your small-minded words, brother." Celebel frowned at him. "Though, if he weren't such an utterly unrepentant *cock,* I might be inclined to agree."

I felt faint.

Celebel's eyes bore into me as we returned to the horses together. Feanim had split off from us as soon as we left the Dragon's sight. Moving down the mountain back into what tree cover remained helped center me.

"Are you going to explain that?" he finally said.

"I pushed things too far. I shouldn't have riled him, but gods *damn,* it was satisfying to watch Feanim eat his words. If it eases you, we spoke mentally just before and Rafael agreed not to actually hurt him."

Celebel paused. "He seemed genuinely angry."

I flicked an ear. "He was. Feanim has been disrespectful to me from our first meeting."

"Please don't make an enemy out of Feanim. I know he's difficult and says awful things sometimes, but he is my oldest friend and we need him as an ally. Whatever happened to you handling it yourself?"

"Hmm, a familiar refrain."

We reached the horses. They waited, groomed, watered, and saddled, swishing their tails in greeting. Celebel's stallion whickered, and he stroked the horse's long nose.

"Cúraniel, please, this is harder than I ever expected. Rafael's moods are quicksilver; his hostility is already nearly impossible to deal with. It hurts to see you pander to his darker impulses. Feanim is also moody and difficult, and I am stuck in the middle of all of it."

I took his hand. "Find your strength, Starshine. It is unlikely to become easier any time soon. You're right, though. It was thoughtless of me. I forget that there is much more at stake here than just our interpersonal relationships, unaccustomed as I am to being in society. Please forgive me."

He pulled me close and kissed my forehead. "I admit the dynamic between you and the Dragon is incredible to watch. How do you stand so steadfast in the face of such instant, terrifying rage?"

"Practice, mostly. He does exactly as he pleases, and it pleases him to tease and banter with me. Most of the time, anyway. He snarls and spits flame, but he's not a mindless monster." Celebel's own fortitude through such targeted opposition impressed me. Few could claim they had stood strong before the Red Dragon's rage, and I had a unique advantage.

"I must learn to manage." He sighed like the combined weight of all our people's struggles pressed on his shoulders, and I hugged him tighter. The edges of his armor pressed into my flesh.

"Thus far, I'd say you are managing quite well. You've remained outwardly calm and haven't yet let him cow you. Sing that melody as long as you are able. The moment you falter, he will escalate his behavior. I know you cannot throw it back on him as I do, but your dignified stoicism is a sound position to maintain."

"Hmm, thank you," he murmured into my hair. "He said something to you right before he left, didn't he? I saw the look on your face."

I bit my lip and looked down at my boots.

Celebel tilted my chin back up to look him in the eye. "What did he say?"

"He said I do indeed have a magic pussy," I said in a small voice, and to my surprise Celebel burst out laughing.

He gathered himself and kissed me. "Your Dragon is awful, but he's not wrong. And you are more impulsive than I would have expected from one your age."

"Focus your ears, eh? I told you I never belonged at court. I am a troublemaker. Age is no indicator of serenity, as Rafael's personality so clearly illustrates. I will try to stifle the troublemaking, though." Leaning back, I smoothed his tabard. "I suppose I should make peace with Feanim." What I wanted to do was feed Feanim to an angry drake, but peace was the better option. Probably.

"It would be wise."

I signed assent, defeated.

"You are truly a marvel." He kissed me again.

We mounted up and rode together in companionable silence. Joining Feanim on his dark liver mare, he looked me over with disdain bordering on hostility. Celebel held Helicos back a little to give us space to talk.

"Son of Melranim, may we begin anew?" I ventured. "We joined our voices on the wrong note. I do not wish to cause more strife. Please accept my apology for provoking Rafael, but know that I will not accept scorn."

His brow creased, but he nodded. "Perhaps I have dismissed you out of turn. A mistake. The Red Dragon seems to hold you in high esteem," he didn't say 'for some reason' but I heard it in his tone, "as does Celebel. I am discomfited by your chosen namelessness, but I will adapt."

"If it would help, I can teach you what I know of drake customs and language. I am also an accomplished healer and seer. I can be of benefit to your cause, but we must have peace between us. And you must never ask me to leave Celebel again."

Celebel started unhappily from the corner of my eye. Feanim considered my speech, then nodded. Good enough. We rode single-file through the earlier meeting place, past the granite pillar broken by Rafael. The horses picked their way carefully over the loose scree.

Feanim pursed his lips, twisting to watch me over his shoulder. "Did you somehow tell Rafael not to strike me?"

Observant. "'Tell' is perhaps a strong word, but yes, I asked him not to hurt you." I stifled a laugh at the idea of *telling* Rafael to do anything and expecting a positive outcome.

"Your connection to him is stronger than average. I was

unaware that any non-elf could do such a thing."

"It is, though we rarely record the feats of other peoples. His mind is as vast as his strength. Do not make the mistake of underestimating his intellect."

"He wouldn't have survived all these thousands of years if he were simple-minded," Feanim said with a sneer. He couldn't seem to help himself.

Cresting the peak, the spires of Férioth came into view.

Chapter 26

Nestled between high granite walls and hewn from granite itself, Araglin's fortress, Férioth, made an imposing sight. It rose as one with the surrounding bedrock, its sharp spires casting long shadows like spears. Parting the curtain of protective spells and glamours hiding it took a combined effort from Feanim and a few others, which they shielded from the prying eyes of a certain drake. It was much less fanciful in construction than our edifices usually were, out of practical necessity. Along the way, Celebel told me of how Araglin, the Astolar elf who'd redesigned it, had initially planned to maintain Férioth's history as a place of monastic study and gathering.

Raising the walls had begun just before the Fomorian raids started in earnest. The hostile territory required much more fortification than he'd expected, especially as elves sought refuge from the attacks and made their way to his remote home. Surrounded by a sheer ravine, only a single high bridge spanned the gap to the front gate.

Celebel and Feanim led the way. We'd taken some time the morning of our arrival to bathe and dress well, and their armor shone in the light. I rode slightly behind them, wrapped in a blanket to prevent sullying my gown. Rafael loped along beside me, his long legs easily keeping pace with the nervous horses. The sentries called out, Feanim answered, and the gates opened. The portcullis, crafted of thorny iron vines and beautiful in its way, rose with a groan.

Serving youth greeted us to take our horses to the stables. For once, I was grateful to walk, as it made observing my surroundings a little easier. The courtyard was broad, paved with flagstones and surrounded by tall battlements. Multiple watch towers had arrow slits facing inward should the worst occur. Not what I would expect from a monastic city. A second portcullis to the interior stood ready to crash down on invaders.

Rafael held back, waiting for my cue with open amusement. I was to send for him once we'd prepared the court for his arrival. He examined the fortress with the faintest wry smile curling the corners of his mouth. Sharp, viperine eyes took stock of every path and street branching off from the main thoroughfare. His posture was as relaxed as it ever got, which I found encouraging for someone wading through enemy territory.

Following Celebel and Feanim, we wound up the path through the main courtyard to the great hall. Its high vaulted ceiling and graceful chandeliers created a sense of grandeur. Even with the practicality of the fortress, there were finely wrought stained glass windows depicting our heroes of old, with intricate tapestries hung between them to absorb sound. A richly patterned green and silver carpet cushioned our footfalls.

Before us, two elves parted the gathered crowd to meet us. The first was a tiny waif of a Lachanaur dressed in layers of wispy, pale green chiffon. Waist-length, tight curls, the soft orange of candlelight, framed a tawny brown face faintly sprinkled with freckles. A high forehead and large, round hazel eyes gave her an appearance of reserved dignity far beyond her small stature. I estimated that the top of her head would barely graze my shoulder.

Feanim had advised me before we'd entered the gates that this elf, his soulmate Nimthil and Queen of the southern Lachanaur, had lost her hearing in utero. The result of a spirit attack during the Breaking of Stones, she'd chosen not to have it restored. I thanked him for the consideration. Deaf elves were rare enough that I'd never met one before isolating myself from our society. I hoped my older version of the common sign would be intelligible to her. My fingers twitched with anticipation.

The second elf to approach was a lanky Astolar with ashen hair so pale it was nearly translucent. Cut unusually short, it ended bluntly at his collar. A narrow face and icy blue-white eyes under brows that turned up at the outer edge gave him the air of a trickster. This must be Feledhor, one of the forerunners for the

Astolar throne, and apparently Queen Nimthil's close companion. He wore a long coat of glimmering white, azure, and pale pink.

The pair led us to the dais where two grand chairs stood and turned. A hush fell on the crowd as the dainty Lachanaur turned, raising graceful hands.

"Well met, Consulate," she signed in large, sweeping gestures as she spoke. Her voice lilted with a unique accent. "We celebrate your safe and victorious return! We had received news that Lord Celebel had fallen in battle. Great is our joy to discover that untruth."

"Well met, Queen Nimthil," Feanim boomed, signing as he spoke. "We have returned triumphant, with Lord Celebel restored, and new, powerful allies at our backs!"

"We welcome your return, oh Consulate," cried the Astolar, also echoing his words in sign.

"You have our thanks for carrying on in our stead, Feledhor," Celebel called back and signed.

They continued on like that. Each congratulated and gave thanks for the next and ritually invoked gratitude for the parents. The next round thanked and named grandparents, and so on farther back, all the way to their ancestral stars. I'd forgotten how tedious court fanfare could be.

My eyes landed on a familiar, haughty face in the crowd. Tall and statuesque, burgundy silk wrapped her body in contrast to the sleek silver hair that fell to her hips. Eyes the color of a winter sky peered from a face almost as pale as mine. Her breathtaking beauty needed no enhancement. I beheld my sister, Silfanië.

Our eyes met, and hers narrowed. I'd expected to find her here, and yet my chest constricted painfully. As one of the oldest members of this court, her opinion would hold considerable weight. Silfanië's mother was nowhere in evidence.

Feledhor gave updates on the state of the fortress. Celebel and Feanim both embraced an Astolar introduced as the famed Araglin. Black eyes sparkled with kindness in his dark umber face, despite a rather serious set to his mouth. A slim diadem set with a glittering heliodor held back his shoulder-length, oak-brown braids, complimented by a scholar's robe in rich yellows and ochres. He spoke at length on the various updates from other parts of the field. His stentorian orator's voice soothed me.

Celebel turned to gesture to me. "Hear ye nobles of the court. I am saved by this woman, my newly discovered soulmate, and have chosen her as my consort. Greet her, Cúraniel, Crescent Moon Woman, formerly of the line of mighty Maelial!"

My skin itched as every pair of ears in the room swiveled to me. I still did not care for flaunting my broken lineage, but I'd bowed to necessity at Celebel's request.

I stepped forward, turning to the crowd, and bowed my most courtly bow, however antiquated it may be. Briefly grateful that I'd fought against my urchin instincts, I'd chosen a floor-length, white silk gown, cut low in the front and slit up the sides for movement. With the sapphire collar Rafael had given covering most of my bosom, and my black hair unbound and falling to my ankles, I made a striking impression. The murmurs started up. A sea of unfriendly eyes raked over me, taking in every tiny detail, stockpiling their ammunition. My sister's lips thinned in disapproval. I moved to Celebel's far side, partly to get a better view of what was about to happen, and partly to get their eyes off of me.

Celebel wove a thrilling tale of his rescue and subsequent healing by me, embellished here and there in minor ways. Significantly, he left out Rafael's involvement. His spirit flowed over the crowd in a subtle manner, gently encouraging their fascination with his words. I needed no spirit to let his story sweep me away, though I'd lived it. He spoke well, with an engaging manner and colorful use of metaphor. His account of the reunion with the camp brought some tears. A lurid description of the ambush that followed at Seregond Pass drew gasps and exclamations of horror.

"Just when all was surely lost and our doom closed in, my lovely Cúraniel saved me yet again. She saved us all. Calling upon a bond forged through her selfless kindness, she pulled our rescue from the very skies!" A neat touch, crediting an elf with the rescue rather than an old enemy. The court stretched their ears toward him as one, with wide eyes, fully enrapt. At a glance from him, I sent to Rafael.

Feanim stepped forward. He'd rehearsed his speech with Celebel on the road. "Hear me, oh nobles of the court. We have made a powerful new ally through this daring salvation. We have struck through ancient enmity to forge new bonds. Greet him, the Red Dragon, Rafael! He has brought the might of drakes to fight by our side!"

Murmurs grew to hissing whispers when the grand doors opened, and Rafael strode silently into the great hall. The crowd shuffled away from him, pressing themselves to the walls as best they could. The susurrus reached a fever pitch as the Dragon stepped up before the dais.

Rafael turned and surveyed the lot of them, assessing and dismissing each one, right hand resting loosely on the pommel of his sword. He made a stark contrast in his black cloak and armor, hair like glowing coals, against the green, silver, and gold of the hall.

Before Rafael could address the group, one of the largest elves I'd ever seen pushed his way through the grumbling crowd. Straight, dark blonde hair and thick brows framed bright green eyes on a square face. Clad in a fine, gold-spun tabard over gilded chain mail, he also made quite a figure. Well-built and tall as he was, the fire drake still had a handspan of height and significantly broader shoulders. The scene resembled something in a tapestry; the shining hero confronting a dark-shrouded villain.

"Foul beast! Cursed Dragon," the man cried, pointing at the impassive drake, "I will have satisfaction! You murdered my family at Sirelon and must answer for your crimes!" He drew his sword, also drawing gasps and shouts from the crowd for the unthinkable breach of hospitality.

I froze, unsure of what to do. The irony of Celebel's earlier question of whether Rafael would allow the drakes to visit violence upon allies made me slightly ill.

"You will not draw steel in this hall," Celebel himself called over the mingled voices. "All our ancient laws forbid this. You risk the very wrath of the gods!"

Rafael pointedly turned his back to the knight. Enraged, the blonde elf leaped forward with a mighty swing of his blade, aiming at the fire drake's neck. I cried out, but the Dragon caught the sword in his hand without looking, the edge not even breaking the skin of his palm. Plucking the sword from the stunned elf's grasp, he neatly folded it in half and tossed it at the knight's feet with a ringing clang.

The gathered elves fell silent as one.

"Stop that," he chided, as if speaking to a naughty child, deep voice carrying through the hall. His eyes flicked over to Feanim. "Are all your people so discourteous?"

The challenging elf's face went stark white with shock. All at once, the crowd erupted. Two major breaches of decorum in one day. I covered my ringing ears. Elves argued and yelled over each other, virtually everyone gesticulating wildly at the Dragon and the two Consuls. Rafael gave me a meaningful look, then turned and strode out of the hall.

"Meet me in the training field if you insist on dying," he called, waving a careless hand without looking back as he reached the door. Naturally, he'd been learning the layout while waiting for the summons during all our big fanfare.

Several nobles bristled and drew swords. Feanim shouted at them, and a few shouted back. One of the younger elves cried out in fear. The din grew to ear-aching proportions as the crowd voiced their complaints and protests. I slipped out in the chaos with a nod from Celebel, readying myself to heal anyone foolish enough to take Rafael up on his offer. Not that there would be many survivors. If any.

I found the training field close to the stables. I hadn't noticed it when we originally rode in. It was an oblong ring, with a layer of sawdust strewn over the dirt, and enclosed by a simple wooden fence. A few small trees provided a bit of shade, and a stand nearby held an assortment of weapons. Targets and well-worn practice forms took up space at the nearest wall. Rafael waited there, leaning against a tree and looking bored, just as he had said. Thankfully, none of the angry nobles had beaten me to him.

"I see no bodies," I said. "Did you incinerate them already?"

He shrugged. "They are cowards. Barking like toothless dogs. What did that one expect, grandstanding in the hall?"

"Do drakes have courtly manners?"

His laugh was a short, choking cough. "We have no court. Nor manners. I called that fool on the breach of his own etiquette for your sake, and the sake of your Consulate. If they cannot manage their people's hatred of me, this will not work."

"I'm surprised you know so much about our etiquette." I leaned on the fence beside him.

"Are you? I have dealt with your kind for millennia. They are predictable. Did they truly perform that group masturbatory act of thanking each other's progenitors into infinity?"

The description startled a laugh out of me. "They did."

"Your historians adore congratulating themselves on a birthright they did not choose." He reached out and touched my necklace, lifting the largest central sapphire to inspect. "It pleases me to see you wear this."

"I'm pleased you shared your hoard with me," I said with a grin.

"Looks better on you than it does locked away. Matches your eyes. Ah, here they come." He looked over my shoulder.

I turned to see the original angry Astolar storming our way with a trail of equally angry nobles, like a hissing goose leading his scrambling, posturing goslings. Feanim and Celebel followed shortly after, along with Nimthil. Araglin was notably absent; perhaps he abhorred bloodshed. The blonde elf threw open the gate to the training field with a dramatic flourish and drew another sword. He'd picked up a shield along the way. Some wicked part of me hoped it was a better blade than the last and immediately felt guilty. The poor man.

"You perish this day, Dragon! Go back to the hells whence you came," he cried, and the nobles behind him cheered as he clanged the sword against his shield. Brightly painted wood, I assumed it showed the crest of his lineage; a golden boar passant on a green field.

"Step away, dove," Rafael murmured to me. "I should hate to get blood on your dress."

I backed up as Galdir approached, crouching low behind his shield. Before he could attack, Rafael flashed forward in a blur. Grabbing hold of the top edge of that shield, he dug his talons into the wood and looked down with a horrible, toothy grin. I gasped as the elf stabbed at him, but the Dragon simply turned his body. He wrenched the shield away with a jerk. The knight's arm wrenched with it in a loud, wet snap. The Astolar screamed, stumbling forward and falling. Blood darkened his tabard as he clutched at the injured arm.

I might not have known much about combat, but that shield snatching move was completely unexpected, mostly because no elf would have been strong enough to pull it off. Nor cared so little about the potential for taking a wound, though Rafael had avoided it.

The drake allowed his opponent to regain his feet. With a macabre expression of amusement, he watched the Astolar grit his teeth in pain and lurch into a new stance. The injured left arm hung at his side. Rafael clearly wanted the audience to witness just how futile this fight was.

Much to my surprise, Celebel strode into the field between the combatants, creating a ripple of shocked murmurs among the gathered crowd.

"Galdir, I *command* you to stand down," he bellowed.

I'd never seen him like that. Even Rafael seemed surprised.

The blonde elf, Galdir, sputtered with rage. "My lord, that is the very demon who slaughtered an entire branch of my family! *Generations* of my lineage fell to his bloody talons. A scant handful remains."

"Galdir, I forbid you to attack an ally on pain of banishment," Celebel declared coldly, eyes flashing.

"*Interesting*," Rafael said, with a calculating look in his eyes that I didn't like.

Galdir panted in pain, swaying on his feet. "Draw your sword, demon," the knight demanded, trying to get past Celebel, who stood planted stubbornly in his way.

"Hrrm, no." The Dragon folded his arms impassively over his chest.

I thought Galdir's eyes might burst from the force of his anger and felt intensely sorry for the man. Here was one who had lost his entire family thanks to my lover, who toyed with him. Circumstances prevented him from even attempting vengeance. A vengeance he surely knew would cost him his life and yet still desperately wanted.

"Galdir, this is your last chance. You will honor our laws of hospitality or be banished forevermore! Continue and no gate will open for you. No elf will provide you succor. You shall be severed from the song, and your name shall be struck from the records, on my authority as Consul," Celebel thundered, and Galdir sagged in defeat. "The same goes for the rest of you, begone from here!"

Hangdog and shaking with impotent fury, Galdir slunk away. The gathered nobles scattered after him like pigeons. I would have followed to offer my assistance if not for the evil look he shot me as he passed.

"I'm surprised you allowed him to live," I said to Rafael.

He shrugged. "I want to see how this farce plays out."

"Did you actually murder that poor man's family?" I still found the tales of Rafael's bloodthirsty acts, even the ones I'd witnessed, difficult to reconcile with the man I knew. The man who grew roses and brought me books.

"Probably." He met my eyes with cold apathy. "I have murdered a great many families. There is nothing distinguishing about his."

"Couldn't you at least try to make it right, in the interest of peace?" I knew better than to appeal to his nonexistent sympathy, but I did it anyway.

He snorted. "I have never been interested in peace."

A tapping on the ground caught our attention. Nimthil stood behind me, clinging to Feanim's arm. "Perhaps with the main rabble rouser gone, trouble will end," she signed. Celebel returned as her hands moved. "After Galdir's defeat, others may lose interest."

"This is a hydra. Cut one head, others grow in its place," the Dragon countered. "I expected no less. Somewhat disappointed that was the best they could manage." He grinned evilly.

She watched his mouth closely before responding, in both sign and speech, "Forgive my intrusion, my lord. I am—"

He cut her off. "I know who you are, Nimthil Tinunith, daughter of the spark, queen of the southern fire elves."

Poor Nimthil blanched with fear, a tremor running through her. Feanim steadied her with a hand on her shoulder and she gave him a grateful look.

"You said you would not fight the nobles." Celebel turned to Rafael.

"I said I would not *start* the fight. I will always finish it. You would do well to remember that," the drake said, menace evident in his voice.

"Spilling blood in our halls provokes the gods. Hospitality is sacrosanct. They may withdraw their blessings!"

I shuddered at Celebel's words. That could mean anything from extinguishing all the witchlights permanently, to depriving us of the very spirit that granted our powers. The former, a minor annoyance. The latter, devastation. Hopefully, the gods would spare us on a technicality, as the spilled blood happened outside of the hall, and Galdir wasn't the one to spill it. I muttered a furtive plea to the Night Mother for mercy as I slipped over the fence and laid a placating hand on Rafael's arm.

"Enough of the threats for today, please, enough," I begged.

He turned and cupped my cheek, brushing an errant strand of hair from my face. A gesture very much at odds with his earlier show of brutality.

"As you wish. I will be among my people this evening, seek me out later." It was not a request. "Others will arrive soon."

"More drakes?"

"My lord Dragon," Feanim interrupted. "May we offer you a suite? You said you wanted to be nearby. I think perhaps—"

"A small room will do. One window. Your grand suites are indefensible." He looked at me. "I will be at the gate at nightfall." He strode off.

Nimthil collapsed against the fence in relief at his absence.

"Could someone *please explain* what occurs?" she signed, motions jerking with frustration. Straightening, she tapped her abdomen. "Can feel his voice in belly. Almost two voices." The reference to the growling chorus of Rafael's speech fascinated me.

"You can hear some of that tone, yes?" Feanim asked.

"More felt." She patted her abdomen again, then smoothed her dress.

He took her by the arm, surprisingly gentle. "Come, heart, lean on me, I'll tell you everything."

I watched them go with wide eyes. Nimthil stood two fingerbreadths taller than Feanim, but her petite stature made her seem less so despite her regal posture.

"Are you truly going among the drakes tonight?" Concern knit Celebel's brow.

I rather looked forward to it, but didn't want to seem too eager in the face of his worry.

"Sounds like I need to. I'd better change out of this." I held up the hem of my dress where it was staining in the dirt of the training field. "It's lovely, but not appropriate for meeting with drakes."

"I didn't realize drakes were prudish." His brows raised with interest.

"They view overt nudity as flaunting vulnerability and therefore an affront." Which had made my early interactions with Rafael more charged than I'd intended. "In particular, I need to select a different color to wear. White is not neutral to them."

"Would you like some help with that?" His eyes sparkled with mischief. "If you don't mind waiting, I need to meet with Feanim and a few others to discuss everything that just occurred here."

"Do I need to be present for it?"

"No. I'll send a serving youth to guide you to my chambers, and I'll join you as soon as I can. This incident will take some time to resolve, and we will not hear the end of it tonight."

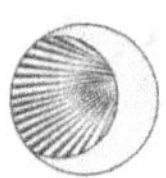

If our tent had been luxurious, Celebel's bedchambers were absolutely lavish. The serving youth, a sweet-faced Talithiri boy, led me directly there with quiet manners, though questions bubbled in his light brown eyes. The antechamber was richly appointed with fine furniture, excellent for lounging and greeting guests, and larger than the interior of my bower all by itself. Other serving youth scurried back and forth, still bringing in Celebel's belongings and setting up the space, but it was extravagant. The discovery of a private attached bathing room dominated by a large copper tub delighted me. Various scented oils and ointments lined a shelf in thoughtfully easy reach from the edge of the tub.

The bedchamber itself, though. Ah, what a sight. A stone fireplace warmed a room that centered on an enormous, completely round bed. Loaded with cushions and draped with filmy veils of curtain, it certainly invited exploration. A heavier curtain, tied back with sumptuous thread-of-silver pulls, promised plenty of comfort through the coldest winter.

I picked through Celebel's wardrobe as the young elves arranged his clothing. Mostly black, shades of blue, white, and silver—lineage colors, as expected—he did have a few pieces in rich purple, earth tones, and various patterns.

Celebel came upon me rifling through a trunk. "Find anything useful?"

"Just satiating my curiosity. How was the meeting?" I straightened.

"I believe I've smoothed the ruffled feathers for now. I've arranged for a gift, or rather a peace offering, since they're odd about gifts, for you to bring when you meet the drakes. It will be waiting for you by the inner gate. You'll understand when you see it."

"Thoughtful, thank you." I shot Celebel a knowing look and hopped onto the bed. "How many people can fit comfortably here?"

He feigned innocence. "Apart from me? Oh, perhaps six or seven? I lost count last time."

"You, sir, are an inveterate lush!" I tossed a pillow at him.

He laughed and swatted it away. "Says the woman with two soulmates!"

"*One* of whom is highly uncooperative." I pouted, and he tossed me backward onto the bed.

"I promise to be extremely cooperative. What kind of cooperation would you like?" He crawled over me and I grabbed his ass with both hands.

"This is a good start." I leaned up to kiss him. He grew hard against my belly. Unwelcome reality intruded, and I rolled away with a groan. "I should abstain for tonight. Otherwise Rafael will scent it and we'll have another incident to deal with. We were only lucky he kept his distance after the last time. I'd rather not have the other drakes weighing in as well."

Celebel made a frustrated noise. "This man is already a plague. At least come and bathe with me?"

I couldn't resist a soak in that glorious tub with him. "I'd greatly like to rinse away all the judgmental stares from earlier, yes. And relax, this restriction is only for tonight."

He washed my hair, reverently teasing away any tangles, and scrubbed my back. Turning, I did the same for him. He splashed me over his shoulder. Then again. The next thing I knew, we were sweeping water at each other and laughing like children. Our peals of mirth echoed off the walls, and we soaked the floor with our silliness. The lighthearted water fight did wonders to loosen the knot in the pit of my belly. When we finally climbed out, he wrapped me in a soft towel and squeezed the water from my hair with firm twists of his hands. I kissed him carefully, gratefully, and dressed to go meet the drakes.

Chapter 27

Rafael waited for me by the main gate. Unarmored, with no sword, thank the Night Mother. Behind me trailed two ponies loaded down with barrels of the peace offering Celebel had promised. The initial sight of it had made me laugh with appreciation. The ponies grew increasingly nervous as I approached the Dragon.

"I have never seen you so frequently and thoroughly covered," he said, appraising my outfit. "Useless leather armor notwithstanding."

The echo of Celebel's sentiment made my heart ache a little, making me wish I could share these things with him. I kept my tone light. "I remembered your instruction. See the neutrals? I do pay attention!"

"Hrrm, indeed. I should like to peel you out of that later." He gave me a slight smile, and I took his arm as we walked.

"Keep being nice to me and you may get the chance." As though my knees didn't quiver at the thought. How long would he continue to keep me an ear length away? "Why don't you wear your clan colors?"

"I have no clan." His eyes glittered with mischief. "And I have always worn black."

I tugged an earlobe. "Best suited to hiding blood stains, I imagine. And you forced the others to adapt their expectations?" Rafael's silence was answer enough.

We left the ponies, shivering with fear, on the near side of the bridge just before reaching the thin smattering of trees. I murmured soothing words to them, to no avail. The animals huddled together with wide, terrified eyes, nostrils flaring.

Quite a few more drakes had arrived. They'd gathered in what could only loosely be called a camp. There were no tents or mounts. Occasional campfires dotted the darkness, but most seemed to be used solely for warmth, with no sign of cooking utensils or pots. I was faintly shocked to realize that, despite his great height and build, Rafael was actually among the smallest of them.

Most of the drakes wore hulking reptilian forms, long dragon faces swinging round to stare at us as he guided me confidently into their midst. A few had more recognizable elf-like faces. Those wore clothing, the rest wore only scales. They were a wild cacophony of colorful hides and deep, rasping voices, hisses, and growls.

Some tussled as we passed, some watched us, and others seemed to be involved in some kind of carnal activities. Despite my curiosity, I decided not to look too closely in case they might take umbrage. A few others were sound asleep in a pile of scales, wings, and tails, some actually sprawled on top of still-smoldering campfire embers. That answered my lingering questions about drakes and casual touch; Rafael was an outlier there.

What seemed like a vast army of drakes was in actuality probably only two dozen, but they took up enough space to seem much more plentiful. To my uneducated eyes, many of their dragonish faces looked similar, making it difficult for me to pick out individuals of the same color scales. Shades of green were among the most prevalent. Had any elf ever observed so many drakes in proximity and lived to speak of it?

Rafael rolled his sleeves up to his elbows. Holding his arms up, the exposed skin sprouted keeled scales. He scraped those scaled forearms together and downward in a sharp motion, making a startlingly loud, harsh sound reminiscent of a file rasping over metal. Before my ears stopped twitching, we became the center of attention for a dizzying number of slit-pupiled stares. He spoke draconian, which translated easier than I'd expected. Perhaps because of the same precise manner of speech he used with elvish, only with a more prominent growl.

It went something like, "Listen, you fucking fucks. This elf is mine. Smell her scent, see her face, hear her voice. Know her well. If any of you sun-warmed shits harm a single hair on her head, I will know, and I will kill you and eat your children."

The "eat your children" part had a connotation of crushing eggs. I was mildly shocked at the vulgarity, and even more struck by how he stood out amongst the more reptilian of his kind. I noted that the word he used for "elf" was female-coded, slightly diminutive, and only marginally less possessive than what he would use for a claimed mate.

The drakes rumbled their assent, clicking scales and hissing.

"Did you follow that?" Rafael asked me, in an aside a few moments later, stepping back beside me.

"Yes, may I try to speak to them?"

"As you wish."

I worked my throat, trying to make the correct sounds as best I could. "Warriors, you honor me! How strong you are, how bright and fine your scales, how sharp your teeth! I have brought firewater, let us celebrate your arrival!"

They roared approval, stamping their feet. I tried not to sag with relief. I'd practiced that little speech on the way to Férioth in order to avoid thanking them or implying I was giving a gift.

Rafael indicated it was safe for me to get the ponies. I led the poor terrified things back to the drakes, hoping the whiskey would be met with approval. They approached in a swarm and I backed away. One lifted a cask in a single, powerful arm, swatting the others away. Another bit a pony's flank and it shrieked. The other pony immediately panicked, squealing and kicking. Before I could protest, the drakes cheerfully ripped the screaming animals into bloody pieces. Cracking open the casks of whiskey sounded entirely too much like breaking bones. My stomach heaved, and I turned away to steady myself so they wouldn't witness my moment of weakness over a couple of what they considered prey animals.

"Well done," Rafael said, and I basked in his rare praise, instantly feeling better. "Come, I will introduce you to a few you should know. These three are the strongest apart from myself and one other who will join later. The first two are clan heads. Leaders in their own right."

The first was a burly green drake. Slightly shorter than Rafael, he had a stocky build. Square and wide from shoulder to hip, like a door. If I had to guess, the green drake weighed more based on bulk alone. He had unruly hair a few shades darker green than his hide, and deep ruby eyes that burned over a short, high-bridged nose and wide, almost lipless mouth. His square-jawed face, despite the fine scalation around the jaw and cheek, was much more personable than the majority. Without the scales and odd coloring, he could have been mistaken for a very large human at first glance. He surprised me by introducing himself in elvish.

"I am called Marron." He had a gravelly yet warm bass. The double 'r' sound dropped impossibly low in his throat, and the same chorus growl underscored his words. "I am second here, with my mate, who has not yet arrived. You must be the Cúraniel of the tales. I cannot say I appreciate your healing this old viper just when I thought we were finally rid of him." He made a tight-lipped grin.

I couldn't tell if he was serious. "Ah, so you know about that. There were none more surprised than I. He is the worst patient I have ever had." I smiled sweetly at Rafael, careful not to show my teeth.

Marron boomed with laughter; strikingly open and easygoing. I began to relax.

"I like this one. She has grit," he said.

"You have no idea," Rafael muttered with a wry look at me. I fluttered my eyelashes at him and he sighed.

The next was a blue drake with almost elvish features. He was of a height with Rafael, but a slimmer build. Long, straight, azure hair gathered neatly into a tail at the nape of his neck. Enormous, feline yellow eyes dominated his almost nose-less face, framed with scales similar to the green drake. His face was overall thinner and more pointed. Like Marron, his blue hide was a few shades lighter than his hair. He might have been pretty by elvish standards if he'd had lips.

"Tyldain, of the clan of blue drakes," he said, also in elvish, with a hard lean on the sibilants. There was something vaguely off-putting about the appraising way he looked at me with those venomous eyes. Rafael seemed particularly tense and spiky around this one, so I gave him a bow and we moved along.

I noted Rafael didn't speak to introduce me individually, as he had already done so with his declaration. For their part, the drake introductions were spare and blunt.

The last was a huge bruiser who wore a full drake form and towered over Rafael by not just head and shoulders, but a broad barrel chest, too. Slightly iridescent black scales covered the tip of his snout, his hands, and the length of his spine down to his tail tip. The rest of him was a rich red. He was already well into his very own cask of whiskey and gestured happily when I approached.

"Xxyyxxsss," he said, or at least I thought that was what he said, indicating himself. His voice was such a deep growl I could barely catch it, feeling more in my bones than actually hearing it.

"I hope not to offend with my butchery of your name," I said, and he chuckled, a sound that echoed strangely in my head. "Is it Xyxs?"

He nodded approval, swinging his dragonish face down to meet my eye. His were golden and ringed with black.

"I speak not your bird speech well," he said in draconian.

"Nor I sometimes," I replied, also in draconian, thinking of the hillspeech accent I'd picked up. He roared with laughter, flattening my ears against my head with the force of it.

"I see why *Jxxyssdyfnn* takes to you," he said approvingly. I recognized that jumble of sibilance and consonant sounds and filed it away for later.

"That was your draconian name," I said to Rafael as he escorted me back to the fortress. I'd wanted to stay longer and meet more of them, but he'd steered me away, claiming that limited exposure was safer.

"Yes."

"I wish I could say it properly." I'd given up on prompting him to repeat it slowly for me several dozen years ago, but I still had to try on occasion. My inability to even correctly perceive the sounds was a constant source of frustration. I'd never encountered anything like that, and it bruised my elvish pride.

"You cannot." Amusement colored his voice.

The surrounding forest echoed with the dull booms of draconic voices, drowning out the usual nighttime sounds. Occasionally, a rattling thud shook the ground as they tussled with each other. Such a contrast to the silence of elvish camps. Drakes had no fear of discovery whatsoever. Rafael stood apart from the rest, silent even when wearing his full drake form, only punctuated by the rumble of his breath. His ambushes on the hill were a feat that should have been impossible, given my sensitive hearing. Another blow to my pride.

"How does your name translate?" Why hadn't I thought to ask sooner?

"'Dark Fire,' essentially," he said. "A title. It references the ability you witnessed at Seregond Pass."

"Seems a rather long name just for that. Those I've met so far have shorter names." *Marron, Tyldain, Xyxs,* I repeated in my head. Two syllables each, according to my rough pronunciation, even though Xyxs had drawn out the sounds.

"Clan names are shorter than titles. The full title is 'Brings the Dark Fire, End of Days'."

"Why so dramatic?"

He exhaled, a huff of amusement. "The way I rose to power was… hrrm, unpopular." That struck me as quite an understatement.

"You've never told me your clan name, either." All that time he'd been taunting me over a title and not an actual name. Easier to be miffed at the slight rather than consider the implications of that title.

"No clan. Thus, no clan name. You may hear them call me *Rraysth e,* meaning 'Red One' or 'the Red.' Also something of a title."

"I still prefer 'Jax'." I pulled his arm closer, taking his hand in mine. It sobered me to think that all his names were simply titles given by enemies. He'd once told me that his youth was nameless. At least I could grant him this small affection, even if he did find it irritating.

"Of course you do," he grumbled.

"I admit that Rafael is more lyrical." I grinned at him. "Kind of you to allow us that."

"Tedious elf. What was your impression of the others?"

Overall, the drakes were engaging. They were much more open and straightforward than I'd expected, given my limited experience. Contrasts indeed. We crossed the high bridge. The wind picked up, howling through the ravine below. The stars shone especially bright, singing their subtle songs. I took a breath to look up and appreciate them.

"Marron is the most surprising. He seems friendly." He also seemed like someone I could sit and swap stories with over a whiskey. Nemohee would like him.

"Marron could snap your spine like a twig. I am the only one he has never defeated. He is… reliable."

Reliable. How much subtext did that single word contain? He'd always been so cagey around the concept of friendship. Were they even truly allies, or was it that Marron had no choice in the matter? All questions Rafael would certainly dodge. I decided not to press, it was enough that he was openly giving me any information at all for now.

"Oh, I figured as much, but he's remarkably pleasant. That second one though, the blue…?"

"Tyldain." The Dragon's face hardened.

"Yes, him. There is something about him I do not care for. Clearly you don't either."

He nodded. "Good instincts. He is not at all trustworthy, but he is strong."

"And you don't worry that he might turn on you? Or us?"

We paused at the outer gate. He ran a hand over one of the huge gate doors, examining the quality of the wood and the thick iron banding, giving it an experimental tug that rattled the hinges. Probably he could rip that door free if he tried hard enough, but he seemed satisfied for the moment.

"He has tried before. It is not a mistake he will repeat. He is the head of the largest clan behind Marron's, however."

"Hmph. I mislike him. The third one though, Xyxs—"

Rafael made a face at my pronunciation.

"Spare me your disdain, I lack your vocal cords! Anyway, I liked him too. He also seems reliable." I knew it was probably a mistake to think of the giant drake as a huge, friendly mastiff, but I couldn't help the mental image.

"He is, in his way."

"You are so very different from the others. Not only in appearance, though that is the most outwardly obvious way, but your entire demeanor is unlike theirs. They seem like a very direct people, and you are a labyrinth." I twirled a lock of his hair around my finger, thoughtfully. He watched my face. "What did they think of me? Could you tell?" I'd never been overly concerned about others' opinions of me, but the potential consequences of a negative reaction loomed larger with the drakes.

"They do not understand my choices, but then, they never have. They know not to question me. You won them over, though. My people are charmed by you, my little oddity." He tugged indulgently on the pearls woven through my braids.

The knowledge warmed me. I wanted their approval, after

all. Rafael had more in common with me than I realized. We simply managed our social discomfort in *very* different ways.

I thought over the introductions and each drake's response to me. "Did you not tell them of me on the journey here?"

"Of course, but they will recognize you first by scent. Easier to identify when you no longer reek of horse and travel. And other elves." He cast a sidelong look at me. I kept my face neutral, silently thanking the Night Mother for my forethought in avoiding the prior intimacy with Celebel. "If ever we are caught in battle and you are separated from me, find Marron. He is under strict geas to protect you if I cannot."

"You placed a geas on him?" I shivered.

"Only for your protection. It is a compulsion to assist."

That did nothing to assuage my concern. "A part of me wants to ask how you accomplished that, but perhaps I'd rather not know. Also, I'd like to think that the ambush was a fluke, as I have no plans to fight in any more battles."

"War often takes unpredictable turns," Rafael said, implacable.

I hugged him, holding tight, and he wrapped me in his arms, kissing the top of my head. After the horrors I'd witnessed during that ill-fated clash, I had an entirely new appreciation for his strength. Physical safety had never been a particular concern of mine before, but oh, how I loved the security of his arms around me now.

"I'm very glad you're here," I said into his chest. "I know this is all terribly difficult, but I feel much safer now."

"You will always be safe with me." His voice was a deep purr.

We walked on in companionable silence for a moment and I thought of the connections I had here, both old and new. When we reached the inner gate, I paused again, loathe to part.

"I've missed this, just simple conversation with you." I trailed a hand down his arm. He rumbled acknowledgement, and a new thought occurred to me. "Was it my imagination or were there no female drakes in that group?" The drakes all seemed to have a certain masculinity to them, but perhaps it was the deep voices, muscle, and my own bias.

"There is one. Overall there have always been few females. Marron's mate is one of our fiercest warriors. She would be here, except that he has impregnated her yet again," he said, exasperated. "She will join us after the birth."

I pulled his arms around me again. "I know it's against the drake rules to thank you, but   thank you"" I enjoyed his warmth in the cool night air.

"I make my own rules."

"Yes, that is abundantly clear," I said with a laugh, and he kissed my brow. "I like listening to their voices. It's as though I'm hearing the mountains speak."

"Very different from all the little birds chirping at your court." He mimicked a bird's beak opening and closing with his hand and I laughed again.

"Yes, very! And you are by far the most comely of all of them." I stroked his face, tracing his lips.

He snorted. "You say that only because I look the most like your kind."

Taking a moment to examine my reflexive denial, I replied, "Actually, I would say Tyldain looks the most elvish, if a strange sort. How often must I kiss you to convince you that I do not care for such a narrow concept of beauty? You are in a class all your own."

"Your taste is questionable at best." Rafael leaned down to accept my offer of kisses.

"As is yours," I replied against his lips, and he rumbled in agreement. I tried to tempt him by tugging his hands under my coat, but he resisted.

Chapter 28

Celebel paced in our now-shared chambers, an ice-blue dressing gown flung about his shoulders. He wrapped me in a huge embrace the moment I stepped through the portal into the antechamber.

"Ah, my love, I am relieved to see you in one piece!"

"No need for the dramatics. Rafael would never allow them to hurt me," I said gently.

"What was it like, being surrounded by monsters?" He held me at arm's length, looking me over.

"Do not call them that. It is derogatory. They are people too."

Celebel acknowledged my words with a shrug, leading me to sit with him on a chaise lounge by the fireplace. "Forgive me, love, it is only my nerves speaking. Tell me everything. And tell it again to Feanim tomorrow. He will need to know what you saw."

I allowed him grace this once and took my time describing my impressions and the drakes' overall reactions to me. Celebel was enrapt, only interrupting me occasionally to clarify a point here and there.

"Truly, you are the bravest among us," he said when I was done.

I laughed. "It is easy to be brave when you have the world's most famed killer at your back. They are a fascinating people, though. I am eager to learn more. Oh, ah, unfortunately they ate the ponies. I should have anticipated that."

Celebel grimaced. "Ah, that's too bad, poor things. We'll be better prepared next time." He paused. "You should be cautious in your dealings with the Dragon. The rumor mill here is an efficient machine, and jealous nobles will seek to discredit you, to root you out."

"I believe they will find I am far better-rooted than they

expect," I said archly, and he took me in his arms again, laughing. "They are surely already aware of a connection between us."

He sobered as he explained how, in my absence, he and Feanim still had to corral the remaining disgruntled nobles, despite their first attempts to sow peace.

"We had several tense discussions about why attacking Rafael in numbers would only end in tragedy all around. And sharp reminders of the gods' expectations around the hospitality we offer to allies. I tried to lean on the historic nature of this alliance, for what good it engendered. Several called us traitors for accepting the God of Carnage into our midst without challenge."

I winced. It must have been a highly unpleasant experience. Celebel paced around the chamber as he spoke.

"I said to Galdir and the rest, 'I saved your life. You may not wish to recognize such an act, but in doing so, I protected the integrity of our sacred laws of hospitality you so flagrantly disregarded. I want no conspiracies against Rafael. Do not attempt to band together to take him down. These beasts are our allies whether we like it or not. The war is at our doorstep, and you will see I have the right of it before long. If you do not wish to accept my word, ask any of us who were present at the pass of Seregond. We have witnessed his terrible power firsthand. Any attack on the Red Dragon would spell doom for us all.' I also reinforced that dissenters and rabble rousers will face banishment if they go against my word." He sighed, running a weary hand through his hair.

I let his use of 'beasts' as a descriptor pass without remark. "Indeed, that is quite a speech. Do you think they heard you?"

"It is impossible to know. Some seemed to accept our words, at least. Others… well. They wish to witness the drakes' usefulness for themselves. Battle-hungry, in that regard. The most important thing is that no more blood was spilled today."

"Has Galdir been treated? I would offer, but I doubt he would care for my presence."

Celebel grimaced. "Yes, we have other healers here. They

saved the arm, though he will be in recovery for some time, and may never regain full use."

A shame. If I'd been able to lay hands on Galdir immediately, I could have guaranteed a thorough healing. That brought to mind Celebel's righteous intervention.

"I've never seen you get angry like that. It was kind of sexy. Even Rafael was surprised."

"Ah, so *that's* why you're so taken with the Dragon. Rage issues fan your flames." He lunged forward and tickled me. I dissolved into helpless laughter, unable to fend him off. He finally had mercy and released me. "We should sleep now. I have meetings starting at dawn that would benefit from your presence."

Dawn came far too quickly. Rafael and Feanim were already conversing in the war room when we arrived; or rather, Feanim talked and gesticulated while Rafael listened. The Dragon leaned against the right wall, examining the maps.

Nimthil was present as well, sitting so quietly I almost overlooked her at first, as far from Rafael as she could get in that space. Her vantage point allowed her to easily observe everyone's lips. Another elf, Araglin the scholar, entered as we did. He stood beside Nimthil, watching the exchange with a creased brow. He wore similar robes to what I'd seen before, rather than Feanim's more martial-looking leathers.

The room itself was claustrophobically small for the intended purpose, or perhaps Rafael's looming presence merely made it seem so. With floor-to-ceiling windows on the far wall, and a huge central table covered by a topographical map cluttered with various indicators, it was clearly a space well-used. A single large chandelier dangled over the table, and witchlight sconces nestled between tapestries of great battles. In a few places, more charts were pinned over those tapestries.

The moment I entered, it was as if Feanim ceased to exist;

the Dragon focused entirely on me, much to the Duedellen's irritation. Nimthil and Araglin watched the silent exchange with appraising eyes, brows rising in unison.

I nodded a greeting and went to Rafael's side before he started any trouble. Celebel had discussed this approach with me, and we'd agreed it safer versus chancing a pointless confrontation. The present company already knew our situation, barring Araglin, and so posed little risk of court upheaval. My connection to Celebel twinged on cue, and I tried to send back comfort. I didn't need to be present for these discussions. My role was to provide a buffer.

Rafael didn't bother to hide the softness in his eyes as he looked me over. Deliberate, but I didn't know why.

"Did you already tell them about the drakes you introduced me to last night?" I asked him.

"We've discussed it. We've been here since well before dawn," Feanim interrupted. He turned to Celebel. "I've explained our troop movements, where we've sighted the enemy, and our next planned moves. All of it." He waved a dismissive hand. "We're caught up."

"Why did you summon us then?" Celebel asked.

"He believes more eyes on me will ensure good behavior," Rafael interjected with an amused rumble. A vision of his pulling the War Crow's head off popped into my mind and I shooed it away. "That one is too fearful to leave her mate's side, and that one has a terminal sense of curiosity." He nodded at Nimthil and Araglin, respectively. That neither squirmed under his gaze was a point in their favor.

"There is also the Carnyx of Calling to be discussed," Araglin said. He had the voice of an orator, melodious and resonant.

My ears perked as Celebel responded. "Based on your research, we've dispatched a small group to locate it. Thank you, Lord Araglin. This could be the very thing that turns the tide for us."

"What does it do?" I couldn't help myself.

Feanim rounded on me with a sneer, but Araglin answered. "It is an object of power; a battle horn that compels enemies to gather. Only one with sidhe blood may sound it, but it is said to be irresistible. If we can secure it, we may finally draw the Fomorians out into proper battle rather than these henpeck tactics. Get a sense of their actual numbers to determine the true strength of our foes." Sidhe blood, interesting. A few elves had it, mostly Lachanaur. Doubtful that any full-blooded sidhe would willingly aid us.

"I shall not fully commit my people to war until we have a clear sense of our opposition," Nimthil added, hands moving to echo her words, as though she'd heard my thoughts.

Rafael snorted. "Good to know your entire strategy depends on a magic trumpet." I stifled a laugh, not wishing to encourage him.

Feanim ignored the jab, addressing Celebel. "Did you know the Lord Dragon is also a smith? His ability to control his dragonfire will be perfect for certain projects we've been planning if he's amenable. Þilvor has always been tricky to work, needing such sustained high temperatures."

That last comment piqued the Dragon's interest, and he nodded cautious assent. He rested a hand on my shoulder as he listened to the Duedellen's speech about new ways to forge.

Araglin interrupted smoothly. "Yes, well said, but what other properties have we overlooked in incorporating said dragonfire? What of the potential for unseen pitfalls?"

"Save your moralizing, I'll have none of it today," Feanim snapped. It had the cadence of an old argument.

"If you wish to utilize my forge, you'll simply have to tolerate a bit of moralizing," Araglin replied, serene. "I mean no offense, my Lord Dragon." I decided I liked him.

Rafael gave the Astolar an appraising look, just long enough for the others to shift with discomfort. "An intelligent question. It would take far too much effort to imbue each piece with enough power to exert any real influence. Nor do I have any desire to do so. No unnatural flame. You have my word."

Araglin nodded, evidently satisfied, folding his hands into

his sleeves.

Feanim plucked at an earlobe in his annoyance. "Here, I have discovered this moranga, the mythic demon ore. It was a long and arduous mission to find it."

He brandished a small, black dagger that created instant discomfort. It seemed to drink in all the energy of the room along with the light, and made my skin crawl. I wasn't alone in that sentiment. Something passed over Celebel's face, too quickly for me to decipher. Araglin's nose crinkled. Nimthil looked down at her lap. Rafael, however… His eyes lit with a particularly draconic greed, pupils dilating in a disturbing manner.

"Forging it is very difficult, but I have managed this one piece." The Duedellen raised it higher.

Rafael leaned across the table and neatly plucked the dagger from Feanim's startled hand. I scooted away from the Dragon as he turned it back and forth, inspecting it, hefting and smelling it. Then he shocked us all by using the blade to cut three fine, bleeding, steaming lines into the back of his right hand. Araglin stammered something about not absorbing demonic curses, but Rafael paid no heed. Seemingly impressed, he nodded approval to Feanim, and then disappeared the dagger up his sleeve.

Thunderstruck, Feanim managed to stammer out, "*Give that back!*"

It must have been the very dagger Feanim had initially thought to offer to Rafael as a gift. I caught Celebel's eyes and managed to stifle a snicker. Celebel pressed his lips together, ears twitching.

"Take it from me," Rafael said in a laconic purr. "Where is the rest of this ore?" Feanim only stared until the big drake leaned forward and growled, "Tell me."

I laid a placating hand on his arm. "Easy, Dragon. We already had plans to share it with you. *Right*, Feanim?"

"Yes. Yes, of course."

I eyed the sleeve where the dagger had disappeared. Not an outline, no trace. "Does it truly hold such power?"

"Moranga is a siphoning enhancer for those strong enough to master it." Rafael's gaze flicked disdainfully over Celebel. Siphoning of what? Enhancing how? A melody fraught with discordant possibility.

Nimthil tapped the table and spoke, hands flashing. "What evidence have we that you will not use this demonic material to conquer the rest of Vaeda?"

The Dragon coughed a throaty laugh, startling the others. "Why the fuck would I want to rule this great conflagration of fools? I never even wished to lead my own people. A side-effect of gathering power, not a goal."

Nimthil frowned prettily. I agreed with her sentiment; not exactly a comforting statement.

Rafael's gaze shifted back to Feanim. "I will not ask you again."

"I will show you the ore when we are done here," the Duedellen said.

"You will show me *now*," Rafael rumbled, and Feanim sighed in defeat.

He turned and led Rafael from the room. The Dragon imperiously demanded answers about how and where Feanim had found the moranga, and how he'd kept it shielded so well. Celebel lingered in the doorway, fingers tapping away on his arms.

"The implements of war are beyond my expertise," Araglin said, excusing himself from the room in the opposite direction, robes swishing.

"Should I chaperone them?" I asked the ceiling.

"Please keep my soulmate safe from his talons, if you are able." Nimthil's lilting voice caught my attention. Open fear registered in her eyes.

I couldn't resist a plea to help a soulmate. "I know Rafael is... a lot to accept. But if it puts your mind at ease, I know him well, and he is here to help us."

"He frightens me," she signed, the motions compact. A whisper.

"Your fears are not unfounded, but I will do what I may to assuage them." Clumsy in their signing, my thumbs and forefingers almost stuck, but Nimthil nodded with palms pressed together in gratitude.

Celebel led me to the armory. "There isn't much moranga to show, as far as I'm aware. Feanim had only a small stash. Enough for perhaps a suit of armor and some blades."

The Dragon's rumbling bass carried, bouncing off the stone walls long before we came upon him.

"All garbage, why are you keeping these?" followed by a twanging crash, and a dismayed cry from Feanim. We rushed through the door to see Rafael ruthlessly pulling swords off their stands and discarding all but a few into a large pile at his feet. Feanim looked as though he might be sick.

"What are you doing?" I demanded.

"Clearing out the trash," Rafael replied without stopping. "We will make more, and better. I will bring adequate substitutions in the meantime." He tossed another sword on the ground and Feanim groaned.

"First you abscond with my ore, and now you wreck our weapons?"

Rafael ripped an entire rack off the wall, dumping it on the pile with a crash that hurt my ears. "I will work with you, but only on my terms. Where is the rest?"

"Stowed in another fortress for safety."

He paused. "Your idea of safety is laughable. Moranga has resonance. The wards here were adequate, but they require proximity to maintain. Otherwise, you will attract demons."

"Demons?" Celebel's eyes went huge. "What exactly is wrong with these swords?"

The fire drake straightened, rolling up a sleeve to expose

his corded forearm, and drew one of the discarded swords sharply across it with an awful screech. His skin remained perfectly unmarred, and the edge of the blade was ruined.

"Tell me, was your mighty warrior's sword a family heirloom, or a recent acquisition?"

Feanim shrugged. After a moment Celebel supplied, "Recent."

Rafael's gaze flicked to his face and back to Feanim's. "And have you been forging from pure þilvor, or alloying to stretch your materials?"

"Alloys, of course," Feanim said, realization dawning. "So you believe a blade is worthless if it cannot part your skin. And to do so, must it be pure þilvor?" His brows raised in incredulity. "These work perfectly well on Fomorians."

"Moranga will also work, or weapons fashioned from our scales, teeth, and talons." Rafael sneered, explaining as though speaking to a child. "Am I the only drake in existence? Do you suppose every last one of my people will follow my direction without fail? If your swords cannot cut through a dragon's scales, then yes, they are worthless." He tossed the rejected blade back on the pile.

"You have scales currently?" Feanim asked just as I said, "What about all those weapons you left with me?"

The Dragon paused, turning his disdainful glare on me. "The blades you had carelessly piled into that trunk?"

Celebel also gave me a hard look, which I ignored. My ears flicked.

"I took them back." Rafael turned again to his task, casting another sword into the rejects. One he eyed thoughtfully, and set aside.

"You took them back? You've been to my bower?" The thought of it tightened my chest. I missed my cozy home with sudden fervor. How had the Tree reacted to Rafael approaching without me?

"You did not deserve them, treating them so shamefully.

We will make better use of them here."

I yanked at my lobes in exasperation, hardly able to focus through the acrid tang of so much metal. "I never wanted them in the first place. You simply dumped them all at my feet!"

"Then you should appreciate their reclamation," he said with an infuriating smirk. The few remaining blades on the wall, mostly pikes and halberds, rose behind his head like a deadly crown.

"Would you two cease flirting long enough for us to make some kind of plan?" Feanim cut in.

Rafael instantly rounded on him with a snarl. "Keep going, *Inuriterrege*."

I stepped between them and put a hand on the Dragon's chest; futile, but it made a point. "Stop it, Dragon. Yes, he's an ass, we all know he's an ass—*not unlike you*," I poked his chest with my finger, "but we will never gain ground if you keep threatening to murder all our allies. Can we have a truce, please? *Both* of you?" I turned, with my hand still on Rafael's chest, to glare at Feanim as well.

The Dragon huffed but relaxed. I let my hand fall. Feanim gave me a sour look and nodded.

"Shall we tour the forge? If you can stop yourself from tearing apart my armory for a few moments," the Duedellen said. "I will also show you where I'm keeping the rest of the ore."

"Can I trust you boys to play nice or are you going to make me escort you? I have no desire to be near that ore. It turns my stomach." I shivered.

Rafael gave me a wry look. "If I promise not to eat him *today*, will you stop fussing?"

"Good enough for me." Privately, I sent, '*What does Inuriterrege mean?*'

'*Anthill king*,' Rafael sent back, and I bit my lip to keep my laughter in check. He came up with the most disdainful nicknames. Even 'dove' wasn't entirely complimentary, given his chirping birds analogy.

After the Dragon ducked through a door after Feanim, Celebel let out a long, gusty sigh.

"Why do I have the terrible feeling that those two are going to end up friends, to the detriment of the rest of us?"

Chapter 29

I shifted in my seat beside my Consul's throne. Despite the velvet cushions, the cold seeped into my joints. Celebel had insisted I join him at court to understand the scope of his responsibilities, and also to show solidarity by placing me visibly at his side. That second bit was a bold move on his part, to raise a nameless elf to such a coveted position. The nobles would naturally assume I was attempting to regain my rejected power and status, though that couldn't be farther from the truth. All I desired was to work with patients and help keep Rafael's violent tendencies in check, assuming that was even possible.

Dressing the part of consort proved tricky to navigate. Clothing of the same finery and elaborate design as Celebel wore would indicate similar status, which I did not wish to claim. Wearing my usual knotted bolts of sheer silk gauze was also not an option. I'd opted for an unadorned gown, long enough to conceal my bare feet, and chose a braiding pattern that would not hearken to my former lineage.

I said little and heard much. From my vantage point on the dais, I observed the audience's reactions to the speakers quite well, and entertained myself watching how the large stained glass windows painted them with color, as well as cataloging the new, more casual styles.

Celebel donned a floor-length skirt of finest silk, gathered with just a few pleats in the front, under a long, tailored, silk brocade coat. I loved the way clothes draped over his body, and enjoyed helping him dress. He could make any garment enticing.

Feanim dressed more casually. He favored a dark green, quilted tunic with pleated sleeves, open at the front to show a white linen shirt and gold jewelry, with loosely-fitted leather trousers, and a visible blade at his belt. It gave off a militaristic rather than regal air.

Most elves donned delicate þilvor hair and ear nets set with smaller, sparkling gems, versus the old larger, heavier, jewel-forward pieces. Perhaps the newer, finer jewelry was a result of repurposing some of the heavier þilvor pieces into armament due to the war.

Beginning at dawn's light, the first court day involved one noble after another with a litany of unfounded fears and biases about the drakes at the gates. This one ate livestock it wasn't supposed to, that one scared away a band of refugees. What if they snuck inside at night and devoured the serving youth? On and on. When prompted, I advised where I could.

Celebel proved to be fair-minded, resolving disputes to leave both parties satisfied. He had a way of intensely focusing his ears on a speaker that made them feel valued. At the end of such hearings, he mingled with the remaining audience and exchanged greetings and personal pleasantries.

I played a more active role in the social portion, trying to assess potential allies and pitfalls. As expected, the nobles were chilly but polite to my face, so long as I remained in Celebel's earshot. Lineage-breakers were rare enough, as it generally only happened through banishment, and they had a hard time accepting that I'd done it of my own accord. Strange, to be treated as a criminal when my only "crime" was to choose an existence outside of social norms. At least the younger, less socially important elves tended to be a bit friendlier and more curious than judgmental. Perhaps I fascinated them with my wildness.

A striking Lachanaur woman parted the crowd that first afternoon when our session ended and we mingled with the audience. She stalked over to us with an unreadable expression on her tanned, freckled face. The skirt of her purple silk dress swirled about her long legs. From his description, I knew at once that this must be Recarmial. Taller than me, nearly of a height with Celebel, she moved with a sort of raw-boned grace. Her eggplant brocade bodice, dotted with pearls and laced tight with shimmering white ribbon, emphasized a bosom similar in size to my own. A delicate collar of enamel leaves in warm pastels graced her neck. I loved the style and color choices; the whole ensemble played up her features to dazzling effect.

Her liquid brown eyes scraped across his family talisman dangling from my ear, as she drifted over. With a practiced, seductive smoothness, she tucked a note into the collar of his robe as her gaze lingered on me. Then she swished away, long auburn braid lashing like an angry cat's tail behind her.

Such a casual hairstyle would have been controversial back when I'd held real status. I took it in with rapt interest. Our fashions typically changed much slower than the other peoples of this world, but they did eventually change. Did drakes have similar trends?

"I should have sought her out before making our arrangement public, out of consideration." Celebel grimaced, watching her glide across the plush green and silver carpet of the great hall. "She did not accept the change in perceived status with grace, though we never once exchanged any declarations of love or devotion."

I sighed. "Unfortunate. I would like to avoid making an enemy of her. What did she give you?"

He unfolded the note. "An invitation to a welcoming celebration for my healthy return. We are the guests of honor."

"Is this a play, do you think?" It certainly felt like one.

"They may disapprove of your circumstance, but they are still wildly curious about you." Drumming his fingers for a moment, he pursed his lips in thought. "Do you suppose your pet Dragon would attack any who pay attention to you, or am I a special case?"

I sucked in a breath. "I wouldn't like to test his limits. Nor should anyone else find out the hard way, I think." I could too easily imagine Rafael's display of incandescent rage if I even marginally participated in such a thing. He might very well pull the fortress itself down around our ears. "Pity we can't simply bring him along."

Celebel let out a sharp bark of laughter. "That would be most educational, yes. For everyone involved."

"Seems a shame to miss out on getting to know everyone.

It might have been a chance to give them some comfort and insight about my presence here. To let them taste my spirit and hear my song." I sighed. "An orgy is simply too risky, given the circumstances. I've barely gotten him to accept my intimacy with you, and only because I shield the bond so heavily."

Frowning prettily, Celebel's fingers tapped the rhythm of his thoughts. "Honestly, these things can be tedious and I'd rather spend the time with you. I'll find a graceful way to bow out."

I twined my arm in his. "Let us perform our own rituals then."

We rinsed and anointed each other with oils, plaiting fresh braids into unruly hair, and draping each other in silks.

"I'm grateful to find a lack of stiff brocade, high necks, and the hats with those ridiculous veils. The stodgy old court resembled a dreary field of dying flowers in the last light of late autumn." Except for our earrings and the pearls I kept knotted into my hair, we wore no other jewelry. "These colors are much kinder on the eyes."

Celebel dressed as the sky of summer sun. I appreciated the way his fine, royal blue watered silk robe clung to his body, pouring over his shapely buttocks and thighs, to splash at his feet. He chose an icy blue silk for me, patterned with glimpses of opalescent thread to resemble the wispy clouds of a bright, frigid day.

"The relief of sun in deepest winter," he said, drawing it around me.

Cut from a single bolt each, the robes tied once at the waist, for ease of removal. We'd decided to at least wear the trappings of a formal orgy, even if we couldn't participate.

Celebel grabbed me the moment I turned away, pressing me into the door frame from behind, his erection hot and heavy against my ass. He brushed my hair to the side to lick my ear and the side of my neck, making me shiver. I leaned into him, savoring his soft lips on my skin, and reached behind me to grab his cock.

"You are distractingly beautiful," he murmured, nipping along my lobe and cupping my breasts. "There will be a great outcry of sadness at the denied opportunity to sample your loveliness."

"There would be even greater sadness if I'd granted that opportunity and then the Dragon caught the melody." I arched my back, enjoying the sensation of his cock rubbing between my buttocks. "I am striving to make amends with him, remember?"

"Mmm, I'll keep that in mind if I never need a swift removal of political enemies."

"Celebel!" I laughed in delighted horror. "I never knew such wickedness dwelled in your heart."

He chuckled, deep and throaty. "Does it make you wet?"

"Which part? Your wickedness or the idea of letting your political opponents fuck me for your gain and their imminent death?" It did indeed make me wet. I liked this game of teasing the darkness. With him, it remained confined to fantasy. I could not risk toying with Rafael in the same way. Spreading my legs, I encouraged Celebel to maneuver his cock into teasing my vulva. "I have to admit, the more you arouse me, the more suggestible I become."

Tugging at my earrings with his teeth, he penetrated me as he thumbed my nipples, making me whimper with pleasure. "I'll have to keep that in mind. I do like the idea of simply watching you. Your arousal is a powerful intoxicant."

I moaned and tried to force him deeper inside of me, thinking of the last time I sat on Rafael's face, and imagining Celebel there, stroking his cock. A dam broke in me. The intensity of the image sent my arousal flood down my legs. Celebel moaned in response, thrusting faster. Oh, how I'd love to have his pretty cock in my mouth while the Dragon made me scream with that long tongue!

Sudden tension, thrumming like a fired bowstring, seared along my connection to Rafael, and I quickly clamped down on those thoughts. Gods, I would have to be more careful. It almost took me completely out of the moment, and I certainly needed no more complications.

Fortunately, Celebel's lustful nature proved strong enough to sustain both of us. "What about you? Would you like to watch me suck a hard cock?" He punctuated his words with a sharp thrust and I writhed against him.

"You're going to get us both killed," I laughed, and then gasped as he gave me a forceful thrust. "... Do I get to pick the cock?"

He laughed in my ear. "Is it attached to someone amenable?"

"Define 'amenable'." That telltale tension rose again, and I shoved the mental images back down where they'd be safe.

"I admit a certain lascivious curiosity. How unfortunate for both of us he remains so closed off."

Celebel pulled out of me suddenly, and I whined, turning to face him. He bent low and scooped me into his arms, carrying me to the bed. I waited for him to show me his plan rather than ask, running my hands over his shoulders and ears. Laying me gently on my back, he climbed over me in the opposite direction, and I gratefully accepted his cock into my mouth as he began to lick and suck my throbbing clit.

I'd always loved taking a cock that way; the feel of the velvety skin on my tongue, the scent of arousal, the pulsing. Drawing out the climax, pouring down my throat. I liked to stroke and tug at the testicles while I sucked, enjoying how they tightened against the body. Even better if I could manage to orgasm at the very moment of ejaculation, as it made my climax so much sweeter.

His fingers teased my labia apart, making my breath come faster and my heart hammer in my chest as he slipped a few inside. With his persistent tongue on my clit, my orgasm crested. As I sucked hard and he gleefully thrust into my mouth, I licked a finger, coating it as best I could, and pressed it gently into his anus. With a sharp cry, his cock pulsed, and he climaxed, gushing into my throat. I drank him down eagerly and he twisted his fingers inside me, pushing me hard, right over the edge, to join him in muffled moans of ecstasy.

I rolled him so I perched on top, and began anew. My saliva ran down between the globes of his luscious ass and he panted into my cunt. That delicious cock twitched fully back to life when I fingered his anus again. He relaxed, and I worked more fingers inside of him. A hand drew along my own rosebud, working my juices in for comfort.

As his cock pulsed again, I hit a muffled high note, and we crashed together in our waves of bliss.

When I flopped down beside him, I rubbed his feet and he tickled mine.

"Would you like some wine, or a light meal, before we go for the next movement in today's symphony?" he asked, as I giggled and rolled away from him. "I have too many possibilities running through my head to hear you sing only twice."

Chapter 30

The morning after the welcoming celebration, I attempted to speak to Silfanië. A serving youth directed me to where she sat in a small courtyard, fingers gliding through sweet chords on an elegant, cross-strung harp with a gilded frame. A traditional piece, austere as its player, she performed it with serene detachment. Framed with bright sun and the sweeping branches of cultivated willows, it could have been a scene from a stained glass window.

Recarmial and Feledhor made up her audience. Their eyes drifted to me the moment I emerged from the hall. At a subtle twitch of the ear from Silfanië, they departed without a word. Interesting to note the pecking order. I settled across from my sister, where the other elves had been, and waited patiently for her to finish her concert. She played through two more songs before turning away from her harp. And from me.

"Sil—" I began, but she raised a stern hand, shoulders tightening.

"Do not speak my name." With her back to me, her voice chimed like winter wind. "You have no rights here."

"Nor do I intend to claim any. I seek only peace between us, sister." I kept my tone mild.

"As you kept peace by stealing my birthright when you knew you had no desire to use it? As you kept peace by revealing our location to outsiders?" She wheeled, hair cascading around her in a shining wave, fury sparking in her eyes. "You are no sister of mine. Who is to say these monstrous attacks are not the direct result of your carelessness? Perhaps you are the very reason Leyúduin fell!"

Her words knocked the breath from my lungs. Gods, was all of this was my fault? I dropped my eyes in an attempt to control the sudden trembling of my limbs.

She stared me down as though I were a blighted contaminant,

nose wrinkling daintily in disgust. My heart hammered loud enough for her ears to twitch with the rhythm, deepening her contempt.

"Keep your distance, *Crescent Moon Woman*." The dripping scorn could have burned holes through the flagstones. "And keep those monstrosities of yours properly muzzled and leashed."

She swept away before I could speak her name. As she had refused to speak my proper chosen one. I'd relinquished my birth name with my lineage. It would have been long struck from record. Deliberate, that pointed reminder.

What if Silfanië had the right of it? What had I done? The refrain circled over my head like the dark, implacable wings of vultures.

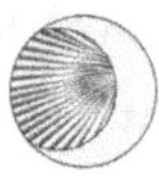

"We'll ease you in to the state dinners, starting with the small, private ones I regularly share with Feanim and Nimthil. Araglin joins on occasion," Celebel said. "We dine in a room close to our chambers, so you can flee if you wish."

I gave him a grateful look.

He wore a long, royal blue robe with a white hem. I chose a sheer silk dress the shifting blue-green of a summer beetle's wing. It draped perfectly, both revealing and demure. I braided Rafael's pearls into my hair in the usual manner, and my lover gave me a measured look.

"Would you have me adorned another way?" I teased.

"Merely an idea for enhancement."

He went to one of the tall wardrobes, revealing an intricately carved case with many small compartments. From the top section, he presented me with a thin þilvor circlet, glimmering bright silver in the light. Suspended via a charm imbued into the metal dangled a single large, rose cut diamond drop, with a vivid blue-green hue of its own. I knew this sparkling gem. Fallëvaethil, the 'Rain Jewel,' had graced more than one royal crown over its long history. A truly priceless relic.

"Would you honor me thus?" he asked formally. I bowed and kissed his knuckles.

"Of course, my love. It is you who confer the honor."

He settled the circlet on my brow and Fallëvaethil hummed to life, buzzing pleasantly against my skin. Its tacit acknowledgment after my sister's accusations lightened my heart. The diamond cast scintillating colors on the walls as I gave Celebel a twirl, making the royal jewel sing. He whistled appreciatively, and I fell into his arms, laughing.

"Come now, we can have a tumble after dinner. We're going to be late," he said.

I followed him with my best pout, silver slippers tapping deliberately on the flagstones. He slipped an arm about my waist, letting his hand rest lightly on my rear.

The dining room was surprisingly comfortable, a smallish space set apart from the formal dining hall. It had a low ceiling with a warmly lit crystal chandelier that cast dancing lights over a simple oaken table, and reflected off a couple of cleverly placed mirrors set to brighten the space. No windows adorned the chamber, and a thick veil of dampening emphasized privacy over aesthetics. Thick tapestries, spelling out a millennia of genealogies, padded the walls.

Feanim and Nimthil were already seated side-by-side when we arrived. No Araglin this night, apparently. Celebel settled in front of the Duedellen; his customary spot. I pulled up the chair across from Nimthil. She was subtle about it, but she eyed the diamond on my brow with mild disapproval. The Lachanaur Queen herself was dressed in a simple white, scoop-necked shift, with sage green stitching at the sleeves, under a forest green, sleeveless robe that laced over her small bust. Fine þilvor chains draped her ears, glittering fetchingly against her soft candlelight hair. Feanim wore an unadorned black surcoat over a black shirt.

Dinner consisted of a rich persimmon and honey stew, filled with black currants and root vegetables, and paired with a nectar wine in graceful art glass stemware. I recalled Rafael's opinions about what he considered "overly sweet" elvish wine and smiled to myself.

The serving youth interrupted us only once, to remove our plates and bring a palate cleanser of mint in a light cheese. I savored every bite. It had been a literal age since I'd had such refined fare, even in this simplified version. I noted that Feanim almost crouched over his plate while Nimthil picked daintily at her food with perfect manners. Celebel was the only one who seemed truly at ease.

"I am not entirely sure what keeping these drakes fed is going to entail," Celebel said, signing along. "It's not as if we keep large flocks to cull easily." He swirled his glass, frowning.

Feanim gestured idly with a knife as he spoke. He did not sign, and Nimthil had to lean forward to see his lips. "I can't imagine they need to eat that often. I've read that their bodies are very efficient, depending on the blood mix. The closer to the true dragons, the less they need to sustain themselves apart from rapid or frequent shapeshifting. I have some contacts over by Ira Belanore who've agreed to send some hoofstock in the meantime." He raised his brows, waiting for my input.

I set down my wine to use my hands. "Nimthil, please tell me if my signing seems strange. It looks to have evolved since I learned it." She nodded. "I frankly haven't any idea of a drake's regular diet. Rafael rarely expresses any need for sustenance, but he is not typical."

"What does that mean?" Feanim probed.

"You'll notice it most clearly when he's among them. It's more than just looks; he acts very differently. The rest are more... well, more overtly draconian, for lack of a better word. They seem very straightforward for the most part."

Nimthil tapped the table. "Why did you go to their camp?" Her golden brown face paled, making her freckles stand out in relief.

"Rafael wanted to introduce me so that there would be

no question of 'accidental' devouring." I laughed, stifling it when Feanim and Nimthil both shifted uncomfortably.

"With your confidence in these supposed allies, I find no reason to call more of my people here." Nimthil's fingers danced above her plate as she addressed the two Consuls. "Originally, you requested their presence, citing safety in numbers, both here and on the battlefield. Now, you have all the muscle you need, and I will not subject them to increased risk."

Celebel drummed on his arm. "If we do locate the Carnyx—and recent reports indicate we are closing in on it—we will need every soldier we can muster out on the field."

"Be realistic." Feanim sneered. "We have the fucking *Red Dragon* on our side, and you think we need more elves? Like adding candles to a wildfire. We may as well sit out the next battle and have tea."

Nimthil tugged a lobe and I echoed the sentiment. "You would have us pin all our hopes on these beasts?" She combined the sign for 'beast' with a huff of expelled breath.

"They are not beasts." My protest clattered to the floor, unacknowledged. Much to my annoyance.

"You cannot sing both melodies," Feanim said. "Either your people join in the fight, or we rely on the strength of our allies. Which is it?"

She folded her hands and stilled her face.

Celebel nodded. "Understood. I, too, am hesitant to put all my faith in an ally who wishes me dead."

Feanim waved a hand. "We know the Carnyx will work. The Fomorians already use smaller versions of it in their current attacks to draw up their forces. It's a matter of properly positioning ourselves to appear vulnerable, and the drakes to easily drop in. No need for the padding."

Assuming the drakes cooperated. Rafael reacted poorly to that kind of unearned confidence. His great love of subverting expectations could pose a serious problem. How did the other drakes even feel about being here?

"The Fomorians also attack in hordes, seemingly without centralized leadership." Celebel swirled his wine, frowning. "No generals to target, nor even captains. They do not adapt to our tactics as I would expect. We can use that to our advantage, as the horn will allow us to pick the field."

Nimthil signed reluctant agreement, and Feanim laid a hand on her arm. It still jarred me to see him go soft for her.

"We can discuss it at length later," Celebel continued. "As it stands, we have a more pressing issue. How do we approach hospitality with Rafael at the upcoming banquet?" A grand dinner—another gesture of celebration for Celebel's recovery and the others' safe return—loomed on the horizon. Ostensibly, it should also serve as welcome for Rafael's allegiance, as we would hold a feast for any other ally.

Feanim twirled his knife, walking it across his fingers. "I am surprised you have a care for his comfort. He certainly has none for yours."

Privately, I echoed the sentiment.

Celebel leaned back in his chair. "This is not for my personal edification. We have already come far too close to breaking hospitality with his involvement. Do you truly wish to risk it again?" Silence stretched for a moment, and he looked to me. "Again, you are the expert here. How should we serve him? Where should he sit? Must we send hunters to find game for him?"

Nimthil slammed her hands down, making me and her wine glass jump. "Not my table." Her signs grew larger, more exaggerated. "No dead flesh!"

"I sincerely doubt Rafael would expect to dine with us," I said. "If I am mistaken, I will accept that responsibility. I do not, however, think this wise."

"He is a foreign dignitary." Celebel rubbed his face, hiding a scowl. "We cannot exclude him, it would be an affront! The laws of hospitality demand that we host him."

My ears drooped. He had a point. Perhaps we were damned either way, but better not to make the choice that constituted a deliberate snub. "Very well. I cannot guarantee my ability to curtail his response if provoked, but I will do my best." The connection to my Dragon jangled in warning, and I put more effort into guarding my thoughts. "Just, please ensure he has a chair suitable for his stature. After dragging him up that hill, I can say with certainty that he is even heavier than he looks."

"He looks quite solid," Feanim said with a smirk, and Nimthil surreptitiously poked him. We hashed out a basic seating arrangement, and the conversation drifted to more pleasant topics.

Nimthil pulled me aside in the hall as we left to return to our chambers. The Consulate walked ahead, deep in conversation, and did not spare us a glance backward.

She gave me a hard look and said, "I do not care for you." I stared at her seemingly uncharacteristic bluntness. "There has been nothing but unrest since you arrived and brought that… *beast*."

"We would have died without—" I began, but she made a cutting motion in the air, jabbing a finger at me.

"*You* brought him *here*." Her hands repeated the words, the exaggerated motions rolling her shoulders. "I do not approve. But I am told you are a skillful healer and I am grateful for Celebel's safe return. We may never be friends, Cúraniel of the Crescent Moon. I will never forgive you for what your pet monster has done to our people, for what he's doing to our court. However, also know that I will never impede your work."

"Good enough."

We locked eyes for a moment, assessing each other. I saw her hidden steel, for the first time understanding how someone so outwardly delicate could rise to Queen of the fiery Lachanaur. Then she signed "yes-yes" and swept away with a practiced flourish of her robe.

I appreciated her directness, if not the sentiment behind it. Interesting that she blamed me for all of Rafael's actions, past and present. I should strive to be so powerful.

Chapter 31

The formal dining hall was a sight to behold. Massive crystal chandeliers hung sparkling from its high vaulted ceilings, casting prisms on the table and floors. The walls and floor were crafted from gold-in-quartz, and golden trim accented the tall, faceted windows on the west side. The table itself was absurdly long and grand, crafted from a pale grey larch wood in flowing lines. A spirit-fed river bubbled up from the head of the table and flowed through a channel in the center, branching off to each seat.

Two stately thrones stood side-by-side for the Consulate. Also wrought from gold-in-quartz, pierced in an exquisite lattice pattern down their tall backs and laden with velvet cushions, they lent a regal presence. Behind the grand table and thrones spread a decent-sized marquetry floor, clearly meant for dancing. Musicians perched in raised platforms at regular intervals along the walls.

That Araglin chose not to take the position of highest honor at his own table made me curious. How much of this had been built or brought in since the Fomorian raids began? I didn't know him well, but it seemed ostentatious for a monastic scholar. In contrast to the great hall and this one, most of Férioth held an elegantly understated aesthetic.

Feanim sat in the left of the two thrones, with Nimthil at his right hand and Feledhor beside her. My sister, much to my chagrin, sat to Feledhor's right. At least Recarmial was not among the cadre of my opponents for the night. Nor was the unfortunate Galdir. Eledom and Lamirië, along with two other guards I did not recognize, stood behind the thrones. Eledom winked when I made eye contact, but Lamirië pretended I didn't exist. Celebel, positioned on the right throne, had me at his left, directly across from Nimthil.

Rafael was to be seated beside me on my left, but he instead stood behind me like a dark shadow. Unsurprisingly, I'd had to cajole him into attending. He wore his typical simple black leather and wool, but at least agreed to leave off the armor and sword. Not that he was ever truly unarmed. I sensed his discomfort at having his back to the doorway where the serving youth passed, and cursed my lack of familiarity with the layout. There was no easy solution. Fucking politics. Though he emanated mostly watchfulness, threat lingered in the living flame of his hair and eyes.

Poor Araglin had begrudgingly agreed, after several discussions, that he would be the least likely to accidentally offend the God of Carnage. He moved to the left of the Dragon's ironwood bench. It crouched like a reptile among the rest of the delicate vining seats. We ensured plenty of space in the seating arrangement so that the scholar would at least be out of immediate reach.

Warring scents nearly overwhelmed me, especially combined with music winding through the rising conversation. Ill-prepared as I was for my abrupt return to society, all the delicious possibilities now within reach helped me regain some lost footing. I'd grown accustomed to lengthy fasts during my years of isolation, and had discovered a newfound appreciation for culinary arts. Despite that, worry over Rafael's presence made it difficult for me to find my appetite.

Already laden with intricate fruit sculptures rising far above the heads of the guests, serving youth carried steaming trays of roasted vegetables, great tureens of soups, and baskets of fragrant bread. Wrought from leaves, bark, and starchy reductions, the vessels were as much a part of the meal, as the preparations they carried. The crude carved wooden cups and bowls I'd used at my bower would come as a shocking lowering of standards to these folks. The youth laid each vessel on the bubbling channel, and a parade of artful food floated down the table.

We all stood as Feanim and Celebel traded lengthy songs about Celebel's return to the court. The guests took it in with rapt attention. Well, most guests. Rafael's gaze roamed over the crowd. Eventually, the Consulate chimed knives together in unison, the signal to begin. We sat as they did, all except for the Dragon. The Consulate poured wine and served each other, then did the same for Nimthil and myself; symbolic of their ability to serve their people.

Using the birch fork provided, I hooked a floating basket, and a ladled a thick mushroom soup over a portion of seeded bread. Birch proved a good choice, adding a delicate flavor to each bite. I pushed the remaining soup back into the center current. Serving youth filled our goblets, skirting around the drake as far as they could without being accused of discourtesy.

Turning in my seat, I sent, *'Please stop lurking like a gargoyle and sit. I promise they are all suitably terrified of you.'*

He gave me a sardonic look, and sank onto the bench beside me, his back straight as a redwood. I chatted with him in a bid to get him to relax, and also show the others that he was perfectly capable of carrying on an intelligent conversation without resorting to violence.

"Earlier we attempted to work out how to keep your people fed."

"Feanim approached us." That surprised me. "He is fortunate Marron reached him first." Rafael pitched his voice low. The quiet *whoosh* of every ear in the room swiveling to hear his words put a shiver down my spine. "Xyxs would have eaten him without a thought."

"Gods. Is that typical?"

He snorted. "Xyxs has more muscle than sense. Marron marched your little Consul over to me for translation." I stifled a laugh. The green drake spoke perfect elvish.

'Was that coordinated?' I sent, sipping at my soup.

'No, he simply does not care for elvish hubris.' The corner of Rafael's mouth curled sardonically.

Did the others actually prefer me or were simply responding to the acceptance forced on them by my intimidating soulmate?

Either way I had an unexpected advantage on Feanim.

"That one," Rafael's viperine eyes flicked over to the Duedellen, "presented me with an acceptable arrangement. I consider the matter settled."

One less worry made my food more palatable. Conversation rose tentatively around us as the Dragon lapsed into silence. I selected a blossom bowl for my next course. Breathing on the hand-sized flower—a lovely pinkish-orange peony—it unfurled to reveal a bed of steamed, honeyed seeds. I plucked a bitter petal and scooped a few seeds into my mouth. Bliss!

Araglin leaned forward and steepled his fingers, braids falling over his shoulders as he caught my eye. "I understand that you healed the great Red Dragon." His voice remained impressively mild as he glanced up at the looming figure beside him. "She saved your life?"

"You understand correctly," I replied, blowing on the steaming seeds.

Araglin chewed thoughtfully on a candied pansy, nodding and waving a birch fork along with his words. "How do you reconcile being a healer, ostensibly wishing to save lives, with rescuing a most notorious killer? Please let me say that I mean no disrespect, Lord Dragon."

Rafael rumbled agreement, resting a hand on my bare skin, talons curling possessively over my shoulder. "It is only truth. I have asked similar questions." The Astolar's ears relaxed. Rafael's questions along that subject had been quite a bit more pointed.

"I cannot save the world, my lord Araglin. I can only save the life in front of me, and the Night Mother herself bade me rescue any soul who could reach my hill. Where would you draw your limits? Who am I to decide who is worthy of life?" I smiled to take the edge from my words.

"Who indeed," Rafael said, and I tensed, waiting for him to start trouble. "Simple enough. Kill the threats, eat the prey, cull the weak."

"'Cull the weak?' To what end?" Araglin peered curiously

at him, fiddling with the long sleeve of his marigold velvet robe. "What constitutes weakness in your eyes, my Lord Dragon?"

"Resource drains; those who take much and contribute nothing. Those who cannot defend themselves." His talons tapped lightly on the table.

"If 'weak' means 'anyone who cannot defend themselves against you,' then you should have culled all of Vaeda. But you would also die, having destroyed the one person in a position to save you." Pique heated my face.

Rafael arched a brow at me. "Why did I agree to this? Did you expect to change my world view over dinner?"

"Stop being so spiky, please." I would have laid a hand on his arm, but Araglin watched our exchange with unfettered fascination. He wasn't the only one.

"You have never been surrounded by those who would celebrate your death. Though perhaps you are beginning to understand, given the number of hostile glares currently cast your way." He raked a burning gaze across the table, and every elf in his line of sight immediately averted their eyes. *Imagine if I wore larger scales.* Venom laced his tone.

Not everyone here is your enemy, Dragon. I shrugged and his mouth twisted, but he finally relented with a dramatic sigh. Eyes bore into us from all around as Rafael settled back beside me. Celebel's gaze pressed most keenly. I didn't dare turn my attention to him. Not yet.

"Surely you can see the value in noncombatants," Araglin tried again. "Scholars, artisans, botanists—"

"I am all of those things," Rafael interrupted, turning that burning gaze on Araglin. "And yet, there are none among you who may match swords with me. What, then, do I gain from tolerating weakness?"

Araglin didn't back down. "Why have you come to our aid, then? Why grant your favor to a healer?" His tone remained calm, conversational. Respectful.

I surreptitiously poked Rafael in the side as I leaned forward.

'*Because you're a contentious blighter who likes to pick fights.*' Out loud, I said to Araglin, "Despite his unpleasant demeanor, he cares about my well-being." I gave Rafael a sour look. "Or are you only keeping me alive, keeping your word, as long as I entertain you?"

Infuriatingly, he smiled at me. "Perhaps."

'*Ah, so you think this is all foolishness, and since you don't wish to be here, your aim is to make us all as uncomfortable as possible,*' I sent, trying not to flatten my ears.

'*Of course.*'

I couldn't see the sharp teeth behind the grin, but I could certainly feel them. '*Wonderful. Very helpful.*'

'*At your service, my lady.*'

My palms itched to slap him. His eyes only brightened with malice.

To Araglin, he said, "I did not grant her my favor. She won it. Cúraniel is the strongest among you." He folded his arms and leaned back. From all the scowls, it felt more like he'd painted a target on my head than offered praise.

"Lord Dragon," Nimthil ventured from across the wide table. Her dress was a simple jade silk with belled sleeves. Green, again. "You honor us with your presence. Please partake of our feast." She signed as she spoke, indicating a tray laden with steaming fruits and flowers, and the distinctly empty place setting before him. "Please allow us to serve you."

Rafael snorted. "Lady, I am a carnivore. There is nothing here for me."

I poked him again. '*Be courteous!*'

'*How do you invite a fucking* dragon *to your table without providing meat?*'

I had to bite my lip to keep from speaking aloud, almost hard enough to draw blood. '*Blame that misstep on me. I did not think you would want to partake, and the presentation of meat would offend the Queen.*' I speared a petal with my fork, shredding it.

To my surprise, Rafael relented. '*You were correct. It is the demand that I join you in eating flowers that I find offensive.'*

Feledhor leaned in, looking at the Lachanaur queen. "Witness how he refuses our hospitality, Lady Nimthil." Implying that Rafael's rejection of our offered peace meant the provocation of the gods. I sucked in a breath. "If Beredhel were here, he never would have tolerated such a thing."

Murmurs rose like wind and I decided right then and there that I disliked Feledhor. From the way Rafael speared the pale elf with his hostile stare, he felt the same. Silfanië shifted uncomfortably at the troublemaker's side, looking everywhere except across the table to avoid the Dragon's penetrating gaze.

Feanim's knuckles turned white around his knife, and for a moment I thought he would lunge. "Do not speak of my brother." He bit the words off.

A sore point, indeed. Rafael's eyes flickered, taking in Feanim's reaction.

My elvish soulmate intervened at that moment, standing and catching the attention of the room. A vining wreath of þilvor set with tiny, glimmering sapphires complimented the shining streaks in his hair. Black velvet sleeves embroidered with constellations billowed out as he raised his arms in supplication. Calming spirit flowed so subtly from him I almost didn't perceive it.

"My lords and ladies, I know we hold ancient enmity, but the time has come to put our differences aside and bind together, lest we are all swept away by the mighty tide of this war. As you know, the Red Dragon has been more than generous in his aid. Indeed, Lord Feanim and myself, as well as my Lady Cúraniel, and the rest of our company would have been decimated without his timely intervention. We owe him a debt of gratitude which surely includes our sincere attempts to breach the gulf of our differences. We must find harmony." Celebel's influence had an effect, as some elves relaxed. He leaned over and took my hand, pulling me gently to my feet. "To my love, Lady Cúraniel of the Crescent Moon, we also owe our thanks. It was her *friendship* with the Red Dragon that allowed us to call upon him in our time of need."

I bowed to the cold stares of the nobles, and considered the way Celebel had leaned on the word "friendship." Either a deliberate undermining, or a well-meaning but naïve attempt to provide protection from the court. For his part, Rafael utterly ignored Celebel, opting instead to look over my butterfly-wing silk with frank appreciation.

'I like the dress. It accentuates your curves nicely. Looks as though it could slide right off.' He made a subtle gesture, and I had to grab the jet bead strap of my dress to keep it from slipping off my shoulder as I sat. I didn't mind baring my breasts in public, but only on my terms.

'Stop that, you lech!' Much as I loved his blatant flirtation, I couldn't allow it here.

He gave me a small grin. Ah, there were the teeth. Celebel tensed beside me, observing our exchange, and I squeezed his hand as I sat back down.

"What goes between you two?" he signed, just under the table. He risked being called rude for hiding his hands, but given the circumstances, it was understandable.

"Forgive this. I try to stop trouble," I signed back. *'Speak mind-to-mind for safety. Rafael may know a goodly number of our signs, with his interest in language, but I can block him from my thoughts if I concentrate.'*

Celebel grimaced and indicated to Rafael that he should address the table. The Dragon gave Celebel a hard look and placed a possessive hand back on my shoulder. This time it was the same shoulder with the strap holding the top part of my dress in place—the strap which he hooked a threatening talon underneath. Surreptitiously, I tried to wrest his hand away, but he wouldn't let me budge it. He continued to ignore Celebel's increasingly meaningful glances, as well as the rest of the dinner guests.

Sighing, I surrendered, poking at a steaming golden sweet potato stuffed with goat cheese on my plate. My guts were now wound too tightly to make space for my appetite, but I tried to make a show of it.

Feanim's clipped tenor got my attention. He wore a fine, short coat of olive green wool that matched his eyes, over a pair of dark brown woolen trousers tucked into high boots.

"Soon enough we shall return to the field of battle," he was saying. "We must draw the Fomorians into direct confrontation. I know it may perturb some of you to fight side-by-side with the drakes, but truthfully, we need their might to combine with our own. We shall take precautions to keep our forces separate to avoid potential incident."

A chorus of protesting voices rose from the gathering. I looked at Rafael and he mimicked birds chirping with his hand under the table. I had to bite back laughter. A particular stare drilled into me, and I looked across the table into Feledhor's icy blue eyes.

I raised my eyebrows. "May I assist you in some way?"

The pale Astolar smiled broadly. "The pearls in your hair. A lost Maraiya treasure, are they not?"

A note of dread crept along my spine. "I believe so."

Feledhor smiled nastily. "Yes, yes, there is a song about these famed pearls. And how they were lost to dragon fire."

"You are welcome to direct your complaints to the corpse of the dragon who stole them," Rafael said, inspecting his talons. "His name was Skeffynthir. I took them from his hoard after I slew him." The implications of his words rippled through the table. Blue Skeffynthir had many tales of destruction and woe attributed to his name. "If you prefer, you may also confront his descendent. Tyldain waits just outside your walls."

"Why does *she* now wear them?" The voice belonged to Silfanië. "What right has the nameless one to the lost jewels of our kin?" Though I detected a faint quiver in her ears, she fixed me with a hard stare. I appreciated Araglin's horrified gasp. Perhaps I'd made at least one ally.

"It pleases me." Rafael's voice went low and deadly as his chorusing growl rose. "The right I claim. If Skeffynthir lived, you would have no pearls to whine about, and a true dragon free to burn your cities and eat your children. Where is your gratitude for the salvation of your kin? Or do only my perceived sins count in your histories?"

My sister's throat worked silently.

The Dragon continued, his hackles truly rising now. "Cúraniel did me a great service." I appreciated his unusually tactful word choice. "I gave her the pearls. They belong to her now. Take them back, if the sight offends you. If you are able."

"The sight of them on a nameless elf sullies their history—" Feledhor chimed in. And froze.

Rafael was on his feet, jagged teeth bared in a snarl and red murder in his eyes. Like a candle snuffed out, the whole table went silent. I grabbed his sleeve. He ignored me.

"Perhaps I have found an appetite after all." His thunderous growl raised the fine hairs on the back of my neck. "It has been many a year since I last tasted elf flesh."

'Please, don't do this! Please,' I begged him. The muscles of his arm rippled under my hand, readying to crush the life out of the insolent shitheel sitting across from us. A not-insignificant part of me *really* wanted to see it happen. Instead, I leaped to my feet.

"Shall we dance, my lord?" I called out in desperation.

Tugging on his hand, I tried to pull his focus away from an increasingly sweaty Feledhor. I had no plan, only a vain hope that someone would back me up. Luckily Feanim was quick on the draw, rising to his feet with Nimthil's hand in his and gesturing for the musicians seated on the nearby platform to play. Tentative at first, the others joined in and the music swelled around us in a wave.

Shaking the tension from his broad shoulders, Rafael exhaled a blistering breath that scorched the food directly in front of him, drawing gasps from those seated nearby and a puff of steam from the center channel.

He leaned over the table. "Insult her again, and I will extinguish your entire pathetic line." The growl rose from deep in his chest. The Dragon maintained eye contact with the pale

Astolar and clicked his sharp teeth together.

I hadn't thought it possible for Feledhor to get any paler. Sweat rolled freely down his forehead, plastering his cornsilk hair to his skin, and he didn't dare move to wipe it away. The Dragon finally released him from the glare, breaking the tension, and the gathering collectively slumped with relief.

'*You owe me for this.*' His tone held a sharp edge.

'*I owe you for a great many things. Dance with me?*'

Rafael responded by spinning me into his arms and let me pull him over to the marquetry dance floor. Much to the shock of the onlooking elves, he danced with every bit of the effortless, liquid grace that we so prided ourselves on. He lifted and twirled me around him as though I weighed no more than a silk scarf. I laughed with the sheer pleasure of it, enjoying his strength used in such a gentle, almost playful manner. Strings hummed, pipes lilted, hand drums thumped. The music moved through us, and we with it. The sensuality of his perfect control brought a flush to the tips of my ears and quickened my breath. No one else dared come near. For the length of a song, we were alone in all the world.

On the hill, he'd quietly watched me dance and sing to myself for years. One day, as I grew frustrated with yet another unproductive sparring session, he'd unexpectedly spun me in his arms. Just like that, we were dancing together. I smiled at the memory and wondered how Celebel would react if he ever heard the Dragon sing.

When Rafael finally set me back on my feet, I debated kissing him in front of everyone. A light tap landed on my shoulder. Celebel stood behind me, wearing a look of expectation.

"May I?"

Rafael relinquished me with a challenging glare, and Celebel bowed, taking my hand. We danced across the floor with linked arms, swaying to the music.

"I had no idea he could dance so well, did you teach him?" Celebel's voice held a note of disbelief. "A man with shoulders like that has no right to be so graceful." It was almost a pout, which I found absurdly endearing.

"I keep telling you he's full of surprises. You've seen how he moves even when walking, was it truly such a stretch? I taught him our steps, but he already knew how to dance."

"Imagine, drakes dancing," he scoffed, spinning me.

"You just saw one dance and commented on his grace! You do yourself a great disservice to underestimate their culture." I smoothed his hair from his face. He dipped me, and I kicked a toe to the ceiling. "Do not make the mistakes of your ancestors."

As Nimthil and Feledhor swept by arm-in-arm, I glanced over to see Rafael involved in some heated discussion with Feanim. They glanced at me in unison, making me uneasy.

"Great, they're plotting something," I said and Celebel murmured assent.

I enjoyed the light pressure of his hand in the small of my back as he guided me through the repeated spins of the dance. His easy smile eased me as well, and I leaned into him; we moved as one.

Feanim and Celebel danced the next set together, and I rejoined Rafael. He had stationed himself as close to the door as he could manage without actually leaving. More than one serving youth swerved in a wide arc around him as they filtered in and out.

"Was that truly so torturous?"

"That little shit actually had the courage to ask *me* to dance." He was so obviously put out, I almost felt bad for him. And yet.

"Who, *Feanim?*" I couldn't hide my shocked delight, and looked over as Celebel and the Duedellen spun around each other. They were smiling, and had obviously practiced the dance together many times. The Dragon grumbled and folded his arms over his chest.

"Oh, come now, why didn't you accept?" I sidled up to him, grinning, and prodded him in the ribs.

"Yours is the only touch I will tolerate," he growled. "And if you do not stop poking me, I will bite that finger off."

"Yes, yes. Big mean fire drake. Fearsome! You are a bit too

easy to bait, you know." That garnered me a brow arch. "It was nice to dance with you again. I hope you enjoyed it. I certainly did."

Chapter 32

The banquet ended as the sun rose. Rafael departed first, well before the others. Celebel lingered to speak with various elves. I headed back to our shared chambers, aflame after the dance. Rafael's hands on my body, the way his hips moved against mine, nearly choked me with need. Digging in a trunk filled with my scant belongings from the hill, I located the red implement. The smooth heft of it tightened my nipples with anticipation.

Climbing into the expansive bed, I settled myself on my back in the dead center, propped on pillows. I licked the implement thoroughly, my cunt already slick, before sliding it between my legs. One hand guided the implement, carefully working the girthy piece into me. The other hand toyed with my clit, and I let my imagination fly free. I wanted to worship.

The impact of landing threw me to the ground, and the Red Dragon loomed over me. His massive body filled my vision, so vast the underside of his tightly muscled, scaled belly became my sky, his hind legs pillars to the heavens. A rumbling growl shook the ground, bouncing me along with the surrounding rocks. The rising incense musk of his arousal intoxicated me.

"Dragon! Let me worship at the altar of your cock," I cried, climbing to my feet and reaching to that red sky. He roared, shaking the world apart.

Rafael dodged intimate questions about his other forms with the same adroit skill he used to slap me into the ground during our training sessions. It only strengthened my carnal curiosity. I didn't actually know what his genitals looked like in his full dragon form, and I'd never seen his bare erection in any of them, but that didn't interrupt my fantasizing. My mental conjuring would simply have to suffice.

A bulge appeared at the seam between those mighty legs, and the scales slid apart. His cock emerged, hard and ready, and larger than my entire person. With a somewhat pointed head, and a textured ridge running up the top side, the sight made me writhe beneath him. Flesh darkened with blood flow, especially at the head. That awe-inspiring erection offered little contrast to his deep crimson scales. A pearl appeared at the tip and my clit throbbed in response, watching it roll downward.

"Anoint me with your pleasure." I stretched as far as I could, still well shy of reaching him. No end suited me better than complete annihilation by dragon orgasm. If I had to die to bring him to completion, I would count my life worthy and my lascivious nature finally appeased.

He crouched low, and I leaped, wrapping my arms around his shaft. With a heave, I flung my legs around him as well, and held tight. I pressed my breasts, my belly, my wet, needy cunt against that glorious, utterly enormous cock. My hands and feet could not reach all the way around, and I worked against muscle fatigue to achieve my goals.

Pressing my face into the seam in the head, far larger than my skull, I licked at the steady issue of his desire. Hot, salty, and spiced in my mouth, I urged his release with every stroke of my tongue. Raking my teeth along his skin made him rumble. Biting the edges of the head made him hiss, and his cock jumped in response.

Pounding myself with the implement and flicking my sensitized clit at the image, the pressure grew at the base of my spine. I did not dampen my connection to Rafael. In that moment, I hoped my stubborn soulmate could feel every detail of my lurid thoughts. Hoped he missed me with the same all-consuming need.

The Dragon's groan of pleasure shook me free. I landed on my back with a huff of expelled breath. The tip of his cock dragged down my body, pulling cries of ecstasy from my throat. He paused, and a visible pulse ran the length of his shaft.

"Yes, my Dragon! Come for me. Give it to me, drown me in it!" I arched my back off the ground, raising my hips as high as I could, offering my desperate cunt. If he split me open in that

moment, so be it. A death worth having.

His red cock pulsed again. Once, twice, then came the flood with an earthshaking roar. The ground split open around me and so did the delicate membranes of my ears. A deluge of searing seed knocked me flat, rolling me in its current. I choked on his issue. It burned my skin, almost as hot as his blood, turning my cries into screams. Begging for him to stop, for him to give me more. I drank down more than my belly could hold. It streamed from my nose and mouth. Each pulse of that massive cock sent another tidal wave over me.

I gasped and whimpered with the strength of the orgasm that rocked my body, arching off the bed, slamming the implement home hard enough to bruise.

Finally, the flow ceased. I wiped the sticky, steaming liquid from my eyes in time to see a second, slightly smaller cock emerge from the slit between his legs. 'Smaller' meant only that I might encircle it with my arms. This one had a more distinctly knobbed ridge.

Everything I'd read about dragon anatomy mentioned a certain similarity to reptiles with their hemipenes: two fully functional cocks. I'd already lost myself. My mind ran wild with the possibilities.

Rafael lowered the second cock. Once more, I wrapped my arms and legs around the shaft. My fingers barely touched on the other side. The Dragon moved with rhythmic jerks, using the lubrication of his spent semen to glide through the circle of my limbs—

Celebel watched from the opening of the bed curtains. My concentration shattered, and I froze, implement halfway inserted. A sly grin crept across his face. "Please, don't stop on my account. I'm rather enjoying the show!"

I took in the sight of him. He removed the þilvor circlet and shook out his hair. Next, he opened the front of the velvet coat and pulled out his already hard cock. I shuffled around to give him a better view, spreading my legs wide, and he hummed with appreciation. Climbing into the bed, he paused at my feet.

"I assume you've been thinking of *him*. Given the appearance of this tool." The relaxed posture of his ears reassured me.

My throat worked for a moment before words emerged. "Does that bother you?"

Celebel grinned. "Not unless I'm barred from appreciating the side-effects. I could surely use the pressure release after all that. Tell me about your imaginings."

I was all too happy to fling open the book of my mind, but Rafael, being quite the opposite, gave me pause. Celebel picked up my hesitation and nodded.

"Not yet. Very well, perhaps it is a future goal to work toward. Will you tell me how to assist you? I cannot very well leave my precious soulmate unfulfilled." The wicked sparkle in his eye sent a tingle of anticipation down my spine.

"Climb over me and come on my chest," I commanded. "Keep your clothes on."

Celebel straddled me without another word and pulled his erection free. "Ah, in your mind, this is not the first shower of the night."

My ears flushed with heat, traveling to my cheeks and down my chest. His grin broadened.

"Indeed. And you want me clothed… As he was clothed? No… not clothing. Scales?"

I couldn't hold his gaze. His teasing fogged my mind with need.

"Scales then. What a deviant you are."

"If only you knew," I murmured, and his eyes lit with salacious glee.

He moaned and went to work, pumping his hand slowly over his shaft. Leaning back, his other hand joining mine in working my clit. I resumed fucking myself with the implement.

With the delicious sight of Celebel pleasuring himself, the sounds of his rising climax, and the vision of the Dragon's huge cock sliding against my body, I peaked again almost immediately.

Celebel groaned, pausing his strokes as he painted my breasts with his pleasure, and my orgasm followed. I bucked under him, shrieking, and he laughed as he finished.

Chapter 33

By the next evening, the first pamphlets appeared. A simple trifold design, they scattered across the hallways. Parchment copies made from a single original through a linking spell, they'd been subtly crafted to hide the author's spirit. I'd never encountered myself drawn in caricature before. Depicted nude with breasts too large for me to see over, dirty feet, and a wild tangle of hair that tripped me; I loved it immediately.

The author made light of my 'uncouth' accent with barely legible scratching. They showed me using my wild ways to ensnare a sweet, innocent Celebel. Rafael's caricature, playing up his non-elvish features in clear bias, lurked in the shadows. Absurdly villainous, overly simplified thoughts floated in a black cloud above him.

I came upon the Dragon himself in the corridor, leaning against the wall and reading one of them with a look of bemusement. He held up the pamphlet.

"Apparently, I am too tall and have a large nose. How enlightening."

I laughed, more than a little relieved at his mild reaction to the childish mockery. "Your large nose suits you."

"My voice holds a barbarous tone as well." He growled for emphasis, the sound echoing down the hall.

I slid my arms around his waist. "How dare they criticize your best features! They could have said something useful about your viciously sharp tongue and foul temper instead."

"They have plenty to say about your startling lack of sanity." He snorted. "I expected better insults."

Thanks to the intense wards Rafael wove around it, his room was the perfect place to hide from unfriendly eyes. He'd keyed the wards to allow only the two of us to pass. The room itself was surprisingly small and simple, as he'd requested, and located on the opposite end of the fortress from Celebel's chambers. A single window illuminated a large, ironwood-framed bed pushed against the far wall. The mattress was fitted with perpetually ignored, plain grey sheets. Beside it stood a writing desk with a matching chair, both stacked with pilfered books, scrolls, and his own notes. Across from that was a tall wardrobe filled to the brim with precisely organized weapons. Sconces held bare witchlights that he never bothered to light.

Curiosity got the better of me when I spied his journals. A few were full of writing in a language I did not recognize, but his neat, spiky penmanship was unmistakable. Another held diagrams of weapons and armor that no longer fled from my eyes. A last one… oh, the last held life drawings. Some were innocent enough, such as interesting landscapes or flora and fauna, but the rest were of me. Mostly in rather compromising positions. Unfortunately, there were no portraits of the two of us together, but his depictions of me were painstakingly detailed. Though he never would, the idea of Rafael stroking his cock to my image intensely aroused me.

"It is not the color of my scales."

Startled, I hugged the journal I'd been flipping through to my chest. Rafael leaned against the door frame with an amused quirk to his mouth.

"What is not… *oh*." He'd gotten a dose of my lurid fantasies after all. I opened my mouth to ask, and he gave me a look. I promptly closed it again.

He approached and plucked the journal out of my hands, casting an eye over the various works strewn around me. "Make yourself comfortable."

"I hope you don't mind my presence here." Unusually shy before him, I had never infringed on his private space the way he always did mine.

"How much of this do you understand?" He held up a journal of diagrams.

"I prefer this one, so *naughty*." I slid the book of lascivious drawings toward him.

He rumbled and picked it up. "Of course you do. You were put into this world to test my patience."

"If yer aff tae sass me lik' that ye better at least pull tha' shirt aff!" I threw a pillow at him and he batted it away with a deep rasp of laughter.

To my surprised delight, he cooperated, unbuckling his belt and setting it aside with his sword. He unbuttoned his leather jerkin, shrugging it off, and then slowly unlaced his shirt to pull it off over his head. I drank in the sight of his muscular body; the movement of his abs as he tossed the clothes over the back of the chair, the ripple of his shoulders as he bent and kicked off his boots. Stretching, he placed both palms flat on the ceiling.

His intoxicating scent intensified. I sucked in a breath at his powerful shoulders, the heavy muscles of his chest, his sculpted abdomen and slim hips, the intimidating outline of his cock under the thick leather. I bit my lower lip.

"I will never understand your limitless desire to observe my form, but I appreciate it." He curled sinuously around me on the bed, pulling me close.

"I was so cold in here without you," I said against his lips, running my hands over his corded arms and twining my legs around his. "I've missed you terribly."

"Take as much of my heat as you desire. I am at your mercy."

"Am I forgiven then?" I dared pull back to look him in the eye. The pupils rounded. He touched my lips, my brows, the length of my ears. "Have I atoned?"

"I love you as the moon loves the night." He kissed my

forehead and my breath caught. "I forgive you. You are the first and only to hear those words from me."

I blinked back tears, a deep-seated knot in my belly finally releasing. "Oh, my love. It is good to be in harmony with you." For the first time since I'd confronted him on the hill, I could take a full breath. I rolled onto my back, and he trapped me under his body with a long, deep kiss. My spirit rose to mingle with his and my thighs slicked with desire. In that shared breath, his darkness and hellfire wove my tattered pieces back together.

We took our time getting reacquainted, carefully exploring each other. It seemed like an age had passed since we could indulge. Millennia since the last time he had brought me to climax. Desire made me giddy, and the dance had only fanned the flames. Like a fever, the need for him burned me up.

Rafael took care to smooth away the rough directionality of his hide so I could kiss and lick him without hurting myself. With my tongue, I traced the hard lines of every muscle I could reach. Savoring his skin, his heat. When I bit his nipple, he moaned and gripped my ass, squeezing with both hands. Encouraged, I dragged my teeth over his skin, brushing the tips of my breasts against him as I moved. No matter how hard I raked and bit, testing the durability of my teeth, I could never leave a mark on my Dragon. He rumbled encouragement.

He teased my nipples through my gown, first with light flicks of his fingers, then with slow swipes of his tongue. The silk dampened, adhering to my sensitized flesh, and he lowered his head to suck. I reached between my legs to relieve myself and he caught my hand with a growl.

"No. I will decide when you climax." Rising above me on his knees, he ripped my gown down the middle. My wetness soaked the sheet beneath me. Gods, I loved it when he bared my breasts. He ran that exquisite tongue along my ears, my throat, all the way down my body and back up. A river of fire stealing my breath, my wits. I writhed beneath him, clawing at his back, unable to even beg him to fuck me in my lust.

Mindless in my delirium, my hand slid too low, brushing his buttocks. He immediately sat up and swung his legs over the side of the bed.

Panic surged. "Gods, I'm sorry! I—"

He cut me off mid-squeak. Grabbing a fistful of hair on the back of my head, he dragged me over his lap, face-down. The pressure on my scalp shot straight to my cunt, just he knew it would. He tore the rest of my gown tore away.

"Actions have consequences, Cúraniel," he hissed. "You cuckold and tease me. You invade my privacy. Now you would touch me without consent?"

"It was an accident!" I squirmed with alarm, twisting to look at him. Rafael smiled that false, predatory smile, lips pulling away from jagged teeth, and leaned in close.

His dark growl caressed my ears. "I know."

A palm connected with my ass. I yelped at the unexpected sting, and he swatted me again. Heat spread from the contact. My clit throbbed with the exquisite edge of pain. The lightest controlled blows from him rippled all the way through my body. I fixated on how easily he could shatter my spine, fear blending into delicious ecstasy. His rumbling breath, his scent, his heat, his terrible strength; I wanted all of it. Every slap rolled my belly across his leather-bound erection, and I drove myself wild, hoping he'd finally orgasm that way.

Almost involuntarily, I braced myself and lifted my rear for better access. The next blow landed with blunted talons, and I gasped. Each impact swept me deeper into the rip current of desperate need.

"Harder. Bruise me. I want to feel you with me every time I move." My lust spoke with its own voice, leaving me to tumble in the waves of orgiastic pain.

He rumbled a laugh. Slapping my ass again, he dipped his fingers between my legs to sample my wetness. "So needy."

The strikes picked up speed and intensity until I whimpered in counterpoint. The flesh of my buttocks dimpled and burned.

Deep, throbbing, delectable pain. I trembled with the force of it. He brought me to the edge, dragging my very spirit right to the surface, and stopped. I begged him to keep going, to hit harder.

"No, my lovely one. Much as I admire my handprints on your flesh, you have reached your limit."

I whined in protest, arching my back. "I want you to destroy me!"

Rafael laughed softly and gathered me up. "You do not. I know my strength, dove. Any more and you will have lasting injury. Enough."

He arranged me face-down on the pillow with my battered ass in the air. Moving between my thighs, the heat of his breath along my throbbing clit was almost enough to push me over. He paused, blowing gently on my vulva. I cursed and writhed, grabbing fistfuls of the sheets and rocking backward, trying unsuccessfully to push his face into my crotch. Even if he bit me and rent my flesh in that moment, I would keep begging. Finally, he plunged his tongue into me. I orgasmed immediately, bucking against his mouth as I cried out. The force of it made tears spring to my eyes.

He squeezed my ass, and the bruises throbbed. "I doubt you have learned a single lesson."

Only inarticulate sounds left my throat.

He coughed another laugh and nuzzled my inner thigh. "How many more times shall I make you orgasm? Nine, I think. To start."

I lost count. Relentless in his hunger, Rafael brought me to climax over and over, barely allowing me to catch my breath before starting again. As ever, he held himself back, focused solely, frustratingly, on my pleasure. No matter how I pleaded for his cock. Along with his tongue, he slid fingers deep into my cunt, stretching me to capacity. I shattered around him. When my legs trembled with fatigue, he flipped me over and continued. Just before the ultimate peak of ecstasy, I had a lucid, very unwelcome, and practical thought.

"Did you put a dampening field on this room? For—*mmph*

keep doing that! For sound?”

He glanced up from between my thighs with an absolutely evil grin. “No,” he said, and thrust his tongue deep into me with a guttural roar that vibrated my clitoris so hard I immediately came screaming.

Rafael stretched out beside me, taking me in his arms. As I lay nestled against his chest, spent, he rubbed my ass to soothe away the worst of the damage. Stroking my back, combing his fingers through my hair. Safe, secure. Home.

I almost choked when the frantic pounding on the door started. “Oh gods, they think you’ve slain me!”

“Haven’t I?” he purred, pleased with himself.

“Wicked beast!” Swatting his hard shoulder with a laugh, my hand stung like I’d slapped a rock. “I am unharmed,” I called, pitching my voice to the guards outside.

An anxious voice called back, “Are you sure?” Lámirië. Crow, I’d need to come up with a sufficient apology for her later.

“Quite.” I tried to stifle my giggles.

“Ah, uh, sorry to bother—”

“*FUCK OFF!*” Rafael bellowed, rattling the door on its hinges, and I heard the guards scrambling to get away. I collapsed in helpless laughter, clutching my aching ears.

I would have skipped back to the bedchamber I shared with Celebel if my ass hadn’t been so sore. Right away, I should have known something was off. He stared out the far window into the night sky, hands clasped behind his back. I, however, was too delirious in the afterglow of a veritable storm of orgasms to notice.

“Hellloooo, Starshine,” I sang, approaching him with a sway in my hips. “Guess where I’ve been?”

“I know. The whole damned fortress knows,” he said slowly, in a voice gone frosty.

“You’re angry?” I was stunned. “Are you upset that I fucked

him without asking permission first?" I'd been expecting him to be interested in, or even aroused by, my liaison. As he had indicated before.

"Do not be silly." Celebel turned to me. "Cúraniel, how could you be so foolish as to lie with him unshielded? I just sent the captain of the guard away!"

I'd never heard him sound so distant and imperious. So utterly, judgmentally elvish.

"I presumed he would have a dampening field among his wards. I didn't think—"

"Precisely!"

I stopped in my tracks at the anger blazing in his eyes.

"I am utterly drained from assuaging the others. Peace between the Dragon and the court is tenuous and requires the most delicate diplomacy to maintain. That balance is shaken, perhaps broken, through this act of negligence," he hissed. He had pressure, yes, but he'd hardly spoken of it to me. The sudden turn knocked the breath from my lungs. "The previously quiet whispers about you will become confident voices. Your detractors will grow and be emboldened to work openly against us. How much more difficult will our lives become now, all because you were thinking with your cunt instead of your head?"

"How fucking *dare* you!" My shock bled instantly into anger. "There is no dampening field over our own chambers, nor have you ever mentioned one! Of course Rafael can hear us, but that hasn't bothered you one bit. How can you ask of him what you yourself were not willing to provide? How *dare* you try to yoke me when the expression of my love for him inconveniences you!"

"Cúraniel, focus." He gestured to an ear, the motion sharp. "Everything he does is calculated. He left out the dampening field intentionally, knowing your cries of pleasure would sow chaos and apply pressure on our relationship. And you walked right into it. He *used* you, can you not see it? I have tried my best to offer him grace and am thanked with nothing but his scheming!"

"No. No, Celebel." I was defiant in my fury. "We should not

be made smaller by the limited minds of petty social climbers! You are perfectly happy to take advantage of my longing for Rafael, to take advantage of his might, when it suits you. And yet you still insist on treating him as lesser. I have waited *years* to reconnect with my Dragon, to forge true peace with him, and you would steal my joy for hateful pissants. I should not have to hide my love for my fucking *soulmate*, just as we do not hide ours!"

"Should? No. We *should* not have to care what the court thinks. We *should* not be fighting a senseless war. We *should* not have to hide anything, but here we are, in this reality. Every influence works against our relationship, every institution wishes to dissolve it, almost every friend questions it, whether quietly or openly. That pressure will only amplify now. I feel alone in my fight to love you, Cúraniel. What hurts me, though, is feeling unconsidered by you in that fight. It feels as if I will be forced to choose between you and everything I was raised with."

"Then *do* it!" Tears of helpless rage streamed down my face. "Choose as I did! I left the court long before you were a twinkle in your grandmother's sky, little star. Society was horseshit then and it is no different now. Nothing is forcing you to be here, whatever you may think. Choose! Be untethered! Run away with me and forget all the pressures weighing on your heart! Or perhaps I shall. Rafael's offer to spirit me away still stands! He would burn the world for me and all its people with it. You refuse to even stand up to some petty, small-minded gossip."

"Cúraniel, I—" Celebel's words were soft, suddenly caught out.

"Choose, coward," I demanded. "I gave up my entire life for you."

"I, I cannot abandon our people in our time of need. You of all people can appreciate—"

I stared him down, boring into him with all the rising fury and outrage I could muster. The air shivered with dread, witchlights dimming around us. The sudden weakness and uncertainty I saw there threatened to break me, and I made my own choice. Turning and storming out of the room, I slammed the door behind me.

Part 3

Chapter 34

A short time later I was rapping at the Dragon's door and valiantly fighting back tears. I'd kept a tight rein on my connection to Rafael. The last thing I needed was for him to go after Celebel. Much as I wanted his comfort, I didn't trust his temper. Wandering about the unwelcoming fortress hadn't calmed my heart, nor even digging my bare feet into what little grass remained. Normally, that type of grounding worked wonders for my steadiness. Not this time. I needed his arms around me.

The door swung open at some nonverbal command. Rafael still reclined on the bed, writing in a journal. He'd put his shirt back on. At the look on my face, he sat up immediately, flinging the journal aside.

"My dove, what has happened?"

Always ready to fight. At least it was on my behalf, but I had no emotional fortitude to intervene. I shook my head and climbed into the bed next to him, pulling open the laces of his shirt and burying my face in his chest. He held me, gently kissing the top of my head, but his hands tensed.

"That fucking flower-eater has upset you." A growl rose, tremoring through me. I shook my head again; I couldn't allow him even a hint of permission to wreak his havoc or there would be no return for us.

"Please, I just need comfort." I sniffled in spite of my best efforts. "Will you pull a dampening field around us? I've never been able to manage it properly."

Rafael grumbled, but did as I asked. Wrapping his long, nimble dragon's toes around my feet, he held them, reminding me of all the times he'd done it in my bower. An odd gesture that I found terribly endearing. He once told me it was because my feet were always cold and he wanted to keep them warm—an excellent way to get anything he wanted out of me. He hummed a melody low in his throat as he held me, the thrumming vibrations soothing me into a half-dreaming state.

Morning rays gave his skin a golden burnish by the time I stirred.

"Tell me what happened." He gently brushed a strand of hair from my face.

"Try to listen without getting angry?" I looked up at him.

He sighed and stroked my cheek with the back of his hand, lips compressing into a thin line.

I looked away again. Easier not to meet his eyes. "I had an argument with Celebel. Evidently those guards weren't the only ones who heard you and me."

Rafael snorted. "What of it?"

"Focus your ears, please. Celebel was upset with me. He said that because I hadn't thought of a dampening field before we made love, I did not consider the impact it would have on him. Already the nobles had shown disdain for his relationship with me based purely on rumors. Now they'll truly have the fuel to undermine him. He claims you did this on purpose, using me to humiliate him, and that I should have expected it." The tears came again and I scrubbed angrily at my cheeks.

Rafael lifted my chin up to look in my eyes. A wildfire burned in his, barely contained.

"Are you ashamed of me?" His voice was carefully neutral.

"Of course not! I love you. You are my soulmate and I should not have to hide that."

"Then why should you and I censor ourselves? *Celebel* has certainly never bothered." He spat the name like a curse.

"I pointed that out. Unfair, that he hasn't used a dampening field on the chambers I share with him and yet expected it of you. Without ever expressing as much, I assume?"

A muscle twitched in his jaw as he clicked his teeth together, a habit of frustrated annoyance. All the answer I needed.

"I understand the need for caution." I twisted the pearl strands in my hands, the shimmering nacre flashing in the sunlight.

"The court is difficult to navigate at the best of times, but they are no fools. No one who witnessed the way you danced with me would mistake that for anything other than what it was."

"Hrrm. You may not always agree with my requests, but have I ever asked you to change yourself? Have I ever demanded that you edit yourself to be more socially acceptable to my people?"

"You have not. You've only taught me the particulars of your culture."

"Then who *the fuck* is he to make such demands?" Rage simmered in his eyes. "Do you think I know nothing of his little 'welcome home' orgy? Has he ever, even once, paused to consider my position? My people have raised no outcry over my involvement with someone they consider well-spoken prey. Flaunt that disrespect and it all changes." The growl in his voice raised the fine hairs on my arms. "Does he understand just how many drakes I would have to kill if you had not bowed out?" The threat hung between us.

I attempted to breathe evenly in spite of the growing knot in my chest. "I know how hard this is for you to hear, and I truly do not mean to be hurtful, but I love Celebel. I love him, Rafael. Just as I do you. I know you think he's some pretty boy dalliance that I'll tire of eventually, but please hear me. Just as much as you are my soulmate, so is he, and I am perpetually pulled in two. I wish with all my heart that things were not so complicated. If only you could speak with him, work things out—"

Rafael exhaled slowly. Aimed at the ceiling, his breath shimmered with heat. He really was trying hard to contain his wrath.

"That… may be so, but still does not answer my question. Who *the fuck* is he to demand that you diminish any part of yourself for his comfort? To demand that you deny *me*, when *I* have made accommodations for that… hrrm…" The clicking of his teeth grew louder.

"Will you at least try to talk—"

"No," he said bluntly.

"Rafael, please."

"I said no." The message in his flinty eyes was clear: he considered Celebel fortunate to still draw breath. Riled as he was, I didn't want to cause an incident, and backed off.

I sighed and rubbed my achy forehead. "I understand his concern, though. Unfair as it is that he didn't first extend a gesture of his own, Celebel is not wrong. This will absolutely make both of our lives in court more difficult."

"Again, my offer stands to take you away from here. I will claim you as my mate, Cúraniel."

Gods, it was tempting. I caressed his saturnine face, tracing his arched brows, the bridge of his long, hooked nose, the bow of his lips, the slight cleft of his chin. "And then what, my Dragon? You'll secret me away in some far-flung castle and feign that I'll never need my other soulmate again? That I won't slowly shrivel and diminish and die in his absence? As though the other drakes won't try to use me as leverage against you? You cannot claim that it would be an easier life. Remember that I chose to come here for a reason."

He looked away, staring over my head out the window. "I cannot see you hurt. I will not."

"It is a part of life, you know that. How many times have you yourself hurt me, and yet I survive? I am not some fragile doll made of spun glass."

"Oh, my dove, but you are. Your body is too delicate, far too easy to harm. If you fought only humans, I would not say so, however…" He gripped my arm and I suddenly understood. For the first time, real fear flashed in his eyes. Not of his past terrors, but for me, for my safety.

I stretched up and kissed the corners of his mouth. "I know you will protect me, and I vow not to be foolish with my well-being. As much as I may control such things."

He shifted me in his arms, laying me on my back and cradling my head in the crook of his elbow. "My strength is yours, always. Before you, I believed the only purpose for strength was to conquer, to fight, to take whatever I desired by force."

"Have I changed you so much, then? Did I diminish you?" I twisted my fingers into his curls, admiring the texture and color.

"No, my dove, you merely taught me new ways to use such strength. I have grown because of you. Never before have I wished to protect another, nor have I concerned myself with others' opinions. I have lived a long, long time in complete solitude, but for the first time in all these years, I am not alone." His eyes were bright with emotion, voice tight. "I was a great fool to run from your love. The very moment I realized the extent of that foolishness was the moment you finally *rightfully* reached your limits and left me. And now here you are, in constant danger, in another man's bed, and *he* wishes to change *you*?" He closed his eyes with a deepening scowl and I kissed him again.

"Recall that Celebel and I have known each other barely a season, with the added pressures of war and the disapproval of courts and dragons alike. It took you almost a century to overcome your own foolishness, as you put it. I beg you for similar leeway; I am as trapped by fate as either of you."

He response by covering my body with his, wrapping his long limbs around me as though daring me to break free. "You are my dove," he growled. "Mine!"

"I am," I agreed. "The incident with the guards *was* hilarious, though."

"It was." With that catlike smile, he kissed my forehead.

I remained ensconced in Rafael's room for several days, emerging only for food and necessities. The quiet space helped me process my complex emotions, including my utter unpreparedness for the reality of the court in my current state. I'd lived by my own whims for so long that abiding by the rules of others stifled me almost beyond what I could bear.

Along a different melody, I didn't want to cause Celebel's downfall with my shortsightedness. After so much upheaval, the new distance between us stretched me thin almost immediately. The Night Mother offered me no insight on how to balance the needs of my diametrically opposed soulmates without losing myself.

The Dragon lingered most of the time, disappearing twice on whatever mysterious dragon business he always got up to. Probably more arguing with Feanim about metal. When Rafael was around, I made it a point to keep in constant physical contact with him. His solid body and stifling heat comforted me. I relished in his maintained calm, wanting to make it last as long as possible.

I talked him into reclining on the bed while he wrote in his journals so that I could more easily drape myself across him. He stroked my hair with his right hand as he scribbled away with his left, propping the journal on one knee.

"Why do you write so much?" With his flawless memory, it seemed redundant to take constant notes.

"I enjoy writing and archives are useful," he said. "I do not need drawings to remember your face either and yet." He shrugged, the movement rippling down his body.

"Didn't seem like you were too focused on my face in most of those."

He tapped my lips with the feather of his quill. "Happy little distraction, I need to finish this for the morning."

"What happens tomorrow?" I stretched, trying to see the journal page. He tilted it to me, showing neat columns of numbers and some quick, labeled drawings of blades.

"More testing. This is a record of the temperatures and duration of the various flames used on moranga, and how it behaves with each."

"Ah, boring charts for Feanim, I see. Wake me when you're drawing pornography again." I yawned. "Or at least translating something interesting."

The Dragon rumbled something like a laugh. Good enough

for me. I opened the laces at his throat to rest my cheek on his skin instead of the scratchy black wool of his shirt. He resumed stroking my hair as he wrote.

When I slept, I kept my back to his chest, wrapped in his powerful arms and listening to the slow rumble of his breath. It reminded me of my hill. Of familiarity. Safety.

I tried to read through his hoard of books to keep my mind off of my heartache. I learned absolutely nothing about tactics, a little about smithing, quite a bit more about various individualistic species such as kelpies and unicorns, and a lot about the history of dragons as viewed through an elvish lens. A certain Red Dragon was mentioned several times, with a long list of atrocities pinned to his name. Perhaps he used it as a checklist for accuracy. Or worse, inspiration.

The third evening Rafael surprised me by asking if I wanted to sit on the roof with him. I had barely agreed when he kicked his boots off and scooped me up under one arm. Opening the window, he scaled straight up the side of the fortress with ease. Once my heart stopped pounding, the view was incredible. It was an excellent spot for stargazing. Galaxies draped over the dim ridges surrounding the fortress like a sparkling mantle. He held me close in the windy night while I compared elvish names for the constellations with his own draconic versions. The soft whirring of night insects wreathed us in gentle sound.

It meant a lot that he tried so hard to keep my spirits up, especially as I could sense his resentment for Celebel simmering just below the surface. How long would this good behavior last?

"I have a gift for you." Rafael surprised me further with a small package.

"An actual gift or another hoard-extension?" I teased.

"Ungrateful wretch." He snatched it back out of my reach.

"No, no, let me see!"

He relented and let me take the package from his hand. It was wrapped in a lovely antique silk that snagged as I unwrapped it. My breath caught in my throat. It was a single, blood red, heavily keeled and serrated scale, in somewhat of a teardrop shape, and just under the length of my palm. None of his scales were quite so large in his scaled drake form. He'd plucked it from his full dragon form. How long had he been holding onto it?

On the hill, he'd taken studious care to prevent any part of his person from falling into another's hands. He'd never left even a single hair behind. This was a tremendous show of trust.

"It's so beautiful," I breathed, turning it over in my hands and examining the way the moonlight shone on the surfaces.

"It pleases you, then?" He seemed almost shy all of a sudden.

I threw my arms about his neck and kissed him fervently, being sure to keep a grip on the precious scale.

"It is pierced." He indicated the root of the scale where a small, perfect hole was drilled. "I would like for you to wear it around your neck, for protection. To keep me close."

"Protection in the literal or figurative sense?"

He cupped my hands around it. "Can you feel my flame?"

Closing my eyes, I concentrated. The scale grew warm in my hand.

His voice was at once far away and rooted deep within me. "Pull it around you, like a cloak."

I pulled at that warmth, and heat *whooshed* around me. Opening my eyes, I gasped at the dancing wall of flame now surrounding us. Atavistic fear warred with fascination.

"You spoke to me of sharing power between soulmates. You could always do this," he said, with a wry smile. "The scale merely provides a focal point. And a cutting edge, should you need one."

All that time, he'd recognized the connection between us, after all. I pushed those thoughts aside to examine later. "This is the sweetest gift you could ever give me. I will wear it with pride." Fuck the court.

He produced a fine braided cord of what I initially thought was deep red silk. As he threaded the scale, fastening it at the nape of my neck, I realized the cord was made of his own hair. Of course. His hair would be sturdy enough not to be worn away by one of his own scales. The enormity of the gesture overwhelmed me.

"One other request," he ventured, still self-conscious.

"Anything." I beamed. And hoped I wouldn't regret my word choice.

"When… when you are with *him*, be sure to take it off. I cannot bear…" He could not meet my eyes, turning his face into the moonlight that limned his profile. *He does have a noble face,* I thought, perhaps a bit moon-eyed myself.

"Oh, my love, I would not disrespect you like that." I stroked his hair, careful not to tangle my fingers in the loose curls.

The sadness was palpable in his next words. "I know you are readying to go back to him. I can feel the shift in you. I… wanted you to have a piece of me."

"You have been so good to me these past few days. I wish it were always so easy between us."

"We can still leave this place." He glanced at me from the corner of his eye.

"You're never going to give that up, are you."

"Would you?" He arched a brow.

I kissed his cheek. "Who do you think they hate more these days, you or me?"

"Me, but you are a close second."

He let me push him down onto his back as I climbed over him and straddled his waist. I pulled my blouse off so he could better admire his gift. All signs of self-consciousness fled. Concentrating again, I pulled his flames around us, and his eyes lit with fierce desire. His hands rose to heft my breasts. The garnet scale stood out against my skin, like a blood spot.

"A cutting edge, eh?" I hefted the scale. "Will it cut you?"

"Yes," the Dragon rumbled. "Carve me into portions if it pleases you."

"Would you—" Before I could finish my request, he spun

up a dampening field around us with a humid buzz. I nodded my gratitude and drew the edge of the scale down the back of his hand, careful to avoid the tendons.

He huffed. "Use more pressure."

"Take your shirt off," I countered.

He flashed teeth at me, briefly, before cooperating. I enjoyed the way he moved under me, clamping my thighs around him. His hands found their purchase again, squeezing my breasts just shy of bruising, rolling my tight nipples with his thumbs. I squirmed over him, slicking his belly with my need. The urge rose to slice away the leather wrapping his powerful thighs, encasing that delicious cock, and I shoved it back down. Perhaps someday he would indulge me.

Leaning into his hands for a moment, I lifted the cord over my head, careful not to snag it on my ears. With a sharp motion, I sliced the scale across his forearm. A thin, steaming line appeared, and he rumbled encouragement. I traced the line of his pecs with the serrated edge, pressing just hard enough to part the skin, but not enough to bite deep. His lips parted as he watched my face, relaxing his grip to allow my free movement. Using the scale, I outlined the dense muscles of his abdomen the same way, taking care not to dip below his waist. Steam rose with the beads of blood.

"Shall I draw a complete portrait of this beautiful body?" I hefted the scale, dragging it across his clavicles.

He hissed approval, blood plinking onto the tiled roof in a counterpoint. From somewhere within, near the source of our connection, his power held against his body's urge to heal immediately.

I bent and kissed the notch at the base of his throat, heedless of his burning blood. The stinging bite into my skin only heightened me. He crushed me against him, smearing me in crimson, in heat. Sitting us up, he pulled my head back by my hair. I cut his cheek, and he grinned wickedly. That long tongue slid out, licking the blood away. Gods, this man would be the death of me. I moaned at the sight and ground my hips against him. Gripping my jaw, he forced my mouth open and shoved his tongue into it. I sucked hard, the tang and familiar spice of his blood strong. Did the overwhelming urge to consume him come from him or from me?

Rafael bit my lip, just hard enough to pull a drop of my own blood and mingle it with his. I threw myself into the kiss, digging the point of the scale into the thick muscle of his shoulder. Rocking my hips against him couldn't quite get the angle I needed to provide relief for my aching clit. Pulling back, he considered me for a moment, then lifted me off of his lap.

"What are you—" I started, and he turned, putting his back to me. That odd line of extra muscle along his spine flexed, and his wings burst forth.

I immediately clapped myself to the Dragon's back, running my hands along the appendages as he stretched them. He rarely let me touch his wings. They proved much more flexible than I expected, sweeping back and scooping me up from underneath. The clawed thumb joints met just under my dripping cunt. I barely had time to cry out before he pushed them both into me at the same time, stretching me wide. Not as deep as the usual penetrative methods he employed, but no less intense.

I stabbed into the meat of his shoulder blade in retaliation, and he snarled at me, grinning. Encouraged, I rode the wing joints and sliced along the lines of his back. For every drop of blood I spilled, he encouraged me, making sounds somewhere near ecstasy. His talons screeched along the roof tiles, flattening my ears.

The voice given to his gratification, his expression of coming undone, drove me to a frenzy. Raising and dropping my body onto the wing joints, I pressed my breasts into his back, biting the short tip of his ear.

"I never get to see you this way," I panted, reaching around him to cup his pecs. "I love the sounds you make. Gods, you make me wild with need."

He grabbed the hand with the scale and cut deep into the

flesh of his breast. Blood sheeted down his body and he sighed. "Sing for me. Sing away my darkness." The dark burr in his voice thrummed straight into my cunt.

The wing joints thrust upward, hard, working in counterpoint. The orgasm burst forth, roaring free, and I cried out, burying my face in his hair. I scratched haphazard lines across his chest as the waves took me, clawing with my useless nails and scrabbling with the scale. Jerking and shuddering, I clung to him as he thumped those wing claws into me with enough force to knock me off my feet. I think I screamed his drake name. I may have even pronounced it correctly.

He took pity on me and finally withdrew the claws, twisting back and pulling me into his arms. His wings wrapped me in a leathery blanket. Keeping eye contact with me, he licked my juices off of the wing claws. Then he bent and kissed me.

"We are both perverts," I said against his lips. Rafael made a contented rumble.

Chapter 35

The next time I slunk into the kitchens, Celebel waited for me. Dark circles pooled under his eyes and his normally sleek, perfect hair dulled in its disarray.

"May I speak with you?" he asked tentatively.

Seeing him again made my heart clench so hard it seemed my skin was on too tight. I wasn't prepared, but decided against my urge to take a note from Rafael's book when confronted with too much emotion. Enough of being diminished.

"Lead the melody." I held out a hand. He took it cautiously, checking my face for permission, and led me away from the kitchens. I snagged a fruit tart on the way out.

Instead of taking me to our chambers, he surprised me by going to an open balcony that overlooked the stables and training field. Below, Feanim and Rafael traded off exercises with a moranga blade. The Dragon demonstrated a move, then handed the blade to Feanim. The **Duedellen** attempted to copy it and Rafael snapped at him, snatching the sword back. This seemed to be an ongoing process. I let myself be absorbed in their back-and-forth argument, stalling. How long would it take the big drake to kick his training partner into the dirt? My ribs twinged in sympathy from old memories.

Celebel sighed like a rusty gate in a breeze, and I turned to him.

"My love, I must apologize from the depths of my being." His eyes shone bright with emotion. "I should never have spoken to you that way. I do not wish to diminish your light; let me never become the kind of man who sees something beautiful and crushes it down into a trophy on a shelf. That was never my intention."

I looked deep into his eyes, seeing the truth there, and the hurt that remained.

"Explain your intention then." I resisted the urge to call to the Dragon below. Had Celebel chosen this place deliberately so Rafael would see our reconciliation? The thought worsened my discomfort.

"I wished… I wished only for you to understand the impact that your actions have on me, what they mean for our shared life here. To consider me in the choices you make, that I might always be on your mind. I felt disregarded, and I lashed out because of it." Celebel's ears drooped. His voice was contrite.

"I understand your concern, but not the strength of your reaction. If it had truly mattered so greatly, why would you not lead by example and extend Rafael the same consideration you demanded?" My desire for peace threatened to engulf my questions if I didn't force them all out.

Celebel blew out a breath, fingers drumming on the balcony rail. "Truthfully, I allowed myself to funnel all of my pent up frustration from myriad sources at a safe target. I never should have done so." His eyes dropped.

"It took me aback, attempting to share my joy with you, only to be named selfish and a fool. I loved Rafael *first*." I bit my lip to stop the tears. "How many dozens of years have I pined, longing for him to mingle emotion with physicality? For you to call it a cheap manipulation hurts in a way that is difficult to articulate."

"I hear the cruelty of my words now." Celebel bowed his head, stretching back from the rail. "I should have chosen a different approach. Lámirië told me there were elves in a panic all over Férioth after hearing your cries. Many assumed Rafael had attacked and killed you, and the rest would be next. I had to use all my spirit to calm the masses after that confrontation with you; I even borrowed an amplifier from Feanim."

It explained some of his haggard appearance. I took a deep breath. "That is truly unfortunate. And yes, Rafael was surely well aware of the effect he would have. I hold that both of our perspectives are true. My influence extends much farther than I am accustomed to these days, and I apologize for not recognizing it as such. So, how do we move forward from here?"

Celebel's fingers danced on the rail. He did not meet my eyes. "Do you truly wish me to abandon my position?"

I sighed. "No. That was ill-considered. Much as I long to flee back to my simpler life, no one can outrun time. Even Rafael admitted the war would have reached my hill eventually."

He nodded. The sun picked up the subtle thread of gold woven through his rosy pink coat. Unusual colors for him, though it gave his skin a false blush of health. "The obvious truce involves each of us utilizing a dampening field whenever we're intimately involved with you."

"At a minimum." I braced myself. "I wish to announce my relationship with him. Formally, before the court. As you have with me."

He pressed a hand over his eyes with a heavy sigh. "What you're suggesting would require—"

"Courage? Fortitude? From what I can tell, Rafael has made no attempt to keep my arrangement a secret from the other drakes."

He hugged himself, mouth pursed in thought. It would have been endearing under other circumstances. "I mislike where this could lead, but I cannot command you otherwise."

I'd much rather handle the blowback than suffer the anxiety gnawing at my belly, but I understood his position.""Rafael confirmed that if we'd taken part in that orgiastic gathering, it would have been catastrophic in ways I didn't predict." Celebel's hand lifted from his brow, eyes flashing. "If the other drakes found out, it would have been a bloody fight to maintain his status. You aren't the only one with politics to navigate or people at risk."

On the field, the Dragon moved with his usual predatory grace. Feanim's movements grew harried, defensive.

I frowned. "Tell me, did you pick this spot to ensure Rafael will see us together? He has been very kind to me these last days and I am loath to part with him in such a rare good mood. I won't have him hurt again."

My elvish soulmate blanched. "No, love. I wished to have

you join me in this place where I have been coming to observe him from some semblance of a safe distance." His gaze shifted back to the training ground. "Understanding your connection to him begins with trying to understand him personally, on whatever terms I may find."

"Oh? And what have you observed?" My ears twitched.

"That he bristles at my gaze, but is too stalwart, or proud, perhaps, to turn away. His energy resists my contemplation like spiny thorns repulsing touch. He is guarded beyond anyone I have ever encountered." Celebel frowned. "Also, his stature is difficult to describe. Even far below, he seems to tower over us still."

"So you've discovered he's tall, spiky, and does not care for you. Not much of a revelation." Sarcasm laced my voice, despite my intentions.

"Indeed. I require a harmonizing voice to soften his defenses. If you trust my sincerity." He twined his fingers in mine, a beseeching gesture. His eyes were as blue as the sky after a passing rain. My heart fluttered, longing to return to him. Even that simple contact swelled my spirit.

I closed my eyes and exhaled slowly. "All right, stop soul-gazing, pretty boy. I believe you, and I should have been more thoughtful. I never intended to hurt you or make anything more difficult. Please recall that I haven't had to consider social norms since before the elders left, and even then I often failed to follow them adequately. I shall try my best from now on." I took a deep, steadying breath. "And if you ever disrespect me like that again, I'll *ask* him to eat you."

Celebel looked out just in time to see Rafael lobbing the Duedellen across the training field like a javelin. Ah, there it was. Celebel winced.

"Point taken. And yes, I spoke deplorably to you. I hate myself for it. Can you forgive me? Will you?"

"I never wish you to hate yourself. We all have moments where we act poorly. I've certainly had my share." Pausing, I asked my heart what she wanted, and reached for Celebel. He wrapped me in a crushing embrace. We kissed for a long while, tangled together in the sun. When we parted, he gestured toward his tousled braids.

"It seems I am no longer interested in properly maintaining my hair without your assistance. Perhaps you could join me in my chambers to help?" He suggested with a twinkle in his eye.

"I haven't fully forgiven you yet, but I no longer wish us to be parted," I said. Good enough for him.

When I glanced back over my shoulder at the training field, Rafael had stopped his training and watched me intently. Feanim made demands for his attention, and based on the increasing drama of the Duedellen's gestures, grew frustrated at being ignored. The Dragon's mournful sadness tugged at our connection.

"Rafael truly has been on his best behavior while I was away from you," I said as we walked. A bit of a jab, but mostly I wished to be honest. Rafael had kept me sane, and he deserved credit for it. "Speaking openly about his feelings, keeping his temper in check; the growth is nothing short of amazing. I wish you could see that side of him. He can be surprisingly sentimental. Even carried me up to the roof to stargaze and gave me this." I pulled the scale from under my robe and it flashed in the witchlights.

Celebel's ears twitched. I could tell it bothered him, but he made a valiant effort to be receptive. "Trying to win you over, eh? I suppose he's the favorite currently."

"At the moment, yes, but I have a feeling you're about to try and win me back," I teased, and he gave me a sly grin. I tucked the scale talisman into my robe pocket and took Celebel's hand. "Some of this stems from Rafael's desire to pull me away from here. I am not such a fool as to accept his gifts uncritically, or believe he will always behave as well as he has recently. I know my Dragon. Let him feel cornered and witness how quickly that changes. But I am grateful for the peace with him. It gives me hope for eventual reconciliation."

Celebel kissed the backs of my hands. I kissed his. We peeled our clothes off by the time we got to the antechamber. A dampening field's familiar buzz shivered my skin as we entered. Good. Except, no, something sounded off…

Ah, we were not alone.

"Celllebellll, come and join us," a singsong voice called out from the bedchamber.

Celebel's face went slack with shock. A perfectly matched, perfectly naked set of fair-skinned high elves, with long golden locks and equally golden eyes, lounged on our bed; male and female Astolar bookends. The same ones who'd wailed at his feet in the camp.

The woman looked me up and down with a disgusted expression. "My lord, surely you cannot prefer her attentions to our own. You know how good we can make you feel!"

"Is this how you've been entertaining yourself in my absence?" I asked drolly.

Celebel immediately raised his hands in supplication. "No, I swear to you—"

"Relax, Starshine," I laughed. "Rafael is the jealous one, not I."

The golden man climbed off the bed, shouldering past me to reach for Celebel. "My lord, let us remove this filthy *monsterfucker* from your presence and show you true pleasure," he leered. "Surely you no longer desire this nameless one for a consort after all of Férioth heard her coupling with that *animal*."

Rage whipped through me, hot and furious. I grabbed the man's ear, wrenching hard, and using the leverage to pull him into a headlock. Just as Rafael had once shown me. The man screeched in mingled horror and pain, flailing helplessly to dislodge my grip. I bustled him over to the window, unlatched it, and neatly boosted him over the sill and out. He shrieked like a dying peacock, the dramatic fool. The fall wouldn't hurt him, being only a single story above the gardens and a nice cushy bed of spiraling bridalwreath.

It would do wonders for an attitude adjustment, however.

His female counterpart screamed and flew at me. Celebel caught her, pulling her arm behind her back in a firm hold. She screeched and thrashed in his grip, hurling invective. I appreciated her creativity, having no family name to curse.

"You both deserve that treatment for the disrespect you have shown tonight." He marched her to the door. "Get out of my sight and never return! You are hereby banned from attending court." He shoved her, protesting, into the hall and slammed the door in her face.

Panting, Celebel turned back to me with new regard in his eyes. "Remind me never to cross you. Did *he* teach you that ear-wrenching move?"

I grinned wickedly. "He surely did. Our taboos mean nothing to a drake."

"I want to reiterate that I did nothing with those—"

"Celebel, my love, it does not matter. Truly. We can discuss it later if we must. Now, where did we leave off?" I slid my arms around his waist and kissed his neck. He melded to me instantly.

"You are a wonder. Have I said that recently? Now, show me everywhere the Dragon has touched you. I need to reclaim my territory," Celebel said in a husky voice.

"Oh, it's like that, is it? I approve of this game." I drank in the sight of his naked body; his supple muscle, lithe figure, the flawless pale skin. His beautiful, hard cock. I kissed and bit his luscious lips, running my hands through his hair, down his back, and over his shapely, round buttocks.

"You have such a nice ass." I grabbed two handfuls.

He laughed and flung me back onto our bed.

I sat up and cupped my breasts. "You'll want to start here."

He eagerly complied. Our bodies fit together perfectly in our ecstasy.

Fucking until we both shook from exertion, we rested briefly and began anew. The day came and went. We focused only on each other. Making peace with Celebel renewed my soul. We anointed every piece of furniture in those chambers with our bliss, then the floors in each room, and finally landed in the copper tub.

He held me against his chest while I splashed my toes in the jasmine-scented water.

"Did I miss any spots?" he murmured against my neck.

"I think not, but you may always check again."

His tone turned serious. "I do wish *he* wasn't so gods damned hostile toward me. Based on your stories, your Dragon seems quite the attentive lover despite his, ah, limitations. Such a shame that we must be at war instead of working in tandem for your pleasure."

A thrill ran through me and I glanced wistfully over his shoulder at the giant, empty bed. A bed that could easily accommodate Rafael's frame, with room to spare.

"I quite agree." I wriggled closer, pressing my body against his, and he cheerfully complied with my unspoken wishes.

A furious pounding on the door startled us away from our intertwined relaxation. Feanim's voice pierced the peace.

"Celebel, quit fucking her and get out here. We need to discuss our next moves," he shouted. "I've been waiting all day!"

Celebel rolled his eyes and gently disentangled himself, splashing water over the side of the tub. "My apologies, love, I have tarried for too long."

"Not long enough. I like it when you tarry." I tugged at his cock. "You're very talented in your tarrying."

He laughed and swatted my hand away as he dried off and pulled on his trousers. I stretched lazily, admiring the view.

I reached the war room just as a furious Rafael dragged a naked, screaming Lachanaur girl in by the hair. He tossed her at Feanim's feet and stormed off before I could ask questions. The girl dissolved into hysterical, hiccupping tears. Rather than comfort her, Feanim had the utter gall to look annoyed.

"What the fuck is happening here?" I demanded.

He scowled at me, and Celebel interrupted to explain. "Apparently, my *genius* companion decided that Rafael's moodiness could be rectified by throwing women at him."

Thunderstruck, I could only stare at Feanim in uncomprehending shock. The Duedellen sneered but would not meet my gaze.

"Are you fucking *mad?* You sent this poor girl to do what? *Seduce* Rafael?" I could scarcely believe it. Celebel had told me Feanim was callus, but this was an act of pure endangerment. "What if he had killed her? Given what he did to the last person who propositioned him uninvited, you are both fortunate to still draw breath. The fucking audacity."

The girl wailed. I kneeled, pulling her into my arms. "Oh, you poor thing. You must be terrified!" She clung to me, trembling, and I cradled her head against my shoulder. "Hush hush. None of this is your fault."

"I had to do *something*. Rafael has been in an utterly foul mood these past few days. I couldn't get him to focus on anything but *you*," Feanim snarled, unrepentant. "A fresh piece of ass would do him some good. Calm down, she was perfectly willing."

"*He* was not! But you didn't ask him, did you? No, you threw this poor unsuspecting girl straight into the path of his rage." My fury at Feanim's thoughtlessness nearly choked me.

"Am, am I *ugly*?" the girl stammered through her tears. "Is that why he was so angry?"

I would have laughed if she were not so distraught. Here was a strikingly beautiful young woman, barely into her majority, with long twists of gold-shot burgundy hair. Lengthy, lovely ears framed a heart-shaped face. Voluminous, shapely lips and large, dark eyes stood out from flawless, walnut-brown skin that stretched smoothly over a supple figure. More tears sparkled on her thick red lashes as she gazed at me with a quiver in her lower lip. Charms laced through her twists tinkled softly as she moved.

"No, little one, you are quite alluring and not at all the cause of his anger." I stroked her frightened face. "I assure you, your appearance is definitely not the issue here. Rafael is not like us. He does not give of himself easily, nor is he easily approached. I have a unique advantage. He is my soulmate, and we have built a slow history together. No, the fault is entirely with this thoughtless, blighting *shitheel*." I jabbed a finger at Feanim. "He wrongfully assumes everyone is replaceable. And he put you in danger with his carelessness."

Feanim snorted, and I ignored him.

"Lord Rafael could have simply said no," she sniffled, beginning to relax.

I made the connection between this girl's experience, and the twins in our chambers, catching Celebel's eye. The grim look on his face confirmed he had been thinking the same.

"He *should* have been mightily flattered. If he were anyone else, he would have been. Drakes are a testy lot. Come, lovely, let's get you a nice cup of tea and some soft clothing." I helped her to her feet, putting my coat over her shoulders, and she steadied herself on my arm. On the way out, I turned to Feanim and mouthed '*fuck you*' over my shoulder.

Celebel started in on his thoughtless compatriot as we made our slow way down to the kitchens. The door closed off their heated argument.

"Would you really have tried to bed him?" I asked, after I'd gotten her wrapped in warm blankets and ensconced in front of the hearth fire beside the main food preparation area. A serving youth brought over a tea service with earthen pots of herbs at my request.

"The Red Dragon? Y-yes, or so I thought. He is terrifying, but there is a certain mystique. A sensuality. The way you danced together... I like the way he moves." She looked at her feet.

"So do I," I laughed. "We have rarified taste, it would seem."

"My name is Carafindrien." Her voice brightened once she realized I was not angry with her.

"Cúraniel." I handed her a mug of rose and licorice root tea.

"I know. You are most beautiful, Lady Cúraniel." She reached to brush my lips.

I caught her hand and redirected it to her cup of tea. "Let's not borrow any more trouble today, and I carry no title." I gave her a wink and tug of the earlobe. "I already have more lovers than I can manage."

She wilted, the tips of her shapely ears dipping almost to her shoulders. "Never have I been refused, let alone twice in one day," she said, despairing.

"Oh, lovely Carafindrien, please do not take insult. Were I not so thoroughly entangled already, I would happily invite you into my bed." I kissed her lightly on the temple. "You have the misfortune of bad timing, that is all. Perhaps we can still be friends?"

She beamed at me. "I would like that. The way some others whisper about you seems terribly unfair. You've been kind to me." Blowing on her tea, her brows knit. "Is the Red Dragon truly your soulmate?"

"He is. You have no reason to grant me a boon, but please keep this knowledge to yourself for now."

Her dark eyes went wide as she signed assent. "You must be very brave. Did he react to you the same way?" She clutched at her tea as though it would shield her.

"You know, it was not so different. Rafael was truly horrible in the beginning! I will speak to him so that you need not fear. Feanim will bear the brunt of his wrath, and rightfully so."

"May I flirt with the Dragon?" She bit her lower lip, eyes sparkling with mischief.

I laughed. "You cheeky thing! I'd love to see him catch a good flirt from someone other than me, but alas. As he does not know how to manage such things, he'll react poorly again. I'll have to advise against it."

"May I flirt with you in front of him?" She wiggled her hips seductively, dropping the blankets from her shoulders.

I laughed harder. "I find your boldness grand, but he'll most definitely react badly, so please refrain. Drakes have different ways, and Rafael is quite possessive of me."

Carafindrien sighed with relief, leaning into me. "I have little enough influence in court, but I shall surely inform my friends of your kindness." She beamed. "You have an ally in me for life."

Chapter 36

Rafael's wrath hummed through our connection like a single discordant note struck over and over on a lute string. Predictably, he was out on the training field, flowing through forms, anger radiating off his body in waves. At least he hadn't gone off to break faces instead. Perhaps this was progress. The early morning light glowed on his hair gone to flame, and he was beautiful in his controlled fury.

"Dragon," I called out.

He finished a graceful swooping move and turned to me, his face a mask of disgust, eyes burning. "You witnessed it, then." The ever present growl in his voice moved to the forefront.

"I did. Fucking buffoonery from Feanim. Thank you for not harming that girl, it was not her fault. Please don't think ill of her, she did nothing to deserve any of this. She's a sweet thing, really, and very young. I have to give her credit for her taste." I looked him up and down with open appreciation.

"Only you would say so. As long as there are no repeat performances of stupidity, she is safe from me." Rafael joined me at the fence. "I hear you tossed a little bird of your own out of the window. A flightless bird, it would seem."

"You taught me that throw." I grinned.

"Ha! Well done." His answering grin was terrible, all jagged teeth and promise of death.

"I *was* paying attention during your lessons!"

He poked my arm with a blunted talon. "Time for more. How soft you have grown."

I spun away with a laugh. "You rotten beast. I'm not sparring with you when you're in such a mood. I have better sense than that!" Not to mention a lack of inclination to ruin my fine silks in the inevitable thrashing that would follow his idea of a lesson.

"Heavens witness how she spurns me!" He tossed his head

back to the sky with open arms.

"Stop being so dramatic. You just want to beat some revenge into me for spending so much time with Celebel."

"Tempting." He sobered then. "Battle is coming, my dove. Very soon. I would have you prepared."

"I doubt I'll ever be prepared to your standards."

'Cúraniel, will you join us in the war room?' Celebel's voice sounded in my mind. *'You will wish to be present for this.'*

I blinked in surprise, sending back assent and explaining to Rafael. He insisted on following me. Moving through the halls, I kept a slight distance from him. There were enough hostile glares as we passed. He rankled behind me and I sent soothing energy along our connection.

Feanim and Celebel sat at opposite sides of the room, tension humming between them. Araglin took up a position near Celebel. Rafael scowled horribly when he saw the Duedellen. I strengthened the soothing energies, and he acknowledged me with a sigh.

Just inside the doorway, a tall, slim, carved bone horn leaned against the wall. Its bell, a stylized boar's head with a tusked, open mouth, almost scraped the ceiling. Beside it stood a very familiar Lachanaur, with an androgynous pointed face, shorter ears than most elves, and a body taut with ropey muscle. The newcomer wore a longsword at the hip with practiced ease. The hair, though. That fiery hair had been cropped close to the scalp; a symbol of mourning.

"*Nemohee*," I squealed. Throwing all decorum to the wind, I also threw my arms about my friend. "Why did you cut your hair off?"

Nemohee grabbed me and spun me around, silver eyes flashing. "Moon Lady," þey bellowed back. "How the bugger did you get here?" I didn't miss the way þey deliberately ignored my question.

We nearly fell to the floor before þey finally set me back down. Briefly, under the cover of a cloak, þeir hands flashed,

"Much tell. Nothing good." My heart rate picked up, but I schooled my face to calm.

Sketching a perfunctory bow, þey tossed an arm over my shoulders before addressing the Consulate. "Melords, A've fetched yer blightin' horn." Nemohee paused, realizing no one but me followed þeir thick hillspeech accent. Enunciating carefully, þey repeated the words. "I've found your Carnyx of Calling, at great bloody cost to our company. I am the only survivor. The rest were taken or killed. If it please you, I'd dearly like a drink and to sleep through the next moon." *Taken?*

"Our great thanks for your service," Celebel replied. "Had I known your identity, I would have sent word sooner."

Araglin and Feanim moved to inspect the horn, the Duedellen running his hands over its surface. Rafael rumbled with interest, drawing Nemohee's eye.

Þeir shorter ears twitched wildly. "*What*? The Big Red Menace is here too? What kind of drinking party is this? *What* have I been missing?"

The Dragon arched a brow but acknowledged the address with a slight inclination of his head.

"You truly didn't notice all the drakes camped right outside?" I pointed out.

"Came in the back way, but I wouldn't have seen a stone giant if it knocked me head clean off the shoulders I'm so fecking done in. You're telling me there are *more* drakes here?"

"There's a whole bushel of them right outside the gates, rockhead!"

Nemohee's eyes went huge and þey pantomimed þeir head melting.

"What's this about drakes at the gates?" a gravelly voice said. Marron appeared in the doorway, taking up most of it with his bulky frame. I'd ignored his approach in my joy over my reunion, though he did not step lightly. We elves went silent. His ruby eyes flitted about the room, taking in the reactions. "Did I frighten you? I forget how sensitive you folk are. All those long ears perked up like alarmed rabbits."

None of us missed the prey reference.

Rafael rumbled with amusement and our ears shifted to him. "Not yet adjusted to my presence either, these," he said in draconian, to a snort from the green drake.

"Difficult as you are, Rraysth?" Marron replied in kind. My ears twitched with interest. So the drakes did push back against Rafael.

In elvish, my Dragon addressed the room. "Marron will join us at all future councils."

"Why didn't you clear this with us first?" Feanim shot Rafael a dirty look, ears flattened.

My only protest came at the overwhelming amount of masculine energy making all the major decisions. I didn't expect to miss Nimthil's presence, but the room felt very different without her. Otherwise, Marron made a positive addition.

The green drake rasped the backs of his scaly hands together, drawing attention. "Why did you enter our camp unescorted?" He stared down the much shorter elf. His posture didn't visibly change, but something hardened in those crimson eyes. "There are two Consuls. Why should we be limited to only one voice? When my mate joins us, we'll make a nice symmetry." He turned to me and grinned, lips stretching taut over his square face. "I'm the easy one. She's mixed red; they are all unquenchable, tempering fire."

Rafael snorted. I laughed, and the tension dissolved.

Celebel smoothly redirected the attention. "Nemohee has a report of utmost urgency, and this way you'll have it firsthand."

Marron raised a brow at the honorific, but said nothing.

My friend sobered at once, standing tall. Þeir freshly shorn hair stuck out at odd angles, like a sputtering candle. "I'll state this here as you all need to know it. As they're able, the Fomorians aren't raiding to kill. They're capturing elves, taking us alive whenever possible. I doubt it's for consumption or they'd tear into us on the field. I've proof that some of us live still, in their clutches."

Soft exclamations of shock ran through the gathered elves, myself included. Nemohee's statement confirmed my fears about the ambush. I looked to Rafael, and he gave me a blink.

'*Did you already know?*' I sent.

'*I did not wish to alarm you. The Consulate suspected as much. They chose not to make it common knowledge to prevent a panic in the flock.*'

"This the magic trumpet, I take it?" Marron appraised the Carnyx leaning against the wall.

"The very one," Nemohee said.

The green drake huffed acknowledgement.

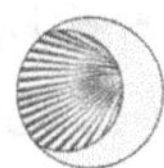

I drifted over to the library. It was compact, due to the limited space in the fortress, but well-appointed. Books lined graceful shelves of organic design up into the high vaulted ceilings, with vining ladders attached for easy access. Stained glass windows lit the rooms well, casting vivid shapes on the carpeted floors. Witchlights floated overhead, much safer than torches around the valuable collection. My whole body twitched with excitement at the free access to so much bounty.

I selected a beautifully illustrated history of the first elves and curled up on an overstuffed pouf, arranging my dress around me for maximum comfort. Swiftly, I lost myself in the reading, drawn in by the delicate watercolors and the author's fanciful flourishes.

Sometime later, a kick to the back of my pouf startled me into nearly dropping the book. Despite my sharp hearing, I'd always focused so hard when reading I often blocked out the rest of the world. I whipped around to Nemohee's face. There was a curious flatness to þeir normally bright eyes that I misliked.

"C'mon, back to my rooms. I've sommat to speak on," þey said. "You ken I've brought whiskey as well."

"Of course you've brought whiskey and *of course* you have

gossip." I gave a nervous laugh, sensing impending bad tidings. "All right, I'm coming."

I trailed after Nem, who nearly jogged along the halls on the way to þeir chambers, well-worn green and gold leathers creaking softly. Þeir freshly cropped hair bobbed about þeir head like a spray of flame, almost white at the roots and darkening to burgundy at the very tips. I'd always admired the unusual ombre effect of þeir hair, ever present regardless of length.

"I thought y'were tired," I teased.

Nemohee merely cast a look over one shoulder. Þey opened the door on modest but well-appointed quarters, with a small antechamber leading into a slightly larger bed chamber. There must have been a shared bathing space somewhere, as no wash room adjoined it. After grabbing a bottle and two glasses, þey plopped down on a rust-brown chaise and kicked off þeir dusty boots, sighing. I poured for the two of us and we clinked glasses before both tossing back the first draught in one great swallow.

"Phew, this one bites," I said. "It's been so long! Did you get my note?"

"Aye." A discomfiting silence stretched between us. Normally we chattered up a storm whenever we occupied the same space. Nemohee finally blew out a breath, rubbing a hand over þeir short hair. "May as well speak it, though it takes a bite of me every time."

"Nem, what has happened?" I leaned in.

Þey held my eyes for a long moment, then looked at þeir feet with a gusty sigh. "Cael was taken."

I sat bolt upright, ears flattening. "No! By the Fomorians?"

Þey nodded miserably. "He lives. I feel him still." Þey gestured over þeir chest. "But he is… changed, somehow. Twisted up inside. I cannot explain it. Tried to speak to him, the mindspeech, but it's hollering through mud. No sense to be made of it."

I poured another draught. "Gods, Nem, my heart breaks for you."

Þey'd never been so happy as when Cael first came into þeir life. Imagining Celebel taken in such a way shook me to the very core and my breath quickened. No wonder Nemohee had cut off þeir hair. Not a full shave, but an acknowledgement of loss.

"Nah, come now. He lives yet, gives me hope." The Lachanaur's ears twitched.

"How were you selected for such a dangerous mission?"

"Half leanan sidhe, eh? Needed someone with fae blood to find the Carnyx, and only fae blood can use it. It's a sidhe artifact and guarded by their spirit. Had to go underhill." The look on þeir face sang a melody of disgust. Sometimes I forgot about Nemohee's fae parentage until þey grinned and showed the exaggerated points of their canine teeth. "I could get us that far at least. We expected a scrap, but not the blighting flood of Fomorians that followed."

Þey sniffed and took another draught of whiskey. "Now, tell me about this fresh boy and how the auld beast took it? I confess, I always figured the Dragon would murder any contest. How did he wind up here with the both of you?"

I made a show of taking another great gulp of whiskey. Nem laughed in appreciation, a hollow, strained sound.

"That ill, eh?"

"Worse." I sat on a low settee. As þey listened to my tale, only moving to take the occasional swallow of whiskey, þeir brow gathered great storm clouds of worry. Especially at the mention of the ambush and all that followed.

"And you're positively certain that both are soulmates?"

"I am. When Celebel showed up bleeding to death at the base of my hill, of course I had to heal him."

Nemohee raised þeir silver eyes to the ceiling and tugged an earlobe. "Of course."

"Hush, you ken my code." The more we spoke, the more I lapsed into the comfortable hillspeech. It reminded me of home. "I healed him, and felt it straightaway, that spark, that powerful soul connection. I didn't want it to be true, didn't want the complication, but here we are. You ken how it feels, punctured straight through the heart." The vision of Celebel's eyes flitted through my mind.

"Aye." Nem looked down. I reached out, taking one callused hand in mine.

"Forgive me. If it's too painful to hear my concerns laid atop your own—"

Þey cut me off with a wave over þeir ears and a wan smile. "Nah, I did ask. I'm wanting to ken. I'm frankly shocked to see the auld Red Menace here, playing so nice. Truly would have expected a slaughter by now. Have you trimmed his claws then?"

"Frankly, I expected the same." I told þem of Rafael's reception at the court, and all that followed, finishing with, "He vowed he would not harm Celebel, lest I never speak to him again. He also offered to win the war for us if I would let him claim me as his mate."

Nem's eyes widened again in shock, a ripple effect that flowed down þeir strong shoulders. "And you agreed?"

"Nah, I said I would consider it. Surprisingly, he left off with that."

Þey whistled in appreciation. "I had my doubts afore, serious doubts, but he does pure love you."

"He does. I only wish it weren't so hard for him to simply *talk* to Celebel. Work things out. Celebel's perfectly willing, but it would take a miracle for Rafael to agree." I sighed, rubbing my forehead. Nem proffered the bottle of whiskey and I gratefully refilled my glass. "I'm grateful to have your voice in my ears. I needed just *one* person here not trying to either fuck or fight me!"

Nemohee howled with mirth, stamping the floor. Þey settled in and spoke on how þeir company had tracked down the Carnyx of Calling and the terrific fight that ensued. Animated with the telling, Nem dashed around the room, jumping on and off the furniture to illustrate the finer points of the battle. I laughed until tears flowed down my cheeks. Quite sure þeir strident voice carried through the walls, I hoped those quartered nearby found the same amusement in Nem's overwrought descriptions.

Þey were clearly using humor to mask the pain. Even apart from the shorn hair, I caught it in quiet moments; the dullness of eyes gone grey, the grim set of þeir shoulders, and a certain tension in þeir hands. Much as I wanted to draw þem out, I knew better than to prod at such a fresh wound.

In the end, Nemohee had barely escaped with both the horn and þeir life. Following those taken had proven to be too great a challenge; the Fomorians retreated to their mysterious lairs, sealing the ways behind them. Most of Nemohee's days since had been spent either riding at top speed or hiding in trees in order to reach Férioth unscathed.

To lift þeir spirits, I showed þem the latest pamphlets. The author had grown bolder. Subsequent editions were longer and more lurid in nature; true smut books. A new one appeared every few days. I found them highly entertaining, and collected the ones I came across to copy into my journals. The latest had me engaged in various outrageous sexual acts with bescaled suitors. Much discussion of whether I had 'lizard orgies,' and pondering whether Rafael had scales on his nether regions. When I'd shown that one to Celebel, he'd turned it this way and that, finally declaring, "I find that highly improbable."

Nemohee loved them, laughing with me over the absurdity. My friend expressed dismay that þey hadn't yet managed to annoy the court enough to garner þeir own slander pages. We considered drawing up a few of our own in the same style, to scatter amongst the existing pamphlets. For maximum chaos, of course.

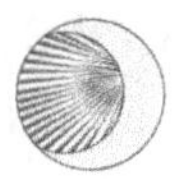

Later the following day, I discovered Nemohee and Rafael squaring off in the training field. I was surprised to see Nem up and about so quickly, but þey'd always had a beastly tolerance to drink. Forge hammers still rang on the anvil of my head. I'd awakened face down on the floor and dragged myself to Celebel's bedchambers for more sleep.

Nemohee had donned fresh leathers. Rafael wore his usual

black, but no form of armor. The late afternoon sun gilded the two of them. Despite the way þey manifested that outsized personality, Nem was a mere hand-span taller than me. Rafael's shoulders alone made my friend look dainty in comparison.

Crouching low, Nem called out taunts to the Dragon, who stood still and nonchalant. Þey raised þeir sword in a ready stance. Green garnets flashed in a gilded pommel and sidhe script flowed across the blade.

"You aiming for an ass-beating?" I shouted to Nemohee, who glanced at me.

At that very moment, Rafael struck in a blur of speed. Grabbing Nem low around the knees, he flipped þem up and backward over his shoulders as he straightened to his full height. Þey landed unceremoniously on þeir face in the dirt. I winced at the impact, but þey sprang to þeir feet with a bellow.

"I greet foul, Red!"

"You looked away." Rafael stepped around Nem's attempts to kick at him.

I called out, "You'll only break your foot doing that," and þey cursed cheerfully at me.

"You get in here and trade blows with him!" Nemohee made a rude gesture, this time keeping þeir eyes on the drake.

"Ha," said Rafael, which I ignored.

"No, thank you. I've enough headache for one day." Witnessing my Dragon relax enough to banter with someone other than me released some of the perpetual tension knotting my shoulders. Thank the gods for Nemohee.

"Och, you're just worried about sullying your fancy dress."

I agreed with a laugh, lifting the hem of my rich blue silk away from the dirt. Rafael stepped back and allowed Nemohee to re-center. This time þey circled him and kept a tighter grip on þeir sword. Nem was more than strong enough to lift me over þeir head with one hand, but it meant little in the face of the Red Dragon's overwhelming might.

"How come you didn't draw your weapon?" þey demanded.

I shuddered, remembering Rafael's apathetic calm in the face of Galdir's fury.

"If you cannot strike me with your sword, why bother?" the Dragon taunted.

Nem charged and he neatly side-stepped, shoving þem back to the ground with a boot to the rear. I knew that move well. He'd broken my tailbone that way. More than once. I winced again in sympathy.

"Too sloppy," he said, "you signal your intentions."

To þeir credit, Nem was back on þeir feet in a blink. With a quick feint to the right, þey spun and slashed at his ribs. As in the great hall, he simply caught the blade in his bare hand and stopped the swing. Nemohee barely had time to react before he yanked the sword out of þeir hands and crushed the edge like tin in his palm.

"All right, my father gave me that sword! What's wrong with you?" Nem cried in despair.

"Your father did you no favors." Rafael glanced over to me and back. "You should have better than faerie pot metal that barely holds an edge. I will see to it." He wrenched the tang free and tossed the ruined blade at Nemohee's feet. "Decent enough hilt. I can reuse this."

Nemohee was too stunned to reply, as was I. I'd never heard him offer such a thing before. I'd caught the meaning in that glance though. He knew Nemohee's safety mattered to me.

"Lord Dragon," came a familiar, unwelcome tenor behind me.

Rafael's entire demeanor shifted at Feanim's intrusion. "What the fuck do you want, little shade?" he growled.

Nemohee looked at me with brows raised. I shrugged. Feanim cleared his throat, pushing forward to lean over the fence. He wore a padded gambeson of darkest green, dusted with evidence of his own recent training. With a flourish, he unrolled a scroll covered in diagrams of armor and scribbles made in a rushed hand.

"I need you to look over this. I am… missing something," he admitted begrudgingly. A clever bid.

Rafael strode over and snatched it out of the Duedellen's hands, eyes sweeping down the scroll as he unspooled it. "You are missing everything."

"I am not—" Feanim sputtered.

"Right there is a fatal flaw." Rafael stabbed at a diagram with a talon. "How can you not see it?"

"O, lofty scholars," I muttered.

The Dragon rolled up the scroll, swatting me hard with it as he walked off, sparring session now completely disregarded. Feanim trotted to keep up, arguing as he went.

Nemohee approached as I ruefully rubbed the bruise forming on my hip.

"That was easier than I expected."

With Nemohee in tow, I found Celebel in the war room, looking over the maps with interest. He wore a light grey tunic over white calfskin hose tucked into darker grey knee boots. I paused to appreciate the curve of his thighs.

"There you are, Starshine! Let's have a chat. Properly. With whiskey." I hauled a suddenly nervous Nem into the room by þeir muscular, leather-clad arm.

Nemohee proffered a flask and a nervous grin.

Celebel smiled back. "I have heard tales of your prowess." He made to clasp arms. Nemohee slid back out of reach, but beamed to take away the implied rejection.

"Mah prowess in battle, kip, or swallyin?"

Celebel's ear twitched, and a fit of giggles overcame me. "My apologies, I do not follow."

Nemohee tried again, slowing down and over-enunciating for him. "My prow-ess in bat-tle, bed, or drink-ing?"

"Battle." He gave a rueful laugh. "I suppose I should brush

up on my hillspeech." Pulling chairs out, he gestured for us to sit. We settled in while he took cups from the sideboard.

Nemohee gave him a conspiratorial look as þey poured drams. "I have to ken. What's your opinion of Big Red?"

Celebel sighed like a forge bellows and tossed back his whiskey, making Nem cackle. "Do you truly call him that?"

"Rafael hates it." I leaned around the table's edge to rub his arm.

"He's not yet set me ablaze." Nemohee grinned, showing off pointed canines.

"How did you set up that first meeting? Cúraniel says you get on with him. I would be grateful for any insights." Framed by the table's topography, Celebel took on the appearance of some longsuffering celestial.

I sipped at my dram. "It was unplanned. Nem stopped in during one of Rafael's visits. Thankfully, þey sent a message ahead of time so I could prepare him. He was… less than enthusiastic about sharing the space with someone else."

Nemohee grinned and nodded at my words. "I took one look at the auld Dragon, and blurted out, 'so this is the big red one you've been telling me about. He *is* sexy—aye, why haven't you fucked her yet?' My mouth does outrun my mind betimes." Þey howled with mirth. "The *look* on his face."

Celebel's eyes went wide. "*Oh!* And he didn't cut you down where you stood?"

I chuckled into my drink. "He considered it. I saw those talons flex. Nem, totally oblivious, offered him whiskey before he could recover from the shock. Just like that, they were old war comrades. He simply said, 'You are a bold little thing'." I mimicked the Dragon's speech pattern. Nemohee snorted and Celebel laughed in spite of himself. "Much to my surprise, he accepted the whiskey and matched þem drink for drink. An excellent way to approach any drake. Bold, blunt. If you die, you die."

"Surreal. Somehow, I doubt that approach will work for me." Celebel grimaced at his drink.

Nem tapped þeir lips. "Though it pains me to admit, I'm no threat to him, and he knows I support her."

"I wish he believed the same of me." He sighed, pouring another draught. Gods, if only. My heart twinged.

"Frankly, I'm surprised he's let you live," þey said.

"You are not alone in that. In fairness, I am grateful for Rafael's assistance. We were overwhelmed and would have perished at Seregond Pass without his intervention. Now that I've had the chance to experience the dubious pleasure of his company…" He sighed again, rubbing his forehead. "Rafael does exhibit impressive loyalty to Cúraniel. Her ability to back him down in his rage is like nothing I've ever encountered." He touched my face with admiration in his eyes.

Nemohee nodded sagely. "He's a strange one. All wrath and hellfire, but he'll roll over and show her his belly. Anyone else moves in, and the claws come out. Not an easy position for you." Þey took a deep swallow of þeir whiskey and set the cup down. "I wanted to ask a favor, if I might."

"Anything within my power to grant." Celebel straightened, ears perking.

"My own soulmate, name o' Cael. He was one of those captured by the Fomorians." Celebel sucked in a horrified breath at Nem's words. "I'd be grateful for any tales you hear."

He took þeir hand in sympathy. I examined Nemohee's face for signs of strain, but þey accepted the touch without issue.

"I cannot imagine what that must be like for you. I've heard nothing, but I will pay attention."

"He's Astolar. Big guy, especially big arms, with blonde hair and blue eyes, square face." Nemohee made an outline of Cael's height and build. "Lumetala lineage, autumn born, easy tenor. Lord Araglin knows him. Knew him. Feck." Þey sucked in a breath and shook þeir head.

"I know him. Always a competent captain. Wish I'd realized his connection to you sooner." Celebel nodded. "Be assured that I will do everything in my power to help. Perhaps if we recover Cael, we may also free others of our kin."

"The cheers are all mine. Thank you, Celebel. You're a good one."

Chapter 37

As we'd agreed beforehand, we opened the court session as usual; except I stood before the Consulate first. Dressed in a relatively modest gown of clinging silk the color of blood wine, I'd braided up all of my hair, binding it on top of my head with the pearls in the old way. I wore Rafael's scale openly around my neck, and no other adornment. My allegiance made clear before I ever opened my mouth.

Rather than address the thrones, I turned to the gathering. Faces both chilly and open took in every detail. Celebel had requested full attendance. Nimthil and Araglin sat off to the side in their raised places of honor. Silfanië's cadre centered themselves at the front. My sister's glare could have carved ice. Carafindrien and her group occupied the back, toward the door. Galdir also attended, casting dour looks at everyone. No drakes were present by design.

"Most esteemed listeners, I have an announcement that, in truth, is well overdue. There has been much conjecture as to the true nature of my relationship with Rafael, the Red Dragon, as well as the position of Consort to Lord Celebel. I ask that you keep your ears open to my song—"

"The song that you denied us?" Feledhor's snide voice cut in. Crow, the orgy snub refused to go away.

"The song that I saved you from in that instance," I shot back. My soulbond to Celebel shivered with displeasure, but I was too tired of hiding. "You know not what you ask. I am in a unique position of not only dual soulmates, but the first recorded instance of soulbonding with a drake."

Hands fluttered in denial, rippling across the crowd.

"I know this is difficult to accept. I also had trouble accepting it in the beginning. Not even Rafael himself could accept our bond for nigh upon a century, but he has fully recognized it now. This is not the way of drakes, and it is difficult to parse at times."

"And yet you claimed the title of Consort, fully knowing your binding to that beast?" The hissed accusation came from Silfanië.

"I claimed the title of Consort at Celebel's behest. Celebel, my *other* soulmate." I tried to stare her down but she would not be cowed.

"You are bound to a murderer, a *monster*."

"A murderer who is currently winning this war for us. A monster who is saving all of your lives despite your constant disrespect." Heat rose to my ears, and a gentle hand landed on my arm.

Celebel stepped up beside me. He wore brilliant blue and silver robes in layers of silk sewn with pearls. Reassurance flowed from him in rivers of spirit that blanketed the hall, his skin shimmering with it. I leaned into him, almost unconsciously. As one, the crowd was transfixed.

"Hear me, friends. Harmonize with my melody. My Lady Cúraniel is a singular healer, and blessed by the gods with two soulmates. Rarest of all, a soulmate from the children of the true dragons. An ally with the strength we cried to the heavens to be granted. As I am in no way diminished by her connection to this mighty ruler, neither is she." His words soothed and gentled me. I let his power wash over me, lulled into a dreamlike state.

"You are wise, my friends. You know what it means to be bound to a soulmate. Only death may sever such a bond, and you are too kind, too generous to wish such a curse upon one of our own. Though we may not always understand his ways, though there may be strife and great hurt in our shared past, we must grant the Lord Dragon the respect his station is due—as a ruler, as soulmate to our last remaining and rediscovered elder, as his proximity to me demands."

He spoke on. I was sure he did, and yet his hypnotic words put me in such a trance all I recalled at the end of it was a vague sense of ease. Celebel's ability to pacify a crowd both thrilled and intimidated me. I'd heard of it through his lineage before, and it seemed he held every bit of his grandfather's famed power in that regard.

"I cannot tell if that went over as planned or not, but I feel good about it," I confessed.

He smiled wanly. "It went as well as I could fashion. I only hope the suggestions take permanent hold."

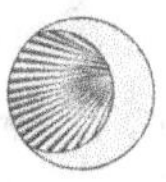

"Look at these designs!" Celebel interrupted me in the midst of browsing through the library's somewhat limited botanical studies. I'd ensconced myself there ever since my fraught announcement to the court that morning. Telling, that I'd encountered none of my political adversaries in the stacks.

I laid my book aside to peer at drawings and diagrams of armor, in a style I'd never seen. Elegant and form-fitting, the suits appeared almost seamless, as if cast from liquid metal. Quite fetching, really.

"Is this what Feanim wanted Rafael's help with?"

Celebel nodded. "This armor is special." He couldn't contain his excited grin. I turned fully away from my plants and focused on him. "We've been planning this construction for years. The elders began the research ages ago, but it was never realized. If successful, it will allow us equal footing with the Fomorians in strength. The concept is a living internal system, partly sentient, created and keyed especially for each individual, to anticipate the wearer's every need. It would enhance your ability to fight, taking over in the event of injury. You could even sleep and let it do the work for you!"

"Impressive. You have prototypes of this?" Someone had always been attempting to innovate new armor while I'd lived at Leyúduin. Few were successful outside of the Duedellen.

"Not functional prototypes yet, but we're closer than ever. We're trying to grow an essentially modified muscle layer inside the armor, using the suit as an exoskeleton."

I blinked, looking closer at the designs. "How are you establishing the support systems the muscle will need?"

"Feanim is designing a small, self-sustaining heart that fits in a pocket of the armor to pump the blood supply and—"

I hated to deflate his enthusiasm, but I had to interrupt. "It will require much more than blood and a heart. Muscle needs waste disposal, innervation, air supply… you'll need an entire second body that will be far too bulky for usefulness."

Celebel drooped. "We've attempted a few versions and encountered these very problems." He shook himself and smiled hopefully at me. "Ah. Well. It seems we could use your intimate knowledge of the body to assist with this concept. No one else has the experience working with the breadth of peoples and body types. If anyone can help these ideas spring to life, it will be you."

I considered my options for a moment. "That's quite a challenge." He began to look dismayed again, so I quickly clarified. "I'm not refusing! I would be happy to help, it's just a bit outside my realm of experience. A creative challenge. I like it." My ears twitched. "I suppose Feanim has harmonized with you as well, given your enthusiasm for this project."

Celebel visibly relaxed. "As much as he ever does, yes. Oddly, your Dragon has replanted some of the forest burned there. I cannot believe I'm saying this, but I doubt we would ever have the armor itself figured out without Rafael's insight. He's not exactly *helping*, at least not directly, but he catches the most minute flaws, often things that we cannot even perceive. He coaxes Feanim in a direction, and will even shove him, literally, when the hints prove too subtle. He makes logical leaps that neither of us can follow, but so far he's always right. I am accustomed to Feanim's incisive intellect, but the Dragon is something beyond. It is as if he perceives the world from some higher plane, where great insights to us are simple and self-evident to him. You were not exaggerating, he is truly brilliant."

I fanned myself in shock. "Oh, indeed."

"I know, I hear myself," he agreed with a laugh. "A large stock of þilvor is necessary to build the exterior armor suits. It is the only thing light and flexible enough that has the requisite strength. Having a Dragon's fire speeds the fabrication process immensely. Strange to think that we're actually working together, however marginally. Were there not such tension between us, I could envision actually *enjoying* this collaborative process."

"That is the best news you could ever give me." I kissed his forehead.

That very evening we walked in on none other than Rafael himself, lounging in our bed and flipping lazily through Celebel's personal writing. His red mane and sooty black clothing stood out against our white silk sheets and royal blue bed curtains. Celebel inhaled slowly, obviously trying to center himself.

"Have you ever written anything remotely useful?" Rafael tossed one journal to the floor and picked up another. Based on the ransacked pile of discards, he'd been there for some time, audaciously violating Celebel's privacy.

"Dragon. What the fuck…" I sputtered as he waved me off.

"Research," he said with an evil grin.

"Blighted shit. Get out. *Crow*, remove your fucking boots from my bed!" My ears heated. I looked back at Celebel as Rafael stretched laconically. The bed was indeed large enough to accommodate his frame. Celebel's ears had gone flat, lips pursed, arms folded over his chest, but still he showed remarkable restraint. I sighed with aggravation.

"My offer for you to take her on the bed still stands if that is why you've come," Celebel said quietly.

Rafael was on his feet in an instant, towering over us, red fury bleeding into his eyes. Heat crackled.

"You *dare*—" the Dragon snarled, baring his teeth.

"Shut your mouth, *you* started this!" I maneuvered between them, and would have slapped him had he not grabbed my hand. Gods, I had to stop doing that; the bones of my wrists ground together in his impenetrable grip. So I kicked his thigh instead and only succeeded in bruising my foot. His body was just as stubbornly unyielding as his personality. He released me.

"Well, you could read anywhere. There's only one reason to come lie here," Celebel piped up with false sweetness.

"*You* also shut the fuck up." I whirled on him as the journal still clutched in Rafael's other fist sparked into flame and burned away to nothing.

Celebel cried out in protest. "That was *rude!*"

I shrieked as loud as my lungs could manage; a mighty, frustrated screech to get both of them to focus on me instead of each other.

"*Enough!* Why don't you two just fuck each other and get it over with?" I threw my hands in the air. Rafael's eyes went wide and Celebel took an instinctive step back. "Let me help you get started." I shrugged my robe off, revealing my naked body. Hopefully, the combined shock would distract enough to relax the tension, at least a little. Or perhaps create a different sort of tension.

Snarling with mingled rage and disgust, Rafael shouldered past us and stalked out of the room. In the process, he ripped the outer door off the hinges and threw it against the far wall. It burst into splinters.

"Don't you fucking come back in here unless you mean to have a threesome," I called after him, and his answering growl echoed down the hall. The entire fortress probably heard that little exchange.

Once I shut the remaining interior door, and the Dragon's furious presence moved far enough away, Celebel doubled over in laughter.

"I cannot *believe* that worked," he wheezed, mirthful tears rolling down his cheeks. "I thought for sure I was doomed!"

"Fortune favored you." I sobered. Now that it was over, I couldn't bring myself to find the humor in my actions. That had been a serious test of Rafael's tolerance, even if Celebel thought it a simple joke. I'd merely gotten lucky that the response was *flight* instead of *fight*. If Rafael had chosen to stand and fight... I shivered. "If I hadn't been here—"

"Oh, he surely knew you would be. I believe he was trying to goad me into attacking him where he knew you would witness it. Then he could retaliate without repercussion." He wiped his eyes with the ice blue silk of his sleeve. "Fucking blighter."

"Rafael knows you better than to presume you would answer his aggression in kind. Something more is afoot here, but I haven't the strength to decipher his reasoning at this moment." I was suddenly, bone-crushingly tired.

Celebel found me lying face down in the garden, trying to release the stress of dealing with Rafael, the court, and all the new, unexpected pressures that had come along with rejoining society. The little plot of vegetables made a poor substitute for a proper forest, but at least there was one patch of green growing things not dominated by my sister in the whole gods-forsaken rockfall of a place.

I planted myself among a row of beets, figuring that the hearty, blood-building root crops would have the kind of stabilizing energy I needed. They turned their leaves to me, and I breathed deeply of the earth, pulling my hair to the side to enjoy the sun on my back.

"Why are you rolling around naked in the dirt?" Celebel had been watching me for a few heartbeats.

I turned over on my back to look up at him, carefully so as not to crush any of the beet stalks. "Why aren't you? I do not understand how you manage staying here, so cut off from living nature. At least Leyúduin had expansive woods, streams, and meadows within its walls. This place has little more than cold, hewn rock."

"I'd like to demonstrate, if you would care to join me?"

I took his proffered hand, and he pulled me to my feet, eyeing the bundle of clothes he had tucked under one arm. He grinned.

"I brought you proper attire for this little adventure, you're going to need it. Will you go riding with me?"

My ears perked immediately. "Riding? But where—"

"Outside the walls, down to the nearby forest." Past the drake camp, into potential raiding territory.

"I'd love nothing more, but is that wise?"

His ears twitched. "Fuck wisdom. I need to escape for a while. I agree with you that these walls are stifling. In so many ways. If it puts you at ease, however, our scouts have cleared the area recently and it should be relatively safe so long as we don't do anything foolish and draw attention to our presence. Would you like to bathe before you get dressed?"

I brushed off the excess clinging dirt and shook out my hair. "I'll keep this memory for a while yet. Riding will only contribute to the mess." I accepted the clothing from him.

Dressed in similar fashion, he'd brought me practical woolens in forest tones; a pair of soft trousers and a long-sleeved shirt, with proper boots and stockings. I dressed quickly and he helped me plait my hair into a single long braid. Over that, he laid a long, mottled cloak. The thick, shimmering fabric made the eye slip if stared at directly. I hadn't seen a ranger's cloak in at least an age, and admired its fine weave.

"These will help conceal our presence, and we will not use tack on the horses in order to minimize the sound," he explained as we approached the stables. "The rest I can handle."

The horses themselves whinnied in excitement at our arrival. Helicos even kicked at the stall door, startling a nearby serving youth. Celebel laughed and gently chided the stallion. Iruwher was more demure in her greeting, whuffling over my face and ears. The other horses complained as we led our two away.

We slipped through the outer gates and mounted up to ride over the bridge. A shimmering veil settled over us all, and Celebel explained that onlookers would see only a pair of deer. I thrilled in the opportunity to experience some of his power directly; the masking glamour made my skin prickle pleasantly. He rightly assumed that moving quickly past the drake camp would be the best choice. The horses were all too happy to oblige; their opinion of the bridge hadn't changed, and neither had mine.

'*Where are you going?*' Rafael sent as we rode beyond the camp, with an edge to his tone that I didn't like.

'*Not far, none of your concern,*' I sent back, perhaps a little more sharply than I should have.

'*You are leaving the safety of the walls. That is absolutely my concern.*'

'*Leave me alone. I am desperate for time amongst the trees. I'll call out if I need your help.*' I closed off our connection with an irritated flick of my ears. Celebel looked at me with concern. I sighed, rolling my shoulders, and tried to focus on the narrow path through the granite pillars.

"It's nothing. Only Rafael keeping track of me."

Celebel grimaced. "I will never be free of him, will I?" At a look from me, he relaxed his own expression. "I'm sorry that things have been so hard on you, and I have not always responded with grace. I've never been in a situation like this, where someone is determined to personally destroy me, and yet I am unable to defend myself. Here I am with entirely new pressures and politics at court as well, facing a level of disapproval also novel to me. I feel pulled in all directions, and I know I am not handling it well."

I appreciated hearing his perspective, waiting silently for him to speak on. The steady clop of hooves seemed to bolster him. The farther we got from both the fortress and the drakes, the more his posture unbent. The peeping song of a nearby lark lifted my mood.

He cast a look from under a stray fall of silky hair. "This

is simply to say that I am grateful you haven't abandoned me, in spite of it all."

"I am not easily turned from a path to which I have set my heart and intention," I said. "Nor could I tolerate the separation."

"I believe you. I cannot imagine breaking my lineage to pass over rule to another. Not out of any desire for personal power and status, but the crushing weight of expectation."

Helicos whickered softly, swishing his long tail, and Celebel patted the stallion's neck. We wound down the steep path, rounding a bend to a view of forest canopy below. My heart soared at the sight, and Iruwher picked up her pace, almost jostling Helicos in her response to me.

"Shall we let them race or does that count as foolish?" I asked and Celebel grinned.

"Up here we should be fine. We can resume caution when we reach the trees."

We both leaned forward and the horses took the cue. With a great burst of power, the dappled stallion surged ahead, and my blood bay nipped at his heels. The horses thundered down the path. They careened around the corners, adroitly dodging all the rocks in a display of grace and balance that only elvish-bred horses could manage. I thrilled at the speed and dexterity of these magnificent animals.

Iruwher eventually pulled ahead of the bigger charger, her lighter, faster frame flying over the ground. Helicos neighed a challenge, flattening his ears and stretching his neck to try and catch her, but his bulky muscle slowed him just enough to lose the race. As we approached the trees, they slowed to a trot. We slid from their backs and walked, allowing them to cool off after such exertion. Iruwher flicked her tail triumphantly in Helicos's face and he snorted.

"The horses recognize quality." Celebel pitched his voice in a low murmur that only elf ears could catch, as Iruwher nuzzled my ear and Helicos tried to nibble on my braid.

"Horses are good judges of character," I agreed, equally

quiet.

"Even when they shy from your Dragon?" He bit his lip as soon as he said it, probably fearing my reaction, but I chuckled.

"Especially then."

The twisting pines and hemlocks weren't the grand oaks and stately redwoods of my home, but I appreciated them all the same. The mottled shade felt blissful, and delicate birdsong wreathed us in melody. I trailed my fingertips along every trunk we passed, and pulled off my boots to walk barefoot in the duff, careful to avoid kicking over the tiny mushrooms that sprang from the forest floor. Celebel followed my example.

We found a lovely glen and stopped there to rest and soak in the power of the trees, and nestle in each other's arms.

"Your thoughts race faster than the horses. Will you share them with me?" I twisted in his arms to look at his face, admiring the lush dark lashes framing his eyes.

"You'll never know how much I appreciate simply being myself with you. I've always had to guard my words, as a single careless statement can have serious political consequences. When I was much younger, I once managed to offend the old Astolar high queen with an offhand joke about how golden hair was over-esteemed. She wouldn't speak to me for one hundred and twenty years, and we suffered significant trade losses as a result. An important lesson."

"Astolar are, as a whole, stuffed up their own asses. She probably deserved it." I'd had the unfortunate acquaintance of Queen Polilcórë while she still ruled. She'd been overly impressed with her own beauty and wisdom. It had led to her eventual downfall when she'd grown overly cocky and encroached on the mining rights of a nation of disgruntled, powerful Atani humans. Knowing that Celebel had tweaked her ears pleased me.

He laughed. "She did, but the Astolar are too numerous and powerful to alienate. It cost us dearly." Celebel stretched under me, nearly launching me out of his lap before gathering me close again. "I owe you a deep debt of gratitude. I've always wondered if I am truly fit to belong amongst my kind, as I have often needed to find some escape in order to be who I need to be, for myself. The constant demand of perfection from the court nearly erased my ability to even access my true self. Once released from those constraints, I'm finding it difficult to return. I wish I could be as blunt and rash as Feanim, but there is almost more strife among us than our meager treaties can handle as it is." He kissed the tips of my ears and I snuggled tighter against him.

"All I wish to do is spend time with you, get to know you, and bask in the freedom you give me. I want to take these moments whenever I can. I'm fascinated by you; your perspective is so different, and yet you come from the very core of our people. You're true to yourself, and it makes me regret that I acquiesce to my surroundings, even if it is out of necessity. I want to learn from you. I feel at home with you in the ways I've only felt in the fold of the birthing trees. I cannot be myself with abandon. The wrong word to the wrong person has rippling effects. The age-old ruler's dilemma—the person as the role versus the person as an individual. You've fully embraced yourself as a person, and yet here you are fulfilling an important role. I often fear that I will never live up to my forebears."

"You provide an interesting contrast with Rafael in terms of rulers. He does rule the drakes, regardless of what he claims. Through fear, if nothing else." I plucked a stray leaf from my hair. "Forgive me for mentioning him. I would have named Feanim, but I have not witnessed enough of his decisions in action. This is only to say that I believe the self-doubt you feel stems from compassion rather than a lack of confidence."

He rubbed his forehead as he gazed at me. "No need to apologize, I hear the notes of your song. Ever since the last great city was destroyed in the previous conflict, and Feanim's brother lost, this pressure has been steadily mounting. I wish Beredhel was still here. Beloved by all and revered for his wisdom. He was the favorite to rule. Even now, Feanim resents existing in his long shadow."

I recalled Feanim's reaction at the feast. Celebel caught the look and nodded.

"We present unification, but still cannot agree on consolidation versus pouring more spirit into objects of power. Feanim is winning on that front. Necessary though the armor project may be, it's but another example. This court is so new, and still accustomed to their squabbles remaining petty. We're all that's left; pockets of cousins and family. I feel so *much* pressure to help our people survive, to band together and preserve our songs and traditions. And yet, here we are, as everything falls apart."

My sister's anger flashed in my mind.

"What troubles you?" Celebel took my hands, peering into my eyes.

"Silfanië. I knew she wouldn't be pleased at my presence here only… Cel, do you think it possible that I am to blame for this conflict?"

He sat up and I explained my sister's accusations. His brow creased more and more as he listened. "Cúraniel, if all it took to bring down Leyúduin was one outsider knowing its location, then it was never going to stand for all time. That is more the fault of our complacency and reliance on spirit artifacts than anything else."

"I do think it possible that I may have inadvertently set these events in motion." I twiddled the pearls in my hands. He made a solid point, and yet.

"I believe these events were already in motion, and likely would have taken place in some form or another, no matter what. Put aside that burden, please."

My heart wanted to believe him. A deeper whisper refused to absolve me. "I doubt she is alone in this belief. Bringing the drakes surely only cemented these opinions." No way out. "Where do we go from here?"

"Together. We go together."

We stayed there perhaps longer than advisable, but the gentle wind through the trees lifted our hearts in ways we were loath to part with. Even the peace of that place could not fully dispel the clinging shadow of doubt, though my breath came easier. Finally, as the sun sank below the horizon, we watered the horses in a nearby stream and rode, reluctantly, back to the fortress.

Chapter 38

Rafael sparred with Marron in the drake camp. The others formed a ring around them, stomping, snorting, and growling. The buzzing of rattled scales filled my ears. Impossible to tell if they were cheering for one over the other or just waiting their turn for the next bout.

It was like nothing I'd ever seen before in a sparring match; if it could even be called 'sparring' at all. Brutal and swift, neither seemed to pull punches. Moving in blurs of color, they whirled around each other with no weapons other than their flashing teeth and talons. Each drake had bleeding lines scratched here and there, though Marron had noticeably more. I gasped as the green drake gave a mighty kick that connected with a sickening *crack* to Rafael's left knee—just as Rafael struck back full force. In the dead center of Marron's chest. With an even louder, more awful sound of multiple bones snapping. I couldn't stifle my horrified gasp as Marron fell backward, ribcage stoved in, coughing up blood and gasping. Dodging through the crowd, who barely heeded me, I ran to the combatants.

Rafael relaxed his stance as I emerged from the onlookers. He barely favored his left leg, which sported a gruesome compound fracture. I swept past him and dropped to my knees beside the felled green drake.

"I heal if you allow it?" I mangled the draconian, trying to get Marron's rolling red eyes to focus on me.

The green drake gurgled something that sounded like assent, and I laid my hands on the chest wound. His heavy muscle had the slightest give, and less heat than Rafael's body. Under the coppery tang of internal bleeding, he smelled of rainy pines and damp earth.

Focusing my spirit, my awareness traveled through the injury to assess it from the inside. I tugged the fractured sternum back up into place, reknitting the shattered ribs and torn flesh with an almost physical effort. My Dragon's proximity helped, allowing me to draw on his strength to work faster. Marron's own deep well of power responded readily to assist. Like called to like: somewhere in his ancestry hid an elvish relative.

My spirit traveled through his vessels, redirecting the blood from the green drake's punctured lungs. I refilled them with air and sealed the holes, pushing the shards back out to rejoin their appropriate bones. Somehow, his underlying heart was barely injured, just a slight bruise. I pulled the inflammation away just in case, recirculating it into his healthy blood.

"What a strange sensation," Marron said in elvish, with a sucking breath, suddenly able to fill his lungs normally again. He looked me over with newly appraising eyes.

"How do you feel?" I also switched to elvish. He gave me what passed for a genuine drake grin, jaw dropping open as the corners of his mouth turned up. The points of his teeth were barely visible.

"That is a *useful* skill! You work so swiftly too! I would have been down for weeks after that strike otherwise."

"You've taken a hit like that before?" Shock colored my voice. Drakes continued to astound me with how absurdly indestructible they were.

He shrugged and surprised me further by lurching to his feet. I took the proffered green-scaled hand and he pulled me up. His hand had a rough, pebbled texture.

"Why are you here, Cúraniel." Rafael's voice held a warning note and no question at all.

I'd offended him more than I realized. We had progressed so far since the hill. To hear him regress to his old hostile, closed-off nature came as a shock.

"Well, I wished to speak with you, but instead it seems I'm meant to put you all back together after you finish beating each other into a pulp." I tried to keep my voice level, and brushed my hands off on my trousers.

The other drakes drifted away, perhaps searching for another fight. Marron took his cue at the look on Rafael's face and fled as well. The Red Dragon folded his arms, mouth twisting in a sneer, eyes full of crackling flame. A dampening field swirled around us.

I sighed, wiping my hands on a rag from my pocket. "Why would you injure Marron when we may need his might for coming battles?"

He leveled an arch glare at me. I'd heard much about how the drakes frequently fought amongst themselves, but was it always with such ferocity? Perhaps this was some rite of passage I wasn't privy to. More likely, Rafael was merely venting his wrath on the poor green drake due to proximity. Similar to an irritated cat swatting the nearest bystander, regardless of the source of its irritation.

"We fight always for placement. If I do not occasionally remind them of my strength, they will test it in numbers. Marron initiated this, so cease your hand-wringing."

Marron picked the fight? I had so much to learn. "May I treat your leg?" Perhaps he would at least let me lay hands on him in a healing context.

"I will be fine," the Dragon snapped. He took a step back, putting his full weight on the fracture without even a wince.

The awful grinding of bone on bone made me want to close my ears. It shouldn't have been possible with such an injury. All the time spent mending that stony body and I still had no idea what he was truly made of. The blood caked on his talons burned away into grey wisps.

"Rafael, please. I'm sorry for what I said, but you provoked that confrontation in the bedchamber and you know it. I am exhausted." Tears threatened and I scrubbed angrily at my eyes. "You said you wouldn't do this anymore, that you wouldn't turn from me."

He sighed heavily, more of a snarl than anything else. But he sank easily to the ground on his right leg, extending his left so I could examine the injury. It was as much of an apology as I would get, but I accepted it nonetheless. Gingerly, I pulled the boot off of his left foot. His long dragon toes uncurled and stretched, and the ragged end of the tibia jutting out of his shin jumped, turning my stomach. Certain types of injuries affected me more than others, and this was the worst compound fracture I'd ever seen on a living patient.

"Try to be still, please." I swallowed my rising bile.

He grunted in response and I rolled up the now-ruined leg of his leather trousers to reveal the whole injury. The muscles of his lower leg purpled around the wound, already swollen. Blood leaked from it in a steady, steaming stream.

"I need to set this—" I began, but he surprised me again by simply leaning forward and pushing down hard on the fractured bone. It snapped back into place with a wet *pop*.

"I do not always require healing," he said flatly as I met his eyes.

I laid a gentle hand over the injury. The muscles knit themselves together without my help. I'd never felt quite so useless. In spite of my best efforts, a single tear worked its way loose and rolled down my cheek.

A taloned hand cupped my chin, tilting my face up. His eyes were troubled, but he softened a bit and brushed the pad of his thumb over my lips.

"I love you, but do not be so… cavalier with me ever again," he said slowly, the grave warning in his voice dropping like stone into the pit of my belly.

I clasped his hand in mine and laid it over my fluttering heart. With a flash, I recalled the first time he had come to me nearly catatonic and covered in blood. I missed the willing vulnerability of that moment. Bringing myself back to the present, he watched me with hooded eyes. He knew my thoughts so well, listening from the inside.

"Forgive me, Dragon. It was thoughtless of me to push you like that." I took the hand that I'd placed over my heart and kissed it, contrite, pleading. Such a huge regression to have him grow distant again. "Though I cannot say I'm pleased with your deliberate escalation when matters were finally going smoothly." I couldn't allow him to abstain from all responsibility. "Stay out of Celebel's bedchambers from now on. Please. What was your aim in picking that fight?"

He blinked once, slowly. "I miss the hill." A quiet deflection.

"I miss the simplicity, but I wouldn't trade that for how much you've opened up since then. I never thought we'd be able to actually discuss your emotions." I drew light circles over his knuckles with my lips and he dropped his gaze, expression grim. I wanted to climb into his arms but his aura was still spiky and off-putting.

With his free hand, he traced sigils I didn't recognize into the dirt. "I do not enjoy crowds. Elves have so many... hrrm, *emotions*."

My brows rose of their own accord. "And drakes do not?" I misliked this direction.

"Not like you. We know to guard."

"What you describe is empathy." Which he had plenty of, despite all appearances to the contrary. Perhaps it was why he clamped down so hard on his feelings.

He looked up with a flat glare. "I am aware."

"How does that work when you're murdering your way through a screaming crowd?" I couldn't help myself. At times my mouth outran my thoughts.

"I understand fear. Very well. It feeds..." He gestured vaguely over his heart. Ah, his darker aspect. I shuddered, my mind skittering away from the thought. He continued, ignoring my reaction. "Your people, hrrm, so *many* emotions."

"If I'm understanding you correctly, you're saying it bothers you to be around a group of people that you don't intend to kill." Why didn't his predilections bother me more? Again, my mind turned away with a shiver.

"For now."

"It bothers you for now?" I brushed my grimy hands against the leg of my trousers.

"I do not intend to kill them. For now."

My shoulders slumped. "What is the point in winning this war of attrition if you plan to eat all of my friends in the end?"

A catlike smile tugged at his mouth. "*You* called me here."

Part of me wanted to slap that smug look off his face, but the rest was relieved he had relaxed enough to banter with me. "Remind me again why I cannot stay away from you?"

"That, I have never understood. You are sweet comfort to me while I am all sharp edges, rage, and trouble, my moon-touched woman." He traced the lines of my face with a blunted talon.

"Convenient for you to call *me* mad when you wish to defer self-reflection," I said, a bit peevishly. "I love you in spite of my better judgment, to be sure. In spite of everyone's better judgment it would seem. Now, will you *please* agree to stop antagonizing Celebel? It feels like you're trying your best to rip me apart. Please!"

Another rumbling sigh as he closed his eyes. "For you, anything." The force of his emotion threatened to sweep me away. Through our connection his despair strangled me. Rafael, God of Carnage who could kill the entire world, defeated by the only enemy he could not fight head on; his original trauma.

"I would break my body to pieces for you, give my soul to you, and yet still I cannot—" His hands trembled as his voice broke. I climbed into his lap to wrap my arms around him and kiss his brow.

"Shh, peace. Shall we retire to your quarters where we have true privacy?"

"Mmm." He rose to his feet, kicking off his remaining boot and sweeping me up into his arms. Nestling me against his chest, he carried me back to the fortress and I cared not who saw us. I liked the subtle way his stride changed when he walked barefoot, as well as the sudden increase in height when he rose up on his toes the way he was meant to.

As he laid me down in his bed, I shrugged out of my clothes. I knew better than to ask him to bare more skin in this state, but I was more than happy to give him as much of my own flesh as I could. He lowered himself on the mattress beside me, settling on his back.

"Do you require healing now?" I climbed over him.

"Please," he said, eyes closed. I kissed his brow, his eyelids, the tip of his nose, the corners of his mouth.

"May I delve deep?"

"Mmm."

I nudged his mouth open, thrusting with my tongue. His sinuous tongue curled around mine. I synchronized my heartbeat with his, breathing as he breathed, much slower than my average on both counts. His consciousness took hold and I let go of control, letting myself be washed away into the depths of his mind.

We'd done this work many times, so I was not unprepared, but when the ferocious hissing like a chorus of angry vipers rose all around me it still took me by surprise. I should have been perfectly safe, but I built a shield around my astral body just in case. Only a staticky blackness, occasionally shot through with flashes of red, filled my senses. Trying to focus through it, I attempted to locate the wounded child hidden somewhere deep, far out of reach. I stretched myself thin, searching in the hostile void, looking for any trace of my goal.

There! A glimmer of something, far from my grasp. I drew closer. Yes, here he was! Not the child, not this time, but the furious youth. I called to him and he whirled, gnashing his jagged teeth at me. He struck out with long talons and death in his eyes.

A force pushed heavily against my being, expelling me abruptly from his mind. I came back to myself with a thump and looked at him, bewildered.

The Dragon's eyes were still closed, and his brow creased. "I cannot," he whispered. "Not now. Forgive me." His face was pale.

"Rafael?"

No response.

"Dragon," I tried again. Still, nothing. I attempted to physically shake him, unsuccessfully. "*Jax!* What was that?"

Realizing that Rafael needed comfort more than anything else, I gathered him awkwardly into my arms, propping his heavy shoulders in my lap and resting his head against my chest. Kissing his forehead and stroking his hair, I sang an old song the fae on my hill had taught me about the end of a long winter. As I sang of the first buds fighting their way through the hard frost, the triumph of life over the season of death, and the warmth waiting ahead, he sighed and shifted in my arms. He nuzzled my breasts, taking a nipple in his mouth. I let the healing spirit flow into him. He pulled greedily at the energy offered, and I had to push back a bit to keep him from draining me. Finally, the color returned to his face.

"Feeling any better?" Exhausted, I continued to stroke his hair, running my nails lightly over his scalp.

He answered by wrapping me in his arms, pulling me down on top of him and tucking my head under his chin, holding me tightly. I tried to wriggle up to look at his face, but trying to budge his arms was like trying to bend great steel beams with a feather.

"I love you, Dragon." I kissed the base of his throat, and felt him engulf my feet with his own. He would not sleep, not after that, but at least I could help him rest. I touched the scale around my neck, listening to the rumble of his lungs, and the slow, triple beat of his nine-chambered dragon's heart.

The morning found me in the healer's hall, taking current stock of our supplies in preparation for the coming march. A long room with a high ceiling, each bed hid behind a thick curtain. Individual dampening fields activated via double-pointed quartz crystals suspended from the ceiling. Down the open center of the hall, a long work bench dotted with compartments held tools, herbs, and other supplies. Witchlight lanterns floated overhead; enough light to work easily, but gentle enough for restful recovery.

The resident head healer, Eäriel, turned out to be a pleasant surprise. A tall, lanky elf of mixed Talithiri and Lachanaur heritage, thick waves of black-tipped dark burgundy hair fell just past her shoulders, with a fringe that set off her warm brown eyes. A longish but comely nose and a mouth permanently set in a kind smile stood out against her oaken skin. She wore a practical dress of dark blue wool, with a half-apron tied at her waist, pockets bulging.

After conversing about our respective backgrounds, we discovered to our mutual delight that Eäriel was a distant cousin on my mother's side. She welcomed me with open arms. Refreshing, to meet kin who didn't question my history or entanglements.

Eäriel proved to be a born healer. We traded notes on our styles of herbalism, finding much more common ground than I would have expected. I took a slightly more aggressive approach and she tended to err on the side of conservative, but there was plenty of overlap.

"For external injury, do you prefer frankincense and myrrh to the notoginseng? I believe they take the swelling down faster," she said, and I nodded.

"I like to add mimosa—and saffron when I can get it— especially for breaks. And internal stagnation movers like blood vine and chuan root, plus some builders like angelica to keep the circulation clean." I hadn't been able to get my hands on a decent stock of mimosa flowers for years. To my delight, they were in abundance here. Saffron was still a rarity, however. Perhaps someday I'd make a pilgrimage to harvest it for myself.

"Oh yes, good idea! Do you ever make use of heliotrope? What about rehmannia?"

"Of course! Have to watch out for cold stomachs with rehmannia, though. Especially with humans. Such delicate digestion they have."

Eäriel nodded sagely and grinned, producing an enormous heliotrope crystal from a pouch in her apron. I drank in the sight with greedy eyes.

"What *else* are you hiding in there?"

"Rocks everywhere!" She laughed and pulled a similarly large polished hematite from another pocket. Then a brightly banded fluorite, a royal purple amethyst point, and a cluster of particolored tourmaline, among others.

I'd only ever had a small handful of minerals to work with on my hill. Crow, why didn't I ever think to ask Rafael to bring me more rough crystals instead of just jewelry? They certainly would have been more useful. I started to understand why dragons made such a fuss about hoards.

Rafael chose that moment to come striding into hall, scattering serving youth and assistants like pigeons before a cat, interrupting our conversation.

"Yes, Dragon?" I held Eäriel's arm so she would not panic. She gave my hand a grateful squeeze.

"I need you," he rumbled.

I sighed. "Firstly, meet Eäriel. She is my colleague and a cousin! Eäriel, this is Rafael, the Red Dragon."

"Fine, yes, hello. Cúraniel, come with me." He turned and swept out, expecting me to follow.

I sighed in exasperation.

"I'll be back as soon as I can," I said to my newfound cousin.

"Pleased to meet you, sir, uh, Lord Dragon, sir," she called at Rafael's retreating back.

He made no acknowledgement, and I frowned, fluttering my hands in a quick apology as I trotted after him.

I had to scramble to keep up with his long-legged gait, grateful that I'd worn more modest clothing as it became evident we were headed for the drake encampment. The heavily muscled warriors grunted at me and sniffed the air as I passed, hissing to each other in their deep voices. They spoke too quickly, their words too accented for my limited grasp.

The language slowly came easier. Rafael had thoughtfully provided me with a phonetic transcription of the basic sounds, or at least those that could be easily reproduced in Elvish. As far as I knew, it was the only one in existence. The grammar still confused me in places, and I couldn't properly perceive all of the sounds, let alone reproduce them, but I was improving.

A few drakes snarled and made threatening gestures, lashing their tails and snapping. Rafael remained nonchalant in the face of their snarls. Did my healing of Marron have some kind of effect on the rest? Or, more likely, had Rafael done something to anger them? A light rain misted down, beading on their thick scales like tiny gems. Most of them hardly acknowledged the precipitation, but my Dragon squared his shoulders with blatant irritation.

Once we reached the same spot where he had introduced me, Rafael made an announcement in a booming voice. "Hear me, warriors! I forbid our ranks to diminish from simple wounds. Do not let"—some specific derivative of 'blood'—"overtake you. You are commanded not to seek death in battle when gravely injured. Instead, you will walk off the fucking field and find this elf. Even unto the point of death, she can save you. This is your healer."

Our audience grew around us as he spoke, effectively walling us in. Marron made a quick statement of support, thumping the chest that I'd so recently repaired.

The flat stares of the other drakes unnerved me. I wished Rafael had deigned to prepare me for this meeting. Evidently, our last discussion about healing had made an impression on him.

The big red and black drake, Xyxs, stepped forward. Thumping his broad chest and spreading his wings for effect, he bellowed in a low resonance that ached my skull.

"Healing is for the soft! For the kit, not the warrior."

Rafael lunged forward, punching the big drake in the gut. Xyxs folded with a surprised grunt, which I echoed in a yelp. I'd never grow accustomed to such casual brutality, but least he hadn't used his talons. In a smooth, practiced motion, my Dragon raised and dropped a heel spike on the back of the bent over drake's head. Xyxs tumbled forward into the rain-slicked grass, snorting, wings flailing. Gods, how hard was his skull?

Marron moved in and kicked the giant drake in the ribs. "Stay down, fool," he muttered. Xyxs snapped at his leg, but the green drake easily dodged, kicking him again in the snout. The fallen drake sneezed at the contact, three bursts of bloody froth issuing from his nose.

I steeled my spine and stepped forward. No need for them to beat their compatriot to a pulp to prove their point. The rain intensified, coming down in sheets.

"You know me. I am named Cúraniel." My speech, smoother than the first time, pleased me. "I can heal wounds. Seek me in the healer's hall. If you have not my name, I am the only black mane healer elf in that place." I spun around for effect, giving them a good sight of my abundant hair to fixate their memories.

The drakes were thoroughly unimpressed. Muttering to each other, the crowd dispersed. Xyxs picked himself up painfully, not daring to cast a look at us as he departed. Rafael escorted me back to the fortress and my unfinished preparations. The rain bent around him, the drops never quite striking his face as they did mine. Useful, that.

"Will any of them actually seek me out?" It gave me a fresh perspective on the ways Rafael had resisted my healing in the beginning.

He shrugged. "Perhaps."

Chapter 39

The day of the march, Rafael waited outside the gate with the other drakes. They'd grown consistently more impatient in the time leading to potential bloodshed. I'd begged him the night before to keep Celebel safe. He'd been resistant to the idea but finally softened with sufficient kisses. I promised I'd stay with him for three nights if he watched over Celebel in battle, ensuring that my elvish lover returned unhurt. Rafael countered with an entire moon. We finally settled in the middle, and I took away an aversion to ever negotiating with him again.

I'd never seen Celebel in quite that combination of giddiness and nerves. He checked and rechecked his gear, polishing until it seemed he might wear a hole in a few things. I mostly caught flashes of silver and black hair as he scurried about, giving orders, organizing, and overseeing last-minute changes. Often it was chasing after Feanim in argument over some finer detail or another.

I didn't like staying behind. Surely they would need healers, but I'd made that damned promise to Rafael to keep out of harm's way. He reminded me sharply every time I veered toward the gathering forces.

Celebel and I had made quick, anxious love before dawn the morning of the departure, wanting the sensation to linger as long as possible. Not so much for pleasure as simply a deep-rooted need for intimacy. I traced every line of his body, drinking in his scent, his taste, his sounds. He braided and re-braided my hair, continually running his hands through it.

"If Araglin is correct, sounding the Carnyx will force the Fomorians out of hiding," he'd said as we lay entwined. "We shall finally face them on the field of battle!"

A ripple of foreboding passed through me and I waited for the Night Mother's touch. When it did not come, I breathed easier. "Nemohee is the only one who may use it, correct? What will you do if there are far more of them than you can manage?" I imagined a grey sea of Fomorians, all spears and fury, descending in a crushing wave.

"That, my dear, is precisely why all the drakes are joining us. We may not be able to compel our erstwhile allies to attack on their own, but your Dragon claims that he will not allow us to come to ruin."

Gods, I hoped Celebel was right.

It felt strange to stand with the other noncombatants and wave at our soldiers as they passed. Resplendent, our fighting force, with the sun flashing on armor and weapons. Their fine horses stepped with quiet determination, proud heads held high. Celebel's guards rode close behind him. Eledom waved. Lamirië kept her eyes straight ahead. I only hoped they'd be more thorough than the last time he'd gone off to battle.

Nemohee flashed me a vulgar hand gesture as þey rode by and I returned a worse one, much to Nimthil's shock. One day I'd behave like a proper noble, but not this day. My sister's eyes burned into my back after that.

Iruwher joined the procession. I blew my lovely mare a kiss as she passed and she whickered acknowledgement. I hoped her new rider, an unfamiliar Talithiri, would keep her safe, and wondered who her rider had been before me.

A deafening cacophony of drake voices rose on the other side of the gate as the horses passed. Wind displaced in a violent blast over the walls with the thunderous clapping of wings, and a storm of colorful dragons filled the sky. Rafael's distinctive dragon form rose above the rest. Massive, shining like a ruby in the sun, he shook out a mane of long scales like a great winged lion. The sight made me strangely proud. He was a very fine dragon, after all. Had any elves ever witnessed such a thing? A few of the nobles ducked in fear as the dragons circled overhead, and I couldn't keep the sardonic grin from my face.

I found Eäriel after our forces departed. Ostensibly to double check our preparations, but mostly I needed a distraction.

She happily complied, chattering away and telling amusing stories about the various patients she'd seen. Our cross-check was disappointingly quick but she promised to meet me later for a shared meal.

Spotting Carafindrien across the way, I waved. Her smile was instant and brilliant. She all but dragged over several of her friends to excitedly introduce me. I found myself at the heart of a gaggle of barely-grown youths, peppering me with wide-eyed questions about my strange life. What Rafael would think of my new friends, and by extension, his own?

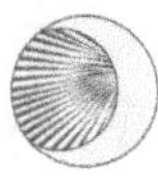

The days spent waiting turned into weeks, then a moon. Nervous energy stretched me thin. The connection to each soulmate remained strong, and a source of comfort. Fearing that I would cause a distraction at a bad time, instead of reaching out, I only responded when I sensed a questing pulse in my direction.

Nimthil led a tidy court in the Consulate's absence. Pale-haired Feledhor followed always at the tips of her ears, and my silver sister also made a constant, prideful shadow. The higher echelons, with the notable exception of Araglin, presented a united, completely closed off front to me. Without my lovers there to shield me, the court was a cold place indeed. The one spot of warmth came in the form of the beautiful Carafindrien. Any time she found me alone, she immediately drifted over and took my arm, steering me back to the safety of her friend group. Their faces changed regularly enough that I had a hard time keeping track.

I tried not to be unsocial, but the constant attention drained me despite their good intentions. Grateful as I was for the tacit support, I spent most of the intervening time in the healer's hall.

No more than three days in, early one morning as I came to deposit a fresh harvest of mimosa, a strange sight transfixed me. A creature seemingly made entirely of swamp detritus shuffled through the herbal stores. It lifted the lid of each jar and took a deep whiff, occasionally flicking out a pointed tongue for a quick taste. I couldn't tell if it wore actual clothing or if the covering on its body sprouted directly from its flesh.

"Is there a particular herb I can help you find?" I ventured, clutching the bundle of powder puff flowers to my chest. Supposedly no greater fae inhabited the fortress, but one could never be too careful.

The creature wheeled, nearly dropping the jar of ephedra. "Heh-heh! This is the one," the newcomer said in an oddly high-pitched draconian. A drake? It did have a vaguely draconic shape, with that long, toothy snout.

Confused, I repeated my question in draconian, and the drake perked up, fins raising like ears on either side of his reptilian head.

"This one makes me tingle, I like it. Heh!" He shoved his long snout into the jar and grabbed a mouthful of the slender dried grasses. "Call me Boshkt."

Significantly smaller than the other drakes, he was only slightly taller than me despite his long, stooped neck. Overall wiry and thin, he had oversized shoulders and distinctly muscular arms and legs. Mottled grey, green, and pale yellow scales blended seamlessly with a mossy beard, fins that spread from his head down his back, and lichenous growths. No wings, but a long tail curled around his feet. What must his dragon form look like?

"That one speeds the heart. Have a care." I settled on a tall stool near the central workbench. Did drakes ever get congested? It worked beautifully on humans. We rarely used it for ourselves.

Boshkt grinned a lolling drake grin, parting his jaws. He had one bright blue and one green, with pupils oriented horizontally. Like a goat. Or perhaps a giant toad. "I feel it. Told me to watch you, the Red did."

"Rafael sent you?" That he'd left a guard behind just for me both touched my heart and annoyed me. Something about the odd stranger did put me at ease.

The mossy drake set the jar down. "Wasn't to interfere unless you were in danger. Got bored. Can't even spar."

I cast about for some way to entertain him. Surely a bored drake was a troublesome drake. "You want a…" the word evaded me for a moment, "an introduction? Tour! You want a tour?"

"You know herbs, yes?"

"Yes, but not their actions on your kind."

He clapped, with a barking laugh. "Heh! You test them on me. I volunteer! Teach the Red something new, we will."

I laughed with him. "Agreed!"

Eäriel invited me to teach the assistants my particular style of herbalism. Getting to know her proved a much-needed balm. Between her effusive positivity, Carafindrien's soft acceptance, and Boshkt's quirky watchfulness, the isolation began to thaw.

One afternoon, as I led a demonstration on the proper way to vinegar-fry, a serving youth appeared, nervously waiting. I called a short break for the assistants as the youth addressed me.

"My Lord Celebel has entrusted me to deliver this message at the appointed time." The youth was a slight Siltaur adolescent with curly mahogany hair a few shades off of þeir skin. "My lord instructed me to say that it is 'important, but not urgent'." Þeir dark eyes widened. "Oh, and to save it for when you should need good cheer."

Þey shyly handed me a vellum scroll sealed with Celebel's house signet.

"Seems we could all take a moment for good cheer," I said, thanking the youth.

Þey bowed but did not retreat, obviously curious about this important-but-not-urgent message. I carefully cracked the seal and unrolled the scroll. Inside was a single lovingly rendered and highly detailed portrait. Of his hard, erect cock.

I almost dropped the scroll directly on my frying pan, doubling over with a surprised cackle of glee. Startled, the youth backed away, and Eäriel immediately demanded to see it. Wordless, still clutching my belly, I handed over the scroll. Her eyes went huge, ears twitching, and helpless peals of laughter caught her as well. We let the mirth flatten us until tears rolled down our cheeks and we gasped for breath. I resolved to demonstrate, in great detail, my gratitude to Celebel for breaking the wire of tension around my heart when he returned.

I split my nights between Celebel's chambers and Rafael's, breathing in the scents left behind in the sheets and trying to soothe my nervous heart. I told myself that both of them had seen countless battles before I ever knew either existed. Rafael in particular, indestructible blighter that he was, surely needed none of my worry. The grievous wounds that had brought them each to me were a rare and fateful occurrence.

It didn't make the waiting pass any faster.

One evening I attempted to climb out through the window of Rafael's room onto the roof as he had done. As my feet slipped on the smooth granite walls, I cursed my lack of talons. His room was a dizzying height off the ground. I scolded myself. What good was a smashed up healer? When my feet touched the floor inside, the Night Mother moved. A vision dragged me down.

Rafael stood alone, covered in blood atop a veritable mountain of bodies. The world around him stilled, eerily silent. Who could stand before the Red Dragon, the God of Carnage? The scene blurred. Now inside dark walls, he cast his sword away. Faces floated in the gloom around him, but no features resolved. Voices spoke, wordless. Kneeling, he bowed his head.

When I opened my eyes, I was flat on my back on the floor with tears streaming down my face. I'd had this same vision before. It had first come to me in my early days of knowing Rafael. He had, of course, scoffed when I told him. Recurrence indicated importance. Not for the first time, I wished I could force myself to have another, newer vision. I wanted to see Celebel, to know what Dûemer made of his fate as well.

Chapter 40

Our people returned in triumph, sooner than I expected. The Fomorians had indeed massed when the Carnyx sounded, just as planned. With the aid of the drakes, the enemy had broken and routed, their ranks decimated. For all the good news, the company seemed remarkably somber.

Those of us who gathered to receive them cheered as they rode past the courtyard, but I observed more grim faces in the company than jubilant. Difficult as it was not to fling myself into Celebel's arms as he passed—we could only blow each other kisses before he crossed into the great hall—I had to stay focused on my duties. Enough patients lined the beds in the healers' hall to demand my attention. They'd been patched up well enough in the field to survive the journey back, but now they needed intensive care.

Celebel had let me know through our connection that he was returning unscathed, and yet he seemed oddly troubled. I resolved that the quicker I could heal our people, the quicker I could run to my lover's comfort. Rafael was not among the company, but that came as no surprise. None of the drakes were present. His presence held strong just outside the walls.

To my somewhat surprised disappointment, Boshkt also rejoined the drakes in their camp as soon as they returned. I'd enjoyed the odd drake's company. He'd been a quick study with herbalism. Never seeming to sleep, he'd greet me just outside my chambers daily. I missed the pleasant routine of strolling to the healer's hall and digging through the stacks of materia medica together. He genuinely seemed to enjoy eating herbs just to see what they would do to him. Mostly nothing, but I took copious notes all the same.

As it turned out, we were over-prepared for the amount of care needed. Most simply needed an extended rest to recover their strength, and the other beds emptied quickly. Between Eäriel, myself, and a few trained assistants, we managed easily. The wounded were mostly simple, straightforward cases. The lack of critical patients seemed strange, but perhaps the battle had progressed more easily than expected. There were some broken limbs to knit, lots of piercing and slash wounds to finish healing, a couple of head injuries that weren't too serious… and one notable exception.

Commotion outside led me to emerge onto a chaotic scene in the inner courtyard. A giant black and red drake moved purposefully toward the entrance of the hall as serving youth scattered and soldiers protested loudly. His nostrils flared as he twisted his long neck back and forth, evidently trying to catch my scent among the others. I waved to him and his golden eyes lit up.

"Xyxs, here," I called in draconian; much improved after all the practice with Boshkt. "What is needed?"

His head swiveled and he approached me, much to the horror of everyone else. By way of greeting, he turned and sank down on a knee. Folding the opposite wing revealed a broken-off shaft buried deep at the joint where it connected to his muscular back. He'd had to kneel for me to even be able to see the injury, as his wing joints normally rode well above my head. I chuckled internally at the loudest detractor becoming the first the seek me for aid.

"Cannot reach this," Xyxs boomed. "Itches, it does!" He turned his reptilian snout to face me, angling his head over his shoulder in a disconcerting way only that long neck would allow.

Itches indeed, what a uniquely draconian thing to say. Fortunately, from the angle of it, his lungs were likely unaffected. A simple wound to patch up, but the actual removal of the shaft could be tricky.

"I see this. Can you lie flat?" I indicated lying on his belly.

Xyxs huffed, spreading himself on the ground like an enormous, winged crocodile.

"Don't move!" I sprinted over to the stables. Searching

amongst the farrier's tools, I finally put my hands on a pair of pliers that looked large enough to do the job. Serving youth watched me with wide eyes, staying carefully out of my way. I thanked them before jogging back to my prone patient.

"Sorry for the delay," I said, and he huffed again.

"Sun is warm on the stones," the big drake replied mildly.

I hoped it would soothe him for what I was about to do. He twisted his head to watch me as I climbed carefully over the shiny black spikes of his spinal ridge. A familiar presence made my ears tingle, but I could only focus on my unusual patient.

"This will hurt, make ready," I said, and he huffed again, a strong exhalation of breath through his nose that blew my hair back from my face.

I touched the entry wound with a light hand, pulling away some inflammation to help the broken shaft emerge a bit from his hide. His scales were not serrated like Rafael's, but they did have black-tipped points. I nicked my fingers a few times as I pushed at the flesh, trying to make enough space to grab the broken shaft with the pliers.

An elf would have already been squirming and perhaps crying out with pain. Most humans would have passed out by this point. Xyxs, however, gave no indication that he even noticed. I opened the pliers, found purchase, planted one foot on the ground and one just beneath his shoulder, and heaved. The bolt inched upward and steaming blood dribbled from the wound.

"You are well?" I asked the drake.

Noncommittal huff. All right.

I yanked again and the shaft was almost all the way out when it got hung up on the wing joint. This revealed the head of a vicious, twisted spear. I winced. At least it wasn't very wide, but there was no avoiding the tissue damage.

"Still good?" I asked. Xyxs grunted assent, making my ears buzz.

Putting my back into it, I heaved with all my might. The spearhead tore free with a lurch and an arc of sizzling blood.

Some of it burned where it landed on my arms in a light spray, but nothing serious. Xyxs sighed in obvious relief.

"Better." He rose to his feet, shrugging me off his back as he worked the bleeding joint, moving his wing with his opposite hand. The courtyard had cleared of elves. No one wanted to be in his way.

"Wait, I heal the wound!"

"You did good. Good elf." He patted me on the head with a heavy thump of one huge paw, nearly knocking me off my feet. The bleeding slowed before my eyes. Incredible drake physiology.

As I watched him slink off, the familiar presence I had ignored earlier flared in my senses. I looked over to see Rafael watching me intently. He picked up the spearhead where I had cast it aside, disappearing it into the folds of his cloak. Tossing away my bloody, ruined apron, I ran to him. He wrapped me in his arms, pulling me close.

"Were you watching to make sure I didn't get eaten, or to criticize my methods?" I teased, kissing him.

"Only to correct your grammar," the Dragon said loftily, and I laughed in spite of myself.

Watching the massive drake stomp off through the gates, leaving a trail of steaming blood in his wake, I said, "Xyxs doesn't seem like the conversational type."

"That one barely speaks more draconian than you. Rocks in his head." His mouth twisted in disdain, and I laughed again.

"I'm amazed there are so few wounded! The battle must have gone remarkably well." I twined my arms around Rafael's neck.

"Hrrm, yes." He looked away. That gave me pause.

"What does that mean? What are you not telling me?" His silence made my nerves twinge with alarm. "We are going to find Celebel. Now!"

The Dragon arched a brow, but relented and led me into the fortress proper. I had to trot to keep up with this stride. In typical fashion, he did not bother to slow for my shorter legs. As we reached the war room, we came into the midst of an argument between Celebel and Feanim. Marron stood off to one side, burly arms folded. With his mouth pressed into a thin line, it was the most outwardly annoyed expression I'd ever seen on the green drake.

"Cel, come off it, we won," Feanim was saying. Somewhere between their arrival and this meeting, they'd both had time to change out of their armor, bathe, and find fresh clothing.

Before Celebel could respond, I bounded across the room and threw my arms around him. Surprised but catching me easily, we kissed for a long moment. Rafael's growing displeasure burrowed into my back, but I ignored it. I'd honor the deal I'd made, but I needed my own reassurances. When our lips parted, Celebel looked deep into my eyes. His own were stormy with concern.

'*That one is a true monster,*' Celebel sent, mouth taut, indicating the Dragon with his eyes.

'*Speak aloud,*' I sent back, then followed my own lead by asking the room what had happened.

Celebel cleared his throat. "Our supposed *ally* and his monstrous people consumed our dead *and* most of the grievously wounded!" Barely suppressed horror tightened his voice. My stomach dropped to my feet.

Rafael remained impassive. "We devoured your enemies also. Are you going to weep over them?"

I wheeled on him, tugging the tips of my ears down. "You did *what*?"

"*I* did nothing. It is our way to consume the fallen in battle. Your sensitive little flower-eaters could not handle the sight." The Dragon leaned on the table and examined his talons.

"You *ate* our people?" Panic rose, squeezing the breath from my lungs. I forced myself to center, to calm, still pulling on my ears.

"I told you before that I would no longer devour elves." He arched a brow. "I simply did not impede the individual actions of my people."

"I ate a few," Marron volunteered with a shrug. "They weren't going to complain, and we needed the energy after all that shifting."

For a moment no one spoke, tension crackling in the air. Celebel banged a fist on the table, making me jump. "That wasn't a battle, it was a *massacre!* I've never seen anything like it."

"Celebel, we *won*," Feanim cut in. "Winning matters more than sensibilities. The drakes saved us from a huge amount of casualties. This changes everything!"

Rafael gave the Duedellen a wry look. My stomach sank further; through the very floor.

With an effort, I released my ears and steadied my breathing. I made a concerted attempt to lift the mood. "We won? We should be celebrating. That means the horn worked, right? We were able to draw them out? I assume that also means the numbers were manageable."

Celebel wasn't having it, more storm clouds gathering on his brow. "If we act no better than our enemies, what is the value in winning? Fewer, but still far more casualties than were necessary! We could have saved our wounded soldiers. I brought another *healer* here for fuck's sake!"

"I brought myself here, thank you," I said pertly. "I thought the Fomorians were capturing us, not eating us, correct?" Celebel frowned with a tense nod. I turned to Rafael. "But he's right, you cannot allow your people to eat our wounded! I won't offer my services to your people if you deny the opportunity to my own."

"*I* cannot?" Rafael bristled. "Your people would all be dead if not for us, if not for *me*. Your little *plaything* would be dead." Scorn dripped from his words. "They are weak. *Soft!*"

"No. Don't you dare act the bully about this. You *knew* I would be upset." I glared up at the Dragon. At least he could direct his rage at me and not Celebel.

"Why am I here, Cúraniel?" he said, voiced pitched dangerously low. "Am I to slaughter your enemies or make you all *feel* better about your impending doom?"

"*Why* is this an argument?" Feanim shouted, and we all turned to look at him. "We are making better armor, better weapons, and now that we know what to expect from each other in battle, it will go more smoothly next time! We'll simply remove the wounded as swiftly as possible. Strategically, this must be addressed for morale, yes, understood. Dead is still dead. Now all of you shut the fuck up about it. We have more important things to discuss, such as repairing the Carnyx."

Repairing it? I frowned in confusion.

Rafael tossed the spearhead I'd freed on the table with a clank, heedless of the blood smearing the maps, and effectively changing the subject. "Have you found weapons like this amongst the Fomorians before?"

Feanim hefted it, rotating the head in the light. "Feels like pure þilvor. Where did you find this?"

"I pulled it out of Xyxs." Of course it had to be þilvor; it had pierced his scales. I mentally kicked myself for not noticing. At the blank elvish stares, I added, "The big red and black drake. He came to me asking for help." Their ears flicked in recognition.

"I've only noted Fomorians carrying blades of bronze or obsidian." Celebel leaned in, his complaints momentarily forgotten. "Perhaps a few with ice."

"Mistaken identity, I'd warrant," Marron said. We all turned to him and he blinked in surprise. "You mean to say any of you would have known the difference between two drakes with similar coloration? Without prior introduction? You two didn't even know his name, and he's earned quite a reputation in the last few centuries. Rose to power fast." He sucked his teeth and raised a scaly eyebrow. Good point. "Xyxs is damn big target in that form."

Rafael snorted, lip curling. No doubt taking offense at the comparison. Feanim watched the Dragon's reaction for a moment, nodding thoughtfully. I described the wound.

"Could have been a practice run. We may need to reconsider your placement in the next battle." The Duedellen tapped the side of the spear against his hand.

"I can tell you from experience that one little spear is not enough to take this one out." Wry humor colored Marron's voice.

"Our misfortune," Celebel signed, and Rafael fixed a vicious glare on him. Celebel returned the challenging look.

The Dragon's gaze settled on me. "You owe me a debt."

"I will discuss it with you later." I moved to cross the room, thinking to join Celebel.

"You will discuss it *now*." His viperine eyes flashed.

Suddenly, I was lifted into the air and tossed over a broad shoulder, like a dishrag.

"Gods *dammit* Rafael, put me *down!*" I kicked and squirmed, trying unsuccessfully to writhe my way out of his steely grip.

"No," he growled. "You made a deal. I am collecting on it. Your *nekarazzi* is unharmed."

Cold fury blazed in Celebel's eyes. "What deal?" he demanded first to the Dragon's back and then to me. "Cúraniel, what deal?"

I heard Feanim say to Celebel that he should just let Rafael have me as I rounded the corner against my will. Uselessly, I fought the Dragon all the way back to his room, yelling, kicking, trying to bite. Once, I managed to snag one of the tapestries lining the walls and knock it down. His only response was to slap my ass hard enough to make me gasp and say, "Enough, settle down." Which only further enraged me.

By the time he swept away the books I'd left scattered on his bed and dumped me on it, I was so furious my ears burned. To my surprise, he knelt before me, taking my hand. I slapped him with the free one.

"I suppose you think I deserve that," he rumbled.

"You should be grateful I'm not as strong as you." I shook out my stinging palm, and slapped him again. He caught the hand as I readied a third slap.

"Stop. You will hurt yourself."

"You have no respect for me, treating me thus! I am not a bauble for you to haul around at your leisure, you gods damned brute." My teeth ground in frustration. "I hate you so much at times. I love you for bringing Celebel back safely, for keeping your word, but otherwise I fucking *hate* you right now!"

Rafael accepted my wrath with calm detachment. Where had that earlier anger gone? I wanted him to roar and rage at me, to give me a better target. Yelling at a stoic Dragon felt wrong, somehow.

"Do you truly?" he asked quietly, and the fight went right out of me. Almost as though… The calm settled so heavily, perhaps it was merely fatigue.

Sometimes his nature seemed impossibly at odds with my own, but I never meant to actually wound him in my anger. I relaxed, and he released my hands. I leaned forward, winding my fingers into his hair, and sighed.

"No, of course not. Sometimes I wish I could hate you, you make me so angry." I tugged at his hair, eliciting a smirk from him. "There it is again, you are *trying* to drive me mad!"

"Your strikes are getting faster. Who taught you that?" His eyes glittered with amusement.

"One day I'll land hit that actually gets your attention." I scowled at the emptiness of my threat.

"You could drive your thumbs into my eyes," he said helpfully. "You may be fast enough now to get at least one."

"Quit trying to distract me, you awful creature. I want to settle this between us."

His expression turned serious again. "I did not consume any elves."

"You swear to me?" I raised an eyebrow.

He'd always kept his word. Even when he had no reason, even when he found loopholes. I still had to ask. He covered his heart with his hands, then extended his palms to me, maintaining eye contact.

"All right, I accept your word." I touched my palms to his, then paced mine over my own heart. "Can you enforce the idea with the other drakes? Let them devour the enemy all they want, but leave our dead and wounded for us to tend."

"It will not be popular. They will see it as egregious waste." Rafael leaned forward and propped his chin on my knee, looking up at me. I enjoyed the change in perspective; I didn't often look down at him. I stroked his hair and he rumbled with pleasure, sliding his arms around my legs.

"Since when have you cared about popularity? Please try. For me. Maybe they will understand if you explain it the same way you did the concept of seeking a healer." The locks of his hair mimicked bloody slashes on my thighs. How appropriate. "If you can convince at least Marron, it seems the others will listen based on how Xyxs altered his song."

Rafael's look was measured. Fine, that was the best I could hope for.

"Also, don't ever toss me around like that in front of others again. It's humiliating!" I yanked on his hair for emphasis. He gave me a knowing smile, heavy with meaning. "I will not be treated like a haunch of mutton!"

"You will forgive me," he said.

"I will not!" I was indignant.

"You always do." The Dragon practically purred, the self-satisfied blighter. "You like it when I toss you around."

Most infuriatingly, he was right. I did like it, and I *did* always forgive him. I needed to examine that problem later. Damn him.

"I most definitely do *not* like being tossed around in front of others," I protested. "It is disrespectful."

"If I had no respect for you, my dove, I would have killed you upon our first meeting. Or at any of the many times you have crossed me since." He said it frankly, but without heat. No surprises there. Rafael paused, with an evil grin. "And your scent names you a liar."

He pushed my knees apart and buried his face in my crotch, inhaling. Gods *damn* him. I pulled his hair, and he rumbled happily.

"I hate you." Exasperated laughter escaped me. "I hate that I cannot even stay properly angry with you!"

"Mmm hmm." He pushed my skirt up to my waist and over his head.

"Rafael! No more tossing me around in public!" I pushed unsuccessfully at his broad shoulders. "I enjoy your salacious flirting up until the point where you overpower me. Then it becomes degrading."

"Hrrrm, as you wish," he said into my vulva, and then I could only cling to the bed for dear life.

Chapter 41

Celebel requested that I take a meal alone with him, so I made my way to his rooms. He immediately swept me into a tight embrace when I stepped into the antechamber.

"Ah, my love, I was so worried! What did he do to you?" He clasped my face in his hands, studying me carefully for signs of injury.

"Be at ease, Starshine. Just more of Rafael's flair for the dramatic. He makes me angry at times—yes, frequently, don't look at me that way—and his ability to control the conversation in that manner is unfair. There was little I could do in the moment. I've since set a new boundary: no more throwing me around in public." I stalled, tensing. For a moment I considered sidling closer to the steaming tray of food on the sidebar, but Celebel left no room to maneuver in his arms.

"What did he mean by a 'deal'?" My lover's brow knit, eyes darkening.

I took a deep breath and braced myself. "I asked him to watch over you—"

"You *what*?" His ears flattened.

"Just focus your ears, please. I asked him to make sure that you returned to me safely, and agreed to stay with him for a dozen nights if he did."

Celebel took his own deep breath, clearly trying to wrestle down his growing fury. "Why would you do such a thing? I want no deals made with that fucking abomination!"

I pulled away with a sharp look. "Do not speak of *my soulmate* that way. And I care about your safety more than I care about your pride. Rafael kept his word."

"We had that battle well in hand. I am no green youth," he retorted, nostrils flaring. "He's exploited your concern as yet another way to keep us apart. You, yourself said to be wary of making any deals with him. How could you do this without even *consulting* me?"

"Celebel—"

"No, *you* focus your ears! You were not there, you did not witness his atrocities. You make allowances for this villain that you would never make for another! You've heard him growl and threaten and posture, but breathing his flame from a distance is a very different thing. Until you have watched him cut through a wall of bodies like a cyclone through a straw hut, how can you possibly understand? He is a *monster*, Cúraniel." Celebel's eyes flashed as he spoke, pacing in front of me. "He's perfectly serious when he says he cares nothing for any life but yours. You would do well to start truly hearing his words.

"I want you present next time. We could use your help with the wounded, and I want you to witness the whole truth of this fiend you've taken into your bed. I insist. You must see for yourself what he does to foes, what he has done to our own people for thousands of years. What he would cheerfully do to *me* if given half a chance! There is war, and then there is… *Rafael*. The elders were no fools to name him thus. He is truly godlike in his carnage."

The pit in my belly grew heavier with each word. I knew he wasn't wrong. It was another facet of what Rafael himself had said earlier; that I always forgave his bad behavior. Had I cursed everyone by coming here?

"Do you regret meeting me?" I said in a small voice, and he stopped in his tracks. "Apart from being healed, do you regret the rest?"

Celebel took my hands. "I love you more than I ever thought it possible to love. And yet I feel such anguish because of it. I am torn between duty and love, just as you are torn between the two of us. I am resilient though, my dear, and am prepared to love you beyond the mountains weathering to silt in the sea. I would only regret loving you if you refused to see what it asks of me."

An honest answer. "Very well. I make a decent field medic if it comes to that. I've never worked during a conflict apart from the ambush, but I have plenty of experience with trauma care after natural disasters. " I kissed his hands. "I know I've asked impossible things of you, and I wish I never felt the need. You've been far more patient than anyone should have to be. Tell me, did Rafael do anything to antagonize you in the field? He has his version of events, but I'd rather hear it from you."

Celebel sat beside me, putting his arms around me. "I want to show you what I witnessed, for you to understand how I feel. Do you agree?"

"Is that necessary, since you also want me to witness this in person?" It would surely be upsetting. My stomach was strong enough, but my heart quavered.

"It would be cathartic for me, at the very least." His eyes were so troubled, I couldn't resist.

I inclined my head, and he pressed his forehead to mine for a moment. Then he stepped back and began to weave the image. Colors took shape first, then sound. Then the scene coalesced.

Celebel stood in his armor on the battlefield with a small group, including his bodyguards, and Feanim. On the adjacent hillock Nemohee waited with the Carnyx of Calling. The huge horn stretched and curled overhead like an ominous standard. Machi, Nemohee's blue roan, waited saddled and ready nearby. A few paces ahead, a line of archers watched the trees. To the rear stood the infantry, and to either side, the cavalry.

Nemohee rolled and stretched þeir shoulders. Þey stepped to the horn, inhaled deeply, and blew a single, long, mournful note. The eerie call floated across the rolling hills where it faded. When the last lingering sound faded, the horn burst apart from mouthpiece to bell with a great, echoing crack!

"Wrong seeming," Nemohee signed with large, exaggerated movements. "Accident?"

Celebel raised a hand for stillness. Horses whickered with discomfort and the archers looked all about. For a long moment, silence reigned. With tight shoulders, the group surveyed the area.

It began as a faint rumble. Weapons slid from sheaths and scabbards, archers readied their bows. Slowly, slowly, the sound grew louder. The horses danced, their barding chiming with the movements.

The Fomorians answered the call. And they did so in force; erupting from the hills themselves on all sides. For a few heartbeats, all was chaos and terror. The enemy stampeded toward the Carnyx, disregarding all else in their mad rush. Nemohee grabbed the pieces of the horn and leaped onto Machi's back. The stallion took off into the protection of the gathered elvish forces.

The elves responded, regrouping swiftly to go on the offensive. The Fomorians weren't nearly as swift, but in such great numbers, they didn't have to be. The ground rumbled under the weight of all their boots.

Archers cut down wave after wave. Cavalry danced a bloody swathe through the advancing enemy, aided by the infantry pikes. The battle roared with a voice of its own.

Feanim clinked his gauntlets for attention in the face of the charging foes. "Where is he? Too close," he signed.

"Celebrating our death, likely," Celebel signed back, with a sour look. The elves braced themselves, assuming their ready stances. Fomorians swarmed toward them.

A thin gout of flame seared through the first wave of enemies from above. They fell, shrieking and clawing at their faces. The entire forward charge of the Fomorians tripped and stumbled over that first line of fallen comrades. Rafael landed hard, taloned feet first, on the skull of the Fomorian directly in front of the party, bearing it straight into the ground with a crunch. He straightened, almost casually, and looked Celebel dead in the face for a tense breath before drawing his sword—and driving it into the ground, up to the hilt. The Dragon's eyes burned red, his hair streaming flame. His talons flexed.

With a mighty swipe, he cut cleanly through the body of the next nearest foe. The field exploded in pandemonium as the other drakes hit. Four more of the big warriors landed heavily, wielding their bodies as effectively as their chosen weapons. Each cleared a space around themselves as they took to the fight. Marron laid about with sword and talon, fighting with calm efficiency. Tyldain fought with a slender sword and dagger, slashing with deadly fast precision, occasionally spitting small bursts of flame into the faces of his opponents. Xyxs eschewed external weapons entirely, swinging his tail like a club as he bit into Fomorians with his long jaws. The last drake held a somewhat avian form. Yellow scales with a green dorsal stripe and a bony crest, that one utilized powerful kicks from scythe-like taloned feet.

Rafael himself became a whirling, snapping, snarling tornado of death. Bodies and limbs flung into the sky with arcs of fountaining blood marked the Dragon's passage. He ripped his way through the massed Fomorians like a saw through silk, untouchable. Before long, the enemy fell over themselves, trying to escape.

As the cavalry charged forth, the party overcame their initial shock and joined the fray. Crossing swords with the bewildered Fomorians, who kept looking to the sky as if waiting for more drakes to fall on their heads, made them significantly easier to defeat. Celebel worked into a rhythm. Thrust, cut, block, lunge forward, dodge. He and Feanim watched each other's flanks, and Celebel's bodyguards watched them both.

At least until Celebel came upon a colossal Fomorian, keenly intent on taking his head off with a flint greataxe. It shoved away all other combatants to focus on the lone Consul. Celebel barely dodged the first whistling swing, readying himself for the next, when the Fomorian's pale eyes bulged strangely. A bloody something tore through the creature's chest from behind… a hand! A taloned hand punched through the huge Fomorian's torso from the back before twisting into a distinctly rude gesture, then withdrawing.

Thunderstruck, Celebel froze as the Fomorian toppled over, grasping at the gaping hole in its chest, revealing a blood-soaked Rafael standing behind it like a grinning vision of death. Blood streaked the drake's jagged teeth, bits of rent flesh dangling from his lips. Some unholy fire lit his eyes.

"Run, little elf. Run back to your camp. Lest I forget myself and mistake you for prey," the Dragon growled, with a slow, menacing sway of his head.

Another Fomorian charged into the drake, and he caught it by the neck. Keeping his eyes locked on Celebel, he lifted the Fomorian until its feet dangled helplessly off the ground. It scrabbled at the Dragon's grip, gasping for breath. With a sudden upward toss, Rafael changed his hold on the creature, snatching first one arm from the socket, then the other, with sharp pops as the joints pulled free. The Fomorian howled raggedly, dropping its cleaver from a nerveless hand. Twisting the Fomorian's now-useless arms behind its back, the Dragon leaned in, almost intimately close to its frantically snapping teeth. With a deliberate blink at Celebel, he turned and sank his own teeth into the Fomorian's throat, ripping it free with a jerk of his head and a spray of blood. He let the body fall and spit the gobbet of flesh at Celebel's feet.

Celebel took a few steps back, and Rafael coughed a laugh that grew into a deafening roar. Drums sounded all around them, pounding a call of doom.

Celebel released me with a face gone pale and taut. The drumming I'd heard was my own heartbeat in my ears. We looked together at the now-cooled tray of food set out for our supposed shared meal, my previous hunger thoroughly diminished.

I sank onto the chaise. "I've seen some of this before, from his perspective." Fiddling with the pearls in my braid, unsure of what else to say. Most of the emotion I'd felt was Celebel's, mingled with the fear of seeing him hurt. "Taunting you so… I find that unacceptable. I'll speak to him."

"I couldn't, in all honesty, tell you if he was fully in control of his faculties. He looked absolutely mad, Cúraniel. Like a gods damned demon."

I nearly choked on my saliva, but my mind turned away.

"Drakes experience bloodlust, and Rafael's is particularly intense from what he's told me. He shouldn't have gone anywhere near you like that. I don't appreciate that kind of risk." Crow, I should have been more specific in my request that Rafael watch over Celebel. I knew better. "But we wanted the might of the drakes and we bloody well have it now. We cannot now fault him for providing the very thing we requested, even if you find his methods distasteful. Yes, it is difficult to watch, but he hasn't committed any particular wrong." No longer able to ignore the growling of my belly, I broke down and nibbled at a candied taro root despite my upset.

Celebel sighed in defeat, but followed suit. "I understand now why you call him feline. He put me in mind of a cat ruthlessly tormenting its helpless prey."

I nodded in agreement. "Yes, very much so. On another note, does this mean the war is over? It seems you've defeated quite a large number of Fomorians."

"Would that it were so. There were several minor skirmishes during our return, and word from outlying Siltaur camps that the attacks are still worsening. We truly have no way of knowing our enemies' numbers until we can locate their strongholds and meet them at their own gates."

"Every conflict resolved seems to generate more. Both on the field and between the three of us." I smoothed my braids and wished I could run away. If only to stand in the warm summer rain down by my creek and smell the lilies.

"I have one question for you," Celebel said, between bites of a roasted parsnip. "How can you love Rafael and despise Feanim? Haven't you noticed they are remarkably similar in temperament? The biggest difference is Feanim doesn't threaten violence at any given moment."

"The biggest difference is that I trust Rafael to keep his word, even if he's occasionally infuriating. Feanim would cheerfully kick anyone's dead body on the way to his next goal. He's incurably biased against me due to my lack of status and my proximity to the people he wants most." I crossed my arms, defensive.

"Again, this sounds familiar." Celebel's mouth twisted.

"I also mislike the disrespectful way Feanim treats Nimthil."

"Disrespectful?"

"Do you truly not notice how often he excludes Nimthil from the conversation with his lack of signing? He also makes her publicly uncomfortable with his fixation on Rafael. Doting on her doesn't reconcile the lack of basic courtesy. Rafael has his issues, but he allows no slight against me." I wasn't perfect either, but I tried. Feanim's carelessness rankled. I held no love for Nimthil, but she deserved better.

Celebel winced. "Fair. Do you hear the notes of this melody, though? You make allowances for Rafael that you never would for Feanim. Imagine if Feanim raised his hostility to the level your Dragon aims at me and had the means to follow through."

I shuddered. "I take your point. You've mostly only heard us banter or argue, but I genuinely enjoy spending time with Rafael. Not only in a sexual context; I like him as a person. We bicker and snarl and come to eventual understanding. It is a ritual at this point. Frankly, I find it refreshing to unleash my darker emotions upon one who never holds such expression against me.

"My Dragon has grown since we left the hill, despite everything. Without a comparison, I understand why you do not perceive the change. You must remember that Rafael is ancient, and very much alone in his power. When has he ever been forced to compromise on anything at all? Who could have predicted that he would ever willingly *aid* elves in battle? These changes take time. He has made many concessions, little by little. Although he is quick to anger, he backs down if I grow truly upset." I clutched the scale around my neck. I'd forgotten to take it off when I entered the chambers, but since I wasn't intending to dally, I hoped the Dragon wouldn't mind.

"Precisely. Rafael upsets you. He does it frequently and without remorse. He wouldn't have to back down if he weren't so relentlessly, needlessly aggressive. And it is only the peak of a very large volcano. Maybe you'll finally recognize it once you've witnessed him crush a few skulls with the same hands that caress you. He is an inherently violent creature, and I cannot trust that any of us are safe from him. Not even you." Celebel's ears flattened. I kept mine aloft with a concerted effort. "And I never claimed your connection was only sexual. Though we all witness the way you fall at his feet whenever he beckons."

"Your ears must be blocked if you think his constant acquiescing to my requests is typical for him. Rafael is not remorseless, but it is a private matter. He's trying harder than you know to accommodate all these changes." I eyed a poached pear with a slice of aged cheese. Agitation clamped my belly, and I thought better of it. "*And* he's right that we would all have died without him. The other drakes' contribution toward this latest victory is not insignificant, either. You know dead is dead. What is the difference in how you kill the enemy and how Rafael kills the enemy? They are still dead in the end."

That gave him pause. "Feanim's words from your mouth," he said with an amused breath, but his eyes were serious. "Perhaps you are right and my sense of honor is naïve, yet I still believe in honorable battle."

"I would not besmirch your honor. But you must understand that using a sword makes you no less of a killer."

Tiring, that these conversations always devolved into good versus evil, honor versus dishonor. It left little space for nuance. Rafael existed almost entirely in the grey, or perhaps just shy of midnight. I grew weary of constantly having to defend him. Appealing to another's better nature erroneously assumed the other had the same moral basis as oneself.

Celebel's fingers drummed on his arms. "Do you realize how quickly you defended your own autonomy and yet so blithely handed mine away?" His eyes had gone stormy again. "You spoke up immediately to correct me in saying you brought yourself here, and yet you had already handed control of *my* choices directly to someone who *loathes* me. You hate being controlled; why would you ever think I would appreciate it? And now I cannot even be with you upon my return. I have missed you terribly and here I am sleeping alone!"

I exhaled slowly. He wasn't wrong. I had been selfish in my anxiety. Though eclipsed by the legendary strength of the Red Dragon, Celebel was by no means a weak man. Truth be told, no elf was particularly fragile, except by comparison to a drake.

"I should not make decisions rooted in fear. You have every right to be angry with me. Sometimes it seems I am almost as talented at making you angry as he is." I looked around the room, anywhere but his eyes. A spinach tart beckoned. "I keep forgetting I came here to eat."

"Eat, my love."

"Am I still your love? Each of these conflicts over Rafael grows more sharp-edged, more strained." I watched Celebel's face anxiously.

His eyes widened, and he pulled me close. "Yes, of course. I'm merely shaken by the battle and concerned for you. When he hauled you off in a rage, it frightened me. I kept recalling the battle. Gods, I never thought I'd feel sorry for the blighting *Fomorians*."

I kissed him, long and hard. "Starshine, I have lived a long time and survived much worse than a bruised ego. Please trust me. I'm doing the best I can in a bad situation. You're never going to convince me to stop loving him. He might, perhaps, but you cannot. Just as he cannot talk me into letting you go. No more of that, please. Yes, he's often terrible. I know it. He knows it too. I love him anyway."

Celebel looked at me for a long moment. "Does he make you happy?"

I'd never truly considered happiness before; such a nebulous concept. Like love. I thought of the way Rafael had held me after I'd fought with Celebel. All of the peaceful times together; on the hill, in his room, on the roof. Dancing together. The small, slow triumphs in getting him to accept his sexuality. His hidden sweetness. The wicked glint in his eye whenever he said something hilariously awful. The *thrumming.*

"When we are alone, yes. He looks at me and the rest of the world vanishes. Otherwise, well… Rafael is who he is. Here, we have enormous pressure attempting to split us apart. I know you feel it in similar ways. Everyone considers my relationship with him to be, at best, a perversion of nature." Sadness crept up my spine and into of my voice. "At worst, they consider me a traitor. I brought the strongest ally our people have ever known directly to their side, and they hate me for it."

Celebel thought for a while, smoothing the sleeves of his cornflower blue tunic, then said, "You may go now, love. I was eager to return here to your embrace. Now I am eager for the nights you have forfeited to pass quickly. This, you will have to atone for if you wish to make *me* happy." He spoke sternly, but with a flirtatious undertone.

His frustration was understandable; I felt it too. Being in his presence and yet unable to fully appreciate it made me want to kick myself yet again.

"I'm looking forward to thanking you in particular for that surprise message you sent." I'd kept the cock drawing in one of my journals.

"Did it raise your spirits?" He gave me a flirtatious smile.

"It certainly raised some eyebrows."

Chapter 42

Jfound Rafael in the library, deep in conversation with Araglin. The Dragon had settled on a chaise of green velvet-upholstered ironwood, carved in swooping lines that mirrored the style of the ladders. Surprisingly casual in posture, his long legs stretched out, and the usual stack of books rested at his feet. Araglin sat across from him in a high-backed chair, his own back stiff, but still openly engaged.

Light from the windows cast Rafael in shadow and illuminated the scholar, as though picking sides. Araglin's slightly soft, tall frame, outfitted in amber robes that complimented his dark skin, made quite a contrast with the Dragon's aggressively muscular bulk wrapped in practical black wool and leather. Without looking my way, Rafael gestured for me to join him.

A flagon of wine stood on a circular table between them, along with two ornate, gold-in-quartz goblets. Someone here evidently loved gold-in-quartz, perhaps Araglin himself. One goblet held nectar wine, and the other stood conspicuously empty. Hopefully, Araglin didn't consider it a slight for Rafael to refuse the sweet drink.

The Astolar poured the second goblet and handed it to me. I accepted it with a bow and padded to the Dragon's side. He moved his legs to make space for me without taking his eyes off of Araglin.

Rafael's deep voice resonated in the space, the chorus growl a rich velvet in my ears. "Ah, elves. Always so assured of their own superiority. Your very origin myth reflects it."

"You know our creation story?" The scholar's eyes brightened.

"Each nation adds its own embellishments, but the basis remains the same." The Dragon's talons flashed in the filtered light as he waved an airy hand. "The starlight coalesced into one

'Great Tree' whose branches then became the sun and moon. Its trunk formed the world, and the roots birthed your kind. Direct descendants of the stars, naturally, while the rest of us *lesser beings* arose from rocks and dirt." A sardonic brow raised.

Araglin huffed, lacing his fingers over his chest. The charms at the ends of his braids chimed with the movement. Trust a theological scholar to be offended rather than overawed. "That's a bit reductionist—"

"Is it?" Rafael's eyes were sharp.

I sipped quietly on my wine; I'd gone many rounds with him on the subject in the past. Ear-perking, to be sure.

The scholar gestured with his goblet as he spoke. "The stars gained awareness as gods, who then sang the tree into being, out of love."

"Love." Rafael snorted. "Who first awakened in this world?"

"Dhraxael." I couldn't help but interject. Rafael swept a hand toward me and I allowed myself a tiny amount of satisfaction at his validation. A few of our historians, those known more for self-aggrandizement than academic rigor, loudly argued for elves as the first.

"A *dragon*. Why?" He leaned forward, pinning Araglin with his gaze.

"The formation of Vaeda required balance, creating such upheaval that the churning pressed a fell beast into being… ah, beg pardon." His ears quivered with realization.

Rafael waved away the insult and Araglin's ears relaxed. "Incorrect. 'Dhraxael,' as you call him, was born of the sun itself, fighting free in a mighty flare that hurled him into the void. Extant long before your world tree mythos."

The scholar steepled his hands, brows drawing together as he leaned forward. "Then how do drakes explain the creation of this world?"

"Dhraxael was a creature of magma and flame, as were all the first dragons. He built a lair from his exhalations, that he may have a place to warm himself and rest his wings. A 'haven' indeed, this world you name 'Vaeda'." Rafael paused, examining the look on Araglin's face—it teetered between fascination and denial. "You call yourself learned. Is this the first time you are hearing of it?"

The scholar poured another glass of wine, swirling the amber liquid thoughtfully in his goblet before answering. "I have heard some iteration of this concept, though not as well-delineated. Would you mind if I noted your words? I had never thought to have such discussions in my life."

"With a mindless, barbarian lizard, you mean." Rafael's eyes glinted. I poked him, recalling the similar way he'd baited me. He ignored my reaction.

Araglin nearly dropped his goblet. "Certainly not! I beg of you, Lord Dragon, please do not assign contempt to my speech. I confess I may struggle to bridge these gaps in understanding, but I have always held you in intellectual regard despite our moral quandary. Even before I had the, ah, pleasure of introduction, I always found the tales of your shrewdness in battle quite compelling."

"Flattery now?"

I cut in before he made the poor scholar faint. "Rafael, stop being a pest. You know very well that Lord Araglin speaks in earnest."

The Dragon gave me a sidelong glare for ruining his entertainment. "Hrrm, very well. Continue."

Araglin recovered his composure smoothly and produced a small journal from a pocket somewhere in his voluminous gold velvet robes.

"What do your people call Dhraxael, if I may ask?"

"Xuatae Aitzindrerrelehen." A title, not a clan name, if I understood him correctly. Damn that double-rr throat drop. I tried to mimic the mechanics of it without making a sound and quickly surrendered.

Araglin blinked. "I confess, I cannot quite—"

"'Progenitor of the First Flame'."

"Ah." His quill scratched across the page. "So then, if your progenitor created the world, whence did its peoples spring?"

"Fire is the element of creation. You are aware that even your stars are cold fire, yes?"

Araglin nodded, the charms in his braids chiming again as he took notes. I sipped my wine, enjoying the deep rumble of Rafael's voice in the cozy library and his heat at my side.

"The Progenitor's flame, carried from the sun itself, sparked the fires necessary to develop life in this world. A very slow, meandering process, unlike what your mythos would have you believe." He held up a hand to forestall Araglin's interjection. "Yes, the stars are involved in the origin of elves, tree birth and all. I do not deny that. It is a fallacy, however, to claim that you are the only peoples of Vaeda with direct celestial origin. In a sense, we are all descended from the heavens."

Araglin tapped his full lips with the feathered end of his quill. "Much to cogitate upon, fascinating. Did the other true dragons also emerge from the sun?"

"Other suns. The Progenitor built a very attractive lair, drawing many of them in over time. In the end, some returned to those suns rather than become a part of this world."

"Truly fascinating. What is the origin of the moon, according to your mythos?"

Rafael turned to me, running a hand through my hair. He took hold of a pearl from the strand, rotating it to admire the shifting iridescence of the nacre.

"Some say she was formed from the shell of the first egg, shining with the light of new life, but I prefer another version. During that first mating battle, part of the progenitor's lair was struck free; a great mountain that fractured and spun into the void. The stars found her among them and mended her broken edges. She collected their light and awoke as the moon, to heal Xuatae Aitzindrerrelehen as he lay dying. She has followed ever after. The sun birthed us and gave us our power, but it is the moon who guards us in our repose."

Interesting. I'd never heard that version of the tale, only the eggshell rendition. Much more romantic. And relatable.

'*A wild creature is the moon, and yet reliable,*' he sent, replying to my stray thought.

"Oh, a battle was it?" I grinned at him and his mouth twitched in response. Everything came down to battle.

Araglin watched our exchange with a studiously neutral expression, but the shine of his mild black eyes and the twitch of his ears gave away his curiosity.

"Go on, ask," I said, "before the questions burrow out of your mouth."

His ears twitched again as he looked to Rafael for confirmation.

"If Cúraniel gives her permission, you do not need mine," he said a little sharply, and Araglin raised his hands in surrender.

"Would you be willing to elucidate on the nature of your, ah, relationship?"

"Our soulbond, you mean," I said, and Araglin's brows shot up.

Rafael circled a protective arm around my shoulders. "Any reformation you find in me is due to her direct intervention," he said in a purr that absolutely melted me. "I lay dying, she healed me, and I awoke ensnared."

"'Ensnared'," I scoffed. "He was a hellbeast upon waking. Took him dozens of years to relax."

Araglin took a deep breath, setting his goblet aside and closing his journal. "I must say, Lord Dragon, your sudden allegiance shift makes significantly more sense after Lady Cúraniel's court announcement. Observing the pair of you at that first dinner, it struck me that you are comfortable with each other in the way that only intimacy provides."

The Dragon rumbled, tightening his arm around me.

"It hasn't been without its pitfalls," I said.

"I am horrible," Rafael agreed, with something approaching cheer. Araglin's ears twitched wildly, though none of his thoughts showed on his face.

"You are drawn to horrible like moths to a candle, yes." I leaned into him, somehow both nervous and relieved to be so open.

Rafael pressed the tip of my ear to his lips. Araglin chuckled and caught himself with a nervous grimace.

"You may laugh. We've been teasing each other like this for almost a century." I smiled to put him at ease. "I appreciate your courtesy in the face of such strangeness."

"I do try to keep my ears open to new songs," Araglin said, rising. "My thanks for sharing it with me. Ah, the gratitude is for the Lady Cúraniel. I know the rule about thanking drakes!"

As he took his leave, I turned back to Rafael. "How exactly did you end up in conversation with him? I hope you didn't say anything terrible. Araglin is one of the few who have been accepting."

The Dragon indicated the books piled at his feet. "He came in search of a tome I had already selected, and was *overcome* with surprise to encounter me here." His mouth tightened for a moment. For once his thoughts were plain on his face. Rafael hated the assumption that he must be an ignorant spear-rattler. It stung his pride. "That one has no guile about him whatsoever. Thus, I invited him to speak his mind."

"He does seem quite genuine," I agreed. "What were you discussing before I came in?"

"Morality. What theologian can resist the urge to question their 'Evil Incarnate'"" His teeth flashed briefly in a wicked grin. "He has a particular interest in the demon realm."

Demons. I shivered. "And did you come to any accord? No, of course not. I'm surprised you were so civil with him." Even more surprising that Araglin hadn't backed down in the face of Rafael's intimidating presence. The gentle scholar had more steel in his spine than I'd given him credit for. The thought gave me a twinge of guilt about my assumptions regarding the court at large.

"Are elves the sole arbiters of civility now?"

I tugged my earlobe, shifting my weight on the settee.

"Cease your caginess for once. Why are you playing nice?"

Rafael watched my face for a moment, the fires that lit his eyes flickering strangely. "Do you understand how vastly entertaining all this is? To be formally invited inside an elvish fortress and watch them fall over themselves in their efforts to both appease and avoid me?"

"A cat among the mice, I'd imagine." I tried, and failed, to keep the snide tone out of my voice.

"A *dragon* among the mice," he corrected with that infuriating smile. "See how they squeak and run for cover? Do they also devour their own young in the face of adversity?"

I stood. "Couldn't provoke Araglin and now I'm your target?" No use talking to him when he was so clearly trying to irritate me.

He caught my hand, tugging me back down on the settee. "Come now, I do not think of *you* as a rodent."

"Oh, how you flatter me." Blighter. He was still deliberately tweaking my ears, but I couldn't resist. "I came in search of a particular herbal treatise, perhaps you've seen it. I need it for a particular project."

"This one, yes?" He pulled a book from his stack and showed me the cover, embossed in gold leaf with the author's sigil.

"How did you—"

Rafael stopped my words with a kiss. The scent of him and the way he brushed his lips ever so lightly over mine sped my heart rate.

"How well I know the holes in your little personal library," he murmured against my mouth, and I twined my arms around his neck. "This one eluded me as well until now."

"I'm not going to steal it," I protested, laughing.

"I am. Now it is yours; a gift." He smiled that cat smile.

My heart fluttered, and I sighed in consternation, more at myself than at him. "Gods damn it, Rafael. How are you such a romantic and yet *so* infuriating at the same time?"

"Do my gifts not please you?" he rumbled, giving me a sidelong glare.

"Oh, be quiet." I kissed him back.

Chapter 43

The hissing of the gossip snakes became a dull roar. I found backs turned everywhere I went, when I wasn't lounging in Rafael's quarters. He often disappeared during the day, leaving me to my own devices. He'd made no stipulations about my freedom, only the insistence that I remain available to him at night.

I devoted my down time to studying Celebel's request to help with the membrane layer of the armor. As I began to hate the stifling enclosure of the fortress more and more, I took to dragging my books with me outside. Plopping under a tree near the training field gave me the opportunity to observe the new armor testing in the fresh air.

Based on my research, I quickly realized the need to forage for materials, which meant a need to leave the protection of the fortress. Rafael granted my request, with the caveat that he would be watching. Nemohee was easy to recruit for some extra hands, and Eäriel cheerfully volunteered to join when she caught the melody of my plans. We decided to stock up on a few medicinals as well, since she wanted to learn more about my use of fungus.

Nemohee scouted for us first, finding a nice, damp copse of trees, where we could forage in peace without wandering too far from the walls. Eäriel and I met þem at the gates. It felt so good to be out under the trees that I immediately kicked off my boots and stuffed them in my pack. My soul immediately felt lighter, and Nem gave me a knowing look.

"Feels good to be out of that cage, eh?"

I dug my toes into the earth, relishing the connection to root and mycelium, rock, and burrowing creature. It was the most grounded and centered I'd felt since leaving my hill. No relationship drama, no courtly pressures. The trees swayed overhead, whispering their greeting with rustling branches, and the birds joined the gentle chorus.

Nemohee wore dappled brown and green leathers. If it weren't for þeir fiery hair and milk-pale skin, þey would have easily disappeared into the brambles. Þey kept a hand on the pommel of þeir sword, with a small crossbow close by as well, while Eäriel and I searched in the leaf litter. I couldn't hear or see Rafael, but his presence loomed as surely as if he stood right behind me.

I spied a familiar gnarl high up in a birch and shimmied up to cut it free. The tree sighed with relief under my hands, the fresh scent of its sap tickling my nose.

"Chaga," I cried in triumph.

Eäriel's eyes sparkled. "Does it make you fluttery?" She waggled her fingers.

I slid down the trunk with a laugh. "No, this is for painful joints. Works well for bringing down inflammation. Not my target but it's an auspicious find."

"*These* make you fluttery." She grinned, producing some bright, red-capped mushrooms with white speckles.

"Amanita is certainly good for talking to whatever ancestors met the tree that it grew on, but let me show you something more entertaining. We'll need to find hoofstock, though."

"This is wondrous," Nemohee said, watching us. "Did you pure bring me out here just to find hallucinogens?"

I laughed. "No, no. It is only a happy side benefit of mushroom hunting. Oh, there we are!" I scooped up a gelatinous yellow blob hiding under a branch. "Find me more of these! I need them for experiments."

Nemohee turned out to be especially good at finding my target species, and soon had a bucket full of the colorful mucoid molds. I showed Eäriel how to use a specific puffball mushroom for treating throat and facial swelling, and she showed me how to find the best damp-draining fungus.

Along the way, I located innocuous-looking little brown mushrooms sprouting from a pile of old horse dung. I plucked them carefully, giving a shake to spread the spores. Rinsing with a little of Nem's pocket flask whiskey and wiping them clean, I handed the majority to Eäriel.

"My favorite way to take these is in tea with a little honey to tonify the middle, and lemon to strengthen the branching nature of the wood element. For now, we can eat them raw. May I recommend stargazing while we do?"

A ripple ran along my connection to Rafael; amusement.

The healer accepted the mushrooms with grace. "Gorgeous, thank you!"

"Here now, I'm wanting to have a go," Nemohee protested.

I laughed and clapped þem on the shoulder.

"Have no fear, faithful sword. I saved some for you!" I turned over half of the remainder with a flourish. "Now, let's go get bendy and talk to the heavens. '''ve earned it." That should offer Rafael some entertainment.

Giggling like children, the three of us unpacked our gear and foraged treasures. Together, we climbed up on top of the stables, stuffing mushroom caps in our mouths as we went. Community acceptance, however small, soothed a rift in my heart I hadn't previously recognized. Perhaps I simply hadn't been willing to acknowledge it before.

Rafael's presence lapped at me like a warm ocean in that state. I smiled and laughed freely more in that evening than I had in years. The sunset colors laughed with us, dancing before our eyes. Later, the stars waved a greeting. We waved back.

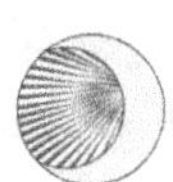

Rafael found me sitting on the library floor, scowling over books strewn around me, trying to make sense of my notes versus my reading. In concept, my idea for establishing the functional layer for the armor should work, but I couldn't find a tangible record to back it up. Nor could I find a guide through the next stage of development, though I did have at least a vague melody to follow. I'd simply have to put my faith in trial and error.

With Eäriel's help, I'd developed a simple nutrient paste from oats with a little spirit to maintain my experiments. Nemohee struck upon the brilliant idea of holding races to determine the most responsive of the colorful plasmodiums we'd collected in the woods. It started easily enough; just a reward of the nutrient paste painted a short distance directly across from the line of test subjects.

Nem immediately declared for a bright orange specimen. Naturally, a fiery Lachanaur would choose one that matched þeir hair. I preferred a bluish, more reactive one. Eäriel made what turned out to be the most practical choice. The largest plasmodium, it was a pale, almost colorless specimen. Her champion covered the distance faster than the others. Mine waited a bit before starting out, putting it in a solid fourth place, out of twelve. Nemohee's came in second-to-last.

The next step came in the form of a simple maze. We set up barriers between the gelatinous specimens and their target. Again, Eäriel's large, pale specimen outperformed the others by a significant margin. We tested them repeatedly, changing the level and type of challenge with each step. Eäriel's choice repeatedly bested the competition.

The winner received its own special smoked-glass jar with plenty of nutrient paste. I propagated it for broad use in the next phase of testing, which would be significantly more complex and time-consuming.

We'd released the rest of the specimens into the garden. All except one. Nemohee insisted on keeping the orange plasmodium in a little jar around þeir neck, naming it 'Speedy' and claiming it just needed more training.

"Quite a nest you have here." The Dragon crouched beside me.

"I am seeking precedent for a project. Not much to be found, it seems." I flipped through the book in front of me, frustrated at the author's lack of useful observations. "At this point, I might as well gather a sample and move forward with testing."

His eyes glittered, interest peaked. "A sample?"

Mostly muttering to myself, I pulled a different book from the pile. "Yes. I need some blood and a little flesh to test my idea. Preferably Feanim's, in case it goes wrong. His prototype is the most advanced, and most prone to failure if this doesn't take. I know he won't entrust it to me without a challenge, though, so damned stubborn. And yet I need a functional test subject to prove myself." I frowned, rifling back to a page I thought I'd seen. Some writer somewhere must have a suggestion of how to bond a living specimen to another's body. "That foolish muscle growth idea he has will never work."

Discarding that one, I pulled another book; a treatise on comparative anatomy between elves and various forms of flora and fungi. It looked more promising.

"How much do you require?" The Dragon's voice rumbled above me.

"Not much. Only a few drops of blood and the merest slice of skin, preferably with a little meat on it," I said off-hand, still focused on my reading.

Rafael's leaned over and kissed my temple. "Done."

Oh no. I dropped the book and looked at him. "Do not."

He grinned wickedly.

"What have I done? *Ask* him first, please. He may simply agree to it coming from you." An evil little voice wanted Rafael to snap a finger off the rude Duedellen, but I tried to stifle it. The Dragon looked entirely too entertained by this idea, which never boded well. I watched him leave with terrible misgivings about what I'd just set in motion. I appreciated his immediate willingness to take my word for my findings and yet…

Not a fingerbreadth on a candle later, Rafael returned. He took my hand and deposited in it a small, stoppered bottle filled to the brim with blood. It also contained a floating, neatly excised curl of flesh. I laughed with nervous horror, nearly dropping the sample.

"You ah. How did he… That's… Well done?"

Rafael merely made a brief, sarcastic bow and left me to my work.

Chapter 44

Rafael stormed into the healer's ward, eyes flashing. Taking a break from my experiments, I'd been working with Eäriel on a batch of topical liniments. Together we demonstrated the process to a group of assistants. They scattered from the path of the Dragon's ire. Eäriel cast a worried look over her shoulder as she followed.

"Have you seen this filth?" Rafael demanded, slamming a smut book on the table with enough force to blow my herbs off onto the floor, in a swirl of powders and leaves.

My stomach dropped when he opened it to a page that depicted him with various types of highly detailed, monstrous genitalia. He flipped to the next—a caricature of him involved in graphic sexual acts with reptiles. Each page grew successively worse and more offensive. The last page showed a disturbing image of me, crying and struggling, begging a slavering Rafael to stop what was clearly meant to be assault. It was even labeled "The Rape of Elvish Culture" to remove all ambiguity. I snatched my hands away as though burned by the pages.

"Forgive me, Dragon. This is much worse than the others. It goes much too far. But what can we do about it? I have no idea who's writing these." My heart pounded, his heightened state feeding my own.

Rafael glared at the smut book for a moment. Picking it up, he held it close to his face. Slowly, deliberately, he exhaled a black smoke over the pamphlet. Something about it made me shiver with dread. The smoke sank into the parchment. Inhaling deeply, his eyes narrowed to venomous slits.

"I do." His growl raised the fine hairs all along my body. "This edition came from a single individual. The others were a group effort."

"Dragon, please. These folk know nothing of your past. I'm

certain they are only trying to tweak our ears."

"Then I shall have to congratulate them on their success. In person." His teeth clicked together.

"Rafael, please." Knowing what was coming, words failed. Much as it distressed me, I couldn't rightfully stop him. The fools. Let it serve as an important reminder not to continually offend someone *we as a people* had named 'God of Carnage.'

"This is not an ally," Rafael said in a dark tone.

I sighed. He'd found a loophole in our agreement.

"What if this provocation serves some other purpose? An attempt to destroy this tenuous alliance by demonstrating to the others that you are indeed the monster they fear?"

"I have never ceased to be that monster." His eyes flickered. *'Better this than your entire population, should my people learn that I let such insult pass unchallenged.'*

"I understand." I shoved down my growing dread. "Please, try to be discreet."

He crumpled the pamphlet in his fist, burning it to ash, and stalked away.

'Come.' Celebel's voice rippled through my mind, lifting me from slumber before dawn. The tension in his tone had me instantly alert, tossing on clothes and rushing to meet him. Locating him through the bond was simple. His presence drew me to the great hall.

Passing through the great doors and few distressed serving youth milling about, I came upon Celebel and Feanim staring at a macabre tableau. A body had been strung up between the thrones of the Consulate.

I gasped, turning heads. Celebel shot me a tight-lipped glare. As though I'd committed this atrocity myself. Dûemer's celestial mantle of calm settled around me, naturally lingering in the presence such transition. I murmured a prayer of gratitude to the goddess.

Barely recognizable as an elf, the stripped corpse hung suspended by the neck from a wire attached to the high ceiling. Another wrapped each ankle, tacking the legs wide to either side of the thrones. The victim's belly was split open and emptied. Beneath it, entrails carefully spelled out a single word in the ancient high court elvish script: DISRESPECT. Severed ears marked the accents.

I circled it cautiously, trying to keep my gorge down. Smut book pamphlets folded into neat rosettes burst from empty eye sockets in a hideous paper bouquet. More pamphlets had been forced into the shorn-off ears, as well as the mouth, and anus. Where was the blood? None pooled on the floor, though the offal stained the carpet.

Celebel conferred with his fellow Consul as I absorbed the scene. "We must carry the body and wash it ourselves." His voice held a hollow, carefully detached tone. "We cannot ask this of the serving youth." Together they cut the corpse down, rolling it carefully in a sheet to contain the viscera.

A strange numbness held my emotions in check. "Gods damn it all. I never thought he would go this far." Crow, he'd been thorough, and must have worked quickly. *Shouldn't I be more appalled?* My mind skittered away from the thought.

Feanim turned to face me. "Rafael's doing."

"Yes, obviously. He must have chosen this clean, methodical dissection to remind us that he is no wild beast." The ear placement also displayed his twisted sense of humor. I rubbed my temples, already overwhelmed with the coming storm. "Who is the victim?"

"We aren't entirely certain, but we believe it to be Unarimë, a young Astolar, based on what spirit lingers within him. Minor lineage. My… former acolyte." Araglin's quiet voice startled me. I hadn't noticed him off to the side. His normally rich brown skin had a greenish tinge, the kindness gone from his eyes. He hugged himself, looking anywhere but at the gruesome scene. "If only we'd discovered him sooner, put a stop to his behavior before... this."

Celebel shook his head. "So, you condoned this retaliation in advance?"

I bristled. "Rafael came to me in a fury. I condoned nothing."

"I thought at most he would be annoyed at these silly drawings. But this..."

"I thought the same until he showed me the latest one. It was much, much worse than the others. One page overtly depicted Rafael forcing me, drawn and labeled in graphic detail. He would never let that stand."

"And you approved *murder*?" Celebel's brow pinched.

"It's not as though he asked my permission! You grant me far too much power." I exhaled through my nose, trying to stay calm. Trying not to stare at the cocooned body lying on the ruined, once-verdant carpet between the thrones. "Frankly, we're fortunate the walls yet stand."

"You could have warned us," my soulmate persisted.

"To what end? More dead?" I yanked at my earlobes, and he looked away with a scowl.

Feanim clicked his tongue against his teeth. "The talisman earring is gone, too. Rafael has certainly sung a compelling melody. The serving youth who discovered the body couldn't read the ancient script and thought he'd spelled out some gibberish. Took Araglin having a look to decipher it. It's so horrible it's almost fucking funny."

The scholar looked up with a frown. "Inappropriate, Lord Feanim. Your tread crushes the grass. We have lost one of our own, in the very heart of our sanctuary. I find it especially disturbing that the Red Dragon carried out this vile act in our midst and no one heard any of it. The young fool, barely into his majority—" His voice cracked. Feanim bowed his head, momentarily contrite.

Celebel shook himself. "How did Rafael identify the author?"

"By scent, essentially." Some instinct told me to kept the details quiet when he shuddered. "I warned you. The court has been far too complacent, hiding behind a tenuous alliance and thinking themselves safe. They *know* his reputation, and yet they provoke him at every turn." I blew out a frustrated breath. "I tried to dissuade him. I did! He claimed the very presence of the other drakes would have forced his hand even if he hadn't taken offense."

Feanim nodded. "Yes, Rafael would have to answer a direct insult, and in a manner that brooked no argument." He frowned at the body. "Fucking fool had it coming."

"Enough. There must be a tribunal." Araglin's voice cut in. "I will call it after the funeral rites." He swept out of the hall without a glance at me. Celebel watched him go, eyes darkening.

The two Consuls lifted the corpse, and I followed them to healer's hall. Alone in the space, we washed Unarimë and removed the pamphlets. More were buried deep inside the body cavity. The excised organs we stored in porcelain pots. I used a little spirit to reattach his ears. Oddly, the ears disturbed me more than anything else; a final erasure of identity. Once wrapped in fresh linen, Celebel and Feanim cast a preservation on the dead elf. It would do until a ceremony could be held.

"You are less bothered by this than I would expect," Celebel said, once Feanim departed.

"Bothered?"

That blank, numb sensation persisted overall. I'd seen awful things inflicted on myriad bodies, though this was a new type of awful. When balanced against the sheer amount of sexual harassment this Unarimë had deliberately inflicted on my soulmate, however, I couldn't find much compassion in my heart.

"You are a healer. Isn't this kind of violence anathema to you, and that Rafael would make a sick joke of it? I'm a bit surprised at the darkness."

"Cel, I am a healer. Darkness grants us strength. We must embrace it or be drowned by it. If I were the gentle 'love and light' sort, Rafael would have eaten me immediately upon awakening. I do not care for the approach, but all he did was send a clear message about respect. One that you would do well to remember."

He took my hand. "We still have much to learn about each

other. This killing disturbs me profoundly, yet there is truth and balance in shadow. I should not be surprised you are acquainted with that, Moon." We held each other's gaze and sincerity shone in his eyes. This was a man capable of holding love for Feanim despite that elf's darkness. Perhaps some hope persisted.

"I must return to Rafael."

He blinked. "You must attend the funeral rites. Your absence now will send a message you do not intend."

The grim mood settled heavily about my shoulders. "I have a more important role to play in managing Rafael directly. He'll demand these last promised nights regardless of circumstance. It is the only way to be sure he will not interfere with the funeral itself."

Celebel's lips thinned but he did not protest.

Chapter 45

Rafael was, predictably, unrepentant of his crime. A harsh, hissed conversation led to me him, though I understood little of it. As dusk fell, I found him in the same clearing outside the walls near the other drakes. He wore what I thought of as his hellknight form. Covered in keeled scales like armor hewn from garnets, his features remained largely the same. He bore no extra appendages. Two long, white horns swept back from his temples, emphasizing the sharp peak in the center of his hairline. The effect was somehow more intimidating than his more draconic forms, and perhaps perversely, intensely attractive.

Tyldain stood with his back to me, arguing. It involved a lot of scale rattling. At my approach, Rafael sent the other drake away with a snarl. Tyldain cast an unreadable look over his shoulder as he stalked off. My Dragon's lip curled in an answering sneer. Once the blue drake's footsteps faded, I settled on a fallen log nearby.

I meant to confront him about the murder, but instead found myself curious. "Skeffynthir was Tyldain's progenitor, you said. Do drakes hold grudges for kin slaying?"

"Seldom." He leaned against a granite pillar. "Common enough for offspring to kill and supplant their parents in the clan hierarchy."

"What will happen if Tyldain challenges you?"

Rafael snorted. "He will not make that mistake twice. Instead, he will go against Marron and attempt to seize control of the green clan. If he wins the fight, and he may, Marron's mate is next. What she lacks in stature, she compensates with sheer ferocity." A wry smirk curled his lip. "Luck be with Tyldain if he challenges Vaerra head on."

"Marron must outweigh Tyldain by half. Is it really such a close match?" From the size of the green drake's hands alone, he seemed capable of breaking the relatively willowy Tyldain over his knee.

The Dragon cast a disdainful look down his long, scaled nose. "There is far more to ability than the appearance of a single form. Marron's power is based in earth, thus he may counter much of the intensity of my flame. The difference between us comes down to speed and… hrrm, call it adaptability." Something hid in that term, but I couldn't tease it out. "Against Tyldain's storm calling, he is less effective."

"Tyldain calls storms?" I envisioned a hurricane descending upon a battlefield.

"Not with the finesse you imagine. Elemental versus affinity." He demonstrated with a serpent of living flame that coiled about his arms. It slithered across the space between us, wrapping me with an intense warmth that did not burn. "I am elemental fire. He utilizes storm calling through an affinity to water."

"Oh, no you don't." I dispelled the fire snake back to him with a wave of my hands. "You are trying to distract me away from addressing all the problems you've just caused."

Rafael smiled faintly. "Is it working?"

"Every elf in Férioth was at arms when I left to find you." Once the notes of that melody reached the others, the song immediately split into discord. My ears still throbbed from a sea of elves driven to shouting over each other in their distress and anger.

He watched my face closely. "And you?"

How *did* I feel? "Numb. Adrift. Taken aback by the severity of your response. Logically, I understand why you acted with such demonstrative brutality. Emotionally, I am still an elf, and we hold the lives of our people sacred." My heart pounded in my ears. "You think of me as singular, not part of a whole. But these are my people. Their pain is my own." I glanced at the sun. The funeral would be starting any moment. Guilt twisted me into knots.

He swept me off my seat, tilting my chin up. "My people think me soft for tolerating any of this."

"They did not witness your murderous answer!" I could not

erase the mental image of Rafael methodically carving up an elf. Without my protection, that could have been Celebel. My stomach lurched.

"You speak with such surety." He pinned me with that blistering stare until my ears heated and I looked away. "Did you think none of those smut books escaped the walls?" His arms tightened around me, forcing me to breathe in short gasps.

"I hear you. I understand."

"Do you presume only your people felt my wrath?"

"Rafael." I'd intended a sharp reprimand, but only a squeak came out. He released me immediately. I rubbed my arms, trying to catch my breath. The sharp edges of horror embedded in my mind wore away, like broken glass tumbled in sand. Submerged in the ocean of him. Some part of me wondered if I should clutch that memory, hold it in place. His voice redirected my focus.

"Forgive me." He looked away. "It is difficult, hrrm, to divert my aggression when you approach me in this way." During an interaction with another drake, or the grip of past trauma? He did not clarify.

"I am unharmed. How can I help you overcome this?" Nothing about the situation would improve if he couldn't recover his balance.

Rafael held silent for a heartbeat. "There is a private copse of trees."

"Show me."

He led me down the hill to a formation of granite pillars overgrown with stunted conifers. Ducking under a pillar fallen diagonally across two larger ones revealed a cozy, nestlike space, padded with a thick duff of pine needles. He wrapped us in a dampening field. I cast a small witchlight into the branches over our heads, and he draped his cloak across the ground.

"We have two nights left of your bargain." I unbuckled his sword belt and traced a light finger over the scales lining the arch of his cheek. "Tell me what you need, Dragon."

"You. I need you. To know, beyond doubt, that you want

me." Ancient pain flashed in his eyes. "That I am not the same as those who—"

I placed a finger on his armored lips, stopping his spiral. "Quiet those voices, my love. I know you, and I will always want you. Take all the comfort you desire in my body."

I shrugged off my coat, revealing my nudity beneath. He immediately cupped my breasts, thumbing my nipples, and my clit throbbed in response. It took so little for him to light a fever in me. I grabbed hold of his horns as he bent to nuzzle my bosom, wrenching his head back.

"Ah, I like this. You should wear the horns more often. Gives me leverage." I yanked on his horns again for emphasis. "Remove the jerkin."

He gave me an arch look, spiked brow rising. "Remove it yourself."

I pushed him onto his back and straddled him, grabbing one of his hands. He watched with vivid amusement as I used his talons to slice through the thick leather tunic, opening it in the front. Something about the way the leather parted made my cunt ache. I tugged the black wool shirt free of his leather trousers and he cheerfully cut it down the front as well, revealing a torso covered with flat, pebbled scales. His already well-defined muscles took on even more contrast.

"Fuck, you look amazing," I blurted, and he raked a hand backwards through his hair. Perhaps someday he would readily accept physical compliments. I ran both hands over his chest and belly, appreciating the new, added texture.

Crawling over him, I kissed him long and hard. He curled his tongue around mine as I ground my aching clit back and forth over those highly textured abdominal scales. Something about holding that powerful body in place sent frissons of potent desire through me. Obliging, he flexed and relaxed the muscles beneath me, rolling them for me. A moan escaped my lips; climax found me faster than I planned.

I clasped his head to my breast, and he sucked hard on my

nipple as I brought myself to release on his abdomen. His hands cupped my ass as I rocked against him. The orgasm grabbed me in its jaws, wresting a panting cry from me as it wracked my body.

Suddenly, we were both moving. Rafael rolled me onto my back and stood in one smooth motion, pinning me under his foot. From my vantage point on the ground, his horns might graze the stars themselves. He trailed a finger in the glistening juices I'd left on his body, then sucked that finger clean. The sheer eroticism of the gesture wrung the breath from my lungs.

"You delight in my scales," he rumbled, looking me over. "I wonder, will you find the same delight in my talons?"

"You've used your talons on me many times." A horrid thought occurred to me, and I struggled to escape the foot planted on my belly. "Unless you no longer intend to blunt them?"

"Not to worry." His voice held a dark smile. "I will guard you from my cutting edges." A talon at the tip of a long toe tapped my sternum. "Unless you ask nicely." His foot slid down between my legs. The knuckle of a toe slid against my vulva and I shivered. "As I suspected." The smooth edge of a talon circled my clit. I gasped. What was he doing to me? I moved to rise, and he splayed out a hand. "Stay. There."

The command may as well have been a geas, freezing me in place. The Dragon balanced easily on one leg, as though rooted to the spot. Heat shimmered over the foot held aloft, cleansing away any dirt.

"Spread your legs and raise your hips."

I did as he bade, pushing my vulnerability aloft. Anticipation and no small amount of fear made my desire drip to the cloak beneath me. He teased my labia apart, slipping a talon inside. I hissed, tensing, but no pain followed. The first joint of his toe was much larger than a finger, and he eased it in slowly. I watched, enrapt, as the red scales disappeared into my body.

"Always eager for more." The timber of his voice made my nipples stingingly tight.

With a sigh, he raised his hands and sliced open his

forearms.

"No!" Horrified, I cried out, struggling again to reach him. The digit buried inside me pinned me in place.

Rafael paused, blood trickling down his arms. "Be at ease; my mind is not clouded. I merely release the pressure of these gathered shadows, as the past demands. Consider this self-pleasure, if you must."

I held his gaze for a moment. Satisfied with his sincerity, if not his methods, I refocused on this new style of penetration. Another toe joined the first, stretching me. When I moaned, he clawed at his sides, raking steaming lines through the scales. Drops of blistering blood splashed my lower legs and the sudden pain lifted my hips involuntarily. He took advantage of the motion, pushing the third toe into me. Much like fisting, and much more intense.

"You will tear me!" Fear shot up my spine with a warning jolt of pain.

"I have faith in you," he rumbled and pulled his foot back slightly, sparing me for a breath. I relaxed as he caressed my entrance with an undulating motion. Then he thrust deep. I made an inarticulate sound as the talons tapped my cervix. "Your wetness belies your protests. How slick you are." The spear of his digits twisted inside me and I bucked, almost against my will. I squeezed my eyes closed, lost in the delirium of lust, as he began a slow, thumping rhythm. "Your fear is a liar. You enjoy the pain."

I did, oh I did. Droplets of blood burned my belly. I opened my eyes to Rafael looming over me, once again demonstrating his flexibility. He bent to suck my nipple as I writhed. His scales bit into my tenderest flesh and I whimpered, searing pain pushing me toward the brink of a brutal climax. Delirium took me, the edge of agony blunted with the high of bursting pleasure. He raised his hand and bit into it. Blood splashed across me in a burning shower. Smearing it across my breasts took the heat away, and I moaned, shuddering.

"I should fuck you like this on their little thrones," he hissed, "painted in my blood."

"Yes, yes!" I would have agreed to anything he wanted at that moment.

Ruthless, his toes twisted inside me, pulling back and shoving deeper. He forced me into a single long, punishing orgasm. Helpless in the tidal wave of ecstasy, it stole my breath and flashed my vision to white and then black.

When I slumped, still shaking, he carefully withdrew his toes. Laced with my blood, he wiped his foot carefully on my inner thighs. I could barely discern my body fluid from his sanguine scales. He held my eyes as he bent to lick me clean, savoring my mingled blood and juices like a delicacy.

"Gods," I gasped. "What is wrong with me? I really would forgive you anything, as long as you make me climax that hard."

"I know," he purred, eyes bright under his spiked, crimson brow.

Agony seared through me, jolting me awake. Rafael sank his teeth into the back of my neck, right where it met my shoulders. Biting through skin and meat, almost down to the bone, before drawing back.

"Dragon, what the fuck!" To my surprise, though I could staunch the bleeding and the throbbing pain, I could not erase the punctures left by his teeth. A mate claiming mark.

"A memento." He gave me a bloody smile, licking his teeth clean. Sometime in the night, he had shapeshifted back to his usual form.

"You would be furious if I left a mark you couldn't remove." Celebel was going to be livid, at least until he understood that I wasn't truly injured. Rafael could claim it wasn't direct antagonism, and he would be right.

"Would I? You have never tried." He looped a lock of my hair around his finger, casually twirling it in his talons. The sensation shivered along my scalp.

"You could at least stop looking so pleased with yourself. I do not belong to you, and I have not agreed to your claiming. How is it that you are somehow both easier and *far* more difficult to get along with now?"

"You will tire of him eventually." Rafael examined the lock of hair he had captured.

"Excuse me?" I snatched my hair away from him and rolled to my feet, ready to fight.

He sat up and looked at me. In a measured voice, he said, "You hate it here. You hate these people and their ridiculous expectations. Did the incident with the pamphlets teach you nothing? You will tire of this life and of him." The Dragon reached to touch my face, and I swatted his hand away. "I can be patient, Cúraniel. This war will end eventually, and what will hold you then?"

The worst part was how right he was about most of it.

The Dragon's gaze burned into my skin. He looked *into* me. I opened up, showing him my heart freely. His presence settled into every crevice of my being, more intimate than any sexual encounter. And *pulled*, as if yanking my very soul from its seat, and placing himself upon the throne.

Shrieking, voiceless, I thrashed against him. Grasping every shred of his presence, like taking hold of drifting smoke, I thrust him out with all my might. He released me of his own accord, backing away, and I shut him out of my mind, out of our connection.

"No! Not now, not ever. Or you become the very thing you fear." I launched myself backwards, as far from him as the small space allowed. "You will not influence me in that way. *Never* again! I should be angry. Instead, I am only weary and disappointed. This is a major boundary, Rafael. Close your mouth! There is no justification for this." His jaws clicked shut at my demand. "Fucking hells, you are hard to love at times. Either I come with you freely, or not at all. How would I even survive without both of my soulmates?"

Something passed behind Rafael's eyes, sinister and calculating. I forced my pounding heart to slow. My anger and distress would only make things worse, would only feed the growing darkness.

"Come back to yourself, Dragon. I will not allow your shadows to swallow us both." With a steadying breath, I opened our connection again, sending as much of my healing spirit through as I could.

We stared each other down. He finally rumbled and backed off, hands raised in surrender.

"How can you know your own mind so well and yet be so divided?"

I watched for a heartbeat longer, ensuring his energy truly returned to normal. "I did not ask for this. Neither did you, but you made a choice, and so here we are. Now you're learning the hard lesson of being unable to take everything you want by force." I crossed my arms, staring into his eyes.

"You are indeed a trial. I should not love you for it and yet…" Fast as lightning, he grabbed my hands and pulled me, struggling, into his lap. "Do you truly understand how you torment me?" he murmured into my hair as I tried unsuccessfully to push him away.

"I thought you were the expert in torment." I tugged my lobes. "Tell me then, how do I torment you?"

Rafael pulled back to look me steadily in the eye. "Before you, the last time I felt vulnerable was at the hands of a human gang who tried to kick me to death, and took turns raping me," he said bluntly. My heart clenched. The terrified child, then the furious youth, flashed in my mind. Impervious to death at the hands of mortals, but unable to defend himself. "You know the start of it, but escape from the Tárthanë improved little in my life until well after I came into my majority."

"Rafael—"

He laid a finger on my lips, the mirror of my earlier gesture, his eyes haunted. I covered his hand with mine and he cupped my jaw. "Time is no ally to a flawless memory. When I finally began to win the fights, I vowed never to back down, *never* to be degraded, ever again. And so I have fought ever since, and won. It has been nearly a century since I last had a true test of my strength. Before that…" He waved a hand in the air.

The image of him lying in a broken ruin, his chest cavity and abdomen split open, guts spilling out, flashed unwelcome across my mind. The headless body of the War Crow broken at the bottom of the ravine. His blood scalding the skin off of my arms.

"Gods, you were so angry with me for saving you." The murderous look in his eyes when first he awoke. His jagged teeth on my throat, with that reverberating growl, when I'd mistakenly moved within reach. How he had raged and nearly incinerated me on the spot when I'd attempted the healing kiss. "You couldn't hide the despair under all that fury, not from me."

"Needing you." He shook his head, closing his eyes. "Unfathomable. I am still… adjusting to the concept. I thought I had rooted out all weakness, burned and crushed it, and yet here you are."

"Needing another is not weakness." I traced the line of his jaw.

"When it is a trait that can be exploited? Yes, it is weakness." He leaned into my hand, maintaining eye contact. "A weakness I cannot deny myself, it would seem. It is no great thing for me to fight at your behest. The fight is all I have ever known. Aim me like an arrow at the hearts of your enemies and watch them die. But know that I will not be broken again. If I am to fight, I will *win*. If I am to be hobbled on one front, my strength stripped away, still I shall triumph. Do you understand? I will destroy this world and all its people before I will ever let you be *taken* from me." His eyes sharpened, yellow streaking into the blue. "If not for your protests, I would be of a mind to end this little conflict now. I could hunt down and kill every other fucking elf in Vaeda. With your elders gone, not one of you left could stop me."

The blunt truth of his words chilled me. He traced a slow finger across my lips, down my neck, over my breast, as I drew in a shaky breath. That was another loophole in our agreement that I had never considered. I resolved to be grateful that he was telling me instead of acting on it.

"Your people do not know how greatly they owe you," he continued. "In truth, I was considering it before you saved me, before you cast your spell on me. You alone changed my mind." The Dragon paused, gathering my hair in his hand, letting it run through his fingers like dark water, making me tingle. I held my breath. A deliberate test. He exhaled slowly, wreathing me in the heat of his breath. "Sirelon brought about its own doom. I had no intention of attacking elves until they forced my hand."

He'd never spoken about it prior, diverting all my questions. My ears perked with interest. "What happened?"

"I was young, still learning my power. Had yet to discover my own people. Elves tracked me to my lair—at the time, a simple cave in the mountains—and set upon me while I recovered from an extended time in my dragon form. Weakened, unable to shift, they chained me with wards." His eyes closed. "Shot full of arrows, stabbed with bright spears, and yet I would not die."

"How did you escape? This was just after the… after you hunted down your tormentors?" The word 'slaughter' burned on my tongue.

"It was the first time I heard the whispering. The smoke, the shadows…" Rafael tilted his head, as if listening. I could hear nothing, no matter how I stretched my ears. "I followed them out. Hid and gathered strength. When I was ready, I tracked the elves in return; to their precious city." He opened his eyes.

I nodded, rubbing the back of my neck where the mark ached suddenly. Our histories recounted the rest in detail. "We vowed never again to get involved in external affairs after that incident. Before, we had numerous treaties with other peoples, other nations. Trade was open." Though an unpleasant topic, I encouraged it as my Dragon visibly calmed with the telling of it. I'd known the attack was retaliatory in nature, but never why. "You single-handedly closed our culture to the outside. Celebel's grandsire made that edict." The very edict I'd flaunted by revealing Leyúduin to outsiders.

"Would that I could not so easily see what you see in *him*. He is like you; beautiful, steadfast… whole. Adored by those around him. He, who has been showered with grace from his very birth, of course you would turn from me." The bitterness in Rafael's voice broke my heart, and I twined my arms about his neck, peppering him with kisses.

"I love you, my Dragon. You must stop holding so tightly. I will not leave you, but I need to breathe. I need to love Celebel as much as I need to love you. It is the nature of a soulmate!"

"You say that you will not leave just as you turn to go. Every time. Recall how you used to beg me to stay with you? Now I am brought low. Do not go, do not leave me. Please." He drew a shuddering breath and covered his heart. "It hurts."

"Oh my Dragon, my Jax. Spending time with Celebel does not mean that I am leaving you. I wish you would simply *talk* to him." I stroked his hair. "Neither of us wants to hurt you. He is not hurt by my time with you, only by the strife your actions have caused."

"*HE* has everything he wants," Rafael snarled. "Everything! It sickens me to think of his hands on you, that you kiss him as sweetly as you do me, that… that he gives you what I cannot."

Talons screeched against stone as his feet inward, cutting gashes through the cloak. I slid off his lap to kneel before him, pressing my lips to the top of one foot, then the other, wishing I could take his pain away. Here was the root of his sudden turn; acting out of a fear of abandonment, following on the ear tips of greater trauma.

"I want you no less for being with Celebel. I wish you could understand that! My love is not finite and never will be. The reverse is true of what I said—you will never convince me to stop loving him. I cannot say what will happen when this war ends, but if this is so untenable for you, I would rather you be free than miserable. Return as you must, to feed the soulbond and replenish yourself, but I would not hold you hostage."

"My life before you was nothing but misery and death. Why would I ever wish to return? I have slaughtered thousands, I have fought my way to all the power and wealth I could ever want, and it means nothing without you. I would break the world for you, my dove. I will break myself as well if I must, but I will *never* surrender you." His eyes were hot coals.

Chapter 46

The court rippled with hushed excitement at the tribunal. From the fluttering hands and occasional murmur, they expected an end to our alliance with the drakes. And the immediate expulsion of Rafael from their presence. Fools. I cast an eye over the hall. With few exceptions, they were green as saplings in spring, shielded from the ugly reality of war. Even this most recent battle had asked little in the way of sacrifice, and they'd not deigned to mingle with the less illustrious lineages that made up the bulk of our soldiers. I'd cleaned up warriors all my long life. These children of peace had no concept of just how badly we needed the drakes.

Dressed in our most formal attire, I'd picked an elegant black silk gown—a subtle allegiance—with the pearls braided into one long tail. I'd intended to wear Fallëvaethil, but the diamond was missing. Perhaps another elf borrowed it.

Rafael stood facing the dais, a dark shadow on the green carpet. Upon his entrance, he had closed our connection down to a dull background hum. I fixated on him, hoping to anticipate a sudden mood change. No one dared look at him directly.

His eyes had glittered with malice when I'd extended the request for attendance, but he'd appeared without protest. He certainly had no intention of submitting to elvish justice.

Marron sauntering in behind him came as a welcome surprise. Casually dressed in comparison—when was he ever without a light coating of dust on his brown leathers?—he glanced openly around the court. Much to their discomfort. Rafael certainly didn't need his second, but the green drake's solid presence helped soothe my anxious tension.

Araglin stood and read the list of charges from a scroll, describing the murder in detail. Some elves wept, others watched with steely anger. From the set of Feanim's jaw, he placed among the latter, though I couldn't pinpoint the target of his ire. Rafael merely looked bored.

"The Consulate adjudicates. The accused may speak in his own defense, or call upon others to speak. If none will speak, and the accused is deemed guilty of breaking elvish law, rather than banishment, he may request—"

"Yes, yes." Rafael waved an airy hand. I braced myself. "I request trial by combat." A hiss rippled through the room, hands moving rapidly over silk.

"Unnecessary." Celebel stepped forward. "I will speak on his behalf." The hissing gained momentum, and Rafael's eyes narrowed. Every ear stretched to the Consul. Though I'd known what to expect, as we'd discussed strategy that very morning, the ease with which he assumed my usual role impressed me. Especially as it had been somewhat of a heated conversation. "The sacred laws of hospitality were broken. This injustice demands an answer."

A defiant chorus rose from the court. Celebel raised both arms, palms out, and his spirit rose with them. Rolling off his skin in shimmering waves, it washed over us all.

The Dragon's eyes narrowed and I tensed. "Sit down, *nekarazzi*. I need no other mouth. Here is my appointed champion, since you would all protest if I fought." He stepped aside and Marron moved forward. A talon jabbed at Celebel. "*You* brought these charges, I assume you will be the challenger." Both drakes grinned, exposing vicious teeth. Gods fucking *damn* him, I should have known. "Surely the high-minded Lord Celebel would not send another elf to die in his stead."

Fury launched me from my seat, but Celebel held up a hand.

"No need for more violence, Lord Dragon. Hear me well, oh my people. Our laws apply regardless of the perpetrator, and it was Unarimë who first broke them. The Red Dragon's retaliation was justified, if extreme in its expression."

Angry hands and voices mingling in the crowd. Near the back, Galdir stood. With a furious scowl, he clapped both hands over flattened ears with a quick *smack!* I stiffened. I hadn't seen that painful gesture of disdain since I'd quarreled with my father over breaching the walls, and I'd nearly slapped him in response. Instead of picking another losing fight, Galdir turned on a heel and left.

Tension crackled, raising the fine hairs on my arms. Celebel's influence surged, stilling the elves as one. It clung to my skin in a fine mist, forcibly relaxing me. Rafael tilted his head, fiery eyes boring into the Talithiri Consul. His talons flexed at his side, obviously annoyed. I wanted to berate my troublesome soulmate for his attempt to find yet another loophole to harm Celebel, but the influence stilled me, redirecting my attention.

"Unarimë committed an egregious violation of personal autonomy in those pamphlets. A violation that would, of necessity, be answered with force." Celebel's warm baritone took on a hypnotic cadence. "The Red Dragon acted in accordance with the customs of his people, to rightfully defend his honor. Though violence is not our way, had such insult been leveled at either myself or my fellow Consul, banishment would have been the minimum punishment. Severance from the shared song." Feanim signed assent at that, large enough for the entire hall to witness. I held my breath. "Allowing this crime to stand unanswered would offend the gods. We must put aside our personal feelings in this matter. The Red Dragon holds no guilt."

A hush fell over the hall, entranced by Celebel's power. His lineage radiated through him; the very stars made flesh. Whether dazzled by his influence, sheer beauty, or the attraction of watching him claim his true might, I could not say. All around, lips parted and ear tips flushed. Rafael, however, clicked his teeth.

"Lord Celebel has the right of it." Feanim stepped forward, breaking the trance. "The deceased violated sacred hospitality and as such was no longer protected by our laws." For the first time, his presence actually improved a situation. "The Consulate stands in agreement on this judgment."

A muted flutter of angry hands swept the room.

"I suggest a way forward for both of our peoples." Celebel's voice held the faintest note of strain. What did that amount of crowd control cost him? "Lord Dragon, are you willing to bring your grievances to us before enacting violence? We will attempt to resolve the issue on our own to your satisfaction. Swear before the court and the gods, that we may have a formally binding treaty."

"I walked this world long before any of you were a spark in the wind, yet you have the fucking audacity to demand assurances from *me?* You must feel supremely safe, perched in those thrones." Rafael growled low in his throat and I shivered involuntarily.

The hiss of sucked in breath from several sources almost drew my attention away. They had every right to be afraid. With the roiling darkness growing in my soulbond, the court hovered a breath away from slaughter. Celebel's spirit grew with it, in a twinkling fog that hung over the gathering. Fine lines crinkled the corners of his eyes.

"Lord Celebel's request is a reasonable one, I believe." Araglin's melodious voice chimed across the room as he stepped forward. "If you will not swear, will you at least accept?"

Peering around the angry red drake, Marron raised a craggy brow at me. I shrugged, hazy in the grip of Celebel's power.

Araglin bowed, braids chiming. "I personally offer heartfelt apologies for the insult inflicted upon you. Had I but realized what occurred in my home, with my own acolyte, I would have intervened immediately. Long before it had the chance to escalate. I mourn the loss of life, but so too do I mourn the loss of honor."

Rafael glared at the scholar so long even I shifted with discomfort.

"Good enough," my Dragon finally said. He stepped up the dais, stopping just before Celebel to lean in uncomfortably close. Celebel's throat bobbed, but he signed for his bodyguards to stay back. Keeping his motions small, Rafael signed in short, staccato bursts. "Try your influence again, I pop your head like grape." He turned and swept out of the great hall before any of us could react.

"I *told* you he knows our sign," I muttered at Celebel's sharp exhale.

Marron watched Rafael's departure, scaly brows creeping higher. "Oh, he has *changed*," the green drake said. "I expected a bloodbath."

The moment we were safely ensconced in our chambers, Celebel buried his face in my hair and sobbed. Startled, I held him for a long moment, allowing him to catch his breath, before I pulled back to look him in the eye.

"Starshine, speak to me, please! You were glorious today. What has you so distraught?"

"The pressure." Wiping his cheeks, he collected himself. "The pressure, and the distance from you." The contrast of his black brows and lashes against his creamy skin, with emotion brightening the blue of his eyes, caught my breath in my throat for a moment. Even upset, his beauty captivated me. "Your avoidance of the funeral rites was fraught. Raised questions of your loyalty, and by extension, mine. I fear for the future with so much internal strife in the court."

He poured a honeyed wine for us, and I accepted a goblet with gratitude. After the recent time spent ensnared by Rafael's guarded intensity, Celebel's softer earnesty ached with sweetness. He kissed me and I reveled in his lush, velvety lips.

"The war and the expectations of the court were bad enough, but from the moment that damned Dragon planted himself in my path, he's been deliberately trying to force a wedge between us. I've never felt such a mix of excitement and despair. Each moment of elation suffers from anguish following so closely on its heels." His fingers drummed a light rhythm on the bowl of his goblet. "Every move Rafael makes forces me to question myself. Worse, I cannot speak a word out of turn for fear of immediate reprisal, and so I must repress my every reaction to his constant goading. As I stated, I understand the reasoning behind his retaliation, but the action itself remains an atrocity."

He drained the goblet and set it aside. Cupping my face in his hands, he ran his thumbs over my cheeks. I let him speak without interruption, hopefully releasing all the pent-up frustrations that so clearly picked apart his insides.

"Your sister has formed quite a cadre with Feledhor and Recarmial. They've grown vocal in questioning my fitness for leadership, and attempt to draw Nimthil to their cause. Others are listening. Silfanië may well seat herself as Consul before this is over.

"It is no wish to cling to power that concerns me, rather a fear that the divide amongst us will grow." His brow furrowed. "Perhaps your Dragon would better tolerate your own blood in the position?"

I tried to imagine it; my sister's cold eyes glaring down at me from the Consul's throne. "Doubtful. Silfanië makes no secret of her animosity for me. Rafael considers you a rival, despite my best efforts, but he also knows that you would not deliberately allow me to come to harm."

"If his aim is to drive you away from here, would that not accomplish his goals? Perhaps this is merely another step in his convoluted dance."

I eyed my wine, wishing it were something stronger. "Well then. Has Rafael succeeded in putting you off of me yet?"

Celebel barked a laugh, flopping backward onto the bed. I climbed up and draped myself across his lap. He played idly with my hair, combing out my braids with his long, elegant fingers.

"In truth, the harder he tries to put me off, the more determined I become to remain steadfast."

"Perhaps I'll tell him that." I grinned.

Celebel tweaked the tip of my ear. "You *are* a wicked woman!"

"I'm your wicked woman at the moment. What would you like to do with me?"

His blue eyes shone, and for a moment I thought he would

weep again. "Much as I desire the comfort of your flesh, will you simply hold me and sing me to sleep? I have hardly rested since our return from the field. Using so much spirit has left me utterly drained."

One of the problems with a circular bed was the lack of headboard to rest against. I rooted around on the absurdly large mattress for a moment, gathering up a mound of cushions to prop under my back so that I could lounge upright and still hold Celebel. With his back to my belly and his head pillowed on my breasts, I drew my nails lightly over his scalp and ears as I sang. Songs of rest and rejuvenation, deepest winter, when the world quietly gathers its strength. Within only a few verses, he dozed peacefully.

Chapter 47

Relaxing into his touch, focused on dressing for dinner, I forgot about the mark. Celebel combed and braided my hair. As he smoothed his work, weaving in loose ends, his hand slid over the back of my neck. He froze.

"What is this?" Before I could turn away, he lifted the thick rope of braid, revealing barely-closed indentations from a set of vicious teeth. "You proclaim Rafael would never hurt you, and here you are with a wound he inflicted!"

I tugged my hair free to face him. Just as furious as I'd predicted, Celebel's ears flattened against his head.

"Be calm, it is only a love bite. You know my preference for rough sex. It does not hurt." He might very well be horrified at the extent of roughness my draconic lover, and even more so if he understood Rafael's darker desires.

"Surely you do not expect me to believe that this wasn't deliberate. A wound that you cannot heal?"

"Of course it was deliberate, but I promise I am unharmed. It is healed well enough; I simply cannot erase the scar, and I have no desire to fight about it. Please." Unconsciously rubbing the mark, I forced my hand to drop, frustrated with my carelessness. I'd intended to save the inevitable discussion for a better time so that we could simply enjoy each other's company.

Celebel gave me a long, flat stare.

"The more you let Rafael tweak your ears, the more you play right into his hands." I raised a hand as he opened his mouth to protest. "I should have been more prepared for something like this. The smut book incident brought up a lot of old trauma for him and he was bound to act out."

"Trauma which he immediately passed along to us."

"Haven't we ended the tribunal already?" I squeezed my eyes shut against the memory of the desecrated body. Somehow, the severed ears were the hardest to forget. "Whether or not you believe it, only a single kill rather than a slaughter is a remarkable sign of restraint on his part. You heard Marron. Not precisely the growth we desire, but it is growth."

"Yes, very encouraging." Curt, clipped. His eyes took on a stormy grey as he closed off.

We walked in tense silence to the dinner, sitting together but leagues apart. When Feanim and Nimthil joined us, the Duedellen's eyes drifted from my face to Celebel's as he intoned a greeting. Nimthil blithely ignored me. We ate in uncomfortable silence. I wished the room were brighter; the dim flicker of the witchlights did nothing to lift the mood. When the trays were finally removed, and the last wine poured, Feanim swirled his thoughtfully, staring at me. From the quirk of his brows, something awful formulated there.

"What is Rafael like in bed?" he asked, eyes squinting with his mischief. Just like him, to attempt to throw me off balance.

Celebel rounded on him, eager for a target. "Fucking hells, Feanim! Why would you ask such a thing?"

"I am not asking you, I'm asking her. What is he like? How do you deal with all the sharp bits, talons and teeth?" He pantomimed biting and made his hands into claws.

I pinched the bridge of my nose, trying to both calm my anger and stifle a laugh at the horrified look on Nimthil's face. "He blunts his talons." Feanim leaned forward in interest. "Smooths out his scales, and so on," I added.

"He can do that?" The Duedellen grinned with lascivious fascination, flattening his palms on the table. Still not signing, though perhaps that worked to Nimthil's benefit in this case.

"He's a *shapeshifter*, Feanim, of course he can. And he's quite deft with his hands, I can assure you." I smiled sweetly, signing in clear, deliberate motions. Nimthil looked like she might faint. Served her right for her judgment, despite what I'd said earlier. Knowing of her potential allegiance shift stifled my sympathy for her.

"That's enough," Celebel cut in.

"Does it upset you to hear?" Feanim asked him. "I should think you would be well-versed by now." He looked back at me. "Rafael is such a beast, seems like he would have a huge—"

"I said *enough!*" Celebel slammed his glass down on the table, nearly shattering it.

I shouldn't have encouraged Feanim's bad behavior, but rebellion had me in its teeth. 'Enormous,' I mouthed, and he grinned, mischief glinting in his eyes. Celebel tapped my foot under the table with his own. I kicked him back. No more hiding. I was heartily sick of it.

"Celebel is angry because the Dragon marked me."

"Show me!"

I turned in my seat so Feanim could look at the back of my neck. He gave a low whistle of appreciation.

"Damn, he has a lot of teeth."

Nimthil rapped sharply on the table. "All of you, stop this." Her voice was quiet but forceful. "I shall not tolerate discussion of that monster's *proclivities* in my presence." Her hands fluttered, belling out her lace cuffs like an agitated dragonfly's wings.

Feanim reached for her, but she shrugged out of his touch and took her leave. How much of her soulmate's open admiration for a hated enemy did she privately tolerate? The inherent irony sobered me. To be fair, if Rafael himself had overheard any of that exchange, Férioth would already be in flames.

Celebel heaved a great sigh, and I reached for his hand. For a moment, he tensed, then twined his fingers in mine.

To Feanim, he said, "Have you made any recent progress with your research?"

"The next few days are important. We're at a crucial point in this armor development. I've a new prototype to test," Feanim said. "If this works, you and I will each have a full set soon. It would make many things much easier." He indicated Celebel.

"Are only the three of you laboring on this project?"

Feanim's ears twitched, his mouth curling into a sneer—our

little mischievous accord dissolved. "Surely you know the legacy of my lineage."

"Of course. Your family's smithing is legendary. But why limit yourselves to only three perspectives?" Ever since Rafael had ransacked the armory, the forge rang with constant hammering. Blacksmiths worked to remake and improve the weaponry with the recommended þilvor purity.

"We wish to keep the knowledge contained until it is refined enough to share, to avoid dilution of the process," Celebel said. Feanim shot him a dirty look, evidently unhappy that he'd mentioned such things to me. Interesting.

"I am frankly shocked that Rafael is willing to work on armor for you."

"He is not," Celebel replied quickly.

"Rafael is developing his own armor, out of moranga," Feanim added. "It's never been done before! Fascinating to watch. At times, he even eschews a hammer, simply manipulating the heated billets by hand."

I shuddered at the thought of demon armor. "Yours are of þilvor, I assume?"

Feanim waved a dismissive hand at me.

"We've been stockpiling it for a long time," Celebel said, clearly grateful for the subject change. "When the old ones departed, they left a great deal behind. We've repurposed some objects and certain weapons to make better use of them."

"You truly fail to pay attention to anything that doesn't make you come," Feanim jeered.

Celebel slapped the table, echoing Nimthil's gesture. "That is uncalled for!"

"Act with all the vulgarity you can muster. Rafael will never fuck you." I leaned back in my chair, wishing my wine were whiskey. Let Feanim be the one discomfited for once. I stared him down, daring him to reply. With a light tug of my power, I found the edge of a cut along his jaw, and ever so slightly peeled it back. Feanim clapped a hand to his jaw and glared.

Celebel cleared his throat. "We're swiftly approaching the point where we're going to need to test that membrane you're working on."

I nodded, grateful for the tacit support. Rafael's diagrams could indeed be useful.

"What membrane?" Suspicion sharpened Feanim's eyes, and he rubbed again at his jaw.

"I call it Pîntellum, 'little mushroom.' When Celebel told me what you were trying to accomplish, I realized a different approach was needed—" here the Duedellen tried to interrupt, but I simply raised my voice and continued. "So, I searched for an organism that was inoffensive, non-sentient, and yet able to respond to external stimuli." I grinned. "Slime mold! Slime molds are perfect!"

"Are you fucking serious? You're attempting to craft a responsive membrane out of a ball of snot that eats leaf litter?" Feanim sneered, but he paid attention under the veneer of arrogance.

"Sneer away, but it's working," I said. "I separated them and ran a few simple experiments to see which mold was the swiftest and most responsive. The next step utilized a bit of spirit to combine it with elvish tissues and test the response. Feanim, the sample that you provided me with seems to work very well."

His eyes went wide. "What fucking samp… oh gods DAMN it, Rafael!" He rolled his sleeve up to expose a thin red line on his inner arm. "That fucking blighter!"

"I told him to *ask* you!" I barely suppressed the gleeful cackle fighting its way out of my throat. Carefully, I avoided Celebel's eyes, knowing I would lose my grip on my rising hilarity with even a hint of encouragement from him. "No wonder I heard nothing from you after he brought me the sample."

The Duedellen's outrage visibly warred with his curiosity, ears twitching wildly. In the end, curiosity won. "I would have just given it to you had you asked. No need to have your lover grab my arm and skin it like a chicken."

"Indeed, Feanim?" Celebel said. "You rarely cooperate

unless it was your idea first. I also loathe Rafael's bully tactics, but he's effective, I'll give him that. And now you have proof of Lady Cúraniel's trustworthiness, despite your constant antagonism. Now let her finish the melody, please."

Wetting my throat with a sip of wine, I continued. "I've grown a decent-sized Pîntellum, large enough to line at least a set of gauntlets, if you wish to try it. I thought you would like to be first. So far, it seems quite responsive, and all it requires for maintenance is a little nutrient paste."

Feanim's eyes lit up. "Yes, tomorrow, when we put the new prototype to the test. Fucking slime mold, really."

"Nemohee thought the slime mold races were hilarious. Þey placed bets, but unfortunately þeir favorite didn't win. So þey kept it as a pet." No one else seemed to find that as amusing as I did.

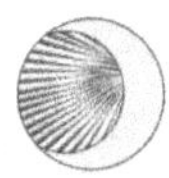

As soon as Feanim departed, a spark of mischief lit Celebel's eye "If that bloody drake gets to toss you about, so do I! I'll take the back stairs so few will witness this act."

Appreciating the shift in his mood, I grinned. "If you think you can catch hold and keep me!" I made to dodge around him.

Celebel immediately crouched and lunged at my legs. I hopped over him, laughing and tweaking an ear as I passed. Without missing a note, Celebel shifted his weight and hooked my leg with his heel. I put an arm out to brace myself rather than fall, and he grabbed me about the waist. Crowing in triumph, he tossed me over his shoulder as I giggled and pretended to struggle.

He marched us to the bedchambers, kicking the doors closed and depositing me on the bed. I landed with a graceless *whumph* into the soft mattress.

"Stay there," he ordered. Rummaging in a trunk, he produced a length of spidersilk rope. "I'd better tie you up to keep you from running off again."

He looped the rope behind my neck and down between my breasts, tying me neatly and efficiently in a harness that pulled my arms behind my back. His hands slid over me with deft attentiveness. Stepping back to admire his work, he maneuvered me by the harness to drop to my knees and lean me forward over the bed. I arched my back in anticipation.

Teasingly, he swatted my ass with the trailing end of the rope. I responded immediately, spreading my legs.

"Ah, at times I underestimate how much you like pain," he murmured in my ear, and a thrill ran down my spine.

"Both giving and receiving." I tossed a smirk over my shoulder.

"Face forward," Celebel barked. "That damned drake took my choice, my control away. He returned you with a fresh bite mark proclaiming you as his, knowing full well it would provoke me. I will take it all back tonight, and leave a few marks of my own." Leaning forward, he nipped at my ear tip. "That is, if you are amenable?"

"I am at your mercy. Do your worst," I said, unable to keep the grin off of my face or the wetness from sliding down my legs.

"How will you indicate if you've reached your limits?"

I laughed. "Sweetness, if the Red Dragon himself did not break me, you surely will not." Rafael never asked; he unerringly observed and adapted. For his own pain tolerance, he had no discernable limits.

Celebel reached around and pinched my nipple, making me yelp. "Give me your sign."

I threw a surge of resistance into our bond. "There, you feel it?"

He stroked my hair. "Yes. Now, confess your crimes to me."

A different kind of tap landed on my buttocks. Unable to control my curiosity, I glanced back just in time to see him swing a riding crop. He brought it down with a smack and I jumped.

"Forward, I said!" He tapped the other side for emphasis.

I obeyed. "I've been with another man." The crop came down with a light *crack*. He dragged it between my legs and I moaned. Gods, I'd missed him and his easy sexuality.

"I allowed him to touch me where you have touched me." *Crack!* That one had more force behind it. I relaxed into the sensation and he worked into a syncopated rhythm of blows. Light, quick taps alternating with harsher blows.

"He makes me so wet." *Crack, crack-crack!*

"I wanted to fuck him so badly." *Crack, crack!*

Celebel paused, rubbing the now-warm globes of my ass. "You flush so quickly. That same violet tinge as your lips and cunt. Is all your blood that color?"

"Keep striking me and find out," I challenged, and he smacked me with an open palm; a stinging slap. I whimpered, playing up my reaction and he laughed wickedly.

"Continue your confession!"

I resettled my knees into the mattress, spreading them farther in invitation. "He uses appendages you don't even have." *Crack!* A long pause, and then rapid blows rained down. *Crack-crack-crack-crack-crack!* I panted through the pain, letting it seep into me, accepting. My clit throbbed with the need to be touched, to be licked.

"Rafael said—ah!" Celebel interrupted my confession with a palm strike. The welcome haze of pain fogged the edges of my mind, lifting me into euphoria. "He said he should fuck me like that on your little thrones." *Crack, crack!*

"How?" Celebel demanded, his voice gone husky.

I was sharing the Dragon's secrets, but I couldn't stop. "With… with his foot—"

Thunderstuck, Celebel stopped the crop swings for a moment. "His *foot?* Talons and all?"

I opened my mouth to explain, and he brought the crop down hard. *CRACK!* I gasped, toes curling.

"Filthy slattern! Wicked woman. What else have you to confess?" He tried to sound stern, but glee rang in his voice.

"I did not fuck you when I should have." *CRACK!* The last blow knocked me forward, and I felt him move closer, pulling my hair and thrusting the pommel of the crop into my cunt.

"Tell me you're sorry for fucking him instead," Celebel hissed in my ear. I gasped, and he thrust harder. The crop worked in and out of me, building a wave of pleasure along with the floating, delirious pain.

I turned to look him in the eye. "No."

He slapped my ass so hard my ears rang and squeezed lightly at my throat. "Say it."

"No! Never!" Giddiness overtook me as his hand tightened and he fucked me with the crop.

"I am going to fuck you in the ass if you don't say it."

I laughed and arched my back again. Just as he'd threatened, he pulled the crop out. Spreading my buttocks wide, he lubricated me liberally with my own juices and teased his fingers slowly into the tight ring of muscle. Hazy in my pain-induced high, I relaxed into his touch.

He withdrew his fingers, moving around behind me, and I heard a cork pop out of a bottle. A hand warmed with oil prodded my anus, and his fingers slid in easily this time.

"Hmm, you feel like you need more." The fingers withdrew, and he plunged his cock into my ass. "Say you're a dirty slattern," he called with a laugh in his voice, pumping hard.

I braced myself as best I could without the use of my arms. "I'm definitely a—AH—a dirty slattern. Filthy and greedy." He whipped the crop down again. "I'd fuck you both at the same time if I could."

I slammed my hips backward, forcing him deep inside me. The crop rubbed against my aching clit. My orgasm arrived, the wave crashing down and dragging me under. I cried out, writhing in his grip. Celebel slammed into me, gripping my hips and spasmed, spilling himself into my cunt with a long groan of pleasure. I loved to hear him voice it. He released for a long time, filling me well.

Finally, he pulled out, moving slowly and carefully. He deftly untied me and I collapsed in a sweaty heap on the bedroll. With a warm, damp rag, he cleaned me as I lay panting. Gradually I came back down from the heights and into full consciousness.

"That was impressive! I did not know you could dominate me like that," I said, gleefully nipping at his ear.

"Ah, we still have so much to learn of each other." His smile was blissful. "I usually prefer to be dominated, but I thank you for your submission. Your pleasure is what arouses me most."

"Mmm, yes, well, you'd better prepare yourself. I am versatile, lover. Perhaps I'll grant you that domination once I recover," I said with a purr, and he pulled me on top of him.

"I am fully yours. Make me your pet." He kissed me fervently.

"Be careful what you wish for. I hope you like pain." I kissed him back. "Because Rafael does, and he's taught me quite a few innovative ways to inflict it."

"Oh fucking hell, Cúraniel—"

"Silence, slattern!" I slapped his face playfully. For an instant shock froze him, then he dissolved into laughter and we wrestled in the blankets.

Chapter 48

emohee found me hiding in the library and dragged another pouf beside mine. I set aside my armor membrane research as the Lachanaur plopped down beside me. A quick glance at the nearest window told me I'd been reading for most of the day already. My eyes needed a rest. Delving into my work padded me from the sting of the court's growing hostility.

"So, this is where you've been hibernating!"

I stretched, mild guilt washing over me. "Some friend I am. Hardly checked in on you after the battle! But here you are, all in one piece."

"Big Red hauled you off afore I could so much as squeak in your direction." Nemohee waved it away. "'Twas a bonnie melody. I played me a tune, the Fomorians came running, and your scaly friends did their bloody work. Though, the horn cracked. Not sure where that will lead.

Þey tapped pursed lips for a moment. "The other drakes fight like the top predators they are. Yours fights like all the hells rise up within him. He laughs as he kills, did you know?" Shifting light from the stained glass windows cast pink and purple shadows across þeir face like the memory of a bruise. "Grateful I am that Rafael is on our side. I wouldn't want to imagine the outcome otherwise."

The calm assessment assuaged my fears. "I asked him to keep the drakes from eating our dead and wounded in the future. He argued they'll view it as waste."

"'Twas a terrible thing, the way they ate up all the bodies, but I note the logic in it. Wounded though… Seemed 'twas only those nigh upon death that fell prey. All the same, I'd rather rattle out me own death rattle, aye?" Þey shuddered. "Worth it to note Rafael did none of the eating. I'm surprised he left off at the tribunal as well."

"As am I." I tried very hard not to imagine what the aftermath would have been otherwise.

"They're all so shocked, but I'll tell you that nary a soldier on that field would be. You're sure he's not a true dragon?"

"Sure as song." Drawing detailed parental information out of him proved even more difficult than seduction, but he'd always been clear about that point.

Nem tapped out the rhythm of a vaguely familiar quadrille on the cover of my book. After a moment, I placed it. The sidhe used it to entrap unsuspecting folk and force them to continue dancing until death. Morbidly appropriate.

Þeir ears perked, signaling some internal decision. "Can't feel too out of sorts when they brought it on themselves. How many times did these fools think they could go on and stab at a gods damned *dragon* before the dragon breathed fire? I didn't know the one killed, did you?"

I shook my head, stretching forward. My braid slipped over my shoulder, revealing the back of my neck.

"Damn, that's for a love bite!" Nemohee whistled just like Feanim had, and I laughed. "You and your man trouble. You pure cannot just pick one? When you first told me of this nonsense, I said to myself, 'Self, we'll pull for fecking *anyone* else, aye?' Yet, here am I, taking up for the auld menace."

"It would be like deciding which limb to chop off. Rafael is remarkably charismatic in spite of himself. He likes you too, though he'll never admit it." My thoughts turned back to my court troubles. "What do you know of Nimthil? She's your queen, eh?"

Nemohee barked a bitter laugh, the usual smile vanishing. "Not my queen, no. She's *a* queen. Never got enough acceptance thanks to me 'murky' fae blood to be allowed into any of the nations. Funny, aye, now that it's needed? They never outright barred me from the cities, simply pushed me to the front lines of every little squabble. 'Aye, we'll miss ol' Nem. Not to worry, we'll have a cracking funeral as thanks for the service'." As often as my friend hid behind humor, occasionally the mask slipped. "Good enough to lose me soulmate finding their damned horn, not good enough for counsel."

We'd always mirrored each other in painful ways. I'd wanted to escape the stifling confines of privilege and power. Nemohee had wanted only to belong.

Þey sighed, dragging a hand through unruly sprouts of bright hair. "I bear Nimthil no particular grudge. No author of any suffering, that one. She rules over the Téraglann Mountain Lachanaur, far from me homelands, such as you might call them. Not any fighter, she. Raised to the politicking, that's her strength. Lineage and influence. Said to be wise, with a fair hand."

I nodded, absorbing the information. Nemohee had been a drifter since I first met þem, until þey settled down with Cael, and preferred not to speak of þeir upbringing. With Cael gone, perhaps forever, who knew where þey would land?

"Whenever I rage at the gods over my own soulmate predicament, I just recall that it could be worse. They could saddle me with Feanim."

Nem made a face and pantomimed wiping muck off þeir sleeves, and we both laughed. Though Nimthil and I lost no love between us, I couldn't help but feel some sorrow for her at that twist of fate. I'd known her type before. She held no real malice toward me. My interference upended her neat worldview farther than she could tolerate. Understandable, at least from an academic perspective.

"Your fresh man is bonny and has a kind smile. I like him."

"Celebel is easy to like," I said. "I know he appreciates your efforts. It's nice to have reliable people at your back, and he's under a lot of stress."

Þey nudged a book on top of my little pile. "'The Application of Slime Mold in Human Wound Care: an Argument for Topical Use.' Riveting stuff."

I tried to push a solid shoulder away. "Leave off, it's for my research!"

Nemohee grinned, thumbing the bottle hanging around þeir

neck. "Speedy's ready whenever you are!"

I spread the Pîntellum experiment out in the small garden, tired of working inside. With the nights growing colder, I took advantage of the sun's warmth as much as possible. The slime mold's movements slowed considerably in frigid weather—something I hoped our body heat would counteract once applied to the armor.

Feanim's sample responded well, growing rapidly with the nutrient paste. I coaxed it to spread over a finely crafted þilvor gauntlet supplied by the Duedellen. Little by little the Pîntellum responded. As I worked, a draconic shadow fell over me.

"Your singular focus has always entertained me," said a voice deep enough to rattle my skeleton. I turned to behold Rafael armored in scales of burnished garnet, wearing a dragon face. Despite the fierce appearance, bristling with horns and spikes, his eyes were blue. A long tail curled around his feet. "Let enemies storm the gates, so long as they do not block Cúraniel from her interests."

I accepted the teasing. He was right. "Why this form today?"

"Your people need the reminder." He crouched, lowering a dragon's muzzle to sniff at the Pîntellum. "This is why you wanted that sample."

I explained the goal and my progress.

"Truly inspired. Why did you not ask for a sample from me?" Almost a pout, which made me laugh, coming from the enormous scaly warrior. I beamed anyway. Of all his rare compliments, those aimed at intellect were the fewest and farthest between.

"Because I do not yet know if it will work or be a big squelching mess. I like Feanim the least. Let him try it out." I made a conspiratorial lobe tug, and he responded with a lolling drake grin. Shifting my weight, I moved to wrap my arms around his neck.

The wind changed, and Rafael's pupils thinned. He backed away from me, standing and stretching to his full, towering height. The top of my head barely cleared his sternal notch in that form.

"Dragon, what—"

"Lavender." He spat the word like a foul taste, scaly lips curling back from his dagger teeth.

"What's wrong with lavender?" I'd been so happy to try the various scented oils in the washroom, as I normally didn't indulge in such things. The thought that I'd accidentally harmed him made me ill.

He shook his head, mane of scales rattling. "It stinks. Why would you wish to cover your natural scent?" His sense of smell was so much sharper than mine. As evidenced by the way he'd tracked down the smut author. I shivered and tried to imagine how Celebel might smell to him, but knew I couldn't ask.

"Does that go for other scents I've worn too, like mint or sweet pea or—"

"I. Hate. Lavender." Rafael bit off the words. A brief flash of his reaction to the drying herbs hanging in my bower, which had contained lavender. Crow, I should have known.

"Forgive me, please. I didn't realize this was the scent that bothered you. I won't wear it again." He nodded acceptance, and I relaxed. "Do I still smell of lilies and petrichor to you?" It had been a long time since he'd mentioned it.

Another grin. "And sex."

"I smell of sex?"

"When you are around me, yes." His eyes glittered as he looked me up and down, appraising. My clit awakened in response. Damn him. "I initially assumed you always smelled of sex until I experienced the way your scent changes around people you do not want to fuck."

"You tease me too much!"

"I am perfectly sincere." He was; it hummed through our

connection.

Gods. I really couldn't hide anything from him. "Go be a menace elsewhere. I'm finally making progress and you're interrupting me!"

He rumbled. Lifting an arm to his maw, he bit into it. Before I could protest, he grabbed an empty bottle from my supplies and spat a bloody gobbet of flesh into it. It sizzled as it hit the glass.

"There. For your next round of experiments." The wound stitched itself closed almost as fast as he'd opened it.

"I feel sorry for the slime mold. Your flesh will likely roast it."

The red drake huffed. "You will find a way."

"You have the strangest manner of flirting I have ever encountered."

He coughed a laugh. Instead of leaving, he curled around a nearby tree and watched me work. Upwind.

I delivered the gauntlet to Feanim with a curious Rafael padding along after me on all fours. The Duedellen's eyes widened at the sight of the Dragon, but he accepted the unexpected appearance with admirable aplomb.

Feanim pulled on the gauntlet. "Feels like old congealed mucus." He wrinkled his nose. "Slimy, but it quickly warms to my skin."

I instructed him on how to imbue it with his spirit and allow it to meld with his consciousness. He took up a blade and made various cuts and feints. Clumsy at first, the Pîntellum adapted as he did, until the motions smoothed. Under Rafael's intense scrutiny, we tested the reflex time of a range of actions with and without the gauntlet. The difference fell starkly in the Pîntellum's favor, and Feanim claimed it gave him better grip strength as well. Very encouraging. Buoyed by my success, I left my Dragon to argue with Feanim over the finer points of how to apply my experiment to armor.

Celebel came upon me scrubbing off the oil in the big copper tub. He perched on the edge.

"Didn't you just bathe this morning?"

"Rafael dislikes this scent." I immediately regretted my mouth running away from me, as Celebel's eyes took on a worrisome glint.

He swirled a hand in the water, sniffing the rising steam. "Lavender puts him off, eh?"

I changed the subject, hoping to distract him. "The Pîntellum experiment is going very well. Would you provide me with a sample?"

He complied. I added one for myself as well, just for balance, though I didn't expect to need it. Good practice for the eventual need to make large batches of them.

Rafael's sample proved just as challenging as its owner. The poor slime mold kept trying to escape to avoid touching his blood. Finally, I melded the two by buffering the mold itself with a heat protectant spirit.

I laid the jars out in our bedchambers, prepped and labeled. They'd need a little nutrient paste each day. I looked up to find Celebel bringing in fresh bundles of lavender. Fuck.

"I'll have to sleep elsewhere if you insist on this. I don't want the scent to cling."

Celebel pursed his lips and set a bundle beside the bed. "Surely he can tolerate a small jab in return for all the harassment."

I scowled until he sighed and took the bundles back into the hall to be removed by serving youth. Rebellious, he broke off a sprig and tucked it into a spray brooch. He presented me with a matching one. I plucked the lavender from it and tossed the offending plant over the balcony.

Lavender spray brooches immediately became all the rage in court. Overnight, many of the nobles, including Nimthil and my own sister, wore them pinned to shoulders and hair. To the higher echelons of the court, it constituted a badge of honor stating their outright disapproval of the Dragon's presence.

Araglin, alone among the higher ranks, remained neutral, but his eyes no longer held the kind sparkle to which I'd grown accustomed. The younger elves, led by Carafindrien and her friends, eschewed the brooches. I thanked them in as many ways for their tacit support as I could find.

I wore the one Celebel gave me only once, with a small lily tucked into it rather than a lavender sprig. Rafael caught me and replaced the lily with one of his roses. Naturally, he dodged my questions about where he'd been hiding such things.

Later that day, I passed Araglin in the halls. Witchlights followed him like a wreath of fireflies.

He stopped me with a hand on my arm. "Have I lost my senses, or is that the Sirelon rose gone red?"

"My lord, I am unsure of the origin." I'd forgotten that Celebel had echoed the same sentiment in my bower. My stomach knotted. Gods, I'd failed yet again at being social. Every small thing I tried to enjoy offended either one of my soulmates or the court at large. The politics of fucking *flowers*, of all things.

Araglin squinted, leaning forward to inhale the delicate scent. "I recall that scent, and the unique petal configuration. Once shimmering white, just as the walls of Sirelon itself, and now stained by the blood of all those who died…" His dark eyes flicked to my face. For the first time, I saw suspicion there. "A gift from the Red Dragon, I presume?"

I wanted to sink through the floor. For a heartbeat, I considered lying. But what good would it do? Araglin was no fool. That was, evidently, my purview.

"Yes, my lord."

Araglin held my gaze for a long moment, before nodding and walking away. Unsure of what to do with myself, I unpinned the rose, crumpling the silky petals in my palm. A thorn pierced my skin.

Chapter 49

A quiet scratching at the empty doorframe revealed Eledom wearing a serious expression. Lámirië hovered just behind him, her dark eyes flitting from corner to corner as if threats hid everywhere. They landed on my face and hardened. I tried not to answer with a glare, but the thought that I couldn't escape judgment even in my own bedchamber soured my stomach. No doubt she'd toss me to the wolves at the first opportunity. At least Eledom gave me an apologetic smile as he stole my soulmate away to confer.

Unfair. I'd had hardly any time alone with Celebel since Rafael relinquished me. Their hands flashed, and I caught a few words; 'Fomorians' and 'raid' featuring primarily among them. Celebel shot me an apologetic look. I gestured for him to follow his bodyguards.

With my hair in a riotous tangle, I shrugged on a robe to meet my future fate in the war room. Silfanië and her little cadre encountered me in the halls; a trio of silken judgment. Witchlights gilded her silver hair, but did nothing to warm her eyes. Feledhor and Recarmial bookended her, glaring daggers. All three wore lavender sprays. I looked beyond them, resisting the urge to increase my pace.

"Monsterfucker," Silfanië hissed as I passed. "Traitor."

"Can't even be bothered to dress properly. Look at her hair, at her dirty bare feet. Like a human street urchin." Recarmial patted her intricate auburn braid where it fell over her emerald dress. Feledhor sneered, looking me up and down with a toss of his white-blonde hair.

Though I schooled my face to calm, a twitch of my ears betrayed me. 'Monsterfucker' was only a rude name for the truth. The urchin comment struck me as silly bigotry, but being called a traitor rankled. I squared my shoulders and kept moving.

The war room hosted a small crowd. Along with the expected trio, Feanim, Rafael, Marron, and Nemohee pored over maps and markers. Nimthil took up her usual position along the wall. I'd expected Araglin as well, and breathed a small sigh of relief that he was absent. Our last encounter had left yet another stone in my belly.

Feanim gestured over the map nearest to him. "We cannot rely on the Carnyx until it's repaired. A discordant note played may have catastrophic consequences. Instruments were never my specialty," the admission came with a pained grimace, "and it's resisted my every attempt. Araglin's put out a call to other Duedellen artisans for help. Could be well over a moon before any of them arrive."

An intricate plan to draw out the enemy took shape, involving a muster and a march, and a lot of feints. We would need to appear weak and disorganized, making ourselves an enticing target to accomplish our end goal. None of the captured elves had yet been located, but we would search for them along the way. Given that Rafael focused more on the upcoming battle plans than his personal animosity with Celebel for once, I stayed only to show my support and watch the dynamics at play.

Nimthil, once again, firmly turned down a request of aid from her people. Marron mostly listened, occasionally asking a question of the two bodyguards. Lámirië consistently jumped at the sound of the green drake's voice. Feanim spoke over Nemohee any time þey made a suggestion, to the point that Rafael snapped at him. That small sign of camaraderie warmed me. Then Celebel got into the logistics and supplies, and my attention couldn't keep pace.

Next thing I knew, I was selecting practical clothing to join Celebel in the field, and making sure Eäriel had everything she needed for our return. I tucked my healing implements into my trunk, along with a few useful reference books. It chilled me to pack my half-moons and falcata. I hoped never to need them.

We rode out together to meet our allies on the far side of the gate. Everyone tacitly agreed to keep the direct mingling with the drakes to a minimum. Happy as I was to be reunited with Iruwher, being at the center of the fanfare discomfited me. Nemohee waved to me from further back in the procession. Eäriel tossed a crystal at me as I passed; a druzy of red garnets on a base of black tourmaline, for courage and protection. I ran my fingers over the rough points to center myself.

When Celebel pulled Helicos away to have a discussion with Feanim, Rafael approached, letting Iruwher take in his scent again before getting too close. Her ears flattened to her skull in warning, but since I was unbothered, she held steady. He had traded his usual boots for armor that freed his dragonish feet. All the better for kicking and heel-hooking with those talons and sharp spurs. He looked more energized than I had seen in a while.

"You should not be here." The Dragon cast a disapproving eye over me.

"Celebel wants me to witness you in active battle. In person." I arranged my coat on the saddle behind me. Admittedly, I was curious to watch him fight. And nervous. "Also, what good is a healer tucked away inside the walls? I need to be where the patients are, and I am a perfectly capable field medic." Filled with nervous, almost giddy energy, the fear of losing loved ones followed right at its ear tips.

He rumbled with displeasure, and Iruwher shied. I laid a calming hand on her dark mane and she quieted.

"If you wished to see me fight, I could have easily arranged that from Férioth," he said in a dark voice.

"Celebel insisted. Stop glaring at me, I will be perfectly safe with the other healers." I thought of all the times he'd come to me caked in old gore, a bizarre habit. "You always claim you'll keep me safe."

Rafael huffed. "Curious to learn if you will be too disgusted to touch me afterward?"

"I very much doubt that. I've seen you in just about every state of horrible except the active one. Surely it will not put me off that much." Perhaps I didn't want to imagine it.

"In some ways you have never seen my true self," he said thoughtfully. "This will be… educational."

"Remember what I said about preventing the drakes from eating our own." I stifled a disgusted shudder. What if I had no patients left to heal? Worse, what if I had to wrest them from the jaws of hungry drakes?

"I do not forget," he snapped, biting off the words.

"Forgive me, love. My anxiety sings loudest at times like these."

"I will keep you safe." He touched my hand briefly, then he was striding off to converse with Feanim. I watched him go, remembering what he'd said about the destruction of elves.

After some days of hard travel, we made a quick camp in the foothills. The camp tenders grew and twisted the meager tree branches with gentle, practiced hands, their swiftness impressive. Soon our dappled tent, small and simplified for easy deconstruction, stood ready. Celebel entered after me.

"You've deigned to stay with me tonight then? What, did the beast put you off?"

"Why are you starting a fight?" My brow creased in consternation. His sharp tone put me on edge.

Celebel's expression grew melancholy. "Forgive me, love. I am perhaps more stressed by the Dragon's presence here than I should be, adding to my other worries. You are not the target of my frustrations." He sighed, running a hand through his hair and shaking his braids loose. "I hate that we've had so little time together."

"Let us have some rest." I pulled him into the bed, curling against his body for comfort.

A grand idea, but anxiety kept me awake. My missteps with flower politics circled into a dizzying spiral. Silfanië's accusations about Leyúduin echoed close behind, regardless of Celebel's assurances. I tossed and turned in the jaws of worry.

In the early hours, just after I'd finally nodded off, Celebel woke me with a cry. I sat up and lit the witchlights, blinking the sleep from my eyes.

"What is it? Are we under attack?" My heart pounded in my ears.

"Something *walked across* me!" His face a mask of confusion; he cast about the tent for the source. "And yet I hear nothing!"

"Something… oh!" I spotted a slightly darker shadow lingering beside one of the tent supports. The outline did not match the witchlight glow. "Oh! You found me," I called out, delighted. The shadow drifted closer.

"Cúraniel, what—"

I waved him into silence. "There!"

The shadow coalesced into a vaguely catlike shape, and two lambent yellow eyes popped into existence. It shook itself and jumped onto the bed next to me, vibrating in silent purr.

"What is that? What *is* that thing? Is this more of Rafael's nonsense?" Celebel sounded more and more unsettled. "Is it fae? Where did it come from, and how did it get in here? That is *not* a house cat!"

"Relax, my little shadow is a friend. It first appeared centuries ago on the hill. I'm thrilled it found me, I assumed I would never see it again. It has always come and gone at will. It loves me! Don't you? I know, I love you too." I cooed and scratched it behind the ears. It squinted happily. Stars twinkled through its form. "Rafael is just as unnerved by it as you are."

"What." Celebel's ears went flat. "Why?"

"Probably doesn't want competition for being the most disturbing entity I know." I laughed, and the voidlet kneaded the blankets, bumping its head against my hand.

"Might as well make a morning of it." Celebel got up, dressing himself.

I followed him out of the tent. We came upon Feanim and the Dragon at the edge of camp. Rafael's eyes widened upon seeing the cat-shaped shadow floating along behind me.

"I told you to stop feeding that thing." He glared at it. "Fucking hells, Cúraniel. It has imprinted on you."

I gathered the creature in my arms and it yawned, revealing galaxies and far too many sharp white teeth. "You sing your own song! This is my little friend." It wiggled happily.

He gave me a look of pure consternation. Celebel watched the exchange with growing trepidation.

"'Feeding it?' What does he mean 'feeding it'? Cúraniel, what *is* that thing?"

"I told you, it's my little friend!" I shrugged. The shadow bobbed its head in agreement.

"That thing is not 'little,' nor your 'friend,' and it certainly is not harmless. It is a piece of the void itself."

"A piece of the void? How?" Fascination lit Feanim's eyes, but Rafael was in no mood to explain.

"Close your ears to the big awful man," I said to the silently purring shadow. "My fluffy little baby voidlet!" I kissed it on its soft forehead. It blepped out an overly pink tongue with a subtle glitter dancing over its surface. The lower half of its 'body' stretched until whatever made up the back paws dangled just above the grass.

Rafael stalked away, shaking his head. "When that abomination swallows half of your camp, do not come running to me for help."

"Is he serious?" Celebel asked me. "He sounds serious."

The creature settled further into my arms, pooling into a blob. I shrugged and swung its little paws back and forth.

"You are so fucking weird," Feanim said.

I grinned, and the voidlet mimicked me, a bright crescent moon splitting the darkness where its face should be.

We struck camp and rode until the forest overtook the granite cliffs. When we were finally among the trees, I breathed easier. Most of the drakes took to the wing, following us in lazy, prismatic circles far above our heads. It gave the nervous horses a reprieve, at least.

At a plateau overlooking a verdant field below, Feanim and Celebel engaged in a furious discussion over a small group of Fomorians they had spotted. Rafael examined the cliff edge nearby. I strained to see what they'd found. There, at the edge of the field, I spied the outlines of elk moving through the trees. Figures perched on their backs.

Since the plan was to tease and draw out the Fomorians along the way to our destination, perhaps it was a good sign. I withheld my opinion, imagining Feanim's biting response. No voidlet shadowed me; it popped in and out of existence without warning.

"We cannot allow them to alert their main force," Feanim said.

"They are well out of bowshot." Celebel frowned, eyes moving over the trees.

Instead of joining in the discussion, Rafael took a few long steps back. He bounded forward, launching himself over the edge with a powerful leap. Leathery red wings sprouted from his back to steady his fall as he stooped toward the enemy like a falcon diving. He breathed a stream of fire at the sheltering trees, flushing out his prey. With an eerie squeal, the elk bounded into the open, Fomorians clinging to their backs in simplified saddles. The last of the fading sun glinted on bronze bits and findings.

Rafael hit the rear elk like a ballista bolt and knocked the poor beast cleanly off its feet. It rolled heavily on top of its rider, who did not rise. Leaping to the next elk, shifting faster than we could perceive, he ripped the head from that Fomorian. Realizing that death was upon them, the rest urged their mounts to top speed, riding hard for the opposite tree line. One bull bugled a challenge. It turned and charged, trying to gore the drake. Rafael simply dodged, grabbing an antler, and broke the elk's neck with its own momentum. The rider lost its face to a flash of talons.

Feanim reined his horse around to make his way toward the unexpected fight. Celebel and I followed. We emerged just in time to see the end of the bloody scene play out at eye level.

Fast as the elk were, Rafael was faster. He'd already downed two more in the time it took us to join him. In his full drake form, he loped easily after the rest on all fours, like a scaly lion. He sprang onto the trailing elk. Easily avoiding its kicks, he crushed it to the ground under his weight and bit through that Fomorian's spine. Turning, he whipped his long tail to catch a second elk heavily on its side. The beast buckled, dropping to its knees and throwing the rider headlong into the grass. The Dragon was on it before the Fomorian could even roll to its feet, skull crunching in draconic jaws.

A flash of color in the sky revealed two other drakes circling the trees. They swooped and spun just above the canopy, ostensibly checking for other Fomorians. No more enemies appeared.

The last rider kicked its elk into a leaping gallop. For a moment, escape looked possible… until Rafael opened his jaws wide and spat a torrent of flame that sheared straight through the mount's legs. Elk and rider went down together, clods of dirt flying with their impact. The Dragon shifted back into his familiar form, approaching to the last enemy scout pinned under its dying elk.

"Hold, don't kill them all," Feanim called. "We need them for—"

"These are peons," Rafael interrupted, lifting the struggling Fomorian by the neck with one hand and looking over at the Duedellen with blistering eyes. "They know nothing."

"I still think we should—"

A sharp crack interrupted the protest. Rafael had broken

the scout's neck, all while maintaining his eye contact with Feanim.

Queasy, I looked away.

"You don't know that! How could you know that?" Frustration tightened Feanim's words.

"*You* cannot smell their meager power. Do not argue with me, little shade." Thunder crackled in the Dragon's voice, and he bared blood-streaked teeth. Celebel gave me a meaningful look. "You can fuck off too, *nekarazzi*," Rafael growled, red eyes spearing into my lover.

I maneuvered my horse between them.

'*Do NOT antagonize him when his blood is up! I do not know if I can calm him,*' I sent to Celebel in a flash, collecting myself with effort.

'*What does* 'nekarazzi' *mean?*'

'*I'll find out later. I need to focus now.*' Aloud, I said, "Thank you for stopping them. I gather we would have trouble if they had gotten away."

Mollified for the moment, the Dragon dropped the corpse. With a flick of his hand, the fire blazing at the edge of the meadow withdrew. It swirled around him like a scarf as he inhaled it. He looked past us and I turned to see Tyldain leading the other drakes toward us.

"Fresh kill, no claim," Rafael said in draconian, and toothy grins split the faces of the approaching warriors. I shivered. Time for us to leave the scene and based on the surrounding expressions, I wasn't the only one of that opinion.

The sickening crunch of bones and fleshy tearing noises followed us as we rode away.

'*Still feel like kissing him?*' Celebel sent, full of disdain.

'*Leave me alone,*' I shot back, trying to wipe the sounds and images from my mind.

Chapter 50

At our next encampment, I sought out the drakes. Celebel had been scarce, locked into long discussions with other martial leaders; he wouldn't miss my presence. A clear night sky greeted me, with a crystalline edge that promised cold on the way.

Rhythmic stomping punctuated by the occasional barking roar filled my ears long before I saw them. The drakes arranged themselves in a loose circle around a blazing bonfire. Drumming the ground with their tails as they stomped, they shook their scales with a buzzing rattle to the beat. They moved in concentric rings that rotated in opposite directions around the fire, occasionally swapping directions. Every once in a while, one leaped directly into the flames while the others roared. They were *dancing!* My mood lifted instantly.

The syncopated rhythm drew me in. Faster and more beat-driven than elvish music, it held a certain driving energy that moved my body of its own accord. The rattling scales made an instrument all on their own. I hadn't realized scales were that mobile.

The Dragon came up behind me, silent as death. "You left your cursed shadow behind. Good."

I pulled his arms around me, pressing my back against him. "The voidlet hasn't been around the last few days. Why didn't you tell me they were dancing?"

The warriors cast looming, twisting shadows as they moved.

"They have only just started."

"May I join?" My hips wiggled with the desire to let the rhythm take me.

He coughed a startled laugh. "Go then, entertain them."

I sidled up to the circle. Xyxs spotted me and made space. The rest paused to watch with open curiosity.

"You dance with us?" the big drake boomed in draconian. "Never seen an elf dance with dragons."

"I will try," I replied in kind. "Teach me?"

His laugh was a thunderclap that flattened my ears. Bending low so he could look me over, Xyxs corrected my posture with a few well-placed thumps. I might be slightly bruised later, but it was worthwhile.

"Like this! Then you step, shake, stomp. Understand?" He demonstrated the rapid way the drakes rotated their forearms back and forth to make their scales buzz.

I tried it and several of the drakes around us roared their laughter, and what sounded like encouragement. Or perhaps mockery. Either way, they were entertained.

"No, this way!" Xyxs boomed another laugh and demonstrated again.

I mimicked him a second time, much to his uproarious approval, though I couldn't tell the difference between that and my first attempt.

A stocky drake with scales the color of fallen leaves set the beat with a thumping tail. Then I was off, stomping and clapping to keep the time with the rest, trying very hard not to grin like a fool and cause offense by showing my teeth. Another drake sang in a resonant, rolling bass growl. I could parse only a few words here and there; it had the cadence of a war song. A few others took up a chant to the rhythm set by the singer and the tail thumper. The circle came alive with the energy of the dance.

After the first round, I spied Marron in the onlookers.

"Green Marron, join us," I called out.

He laughed, holding up his hands. "I am a terrible dancer! I'll just watch," he replied in elvish. "I hate wearing a tail, can't dance properly without."

Marron was right; a lot of the moves the drakes performed with ease were nearly impossible for me without that counterbalance. Not to mention that particular stomping, tail smacking rhythm was difficult to accomplish without that extra appendage.

I turned to Rafael, who was already sighing. "Come dance!"

He let me pull him into the ring, shifting into his full drake form; snout, tail, and added size. Heavily keeled scales sprouted on every bared patch of skin, a crimson gone nearly black in the night. Curling hair became a mane of elongated scales, and pebbled plates slid over the vulnerable underside of his throat. His long dragon's skull bore the distinct hook of his nose and brow arch. Firelight glinted on his white horns. All in the span of a few heartbeats. Despite the change, Xyxs still towered over everyone.

The massive red and black drake set the beat this time, a little faster. I admired Rafael's sleek movements in his drake form. He added little flourishes, more complex than anything I could manage, tossing his mane of scales back and forth to great effect. As the dance sped up, he lifted me onto his spiky shoulders. Laughing, I clung to his spinal ridges and tried not to cut myself. Around me, the drakes spun and stomped in unison. They were a glory to behold, all flashing colorful scales and muscle, sinuously twisting around each other in perfect rhythm.

It was certainly a more lively, pleasant setting than the last time we'd danced together. He seemed to be genuinely enjoying himself for once, and I enjoyed his serpentine grace. Perhaps I simply preferred the company of drakes to elves. As the dance ended, Rafael set me gently on my feet and shifted back into his familiar form. He made it look easy.

One drake passed me a wineskin, but Rafael plucked it from my hands before I could take a sip. When I gave him a questioning look, he shook his head and passed the skin along. Whose blood had they used?

"You dance well enough for a scaleless flower-eater," Marron said, approving. "Need a little more bulk, though. And a tail." He gave me a lolling grin, and I laughed.

A little more bulk, indeed. I had yet to meet a drake who wasn't a solid wall of muscle. Even the slimmer Tyldain seemed struck from rippling stone.

"Do you always speak elvish to me because my draconian is so poor?" I asked, and it was the green drake's turn to laugh.

"Ah, well, I also want to practice. I don't speak with many

elves.”

Nemohee would love this, I thought, watching the dancers. The rest of the camp was dark, as the majority gathered at the dance circle. From the sounds, they'd be at it all night.

“Nemohee has already been out here tonight,” Rafael replied to my musing, startling me out of my reverie. I stopped in my tracks, and he raised a hand. “I would not let þem come to harm.”

“That's uncharacteristically kind of you.” I thumped his arm. “You care for Nem, you just won't admit it.”

“I cannot abide your tears,” he said. “Þey claimed to be going off for more whiskey, should you care to wait.”

Nemohee met me at the edge of camp, hoisting a cask of whiskey on one shoulder. Þeir silver eyes glowed faintly in the darkness as þey loaded me down with jangling bracelets and anklets.

“Where did you get these?” I gave my bangles an experimental rattle.

“Been chatting with Marron. When I learned of the dance, figured I'd make some of our own noisemakers. Kept me hands busy, and best to make merry afore a battle,” þey said.

Nemohee befriending the green drake made perfect sense. Maybe the two had bonded over their infuriating leaders. Rafael waved us on as the fallen-leaf drake approached to ask him a question. Leading with the whiskey like a peace offering between us, we moved deeper into the camp.

A brilliant yellow drake with large green eyes under a bony crest met us first, snatching the whiskey away with a threatening hiss. The same one I'd seen in Celebel's memory. Built like a giant, long-legged bird with a dragon's snout in place of a beak, it was significantly taller than my Dragon. A wide green stripe ran down its back.

“All right, that was rude,” Nemohee protested, reflexively drawing þeir sword.

I grabbed þeir arm too late. The yellow drake's eyes

narrowed, and it lowered its head, pulling scaly lips back from long, recurved teeth.

"No offense meant to you, different are our ways," I stuttered in draconian. My nerves jangled in alarm.

It gave us another low hiss and a stomp. Scythe-like talons twitched. One kick would disembowel, perhaps even shatter a spine. I froze, unsure if I should back away or stand my ground. Nemohee's grip shifted on the sword, muscles tensing.

The yellow drake reared up, as if readying to strike. Instead, it jerked to the left. Thrown to the ground, it landed hard on its side. Rafael appeared behind it, eyes sparking red. He bellowed a roar. The yellow drake shook itself with a clacking rattle of scales, scrambling to its feet.

It whipped around with a snarl and snapped at Rafael's head. He sidestepped the bite with a sharp uppercut, slamming the drake's jaws shut with a *clack*. It dropped to the ground like a pile of dirty laundry.

"Fuck off. She is forbidden to you," he thundered.

Dazed, the birdlike drake struggled to sit up, shaking its head. Pulling its feet beneath it, it rose unsteadily with an answering snarl. Knocked out in one strike, yet still spoiling for a fight. Vicious.

"Go or I will—" Rafael growled something that sounded like 'rip your eggs out and eat them.' A female, then.

After a tense moment, the other drake let out a long, water-kettle hiss and backed away, grumbling and rubbing at its jaw. A feather-tufted tail lashed in its wake.

Rafael closed his eyes for a moment. Our connection hummed with his unrequited bloodlust. I sent soothing energies. Finally, he exhaled in a gust of heat and turned to us.

Sheepish, Nemohee smiled up at him. "Hullo, Big Red. I was only bringing whiskey! I didn't mean to cause a dust up."

He snorted. "Do not start a fight you cannot finish. Put that sword away, it is useless here." Turning, he motioned for us to follow. "Feisty little blighter."

"You said this blade was better than the last," Nem protested.

"The blade is improved, your strength is not."

Nemohee huffed in mock offense.

Marron greeted us at the circle, the cask of whiskey relocated to his side. "Abrrys tried to get greedy, eh? Typical. She's always been a thorn."

"Greedy rude bint," Nemohee agreed, rolling up þeir sleeves to show off the bangles, with a twist that made them rattle.

Marron's ruby eyes widened with delight.

"Makeshift scales. Clever! I want to see this in action."

Rafael stubbornly resisted a second dance, leaning against a tree and watching with amusement. Nemohee and I joined the circle, whooping and laughing, shaking our wrists and ankles as hard as we could to the beat of stomping feet and thrashing tails. The gathered drakes roared unanimous approval when they saw our bangles, making space for us to join in without being trampled. We danced alongside the great scaled warriors until the early hours of morning, leaving our worries and cares behind for just one night.

Nemohee found þeir way back to the elvish camp and I found my way into Rafael's arms. We settled under a tree in the cold night, removed from the others. I curled against his chest, grateful for his warmth. He pulled up a dampening field just as a meteor streaked across the sky just under the waning sliver of moon. The Night Mother had been quiet on portents as of late; I took it as encouragement.

I played over the appearance of the various drakes in my mind, comparing and contrasting them with Rafael. The only other one I'd seen with any red scales was the black-tipped Xyxs. Cagey as he could be about his past, I decided to probe.

"Why are there no other pure red drakes?"

"I killed them." Rafael said it so casually it took me a moment to comprehend the words.

"All of them? Why?" He'd never spoken of kin slaying before. I shivered.

"Call it a difference of opinion." The Dragon's expression grew cold.

"No solid gold or indigo drakes either? Same reason?" Selfishly, I wished I could have seen those drakes. Their scales sounded lovely.

He cast a sharp look at me. "The gold drakes were the dominant clan when I was coming up." Ah. "The remaining indigos I executed because of Byxldurr."

"The one who attacked you on my hill, right? The War Crow?"

The Dragon rumbled assent.

"You've single-handedly wiped out three entire clans and they still accept you as their king?" I tried to imagine what would happen to elvish society in a similar situation. The thought made me shiver.

"We have no kings, and they have no choice. I received some assistance with the gold clan; Marron proved his worth there." That was as close as he'd come to admitting any kind of friendship with the green drake.

"You seem to care for them now."

"I do feel some responsibility for the actions of my youth. We have never been a numerous people. However…" His mouth twisted.

"However, you cannot seem to stop yourself. No wonder you always disappear. Important murdering to do, eh?" Before Rafael, never in my life would I have made light of such things. Perhaps the association with him damaged my morals beyond repair. I changed the subject before the discomfort ruined my mood. "I wish you'd danced with us the second time."

"You two made for quite the spectacle with those ridiculous bracelets."

"How dare you mock me!" At least I danced with grace, if not the same precision as the other drakes.

Rafael rumbled, a low noise of amusement, and stroked my hair. "Your attempts to mingle with my people are charming."

"I rather enjoy spending time with your people. They are much more good-humored than I expected." Well, most of them.

"A contrast, yes?" A smirk curled his lips.

I kissed the corner of his jaw. "You have your moments. Especially when you make me laugh, you cantankerous, awful creature."

"I am horrible," he agreed, echoing his statement to Araglin. "Genuinely foul."

"The very worst." I kissed his lips, twining my fingers into his hair. His hands slid over my rump, lifting and parting my legs to straddle him. Pressed against his rising erection, my arousal answered in kind, and I soaked through the fabric of my trousers.

"What may I do for you, my Dragon? I cannot send you off to battle unfulfilled," I murmured against his mouth, aching to grind my needy clit on him.

"Open your coat," he said, and I complied. Cupped firmly in his hands, he hefted my tender flesh, thumbing my nipples. "Such magnificent breasts." He smiled, a quick flash before it fled. "You taught me to appreciate them. I never cared much before we met."

"I am grateful for your appreciation," I said with a laugh. "Likewise, I never truly appreciated tongues before you."

He bent, the aforementioned tongue swirling around each breast with a slick, gentle squeeze. Taking a nipple in his mouth, he sucked, flicking the point of his tongue rapidly over the sensitive tip.

I sighed with bliss, envisioning his cock trapped in my cleavage. The image of him gliding back and forth, squeezing my breasts together to pleasure himself, made me moan. Rafael paused, releasing my nipple from his mouth with a pop, and tilted his hips away from me.

"Someday, I hope." He sighed, closing his eyes and pressing his face into my chest.

Guilt twinged. "Forgive me, love. You set my imagination alight. I shall try harder to contain it."

"No." My breasts muffled his voice. "No, I do not wish to shy from such things. Voice your desires. Surely, I can at least speak of such things."

That surprised and encouraged me. He so rarely took a step forward of his own accord. "This is growth." I pressed a kiss to the top of his head, enjoying the thick texture of his hair against my lips.

He nuzzled my bosom, his long nose poking into my flesh as he inhaled my scent. "I must force myself to try harder. For you."

"Trying for your own sake matters more." I hated to sour the mood, but I had to be sure this sudden change came from a desire to heal, rather than jealous competition. "Let me be absolutely clear that I do not pit my intimacy with you against what I have with Celebel." He tensed, but I pressed on, raking my nails over his scalp. "This is not a competition. I love the way we fuck. My pleading for your cock when you bring me to the heights in no way indicates a lack of satisfaction. Your healing and your comfort with your body are what I desire most. I am a selfish woman in many ways; I admit that. But, if you decide never to utilize your cock under any circumstances, I will love you all the same. I only want it to be your conscious decision. Not due to some trauma-fueled avoidance."

Rafael lifted his head, studying my face with luminous eyes. Looking into me, weighing my words against his fears. His slit pupils widened and thinned with his guarded thoughts.

"You are kinder to me than I deserve," he said finally, deep voice shivering through the darkness. "I know I do not always… behave. But I would break myself for you."

I traced the sharp line of his cheek. "Oh, my Dragon. You deserve more kindness than I alone may give. No more talk of breaking. How can I help you heal tonight?"

He exhaled, a long, low breath, and laid himself down beside me on his back. "Hrrm, lay your hands on me. Not a caress. Simple touch."

I stretched out beside him. "Whatever you like. Direct my hands. Place them yourself, if you wish."

Rafael took my hand in response, laying my palm over his solid belly, keeping his hand on mine. The muscles of his abdomen jumped in a harsh tense and release.

"Easy, my love. You have all the control here. In this place. I exist only to please you." I kept my voice even and gentle, letting my arm go completely limp in his grasp.

He moved my hand in a small, slow circle, staring, unblinking, at the stars above. Little by little, the muscle twitch ceased, and he relaxed. His eyes closed.

"Touch me at your leisure." He sighed as he released my hand. "Over my clothing. Speak to me as you do so?"

"Happily." I rested my hands on the angular planes of his face. "Shall I speak of my admiration for you? To offset all my teasing? I want you to understand why you are so deserving."

The Dragon rumbled, eyes closed. "As you wish."

"You have such a uniquely handsome face." He exhaled sharply through his nose, and I tapped the tip of it. "Don't you deny me my opinion! I love the intensity of your eyes, suits your personality." I traced the arches of his brow, down the hooked bridge.

"You would truly be a menace if that aloof confidence extended to your appearance." The pad of my thumb outlined his mouth, traveled up the plane of his cheek to the short points of his ears. "I love you for your passion, your intellect, and your sense of humor. Your observant nature." In the moonlight, the lock of his hair I twined in my fingers looked almost as black as my own.

I leaned over him and gripped the top of his shoulders, then his upper arms. "Never have I seen such shoulders in all my life! Your strength awes me. I can hardly fathom it. You are fucking impressive and intimidating and I love how well you know it."

With both hands, I pressed what would be a massage on anyone else down each arm. Taking his hand in both of mine, I spread his long fingers apart, touching his knuckles, his palms. "Such pleasure these hands have granted me. I've always appreciated the sensitivity of your fingers, and the control you have over that terrible strength. Your talons are quite elegant as well. You keep them so clean, and use them with such dexterity. I should be hopeless with talons, I think. Put my eye out or some such."

"Indeed." He rumbled with humor.

I moved to his chest. Palms flat against the heavy muscle, it took effort not to caress him.

"You, too, have a truly magnificent chest." The rumble grew, almost a thrum, encouraging me. Careful to pick my hands up rather than slide them over his body, I cupped his rib cage. "I marvel at the shape of you, as though a divine sculptor set forth to create the perfect incarnation of power."

It took effort not to crawl over him and add kisses when touching his abdomen and hips "Such beautiful lines."

The thrumming stopped.

"Come along, Dragon. I will always find you beautiful. Would you like me to continue downward or work up from your feet?"

"Work up." He kicked his boots off, making me smile. Stretching, he relaxed his feet, and I rubbed the soles.

"I love this stark reminder of your nature. I've a hearty new appreciation for the dexterity of your feet as well."

Rafael sighed and resumed his thrumming. I wrapped my hands around the spurs at his heels, then worked slowly up his calf. Circling his kneecaps with careful hands, I lingered there before moving to his thighs. Here, I used caution. This was usually where he became reactive.

"You have quite shapely legs, you know." I rested my hands on the outside of his thighs, following the swell of the external quadriceps.

He snorted again.

"You do! I am sorry I have not appreciated them enough." I paused. "May I touch your inner thighs?"

"Slowly."

I moved my hands to the tops of his thighs, watching his face. No flinching or brow furrowing. I rested my palms lightly on his inner thighs, fingers pointing inward rather than up at his groin.

"Tell me how you're feeling. I do not want to progress past your comfort." He was doing so well, I almost wanted to cry.

"I need you to keep pushing me." His voice wavered with strain.

"Talk me through it. Tell me exactly what you want. Tell me how it makes you feel, everything you experience. I wish to stop well before it becomes overwhelming for you."

He exhaled through his nose, shifting his weight. "Use one hand, rest it on… on my cock. Palm-down, fingers toward my face. Do not grip."

I hesitated. "Do you wish to place my hand?"

"No." A bitten-off denial.

I followed his instruction, my palm almost floating over him. Even flaccid, his cock was impressively thick under my hand, significantly longer than my entire handspan, and still hard as the rest of him. He shivered, and I almost drew away.

"Speak to me, Dragon. What are you experiencing?"

"I… fracture. Into memory. Their faces, their voices, their ugly scent." He hissed, arching his back and shuddering. I struggled to maintain contact. "I lose myself."

"Is it possible to supplant that memory with me? Open your eyes, look at my face if you are able." I made a sweet, singsong rhythm of my voice, the same as I used for animals.

Rafael cracked one blazing eye. Another tremor ran through him.

"Good, you're doing very well. Stay with me, stay in the present. Shall I take my hand away?"

"Not yet. I need this. I need you." He squeezed his eyes shut again, face contorting with the effort of fighting off the darkness.

"Rafael, my Jax. I'm here. I love you."

"I know. I know. I… ah!" He bared his teeth, snarling, talons raking furrows in the ground. All at once, he sat up and wrapped me in his arms, pulling me on top of him.

I murmured to him, soothing noises. His heart hammered,

palpable through the thick muscle of his chest. I reached through our connection to synchronize it with my own. For a moment, I gasped for breath as his heartbeat bolted away with mine. Pulling hard, I reined it back to a more reasonable pace. He shuddered again, talons splayed.

"You are safe, you are here with me." Over and over. Gradually, the Dragon relaxed. "There you are, my love. How do you feel?"

Rafael heaved a great sigh, lifting me with the rise of his chest. "Lighter."

Chapter 51

A few skirmishes followed, mostly small groups at lower altitudes where they could easily disappear below ground. Our scouts identified the main horde as the Fomorians attacked and retreated in their typical waves. We positioned our forces to "accidentally" encounter their numbers at the greatest concentration.

Harrying them along the way, we fled, and they gave chase. Their forces swelled at every turn, more and more joining the ranks as we passed. We changed course. Heading west rather than farther south, we raced our horses to higher altitude. The drakes took to the wing, striking at the Fomorians on our flank, but staying out of reach. Moving farther into the mountains, we passed the point where the granite offered cave systems.

We reached a valley with a narrow entrance through sheer cliffs rising far above a flat meadow. Waterfalls fed multiple streams that collected in a long, shallow lake. It butted against the remnants of ancient glacial schist at the outflow terminus of the valley. The schist acted as a dam, creating the valley floor. The lake's outlet cascaded over it, and the resulting river tumbled in whitewater through boulders and crags of the lower canyon. Down there, marshy meadows dotted with small stands of trees thickened into dense groves along the edges.

As night fell across the serene lake waters, Feanim directed a camp to be set along the muddy upper bank on a drier hillock. Near a bend where the valley river flowed broad and shallow, the meadow created the ideal place to water and feed the horses. They could go no farther without risking collapse. With no trees for cover, rocks disguised the location.

Celebel loaded me down in uncomfortable armor and perched me at a high vantage point in the crags with a few other medics; close enough to provide rapid aid for those able to leave the field, but not so close as to be embroiled in combat. Rafael kept me company, crouched nearby with his talons lodged in the cliff wall. Archers provided further security.

"No reason for you to join the fighting. If it gets close, take the others and flee. We'll run the horses through and meet you on the far side," Celebel said.

I kissed him thoroughly, trying to rein in my growing anxiety. "Keep yourself safe, please. Don't you go bleeding everywhere like the last time I healed you."

"We'll have the notes of this melody soon enough." He gave me a wink and climbed back down to the valley floor.

Rafael watched him leave with a twist to his mouth, even more imposing than usual in his spiky black armor, hair aflame.

"Where is your helm? I've never seen you wear one."

He arched a brow. "And you never will."

I had a brief, choking flash from him of being restrained with a burlap sack over his head and shivered. "Be careful, please."

He laughed his coughing laugh. Catching my hand, he dragged it up his cheek, against the grain of his skin. The minuscule scales scratched my fingers. Shaking my hand out, I nodded. I tended to forget until he made those scales obvious.

"Your concern is charming." The Dragon turned to look out over the chosen battlefield with a shark-toothed grin. The sudden fierce red joy in his eyes sent a shudder down my spine, and I almost felt sorry for the enemy.

Our swiftest fighters laid in wait with their horses. Nemohee was among them, tightening my gut with more worry. The rest crept away under the cover of darkness. The moon rose and slowly fell. A breeze rippled from the lake. I fidgeted, anxiety mounting as the first light of dawn broke across the peaks, blushing them lotus-pink.

There! Dark shapes emerged from the gap, charging in a great mass to the tents. The Fomorians came billowing out of their cover, easily outnumbering all our combined forces. Dawn glinted on bronze armor and bared blades.

As they neared the tents, the lake's fog rolled over the

attacking force in a thick curtain. Water lapped over their feet, and their movements faltered as they struggled to move in the deepening mud. Confused voices rang out. The enemy howled, spinning about in bewilderment, mere shadows in the cloud bank.

Hidden at the edges of the valley, a few elves worked in tandem, pulling the fog and holding it in place. Others drew the lake itself closer. Those talented in glamour spun a targeted lacing of misdirection to flow along with the fog.

Horses squealed, leaping to their feet. The Fomorians roared in response, some giving chase to the riders darting to safety. I tried in vain to count the hoofbeats, worried that Nemohee hadn't escaped. The principal enemy force remained in place, hacking and slashing wildly at the tents, landing more than a few blows on each other.

There! Campfire-bright hair perched on a blue roan, Nem led the horses away at a gallop. Just navigable enough for the horses, a ravine in the upper valley, where a stream tumbled down from the high elevations, made a predetermined escape route. Given an actual target, the Fomorians gave chase.

The first arrow loosed from an elvish bow skewered an elk-mounted Fomorian directly through its eye. The next volley rained death. Fomorians scattered, desperately raising shields too meager to stop the force of a longbow. Our archers hid along the cliffs, positioned to inflict maximum damage along that path. The impediment allowed the poor tired horses to escape. Watching the progress next to me, Rafael nodded satisfaction.

At the bottom of the ravine, our cavalry served as the hammer to cut off any chase up the ravine path. Able to pin a fly's wings together in a hurricane, elvish archers picked off any Fomorian that tried to push through our rear guard. The cavalry moved and fought at will, arrows zipping around them in a deadly storm, striking their targets with unerring accuracy. I couldn't help a small swell of pride at the archers' mastery. Bodies collapsed, pierced through in myriad places.

The Fomorian force fractured. While they focused on the

escaping horses, we drew the lake out across the dam, cutting off any easy escape. Before they could recover and regroup, the drakes struck.

Lightning lit up the fog, painfully brilliant blooms in the darkness. A crested dragon, yellow as the dawn with an emerald stripe running down the back of a serpentine neck, stooped over the lake above the blanketing cloud. Abrrys screeched, and more lighting pelted the battleground in her wake, streaking down from her broad wings. The bolts struck a few Fomorians directly, arcing through the wet ground to catch others. As they convulsed, I whispered gratitude to the Night Mother that I couldn't smell it from my perch.

With a flash of azure wings, a slender blue dragon swooped over from the south. Tyldain. Wind shears, hail, and driving rain ripped across the lake bed, tearing away the fog cover and flattening bodies into the sucking mud. He lashed a whiplike tail in his wake, flinging any hapless Fomorians unable to dodge halfway across the water, and crushing others.

The blue drake's storm dimmed the growing morning light to a deep gloom. Amidst the cacophony of screeching metal and screaming, the other drakes swooped in from the edges. They fell from the sky like boulders dropped from a cliff, landing amid the enemy with incredible speed. Muck geysered where they landed.

Rafael watched still, eyes bright.

"Aren't you going to join them?" I prodded.

"Waiting for the ground to dry a bit. I hate fighting in mud." He glanced at me. "Calm yourself, they do not need me yet."

"Persnickety creature." Of course he didn't want mud under his talons.

"You go out there and fight, then."

"*You* wouldn't allow me even if I wished it," I retorted, and Rafael grinned. The unexpected humor lightened my worried heart.

Each drake fought independently rather than as a unit, similar to what I'd witnessed in Celebel's memory. Xyxs' great size set him apart, and Fomorians scattered backward out of his long reach. Marron fought near Boshkt and two others; a shiny black drake I hadn't seen before, and the fallen-leaf rhythm keeper. Bodies piled around them. Abrrys and Tyldain, in their full dragon forms, harried the enemy from above, catching Fomorians with each pass over the battlefield. The dragons either hurled their captured prey into the rocks, dropped it from a height, or ripped it to bloody tatters. Eye-watering bursts of flame streaked across the scene, illuminating expressions of abject terror among the Fomorians as they burned.

With a sigh, Rafael pushed off of the cliff wall and dropped. Rather than sprout wings, he banked twice off the rocks and landed at a run. He hit the enemy like a cyclone, standing out from the rest with the sheer carnage he left in his wake. Even at a distance I could see the expression of pure, ferocious joy on his face as he flung broken bodies out of his way. He cut an effortless, bloody swath with sword, talon, and fang. Rarely did he breathe fire; only when his prey moved too far from his gory dance.

Equal parts horrified and fascinated by his awful strength, I couldn't tear my eyes from the field. I'd heard tales of berserker battle rage, but never before witnessed it. Even Celebel's memory weaving muted in comparison to firsthand experience.

Most Fomorians attempted to flee Rafael's carnage, but a courageous few fought back. My Dragon shrugged off hits that should have staggered him like nothing more than the tap of a butterfly's wing. Nightmare made flesh, blood fountained over his head and viscera lined his path. A benediction in death.

Disoriented and beleaguered from all sides, the Fomorians turned to flee back toward the gap. Straight into the arms of our waiting cavalry. Nemohee appeared, regrouped with the rest. The horses danced and pivoted around the slower Fomorians. Waterlogged and battered, the enemy struggled through the sucking mud of the banks. Bright halberds and spears flashed, felling many a foe, and drakes decimated the stragglers.

Regrouping, the Fomorians struck back with renewed vigor

at the sight of their true target. They hurled themselves directly at the cavalry, heedless of the blades shearing through their bodies, until they bore down the foremost horses. Celebel appeared behind those who fell, fighting alongside Feanim. I sucked in a fearful breath. The wave approached.

Then Rafael was there, weaving between horses. He grabbed the Fomorian reaching for my elvish soulmate and flung it away. Celebel repaid him by spearing another Fomorian just past his shoulder. Struck through the eye, it dropped before it could land a cleaver on the Dragon's neck. I thought I saw Rafael give Celebel the slightest nod, and a thrill tingled up my spine.

Marron appeared at the cavalry's left flank, and with the assistance of the two drakes, they pressed the advantage. Hacking, burning, spearing, and trampling, they drove the remaining Fomorians into the clutches of the other drakes. The pincer closed. From a safe distance, longbows twanged, picking off stragglers.

The enemy tried to regroup again and swarm the drakes to overwhelm their individual might with numbers. The scaled warriors shook them off like flies. Swiftly losing morale, several Fomorians scattered and ran. It was difficult to watch. The attempted escape seemed to stir the predatory drive of the drakes to a fever pitch, and they gave chase. The children of the dragons overtook their quarry and tore them to gruesome pieces. And the drakes feasted; all except Rafael. Our cavalry withdrew, singing victory.

Once serene and lovely, the battle reduced the landscape to a steaming ruin. My heart ached at the sight. From the way other elves' ears flattened at the scene, I was not alone in that sentiment. When Tyldain landed near the bank and bent his head to snap up corpses, I finally turned away from the destruction. The awful crunch of bones followed me.

Chapter 52

I joined the other healers at the true encampment, safely hidden behind the granite walls on the other side of the cliff passage. We'd set up a long, wide tent, preparing to receive casualties. Rows of cots lined the walls, and a central workstation featured a bubbling cauldron full of an analgesic, sleep-inducing decoction. A Siltaur woman named Liriadis organized the work flow and directed triage. With her long, chestnut hair streaked gold by the sun and bound into a practical knot at the nape, bright hazel eyes dominated her dark copper face. She wore an expression that brooked no nonsense, but kindness glimmered there, too.

Liriadis led me to a station set up near the entrance for my work, outfitted with any tool I might need, along with a sturdy padded stool and a cot. I recognized the wisdom of placing me a little farther away from the others in case of drake interruptions.

"Get her stabilized." She indicated a young Astolar weakly clutching her right arm. Someone had set it already, but the socket was badly bruised and bled freely. It reminded me of Galdir's confrontation with Rafael, and I hid my scowl.

My patient's face had gone ashen white under her juniper brown complexion and mane of ochre-blonde curls. Green eyes wandered, unfocused. Her pulses were rapid and wiry, with the fluttering of shock. I gave her a pain relieving draught as I examined her, finding a purpling hoof print on her right lower leg. She must have been among the cavalry pulled down. I chattered as I worked, trying to keep her conscious. Clearing the swelling, I staunched the bleeding from the shoulder and reached with spirit to reconnect the torn vessels and nerves. Finally, I applied a ready-made poultice to encourage circulation. Drawing a cup from the large decoction, I helped her drink. She drifted into blissful, safe slumber.

A few patients later, a muscular Lachanaur of indeterminable gender plopped down in front of me.

"Nem, what have you done to yourself?" I smacked þem carefully on the shoulder while examining a shallow head wound.

"I'm braw! Hale and hearty! They forced me to come, anyway. 'Tis just a dunt on the head," þey protested. "Fomorian clipped me coming up out of the tent."

"Hush your nonsense, any little bump on the head can cause problems later. They probably sent you in here because no one can understand your accent and they thought you'd lost your senses."

Luckily, þeir assessment was correct. It was only a surface level abrasion and easily patched up. As usual, þey jokingly complained about my 'fussing' the entire time I worked on þem.

I worked quickly through each patient, noting that I hadn't been trusted with the more serious cases. With no time to dwell on it, I simply accepted the direction. I hummed as I went, to drown out the surrounding noises, and rarely looked up from my work.

With my attention fixed on the patient in front of me, I didn't notice right away when the whole tent went dead silent. The rising anxiety like a shift in the wind finally caught my attention. My patient, a lanky Lachanaur, went white with shock despite his minor injury. I felt *his* presence behind me.

"Rafael. Stop scaring my patients," I called over my shoulder.

"I am your patient," he rumbled.

Out of the corner of my eye, I saw a few of those waiting for care decide that they were perfectly healthy after all and creep away. Everyone else—healer, assistant, and patient alike—went still. They watched with an open mix of fear and fascination.

I finished tying off the herb-soaked bandage on my actual patient, releasing him with a nod, and turned around. No wonder everyone had gone quiet with shock. The Dragon was a bloody horror. Caked in gore from head to foot, only his fiery eyes were clear. And fierce.

"Oh, this again. Are you actually hurt or did you merely wish to bother these poor people?" In that moment, I could put aside my discomfort in favor of protecting my patients.

"*Grievously* wounded." A terrible smile split his face, dried blood around his mouth cracking and flaking away. Unsurprisingly, blood also streaked his jagged teeth. A whimper nearby convinced me to humor him. For now.

"Very well. Sit here on the floor and let me examine you." I didn't trust our small chairs and cots to hold up to his weight.

He obeyed, folding his feet underneath him, and shed his blood-spattered plackart and breastplate. Unlike others, he wore minimal padding under his armor. I sucked in a breath at a dark bloodstain under his arm. He shrugged out of his thin arming jacket and pulled up his shirt, exposing his left side. A broken-off spear lodged under a rib, and his steaming blood leaked steadily. Surely an injury he could heal on his own. More surprising that any Fomorian weapon could even harm him. He rested his left forearm on his head, watching me.

"Why did you need me for this?" I prodded carefully around the wound.

"Heartless woman," Rafael said in a dark, strange voice. He tilted his head. "It is… hrrm, poisoned."

I snatched my hand back. "What do you mean poisoned? I didn't know such things affected you!"

"Touch it, you will understand."

I looked him in the eyes. Yellow ringed and streaked with red, burning with bloodlust as I expected, but something else as well. His pupils constricted to the thinnest slash. In the dimmer light of the tent, something was definitely off. I laid a careful hand on the spearhead and a wave of sickening vertigo struck me. A chorus of voices rose all around me, hissing and jeering. My stomach turned, and I pulled my hand away. Moranga! And… something worse.

"This feels more like… like a *curse*." I shook my tingling hand to rid it of the feeling of *wrongness*. "Is that why you didn't simply remove it on your own?"

He made no response, but I misliked the growing intensity of his stare. His teeth clicked together, rhythmically, and I understood at once. If the enemy could drive Rafael mad and send him back to us, they would never have to worry about another fight. As he himself had said, not a one of us could stand against him.

"Crow. Very well. I'm going to pull this damned thing out," I said, and his teeth clacked. "Do *not* bite me!"

I donned a set of thin leather gloves from my apron. Working my fingers around the edges of the spearhead, I pulled. It hardly budged. Heat rose around us, beading sweat on my skin. I tried to ignore the distant, sibilant voices sliding along our connection. My spine prickled with the creeping sense of being watched by something hostile. With an effort, I kept my focus on the wound. I pulled again, hard, to little effect.

Rafael began to growl. The sound moved through my body, through the floor, rattling the glass jars of herbs on the nearby workbench.

"Easy, easy, Dragon." I slid my hand under his shirt to lay it on the center of his chest, and his eyes flared. His heart beat faster than I could ever remember it. "Stay with me."

Smoke wreathed me, billowing from his parted lips. He shuddered once, and I realized he was holding himself back. Fuck, I had to work faster. Moving more of the swelling away, I got a better grip on the spearhead. This time I braced myself with a foot against his thigh. With a single, swift movement, I yanked, and the weapon tore free. Rafael did not flinch, but his vicious answering hiss scared a nearby assistant into tears.

Taking a risk, I turned from him to wrap the offending item in a rag with a quick muttered charm of containment. Just a minor ward, it should bind whatever malevolent energies the spearhead held, at least for the moment. A sizzling sound and the smell of burning flesh drew me back. Rafael cauterized his own wound with a blue-white flame held in his palm. For the first time since I'd known him, a scar formed when he finished.

"Better?" I chanced a light touch on his forearm. The sibilance in our soulbond died away.

"Much." To my relief, his pupils responded normally to light.

"If I leave to show this to the Consulate do you promise to behave? I don't want to come back here to your signature Rafael chaos."

He seemed tired all of a sudden. "I will go. Do not fear for your precious patients."

I held a hand out to steady him as he rose to his feet, but he waved it away. At a nod from a watchful Liriadis, I followed him out to the trees. "Are you sure you're well?"

Rafael looked down at me. "Well enough. Do not worry." He burned away the blood and strings of flesh embedded under his talons before stroking my cheek. "Tell your Consulate none of the others were similarly afflicted. The spear passed through many hands before reaching me." Had he allowed this simply to discover what would happen? Typical. He turned to go.

'*Like old times, you coming to me all caked in gore,*' I sent, aware of the rapt attention of everyone in the healer's tent. '*Did you deliberately wait to be my last patient?*' An unusual consideration, perhaps even dangerous given his state, and one I was grateful for.

He paused, smiling faintly. More dried blood cracked and flaked off his cheek.

I returned his smile. '*I am grateful that you came to me for help. That you still do.*' He had finally shown me the full truth of him, of his murderous brutality, knowing that it might push me away forever. Yet, somehow, I felt closer to him than before. I had to honor that. '*Did you fear I would no longer love you?*'

'*It was a possibility.*' He shrugged, feigning a nonchalance I knew he did not truly feel. Aloud, he said, "I would embrace you, but you will complain."

"Correct. I am not touching you again without a thorough bath. You're disgusting right now." I looked him over, scrunching my nose at the pungent tang of old blood and tissue. "I do love you, but this is foul. If I have to wash that nastiness out of your hair again, I'm braiding it this time, regardless of your protests!"

He coughed a laugh and disappeared into the trees, but not before I caught the glimmer of relief in his eyes.

I encountered Feanim first, poring over his maps and charts in his tent. Showing him the spearhead, I explained what had happened and my conclusions. His brow furrowed, color draining from his face. He took the spearhead from me, handling it with delicate care and adding another ward to mine. Having it out of my hands freed my breath. I volunteered to fetch Celebel at a nod from the preoccupied Duedellen.

Following our soulbond, I found him among the horses. Celebel gave Helicos one last, fond pat before turning to me. "What drew you out here away from the healer's tent?"

Before I delved into duty, I looked him over. Mud from the battle rimed his tabard and face, but apart from a little blood spatter on his cheek, he looked whole. Hardly a new dent in his armor from what I could see. I breathed a sigh of relief and kissed him. His soft lips soothed me.

"Rafael was my last patient. He came to the tent with a blade stuck in him that doesn't bode well." I explained the spearhead again.

Celebel's brows drew down, lips pressing together. "Another rare ore weapon in the Fomorian's possession? This is troubling."

"At least we know of it now." Together, we rejoined Feanim.

Outside his tent, he sat on a rock with the spearhead cradled in its swaddling. His dark curls obscured his face. For once, he had no pithy comments about my presence.

"Cel. This making speaks to me." Strain stretched his tenor to a higher pitch. "It should be impossible. This is no ancient piece, with lineage stamped in its crystalline structure. Perhaps less than a dozen years old, this forging. Worse, the song it contains... I don't yet know how to interpret these signs."

Celebel crouched beside him. "What do you mean?"

"There is more at play here than we know." He wiped a hand over his brow, succeeding only in smearing the dirt already there. Feanim squinted up at us, green eyes flashing in the fading sun. "This hand is familiar."

Chapter 53

"Let's get this filth washed off of you, I need to examine you for injury." The moment we entered our tent, I tugged at Celebel's soiled padding. He'd left the armor outside on a rack.

Celebel raised a dampening field with a wink. "I would be happy to think about anything other than battles past, present, and future."

This tent was not as lavish as the previous, intended for quick assembly and tear down, but I still had enough space to bring in a couple of buckets of water. Celebel cheerfully let me peel him out of his bloodied, dirty clothing.

"You are a mess." I ran a damp rag over his body and admired the way the water collected on him.

"I am a tired mess." He sat on the floor while I worked on him.

I massaged away his tension as I scrubbed. He relaxed into my touch, leaning back on his elbows while I climbed all over him. I kissed his neck, his chest, the divine hollow of his hips. The feel of his skin, silken on my lips where I bathed him, made me hunger for more. His ears twitched and I captured the length of one, stroking it. He sighed, leaning into my hand as his cock twitched.

I scrubbed myself next, a quick swipe over the worst of it, then I took my time. Slowing where his eyes lingered, I polished my skin to a shine. He took the rag from my hand, looping a pattern over my breasts and teasing my nipples. Tracing the hollow of my throat, the nip of my waist, my inner thighs. Whisper-light, he slid the rag across the seam of my vulva, and I bloomed at his touch.

Deliberately, I removed the scale talisman. "Are you too tired to paint me with your pleasure?" I teased his cock with light fingers. He smiled.

"Never." He rose to kneeling, allowing me better access.

I licked the shaft, and he hardened instantly. Nibbling and

sucking from my hands and knees, I imagined Rafael behind me, fucking me at the same time. Carefully holding that thought crystallized in a part of my mind where the Dragon wouldn't hear it, I indulged in my little fantasy. Rafael's bass growl harmonizing with Celebel's musical baritone, their cries increasing in volume. Stretching to accommodate the Dragon's massive cock while he pounded me into choking on Celebel. My clit throbbed mightily with the force of my arousal, sending it coursing down my thighs to drip on the floor.

"Gods, how wet you are!" Celebel's hips bucked involuntarily. He cradled my head as I licked and sucked.

I imagined Rafael biting the back of my neck as he thrust so deep I felt it in my ribs. The mark grew warm, tingling through me. My nipples tightened in response. What if I pulled Celebel's hips forward and took my mouth away just at the moment of climax, allowing him to coat the Dragon's powerful chest? *Oh gods.* I could lick it away while Celebel drank Rafael's issue from my stretched and gaping cunt.

Hearing my moans, Celebel extended a leg under me, delicately raising and pointing his foot. The reminder of how Rafael penetrated with his me drove me wild. I rubbed myself against the edge of the proffered foot as I sucked his cock with fervor. Pausing for a moment, I licked and dragged my teeth along his deliciously muscular, shapely thighs before returning my attention to his erection. With one hand, I worked the base of his cock, cupping and caressing his testicles with the other.

Sliding against the smooth edge of his foot, I brought myself to a rapid climax. My muffled cries caused his cock to pulse in response. He lowered his foot as I finished and sat back on my knees. Letting his cock slide from my mouth while still holding onto the base of his shaft, I aimed the tip at my breasts. Celebel covered me in gouts of his seed as his forceful climax drew a long, ragged moan from his throat.

He crawled forward, rubbing his issue across my breasts, and dipped his fingers into my mouth. I sucked them clean.

"I need to be fucked," I said, throaty and hoarse.

"Just hearing you say that has my cock springing to life again." Celebel grinned, cupping himself in his hand. "How do you need to be fucked? Roughly, I suppose?"

"Yes. And pull my hair."

He flipped me over, dividing my hair into two thick braids and winding them cross-directionally around my body into a makeshift harness. It effectively pulled my head back and gave him 'straps' to leverage against my hips. The binding of my breasts and waist, and the delicious tension on my scalp, made me instinctively press backward against him, desperate for penetration.

Celebel rubbed his rigid cock between my buttocks. "Perhaps I'll climax this way, spilling myself on your back." He gave my ass a light slap, then a squeeze. "You have such a plush, lovely rear."

I whimpered and tried to maneuver my hips. He stopped me with a yank of my braid harness.

"So impatient," he laughed.

He shifted behind me, and the tip of his cock grazed my sensitized clit. I moaned, reaching underneath to press his erection against me. He tugged on the harness again, forcing me to arch my back and brace with that questing hand.

"Please." I forced the word out between clenched teeth, rocking against him.

"Oh, my needy one. You're going to make me come swiftly if you continue this. Very well."

The head of his cock pushed into me. I gripped it immediately from the inside, using my muscular walls to tug him deeper. He hissed and went along with it, thrusting in tandem with my pull. Just as I opened my mouth to beg him to hit me harder, he withdrew and slammed back into me with a cry. I echoed it, then we were fucking with all our combined might.

Our moans and wails of pleasure drowned out the rhythmic slap of flesh on flesh. He plowed into me and I threw myself onto his cock as hard as I could. Tension humming from his strong arms through my braids, Celebel bowed my back so far I thought it might snap, testing the limits of my flexibility.

"Yes! Fill me to the brink, give me everything," I gasped, squeezing his cock as tightly as I could, ensuring he could no longer completely pull out.

When he pulsed inside me, I screamed and he matched my volume. The angle made each throb of his cock ripple through me, ripping my own orgasm free.

He pressed his forehead to the back of my head and we wove together in ecstasy; the soulbond breathing around us, mingling power and spirit, bliss and love. Unity.

Spent and panting, he carefully untangled my hair before pulling out. I flipped onto my back, eager to watch his every move. Reaching for a rag, he dipped it in the clean water and tenderly washed me, wicking away the sweat and sticky remnants of our lovemaking. Lingering, he kissed my ears, the undersides of my breasts, my belly, and my knees. I combed my hair out as he worked, enjoying his ministrations.

Celebel made a little show of cleaning himself, dancing around the tent, swiveling his hips and tossing his striped hair. Pulling the rag suggestively back and forth between his legs, he maintained eye contact and gave me a salacious grin. I dissolved into giggles and slapped his shapely ass whenever he sauntered close. The lighthearted flirting put me in mind of our time on the hill.

"Am I acceptably uninjured?" he teased, squatting next to me with a brilliant smile, and then sobered. "And do you agree that I am capable of protecting myself?"

"You are a perfect specimen of health. And beauty." I stretched and folded forward to release the mild ache in my back. "Did I imagine it, or did you acknowledge each other for a moment in that battle?"

He nodded, expression relaxing. "No antagonism either. Rafael genuinely did me a good turn, and I repaid it as best I could in the moment. Perhaps this is a fresh start."

My heart swelled. "I dearly hope so." I twirled a shining lock of his hair around my finger. "Will you agree to make an end to protesting his 'monstrous' way of fighting?"

He peered into my eyes, stroking lightly along the length of my ears. "You are a sea of acceptance. Were you so unimpressed by what you witnessed? I may not understand your ability to accommodate your Dragon's brutality, but I shall no longer demure. I'll have to make my own peace." He signed accord, pointing from his head to me, with his other hand rising to match.

I crossed my fists over my heart. "I love you both so much it scares me."

"May we strive always to be worthy of such a blessing."

Chapter 54

Reconnaissance groups returned with no further sign of enemy movement. They brought the welcome news that they'd been able to reach key outposts unmolested. We sang our joy, as was ever our way. Perhaps Rafael made a similar announcement to the drakes, but they kept their distance. We would not return directly to Férioth, not yet. Our route would take us alongside other beleaguered areas, to discover if we could clear them in a similar fashion. I resigned myself to a long wait for my next proper soak.

At one such outpost, a Siltaur roost, we rested and refreshed ourselves, swapping supplies as needed. Deep in the thickly wooded foothills, the sophisticated dwelling hid high in the canopy, spanning many trees. Witchlights floated among them, the drifting motes of light creating their own stars in the branches. Longing for my own Great Tree rose with an ache that threatened to swallow me.

Liriadis approached to request an introduction to the drakes. On the road, she'd conditionally agreed to offer her healing services to them. I studied her face as we walked. I'd eschewed shoes this time, enjoying the soft duff of the forest floor under my feet. Wisely, the drakes camped well away from the flammable roost.

"You don't seem to carry the same instant disapproval of me," I said.

Liriadis shrugged. "Your life, your choices to make. Not the same ones I would, but you'd probably say the same of me. I know the legends of the Red Dragon, everyone does, but I prefer to judge from experience. I believe even the ancients can change with sufficient motivation. He's certainly chosen you as his guiding star, that's plain." She gave me a knowing look. "I doubt you'll have any competition for his attention among your own kind, but Celebel's favor has always been highly sought-after."

"Such luck graces me."

The Siltaur healer laughed at my grimace. "Honestly, having a soulmate seems more burden than boon. No time to sort out your feelings before *wham!*" She brought a fist down on a flat palm. "You're bonded forever. I appreciate the deliberate crafting of my soulbond with the partner of my own choosing."

We emerged from the trees into a meadow. Nodding lupine broke around Rafael and Marron in gentle, purple waves. The two drakes held a conversation about resources, pitched too deep for me to follow easily. Had he informed his second about the spear? More likely, he'd hoard that knowledge along with his other mysteries.

Rafael faced Marron, who leaned casually against a wind-bowed pine, scuffing at the ground with his dragonish feet. They fell silent as we approached. Rafael looked annoyed, but it hardly strayed from his typical expression.

"How do I always meet you first, Green Marron?" I called in draconian.

The green drake answered in elvish. "Your grammar is improving! I stay close to the edges to keep a watch on potential troublemakers. Had to turn away a few overly curious elves and knock a couple of drake skulls looking for an easy brawl." He gave us an appraising look and turned back to Rafael. "Your little collection of elves is growing."

Rafael opened his mouth to say something scathing, but Liriadis beat him to it.

"Piffle, he should be so blessed. I'm already bonded and have a child. I do not need your weird dragon issues, too." She folded her arms and gave Marron a challenging glare.

The green drake dissolved into rasping laughter. "Watch her breathe sparks! These are good elves. Shame we didn't find them ages ago."

She turned to him, staring defiantly up into his ruby eyes. Shorter than me, her head barely cleared elbow height on the green drake. "I have been a field medic for a long time. "

Rafael sighed a long-suffering sigh. "What do you want?"

"Another healer for your people, if they'll accept." I sincerely hoped I wasn't overly testing my luck and his tolerance. "This is Liriadis. She's the chief field medic and the one your people are the most likely to encounter other than me after a battle."

Rafael shrugged.

"Try not to be so thrilled at the offer of help." I thumped his arm. "I am likely to need assistance in the future."

"No hands but yours will ever touch me," he said flatly.

"Oh, fucking hells. I'm not offering to *bed* you!" Liriadis tugged ferociously at her earlobes and I couldn't help laughing. Out of the corner of my eye, Marron tried to control a smirk. "Is he always this difficult?"

Rafael gave me a hard glare, and I smiled sweetly at him. "Yes, yes, he is." A thought occurred to me. "Marron, what does '*nekarazzi*' mean?"

Marron blinked. "The literal translation in your tongue is 'striped pest;' used for 'badger' most commonly. Where did you learn that?"

I glared at my Dragon. Rather than respond, he twisted, looking up and over my head. A breeze ruffled his hair, now alight with that internal flame. Inhaling, his nostrils flared and his posture tensed.

"Rafael, what—"

Marron also lifted his chin, visibly sniffing the air. "Someone comes," he rumbled in draconian.

Rafael's talons flexed at his sides, as if imagining tearing flesh. "Itreynith." A word I did not know. A name, perhaps?

"I beg your pardon, my lords, but could someone explain what is happening?" Liriadis crossed her arms.

Pupils dilating, Rafael's lips parted, sucking air in through his teeth. In draconian, he said, "More, it brings. Your clan and others? A mix." He looked to Marron. At some unspoken communication, the green drake jogged off toward the other drakes. His heavy footfalls echoed.

My Dragon barked an echoing call that sounded like 'Boshkt.' Switching to elvish, he said, "Other drakes approach. You must flee this place. Find your princeling and ride for Férioth."

I blinked in confusion. "Other drakes?"

Rafael took hold of my arm and marched me back into the trees, toward the stabled horses. Liriadis trotted along behind us, bubbling with questions that he ignored. His sudden mood shift made my heart pound with new anxiety.

Elves startled out of Rafael's way as he half-dragged me to my horse. Reclining nearby, Celebel sprang to his feet, his face an open question. Iruwher reared and snorted, trying to dance away from the drake.

"Be *still*," Rafael hissed.

To my surprise, the blood bay mare froze, trembling. Looking briefly into my eyes, he lifted me by the waist and set me on her unsaddled back. I gripped her sides with my thighs, patting her neck.

Boshkt appeared, lichenous brow furrowed in obvious confusion.

Rafael pointed toward my borrowed room in the roost. "Bring their belongings here," he rumbled in draconian. The mottled drake nodded and skittered up the tree, fast as a squirrel.

"Are we under attack?" Celebel's voice got his attention.

With a hand resting on my thigh, Rafael said, "Any moment now. Other drakes fly here in numbers, swift on the wind. Tell your people to scatter. Small groups to avoid becoming a target. Take different routes and get back to the fortress."

"I'll gather the healers and camp tenders." Liriadis sprinted away.

Moments later, Boshkt leaped down from the canopy with a hard thump, bundles under his ropy arms. Rafael took mine, and Celebel accepted his with a stunned expression.

"Keep your blades accessible at all times," he instructed, arranging me and my pack to his liking. Iruwher blew a fearful snort, but tolerated the rough handling. "Do not stop, do not turn back for me."

Frissons of fear shot up my arms at his deadly serious tone. So unlike his usual cocksure attitude regarding all things combat.

"I take it these new drakes are not allies?" Celebel buckled his sword belt.

The Dragon grimaced. "No. Ride hard if you wish to live. And protect her better than your own life."

With that, he slapped Iruwher's rump. She squealed and shot forward. I twisted in the saddle, crying out for him, for both of them. Celebel shouted instructions to his bodyguards and whistled up Helicos, breaking into a run. As Eledom and Lámirië moved to spread the word, the stallion crashed through the trees at a gallop. Grabbing fistfuls of mane, Celebel swung himself onto the charger's bare back.

Rafael held my eyes for the barest breath. *'I love you.'*

'I love you as the trees love rain. Come back to me!'

He turned and loped toward the edge of the woods. Wings burst from his back, red scales covered him in a rippling wave, and his body changed shape, expanding. A tail whipped around, breaking stone and knocking over trees. His face lengthened into a snout, neck curving and sprouting a ridge of spines.

The Red Dragon rose to dominate the sky, light shining through the membranes of his great wings painting the world beneath in shades of blood. He bellowed a roar that nearly knocked our horses to their knees.

"FLEE, LITTLE ELVES. FLEE OR DIE." His voice boomed like a thunderclap, terrifying our mounts into regaining their footing. I clapped my hands over aching ears. Gods, without being privy to our conversation, the others likely thought his bellow a threat aimed at them.

The mountain pass gave us the most direct line to Férioth, if not the easiest; only a few days' hard ride. Celebel had the same thought, pointing Helicos in that direction. Rather than tempering their fright-driven stampede, we gave our mounts their heads, trusting to their instincts. The forest thinned, soil growing rocky as our horses bounded uphill. As they gained altitude, they slowed to a more reasonable pace.

We rounded a bend to a massive green tail blocking the way. To one side lay a rock wall, and the other a tumble of boulders unsuited to horse hooves. As we debated if we could jump it, the tail slid out of sight. The blunted tip of a huge, green muzzle appeared in its place and our steeds trembled. Toothy as a crocodile, those jaws could easily swallow elf and mount in one gulp.

"PASS ON," Marron's gravelly voice thundered. "I WILL HERD OTHERS TO YOU AS I MAY." The muzzle withdrew. With a booming clap of wings and a wind shear that pushed the horses sideways, he launched himself into the air over our heads.

"*Rafael, what is happening?*" Clinging to Iruwher's back as she streaked over the land, I trusted her to find her way without my guidance, keeping pace with Helicos.

An image of a great, craggy white dragon formed in my mind. Tones of arctic blue flashed as it flapped mighty wings. '*I should have killed Itreynith long ago,*' Rafael replied. His casual tone frustrated me. '*White drakes are solitary creatures. This one dwells far to the south, in the ice caps. Strange to see it here.*'

'*Are you in danger?*' I imagined the white drake calling down blizzards and avalanches, freezing all in its path. Anathema to a creature of flame such as my Dragon. '*You were terribly concerned at this drake's approach.*'

Our number swelled as other riders caught up. I heard Celebel explaining the situation to them, but his words barely registered over my fear.

'*My concern is primarily for you, as this fight will be destructive. I faced Itreynith once, when I was much younger. Overconfidence and inexperience is a poor combination. Damned snowbeast humbled me, using its territory to its advantage. I will not repeat my mistakes.*'

Searing cold shuddered along our connection, nearly unseating me. Itreynith roared; the hollow, echoing crack of glaciers calving. A sensation of icy blood in my mouth. My Dragon suffered a direct hit along his side, but he'd also taken a nasty bite out of the white drake.

'*Rafael!*'

'*Peace, my dove.*' Flashes of flame lit the sky behind me. A different dragon trumpeted a low note that ended in a screech. The air currents rushing around the Dragon's body shifted abruptly as he banked and changed directions. Turning instinctively with him nearly toppled me from the saddle, and I pulled my senses back. '*Some of Marron's clan have turned on us, among others. Reinforcements arrive in numbers. Trust no drake appearing in my stead.*'

'*Please be careful. I love you.*' I clutched the scale around my neck hard enough for the edges to bite into my hand. Not much reassurance, but his confident tone helped.

'*Oh, beloved. You alone, in all the world, worry for my safety.*' Warmth embraced me, and our bond went silent as he dampened the connection.

The heavens turned sickly green as clouds gathered in a dark knot where the dragons clashed. Wind rose and trees groaned, bending as we passed. A fat drop of rain spattered on my thigh.

Shaking off the lingering sense of dread, I looked to Celebel at my left. Liriadis and a few other healers and assistants rode behind us. No sign of Nemohee, Feanim, or Celebel's bodyguards.

I gave Celebel a summary. His brow creased.

"Gods, what—" The ground quaked, interrupting his response. Fissures appeared beneath the horses' hooves, spurring them into another terrified bolt. We turned our attention to staying mounted as our steeds careened wildly around turns, leaping over boulders and deadfalls.

What should have been a victorious return to Férioth transformed into a panicked rout. We rode hard, pausing only so horses would not collapse. In several places, the narrowing path forced us into single file and slowing the pace. Sharp drops and sheer walls left little room to maneuver. As much as possible, we stayed under tree or boulder cover. My neck ached from constantly watching the sky. Some slept in the saddle when possible. I could not rest at all, and kept watch to be sure no one tumbled to the ground in their slumber.

Rafael's warning about the destructive nature of the fight rang all too true. The weather reminded me of the huge storms generated by his battle with the War Crow. Sand-blasted hot winds alternated with flooding, freezing rain. Small twisters occasionally forced us off our path, churning dirt, vegetation, and rocks into dangerous projectiles. Helpless, I watched in horror as lightning struck one elf and her mount, killing them both on the spot.

Crossing a broad, open area with little cover, a huge shadow fell like early evening across our party. We looked up as one. A dragon circled overhead, the bright sun behind it casting its scales into darkness.

"Make for that overhang," Celebel called, pointing ahead to a granite outcropping. Our horses needed no encouragement. They bolted as one for safety.

'*Is this an enemy?*' I sent to Rafael, with an image of the potential threat. Anxiety strummed my nerves like a lute.

The sensation of freezing wind, cold striking to the bone, chilled me through our connection. '*Yes,*' came the tired answer. I shivered. That did not bode well for what lay ahead.

We huddled together under the overhang, barely daring to breathe. The one time we needed fog or driving snow for cover, and instead unseasonably hot winds blasted the sky clear. Shadows changed with excruciating slowness as the sun crept across the sky. Finally, after an entire day lost to hiding, the dragon moved on.

With unusual thoughtfulness, Rafael gave me the occasional brief update. The drakes fought throughout our retreat, moving along with us toward the fortified city. Many of the attackers fell, as well as some allies. Itreynith finally turned tail and fled, and the rest of the enemy drakes departed with their leader. A hard-won victory, but victory nonetheless.

Relief flooded me as Férioth came into view. I took the first deep breath in days as our horses plodded across the high bridge. Nimthil ran to greet us through the outer courtyard, serving youth flocking behind her to take our poor, exhausted horses.

"Feanim should be just at the tips of your ears," she said, hands fluttering rapidly. "He took the valley route and rode hard. Sent his crows ahead."

Celebel leaned against me for a moment. "This gladdens my heart. Has anyone else arrived?" His hands echoed the sentiment.

"You are the first. Araglin is in his study, should you wish to confer. He says he is on the verge of a breakthrough on repairing the Carnyx." Nimthil gestured for the serving youth to attend us. They passed around flagons of sweet water and I drank deeply.

Celebel nodded, holding his arms out as two youths peeled him out of his armor and padding. "I shall go consult with him. We must consider how to best seek our remaining people and gather reinforcements should the enemy drakes return." Dropping a kiss on my forehead, he moved toward Araglin's study.

"Drakes attacked us?" Nimthil's eyes went huge. "Feanim did not mention this!"

"Enemy clans attacked our allied drakes." I checked in briefly with my Dragon. "Rafael says they are unlikely to attack here. He is already returning, swift on the wing." I swayed on my feet, fatigue leadening my limbs. My thumbs and forefingers locked up with my clumsy signs. "The battle against the Fomorians was a resounding success, if that eases your mind." The only thing that could possibly ease mine was a long, restful soak in hot water, preferably wedged between my two naked soulmates.

Rafael sent a snort of derision along our connection.

Chapter 55

'*A*raglin *is not in his study,*' Celebel sent. '*Meet me in our chambers instead. I wish to replace this filthy clothing.*'

The promise of a bath buoyed my spirits, and I made my way there. With the majority of our forces still catching up, the fortress felt strangely empty. I cursed the amount of stairs between the courtyard and our rooms, pausing to catch my breath on the landing of our hall.

A sharp spike of surprise hammered through the connection. New panic coursing through my veins lent me a burst of strength. I dashed into the bedchamber—and skidded to a confused halt.

Why was Feledhor in our chambers? Celebel faced away from him, focused on something in front of him I couldn't see from my vantage. The pale Astolar raised a hand, light glinting on metal. I realized, too late, what I witnessed. It wasn't possible, this couldn't be happening.

The blade came down, and Feledhor's dagger sank into Celebel's back.

I screamed. Celebel twisted, knocking the knife from Feledhor's grip, and punched him hard in the ear. The pale elf recoiled with a squeal of pain, clapping a hand to the side of his head. Celebel followed through with an uppercut that slammed the traitor's jaws together hard enough to break teeth. A detached part of my mind noted the lavender spray brooch pinned to the traitor's breast.

The movement revealed Recarmial on Celebel's far side; the subject of his previous focus. She slashed forward with a blade, aiming for Celebel's torso. Frozen in horror, I shouted a warning.

Celebel dodged easily, twisting to bring an elbow down on her shoulder, and kneed her in the gut. Dry-heaving from the blow, her dagger clattered to the floor. Our eyes met as she looked up. I shook my head hard enough to whip my ears around. None of this made sense. Celebel staggered, clutching at his wound.

"Cúraniel, run! Tell the others!"

Rage flooded me, like nothing I'd ever felt, lighting me on fire. I shrieked in wordless fury, surging forward instead. How dare these leeches attack one of our own? How *dare* these blighters attack *my soulmate*? The scale between my breasts burned against my skin, and I drew Rafael's flames around me like a cloak. I did not know what the traitors saw, but their faces paled in unison as I bared my teeth like an angry drake.

"Monsterfucker," Feledhor snarled, pushing past Celebel to leap over the balcony.

Recarmial scrambled to follow the pale Astolar a heartbeat too late. I lunged and caught the tail end of her braid, yanking with all my might. Heavy lavender perfume burned my nose as I tried to haul her up over the banister by her hair.

She screamed, gripping her braid at the base in a vain attempt to ease the pull on her scalp as she dangled. The load proved too much for my fatigued limbs, even throwing my weight backward. The Lachanaur woman slipped slowly down, kicking to free herself.

I settled for hurling insults made incoherent by my spitting wrath. "You blighting, maggot-ridden pustule of rotted, putrid, harpy bile! May your teeth grow inwards, to gnaw your organs from the inside!"

Her hair ripped free in a loud *SHH*. Recarmial dropped with another shriek. She landed in the same bush that had cushioned the golden fool I'd levered off the balcony, what seemed like an age ago now. The hank left in my hand burned to ash. I spat after her, of a mind to leap over myself and give chase.

The thought of raising my hand against another elf with intent to kill sobered me, turning my stomach. Surely Rafael's influence, his flames goading me to violence. I released them, trying to clear my head.

"Gods, Cel. This makes no sense." I turned to my soulmate, who steadied himself on the bed frame. "They've never made a secret of their hatred for me, but to attack you?"

Before he could answer, a Fomorian charged through the open doorframe into the room. Its horned head nearly scraped the ceiling, impossibly tall, canine nose sniffing the air. Pale yellow eyes locked into mine, and it bared flat teeth in a long muzzle. Fumbling, I pulled Rafael's scale from my neck in the vain hope it could do some damage.

Celebel shouted, but the Fomorian paid him no mind. It surged forward, clawed hands reaching for my face. I stabbed out, flailing, forgetting any training I'd ever had. The Fomorian yelped and recoiled as the scale amulet sliced through several fingers. Pressing my slight advantage, I thrust my power into my foe, seeking old injuries to unheal. There; a former twisted knee. I flooded the joint with spirit, searing it apart, and the Fomorian's leg buckled. Leaning into my power, a web of old scars lit up its grey hide. I caught the edge of one and ripped, like pulling a weak seam.

The creature shrieked and burst apart in a spray of blinding power, the force of it knocking me backwards. Dazed, I blinked rapidly until the room came back into focus. My ears rang with the aftereffects. A shape coalesced before me.

Huddled where the Fomorian fell lay a slender man with hair the color of a robin's egg. Fine black antlers formed a crown over short, pointed ears and an equally pointed face. He wore a scintillating tabard over elaborately enameled bronze armor. Silvery-purple blood spread beneath him, leaking from a latticework of wounds.

A sidhe.

"What the *fuck* is happening?" I blinked again, rubbing my eyes. "A Seelie sidhe. Why is there a Seelie sidhe in our room? Are all the Fomorians actually sidhe rather than some other fae? Why are they glamoured that way? And why are the sidhe capturing us?" The babbling rushed out, a leak sprung in a giant dam of panic.

"That is indeed a sidhe. Gods, I wish *someone* hadn't

broken our fucking door." With a hand pressed to his back, strain pulled at the corners of Celebel's eyes, despite his deliberately light tone. "Well done, though." He swayed on his feet, face pale.

I steadied myself. I'd be of no use to him or anyone else if I fell apart now. Or exploded into light like that Fomorian. Sidhe. Whatever it was. I squinted at the body, detecting a faint shimmer like a clinging aura. Glamour upon glamour. The Seelie court always wore one to make themselves more outwardly attractive and less alarming to outsiders. That second-skin glamour came as an inherent power, nearly impossible to break without their permission. Even in death.

Stretching my ears, I heard no evidence of anyone else approaching, and turned my attention fully to Celebel. He sagged against the bed frame. Blood seeped from between his fingers where he clasped his wound. I eased him to the floor on his uninjured side, ripping open the linen shirt. A straightforward stab wound. Gathering up my flagging spirit, I poured it into him, stopped the bleeding, and blunted the pain.

My hands tingled in warning and a feeling of dread ran up my arms. Something else clung to the wound; a miasma of sickness. It would need more care than I could provide through the haze of exhaustion. Bad as it was, the injury wasn't as severe as it could have been. If Feledhor had struck true, he might have severed Celebel's spine. Combined with moranga's soul-sucking power, it would have been beyond my ability to heal.

"Forgive me, I did not expect... we've been betrayed..." Pain and sorrow pinched Celebel's voice.

"Hush, my love, none of this is your fault." I brushed his hair back from his face and kissed his sweat-sticky forehead. "You were stabbed with moranga. The blade may have been cursed, similar to that spearhead I pulled from Rafael. I have tried to dampen its effects, but I need help." Tearing his shirt into stripes, I bound the wound. "If there are Fomorians inside the walls, we have more urgent matters to attend."

A glint of metal on the bedside table caught my eye, and

I went over to investigate. An earring lay winking in the dim light, cobalt blue enamel with a crescent moon wrought in moonstone and diamond. *Silfanië*. The only one with access to my old talisman earring. She had left it deliberately for me to find. An oddly painful gesture, but why? I palmed the talisman, heartily sick of mysteries.

"We must return to Nimthil, to ensure her safety," he wheezed.

"We need Eäriel to attend to your wound. I am too done in to manage more than surface level care."

Celebel waved away my concern, struggling to his feet. His face hardened, taking on his role as a leader once more. "With traitors in our midst, this entire fortress may be compromised. Gather up your Pîntellum jars and the small jewel chest in the wardrobe. Do not overburden yourself in case we are attacked again. We need to be able to move."

I made a makeshift sack from a sheet and wound it around the bottles. At the bottom I placed my favorite herbal treatise and my notes, and stacked the box of jewels on top, slinging it all over one shoulder. Heavier than I would have preferred, but better than leaving it all behind. I sighed at loss of my mortar and pestle, yet again. At least my pearls were still securely braided into my hair; the only jewel I truly cared about.

Celebel leaned on me as I guided him toward the doorway. A wax-sealed scroll, previously unnoticed in all the chaos, rested on a table in the antechamber. He plucked it as we passed.

"This is Araglin's seal." His ears flattened. "I mislike this very much. Help me to the great hall."

Slowly, painfully, we made our way to the others, sending word through the serving youth to gather. Nimthil ran to us the moment we entered through the tall doors, with Eäriel close on the tips of her ears, healing implements rattling together in her many-pocketed apron.

"We are betrayed," Celebel choked out, just as a roar rattled the chandeliers.

The ground vibrated. Moments later, Rafael stormed in,

unease at allying with such an immoral creature as the Red Dragon, I desire to approach our opposition with open arms, in the hopes that an accord can be made from the inside. I have gained knowledge that allows me freedom of movement I will utilize to our benefit. As time and circumstance permit, I shall return.

I remain, as always, faithfully yours.
Araglin

Helpless tears choked me as I pulled the tips of my ears down. My one ally in the court had betrayed us at the most base level, naming Rafael as the cause. Perhaps there was no hope for redemption among my people after all. I threw my arms around Celebel, and we indulged in a moment of shared grief. How much worse must it be for him, to lose a beloved, lifelong advisor in this manner?

Feanim took the scroll from my trembling hands, read it, and threw it to the floor in disgust. "Surely Galdir had a hand in this as well. He has gone missing, and was among those who returned with me."

With a perturbed glance at Feanim, Nimthil bent and plucked the scroll from the floor.

"I told you it was a hydra," Rafael chimed in from the door. "Snivel later, we need to move. Come to the stables."

Several elves spoke at once. Panic rose in a tidal wave, my heart bobbing like a fishing weight in my chest. Unable to do more, I followed my Dragon, Celebel followed me, and we all made our painful way to the stables. To yet another retreat.

Another group of survivors joined us. Lámirië rushed to Celebel's side. Her dark hair had come free from its braids, unusual disarray for the tightly controlled woman.

"Ele—" Her voice broke.

Celebel placed his hands on her shoulders, brow creasing. "Please no. Do not say he has fallen!"

She shook her head. "Worse," she choked out. "He has

eyes and hair blazing. Smoke billowed from his mouth and nose. The gathered elves shrank away from him as he approached.

"Are you hurt?" he demanded, gripping me by the arms and peering into my eyes as though scouring for secrets.

"I'm unharmed, but Celebel was struck. Elves attacked us, and there are Fomorians in the walls! Or sidhe? I am utterly confused." The world spun and I pressed a hand to my head. I could barely fathom my own words. Something twinged through our connection. He kissed my forehead and released me, leaving a wisp of acrid smoke that tickled my nose.

"Traitors abound," the Dragon growled. His eyes landed on Celebel's wound and Eäriel shrank back from her examination. "Try not to let your pretty boy die before I get the chance to kill him."

Celebel chuckled weakly. "How kind of you, to call me 'pretty'." In other circumstances, I would have laughed.

Rafael snorted, ignoring the bait for once. He moved with purpose through the crowd, heedless of their reactions to him as he paused to inhale of each person's scent. Gods help any poor blighter who smelled of lavender now.

Familiar faces entered the hall, looking as bedraggled as I felt. Nimthil raced into Feanim's arms and he held her tightly. Nemohee approached me, purple shadows under þeir eyes casting false color to the silver. We clapped each other in a grateful embrace and I told the newcomers of the dreadful developments.

A choked noise from Celebel grabbed my attention. Tears slid down his cheeks as he read Araglin's scroll, sinking to the plush, green carpet. I darted to his side. Wiping his eyes, he handed me a crumpled letter written in an elegant hand.

My dearest companions,

I know well that you will not comprehend the logic of my decision at this time. Please understand that I have only our peoples' greatest good in mind and heart. Far beyond my deep turned against us. Eledom made a speech about joining a great force who would unify the elves in new power, if only we turned against the Consulate. He spoke of casting out ancient enemies," here she glanced at Rafael, "and a return to our old ways of isolation. Several joined him. Those who wouldn't… Cel, he *attacked* us!"

Celebel made a strangled noise.

"I barely escaped with my life…" She trailed off, shaking her head again. "The traitors must have some sort of deal worked out with the Fomorians. Those creatures parted ranks to allow Eledom and his compatriots to pass before attacking us again."

I could hardly believe it. He had always been easygoing, if not a friend to me. *Eledom* was a traitor? Guilt stabbed me. Lámirië was the one I'd faintly suspected, due to her typical standoffish Duedellen ways. My prejudice had closed my ears to the true traitor, and neglected the faithful ally. She caught my eye and held it, as though hearing my thoughts. I let my shame show on my face.

"Thank you, Lámirië."

She nodded once, a curt acknowledgment. Celebel took her hands and kissed the backs of them, and she bowed to him.

The voidlet popped into existence nearby, floating over as a formless shadow and settling around my shoulders in a weasel-like form. I patted it for comfort. Looking around the group, I tallied up the missing, out of those who should have been accounted for. Feledhor, Recarmial, and Araglin, obviously. Galdir and Eledom. Silfanië. Had she joined the defectors or been caught up in the attack? The thought hit me with unexpected force and I pushed it away. No time to grieve now.

"Amrún," Feanim said, and Celebel grimaced. "It is our only option, and large enough to hold everyone." The Duedellen looked to Rafael. "It is in the high lava fields north of here, over an active fissure vent."

"I know the place," he rumbled.

"Hard ride through mountains," Nimthil signed, her motions small and slow. Melancholic. The letter from Araglin peeked out from the belt at her waist that nipped in her voluminous, impractical skirt.

Wearily, we saddled all the remaining horses, leaving feed bags in place. There were not enough for everyone to ride, meaning our pace would match the slowest walker.

"Collect your weapons and prototypes." Rafael bared his teeth. His voice dripped venom, leveled directly at Celebel. "We will clear the path. Spread the word, little king: any of you flower-eating shits found wearing fucking *lavender* is now dead on sight."

"No," Celebel protested, turning to Feanim. "He will kill innocent people!" This was my doing. My fault. I wanted to vomit.

"Innocence is a myth," Rafael snapped.

"Cel, was Feledhor wearing a brooch? Was Recarmial?" the Duedellen asked. "I trust his instincts." They stared each other down in challenge while Rafael clicked his teeth together with growing impatience. Finally, Celebel relented, a bitter look on his face. Feanim and Nimthil made for the forge, and the Dragon stalked off, moving with deadly intent.

Moments later I heard three loud, eerie caws from the courtyard. I emerged to see Rafael briefly wearing a dragon's head on his body. Marron swooped in on broad green wings, followed closely by the other drakes I knew, and some I did not. Shades of earth, shiny black, a mix of colors, and one shining silver.

I ran to the Dragon's side. "Wait, please don't kill my sister! She may be wearing a brooch. Perhaps she's defected and left this place, I don't know, but please spare her life if you find her. Please!" The tears surprised me.

Rafael paused, assessing, then bent and tore a strip of fabric from my hem.

"Similar scent. Silver mane instead of black." He handed the fabric to Marron. "Bring this one to me." Turning to me, in elvish he said, "If she is here, they will find her."

The other drakes bounded off, talons flashing, and I felt intensely sorry for anyone they might encounter. "You are not joining them?"

"I will not leave your side." For emphasis, he spun on a heel and spat flame at two Fomorians emerging from the shadows behind us.

I scurried to him, wrapping my arms about his waist. A shock of cold stung my flesh, sympathetic pain shivering up my arms.

"You are wounded," I cried. No minor wound either; it ran the entire length of his right side, hidden under his clothes. I squinted, recognizing a stiffness in the way he held that arm.

"Nothing I cannot manage." He motioned for the trickle of elves from the great hall to join us. Only a severe injury could persist against his preternatural ability to heal himself.

Before I could argue, more Fomorians surged around the corner, a cluster of five. Remembering how the one in the bedchamber reacted, I sent out my spirit and took hold of the leading pair. It was easier this time to find the seams. With a sharp tug that also tore something inside me, I pulled.

The explosive flash spooked horses and elves alike. When it cleared, I stood blinking and staring at the other three bewildered Fomorians. Two dead sidhe lay crumpled at their feet. Taking advantage of the distraction, Rafael breathed flame on the remainder.

Eyes bored into me from all sides. I shrugged, and the motion buckled my knees. Rafael caught me before I hit the flagstones.

"We will discuss this later. When you are safe."

At his words, the others looked away. The remaining fighters formed a protective ring around the horses. We began an agonizingly slow mobilization, stopping every few steps to fight. I wanted to help, but I could barely stand. A glance at Celebel's grim expression told me he felt the same, tucked safely in the center of the defenders. Helicos stamped and he patted the charger's neck, swaying a bit in the saddle. With an assessing look, Rafael lifted me onto Iruwher's back. She accepted his presence without complaint.

"Send that thing away." He waved at the voidlet wrapped

around my shoulders.

I sighed, whispering thanks to it and asking it to return later. It trembled for a moment, casting a distinctly malevolent glare at Rafael, who answered with bared teeth. Then the voidlet winked out of existence.

Another wave of Fomorians targeted us. I lost count of the numbers, unable to contribute beyond pointing at them. Somewhere in the fortress, an elf screamed; a high, thin sound. Nemohee took up a position beside me, þeir normally jovial face frozen into a bitter mask. What must it mean to þem to discover the sidhe may be behind this entire bloody farce?

Rafael allowed Nemohee to vent þeir cold fury on any Fomorians foolish enough to venture within reach, only intervening when the numbers threatened to overwhelm. Without even a single taunt leveled þeir way, he demonstrated an unexpected compassion. Nemohee cut a silent, bloody swath around us.

I winced when þey took a cut to the shoulder. When a blow glanced off þeir face, I moved to dismount and help. Rafael grabbed my shoulders, holding me firmly on my horse with a meaningful glare.

'*Let me—*'

His hands tightened. '*You stay out of this.*'

Nemohee shook þeir head, slinging an arc of silver-tinged blood from a broken nose, and charged the offending Fomorian with an ululating cry. Feinting around an axe swing, þey stabbed it in the stomach and cut upward. The Fomorian clutched at its belly. Nemohee shoved þeir blade in farther, harder, until the tip burst from the glamoured fae's back. With a triumphant growl, Nemohee showed a flash of þeir true heritage, and bit down on the dying Fomorian's neck. Þeir fangs sank deep, and þey fed, ignoring a susurrus of shock.

When Nemohee finally tore away from þeir prey, þeir eyes shone like twin moons. A look passed between Rafael and my friend.

"They taste like honeyed shit," he said.

Nemohee nodded, smiling a huge, blood-streaked smile. Somehow both the creepiest and most heartwarming exchange I'd ever witnessed. The glamour even changed the Fomorians' blood to fresh red, rather than the silvered purple of the sidhe, even in death. The others studiously ignored the interaction, focusing outward on the next wave.

Feanim and Nimthil emerged from the direction of the forge carrying a trunk. A pair of Fomorians descended from a rooftop, landing in front of them. Lámirië riddled the attackers with arrows before they could take a step.

Nimthil regained her composure with remarkable grace. With a call, Feanim summoned his crows. They descended on him in a swarm of inky feathers. After a muffled conference, the birds took wing again.

"They'll help us find stragglers." He mounted his ill-tempered liver mare. Nimthil swung up behind him, clasping her hands about his waist.

"The front gate has collapsed," Marron called, trotting into view. "Those shitbeasts are swarming in over the bridge."

"There is another exit, an underground passage." Celebel twisted his fingers in Helicos's steely mane. "Can you destroy the bridge?"

Marron nodded and disappeared in that direction. Celebel guided us to the hidden exit. Feanim joined the defenders, cutting down Fomorians as we passed. Nemohee fought with renewed vigor, with Rafael at þeir back. He conserved motion, lashing out with his talons only when the Fomorians came within reach. The cold pain in his side throbbed through our connection.

Crows called from the battlements, sending a few of our fighters running. They returned with an elf I didn't recognize; a slight, mahogany-haired Talithiri man with pale skin. He expressed tearful gratitude until Rafael approached. Everyone else backed away, leaving the hapless Talithiri alone before the Dragon.

"Interesting choice of jewelry." Rafael plucked a familiar brooch from the man's shoulder. The protests, including my own, died away as Rafael held up a fist. The piece popped and sizzled in his palm, dripping to the ground in a molten splash. "I was clear. This is not an ally."

The man whimpered, cut off as the Dragon's hand wrapped around his throat. Rafael cast a glare at Celebel. "You did this."

Celebel teared up but did not look away as Rafael crushed the elf's neck with a quick squeeze. I wished I had. The Dragon's reasoning was sound, but that made it no easier to watch. Had I already become inured to elvish death? With all the upheaval, surely the stars themselves would rain down upon us soon.

The ground rumbled as he dropped the body. Horses reared and screamed as the flagstones jumped under their hooves, elves trying their best to calm the animals. A booming crash echoed around us. With a groan, a final shockwave rolled across the ground and stilled.

A drake more dust than scales entered the courtyard. "Bridge is down," Marron announced, creasing the dirt on his square face.

Chapter 56

Though large enough to ride half a dozen abreast, we led our horses through the steep underground passage. Poor Iruwher's proud head drooped with weariness. Witchlights danced along the entirety of the tunnel casting moving shadows that made me jumpy. Other than their leader, the rest of the drakes filed in behind us, ostensibly to keep our flank clear. Their voices boomed painfully as they joked and argued with each other. It made me grateful for Rafael's quiet, rumbling breath.

The passage wound all the way down, almost to the bottom of the ravine, before leading us back up to the top of the ridge. A huge elevation change in both directions, and my legs burned with the strain. When I stumbled, Rafael simply lifted me into his arms and carried me. Too tired to argue, I fell asleep with my head resting against his chest. Shadows troubled my dreams, images of the ground itself rearing up to attack, of clouds falling on us, the entire world gone mad.

Daylight woke me as we emerged from the tunnel. Rafael set me on my feet with a faint smile. The short rest rejuvenated me. We were on the other side of the ravine to the west, concealed along the ridge by a copse of firs. Drawn and wan, Celebel sat on a fallen log and discussed next steps with Feanim. Nimthil stood nearby, wringing a scarf in her hand. Marron watched the scene from a short distance away, and other elves watched him warily as they tended the horses. The rest of the drakes passed before us, clearing the way ahead.

Eäriel approached me, an uncharacteristic frown line creasing her forehead. "I cannot fully heal him." She indicated Celebel. "I'm unsure why. It's as though the wound is fouled somehow. Perhaps a poultice will help, but otherwise I am at a loss."

Fortunately, Eäriel still had a few useful herbs in her apron, stocked from when we'd initially called her to the great hall. We fashioned a rough mortar and pestle from a nearby crag and prepped it as best we could. Celebel helpfully removed his coat for us to wrap his injury.

"It smells of moranga," Rafael said. "Herbs alone will not clear that influence."

"You can smell Celebel's wound?" I blinked in surprise. "Can you draw such an influence out of him?" I realized the enormity of my request moments too late.

"No."

Frustration bubbled up. "Rafael, please—"

"It is not a question of will." He leveled a stare at me.

So rare was the admittance that anything lay beyond his power that I simply blinked again. "But you've healed me."

He shook his head. "I merely assisted you in healing yourself. Recall that the ability is unknown amongst my kind. I have no skill in it that you have not provided."

"All this time, you have been drawing on my own power? Through the connection you denied for so long, no doubt."

A rustling interrupted us, gaining intensity. Something approached. As one, we watched the tunnel exit. Footsteps, many footsteps. Harsh breathing. The clank of armored joints.

Howling, a throng of Fomorians burst from the tunnel. The traitors must have sent them after us. Quick on his feet, Feanim darted forward and landed a series of cuts on the belly of the leader. It fell grasping at loops of exposed intestine.

"Down," Rafael bellowed. As one, the elves dove. My Dragon bent forward at the waist and breathed a wide fan of flame. Fomorians crisped and shriveled like rice paper, incinerated. He glanced at Feanim. "Do you have a compelling argument against collapsing the tunnel?"

The Duedellen shrugged, rolling back to standing. "Férioth is lost. Do your worst."

"Marron." Rafael switched to draconian. "Once more?"

The green drake stretched reluctantly, and approached

him. "After this, a year-long sleep," Marron grumbled. "First pick of the spoils, too, for all this trouble."

Spoils. The thought of drakes looting the monastic fortress tightened my chest. Like robbing Araglin's corpse. I shivered.

They positioned themselves at opposite sides of the tunnel exit. Rafael inhaled deeply, broad chest expanding. With a great lurch forward, he exhaled a dazzling, blue-white flame. I couldn't stare at it directly. Marron clapped both hands to the ground and a rumbling started in the distance. It trembled through the ground beneath our feet and the horses stamped in protest.

Heartbeats passed as Rafael maintained his flame. The tunnel exit softened and wavered, stone lighting up with an internal glow as it melted. All at once, the entrance collapsed. The drakes straightened, ceasing their output of power. I had a new appreciation for the sheer destructive force of their cooperation.

Marron sat on his haunches, breathing hard. Strain showed around Rafael's eyes, the circles under them darker, the lines in his face carved deeper.

'*Dragon, let me tend to your wound.*' I approached him with a hand out.

Rafael waved me away. '*It is nothing.*' I frowned but he remained stubborn.

One of the elves—Carafindrien—began to sob. At her tender age, Férioth was likely the only home she'd ever known. In unison, we elves bowed our heads in sorrow. Someone began to keen a mourning song and we lifted our voices to match. I let the melancholy wash over me, freeing my tears and my music. Our melody smoothed the edges off of the horror and betrayal, gentling the riot of emotions. We held each other and wept, singing through the pain. The drakes watched in bemused silence until we finished.

"Fucking hells." Feanim broke the peace, staring at the spires of Férioth.""The library. And my journals. Fuck! My notes!"

Rafael produced a small stack of journals tied with a leather strip from his cloak, and tossed it to Feanim. "Foolish, to leave them behind while you ride off."

Stunned, the Duedellen caught the journals and turned them over in his hands. "When did you do this?"

"Hrrm, when did we begin the last march?"

Feanim sputtered with outrage.

"Right, and what else have you got in there?" I prodded. The Dragon gave me a sidelong look. "Rafael…"

"The chiding I tolerate from you," he muttered. With a sharp exhale, he took my hand, depositing something in my palm and closing my fingers around it. A familiar tingle spread through my flesh and I opened my hand to a sparkle of bluish-green. My eyes went wide.

"Fallëvaethil? Dragon, how did you get the Rain Jewel?" Privately, I sent, '*And why did you return it now*?'

"You should all learn to ward your personal chambers better." A smirk curled his lips. The image of him reclining on Celebel's bed flashed in my mind. Gods damn it! '*I thought it might cheer you. We can recover much of your lost treasures once you are settled in safety. Simple enough to fly back after a rest.*'

"You sticky-fingered blighter." I couldn't help but laugh, more touched than annoyed.

Xyxs chased another Fomorian into our midst, biting through its spine in a spray of blood. The serving youths scattered out of his way, screaming.

"Mount up," Celebel called, giving the big drake a wide berth. "We have to keep moving!"

The enemy harried us with little respite. We moved in a loose, protective formation, with the most vulnerable serving youth and noncombatants in the center with the wagons. Next came a ring of those like myself, not trained fighters but capable of self-defense. Our remaining soldiers encircled us. The drakes made up the furthermost ring, preventing the bulk of attacks from reaching the inner rings.

Nemohee walked beside me. We each led our tired horses, loaded with with what meager items we'd been able to salvage.

"This is a troublesome thing, very troublesome. I simply do not ken how any of us would willingly gang over." Nemohee shook þeir head.

"I wish I could not grasp their motives. It seems they hated Rafael more than they loved their own. I know it was the catalyst. I imagine some of them were disgruntled already and his arrival just pushed them over the edge."

Responsibility weighed heavily on me. Rafael never would have gone there without me. I never would have needed his assistance if we hadn't left my hill when we did. Round and round my thoughts chased their tails.

Nemohee laid a gentle hand on my arm. "'Tis not your fault they're rabbit-hearted cowards." The rare physical touch from my friend warmed me.

I sighed. "I only wonder how long they'd planned this. Thank you."

"You've always stayed true to yourself, 'tis what I admire about you. Don't go giving up now." Þeir expression was kind. "If not for you, how would we ever overcome such numbers set against us? Rafael may be a bundle of problems masquerading as a man, but damn if he isn't the most effective fighter I've ever known."

"I've waded in too deep to give up, and now we are caught in a rip current. So far it seems like staying true to myself only creates problems for everyone else. I was better off isolated on the hill." I hugged my arms.

"Come, you'll have time enough for all your maudlin woes after," Nemohee said, clapping me heartily on the shoulder. "Move along."

"I truly hope Amrún has a good stock of whiskey," I agreed.

Chapter 57

Celebel sank into a deep melancholy. I waited patiently for a day, hoping he would open up on his own, but he only closed off further. I gave up on that tactic and cornered him when we finally stopped to rest. No longer using the elaborate tree tents, we simply huddled under a gnarled pine within earshot of the others.

"I feel the gloom sucking at your soul through our connection. Please talk to me!" I sat behind him, braiding his hair in the way that he so loved, hoping it would ease him enough to speak. The farther we'd moved from Férioth, the thinner and less coherent our bond became, as though moth-eaten.

He sighed heavily, pulling at the tips of his ears.

"Come now, tell me," I prodded, stroking his hair. "Unburden your heart."

He rolled to look at me, pulling a small dampening field around us with eyes gone stormy. "I cannot help but feel as though this is all my fault. As though I do not know what I'm doing. Perhaps I should relinquish my seat to another after all."

I frowned, caressing his cheek. "Starshine, why do you say such things?"

"I only meant to poke at Rafael a bit, with the lavender. Never did I intend for it to grow out of control in such a manner. I thought I had handled the nobles, that I had done the right thing with preventing more violence in our halls. And look where it led us."

I kissed his forehead. "My love, if they genuinely hate Rafael more than they wish to see our own thrive, were they ever truly allies? This stiff-necked, spiteful behavior might be our truest tradition. If we had truly welcomed him, I believe it would all be different. Can you imagine a scenario in which any other person who saved so many elves would be similarly reviled? They never gave him a chance to be anything other than a monster in their eyes and then provoked him until he would no longer tolerate it." I dug my fingers into Celebel's scalp as he turned away, massaging across his skull, the joints of his ears, down his neck.

When he sighed again, I continued. "You could argue this is my fault because I brought him here, or Feanim's fault for courting the idea. You may blame it on Rafael himself if you like. He certainly cares not, except in the ways it directly affects me."

"This is so much harder than I expected," Celebel admitted. "In the beginning, when you told me of Rafael, of this questionable connection you have to our sworn enemy, I thought I only needed to be understanding and we could eventually reach some kind of accord. I mistakenly assumed he would be reasonable. Now, where are we? With no sign that this conflict between us will ever resolve. He still takes every opportunity to provoke me, and he upsets you. I no longer understand the benefit here. I am feeling less and less understanding with each passing day."

"What current conflict? He's left you completely alone since the battle," I pointed out. "His killing of that elf—"

"Pulalvea. His name was Pulalvea."

"—his killing of Pulalvea was distasteful and upsetting, true, but I doubt you can claim with certainty that this was no traitor."

Celebel rubbed his forehead with another gusty sigh.

"Come now. Would any of us have survived an attack by enemy drakes without his protection? Would we have made it out of Férioth alive?" The sudden mood shift surprised me. I'd thought they were finally making some kind of peace.

"Of course you jump to his defense. You always do. I could not attempt even one small push back against his bully tactics without major consequences. I have to just sit back and take it, or risk unleashing his wrath on all of us." His eyes were hot with unshed tears. "Is he even interested in this healing you keep talking about? Or is it just another ploy, another way to make sure you remain in his possession?"

I rubbed the bite mark on the back of my neck. It had faded slightly as it healed, but remained visible. "I defend you to him as well, you know."

His ears flattened. "What is there to defend?"

"Were you not just speaking on the lavender fiasco? Perhaps if you had defended me to the court, or publicly acknowledged my soulbond to him without my prompting, they might have had an easier time with acceptance." Anger rose, heating the tips of my ears. "He hates that I'm here at all, putting myself in danger, and you know that. No matter that it was my decision. I would never have left my hill if not for you. I returned to a court that disdains me, to a life I fled long ago. A life I was clearly unprepared to re-enter." I got to my feet, face flushed, and Celebel clutched at me. I dodged his hands.

"Cúraniel, sit back down. You asked me how I felt and now you're angry at the answer?" Celebel's own anger surfaced in a scowl to rival Rafael's. "Can't you listen to me without immediately reacting?"

I sat, my ire draining away. He was right. "Forgive me, that was unfair. Sometimes I cannot seem to help myself. Underneath all that rage and violence is a very hurt soul, and I defend him out of instinct. Even when he doesn't deserve it. He's certainly never asked it of me. And it's not your fault that the court is awful, nor is it your fault that some of them defected. I shouldn't have implied that."

"You did not answer my question. Is he interested in actually being healed by you?"

I sighed. "Rafael's trauma is extensive and unpredictable. I am learning to navigate it alongside him. We made good progress just before the battle in the mountains, and he's done very well since." Frowning, I paused. "I can tell from the set of your ears that you don't believe me."

Celebel shook his head. "This is all a game to him. He toys with our lives, and we have no control over it. Now friends I've known all my life have turned on me. I find myself siding with a monster, questioning every decision I've ever made." He put his head in his hands.

Cautiously, I reached out and stroked his hair. Celebel's upset surely had more to do with his feelings around the betrayal than anything Rafael had done recently. It made perfect sense to deflect the pain to an easier target.

"Have you spoken to Feanim about all this? What does he say?"

"Feanim is not nearly as emotional about the defection as I am; mostly angry at losing the strategic location. He's already abuzz with plans for the next one." He sighed. "Likely thrilled to have someone more ruthless than he to help test his gruesome weapons and tactical ideas. I am unsure if he values my opinion these days. It feels as if I'm under attack from all sides."

"Even from me?" I hadn't truly considered the effect that Feanim's growing friendship with Rafael would have on Celebel.

"When I cannot express my frustration with a rival who wants me dead? Yes, even you." He looked at me with hard eyes.

"Fair enough. I do not know what to say. I cannot change who Rafael is or the situation." I pulled back, running my hands through my hair.

"Tell me true. Is there a world you can envision in which you would ever give him up?"

His words landed like knives thrown, but I owed it to him to consider them. I tried to imagine it. I'd seen what happened to those who deliberately severed their connection to a soulmate. In every instance, it meant taking a soul-deep wound, and many did not recover. Those that did were forever hollowed and diminished by the experience. Then there was the other complication.

"Even if I could, how do you imagine Rafael would respond? I can guarantee it would not be with compassion and understanding."

"Forget his reaction for a moment. Can you imagine doing it for yourself?"

I remembered how I'd felt right after I told Rafael of my new lover and imagined that crushing heartsickness extending on for the rest of my very long life. Celebel watched me carefully.

He nodded, mouth twisting. "That's what I thought. So, I was wrong in my most basic assumption that you simply had unresolved issues to work out with him, and then we could reach some kind of harmony. It's never going to be finished. If you refuse to break with him, and he refuses to change, where does that leave us? And now we're more reliant than ever on his strength and his people. I'm truly never going to be free of this menace."

"Does it help you to hear that I also can't imagine living in a world without you? He would spirit me away in a heartbeat if I said the word, but I cannot leave you. Whatever else happens with this gods damned war, whether you actually need my help, I cannot tear myself away from you." I tried to breathe through the emotion threatening to choke me. "I hope I haven't saved your life, only to your detriment thereafter. Will you allow me to attend to your wound, at least?"

He grunted, but rolled onto his side. I unbound the latest poultice and gently pried it free. A stench made my eyes water the moment I exposed the wound. Not of rot, but of foul energies. I recoiled. We had chosen our herbs well, but they could never combat a curse like this. Similar to the one inflicted upon Rafael, but more insidious. Perhaps Feledhor planned exactly where he struck. This poison sank into the soulbond itself. Clever, subtle, and terrifying.

Planting my feet in the earth, I grounded myself before beginning, drawing in the Night Mother's presence. I crouched and placed my hands near the wound without touching the edges, delving into Celebel with my spirit. Something dark coiled there just under the surface, waiting to strike. If I looked at it through the focus of spirit, I could see roots spreading throughout my hapless soulmate.

With a flood of power, I took hold of it, like pinning a venomous snake safely behind its head. The darkness thrashed within him, and Celebel's body jerked in response. I pulled hard. It boiled out of the wound and up my arms, into my mouth and nose. Into my ears. My vision went black.

I screamed. Or at least, I think I did. Lashing out with spirit, I punched through the dampening field, reaching for my bond to Rafael. Desperate for his strength, for an anchor, for anything to keep me from being sucked into the darkness. I gasped for breath, clawing at my throat.

Try as I might, I couldn't shake the foul energy. Coughing only hurt my lungs. Any physical movement increased the pain. Gathering all my power, I scraped it away, but it clung like tar. Pouring into me, choking me, a constricting coil that tightened with each labored breath. My heart pounded in my ears, my vessels trembled with the strain. Blinded, deafened, throttled, crushed. Surely my blood would soon boil from the pressure.

Rafael's presence loomed behind me. He wrapped his arms around me and gripped my wrists, enveloping me in his heat. The darkness thrashed again, painfully, but did not release its hold. I felt, rather than heard, his growl.

The Dragon cloaked me in shadow, his own familiar darkness flowing around me. I leaned into him, drawing on his strength to keep my own from extinguishing. Little by little, he took hold of the clinging poison. With a snarl, he ripped it free in one violent motion.

Celebel gasped, arching off the ground. I gagged, crying out with him as Rafael dragged the tainted shadows from deep within us both. The darkness vanished all at once, and Celebel went limp. I checked his pulse and breathing. Both even. I sighed a prayer of thanks. His wound looked much better, though still not fully healed.

"Gods, Rafael," I panted, trying to catch my breath. "That was—"

His arms slid away. I turned to see Rafael slumped over, eyes closed. Stunned, I tried to rouse him. Shaking his shoulder and calling his name did nothing.

Panicked, I opened his jerkin and tore away the shirt beneath. An ugly, greyish wound spread from his collarbone down his left arm and all along his side where the white drake's freezing breath had hit him. The stubborn blighter! All the while, he'd insisted he didn't need my help. That much shapeshifting, fighting, and power expenditure must have left him utterly drained. Worry knotted my stomach. Had I drawn too heavily on his strength and accidentally harmed him? Or worse?

A drake roared nearby, startling me. Metal clanged on metal. Someone screamed. More Fomorians attacking?

I looked from one unconscious man to the other. "Fuck. Now what do I do?" Rafael's enormous greatsword was no use to me. Celebel's sword remained bundled on his horse. All I had was my little braid knife.

Neither of my soulmates answered. Nor did the Night Mother. For the first time in almost a century, I was completely alone.

TO BE CONTINUED IN BOOK 2 OF THE SOULBOUND SONG

Acknowledgements

First and foremost, I have to thank my husband, Henry. Your feedback was instrumental to the construction of this story, and I couldn't have done it without you. You tolerated all of my weird hours, angst, tears, and rambling. Thank you for the gorgeous map and all the language work you did. Vaeda is so much richer because of your contributions. I am very, very fortunate to have such a supportive partner.

Second is my ride-or-die, my sister Charlotte. You hate fantasy, weird sex stuff, and reading in general—and that's ok. Just knowing you've got my back and always believe in me is enough.

My dear friends Sooz, Shelley, Maria, and Becky: I may owe financial compensation for making y'all read my dumpster fire of a first draft. Thank you for not tossing me off a cliff. Nemohee, Machi, Eäriel, and my herbalism jokes just wouldn't be the same without you.

To my Sunset Riders: I still don't know how I weaseled my way in amongst the romance writers, but I'm very grateful for the acceptance. Marie, you were the first one to take a chance on me, and your feedback and support mean the world. Anka, hush up about Rafael's talons. We talked about this (but seriously, your insightful critique really saved me). All of you keep writing and spilling the tea.

A.E.! Where do I even start? You've been such a light in my life, and I am beyond grateful to have met you through this process. Cheers to Sleep Token and Booktok for bringing us together. You talked me down from the cliff more times than I can count. I can't wait to see where your career takes you. I don't know what I would have done without you and our other author bestie (thanks for trying in vain to teach me how commas work. You know who you are).

Azalea Crowley, I appreciate the education, sensitivity reading, and emotional support more than I can ever say. I know I'll be seeing your name in lights someday, because your books are amazing and so are you.

To my most amazing cover artist, Prokaryarts LLC: I'm thrilled to collaborate with you on this cover and all the character art. Your talent blows me away! Thanks for always listening to me chirp about my disaster babies.

R.N. Barbosa, editor extraordinaire: your gentle coaching and enthusiasm for the story came at just the right time. Thanks for all the times you let me firehose worldbuilding and character backstory at you. And for helping me overcome the mental obstacles.

Finally, to all my readers: thank you for coming along on this wild, weird ride with me. There's a whole lot more where this came from.

About the Author

C. A. Chaplin lives in California with her husband, her two black cats, way more carnivorous plants than any one person should own, and the people in her dreams who never leave her alone.

To learn more about upcoming projects, please visit www.cachaplin.com

www.ingramcontent.com/pod-product-compliance
Lightning Source LLC
Chambersburg PA
CBHW070149310726

48976CB00001B/37